Jellybird

Jellybird

LEZANNE CLANNACHAN

First published in Great Britain in 2013 by Orion Books,
an imprint of The Orion Publishing Group Ltd
Orion House, 5 Upper Saint Martin's Lane
London WC2H 9EA

An Hachette Livre UK Company

1 3 5 7 9 10 8 6 4 2

A CIP catalogue record for this book is
available from the British Library.

ISBN (Hardback) 978 1 4091 2657 7
ISBN (Export Trade Paperback) 978 1 4091 2768 0
ISBN (Ebook) 978 1 4091 2767 3

Typeset at The Spartan Press Ltd,
Lymington, Hants

Printed in Great Britain by CPI Group (UK)
Ltd, Croydon, CRO 4YY

The Orion Publishing Group's policy is to use papers that
are natural, renewable and recyclable products and made from
wood grc   uring
pro

To Emily, Carsten and Maia, for the light in my life.

In memory of my father, Allan M. Maltarp.

I

October 2012, Seasalt Holiday Park

Jessica arrives at the caravan park sometime in the night.

'You sure this is the right place?' the taxi driver asks, staring at the closed gates, the blacked-out campsite beyond.

It belongs to my mother, she could explain, if she were able to dredge up the words. The fare shows up in sharp, red lines but the numbers slip about like oily fish in her head. She hands the driver a note, hoping it's enough, and gets out.

When he's gone, she stands in the lane surrounded by blackberry bushes that in summer whisper with a sea breeze but are now frozen still. She'd forgotten how dark it could get. She presses the night bell and waits. Minutes later, torchlight weaves through the mobile homes.

The gates rock back and her mother, nightgown brushing the muddy toes of her wellingtons, fixes the beam in Jessica's face. 'What's happened?'

'I just . . .' Her voice sounds distant, as though someone else is speaking through her. 'Woke up this morning thinking about this place.'

It's not true, but Jessica can't say about the kitchen floor; how she lay on it until the wooden boards pressed bruises like thunderclouds onto her shoulder and hip.

She follows her mother through the unlit park, the night so dense that nothing exists unless the torchlight flashes over it. It makes Jessica feel bodiless, like she could slip outside of the shivering exhaustion and aching limbs. She wants to keep going but then they reach the caravan that is both her mother's home and office.

'You could stay with me, I guess,' her mother says, 'but there's only one room.'

'How about Caravan Nineteen?'

Her mother sniffs as though the choice displeases her. She disappears into her caravan and comes back with a key. A blue enamel flower dangles from it. Her mother made it, years ago, on some course. One for each caravan and an extra one for Jessica, who stops walking, trying to remember when she last saw her key ring. The loss of it is sudden and sharp as gunshot.

'This way. You remember.' The torch in her mother's hand draws fleeting lines on the black gravel.

Inside Caravan Nineteen, her mother slaps dust and dead spiders from the sofa cushions.

'There are extra blankets under the bed.'

'I remember.'

When her mother leaves, Jessica stands in the centre of the snug sitting room, facing the sofa. She flips over one of the seat cushions then kneels before it. Her fingers trace a faint brown outline like a smudged cloud. A washed-out stain. Too old to be certain it is blood.

Hugging her rucksack, she lies down, pressing her cheek to the mark. She doesn't sleep. Before dawn, she walks out of the holiday park.

Opposite the park lies a derelict pleasure garden. A sudden moon has opened up the night, structures emerging – the boarded-up pavilion, the empty lido, her own body. She reaches a gap in the picket fence where a gate used to be. Past it, the raw edge of the cliff and a flight of rickety steps leading to a horseshoe bay. She feels her way down the stairs and onto the beach. The sand creaks with ice beneath her feet.

As she waits for first light, she takes a cuckoo clock out of her rucksack and cradles it in her hands.

From a distance, it is a perfect miniature of an alpine chalet. Up close, its plastic seams become obvious. The walls, once slaughterhouse red, have faded to a hammy pink; the roof bleached in patches like stale chocolate. Jessica no longer winds it up. It had been bought as a joke, after all.

The key is Sellotaped to the bottom. She scratches it free and winds it up. A slow tick starts inside the woodchip walls like a tutting tongue. Jessica moves the minute hand to twelve. Two windows above the clock face spring open. A peg figure appears in each, one in a white dress holding a bunch of painted-on flowers, the other in a funereal black suit. The groom's black eyes peer sideways at his bride as he hovers in his window.

Then they jerk across empty space to knock heads in a clumsy kiss beneath a scroll declaring *You'll Find Love in Longhaven Bay*.

Jessica stares at the peg-man. His eyes, with their sideways glance, now look away from the embrace, over his bride's shoulder at something – or someone – behind her. She takes hold of the little groom, making the clock's mechanism squeal and shiver as it tries to pull him back.

With her thumbnail, she scratches off his eyes.

When the sky opens up in morgue blues and purples, she lifts the cuckoo clock above her head and hurls it at the water as though she's bringing down an axe. It disappears into the ocean with a viscous gulp.

Job done.

Ten minutes later, she arrives at the park in time to see her mother leaving Caravan Nineteen, a lumpy bin bag tucked under her arm. There's a breakfast tray on the kitchen counter.

'How long will you be staying?' her mother asks.

'Just a few days, Birdie.'

They both know that isn't true. 'The Premium and Superior caravans are empty, you know.'

'Here's fine.'

Her mother strides away, the plump pads of her hips wobbling through her fisherman's jumper.

The breakfast tray contains three triangles of toast and a pot of bitty marmalade. It sparks a memory of the French toast her mother used to make on Sunday mornings – cinnamon bread, butter-gold with fried egg

4

and maple syrup. The thought of food nauseates her. Sliding the tray outside, she locks the door.

In the bedroom, she finds her clothes are no longer on the floor where she'd dumped them before walking to the beach. The bin bag under her mother's arm takes on a new significance. Rather than crawling into the bed – narrow and comfortless as a ship's bunk – she has to go in search of her few belongings.

The deserted holiday park is picture-still as she heads to the laundry block. Jessica touches the walls of the boarded-up mobile homes, offering them comfort. The desolation of the place suits her, like stepping into water already wet.

The laundry block is a square cement building with a flat roof and slit windows for ventilation. Years back, her mother, in a flight of artistic fancy, painted one of the walls with a jungle of creepers and exotic birds. The colours have dimmed and the birds have become sinister, blurry-eyed beings among the trees. From inside comes the sound of voices and wet sheets being flapped out.

'The girl's a wreck.' Grannie Mim, her mother's best friend. Jessica recognises the slight wobble in her voice. It isn't age; she has always sounded the same. 'I saw her staggering off to the beach this morning. Dawn, it was.'

'Bit of sleep, that's all Jessica needs.' Her mother, so flat and practical. 'She's tougher than she looks.'

'Why's she here?'

In the pause, Jessica peels off a curl of paint from the body of a fat, blue bird.

'I don't know,' her mother says. 'It's none of my business.'

'But it is, Birdie. She's your youngest.'

'She's twenty-nine.'

'Still your baby.'

'She doesn't want anything from me. Never has.'

'You still have to offer it.' Despite her frail-sounding voice, there's nothing meek about Grannie Mim.

Jessica waits for her mother to respond. When she hears nothing but the accelerated snap of damp linen, she goes back to her caravan, climbs fully dressed into bed. As she drifts off to sleep, a noise startles her. She kneels at the window, convinced she heard a handful of pebbles dashed against the glass. There's no one there. Just a seagull in the sky, suspended against the wind like a kite on a string.

Birdie calls this the dead season.

Jessica sleeps away a whole day and night, waking on her second morning at the park to the blind whiteness of the room, confused, disorientated. She finds her watch on the floor where she has thrown it off at some point. It used to make him laugh, how she'd discard everything in her sleep until she was utterly naked. Her wedding ring often disappeared in that way, found days later in a crack in the floorboards or inside the pillow-case.

You trying to tell me something? he'd tease. *Everyone's honest in their sleep.*

Jessica checks her left hand, and sure enough the ring is gone. Just as she lifts her pillow, she remembers where it is. Making a circle in the gathering dust of a mantelpiece far from here.

She peels off the sheets, damp with sea air and pushes the curtains open with her socked feet. Spotting blue sky, she sits up. At the far end of the park, Grannie Mim is returning from the beach, hair like brittle wool. She follows the shingle path which runs like a corpse's vein through the caravan site, heading straight for Caravan Nineteen. Hearing the front door open, Jessica pulls the sheets back over her, closes her eyes.

Mim doesn't knock; walks straight into the bedroom and grips Jessica's foot through the covers.

'Up you get.' She gives Jessica's foot a shake. 'We can't have you sleeping your life away.'

Retreating to the door, she nudges a parcel of laundered clothes into the bedroom with the toe of her walking boot. 'Your ma's done your clothes.'

Jessica waits for the door to close before getting out of bed and inspecting the bruises that run from shoulder to elbow on her left arm. The flesh feels pulpy and tender. She chooses a thick-knit jumper, loose and concealing, checking her reflection in the window as she dresses. *Clean jumper, tick. Hair brushed, tick.*

In the kitchen, the old lady hands her a mug of tea.

'It's good to come home when you're running low,' she says with a look from under her patchy eyebrows that implies layers of meaning. Grannie Mim's digging.

'It's more your home than mine,' Jessica says. 'How many years have you been at the park now?'

Grannie Mim ignores the question. 'At some point, you have to move on.'

'Someone's been talking.'

'Your ma's said nothing.' Mim sniffs, pinches her nose and wipes her thumb on her trousers. 'At seventy-six you just know these things.'

The tea tastes like milky, boiled water. Jessica drinks it in the hope that she'll be left alone once it's finished.

'I heard sobbing last night.'

Jessica has to smile. 'I haven't shed a tear.'

'Maybe you should.' Grannie Mim leaves her tea untouched. 'I'll wake you again tomorrow.'

After she's gone, Jessica thinks about crying. She pokes about in old memories to see if something might startle her into tears, finally settling on the bedsit in Threepenny Row. Where it all started.

There's a quiet knock at the door.

'Tea.' Birdie holds out a steaming mug, looking straight past Jessica into the caravan as if checking for signs of disorder, something that might need setting right. 'How did you sleep?'

'Badly.' Not her normal answer. It's Grannie Mim's fault. All of a sudden Jessica wants to feel bad. Or at least pretend to, in the hope that a real sensation will follow.

Birdie nods. 'The gale kept me awake as well. There's storm damage to some of the roof shingles.'

Jessica suspects her mother's here on Grannie Mim's insistence. 'It wasn't the storm that kept me awake.'

'Well. I guess you're used to noise from the city.'

'Did I ever tell you about Threepenny Row?'

Her mother goes straight to the cupboard under the

8

sink and finds a duster. 'I visited you there, if you remember?'

Once. And she'd stayed on the doorstep, refusing to come in.

Jessica sits at the breakfast bar. 'It stank of mushrooms and rancid air-freshener, that place. Eau de Plastic Peach, we called it.' Softly to herself, she adds, 'Me and Jacques.'

Her mother, noticing Grannie Mim's mugs by the sink, empties them and starts washing up. 'You can see the water from Caravan Fourteen.'

'I like this one.' Jessica hugs her elbows, looking out over the campsite. The sky is now the same mottled white as the caravans. 'Threepenny Row was a hole. I could lean out of bed and light cigarettes on the gas stove.'

Birdie's nod is the gesture of a conductor, moving things along.

'Jacques was appalled. Said he couldn't sleep at night, imagining me burned to death in my bed. I screamed at him when he moved it.'

'Well, it sounds like a fire hazard.'

'He once took a blue biro and joined up all the freckles on my back.' Jessica discovers the bar stool squeaks, if she shifts her weight. Interesting, how her mother can make her feel five years old again. 'He said I had the star constellation of a leaping salmon between my shoulders.'

Birdie turns her attention to the window above the kitchen sink, rubbing the glass with sweeping arcs that strain her coat's stitching under the arm. 'And where is he now?'

Her mother's words do the trick; Jessica stops talking.

'I could do with some help mending the roofs this afternoon.' Birdie turns to go, then stops. 'I nearly forgot. Someone was looking for you yesterday when you were sleeping.'

'Who?'

'A woman.'

Adrenalin bursts under the shallow surface of Jessica's skin. 'What did she look like?'

She tries to sound casual but it's too late. Birdie must have seen something in her face because she looks away. Her mother is the only person she knows who can pass a car crash without a glance.

'I told her you weren't here,' Birdie says.

'Did she believe you?'

'I think so.'

The tension in Jessica's neck eases, her shoulders drop. 'Thank you.'

She wants to sound grateful but Birdie's merely doing her a favour. One favour requires another in return. 'Let me know when you're going to fix the roofs.'

By the afternoon, an Atlantic gale is blowing. The caravan creaks and judders as Jessica pulls on as many layers as possible under her thin jacket. Her newly laundered clothes smell of hot-ironed soap powder.

She finds her mother balanced on a ladder at Caravan

Two, her ankle-length skirt of tropical greens gathered and tucked between her knees. Thread veins map the contours of her stout calves through beige nylons.

'That looks dangerous,' Jessica says, the ladder shaking with the vigorous jack of her mother's elbow as she crowbars broken shingles off the roof.

Birdie peers through her armpit. 'Hand me the new shingles, if you would. And some nails.'

With a steadying hand on the ladder, Jessica does as she's told. Her mother positions the shingles, humming a tune Jessica doesn't recognise and keeping time with the hammer as she drives the nails in.

'You're actually enjoying yourself, aren't you?' Jessica tries to grind the blood back into her fingers. 'Is there nothing you can't fix?'

'Cars.'

Jessica can't tell if her mother is being serious or not.

'Cars and people,' Birdie adds.

Raindrops, glutinous with unformed snow, burst on Jessica's face and hands. 'I'm not here to be fixed, if that's what you think.'

Her mother drops the crowbar and hammer into the deep pockets of her skirt, gently touching the newly positioned tiles with her fingertips like a blessing, before climbing down. Eyes on her mother's impassive face, Jessica helps gather up the damaged shingles from the sodden ground.

'Like I told you, Jessica.' Birdie straightens. 'Cars and people.'

Jessica clamps her teeth down on her tongue, looking over her mother's shoulder. Beyond Seasalt Park's hedgerow boundary, she can see the sloping roof of the house she grew up in. Purbrook Rise. Smoke wisps out of the chimney, catching and tearing in the wind. A new family in her old home.

'When was it you sold the house? January?'

'March.' Birdie glances across at the roof. 'It feels longer though.'

The thought makes Jessica dizzy. She remembers coming down from London to clear out the few remaining items of her childhood from her old bedroom. It was the day she took the sea-dragon box from its secret place in the chimney flue. If only she'd left it there, she thinks.

Which brings her to Libby. Had she already met her by then? What came first – the box, or Libby? Gnawing the tip of her thumb, she tries to sequence the events. She senses a pattern, a series of incidents that appeared random but were invisibly linked; a net waiting to catch her. If she'd only left the box in its hiding place; if only she'd never met Libby. Jessica squats down, head low to bring the blood back.

Birdie's feet stop in front of her. 'I'm surprised to be saying this, seeing as you slept the whole of yesterday away, but maybe more rest is what you need.'

It's the most her mother has said since she arrived.

'Sleep does wonders,' Jessica says. Her mother's favourite saying when she was a child. She watches Birdie stuff the tube of roofing tar and remaining shingle into her pockets and walk away, the silhouette of her skirt disfigured by sharp angles.

When she was little, Jessica used to fish her hands

into her mother's bottomless pockets, hunting for treasure. On the rare occasion she came up empty-handed, her mother would say, *Oh, but you gave up too soon*, and with a magic flourish of her hand produce a chewy sweet or a marble or a nail bent into an improbable shape.

2

Nine months earlier, January 2012, London

Every surface in the restaurant is a droning white, making Jessica's head ache. In contrast, the sprouting green of her wool dress looks vulgar and her leather boots far too earthy.

The box sits in the middle of the table. Against the starched white of the tablecloth, it too looks cheap and garish, with a swirling oil-on-water pattern of pink and silver; the product of an entire evening trawling through packaging on the internet. She should have chosen something plain.

Through long windows overlooking the restaurant's walled garden, she can see falling snow, the sky a cool metal-grey. The cold looks delicious, making the airless, overheated restaurant suffocating by contrast. The wool against her skin starts to itch.

The woman she is waiting for, Elizabeth Hargreaves – she must get her name right – is late. Five more minutes and she'll leave.

The waiter offers her a choice of rolls in a silver basket, spilling crumbs across the lid of the box. As she brushes them away, a sudden flurry catches her attention. It's not so much a noise as a ripple through the air, like something only animals sense, heads craning. Jessica's first impression is of a violent pink that seems to burn a hole in the restaurant's pristine white. A woman, whose magenta jumper is making Jessica wish she'd worn her green dress with similar audacity, studies the other diners. There's something compellingly physical about the woman's presence that keeps drawing Jessica's eyes. She is tall, wide-shouldered, and her face, framed by a black bob, is strong, almost masculine. Standing among the tables, she is clearly enjoying the attention.

Here comes drama, Jessica thinks, smiling to herself. Then, as the woman's eyes fix with sudden intent in her direction, she experiences a vague sense of panic.

This is Elizabeth Hargreaves.

'You must be Jessica Byrne.' The woman thrusts out her hand as she reaches the table.

'How did you know?' She shakes Elizabeth's cool, dry hand, aware of how unpleasantly damp her own is.

'A clever guess.'

Jessica waits for the woman to sit down, flap out her napkin and smooth it across her lap before pushing the box towards her. 'Here it is.'

Elizabeth ignores it, regarding Jessica instead. Her mouth curls in a small, secretive smile that sends another woollen prickle through Jessica. It reminds her of their telephone conversation a few days earlier. How

Elizabeth had taken her time to say who she was and why she was calling. Jessica had come away with the distinct impression that the woman had enjoyed her confusion.

'I know this must seem odd. I'm sure you've never met your other internet clients before.'

'No.' Jessica nearly adds that her website has only been live for three weeks.

Elizabeth nods. 'I am, after all, interested in your entire Deception range. I can hardly rely on internet pictures alone.'

'Of course not.' Jessica tries to match the woman's smooth, even tone. 'It's a pleasure for me to show you.'

Elizabeth signals the waiter to clear a space for her. Once her plate and cutlery have been removed, she places the box in front of her. Instead of removing the lid, she says, 'Do you know, we have quite a lot in common.'

Jessica holds back a sigh. *Open the box. Just open it.*

'I grew up in Barnestow.'

'Barnestow. I know the place,' Jessica says, trying to concentrate. 'It's about forty minutes from where I grew up.'

'I know. I read the profile on your website.' The box lies forgotten between the woman's hands. 'You must know Seasalt Holiday Park?'

Jessica straightens. 'It's my mother's. I grew up there.'

Elizabeth hides her mouth behind her hand, her eyes wide with astonishment. 'What a coincidence. I used to visit it as a child.'

Jessica smiles, her shoulders released from their tense knot. 'I used to hang out with the Caravan Kids, as my sisters and I called them.'

'Perhaps we played together.' The woman is smiling now, and Jessica is struck by how it transforms and softens her face. She is, in fact, beautiful.

Elizabeth turns her attention to the box and finally lifts off the lid.

'You've taken a lot of trouble with the packaging.'

Inside, each piece of jewellery has been wrapped in black velvet and tied at either end with orange ribbons, like oversized confectionery. Elizabeth takes them out of their nest of shredded tissue paper and lays them in front of her.

In spite of her nerves, Jessica is fascinated by the slow ritual of a client unwrapping and handling her jewellery for the first time. Last night, she had tried to explain to Jacques why she was putting so much care into the packaging when the sale was yet to be agreed.

It's the moment I always imagine but never get to see.

Elizabeth takes her time untying bows and unrolling the velvet, her face severe once more in its lack of expression. Against the pale tablecloth, the glinting oranges and reds of her necklace shout out like a battle-cry. Jessica sighs with pleasure.

It almost doesn't matter what anyone else thinks.

'May I?' Elizabeth takes off her pink jumper, undoes the top two buttons of her white blouse, pulling the collars apart, and clasps the necklace around her neck. 'Do you have a mirror?'

'Sorry, no, I didn't think . . .' Her voice trails off

as Elizabeth gets up. In a bubble of anxiety, Jessica watches her head towards the Ladies.

She studies Elizabeth's face when she reappears, but the woman is busy glancing around the restaurant, the necklace seemingly forgotten.

'According to your reviews,' Elizabeth says, sitting down, 'you're some sort of alchemist.'

'I wouldn't go that far.'

'But you take pieces of rubbish and transform them into treasure?'

Jessica nods, heat rising in her face. In a minute the woman will walk off and she'll be left alone, under the eyes of the other diners, to put it all back in that silly, whimsical container.

'So. Spill the beans. What exactly am I wearing about my neck?'

Jessica thinks she catches a fleeting look of humour, but she can't be sure.

'You want a list of the materials?'

'My friends will ask.'

She takes a breath. *What the hell.*

'Unpolished citrines and topaz. Paste jewellery from old theatre costumes, pieces of broken tile – see those swirling orange and purple pieces? Fool's gold, glazed petals of a fake rose I found in a charity shop, and those shiny yellow-brown bulbs are actually teeth from an old stag's head.'

Elizabeth says nothing. She motions the waiter over. Jessica feels an odd sense of relief. *All over now.* But instead of asking for the bill, she orders a bottle of champagne and then winks at Jessica.

'I think a celebration is in order.'

'You like it?'

Elizabeth reaches forward so abruptly that Jessica almost flinches as her hand is grasped. 'It's fabulous. I can't wait for my friends to gush over it, only to be told it's a load of old rubbish, if you'll excuse the expression.' The fingers of her other hand trail over the necklace's rough surface as she speaks, her face pink with sudden enthusiasm. 'I absolutely love it.'

'If you take it off, I'll show you why it's called Deception.'

Elizabeth hands the necklace to Jessica, who flips it over and points out the row of heart, diamond, spade and club pendants that form its base.

'Fascinating. But you can't see those shapes from the front.'

'Deception,' Jessica says. 'Its true form is hidden because the eye is distracted by all that colour and glitter.'

'Oh, Jessica. You are a genius.'

When the champagne arrives, Elizabeth proposes a toast.

'To us becoming friends.'

As they chink glasses, she adds, 'Oh, and it's Libby, by the way. My friends call me Libby.'

3

February 2012

Jessica can still taste whisky and cigarettes from the
night before. Even with the sour, hollow pit in her
stomach, she's happy to be propelled along by the
late-morning crowd in Columbia Road Market. With
Jacques holding her hand, they walk in awkward single
file through trolleys of fresh-cut flowers and sculpted
trees. She squints in the glare of a brilliant February
sun, drifting along in a dazzled impression of bodies
and foliage, full of aimless well-being. The air smells
crisply green.

Neither of them knows much about plants, and
Jacques is making up names as they wander through
the flower market. 'Moon Roses. Fatboy Dahlias. To
your left, Jessie – the greater-spotted Fernicus Flower.'

'Fornicus Flower, don't you mean?'

'Of course. The *Fornicus* Flower. A favourite of
mine.' Jacques has pulled his woollen hat low over his

eyes. His face – angled and drawn from lack of sleep – softens as he turns to smile at her.

'I need to eat,' he says.

They find a tapas bar at the far end of Columbia Road, away from the crowds and shouting street vendors.

'Let's buy some mini-trees,' Jessica says, once they have sidestepped their way through the busy restaurant to a table by the window.

'Olive and lemon,' Jacques agrees. 'And tomato plants for the roof terrace.'

Last night Jessica had conceded it was time to make their flat more homely. Less crash pad. She suspects this brings them a step closer to the day when Jacques will suggest converting their boxy study into a nursery.

As always, he over-orders. Terracotta bowls of chorizo, garlic prawns, spicy *patatas bravas* and oily sardines arrive; they eat in greedy silence until Jessica sits back. 'I've gone too far. Should've stopped eating ten minutes ago.'

'You need to practise, sweetheart.' Jacques forks a piece of chorizo off her plate. 'Ma Larsson is suspicious of girls with small appetites.'

Jessica pinches his thigh. 'She's had years to get used to my lack of appetite and childbearing hips.'

'She loves you the way you are, you know that.' Orange grease glistens on his bottom lip. 'She just wants grandchildren.'

Jessica reaches across and wipes away the grease with her thumb, bringing it to her mouth afterwards. 'Ma Larsson will just have to wait.'

21

She's smiling as she says it. Her mother-in-law's longing for grandchildren is a comfortable, well-worn carpet of conversation; perfect for hung-over Sundays when the idea of babies is nothing more than the notion of foreign lands yet to be explored.

Right now, she can't bear the thought of sharing Jacques with another living thing.

'Let's go home,' she says.

Her husband leans across the debris of half-eaten food and kisses her. He tastes of spicy sausage and stale alcohol; she opens her mouth, her hands in his hair, pulling him in.

'We mustn't kiss any more. Not after five years of marriage.'

Jacques nods. 'It's downright inappropriate.'

They grin at each other and Jessica feels a squirm of complicit pleasure, the two of them cocooned against the rest of the world.

'Look what I found.' Jacques pulls his wallet from his back pocket, leafs through old receipts until he finds a creased photograph. He holds it up for her.

A figure sits cross-legged on an unmade bed. Legs naked except for thick socks bunched at the ankles, a slight body swallowed up by a grey sweatshirt. Jacques' old walking socks and jumper; the young girl is herself.

'Where did you find it?'

'I was clearing out some of the boxes in the study.'

She decides not to ask why. 'I must have been seventeen. There's that revolting sofa bed in Three-penny Row.'

Jacques turns the photograph back towards himself;

regards it with such tenderness that Jessica feels a pang of envy for her seventeen-year-old self.

'I always loved that look on your face,' he says.

Scraping her chair closer to his, she frowns at the picture. Her face looks wide-eyed and sleepy as a child's, her mouth loose; no words waiting to be spoken. 'I look vacant.'

'Open,' Jacques says.

An electronic melody of bells sounds from under her chair. Jessica scoops up her bag and stirs its contents in search of her mobile. It takes her a moment to place the voice. 'Elizabeth?'

'Libby. I keep telling you. Only my maths teacher called me Elizabeth, and that was to conceal his lust for me.'

'Where are you? It sounds busy.'

'At the flower market,' Libby says. 'I thought you said you'd be here. With Jacques.'

'We're in the tapas bar. Come and join us.'

Jacques mouths, 'Who is it?'

Jessica ends the phone call. 'Elizabeth.' When he looks blank-faced she adds, 'The one who bought my entire Deception range.'

'Ah, yes. Your internet stalker.'

'Best behaviour, please.' Jessica nudges him with the tip of her boot. 'She's on her way now. Hope you don't mind.'

'Not at all, honey.'

'She's been wanting to meet you. Apparently you sound too good to be true.' Jessica is anticipating the look of appreciation on Elizabeth's face when she meets

Jacques. Her new friend is showy and expressive in a way that's alien to Jessica. It intrigues her.

A woman walks past the window, her white coat unbuttoned, billowing in the wake of her stride.

'In fact, that's her now.'

Jacques sits upright, twisting in his chair as though he has a sudden, sharp pain in his side. 'That's your new friend?'

There's something in his voice that makes her glance at him but then the bell above the door rings and Elizabeth walks in. She stops in the centre of the restaurant, looking about her. She's wearing a black trouser suit with a white, masculine shirt that stretches tight at her chest and huge gold earrings like autumn leaves dangling from her black bob. She's like a wave cresting over the room, everyone holding their breath, waiting to be swept away.

Jessica smiles to herself. *Here comes drama.*

'We're over here.' She waves, glances back at Jacques. There's a look on men's faces when they see Libby, she's noticed, something close to greed.

But Jacques is the only person not looking as he frowns out of the window.

'Libby?' he's muttering, and Jessica elbows him.

'Short for Elizabeth. Try to keep up.'

'Jessica, you gorgeous thing.' Libby comes over and they exchange kisses.

Jacques offers a brief handshake without standing up. He's put his hat back on as though preparing to leave. 'Nice to meet you.'

She waits for Jessica to clear their coats off the third

chair and smiles across at Jacques. 'As handsome in the flesh as your wife said you were.'

'Can I get you a coffee?' The cheery rise in his voice sounds like a stumbled attempt at running up a hill. He's looking pale again, which makes the darkness of his stubble stand out like theatre paint.

'Coffee would be lovely, thank you,' Libby says.

Jessica catches his hand as he gets up. 'Are you feeling OK, Jacqy?'

He nods, stroking his knuckles briefly against her cheek. 'Back in a minute.'

Libby gives Jacques an oblique look as he walks away. 'I was expecting a real charmer.'

'We had a messy night at a comedy club in Camden.'

'I guessed as much from the boozy haze.' She gives Jessica's arm a friendly squeeze. 'So now that I've met your husband, it's time for you to meet mine.'

Jessica watches Jacques over her new friend's shoulder, dawdling by the cakes at the counter. By the time he returns, they've agreed a date.

'We're having dinner on Friday the sixteenth,' Libby says as he approaches with a tray of coffee and cakes. 'Your lovely wife has checked the diary and you're both free.'

'Wonderful,' Jacques says but he doesn't smile. 'I'm sure my lovely wife will look forward to it.'

They both sit back. Libby looks amused; Jacques takes off his hat, ruffling his hair. Jessica has an odd sense of having missed something.

'Where shall we go?'

They both look at her blankly.

'Matthew will make a reservation somewhere,' Libby says after a beat. 'He's good at that kind of thing.'

'Matthew being your better half?' Jacques asks.

'My *other* half, yes.'

Sugar is added to coffees, followed by careful stirring and tentative sips. Jacques eats both the carrot cake and the chocolate cake while Jessica tries to think of something to say. She had imagined an instant, easy flow between the two of them.

'I can't remember if I told you, but Libby is a florist. She has her own shop. E.H. Flowers.'

Jacques nods. 'You said.'

The three of them reach simultaneously for their coffees.

When they say their goodbyes outside, Jessica worries that Libby's mouth looks a little tight. Jacques holds his hand up in a short farewell and goes to inspect a row of blue-glazed pots on a nearby stall.

Under her breath, Jessica says, 'I don't know what's got into him today.'

'I'll wear him down, you'll see.' Libby's voice is so low that it draws Jacques' attention. From the corner of her eye, Jessica sees him watching them from under his hat.

Blowing kisses, Libby heads back into the crowded market.

Jacques puts down the vase he was holding. 'Tell me again how you two met?'

'She was my first online customer. You and I disagreed on the price, if you remember.'

'All those hours you spent on it. She pretty much got it for free.'

She can't understand why it's upsetting him now. He'd been delighted when she came home from White's and announced she'd sold the whole range.

'No wonder she's such a fan,' he adds.

Jessica stops walking. 'As opposed to the quality of the workmanship?'

'Sorry.' Jacques takes her hand, still not looking at her. 'I'm sure she loves your jewellery.'

'What's bothering you, Jacqy?'

He is squeezing and kneading her knuckles. 'Why would you want to be friends with a woman like that?'

'A woman like what?' Jessica raises her eyebrows at him. Jacques is the most tolerant, easy-going person she knows.

'I just don't get it.' He drops her hand, pushing his deep into his pockets, shoulders hunched. 'You're a very different person to her.'

'Exactly. I like that.'

'She's all glitz and no substance. You can't trust someone like her.'

The way he is keeping his eyes dead ahead makes Jessica suddenly uncomfortable. 'Is it because you found her attractive?'

'What? Christ, Jessica.' It's Jacques' turn to stop walking. 'I do not find her attractive.'

'You don't have to pretend she's not.'

He shakes his head. 'Can we stop talking about her now?'

She doesn't try to take his arm again and it feels odd walking side by side, not touching. 'Weren't you the one who thought I needed more friends?'

4

March 2012

Clerkenwell Artists' Studio is hidden inside the white, anonymous flanks of a converted warehouse. It faces a water tower protected by a high wire fence. Approaching the studio, Jessica's pace increases. The narrow side street feels both deserted and watched; she always has the sense of unfriendly observation.

She steps over a fresh collection of windblown newspapers and polystyrene cups into a stairwell with white, eczema-patched walls. Skipping up the stairs to the second floor, she pushes open the glass and wire doors to the studio. Light and space envelop her as she catches her breath.

The studio takes up the whole floor, reaching high into the rafters where unbalanced pigeons flap and shit. Morgan, a painter of urban landscapes, sometimes leaves his wet canvases out overnight to catch their white splatters.

The studio is open-plan, roughly divided by the

territorial overspill of tools and workbenches. Five artists share the space. Herself and one other jeweller, Serena; Neil, a potter who looks barely old enough to shave but six years ago became one of the Clerkenwell Studios' founding artists; and two painters, Janey-Sue and Morgan.

This morning their benches are messy with interrupted work and dirty mugs. No one is in.

Jessica sits at her bench with a coffee. Shoves a pile of sketchbooks and loose scraps of unrealised designs under the desk. Today she wants to work with her fingers, to pour herself into the tiny, mundane tasks that give birth piecemeal to the trinkets in her head.

She spends the day soldering links for a charm bracelet and polishing a set of rings, barely registering Morgan's arrival sometime after lunch. As the sun drops below the skylights, she displays her work across the desk and hugs her elbows with satisfaction.

Looking across at Morgan, she says, 'Bitter shandy and a packet of peanuts?'

After such intense, intricate focus, her head feels detached from her body, as though she's viewing everything from far away. She needs the press and noise of other people to pull her back into her physical surroundings before going home to an empty flat.

But Morgan is gnawing his thumbnail, glowering at an unfinished canvas. He shakes his head without looking up.

When she gets home, she finds Jacques in the bedroom, doing sit-ups.

'You're back early.' Leaping on him, she pinions his wrists to the floor. 'Is it my birthday?'

'If only.' His damp hug squeezes the life back into her body. 'Dinner with the Hargreaves, remember?'

'It's a miracle she's not cancelled after your sulk last Wednesday.' Jessica tries not to smile.

'So, I was a little out of sorts.'

'But Jacqy, you are never out of sorts.'

'I hadn't expected to come home from a long day at work to find your new best friend settled in for the night.' He had sat at the desk, facing the window, glass of wine in hand, his silence a great boulder around which Libby and Jessica had been forced to manoeuvre their conversation.

Jessica climbs off him. 'We don't have to go if you really don't want to.'

'I'm happy to do it for you. Just don't get carried away and invite them back for coffee. There's only so much Libby I can stand in one evening.'

He runs a bath, and when it is full they both get in. Jessica hangs her legs over the side of the tub, painting her toenails while Jacques scans work notes, topping up the hot water.

'What is it, exactly, that you don't like about Libby?'

Jacques puts down his work. 'Her best-friend act.'

'Why would it be an act?' Jessica frowns down at him, stepping out of the bath.

'Just seems a bit keen.' He fills his palm with far too much shampoo and lathers up his hair. 'Does she have to see so much of you? Or drop by whenever you can't come out to play?'

Jacques slips below the surface, scrubbing his scalp with such vigour that water slops over the rim of the bath. When he re-emerges, she leans over him, dangling her wet hair in his face.

'What?' he asks, catching her grin.

She kisses his wet face. 'I don't like sharing you either, Jacqy.'

They meet Libby and Matthew in a Highbury steakhouse with long trestle tables and bull heads on the wall. Libby arrives ahead of her husband, a commotion of kisses and hugs and perfume. When they sit down, Jacques slips his foot around Jessica's, ankles touching. There's a slick of Libby's lipstick on his cheek like a small, deep gash. Jessica rubs it away with her thumb.

'A little . . . smut, that's all,' she whispers when he turns to look at her.

Matthew, having parked the car, makes his way through the diners, frowning as if he's woken up in a strange place. Half his shirt hangs over his belt and his jacket hangs boxily off his shoulders, making him appear gaunt. Beside Libby, he looks like an unmade bed. Jessica finds herself studying their casual automatism as Libby holds out her hand for the car keys and Matthew takes her coat. She wants to peek beneath the public skin of their marriage and see what binds them. Wonders how people see her and Jacques.

Once the drinks have been ordered, there's silence as they read their menus. Libby barely glances at hers. Putting it down, she catches Jessica's eye and winks.

Jessica smiles back. 'Chosen already?'

'I'm here for the conversation, not the food.'

Jacques brings his head up sharply. 'Can't live on talk alone.'

Under the table, Jessica squeezes his knee.

'Good point, Jacques.' Libby smiles sweetly at him. 'We need talk *and* kisses to sustain us.'

'I think your work is wonderful.' Matthew shifts his chair to face Jessica. 'So clever the way you use commonplace materials, a little subversive, even. So what does a day in the life of a jewellery designer look like?'

She gives him the bare bones of her day at the studio and though he makes no comment, his eyes don't leave hers. He has a knack, Jessica decides, for listening.

The waiter brings a round of vodka tonics and a bottle of Pinot Noir, after which the evening relaxes into an easier flow.

'What about first love?' Libby poses the question to the whole table. Matthew nods, giving it due attention.

'Alas, my wife's still searching.' Jacques strokes Jessica's earlobe. She loves the way he deflects personal questions.

Libby isn't satisfied.

'How about *your* first love then, Jacques?' She's talking loudly, with her mouth full, somehow making it look adorable. 'If you say Jessica I shall die of boredom.'

And even though Jessica knows it was a girl called Valentina at his junior high school, he says, 'It was Jessica.'

Libby purses her mouth. 'I've been meaning to ask you about your name.'

Jessica stiffens. Libby already knows the story behind Jacques' name. In a moment of weakness, Jessica told Libby a secret that wasn't hers to give away.

'You're American, aren't you?'

'Yes, ma'am,' Jacques says, tipping an invisible cowboy hat. His eyes flicker to Jessica's, and she manages to give him a sympathetic smile while resisting the urge to kick Libby under the table.

'Then why *Jacques*, and not good old stars-and-stripes *Jack*?'

Jessica pictures Libby's expression of scandalised delight when she explained that Jacques' mother told him the truth behind his name's origin on his tenth birthday and then swore him to secrecy. She'd named her son after her first lover, a Parisian exchange student, not – as he'd grown up believing – the famous underwater explorer, Jacques Cousteau. He was never to tell his beloved father and for this very reason, Jessica knows, her husband abhors secrets and dishonesty.

'You know us Yanks,' Jacques drawls out his accent. 'We're suckers for a bit of European sophistication.'

Libby's eyes meet Jessica's for a finger-snap second. 'It's a gorgeous name for a gorgeous man.'

She takes a slow drink of her wine, then leans across the table to stroke Jessica's sleeve.

'Seven weeks ago today I sent you an email saying how much I liked your jewellery, did you know that?' Raising her glass, she says, 'Let's make a toast to how much more fun the world is when we're together.'

Matthew takes a slim camera from inside his jacket and asks the waiter to take a photograph. Jessica pictures how the four of them might look to the outside world. A tight, closed circle. Libby bestows her friendship like a gift; she can't help but be flattered.

The next morning, Jessica potters about the flat in Jacques' green dressing gown. It's her favourite time of day, the flat full of early light, windows open to weed out the smell of sleep and exhaled alcohol. Jacques has gone running, and she has the place to herself. She makes coffee and thinks about the night before.

A touch, she remembers.

Jacques had relaxed enough to tease Libby about her series of car prangs – *Driving 'Near-miss' Daisy* – and Libby had leaned in, laughing as she squeezed his forearm, his shirtsleeve puckering under her nails. The touch fascinated Jessica; she's never been able to touch people so casually.

When Jacques comes home, he is springy with energy, his face raw with cold. He showers, dresses and starts chopping vegetables for the Sunday roast.

Jessica joins him in the kitchen with her sketchpad. 'How's the Arden Group thing going?'

'I want the walls to billow out like sails.'

'Sounds complex.'

'You have no idea.' He puts down the potato peeler so he can cup her face. His fingers smell earthy. 'Buildings don't just . . .'

'. . . grow out of the ground like trees.'

'So you do listen.' Jacques' thumb strokes her temple. 'The structure of a building is as complicated as the human body. Take your eyelashes, for example. They

35

are a particular length, placed at just the right angle to protect your eye without interfering with your vision. It's all measurements and angles.'

'And I thought you just liked green eyes.'

'I never underestimate the influence of colour.' He touches his lips to each of her eyelids then goes back to his vegetables at the kitchen sink. On a blank page, Jessica chases his moving lines in charcoal against the light of the window.

'Honey, I hate to do this but—'

Jessica closes her pad. 'The office?'

'After lunch.' He goes back to her, puts his hands on her waist. 'Don't be upset.'

She kisses his forehead. 'Upset is ripping at your shirt so all the buttons fly off, shouting "liar".' *Upset* was what her mother used to do.

Jacques smiles. 'In that case, I'm grateful you're not upset.'

She almost tells him about the little pad Birdie used to keep, noting down the length of her father's absences. Searching for a pattern.

Jessica rounds on the mess in the kitchen, scrubbing grease off roasting tins with freshly boiled water that leaves her skin red, sensitive to the touch. When the phone rings, she doesn't rush to answer, knowing it's her mother's weekly phone call.

'I'm selling Purbrook Rise.'

Birdie always opens the conversation with a particular piece of news, as if there must be a purpose to their Sunday chats.

'Have you had an offer?' She won't give her mother the satisfaction of sounding shocked.

'Not yet, but my agent says I can add twenty per cent on its actual value and one of your lot will still snap it up.'

'My lot?'

'Londoners.'

'He's probably right.'

'It always was an ugly house.'

Jessica rubs the sore skin on the backs of her hands. 'Where will you go?'

'I'm moving into one of the caravans.' Her mother pauses. 'Han and Lisa have already taken their things.'

'Can it wait for the weekend, so Jacques and I can drive down?'

'A car won't be necessary. You can probably bin most of it.'

Jessica wishes her luck with the viewings, trying to remember where she hid her emergency cigarettes.

She finds a crumpled pack of Marlboro Lights in a pocket of her winter coat. The wind rattles the bedroom window – a sound she suddenly remembers from the bedroom she and Hannah used to share. They used to stuff newspaper in the gaps of the old sash to make it stop.

Putting on the heavy woollen coat, she unlocks a narrow door hidden behind a curtain in their bedroom. It leads to a two-tier flat roof. Lit cigarette in mouth, she climbs the metal ladder to the top level. There's nothing to sit on. In summer they'd furnished it with chairs and pots of geraniums, until the neighbours informed them that planning permission was required to convert the roof into a terrace. Jessica refuses to stop using it. It's her favourite part of the flat. She does a little tap dance for the Silverstons' benefit, in full view of the lit but deserted office blocks. No one's working on a Sunday evening. Except Jacques.

When he comes home a few hours later, she's potting tomatoes in the bathroom. As he walks in, she notices the soil she's spilled on the floor. Before he can comment, she says, 'Birdie's selling her house.'

'You're kidding? Are you OK with it?'

'When did I last even visit?' Jessica shrugs. 'I am going down there tomorrow to sort through my stuff.'

'If you wait until the weekend, I can come with you.'

'Birdie insisted on tomorrow.' A white lie. White lies don't count.

If her mother searches hard enough, she'll find the sea-dragon box and the terrible memories it keeps. The thought makes her nauseous. Even now, seventeen years later, she needs to keep Thomas a secret.

5

The estate agent's yellow sign swings in the wind, standing out like a brilliant weed against the weathered fence. It isn't just the sign that makes Jessica hesitate. The swing her mother made from an old dining-room chair is gone, and the azalea bushes she once played hide-and-seek in have been replaced by neat rockeries.

A man is working at the flowerbeds with a trowel. Seeing her, he winces to his feet and disappears behind the house. Jessica has never known her mother to part with good money for outside help. Another sign of Birdie's determination to be done with the place.

She checks her reflection in the window of a parked car. Her hair is escaping its black plastic grip, falling around her face. *Hair like a firework*, Birdie used to say, tugging a brush through Jessica's night-tangles. She ties her hair back with a rubber band from the bottom of her bag.

Before she can open the gate, Birdie is standing in the front door, arms folded.

'You said the weekend.'

'I thought I'd surprise you.'

'Well. You've done that.' Her mother doesn't smile. 'I've barely touched your room.'

'That's why I'm here. To help.'

Birdie steps aside as Jessica reaches the porch. 'I'll make tea.'

As always, the wooden baldness of the house shocks her. A blue corduroy jacket – presumably the gardener's – has been slung over the banister in the hall, its vibrant colour disturbing the blank room.

In the kitchen, the gardener is washing mud off his trowel in the sink. Instead of telling him off, her mother offers him a cup of tea, her hand hovering above his sleeve, not quite touching.

As he heads out into the garden, Birdie refuses to catch Jessica's eye. They watch him from the kitchen window as he bends to deadhead a small rose bush. It gives Jessica a sudden picture of her father in his shabby red turtleneck, pushing his fringe back as he tended his plants. She turns her back to the window.

'You never mentioned a gardener.'

As her mother lays crockery on a tea tray, Jessica notices cosmetic dust tracing the fine lines of her skin. It springs another memory – of her father scrubbing a flannel across Birdie's cheeks before one of their rare nights out. *Why would you want to hide that beautiful skin?* And her mother submitting, eyes liquid with what Jessica now recognises as love.

Feeling her scrutiny, her mother looks across. 'You take sugar, don't you?'

'Three. Same as ever.'

Birdie carries a mug of black tea out to the gardener while Jessica takes the tray into the sitting room. Standing in the doorway, she tries to remember how it once looked – before her mother threw all the furniture on a huge bonfire. It hits her every time she visits. How she and her sisters adapted to such a changed home. No furniture, and no father.

She notices the apple crate has been replaced by a DIY coffee table in lemon-yellow wood. Jessica puts the tray on it and sits down on a camping stool.

Apart from the cheap coffee table, the room is as bare and unwelcoming as ever. Birdie's collection of birds' eggs has grown, glass jars lining the skirting boards, filled with fragments of blue, cream and speckled eggshell. It wakes another uncomfortable memory; her mother coming home after one of her long walks, an empty blackbird egg cupped in her hand as tenderly as if it were a living thing. The dry sound like a tiny itch as it settled on top of the other broken shells. When no one was looking, Jessica had tipped them out and ground them into the floorboards, the delicious crispness of them under her foot.

'There was always something wrong with this house.' Birdie joins her a few minutes later, standing in the doorway, shaking her head. 'It was never a home.'

'That's not true. Though burning all the furniture didn't help.'

Her mother ignores the remark, sipping her tea. 'I should have trusted my instincts when I first saw the place, but he loved it. I let myself be persuaded.'

He. The reference to her father shocks Jessica into voicing a sudden thought. 'That's why you're selling it now because—'

'He was never coming back, in any case.'

But you hoped. She wonders what happened the day Birdie picked up her post and found the black card with embossed letters looping under the sorrowful weight of their message. A penned scrawl had been added to Jessica's invitation, begging her to attend the funeral. It was that which had prompted the fury of her reply; her words driven in, defacing the discreet gold lettering.

As far as I'm concerned, he's been dead seventeen years already. I didn't mourn him then and I won't now.

Jessica tops up her mug though she is yet to drink from it; the clink of crockery loud against their silence. 'Han, Lisa and I were born here.'

'Too much pain trapped inside these walls.' Her mother sighs. 'At least in hospital everything is scrubbed clean again.'

Birdie can still suck the air out of a room.

'You finally bought a coffee table.'

'The estate agent insisted. Said the crate and camping stools would make it difficult for potential buyers to imagine it as a home.'

'He had a point.'

Her mother lowers herself into a folding camp stool. 'I'm moving into Caravan Thirty-Three.'

Jessica nods, staring into her tea. 'I don't think I ever said sorry about the eggshells.'

Birdie looks at her. Jessica can't tell if she remembers the crushed eggs. 'I felt awful about it straight away.'

'Well.' Her mother gets up again. 'I've left your things in a box. I'll go to the tip later with anything you're not going to take.'

Jessica follows her mother to the bedroom she once shared with her older sister. Except for a large removal box, the room is bare. There are two wine-red rectangles of carpet where their beds used to be.

'The Tesco bag is also yours.' Her mother points to a bag by the doorway. 'Don't forget it. And your secret box is still in the chimney.'

Jessica crosses her arms, digging nails into her closed fists. She listens for her mother's feet on the stairs before kneeling by the hearth. The tiles shine in the pale afternoon light, their hand-painted birds lifting out of the ceramic. They've been polished; no telltale sprinkles of soot to inform her whether the box has been disturbed in its hiding place. She slides the back of her hand inside the flue until her nails touch metal. As she lifts the box off the brick lip onto her spread fingertips, it tips away, almost falling, heavier than she remembered.

The tin is coated in a layer of blackened rust and bird-droppings. The grime hides a painted sea dragon on the lid. Jessica scrapes at the grey droppings. Flakes of rust with a brilliant blue underside come away in her fingers. The sea dragon can't be saved.

'Joss and I are going to the garden centre.' Her mother reappears at the door. They both look down at the box. 'Mind you don't make a mess of the carpet.'

Jessica cradles her box, listening to the low hum of

voices in the hallway, followed by the sound of the front door closing.

A pile of newspapers, crisp with age, lies beside the packing boxes. Jessica folds a yellowed *Selcombe Messenger* around her treasure box before placing it into the bottom of her rucksack. She doesn't bother to look at the rest of her belongings in the packing box. On her way out, she picks up the Tesco bag from the doorway. Another newspaper lies just inside. Before she can discard it, the headline catches her attention.

Local Jeweller Dazzles London

Unfolding the stiff, crackling paper, she discovers a photograph of herself at her first exhibition stand, surrounded by customers craning over her necklaces, oblivious to the photographer. Her face is wide-eyed, wary, as though a noise that no one else could hear had startled her. The force of the moment returns with the flashing camera, the genial pestering of the photographer and her dizzying nerves. Then she spots Jacques, standing close, his head turned away in distraction and yet his hand lifting slightly towards her. Always taking care of her. Jessica smiles; Hannah always said his was a profile fit for a coin.

Folding the newspaper back into the Tesco bag, she draws out an item of clothing folded beneath. The material looks familiar – a man's tweed jacket with velvet elbow patches. The sight of it stops her dead.

Sliding two fingers into the breast pocket, she finds a scrap of paper. Tweezing it out, she flattens it against her knee.

A pint of cream,
streaky bacon,
1 onion,
2 bottles of chianti!!
and you.
xxxx
PS a box of Frosties while you're there!

With trembling fingers, she refolds the little shopping list along its worn lines. Squashing the jacket back into the bag, she ties the handles into a tight knot.

She's an hour early for the afternoon train, and Platform Two is empty. Opposite her, the sea wall keeps the shingle off the tracks, the beach hidden from view. She hears the water hissing against the shoreline. The air is mild and behind the seagull cries, she can hear a blackbird singing. The first sound of spring.

Taking the dragon box out of her rucksack, she holds it on her lap. She has spent all these years trying to forget its contents.

She calls Jacques. 'I'm on my way home.'

'Already, hon?'

'There wasn't much to do.'

He pauses. 'Sweetie, I thought you were going to stay the night? I'm working late, remember?'

'It's OK.' The solid fact of his voice is enough. 'Wake me up when you get in.'

'I hope you didn't let Birdie upset you.'

'I'm fine, Jacqy.' Which isn't true. Seeing Birdie makes her restless in her own skin, like the onset of fever. With a deep breath, she prises open the sea-dragon box.

Newspaper clippings spring up, threatening to over-spill. Topmost is the grainy picture of a young boy sitting on a harbour wall. The sun is hitting him sideways so half his face is in shadow. He looks so young, it hurts her.

She thinks about calling Jacques again for the comfort of his voice. Only she can't tell him about the box and its secrets. Not yet.

In the corner of the tin, she finds a collection of stones. When she scoops them up, they fall into a familiar shape – a bracelet of grey and white beach pebbles strung on blue twine. Pressing the bracelet to her mouth, she roots through loose sketches – the cara-van park, cartoon winter trees – until she finds some-thing red and hard hidden beneath the whispery paper.

A notebook bound in crimson leather – one she's never seen before.

Frowning, she flicks through it and finds a stranger's handwriting, neat and rounded, filling every page. She can't make any sense of it. Putting the book aside, Jessica returns to the picture, staring at it until the boy's face pixelates into black and grey dots.

Thomas.

6

February 1995, Seasalt Holiday Park, Selcombe

Hannah was trying to get out of walking the dog, even though it was her turn.

'I'll give you a quid.'

'Forget it.' Jessica pointed at the overcast sky. 'It's going to rain.'

'Two.'

Jessica closed her homework. 'A week's pocket money or nothing.'

'Fuck's sake,' Hannah mouthed, keeping her eyes on their mum. But Birdie wasn't listening, her hands peeling potatoes in the sink, her head somewhere else. 'Three, then.'

'Done.' What Hannah didn't know was how badly Jessica wanted to get out of the house. The thought of another evening with her mother shadowing her dad, hissing like a cat under her breath, was unbearable.

She made her sister hand over the coins before she left.

'Keep an eye out for Bloody Russian,' Hannah said, crushing a mix of twenty- and fifty-pence pieces into Jessica's palm.

'I'm not scared of that old nutter.'

'You haven't heard what he did to Leona's big sister, then?'

Despite herself, she had to know. 'What?'

Hannah shrugged, her eyes creasing into a fat grin. 'If I tell you now, you won't dare walk Kezy.'

Jessica rattled her fist of coins. 'You're the one who's too scared to go outside.'

Closing the front door on her sister, she felt better, like peeling off a wet jumper. She reminded herself that the tramp hung around the school, not the beach. Tickling the top of Kezy's head, she clipped on the leash. The terrier bounded around Jessica's feet, the flopped triangle of her ears shivering with excitement.

She headed for Crowline Avenue so she could spy on the massive houses with their swimming pools and tennis courts. The lawns had neat rockeries with prim flowers, while her garden sprouted random patches of early daffodils and crocuses. Bloody Russian wouldn't come here. Someone would call the police as soon as they saw his crusty face and broken shoes.

Jessica started to sing, making the Jack Russell glance back, doggy-grinning, flipping out her bad leg.

The last house on the avenue was the Seawitch Nursing Home. Past it, there was nothing but a wasteland of scrub and sand dunes leading to the empty coast. No one ever went there, not even the tourist coaches, because everyone knew it was haunted.

Years ago, when her mother was young, a teenager had vanished there, his body never found. Jessica couldn't bear to think of his lonely bones. She'd be the one to find them – if she ever dared walk that far. She felt it in the same way her mother always knew when it would snow.

Reaching the nursing home, Jessica sat on the low garden wall as Kezy sniffed around her feet. Suddenly the dog darted across the deserted car park.

'Hey. Come back.'

Jessica watched in horror as the terrier nosed her way under the fence and into the gorse; a flash of white wire wool racing through the scrub. By the time she'd taken a few steps past the fence, brambles plucking at her trouser-legs, Kezy seemed impossibly far away. She couldn't bring herself to shout, standing there all alone on the edge of that vast, watchful space.

She'd tell her dad how Kezy had run off, and he'd come back later and find the stupid dog. He'd understand. He wouldn't want his daughter walking alone in that place.

Then the Jack Russell gave a single, shrill bark and Jessica knew she couldn't leave her there. Biting the inside of her cheek to stop the rising tears, she tore deep into the knee-high gorse.

She ran in soundless panic, eyes on the beach ahead, afraid to look down and see what awful things might be sticking out of the ground. Something cut into her ankle, pitching her to her knees, and the silence caught her. Keeping to a crouch, she brushed dirt from her trousers and peered over her shoulder. She was deep into the wasteland, the car park as far from her as the distant stripe of sand. Kezy was nowhere to be seen. The wind made a noise like whispered voices through the dry gorse and she hunched closer to the ground, holding her breath.

Then she spotted Kezy's little brown head bobbing along the dunes and jumped to her feet. Ignoring the twinge in her left ankle, she started to run again. The tight mesh of brambles gave way to sand and seagrass. Fringe glued to her forehead, lungs shrinking, Jessica finally reached the shore.

Kezy leaped at her, paws pattering her legs as she caught her breath. She pushed the dog away. 'Bad girl. Horrid dog.'

She sat down on the cool sand, delaying the walk back across the haunted dunes. A dark hand of cloud pressed down from the sky, squeezing brilliance from the light beneath. A fisherman's boat passed close to the shore, the rumble of its engine sucked out to sea as though the gathering storm had drawn in a huge breath.

It was then that Jessica realised she wasn't alone.

Further along the beach, a boy was standing with his feet in the surf. Stomach tumbling over, she wondered how she hadn't noticed him until now. In the strange light, it was hard to see him clearly, his silhouette blurring against the water like he was made of shadow. He was too tall and skinny to be the Russian tramp.

She'd found the missing boy.

The funny thing is, she didn't feel frightened. He was oblivious to her, trapped in his own place. Standing motionless, he stared into the water that swelled around his shins.

Impressed by her own daring, Jessica watched him. 'It's OK,' she told Kezy. 'He can't see us.'

Then the ghost moved, and she noticed he was holding a stick. He raised it in a slow arc over his head, breaking the motion with a sharp flick of the wrist, and a line caught in the sea. The ghost was fishing.

'This is what the boy must have been doing, Kez. Catching fish off the beach. Then something bad happened to him.'

The ghost lifted his arm again and a large fish swam through the sky. He freed the hook from its mouth in one easy movement, his hands gentle. Then he brought the fish down hard against the surface of the beach. There was no sound.

Kezy trotted towards him before Jessica could call her back. As her dog sniffed the catch, the ghost ruffled her head. The contact shocked Jessica. If he could see the terrier, he could see her too. She sat rigid, afraid to move and catch his attention.

Picking up the fish, he started walking towards her, Kezy at his side. Jessica was furious with the dog all over again. Pushing her fingers into the sand, she watched him from the corner of her eye. As he got closer, she stopped looking, concentrating on digging pebbles from the damp sand. She couldn't help lifting her head when he walked past. He looked down at her with the palest eyes – the colour of bones under the sky.

But he was no ghost: a boy, some years older than

herself. He didn't smile, though she had the feeling he was amused. He'd known she was there all along.

A drop of blood from the fish landed on a pale stone by her shoe. She was struck by how beautiful the red looked against the white. When she was sure the boy had gone, she put the stone in her pocket.

7

March 1995

Jessica tried not to think about the boy on the beach. The more she thought about him, the less real he seemed. She pictured him with brilliant evening light shining through his skin, his eyes blind-white. The drop of fish blood on the pebble had dried to a rust spot, and she wondered if it had been nothing more than a ghost trick.

She could feel the boy watching her; out in the garden at night, peeping through the crack in the cupboard door, behind her closed eyes. When her dad came to kiss her goodnight, she pressed his warm, dry palm across her eyes until the boy disappeared.

Her mother caught her late one night staring out of the bedroom window.

'What are you doing?'

'Nothing.'

'Let's go downstairs.' Birdie nodded at Hannah's

sleeping figure in the next bed. 'I'm making hot chocolate.'

Jessica sat at the kitchen table, thinking how long it had been since her mother had last made hot chocolate.

'Hannah says you haven't been taking your turn to walk Kezy,' her mother said as she heated milk in the pan.

'What about Lisa? How come she doesn't have to walk the dog?'

Birdie put out a single cup, spooned in cocoa powder and poured in the hot milk, slopping some of it down the sides. She sat down, ignoring the spillage. That was how she was these days; careless.

'What's worrying you, Jess?'

'Nothing.'

Her mother nodded, looking up at the clock, and Jessica realised she just wanted company as she waited for Jessica's father to come home. Birdie took a brush from the pocket of her dressing gown. Head tilted to one side, she pulled the bristles through her hair until it undulated like a silk handkerchief. Jessica wanted to wave her hand through it to feel it slip off her skin. Her own hair always split into messy waves.

'Actually I'm scared of going near the sand dunes where that boy disappeared.'

Now she had Birdie's attention. 'Has a boy disappeared?'

'The one you told me about. That boy who went for a walk and all they found were his socks and shoes.'

'That was a long time ago.' Like marbles on a tilting

54

plate, her mother's eyes kept sliding sideways towards the clock.

'Can you tell me the story again?'

Her mother picked loose strands of hair from the brush. 'Well. The strange thing was he'd tied his shoelaces together and walked off barefoot.'

Barefoot. Jessica shuddered. The boy on the beach hadn't been wearing any shoes either. The marbles tilted again. Then her mother sighed, dropping the brush back into her pocket and pulling her sleeves over her wrists. 'I knew him, actually.'

'You knew him? You never said.'

'Not very well.' Birdie took her knitting from a drawer in the dresser where Jessica's dad stacked his vet magazines. 'He used to help his father at the farmer's market in Brigham. He was always laughing at things that weren't funny.'

Jessica's hands had gone cold. She wove her fingers around the mug. 'What did he look like?'

'Plain. Brown hair, blue eyes. He gave me a red paper flower once. He was an odd one.' Her mother's fingers were a little machine she'd switched on and left running. Hands busy, her eyes were free to stare openly at the clock on the wall.

'I'm scared I'll find his skeleton if I take Kezy for a walk.'

'Walk somewhere else then. The forest, or Selcombe Bay.' Birdie was no longer part of the conversation. She'd put her voice on automatic, along with her hands.

'Where's Dad?'

Her mother sat up as if she'd been pinched. 'Work.

There's some kind of virus at the Matthews' farm. Or maybe the pub. He needs to unwind.'

Jessica left her chocolate and went to bed.

The next day the ghost found her.

He was standing under the birch tree opposite the school gates, half hidden beneath the low-slung boughs. Where a heatless February sun dropped through the branches, it lay on him like spatters of white paint. He was smoking a cigarette – a detail which made her a little less afraid. Ghosts don't smoke rollies. He was also wearing shoes. The other girls noticed him as well. His presence was like a sudden breeze through a tree; he had them all flapping and fluttering. Boys at the school gate were always big news. Jessica pretended to look through her school bag, hanging back as her school-mates linked arms, grew bolder in their huddle and tossed looks over their shoulders.

She allowed herself a moment to study him. Everything about him was light and windblown; sand-dune hair spilling over his forehead and ears, almost reaching the neck of his t-shirt. Eyes wide and brilliant with a trace of colour, suspended in the tree's shadow with a light of their own. Like the eyes of a nocturnal animal caught in headlights – a flash of reflected light, a body concealed in darkness.

He was slim and long-limbed, arms hanging loose, cigarette smoke curling up his wrist. His stance lacked the usual, self-conscious posturing of older boys. It made him look poised; ready to run. Or pounce. Jessica shivered and gathered up her bag.

When he spotted her, he lifted his head a little. He didn't smile, so she walked on past him. Once she left the main road where the mothers who didn't work collected their daughters, it became clear she was being followed. Someone was walking behind her, whistling. They were alone now on the lane that led uphill past the rust-pocked sign to the Seasalt Holiday Park. She wasn't afraid. Bloody Russian hadn't been spotted for over a week, and he always made himself obvious when he was there, pretending to lunge at the girls, jabbering in his funny language.

Ghost Boy was following her. She walked all the way home without looking back.

Two days later, he was back at the school gates.

This time she scrabbled up a handful of stones as he followed, throwing a pebble high over her head to see what he might do. The stone never landed. So she threw another and another, grinning all the way home as he caught the stones. The next morning, there was a neat pyramid of pebbles outside the front door.

He followed her home again a week later, on a spring day of such early heat that everyone was red-faced and giddy with the foretaste of summer. She cut through waist-high fields of oilseed rape and into the woods, where she took her time picking red campion and lilac-veined wood sorrel, whose leaves her mother put in salads. There was no sound; just the lazy two-note of a distant cuckoo, and the occasional snap and rustle as Ghost Boy followed behind. Bending to pick flowers, she could see him from the corner of her eye, her heart double-bounding. The sun fell through the trees and poured through her body. She wondered if he was watching the light on her hair.

He was, she imagined, keeping her safe on the long walk to her house.

As soon as she got home, the warm, sleepy feeling vanished. It was an angry heat in her house, thick and airless. That night, with Hannah cursing and kicking at her covers in the bed beside her, Jessica lay perfectly still, listening. Her mother's raised voice seeped into their room through the floorboards like smoke.

'Why does she hate Dad so much?'

'Because she's scared he doesn't love her any more,' her sister said. 'Now shut up. I'm trying to sleep.'

It was the bad feeling in the house that finally made her confront Ghost Boy. The next time he followed her, she got halfway home and stopped dead without looking around, silently daring him. He shuffled grit under his shoes, then came and stood beside her.

'Why are you following me?'

She saw his face up close for the first time. His eyes were as grey as winter sea, and there was a scar like a comma at the corner of his mouth. She wondered how it would feel to the tip of her tongue.

He shrugged. 'I like your red hair.'

'Everyone likes my hair.'

'I'm going to keep following you.'

She smiled for the first time that day.

'I thought you were a ghost when I saw you on the beach,' she said, and he seemed to like that thought.

'I'm Thomas,' he said. 'Sometimes I am a ghost.'

8

Because of gymnastics, Tuesdays were bad days.

Jessica put her jeans over her school tights, pulled a pair of Hannah's hockey socks on top and got back into bed with the covers up to her chin. By the time her mother came to see why she hadn't come down for breakfast, her face was burning.

'I don't feel well,' was all she had to say. Her mother, whose eyes never once missed a trick, just nodded. She didn't even feel her forehead.

'It's changeover at the park today. You'll have to go with your dad on his rounds.' There were three furrows on her mother's brow like stick lines in wet sand. Jessica wanted to rub them out with her thumb.

Before she could shimmy off her jeans beneath the covers, her dad walked in with a glass of water. He shook his closed fist. 'Aspirins, sweetheart.'

With a cool hand he felt the glands under her jaw, asked her to stick out her tongue.

'Is it rabies?' she asked.

'Worse.' He shook his head, frowning. 'Badger flu.'

Jessica giggled, then remembered she was supposed to be ill.

'You're quite hot, though. You should stay in bed. I'll only be gone a few hours.'

Jessica hesitated, then kicked off her covers.

Her dad rubbed his chin. 'I see.'

'Are you going to tell on me?'

'Not this time.' He left her to get dressed.

She decided to wear her denim jacket and Hannah's brooch that said TRUE LOVE in pink, glittery letters. There'd be time to sneak it back in the drawer before her sister came home from school.

'Coast's clear, Jess,' her dad called up. 'Your mum has left the building.'

She found him at the hallway mirror, running a hand through his hair, inspecting his shaving with a funny sideways twist of his mouth.

'Mum's right. You're so vain.'

'Just want to look good for my girl.' He threw her the car keys. 'I'll be out in a moment.'

Jessica unlocked the car. Her dad, who was quite messy about the house, kept the inside of his car spotless so there were no magazines or random flyers to look at while she waited for him.

He came out, swinging his vet's case. As they drove, he fiddled with the radio, humming to snatches of music before twisting the dial again. They stopped in Spentley first, and ordered a wedge of carrot cake with an inch of butter-cream icing.

'So what's new?' Her dad pointed at Hannah's badge. '*Are* you in love?'

'I'm thirteen, Dad.'

'I was in love all the time at your age.'

Jessica rolled her eyes. 'There aren't even any boys at my school.' Then, because he was waiting with his eyebrows raised, she added, 'It's chemistry today. Hate chemistry.'

Which was partly true. She didn't want to have to explain to her dad about gymnastics and the undressing that went with it; her small breasts and long, straight boy's figure under the spotlight of judging eyes.

'But you like school?'

'It's all right.'

'You have friends?'

She thought about Lucy Trelawney, who checked her reflection in every shiny surface and Mary Mickelworth – Micky – who started off fun and quickly became irritating. Friends on the surface; better than spending break alone. 'Yes.'

'And your sisters are happy, aren't they?'

A bubble of anxiety was forming in her stomach though she couldn't say why.

'I guess.'

'Good.' He wasn't eating his share of the cake. 'Great stuff.'

Jessica finished the rest of the carrot cake in two huge mouthfuls before asking, 'Are we going to move away?'

'No love, no. I wouldn't take you out of school when you're happy there.'

'I'm not always.'

'And of course your mother would never sell Seasalt Park, would she?'

'Guess not.'

'Let's get going. Four visits to do today.' Her dad asked for the bill and Jessica studied his face, worrying he was going into one of his distracted moods.

At the car he said, 'I thank you,' and gave a little bow as he opened the door for her. 'The gift of your time is most precious.'

Jessica laughed because he was back to his jokey self again.

At each of the home visits, she was offered something to eat or drink – elderflower water, sticky aniseed balls covered in fluff, freshly baked cinnamon buns. To pass the time, she thought about Thomas. It was now their regular routine to walk through the woods, sometimes as far as the beach on her way home. No one seemed to notice her coming back later and later.

After her dad had treated their yappy dogs and nasty budgies, the pet owners patted her dad's arm, pressed his hands. It irritated Jessica, the way they pawed at him with fingers shiny and crooked as sticks washed up on the beach. How their hearts would have broken to hear him trying to make her laugh once they closed the front door.

Jessie, did you notice Mrs Greencage has got more whiskers than her cat?

It's not Rover that needs flea treatment, it's Mrs Palmer.

After the fourth visit, he rested his arm across her shoulders as they headed back to the car. Jessica tried to take graceful steps so he would forget his arm was there and leave it a while longer.

'Do you think you'll become a vet one day?'

Jessica hesitated. 'I want to be an artist. Mr Schaupetter says I'm not bad. Which is a big compliment, coming from him.'

'Follow your heart.' Her dad nodded to himself. 'That's my one lesson to you. Follow your heart.'

Later, as the car slowed for a red light, he said, 'You know what's missing in this age of modern conveniences and instant gratification?'

'Magic?' She could often guess the kind of answers he was looking for.

He smiled. 'Passion.'

Jessica turned her face to the window. 'People still fall in love.'

'They *think* they do.' The light had changed to green and he wasn't moving. 'Few people ever experience real passion. I don't just mean sex.'

Behind them, a car honked its horn.

'Da-ad.' The conversation was beginning to make her squirm. The car behind overtook them with further horn-blaring, a man's angry face, all jaw and brow, flying past.

'Life and death. The battle to survive. That's the kind of passion that's missing now. It's all too easy and comfortable.'

'What's so good about fighting and dying? Everyone gets hurt.'

'You're not living if you don't experience pain at some point.' He stroked her cheek. 'Let's walk to my next appointment.'

'You said there were only four visits today.'

'Five.'

They stopped outside a semi-detached bungalow in a quiet, tree-lined street. It had red curtains in the window and red flowers in the garden.

'You knock,' he said.

A woman, about her father's age, answered. She had long black hair with grey running through it like streaks of silver lacquer. She was wearing a tight pair of cords with a beautiful beaded belt and a low-buttoned blouse. When she moved her arms, her breasts rose and sank like waves above the stretched material. Jessica tried not to look; her own breasts felt ridiculous and slight under a starter bra that kept slipping upwards.

Unlike the other pet owners, this woman didn't try to touch her father. She stood in her doorway and raised an eyebrow. 'You've brought an assistant today.'

'Jessica,' her father said.

The woman bent forward until her eyes were level with Jessica's. 'And what a beautiful young girl you are, Jessica.'

'Not really.'

The woman laughed as if she'd made a joke and stepped aside to let them in.

There was a moment in the small hallway when everyone seemed to forget what they were doing. The woman was looking at Jessica and her dad was watching the woman, obviously too polite to rush her.

'Mr Peter's in the kitchen,' she finally said. 'Sitting on my clean ironing, as usual, the naughty thing.'

'Who's Mr Peter?' Jessica asked as her dad opened a door leading from the hallway.

'My poor little cat. A car hit him a month ago. Your dad's a miracle-worker.'

Jessica nearly said, *Really? I thought he was a vet.*

'You can wait in here.' She took Jessica's hand – something she would never have allowed Birdie to do – and showed her to the sitting room. 'Touch anything you like.'

The door closed and Jessica was left with the impression that she'd stepped into a dressing-up box.

She perched on a horsehair stool, hands shoved under her thighs, and tried to take everything in. The wall opposite was lined with blank-eyed masquerade masks, the light pearlescent on their porcelain cheeks. Below them, a glass table held a collection of crystals, peacock-brilliant. Drapes of material lay across the furniture, and when Jessica lifted a stiff hem of gold-embroidered fabric, there was something reassuring about the bland, stained sofa beneath; the kind of ordinary sofa they had at home, though the similarity ended there. She got up to inspect the trinkets clustered across a wall of shelves like the haul from an ancient tomb. A gathering of squat, pendulous women carved out of stone, their weight tested in her hand; a felt hat hedgehogged with glass hatpins; a collection of bead-wire crowns, the largest of which shivered with ruby droplets. Jessica lifted it onto her head – and heard her mother's voice.

Don't touch. You girls are always breaking things.

Suddenly the woman's careless offering of her treasures worried her. It was showing off, a kind of superiority. Feeling like she'd been patted on the head, Jessica dropped the crown onto a yellow silk cushion and walked to the window. A dreamcatcher filled most of it, a huge diamond suspended beneath, catching and throwing the light like a disco ball. Jessica took Hannah's brooch off and see-sawed it under the dreamcatcher so the pink plastic gems sparkled.

After a while she just stared at the empty road and the flower-pot gardens on the opposite side.

When the woman returned, she was carrying a black pot with fake gems on the lid and a mirror on a stand, which she placed beneath the dreamcatcher. 'I can't resist.'

She spread clips and hairpins across the sill. Then she began scooping up loose handfuls of Jessica's hair. The clips pinched as they were pushed into place but the stroke of the woman's hands was mesmerising. It made Jessica drowsy.

At one point, Jessica's dad popped his head round the door. 'I think Mr Peter would be less nervous if you were to hold him.'

'He's just fine,' the woman said. When Jessica's dad retreated, she said, 'Now tell me. Who do you take after?'

'I look like my dad.' *Obviously*, Jessica wanted to add.

'You have his colouring.' The woman cocked her head to one side. 'What does your mother look like?'

'All done.' They both ignored Jessica's dad as he reappeared in the doorway.

'Dad calls Mum his little brown robin.'

The woman turned to smile at Jessica's dad. 'How sweet.'

He wasn't looking pleased, and Jessica felt disloyal. A brown robin sounded plain. 'My mum's pretty. She has dark brown hair and blue eyes.'

'She sounds lovely.'

'And she has big boobs.'

'Jessica.' Her father marched into the room. 'That's inappropriate.'

But the woman was laughing. Her hands settled lightly on Jessica's shoulders. 'Now. Don't tell me that's not beautiful?'

'Oh.' Jessica studied the better, older version of herself in the mirror. The woman had worked some sort of magic.

'Look at those eyes.' The woman's face joined her reflection. 'How much they already know, even though you hide them behind all that hair.'

Jessica stood up, holding her neck and head stiff for fear of dislodging the hairgrips.

'No, no,' the woman laughed. 'Always walk like you're trying to shake your hair loose.'

Neither of them spoke as they walked back to the car. By the time they reached the high street, a few drops of rain had started to fall. With a sudden roar, it fell hard. They sheltered in the nearest shop, laughing as they brushed water from their hair.

'We don't have any umbrellas.' A middle-aged man behind the counter pointed at a poster with the charity shop's logo. 'People only ever donate broken ones.'

'In that case, we'd better buy coats, hadn't we, Jessica?'

The shop assistant pointed to a rail listing against the wall, one castor missing. Jessica wrinkled her nose. The shop smelled like dried-up sick.

Her dad was grinning with sudden mischief. 'You choose mine and I'll choose yours.'

So Jessica picked up a thick tweed jacket with green velvet lapels and matching elbow patches. Her dad hooked his thumbs through his trouser pockets and puffed out his chest as he tried it on. 'Quite the country squire, don't you think?'

For Jessica, he chose a white plastic mac with large navy buttons. It was too big and squeaked as she moved. When her dad turned up the collar and tied the belt around her waist, she was again struck by her reflection. The rain had flattened her hair but her better self was still visible.

She wished Thomas could see her now. Arms linked, Jessica and her dad marched down the empty street with the rain washing down. All the way home, she imagined Thomas catching sight of her and being struck by her new-found beauty.

At home, her mother watched without expression as they showed off their new coats.

'Best four pounds I've ever spent.' Jessica's dad held out his sleeve for her mum to feel the material. 'Though it smells like someone died in it.'

68

It was only later, when Jessica was sneaking Hannah's drawer open, that she realised she had left the TRUE LOVE brooch on the windowsill beneath the dreamcatcher.

Weeks later, her mother finally took the coat to be dry-cleaned. Her dad had worn it in the meantime, its mustiness gradually overridden by soap and aftershave. Her mother, always practical, must have checked the pockets before she handed it in because she found a note. A shopping list in a stranger's handwriting, signed with a flourish of small x's.

9

There was shouting. The slam of the front door. Regular night-time sounds that washed over Jessica until an odd hacking noise in the garden shook her from the edge of a dream. Her first thought was Thomas. Tearing back the curtains, she discovered a figure in the darkness, swinging its arms through the air. The wind scraped back the cloud and the thing in its hands caught an edge of moonlight. An axe. Her father's hands.

Jessica dropped to the floor, afraid of being seen. Poked Hannah in the back.

'Why's Dad chopping down Mum's pear tree?'

Her sister only grunted, refusing to be roused from her sleep. Concealed by the curtains, Jessica watched. She'd seen him chopping wood plenty of times – the precise way he'd line up a log followed by an economic sweep of the blade that neatly spliced the wood. This was different. Through the patchy darkness, she could see how wildly he was swinging the blade. The impact bounced the axe off at dangerous and unpredictable angles, making him stagger backwards as if struck. Before he regained his balance, he would rush at the tree again.

'Bloody hell.' Hannah was kneeling on the bed, swaying slightly as she leaned forward to peer out of the window. 'Dad's lost the plot.'

'What's wrong with him?'

'Mum's driving him mad. Something about a note she found.'

They watched him strike the tree so hard the axe was wrenched from his hand, held fast in the bark. Hannah flopped back onto her mattress and wrapped her covers around herself again. 'Hope he doesn't come after us next, like some loony axe-murderer.'

'Very funny.' Jessica could hear his grunt of effort with every hack, growing louder until he was growling. She'd never seen this blind, unthinking fury before.

Light spilled into the garden as her mother darted out in a dressing gown; a fluttering moth that hovered soundlessly before disappearing back into the house, taking the light with her. Jessica's heart was thudding so hard she could feel it through her whole body like the shivering blows to the tree.

He began kicking at the trunk between blows, and it was starting to list and crack. Jessica couldn't bear to see it fall. Getting back into bed, she pulled her covers up and squeezed her eyes shut.

When it fell, it did so quietly. A slow, sad creak of wood followed by the sound of branches brushing the earth as if to catch its fall.

Silence. Then the front door opening and footsteps

stamping up the stairs, along the corridor. Marching past her parents' room. Jessica gave a small shriek as the door flew open. Her dad stood in the doorway – hair flopping in his face, breathing hard, the axe dangling from his hand.

'You chopped Mum's tree down.' Her voice was muffled by the covers. It was as if he hadn't heard her because he didn't move. The sound of his panting filled the room. Then he dropped onto the edge of her bed.

'Do you know where . . .' Catching his breath, trying to whisper. 'Where feelings come from, Jessie-rabbit?'

She didn't want a lesson. She wanted him to go away and return when he'd brushed his hair and put the axe away and explained in his normal, calm voice the perfectly logical reason for hacking down her mother's favourite pear tree in the middle of the night.

'Come on. Think about it.'

'Your head,' she ventured because the heart was too obvious. Her covers were suddenly whipped away as her father snatched at them. She scrambled upright, hugging her ankles.

'Wrong. Emotion comes from the deep cavities inside your body. Spaces you can't control or deny any more than you could ignore a heart attack.' Fury was making his hand shake as he wagged a finger, and yet he wasn't fully present. The anger wasn't for her.

'You can't help what you feel. None of us can. Keeping it in only makes you sick.'

It made sense. The things he said always did. Her mother had changed. Never smiling or singing any

72

more, her face sagging and white. 'It's making Mum sick, isn't it?'

He looked shocked and didn't answer. She could tell she'd surprised him. Sometimes he forgot she wasn't a small child any more.

'Perhaps we are all sick.' With a long, deflating sigh, his spine bowed. He wiped a sleeve across his brow and combed fingers through his hair. The axe in his hand seemed to surprise him; he laid it carefully on the floor behind her bed. When he looked at her this time, it was the father she knew; as if he had woken from sleep-walking and found himself in her room.

'I'm so sorry,' he muttered, and his remorse was more alien and alarming than his frenzied attack on the tree. 'I must have scared you.'

Jessica climbed across the covers and hugged his arm, leaning her face on his shoulder. He smelled of sweat and the pub – tobacco and beer – but he was normal again.

'You're a good girl.' He patted her knee. 'My favourite since the day you were born.'

Jessica glanced at Hannah's lumpish frame. Her sister was making a purring sound that meant she'd been sipping at the little bottle under her mattress. What had started as a bit of fun – Hannah helping herself to the wine and liqueurs guests often gave Birdie, tipping their contents into an empty Jim Beam bottle – was becoming a nightly thing. *My bedtime tipple*, she'd say in Grannie Mim's wobbly voice, and laugh and laugh.

'You can't have favourites, Dad.'

'It's the truth.'

He rose to his feet like an ancient man, staring at the floor. 'Everyone has secrets, even those closest to you.' He was about to walk away when he turned and pressed his lips to her forehead. His stubble prickled her skin but she didn't want to make him more sad by shaking him off. 'It's facing your own secrets that takes the greatest courage. Remember that, Jessica.'

After he left, Jessica dug her hands deep into her stomach, trying to locate the black spaces where sorrow and anger were massing. She didn't want to think about her mother or her father or Hannah.

She decided the next time Thomas came by at night and threw pebbles at her window – as he had started to do – she would climb out of the bedroom window and kiss him. That was what the black spaces in her body wanted.

The next day, her dad went to a vet's conference. So her mother said.

Only he didn't come back.

$\backsim$ 10 $\backsim$

April 2012, London

Alone in the bedroom, Jessica is thinking about a story Jacques once told her.

He and Greg Lamensky had been buddies since school. They'd drunk themselves sick on Mrs Lamensky's home-brewed hooch; competed over girls – once with fists – and slit their thumbs on the triangular mouth of a beer can to become blood brothers. One drunken night while Greg was collecting takeaway pizzas, Jacques had kissed a girl called Nancy who'd been hanging around his friend recently. He didn't mention it, assuming Greg would move on to the next one soon enough. Instead, his friend announced their engagement. Jacques confessed to the kiss, knowing how badly Greg might take it. They never spoke again. He regretted that empty kiss but not his honesty.

It was this story, Jessica thinks, that had brought Jacques into full focus; as if she'd rubbed her eyes and seen him clearly for the first time. He was, quite simply, a good person.

She smooths her thumbs across the creased, red leather of the notebook she found in the sea-dragon box. She hasn't started reading it yet – resisting it has become a test of self-control, like unwrapping a Mars Bar and putting it back in the cupboard uneaten, her mouth watering.

Jessica flicks through the pages. The notebook belonged to a woman called Albertine Callum, a counsellor at Thomas's school. She remembers the name. Bertie, Thomas used to call her, saying she was a friend. Jessica remembers also the mute, clogged feeling in her throat every time he'd been to see the woman. It is only now, with the discovery of the notebook, that she realises the full extent of their contact. Bertie had been counselling Thomas; the transcripts of those sessions were contained in the book she now hugged to her chest.

Pages and pages full of Thomas.

Jacques calls her from the kitchen. 'I'm making eggs, hon. You want some?'

She'd love nothing better than to join him, slipping her arms about his waist as he scrambles eggs in the pan. Only she can't stop thinking about the night before, which is why she's sitting alone in their bedroom, trying to clear her head.

'I'll grab something on the way to work.'

Libby had insisted on a cinema trip to the Odeon in Holloway Road. She'd booked tickets and, once they arrived, engineered the seating: Libby and Jacques in the middle, flanked on either side by Matthew and Jessica. Then the permissive darkness fell as the lights dimmed, full of surreptitious movement – popcorn-eating, shifting in the seats, reaching for a drink. All those little actions occurring just out of sight. Was there a brush of hands, the contact of a straying knee? Jessica's fingers whiten against the notebook.

Something about Libby and Jacques makes her uncomfortable. Put them in a room together and the texture of the air changes. He persists in warning Jessica about getting too close to Libby, and yet the two of them have fallen into unexpected ease in each other's company. The discrepancy unsettles her.

This is Jacques, she keeps telling herself. The man who gave up his best friend rather than live with a small dishonesty.

She has seen the damage a suspicious, questioning nature can inflict on a relationship – it drove her father out of his own home. She will not emulate her mother's behaviour. She will never question.

Hearing footsteps in the corridor, she slips the note-book under her pillow.

'How about a bagel then?' Jacques asks. 'You're wasting away on that coffee diet.' He smiles at her in the mirror as he chooses a tie. 'I'm not leaving until I get proof that you do, in fact, eat these days.'

'Not sure I have time to eat. Someone's got to sort you out.' Jessica pretends to straighten his perfectly knotted tie, brushes invisible scurf from his shoulders and runs a hand through his hair. It's their little joke because he's always pristine and she's like a cat brushed backwards.

Once he's gone, she throws her share of scrambled egg in the bin. He left looking happy, she thinks. As a reward for keeping her faithless nature to herself, she'll start reading Bertie's notes.

The shops haven't opened yet as she catches the tube at Oxford Circus. She finds a seat with no obvious stains, which gives a warm sag as she sits down. The carriage is empty except for two women in identical blue tunics with brass name-tags. Their conversation winds a soft thread around the metal squeal of the track. The rocking carriage makes her sleepy. When her stop arrives, she's reluctant to get up. Perhaps she's a little afraid of the book's contents.

William Mansion's is a ten-minute walk from Green Park. Its black fascia and gold lettering stand out like an ink blot in the pastel row of shop fronts. Four years, she has worked here but every time she pulls back the iron grille and steps into the jeweller's warm, cluttered interior she experiences the same thrill of discovery. There's a good hour before she needs to crack open the shutters and run a duster over the glass counters. Jessica lingers by the confectionery display of necklaces and chandelier earrings until the greater temptation of Bertie's notebook pulls her away.

A warren of stale rooms and corridors runs behind the front of the shop. Jessica takes the narrow, un-carpeted stairs to the staffroom on the top floor – a great, musty hug of a room with mismatched furniture and mouse-droppings which trail the skirting boards. It reminds her of home before the bonfire.

Sitting on the arm of a scruffy blue sofa, she calls Birdie.

Her mother sounds harried. 'Have you forgotten it's Moving Day?'

'A quick question, that's all. Do you remember a red notebook?'

'Jessica, I've got the removal men here. What are you talking about?'

'A leather book full of handwriting.'

'Be careful with them, they're precious,' Birdie calls out, then says to Jessica, 'I gave your books to the local PDSA years ago.'

'It was in my tin with the dragon painted on the lid.'

Her mother makes an *aaah* sound. 'Your little box of secrets.'

Jessica digs her nails into her palm. 'Did you put the notebook in it?'

'If that's where you found it, I must have done.'

'Where did it come from?' The line goes quiet. 'Mum?'

'I'm trying to remember, Jessica. Maybe then I can continue moving house.'

Jessica picks at a tufted hole in the sofa arm.

Then Birdie says, 'Someone put it through the letter box. There was a note with it that said *For Jessica*.'

'A note?' Jessica stops plucking the sofa threads. 'Did you keep it?'

'Of course not. It was what . . . thirteen years ago. Shortly after you ran off.'

'I left home, Birdie, as you were fully aware at the time.' But this is old ground, and the conversation bumps over and past it. 'Is there anything else you can tell me?'

'Actually there is.' Birdie sounds impressed with herself. 'The note was scribbled on the back of a leaflet for a farm shop selling Christmas turkeys. I remember thinking, Well, I won't be needing a turkey this year, now that all my girls are gone.'

Jessica lets her mother return to her packing and opens the first page.

Tape 1 transcript: 22 February 1995

School Counsellor: *Albertine Callum, Sir William Weir's Grammar School*
Pupil: *Thomas Quennell, sixteen years old, Lower Sixth*
Background: *Client referred by Form Tutor Mr Andrew Skeet for initial six-week period following history of violent disturbances on school premises. Regular detention, three class exclusions. Held back a year after failing to attend his GCSEs.*

AC: *Please take a seat, Thomas. I'm the school counsellor. My name is Albertine Callum.*

TQ: *Can I call you Albert for short?*

AC: *Miss Callum is fine.*

TQ: *Miss, not Mrs. Not married then?*

AC: *Let's get started. Now, do you understand why you have been offered these sessions?*

TQ: *Because old Skeeter wouldn't dare have me round his house again.*

AC: *Mr Skeet invited you to his house?*

TQ: *For a chat. To show me . . . what did he say? That not everyone had given up on me.*

AC: *No one has given up on you. The fact that your teacher made time for you out of school hours illustrates that, don't you think?*

TQ: *And does him putting his hand on my leg also illustrate that?*

AC: *Thomas, Mr Skeet is married with three sons of his own. Do you think it's possible you misinterpreted a friendly gesture?*

TQ: *I gave him a friendly gesture of my own.*

AC: *What was that, Thomas?*

TQ: *I held his hand. So hard I could feel the knuckles popping. Funnily enough, he didn't invite me again.*

AC: *Thomas, these are serious allegations.*

TQ: *So forget it. Who's going to believe me anyhow?*

AC: *I think we need to discuss this properly. I—*

TQ: *I this, I that. Why've you got all these little animals on your windowsill?*

AC: *They're animal totems. I collect them.*

TQ: *My grandad collected glass eyeballs. I played marbles with them. What do you do with your animal totems?*

AC: *Native Americans believe each one of us has a guiding animal spirit. Now, I'd like to explain to you the purpose of us meeting here.*

TQ: *It's just another room to put me in. Detention, headmaster's office, now this.*

AC: *You sound like you feel trapped.*

TQ: *I like this – what did you call it, totem? – the seal.*

AC: *I do too. The seal is independent, sometimes fierce, sometimes playful.*

TQ: *Where did you get it?*

AC: *Someone carved it for me.*

TQ: *A boyfriend?*

AC: *I can't discuss my personal life, Thomas.*

TQ: But you can stick your nose in mine, right?

AC: Is that how you see this?

TQ: What's that? Are you taping me?

AC: The tapes act as my notes.

TQ: Who else is going to hear them?

AC: No one.

TQ: Yeah, right. I'm not saying another word.

AC: What you're really asking is whether you can trust me.

TQ: I'm not asking anything. I'm juggling.

AC: You can trust me. Please don't throw the seal so high. It's quite delicate.

TQ: I can catch a minnow with my bare hands. I'm hardly going to drop a piece of wood.

AC: If you wouldn't mind sitting down again, there's still twenty minutes left.

TQ: Can I keep this?

AC: Let's forget for a moment why you're here. Why don't you tell me about something you like?

TQ: I like juggling.

AC: And seals. That makes for an interesting start, don't you think?

Here Thomas refuses to be seated. He stands with his back to me looking out of the window. I let him have this silence so he understands there is no pressure and that the sessions belong to him. He does not attempt to leave until I inform him the session is over. As he is walking out he says:

TQ: You are wasting your time. You can't help me.

~ II ~

Jessica closes the notebook and drops backwards onto the sofa, her legs dangling over the arm. This isn't the Thomas she knew. Angry, aggressive. He sounds so immature. As a thirteen-year-old, she'd been in awe of him. In reality they'd both been playing at adulthood.

She opens the book again and reads the counsellor's notes under the first transcript.

Firstly I am struck by how physically mature Thomas is. He's tall, well developed for his age. Self-esteem or alienation issues among a much younger peer group as a result of his resit? The academic record suggests under-average intelligence — this is not my impression. The incident regarding Mr Skeet worries me. Though I am sure nothing inappropriate occurred, it illustrates how Thomas sees the world around him as a hostile and dangerous place. This is a boy not used to being listened to.

As with many young people labelled 'troublesome', he

84

acts the part expected of him. However, halfway through the session he simply stopped talking. He couldn't be bothered to continue the posturing. Encouraging.

What concerns me is the lack of visible anger. His face was blank even as he went through the motions of testing and provoking. The rage is there as exhibited by frequent, violent encounters with peers and teachers. How deeply buried is it? Is he even fully aware of it?

He took my seal.

An entire book filled with Ms Callum's tidy, considered script – fragments of Thomas captured in time. Jessica fans through the pages, reads on. Within three sessions he had dropped his act and become the Thomas she remembered. His voice comes back to her as strongly as if he'd reached across the last seventeen years and touched her.

She looks for the last entry. It was dated 20 December 1995.

The day after he disappeared.

The day passes in a blur of distraction in which she achieves nothing. She had planned to research the make of an antique fob watch booked in for repair but instead she opens random pages of the counsellor's notes, reading snippets like surreptitious nibbles of a chocolate bar.

As soon as she gets home from work, she walks straight to her bedroom and empties the sea-dragon box on the floor. A fat, wooden seal rolls away from the whispery fall of newspaper clippings.

For you, he'd said. *I carved it myself.*

She hears his laugh – that sudden, rare sound – as she picks up the seal, pressing it to her lips. It doesn't matter. His voice has come back to her.

AC: *Do you remember your mother leaving?*

TQ: *Not really. She was hugging this vase to her chest and my dad tried to pull it out of her arms. Nathan was behind her saying,* Just give it to him, just let him have it. *But she wouldn't let go.*

AC: *Does she keep in touch with you?*

TQ: *She waited for me outside school one day.*

AC: *And what happened then? Did she speak to you?*

TQ: *She had a big present wrapped in green paper.*

AC: *What was in it?*

TQ: *Don't know. I threw a stone at her.*

AC: *You were angry and hurt that she had left you. How did she react?*

TQ: *How do you think? She didn't come back after that.*

AC: *You were just a child. A seven-year-old.*

TQ: *I shouldn't have thrown a stone at her.*

12

April 1995, Selcombe

The next time she saw Thomas it was by the sea wall in Trough. Neither of them spoke much, watching the fishing boats rock in the harbour as a muggy spring storm crept in from the sea.

He had a gash at the edge of his mouth, his bottom lip swollen. Before she could ask what happened, he'd turned away and leaped up onto the wall, daring her to follow as he ran along its narrow length.

She abandoned her plan to kiss him – it was nothing to do with his hurt lip. It just seemed like such an airy dream.

'My dad's not been home in two weeks,' Jessica said, once they'd stopped running. As she spoke, she kept her eyes on the rain clouds hanging low over the horizon.

Thomas was whittling a stick into a sharp point with his penknife. 'Where is he?'

'Don't know. Mum won't even say his name.'

She liked the way Thomas nodded, like these things

happened. He didn't say anything stupid like *He'll be back soon.* The kind of thing people said when they weren't listening or that bothered.

'What're you doing with the stick?'

He held it up to his eye, squinting along its slim length. 'I'm going to catch a rabbit for my dinner.'

'Really?' She couldn't tell if he was serious.

'Or maybe a seal.'

'How did you hurt your lip?'

His tongue flicked over the scab but he said nothing.

'Who did that to you?'

Now he turned to look at her, his face as empty as the grey sky over their heads. 'If you're going to start asking annoying questions like everyone else, I'm not going to hang out with you any more.'

'Fine. Next time I see you, I'll be wearing rabbit ears but don't you dare ask me about them.'

Thomas stared at her, then the uninjured corner of his mouth twitched. 'You're such a jellyhead, Jellybird.'

They sat there a while longer, side by side, their hips not quite touching. She shifted closer, a caterpillar inch of movement which failed to close the gap between them. He was always just out of reach. Sometimes she imagined trying to take his hand, her fingers falling through him, finding nothing but empty air.

When it started to rain, he placed a cigarette in her open palm. 'To keep you going until next time.'

Walking home, Jessica carried the promise of their next meeting as tenderly as she caged the cigarette in her fingers, deep in her cardigan pocket. She had no intention of smoking it – her head still reeling from a last drag on his B&H. She hated the taste, the finger of smoke poking into her lungs; loved the damp filter between her lips where his had touched moments before.

With her head full of Thomas, she crossed the road to the bus stop, barely registering the man on the bench inside the shelter. It was the noise he was making under his breath that caught her attention. It sounded like he was sucking tea over his tongue then breathing out in a whispered laugh.

Ha ha ha, *wet suck*, ha ha ha.

She looked round to see a filthy man with broken shoes and a stained shirt unbuttoned down to his belly. A great gold crucifix lay on his white chest. Bloody Russian. That's what everyone called him – a homeless man with horrid sores around his mouth and chin, always hanging around the schools. Out of his mind.

Disgust must have registered on her face, because it made Bloody Russian say it louder – ha ha ha – bouncing his leg in time with it.

Turning her back to him, she leaned against the metal pole of the bus stop. She couldn't run away because nutters were like dogs and reacted to fear. If you ran, they chased you. Act like nothing.

'Freckles.' He rolled the word off his tongue. 'I lick your freckles. Taste like chocolate.'

Hot panic prickled across her forehead and down her back. She wished she wasn't wearing her school uniform with its unmistakable yellow stag-head logo. Wrapping her school coat tightly around herself, she stepped out into the road.

'Watch out, you silly little girl.' A woman in a brown mac careered across the road on her bicycle. 'You nearly knocked me flying.'

Jessica lifted a hand in hasty apology as she rushed down the street. Somehow the shouting cyclist had made her feel less scared. Until that moment, it had felt like she and the homeless man were alone in the world.

Without looking back, she ran past the chippie and arcades, heading for the next bus stop.

By the time she got home, she wondered what she'd been afraid of. Her cigarette was slightly bent where she'd been holding it in her fist. She wrapped it in cling film and hid it beneath her pillow.

It was Hannah who found the cigarette a few days later.

'Mum,' she shrieked. 'Jessica's been smoking.'

Lunging at Hannah, her nails made contact with her sister's arm as she tried to take Thomas's cigarette back. Hannah ignored the scratches, unbalancing Jessica with a shove to the chest before slamming the bedroom door. She was already in the kitchen by the time Jessica had tiptoed to the landing banisters. All she could see were their feet, her sister's school shoes almost upon their mother's bare toes. From the swirly motion of her mother's skirt, it looked like she was scrubbing the casserole pot from dinner.

'Look what I found under Jessica's pillow.'

Jessica held her breath. The skirt stopped moving but her mother didn't speak.

'Aren't you going to say something to her?' Hannah asked.

Perhaps her mother shook her head, Jessica couldn't tell. The skirt started its swirling motion again and after a brief pause, Hannah walked away.

'Give it back to me.' Jessica met Hannah at the top of the stairs.

Her sister snapped the cigarette in two, grinding it between her fingers and pushed past. 'That's for losing my TRUE LOVE brooch.'

Grabbing a jumper from their bedroom, Hannah ran back down the stairs.

'Hockey practice, Mum,' she shouted on her way out, not bothering to take her kit bag. From the bedroom window, Jessica watched her sister close the garden gate, glancing back at the house before she turned right. The wrong direction for the bus stop. Right only led to the caravan park and the booze stacked in the office cupboard among old curtains and cushions.

Jessica heaved the sash window open; it stuck and squealed, scraps of paint floating down. Her sister would snore out stale wine all night long and in the morning their room would stink of it. *Can't you smell it?* Jessica wanted to scream at her mother. Some things only a grown-up could fix.

A wave of dizziness caught her. She tiptoed to the chest of drawers. Hidden beneath her swimsuit was a spiky triangle of brown glass. Easing her school tights past her thighs, she sat on the edge of the bed, bringing her left heel to her bottom. She placed the glass's smooth face against her inner thigh and slid it down, tender and cool on her skin. A lazy stroke before she turned the sharp edge on herself. She scratched the letter T into the pale flesh – tracing over it until the skin opened up like splitting stitches.

The task swallowed her up. Tears ran down her face, dripped off her chin though she couldn't have said why she was crying. She heard Thomas call her name across a great distance and pressed the glass down harder until her forehead was cold and damp. A bloody T-shape bubbled up under her fingers. She imagined swimming with Thomas in summer. He might spot the jagged scar and touch it.

'Jessica. Are you there?'

She lifted her head, the glass shard slippery in her grip. Hot pain shot from her thigh to her stomach, the way it always hit when she stopped. Black beads dotted the bed sheet beneath her thigh.

'Can you hear me?' The voice was coming from outside.

She threw the glass under her bed. Her tights dragged her raw, cut skin. There was blood on her fingers; she crouched to lick them clean before leaning out of the window.

Thomas was standing in the back garden.

'Climb down,' he called in a low voice, stepping onto the upturned apple crate he'd pushed against the side of the house. He raised his arms.

Jessica pressed her legs together; a nauseous sting in her left thigh, the damp itch of blood prickling through her tights. Sometimes the cuts were deep, the bleeding hard to stem. 'I can't tonight.'

'There's something I want you to see.'

'Tomorrow.'

'Who says there'll be a tomorrow?'

'You're such a bugger.' Jessica hid behind the open cupboard door, peeled off her tights and bunched them in a knot, using it to wipe the cuts. Just when it looked like the blood had stopped, the T would bloat up with fresh drops. She found three crumpled plasters in Hannah's washbag, patched herself up and pulled on her jeans. Climbing onto the windowsill, her back to Thomas, she slipped one leg out at a time, the toe of her trainers scraping down the wall. Hovered a moment with her hip bones balanced on the sill.

'Come on. I've got you.'

Jessica took a deep breath as though she were about to jump into a pool and slipped downwards. Thomas's hands clutched at her clothes as she fell. They stumbled backwards off the crate, which smacked against the house. Running across the garden, they scrambled over the garden wall and dropped onto the chalk path behind.

'Where are we going?' Jessica whispered as they caught their breath.

'A secret place.'

He marched off and she had to quicken her pace to keep up with him. They followed the chalk path into the forest where the warmth of the day was still trapped in the trees. The shadows were purple and rustled with unseen life. She slowed, breathing in. At night, the woods smelled like crushed leaves, like dark secrets.

'Is it far?'

Thomas didn't answer, following a route in his head. She recognised that blinkered look. She might as well not have been there. It took him four strides to notice she'd stopped walking.

'What's the matter?'

Standing there with the night painting her skin purple, prickling with secrets and he didn't even know she was there. She wanted to show him the seeping T on the inside of her thigh. *Look what I did for you.* Instead, she shrugged.

He walked towards her, tilting his head to see her more clearly. 'Have you been crying?'

'No.'

'Is it your mum? Hannah?'

His concern made her feel better. 'No. I thought I heard something in the bushes.'

Thomas pinched her side. 'Little Jellybird.'

They walked on, until the trees gave way to black, gale-flattened gorse which picked at their trouser-legs. Jessica hunched her shoulders against an open palm of wind, keeping her eyes on her misstepping feet. She wondered how much trouble she'd be in if Hannah got back before her, finding her bed empty and the window open. Birdie would tear strips off her, like the time she'd skipped school to go to the cinema and been caught by Mrs Parching.

'Here we are.' They'd reached a picket fence lined with barbed wire. Tacked to one of the posts was a sign. *Danger. Keep Out.* Thomas slid his hands under the wire to grip the wooden plank. One of the spiked metal knots caught the back of his hand. 'Put your feet where I put mine.'

He leaped over and waited on the other side.

'What about the sign?'

'To scare off trespassers.'

A few metres past the fence, the ground ended abruptly and Jessica could hear the sea thundering far below it. 'But there's nothing here.'

'Trust me.' He led her to the edge of the cliff. Below them, on a rocky lip of ground perched a small chapel, its silhouette solid black against the night sky. The only way to reach it was along a steep flight of steps carved out of the cliff. Jessica pressed both hands against the rocky face as she followed Thomas, her feet sliding on the sandy surface.

'No one comes here any more. It's my place now,' Thomas said once they stood in front of the chapel. 'They're scared it will fall into the sea and take a coach-load of tourists with it.'

There were great cracks in the walls. Part of the roof gaped open to the sky and the ground was covered in bits of broken tile and stone. 'Do you think it will?'

'One day.' Thomas spoke close to her ear. 'Maybe it'll take the two of us with it.'

'That's one way of getting out of PE, I guess.'

Instead of trying the door, he walked past the chapel towards the edge of the outcrop where the wind surged up from the sea, buffeting his body. He swayed with it, careless. If he stepped out, the sea would swallow him before she could reach the edge. Jessica moved closer until she could see the water breaking against the rocks below. Foam flecks rose and spun, making her dizzy.

'If you look at the surf for too long, it makes you forget your feet. Then you fall in. That's what happened to Julie Morgan's mum.'

'Drowning's not a bad way to go,' Thomas said. 'When I've had enough of this life, I'm going to go swimming. I'll keep going until I'm so knackered I sink to the bottom.'

He sat down, dropping his legs into empty air like he was sitting on a sofa. Jessica knelt behind him, hand out, her fingertips almost touching his jumper. Ready to catch him.

Thomas plucked at the wild grass. It came away with little showers of loose rock. 'If you're in the water for long enough, your skin becomes soapy, like you're melting.'

'You hallucinate before you die.'

'Yeah, I heard that too.' He turned his head slightly, speaking to her over his shoulder. 'One guy saw an angel coming for him through the water just before they fished him out.'

Jessica studied him. The profile curve of his lips, his wrists where his jumper came up short and the hollow drape of the material from the balls of his shoulders.

'So is this what you wanted to show me? The view?' She tried to sound unimpressed, hoping it would make him get up. It worked. She followed him round to the front of the chapel.

'Have you heard of this place?'

Jessica read the sign, its edges eaten away with sea salt. 'The Chapel of St Francis of Paola. Who's he?'

'Patron saint of souls lost at sea.'

'Looks like a bloody deathtrap.'

Thomas unpicked the loop of blue twine holding the double wooden doors together. He rocked them apart and a yawn of stagnant air reached her. He turned on the threshold and smiled. Such a rare sight that for a moment he looked like a stranger. Taking a small flashlight from his jacket, he lit up the short aisle, five pews and an altar carved from a single block of stone. She followed him inside, slipping on bird shit.

'What do you think?' Thomas leaped like a mountain goat from pew to pew, slamming down his weight so the noise hit the chapel walls. Stones trickled from the cracks in the walls. In her head she kept seeing the cliff breaking into the sea, taking the chapel with it. It made her legs ache.

'I should probably get home before Hannah rats on me.'

Thomas sat cross-legged on the altar and pointed with his torch. 'Look at the wall on your left.'

Jessica followed the torch beam. A gold and azure mosaic blazed from the filthy stone, like a square of brilliant sky through a window. 'That's St Francis as he sailed to this shore. Look at the waves. They're made of little fish pulling him along by the strands of his cloak.'

The saint looked out from the mosaic with light blue eyes, his pale hair lifting in stylised waves around his head.

'He looks like you.' Jessica moved closer, tracing her

fingertips over golden tiles. They were greasy with damp ocean air. 'It must be worth something.'

'I guess. It was hidden under a load of crap. I cleaned it with Fairy Liquid. There are three more to do.'

She pictured him here, scrubbing at the walls, the way he set his top teeth on his bottom lip when he was concentrating. Imagined him stealing a bottle of Fairy Liquid out of his house, maybe hidden under his jumper. It made her want to hug him.

'I could help, if you like, after school. I could even stay late on Thursdays because that's my mum's—'

He shook his head. 'Nah. That's OK.'

Jessica pressed her finger over the sightless orb of a fish's eye. Managed a shrug. Thomas passed behind her in the narrow space between the benches and the wall, somehow not touching her, like he was made of air.

'Look at these panels.' He ran his torch over a wooden board inscribed with names and dates, nailed high on the wall by the entrance. 'Here. Joseph Quennell, 1989. That's my grandad, and here's my uncle, Nicolas Quennell, 1990.'

'Why are their names there?' Jessica joined him in front of the wooden plaque.

He stood behind her, resting the torch on her shoulder. 'It's a list of sailors who have drowned.' The beam flicked to the top of the board where the lettering was shallow with age. 'Fishermen's families used to come here to pray for their safe return during a storm. Those who didn't make it back had their names carved here so

St Francis could find their souls in the water and guide them home.'

Jessica, only half listening, was focusing on the sliver of space caught between his body and hers, growing warm. It made her shiver with delicious nerves.

'One day my name's going to be here, too.'

'Don't say that.'

'Are you cold, Jessie?'

'A little,' she said, to explain away the shivering.

'Let's get you home then.' Thomas stepped away and the chapel's icy breath moved in to fill his vacuum.

He didn't speak the whole way home, his thoughts elsewhere. Again she suffered with the rise and fall of his interest, like the sun dipping in and out of cloud. By the time they reached her house, it was close to midnight. Thomas left her at the garden wall. 'See you.'

She watched him walk away. It never occurred to him to kiss her.

Looking up at her bedroom window, she saw it was now in darkness and her heart skipped. Hannah had arrived home before her. Inside the house, all the lights were off. Her mother was in bed. Holding her breath, she crept along the corridor.

Opening her bedroom door, she found her mother sitting on the bed. Hannah lay facing the wall, covers around her ears. She could tell from her sister's silence that she was awake.

'Hannah says he's an older boy.' Her mother patted the bed.

'I just went for a walk.' Her tongue clicked drily.

Her mother leaned over and lifted Jessica's chin, their

first physical contact in months. 'Have you started your periods yet?'

Jessica bit the insides of her cheeks, eyes straining away from her mother.

'Is that a yes or a no?'

Jessica gave a stiff little nod.

Her mother's hand moved from Jessica's chin to a strand of her hair; it felt like a draught rather than a touch. 'You're so like him.'

Hannah twitched her covers lower and Jessica wanted to shout *Yes? Can I help you?* in her sister's exposed ear.

'With that red hair and those green eyes. Your father's daughter.' Her mother got up and left the room.

Jessica sat still, looking out of the window.

'Sorry.' Hannah's voice was muffled in her duvet.

Jessica took off her shoes and lay down. 'For what?'

AC: *Pretend you are a stranger visiting your home for the first time. What's it like?*

TQ: *Like this massive shipwreck. Looters have done it over.*

AC: *In what way?*

TQ: *There's nothing left except marks on the carpet where there used to be furniture. The man sold everything that wasn't needed.*

AC: *Can you describe more of it?*

TQ: *There's no electricity. Just a wood-burner in the kitchen and the man's bedroom.*

AC: *What's the boy like who lives there?*

TQ: *Don't know.*

AC: *And the man, his dad?*

TQ: *He's in the bath because it helps his sore leg. The boy has to help him in and out of it. Sometimes he has to rub cream into his dad's leg.*

AC: *That's quite a chore for a young boy.*

TQ: *The cream makes his hands greasy. It won't come off even with soap. His dad's leg is really white with no hair because of all the scars. I hate how the skin feels.*

13

A few days after the visit to Thomas's chapel, the T-shaped cut in Jessica's thigh began to burn. Pinching the ragged edge of skin under the bathroom light, she saw pus and tried to wash it with soap, her breath catching. She went downstairs, hoping to distract herself with television.

Moments after she'd turned on *EastEnders*, her mother ghosted in and all Jessica could focus on was Birdie's suffocating silence. She put the remote down.

'I'm going to Grannie Mim's.'

She left Birdie staring out of the window, oblivious to the shouting from the television set. On her way out, she pocketed her mother's dusty turquoise studs that had been sitting, forgotten, on the bathroom sill for months.

Grannie Mim lived all year round in Seasalt Holiday Park. Her full name was Mimosa Blue and she'd once been a West End actress; everyone called her Grannie Mim, which Jessica thought was a shame. Her caravan had three bedrooms and its own name rather than a number like the other mobile homes. *Mimosa Blue*, it said in gold letters that bobbed on scrolling waves.

Last spring Jessica's dad had planted young apple trees in a row, separating Grannie Mim's caravan from the rest of the park. *Because you're more than just a guest,* he'd told her. It was probably also to hide the clutter of boxes and furniture stacked outside. That evening, a dressmaker's dummy stood guard at the bottom of the porch steps, and Jessica had to walk sideways through the open door to get past stacks of shiny books with Elvis on the cover. Compared to her own house, it was like climbing into a toy box and rummaging for treasure.

Despite the warmth of the spring evening, Mimosa was sitting alone by the electric fire, smothered in shawls, a faded pink towel tucked around her lap. If someone unwrapped her, she'd probably be nothing more than a stick figure.

'A smiling Jessica. What a pretty sight.' Grannie Mim squeezed her hand. 'There's carrot soup on the stove, sweetness.'

'Where shall I put these?' Jessica held out the earrings.

'How lovely, dear.' Grannie Mim took the studs and put them in her skirt pocket. 'I'll find a good home for them.'

'What do you do with all the stuff you can't sell?' Jessica looked around at Mimosa's cluttered room, full of people's unwanted chairs, books and vases.

'There's a special place for everything. Same with

people.' And she smiled in a way that made Jessica think she'd missed something. 'I have something for you as well.'

From the same skirt pocket Mimosa took out five gilt horse-head buttons. 'I seem to remember you love horses.'

Jessica actually found horses quite sinister, but didn't say so. The buttons were heavy and clicked like dice in her hands. She sat down in the only place that wasn't growing a bric-a-brac stalagmite, a deep bucket of a chair which forced Jessica constantly to shift position, like a cat settling.

'How's your poor mum coping?' Mimosa was the only person who didn't pretend everything was fine.

'Fine.'

'Is she taking care of you girls?'

'We don't need looking after.' Jessica slung her legs over the armrest. The gash on her thigh felt like a hard, burning stone when she pressed her legs together.

An apple-blossom breeze was blowing in from the open front door. Grannie Mim only closed it during rain or snow. Jessica shuddered. 'Don't you get scared here? All by yourself?'

'I'm never by myself.' She winked at Jessica. 'People are always dropping in.'

'But at night? When you're in bed?'

'Of course not.' Mim's face was suddenly serious. 'There's nothing to be afraid of.'

She said it with the kind of emphasis adults use when speaking to five-year-olds. It made Jessica bristle. 'I am *not* afraid.'

'If anyone was going to see off a burglar, it would be your mum. Your dad, on the other hand, would probably have cowered under the bed.'

Jessica was about to jump to her dad's defence when it occurred to her that it was a trap. If she stood up for him, Mimosa would use it as an excuse to talk badly about him.

She shifted in the chair, aware again of the dull ache in her thigh.

'Hannah needs something for a cut. She got it when she was playing hockey.'

'Has she cleaned it?'

'I guess.'

'Bit of vinegar in water will stop it going bad.'

'It's already infected.'

Grannie Mim got up. It always surprised Jessica how easily she moved when the blankets came off. She wrapped the towel around her shoulders, poking through little tubs and jars on the windowsill.

'It's boiling in here, Grannie Mim.'

'Old people are always freezing to death,' she announced cheerfully, and handed Jessica a plastic pot with a missing lid, the label worn off. Jessica poked the greyish ointment with her little finger. It smelled like boot polish.

'It'll sting like the devil, but you youngsters can cope.'

She put it in her coat pocket. 'Hannah's pretty tough.'

'I must show you something I found the other day.' Grannie Mim disappeared into a bedroom and came back with a bundle of photographs. She held out a black and white print to Jessica. 'Me and Leonard on our wedding day.'

A young woman danced with a man in army uniform. Her black hair lay in styled waves across her forehead. Mimosa Blue smiled into her husband's face like she was looking through an open door and getting ready to step in. Jessica's mother used to look at her dad in the same way. She handed the photograph back. 'You were very pretty.'

Grannie Mim leaned forward to pat her knee. 'He wasn't my first, you know.'

Jessica's cheeks reddened. 'I guess you had lots of admirers.'

'On my wedding night I took a pin when Len was asleep and pricked my thumb so there'd be blood on the sheet. But it was such a tiny drop I had to keep going. My poor fingers.' She threw her hands in the air and laughed. 'There must be a better way, really there must.'

Jessica knew there was supposed to be blood the first time but she'd never heard of people stabbing their fingers with a pin before. Grannie Mim talked to her like she knew grown-up things; she wouldn't spoil it with a silly question. She went through the sheaf of pictures as Grannie Mim pointed over her shoulder, making comments.

'Now Lionel, there was a brilliant trumpeter. You'd have thought such talented lips could kiss a gal to sweet Friday but oh, no. And that's Franny, my cousin. Never married. Eyes only for my Leonard, though she never said.' The woman was sitting on a park bench with her ankles crossed.

'They look like movie stars,' Jessica said. She couldn't imagine her mother going about her daily jobs in a tight fitted skirt and matching jacket that gave her a waist like a Barbie doll.

'People dressed smart in those days.' Grannie Mim sat down and re-rugged herself while Jessica helped herself to a mug of soup from the pot on the stove. She felt warm and sleepy as if she could drift away and Mimosa would watch over her. She could see the sun setting, the sky like wet paper soaking up watercolours.

'Who's your best boy?'

Jessica hesitated. No one knew about Thomas and their night-time walks.

'I have a friend.' She searched for the right words to describe Thomas. 'Not really a boyfriend.'

'Of course not, sweetie. You're only thirteen.'

'Thirteen isn't how you remember it.' Jessica lifted her chin but Grannie Mim didn't smirk to herself the way grown-ups did when they thought they knew better.

Instead she said, 'Thirteen is a beautiful age. You can still dream about what's coming next.'

'My mother spends so much time dreaming she's forgotten how to talk.' Jessica was annoyed the conversation had moved away from Thomas. 'What's so good about dreaming?'

Grannie Mim sighed. 'No, I don't suppose you are a dreamer, peppermint. Not like your sister Lisa.'

'Lisa? She's working in a pub so she can save up and

leave home. Mum thinks she's having piano lessons. Not that she ever asks.'

'I hope it's not that boy giving her silly ideas.'

'What boy?'

'The one that's been hanging around your house after dark. I see him most nights cutting through the park, thinking no one sees him.'

A fish flipped in Jessica's stomach. Scared to give herself away, she asked again, 'What boy?'

'Finn Quennell's son. Looks just like his father. Handsome on the outside, empty inside. Like waxed fruit.'

Jessica jumped up. 'You've never even met him.' Her voice hissed out like fat spitting in a frying pan; it surprised them both.

Grannie Mim's eyebrows lifted. 'A boy like that preys on vulnerable girls.'

Jessica couldn't look at her. With her fist, she scrubbed at the spilled soup running down her leg.

'I've heard things about him, sweetie. You don't know—'

Still looking down, her voice quiet, Jessica said, 'I do know. He *told* me what people say behind his back.' And then the words came out in a rush. 'It's because of the disability benefit his dad gets from the council. Someone painted *Fucking Faker* on the wall of their barn but his dad can't even walk to the toilet by the end of the day. Thomas says he growls like an animal with the pain.'

'I'm not saying the boy's having an easy time of it.'

'You can't always believe what people say, Grannie Mim. You have to ask yourself *why* they're saying it.'

'That's exactly what I'm saying, Jessie.' Mimosa's voice pointed like a finger.

Jessica's throat started to burn. She ran tap water over her soup mug, her hands blurring through furious tears. She'd been wrong. Grannie Mim would never have understood about her and Thomas. Something happened to people when they got old; they started seeing everything through dirty windows.

'It's not Lisa, is it?' Grannie Mim said at the door. 'She's not the one I need to worry about after all.'

Jessica turned away; the rudeness of putting her back to Grannie Mim was both thrilling and awful. Her feet seemed to catch all the bumps in the grass as she walked away. The horse-head buttons fell through her fingers like a trail of Hansel and Gretel crumbs.

14

May 2012, London

*I*s designer Jessica Byrne having a laugh at our (quite
substantial) expense? Someone a little less generous than
myself might call her the practical joker of the jewellery
industry. Next time I feel a bit strapped for cash, I shall be
scrabbling about in my neighbour's bin (they have children
– a useful source of garish junk) for precious materials,
cobbling the whole lot together with superglue and calling it
a necklace. For my efforts (and dry-cleaning bill) I shall
make sure to stick a hefty price-tag on it.

Jessica drops the magazine onto her lap. No matter
how many times she reads the damning review, the
words keep their abrasive rub. She'd shown Jacques
before he left for work.

Rise above it, honey, he'd said. *You and I both know
better.*

A car horn blares in the street. Rolling the magazine
into a tight scroll, she shoves it into the side pocket of
Jacques' canvas sailing bag.

Before she leaves the flat, she writes a message on the kitchen blackboard.

Pear Tree Cottage, Bantham, TY45 2ZH. Remember – no landline, little mobile reception but it's only for three days. Good luck in Moscow xx

Libby's white-and-chrome Mini is parked on a double yellow line. 'Get in,' she shouts from the driver's seat. 'The weekend's ticking away.'

It's a full ten minutes before someone lets them out of John Prince's Street into the Friday-night traffic clogging up Cavendish Square. Water hisses beneath car wheels, the traffic like a slow trudge of debris sluicing down a great drain.

'I love this wet, filthy city,' Jessica says.

'You poor, deprived being.' Libby wrinkles her nose. 'Wait until you see Pear Tree Cottage.'

Jessica settles back and watches the city go by. The late-night delis, kebab shops and flats above are lit up – naked in the darkness – and Jessica peeks in, greedy for snapshots of other people's lives; like a child poking its fingers into sweetie jars.

'Mum and I bought the place a few months ago,' Libby's saying. 'She was going to drop by and meet you, but a friend's invited her to Prague for the weekend instead.'

'She sounds very independent.' It occurs to Jessica that Libby rarely mentions her mother.

'A bit like your mum, I'm guessing.' Libby is applying lipstick in the rear-view mirror. 'Do you think she'll marry again one day?'

Jessica pictures the gardener's coat lying across the banister. 'Who knows?'

'And your dad?'

'He's not around.' Jessica pulls her jacket tightly about herself.

'And yet, you start a lot of sentences with *My dad always says.*'

'I never mention him. You're nosing for dirt.' Jessica smiles to lighten her words but Libby's as hard and shiny as a silver globe. Words slip off her.

The traffic thins as they reach the four-storey, wedding-cake houses of Brook Green. The windows have patterned blinds to block out the surrounding red brick of Earl's Court. There's no one on the streets, nothing to see. Jessica closes her eyes.

It's the silence that wakes her. She's alone in the car, parked outside a blue timber house with large windows which are lighting up one by one as a figure moves through the rooms. Opening the car door, Jessica smells seaweed. She can't see the water through the wild rose bushes flanking the cottage but she hears it as soon as she steps out. Her heart sinks. Libby's holiday home sits directly on the ocean. With its endless memories of Thomas; the ocean, which finally claimed him.

From the doorway, Libby beckons her. 'Time for the tour.'

It isn't what she expected; all sanded wood and angled windows, so new it still smells of sawdust. Upstairs, all three bedrooms face the water. Libby flings back the curtains, saying, 'Can you imagine a more heavenly place?'

Jessica nods because how can she explain that she prefers the sound of rainwater washing through London gutters to the endless surge of surf?

Downstairs, the sitting room's floor-to-ceiling windows overlook a small garden with a globe-shaped fountain and an apple tree hanging over the low fence. A gate leads straight onto a narrow ledge of pebbled beach. Jessica sits down in a saffron-yellow armchair facing the empty wood-burner while Libby slides open the glass doors. The room floods with salty air and gull cries.

'I love your mantelpiece,' Jessica says. A single length of driftwood, long and sensual as a dancer's arm, sits above the wood-burner. Framed pictures of Libby – a single one of her and Matthew – balance along its length. One of the frames has scrolling flowers with petals of rough glass set into the pewter. It resembles an overambitious GCSE project. Frowning, Jessica picks it up.

'This is one of mine. When I was still experimenting.'

Still gazing out at the sea, Libby says, 'Told you I was a fan.'

They eat bacon omelettes and share a bottle of tanniny red in front of the wood-burner, now blasting out a sunburning heat. After the meal, Jessica curls up in the armchair feeling warm and sleepy until the review in *The Jeweller's Design* comes back to her.

'I need to show you something, Libs.' Jessica grabs her rucksack and rummages through it, looking for the magazine. A frown like a pulled thread tightens Libby's brow as she reads.

'The *outrage* of it,' Libby cries, throwing the magazine onto the floor. 'I'm going to call that woman, as one of your many delighted customers, and give her a piece of my mind.'

The vehemence in her friend's voice makes Jessica smile. 'But in a way, she's right. I do take junk and make it into jewellery.'

'What you do,' Libby is shaking her finger at Jessica, 'is far beyond the intellectual grasp of that witch. You told me how each chip of plastic or stone has its own place and meaning within the greater piece. Like the notes of a song, isn't that what you said?'

'Thank you,' Jessica says, and squeezes Libby's hand. 'You're the first person to make me feel better about this.'

'Pure spite or pig ignorance, I can't decide which.' Libby refuses to sit down as Jessica tugs at her arm. 'What did Jacques say?'

'He dismissed it. Said he believes in me, no matter what anyone else says.'

'Typical man-comment.' Libby pulls a wry face. 'Does *he* even get it?'

But you understand, Jessica thinks, and decides she will make Libby a gift; something fabulous, a pair of chandelier earrings, perhaps, or a stack of linking bracelets.

*

'You haven't told me how you and Jacques met.'

Jessica shifts in the yellow armchair where she's been drifting off.

Libby looks far from sleepy, her eyes bright, cheeks red. 'You were very young, weren't you?'

Jessica stretches for the last of her wine, wondering how Libby would know this. 'I was seventeen, and working in a café called the Tea Chest in Bridge.'

'Bridge?' Libby nods. 'Further up the coast. Studenty town?'

'It has a big architectural school. Jacques was an overseas student there.'

Libby winks at her. 'Some of the girls at my school used to travel up there on a Friday night hoping to hook up with a rich student type.'

'Couldn't have been further from my mind.' Jessica rolls her eyes. 'I just wanted to escape.'

'You didn't run very far.'

'I guess not. And you and Matthew?'

Her friend flaps the question away. 'Blind date. Or did I pick him up at a party? I can't remember.'

She empties the bottle into their glasses. 'I want details. Don't tell me Jacques chatted you up over a pastrami sandwich?'

'Something like that.'

Libby sighs. 'You, my dear, need to loosen up.'

She leaves the room, returning with a second bottle of wine and a hairbrush enamelled with ivory swans.

'My mum used to brush my hair whenever I needed a bit of TLC.' She makes Jessica sit on the floor in front of her, adding, 'Don't argue.'

She opens the new bottle, filling their glasses. Then she begins to sweep the brush through Jessica's hair until it falls back from her face like a river.

'I knew this boy once,' Jessica says. 'He was very beautiful, though no one else seemed to notice. His name was Thomas Quennell.'

Libby's hand follows the brush, stroking back from Jessica's forehead along the stream of her hair. Brush, stroke, brush, stroke. Jessica hears her own voice from far away as if someone else is telling her story. The wine has wrapped her in cotton wool.

'I haven't said his name in years.'

'What was he like?'

'When I first saw him on the beach, I thought he was the ghost of a local boy who'd gone missing years ago.'

The brush stops for a moment. 'You fell in love with a ghost.'

'He had strange eyes. Very pale, like the colour of water.'

The brushstrokes are very light now; she can tell Libby's listening intently.

'What happened with this ghost boy?'

Jessica goes quiet. She wants to tell Libby but it has sat like a stone in her mouth all these years; she's learned to talk, even laugh, around it but it won't be so easily spat out. 'We went our separate ways. Who was your first love?'

'Craig Doyle. He ate a lot of tuna fish, which was unfortunate when it came to kissing.'

'What happened to Craig?'

'I got my first period.' Libby laughs softly through

her nose. 'And realised he was just a spotty little twit. Tell me more about the beautiful Thomas.'

Jessica sits away from the brush. Awake now, full of sudden energy. She reaches for her rucksack again, her horizon tilting with red wine as she moves. Libby sees her unsteady movement and laughs, topping up their glasses.

'This is between you and me.' Jessica fishes out the red notebook.

'I'm good at secrets,' Libby says, and Jessica thinks, *Yes, I bet you are.*

She explains about the notebook but before she hands it over, she shows Libby a photograph from the sea-dragon box. 'That's Thomas. The one to my left.'

'He's got that typical teenage-boy look, all bones and angles. But beautiful, I can see that.' Then Libby snaps the photo from Jessica's fingers. 'Who's the tall guy with the dodgy Bros hairdo on your right?'

'Thomas's big brother, Nathan.'

'I know him from somewhere.' Libby looks to Jessica, who can only shrug. 'It'll come to me. Now, hand over the notebook.'

She takes her time leafing through it. 'He sounds . . . challenging. Is that the word?'

'If you read it carefully, you'll understand why. There are things even I didn't know, and I was his best friend.'

'What happened to him?'

Jessica can feel the rough surface of the sea behind her. 'He took his brother's Cornish crabber out and never came back.'

Libby covers her mouth with her hand. 'How awful.'

'They never found his body.' Jessica sighs. Looking up, she catches a glitter of tears in her friend's eyes. 'Bits of the boat washed up on the beach all winter. I was terrified of finding . . . something but I couldn't stay away.'

Libby grips her fingers but Jessica has no feeling in her body, her hand a piece of surplus matter.

'When the local papers lost interest, it was as though he'd never existed.'

'Poor you.' Libby squeezes harder. 'And poor Jacques.'

'Jacques?'

'You're still in love with a ghost after all.'

Jessica gets up, walks over to the open French doors. 'I can't bear to be near the water any more.'

In the darkness, the sea's surface rolls and bulges without breaking, like something is moving beneath it. Jessica shudders.

'Let's go outside,' Libby whispers by her ear. 'I'll go grab some jumpers.'

Jessica doesn't wait. She steps barefoot into grass wet with evening dew. Something pulps through her toes; a rotten apple. With a cry of disgust, she flings it over the fence onto the beach.

Hearing Libby behind her, she unlatches the gate and strides down to the water's edge, standing so close to the surf that it laps over her feet; the cold brings an instant, shocking pain. Picking up a handful of stones, she flings them at the sea, scrabbles up another load, throwing harder. Trying to split open the surface.

Something flies over her head. With a heavy gulp, it

disappears into the water. Jessica looks round to see Libby picking apples off the ground.

'Take that, evil, watery beast.' She lobs an apple like a grenade at the sea. 'Take that, monstrous sea.'

Jessica stares at her. 'What are you doing?'

'You want some more?' Libby shouts at the water, giggling as she catches Jessica's eye. She crouches down, gathering up an armful of small green apples. They tumble over her as she lifts her arms, trying to launch them simultaneously.

Despite herself, Jessica starts to laugh, joining in.

The two of them fighting the sea with rotten fruit, laughing so hard it makes them cry.

Jessica lies in a bath, her feet and fingers burning as the blood throbs through them. Libby has her back against the tub, flicking through a magazine. They pass a bottle of port between them.

'So you've told me about Thomas,' Libby says. 'Now I want to know about Jacques.'

Jessica lifts her head from the bath rim. 'I've already told you how we met.'

Libby flaps her hand over her shoulder. 'I'm not interested in the building blocks. Anyone can see them. I want to see the cement, the stuff that keeps you guys together.'

Jessica takes a long, slow drink of port, its sweetness catching in the back of her throat. 'I guess it's the same thing that holds most people together.'

'That's where you're wrong.' Libby plants herself on the edge of the tub.

Jessica pulls her legs into her chest. 'Pass me a towel, would you?'

Libby ignores her. 'When I was a little girl the thing that used to drive me crazy was watching people, heads together, in conversation that excluded me.'

She stops talking, waiting for a comment but all Jessica can think about is how exposed she feels, even with Libby staring through the window at the blackened sky. Having a bath with another person in the room – other than Jacques – had felt daring, like she was opening herself up to the intimacies of a friendship she'd never had before. Now she feels like a moth in a museum display with a pin through its body.

Oblivious, Libby carries on. 'Sometimes I'd lie in bed thinking about all those shared confidences, the secret interactions that I would never be party to, and it made me feel physically sick.'

Jessica gets out of the bath so quickly that she skids on the polished tiles as she lunges for the towel on the heated rail. Red-faced, she turns away from Libby and dries herself. She attempts to drape the towel over her back as she struggles damp feet through the twisted material of her knickers.

'I see the two of you in your little loved-up nest, and I want to scratch the surface and see what's going on. In fact, I want what you have.'

The towel starts to slip and Jessica gives up, shrugging it off. Pulls on her clean T-shirt and Jacques' cotton shorts and turns back to her friend.

'I guess you could say I'm greedy,' Libby is saying,

tapping her chin with one shiny, pink nail, still blank-eyeing the window.

Jessica puts her head to one side. 'I have no idea what you're talking about, but it's bedtime for me.'

'And me.' Libby gets up. 'Good God, is that really what you wear in bed?'

'I suppose you wear some kind of silk negligee with matching eye-mask?'

'You've been through my drawers.'

As they laugh, Jessica feels silly and prudish for her earlier discomfort.

Once inside her bedroom, Jessica doesn't bother with the light, bumping her way around the unfamiliar space to draw the blinds before crawling into bed. She is almost asleep when there's a soft patter against wood. Then Libby opens the door, light from the hall outlining her dark silhouette. She's wearing a long, high-necked nightie which Jessica is too sleepy to comment on.

'What's wrong?'

Her friend crosses the floor and jumps onto the bed. 'Scoot over.'

'What are you doing?' Jessica asks and turns away, hugging her pillow. She'll never sleep now.

'When I was little,' Libby says, plumping her pillow and wriggling into a comfortable position. 'I used to pretend I had a sister just like you.'

'Weed and home-made booze.' Libby grins. 'I've just placed Nathan.'

They are walking barefoot through flat surf. An

early-morning mist is blurring the divide between water and sky.

Jessica stops walking. 'You knew Nathan?'

'Everyone did. He had the local underage market cornered. Nathan's house was the first stop on a night out. I probably snogged him at a party.'

'What a crazy coincidence.' Jessica skips a flat stone across the water, hiding her face. It rankles; her past – kept private even from Jacques – somehow being shared with Libby.

'There are no coincidences. Only universal signposts.'

At which Jessica laughs. 'God, you sound like my dad.'

The silence sags under the weight of her unguarded comment. As they walk on, Jessica gazes at the water, dredging memories like sea treasure.

'Thomas taught me how to float.'

'You grew up by the sea, and you couldn't swim?'

'Of course I could swim. And float. It was just something I told him so that . . .'

'I see.' Libby looks delighted, linking her arm through Jessica's. 'Womanly wiles at such a tender age.'

Jessica smiles, looks away with her memory.

His fingers curling into her armpits as she kicked her feet off the sea bed. *Look up at the sky.* Moving a hand to cradle her head as she leaned further back, the water creeping over her ears. Shingle scratching in the current, the crunch of Thomas's feet as he moved around her, spreading out her limbs. The blissful lightness of her body.

'Do you ever get those moments of complete happiness?' she asks Libby. 'Over the most ordinary things?'

'Oh, I'm too superficial for that.' Libby squeezes Jessica's arm. 'Though this isn't bad. As moments go.'

They follow the shoreline towards Pear Tree Cottage.

'There's a man in your garden.' As Jessica says it, her stomach is flipping over, her heart vaulting behind her ribs. Something about the man's posture and his hair in the sun. Jessica starts to run.

'Why, look who it is!' Libby catches up at the gate and pushes past, arms open. 'Jacques, darling.'

Jacques returns Libby's hug with a fatherly pat, his eyes on Jessica, who is still standing on the other side of the fence.

'What are you doing here?'

Libby is laughing, an arm draped over his shoulders. 'Your Moscow trip was a ruse to catch us up to no good.'

'Honey?' Jacques disengages himself and walks towards her. 'You look angry.'

'No, no. Confused. I mean, surprised.'

'The flights were all messed up, so the meeting's been postponed. I jumped in the car. On impulse.' He looks away, rubbing the side of his nose with his thumb. A gesture, she realises with shock, he uses when he's uncomfortable.

'I thought it would be a nice surprise.'

'It is, Jacques.'

In the house, Libby has become violently animated. 'First, I'll cook breakfast and then I'll make your bed.'

'His bed?' Jessica removes her hand from Jacques', conscious of her slippery palms.

Libby bursts around the door frame, laughing behind her hand. 'What am I saying? I'm all thrown.'

'Show me to our room,' Jacques says into Jessica's hair as cupboard doors bang in the kitchen.

Jacques collects a sailing bag from the hallway on his way upstairs. It's not the case he uses for work trips; he has packed a new one for the weekend. It makes Jessica smile. 'Not quite impulsive enough to come away without clean t-shirts and casual trousers.'

He responds with a pinch to her bottom and closes the bedroom door, pushing her down onto the bed. She enjoys his kiss, open-mouthed and possessive until Libby's muffled singing rises from the kitchen, peeling them apart.

Jacques inspects the view from the window. Jessica joins him and they both dip their heads from the endless sea as Libby bustles into the garden below, spreading a tartan rug and laying out a pot of tea, glasses of orange juice and bagels. Smiling to herself. For a moment Jessica is tempted to slip her arms about Jacques' waist and lead him back to the double bed, leaving Libby with her picnic and her excitement.

When they go back downstairs, Libby flings her arms about Jacques again.

'I love a man who can master the art of surprise.'

I want what you have.

'I would have called,' Jacques says, spreading cream cheese on his bagel. 'But this place is kind of cut off from the rest of the world.'

'Deliberately so.' Libby bites hugely into her own bagel, adding through a full mouth, 'It's very liberating.'

'From what?' Jessica's voice is a jarring note in an otherwise flowing tune. Libby glances at her but makes no comment. Instead, she lies back on the rug, arms sprawled above her head, seemingly oblivious to the dangerous slide of material as her dress rides up and pools like a fallen parachute about her thighs. She closes her eyes in the sun.

'I'm so glad the three of us are together.'

They go to bed early, sun-tired and content. Jacques gives her a chaste cuddle and rolls away. She stares at his broad, naked back and feels inexplicably bereft. Trails her fingers down his spine until he shivers with goosebumps.

'You're not making this easy,' he murmurs.

'Why shouldn't we?'

'Your friend is probably still awake on the other side of the wall.'

Within minutes, he is asleep. Jessica's eyes keep pinging open. Throughout the day, she has studied Jacques and Libby: over a pub lunch, and later sipping wine in Libby's peppermint-stripe deckchairs as the sun set. Looking for what, she couldn't say. Nor did she find it. But it has left her physically uncomfortable, with an aching head and stiff neck. A Sunday-night kind of dread is swelling in her stomach though she doesn't know why.

When she finally sleeps, she dreams of Thomas.

Sitting on a fallen tree trunk, the way he was always hunched over his busy hands, feet planted wide apart, elbows on his knees. On her hands and knees, she crawls into the hollow space between his arms and legs, his chest curving over her like a roof to keep her safe. She can feel the heat of his leg through his jeans as she rests her cheek on his thigh.

She wakes to find a naked Jacques leaning his elbows on the windowsill, gazing out.

'You used to go sea-kayaking with your dad, didn't you?' Jessica clambers over the bed to wrap her arms around him. 'How's the water looking today?'

He turns, pulling her in. Over his shoulder, she catches sight of a figure on the beach by the water's edge. Libby is standing with her feet in the water wearing an emerald-green bathing suit, an old-fashioned kind that has recently become fashionable again with a cinched-in waist and corseted top. It gives her figure the glamorous curves of a 1950s starlet.

Jacques follows her gaze, craning his head over his shoulder towards the beach. 'Not what you'd call an athletic physique.'

Jessica is struck by his biting tone. Jacques, who is always so generous about everyone.

'I know you didn't come here on a whim, Jacques.'

His gaze returns to her. Sighing, he rests his head on her shoulder and for a moment, she thinks she might be sick. 'I interrupted your girls' weekend.'

Jessica swallows drily. 'You did.'

'I just don't trust her.'

'Still?'

'She's great company and all, but she plays games with people. You see that, don't you?'

'You're mistaken.' Jessica pulls away from the distraction of his stroking hand. 'We were having a lovely time. Becoming closer.'

Jacques drops his head again. 'I'll go, sweetie. Take an extra day here. I'll call William Mansion's and make an excuse for you.'

When she doesn't answer, he starts to collect yesterday's clothes from the back of the chair, folding them into neat squares.

'I'd rather go home with you,' she says.

They agree to leave after breakfast. Jessica sends Jacques to help Libby with the fry-up while she strips the sheets off the bed.

When she goes downstairs, she sees them, framed through the open doorway of the kitchen. It stops her; the way they are standing so close together that Libby's head is tilted back, their eyes bridging the narrow space between them. Jessica steps back, closes her eyes, forehead pressed to the wooden door frame as she tries to fish words out of the strained hush of their voices.

'We want the same thing.' There's a soft, entreating smile in Libby's voice.

'She mustn't be—' Jacques starts to say but she interrupts.

'—hurt. I know.'

Jessica sits on the bottom step, waiting, but the only sound comes from the rush of tap water and chink of crockery. She gets up. She will observe them, see what she can glean from the way they will now move about each other in her presence.

'Coffee, Jessie?' Libby waves a small cafetière.

Jacques strides over to the grill. 'Bacon's almost done.'

'We've burnt the toast, I'm afraid.' Libby pushes a coffee mug into her hands. 'I've put more in the toaster.'

Over breakfast, Jacques apologises again for ruining their weekend.

Libby shakes her head. 'You didn't. I had such a lovely day yesterday. With both of you.' And she takes Jacques' and Jessica's hands. 'Genuine friends are rare.'

'Showboat.' Jacques gives her hand a brief squeeze before continuing to butter his toast.

'I'm afraid Jacques has to get back to town,' Jessica says. 'It makes sense for me to go with him.'

A look passes between Jacques and Libby, so fleeting Jessica wonders if she imagined it; her doubt like the immediate darkness of the sky after a firework.

She excuses herself.

In the tiny downstairs toilet she squares up to herself in the mirror, arms gripping the bowl of the sink as though she would rip it from the wall. Her face is flushed, pupils pinprick-sharp. Feverish.

'I am not my mother.' Her voice is too quiet to lessen the pounding in her head. Picking up a silver, lion-footed soap dish, she positions her thumbnail beneath a claw and presses down. The pain is blunt and nauseating but her body starts paying attention. 'This is Jacques we're talking about. *Jacques.*'

He had written the despised origin of his name into their wedding vows, turning it into a promise. *As my name is Jacques, I will never let you down through deceit or dishonesty.*

Feeling calmer, she replays Jacques' and Libby's conversation – something about wanting the same thing and for her not to get hurt – but it could mean anything. So she considers Jacques' surprise arrival, and therein lies the clue.

He and Libby have been playing tug of war with her attention for some time, their behaviour peaking this weekend; Libby stealing her away and Jacques sabotaging her efforts.

What she must have overheard was a recognition of how harmful their actions are becoming. She witnessed a truce.

Jessica releases the bruising pressure from her thumb and nods at her reflection. She has figured it out without screaming wild accusations or tearing at clothing. She is not her mother.

A knock on the door sends the soap dish clattering into the sink.

'You OK, honey?'

Jessica doesn't reply. She takes her time replacing the soap dish and running the tap before opening the door.

'Is a moment's peace too much to ask for?' It is lightly intended but comes out flat, and Jacques steps away without a word.

As they put their bags into the boot of Jacques' old but pristine Volvo, Libby watches them from the doorway.

There's something lost and forlorn about her silence, reminding Jessica of Libby's fear of being left on the outside.

'Come on, sweetie,' Jacques is urging her. 'We're going to hit Sunday traffic.'

In the side mirror, Libby shrinks until she resembles a child, hands clasped together. Jessica kicks off her boots, crossing her legs in the seat.

Jacques clears his throat. 'I was wrong to discourage your friendship with Libby.'

'What's made you change your mind?'

'I think her friendship is genuine, after all.'

Jessica looks away with a satisfied nod. *I am not my mother.*

15

June 2012

In the hallucinatory space between her sleeping body and waking mind, she sees Thomas. Straight out of the sea; sandy-bodied, hair dark with salt water, that rare grin.

Jessica smiles up at the ceiling. Because it's Thursday – her studio day – she considers going back to sleep, chasing her fading dream.

'I've made coffee,' Jacques calls from the kitchen. 'You up yet, honey?'

Jessica spreads her limbs through the warm nest of the bed. 'Almost.'

Jacques strides into the bedroom, towel about his waist and a swipe of overlooked shaving foam along his jawline. He places a mug on her side-table, bends to kiss her forehead and doesn't notice as she reaches for him. Tucking her hand back under the covers, she watches him opening cupboards and drawers, the day already taking him away. 'Do you have to rush off this morning?'

'Today, yes.'

As if today were an exception, she thinks.

'I have a meeting with the Arden Group, which'll probably extend into lunch, and at some point this morning I have to squeeze in a fitting at the tailor's.'

A gust of wind rattles the window, rain spattering against the glass with the vehemence of a drink tossed in anger.

'I think I'll stay in bed today.' She says it quietly, not meaning it. A small test of his attention. 'It's raining.'

'I would take an umbrella, honey, it's looking pretty wet out.'

He delivers a second kiss and is gone.

Jessica puts on studio clothes; torn jeans and a pink sweatshirt, which has stiffened across the chest with polishing dust. By the time she leaves the flat, the bulging sky has burst and she has forgotten her umbrella. She joins a wet huddle of people at the bus stop. When a taxi splashes past with its yellow sign on, she can't resist flagging it down.

'Lockerstone Street, behind Clerkenwell Town Hall, please.'

She writes the letter T in the condensation of her breath on the window and considers the pieces she is working on: a serpent ring with minute scales of lacquered wood and an orchid pendant powdered in crushed glass. The thought of an unfinished item would normally fill her with energy, her head leaping to materials and processes, but today it merely fatigues her.

'I've changed my mind. Can we go to Bayswater instead? Bartholomew Lanes.'

Libby will lift her flattened mood.

The roads are clotted with buses and delivery trucks. Jessica's impatience spikes with every green light that switches to red before her taxi can reach it. She jumps out early, circumnavigating puddles, head down against the rain. Turning the corner, she looks up to check she is in Bartholomew Lanes and sees Libby's pink-fronted florist's halfway along the row of shops. As she wipes rain from her eyes, she catches a blurred image of a man leaving Libby's under a pale blue golf umbrella. Within a few strides he has vanished into the alleyway opposite the florist's. She is left with the impression of slim, navy trousers and a green mackintosh.

'Jacques?' She breaks into a run, slipping on the wet cobblestones, calling his name.

The alley is empty and there are no pedestrians on the adjacent road. Shaking, Jessica leans against the wall, ignoring the filthy sheet of water washing down the brickwork. She can watch the florist's from here without being seen. Five minutes pass without so much as a glimpse of Libby through the bay window. No one walks in or out of the shop. She's not even sure what she is waiting for.

In a shivery daze, she teeters on the pavement edge, searching for a taxi.

Rain drums against the studio skylights like a giant carwash. Only Serena is at her workstation, the silver halo of her curls shivering with the motion of her hands. When she looks up, the youthful plumpness of her face is always surprising under the premature grey of her hair.

'Byrney. Good to see you.' Serena inclines her head back over a tiny file pinched between thumb and fore-finger. Jessica mutters a greeting and heads for the kitchenette at the back of the studio. The smell of sardines and turps is comforting in its familiarity. She stares through the unbarred window at a small church with flint-embedded walls. Hemmed in by warehouses, their shadows circle it like a sundial with the passing day. Closing her eyes, she leans her forehead against the cool glass.

The man leaving Libby's shop was half hidden by the umbrella, disappearing before she could study the way he walked – without these clues, he is just one of many faceless men in neutral clothing. Jacques is in a meeting with the Arden Group. He wouldn't drop in on Libby's shop without telling Jessica. It just isn't him.

Then she thinks of his distraction and how it had all but rendered her invisible as he prepared for his day ahead.

Opening her eyes, she spots a man in an oversized raincoat standing beside the church wall. Staring up at her. She pushes back from the window, watching as he covers his face, pulling his hood up, and stalks away.

Recognition flips in Jessica's stomach – the man looks like Matthew.

'I'm losing my mind,' she mumbles, pressing cold palms to her cheeks.

Back at her desk, Jessica forces her attention to the

miniature landscape before her. Brassy stacks of mock-up rings; plastic chips, aqua-hued, pooling together; opaque sea glass. Incidental placing of materials can spark unexpected chemistry. A fake cabochon ruby – smooth as a drop of fossilised blood – has found an intriguing counterpart in a torn sheet of sandpaper.

The rough with the smooth, Jessica thinks. Trying to remind herself that Jacques wasn't a man of contrasts – his words and actions as constant as the rising sun.

The rain keeps Jessica company long after Serena has wheeled her bicycle out of the studio. When her mobile rings, she ignores it, fending off the outside world. She barely registers the creak and shuffle of the door opening behind her.

A hand on her shoulder makes her jump, her cry spiralling two pigeons off the steel girders above. Matthew bends over her, dripping water from his raincoat onto her workbench.

'What are you doing here?' She glances past his shoulder. 'Is Libby with you?'

'No, it's just me. I'm so sorry I startled you.'

Jessica stands up, folding her arms about her. Asks again, 'Why are you here?'

'I hope this isn't inappropriate, my arriving at your studio like this. I tried to call.'

'What's wrong, Matthew?'

He brushes back his wet hair with both hands, grave eyes roaming the studio. A shaft of evening sun has broken through the rain, slanting across his face. It accentuates his pallor and the dark smudges beneath his eyes. 'May I?' He indicates the chair beside him, fingers stretched and precise as a salute, his formality clashing with his baggy-kneed cords and slouching coat.

'Of course. You don't have to ask.'

Before he sits, he unfolds a square of paper from his trouser pocket. A sketchy necklace has been drawn in blue biro. 'I designed it myself. Badly, of course. I was hoping you could make it as an anniversary present for Libby.'

'You want me to make her a pendant?'

Matthew sits forward to point out various scribbles and arrows. 'It's a hollow, filigree globe which was popular with court ladies during Marie Antoinette's time. They used to fill them with pot pourri or secret charms.'

'Libby calls you the Human Encyclopedia.' Jessica smiles, tracing her nail across the design. Twists of silver thread and secret catches start to take shape under the motion of her finger. 'What shall we put inside?'

'A glass flower, I was thinking. Or a tiny figure of a guardian angel.'

Jessica shivers. 'I've never really understood the appeal of guardian angels. That idea of being invisibly watched.' A beat of silence passes as they study the picture. Matthew is staring at her when she looks up. Something about his stiff posture and the awkward knot of his fingers makes her touch his arm. 'What is it?'

'French courtiers sometimes sealed a tiny lock and key inside as a charm to keep their lady-love faithful.'

A chill sweeps through her. 'Is that what you want to put inside?'

'You know she has affairs?' Even though the studio is empty, he is whispering. She leans in, their bodies forming a conspiratorial triangle over the diagram.

'Since the second year of our marriage.'

'Who?' Sees again the man under the blue golf umbrella leaving Libby's shop.

'That's not relevant.' Matthew draws back, breaking the triangle. 'It's my fault, you see, so I don't interfere.'

'How can it be your fault?' Outrage raises her voice. Seeing him away from Libby's shadow, in his own light, Jessica is struck by how gentle and kind he is. Handsome, even, in an accidental fashion. If she were better at expressing herself, she would tell him so. 'I don't understand.'

'No man had resisted her before I came along. I could see she was beautiful and exciting and vivacious, but I'm simply not equipped to deal with all that drama.'

Here comes drama. Jessica encourages him with a nod and Matthew sighs.

'You can imagine what a red rag *that* was.'

'But she won.'

He spreads the folds of paper with his palms. 'Not really. It hurts her, knowing she is not my perfect fit.'

'And yet her affairs are hurting you. If you're jealous, it's because you care.'

'I do love her.' Matthew pulls his coat back on. 'I just don't worship her, and that's what my wife craves.' He shakes his head, combing his fingers through his hair again. 'She is much sweeter and calmer when she is not in the grip of some passing infatuation. So yes, I'd like her affairs to stop.'

Jessica walks him to the door and surprises them both by suggesting a drink.

The Floss and Junket is a crooked, black-beamed pub squashed between converted warehouses. Its smoke-stained interior is empty apart from two men at the billiard table; one in a pinstripe suit with stripes too fat to be conventional City-wear, his companion with a foxy red beard and harem pants in grey wool.

As Jessica sits down at a battered table held together by what looks like the pewter wheel rim of a cart, something tugs at her sleeve. A splinter of torn metal is lifting away from the table's edge. Plucking at her snagged thread, Jessica wonders what she and Matthew will talk about without Jacques and Libby dominating the conversation. When he returns with two large vodkas, she asks if he passed her building earlier.

'Ah. I wondered if you'd seen me.'

'Why didn't you come in then?'

'You looked,' here he shrugs, embarrassed, 'as though you might have had things on your mind.'

Jessica doesn't answer. Swallows a large mouthful of her drink, the tonic fizzing sweetly acid in the back of her throat.

'So how did you and Libby meet?'

Matthew smiles, shaking his head. 'I was at a restaurant with a new girlfriend. On the table beside us was this striking woman with a couple of friends. I was rather mystified by the way she kept making eye contact with me. When my companion went to the Ladies, she leaned over to me and said, *Why don't you send your little friend home now so we can stop wasting our time?'*

'You have to admire Libby's boundless confidence.' Jessica shifts in her seat, her arm catching once again at the ragged table-edge. 'I assume you complied?'

'I admit I let her take my phone number.' He shrugs one shoulder, no longer smiling. 'Of course then I felt ashamed and refused to return her calls. I was quite unprepared for the aggression – no let's call it the vigour – of her pursuit.'

Jessica takes a spiky gulp of vodka. Looks down at her lap, fighting an overwhelming desire to tell him she saw Jacques leaving Libby's shop this morning. Or thought she saw. The metal splinter has a beautiful shape, she notices; the edge rippling into a lethal apex. With the pad of her thumb she discovers its pleasing slice.

'You and Jacques seem to get on well.'

Matthew, mid-drink, points with his glass, slopping liquid over his fingers. 'I like that man of yours. He's decent, straightforward. Exactly what it says on the tin.' He leans forward, elbows bumping onto the table, almost knocking Jessica's drink sideways. 'And the thing that makes me chuckle is that my wife is fairly taken with him and he doesn't even notice.'

A delicious, red-embered needle of pain slides under Jessica's nail and deep into her arm as she pushes the metal splinter into her thumb. It makes her breath catch, bringing tears to her eyes. Matthew's eyebrows rise in concern. He digs a creased handkerchief from his pocket.

'I've upset you. I only meant Libby expects a certain male reaction. A bit of harmless flirtation.'

A polished bead gathers on her thumb-tip, swelling until it spills like melted candle wax down to her wrist. 'Jacques would never want to hurt me.'

'I've noticed how protective he is of you.' Matthew nods in vigorous agreement, and the shadows of his face are released. 'Libby and I have often commented on your . . . togetherness, for want of a better word. It's a rare thing these days.'

Jessica's injured thumb begins to throb, her heartbeat slowing to match its pulsing ache. Blood-letting, she thinks. Letting the bad blood flow away.

'You have no idea what your friendship means to Libby.' Matthew blinks, looks away, embarrassed perhaps at having said too much.

Jessica sits back in her chair, noticing how the lights in the pub are leaving streaks in the air. She hasn't eaten since a mid-morning snack of stale pretzels, and the double vodka is singing in her head. She fixes her wavering gaze on the solid bulk of the bar. 'I managed to avoid the best-friend thing throughout my childhood. It's funny, really . . .'

They finish their drinks in silence before Matthew offers to get a second. Jessica inspects her thumb as his back is turned and realises she has been staunching it with Matthew's handkerchief, which is now wet with blood. Scrunching it into a ball in her rucksack, she hopes he will forget to ask for it back.

By the time they leave the pub, the streetlights are on and a rinsed breeze makes the night smell organic and pure. As they walk to the tube, bumping companionably, Jessica says, 'I know exactly what we'll put inside Libby's pendant.'

'Tell me.' Matthew's head looms unsteadily towards her.

'A smaller globe, and then another one inside that, and another, like a Russian doll.' The idea elates her. 'It's perfect, don't you see?'

He is nodding but frowning.

'It's about layers, Matthew. Secret layers.'

By the time Jessica gets home, her actions feel thick and swollen but her mood is buoyant. The first thing she sees is a bright red umbrella with a white Arden Group logo leaning against the wall. Not a pale blue golf umbrella. Running her hand along the material, she catches a last few drops of rain. The television is on. Jacques has waited up for her. Light with relief, she skips along the hall. At the sitting-room door, she realises it's not the sound of the television but murmuring; a low voice and a light one threaded together.

She tries to pick out individual words over the sousing blood in her ears but it's like trying to scoop leaves out of rushing water. With the pads of her fingers, she nudges the door open, knowing exactly what she'll see.

On the sofa, Libby sits cross-legged facing Jacques, who has an arm slung over the back of the cushions above her shoulders but not touching. Not touching.

The scene is so comfortable, so natural, it feels as if she's seen it before, or imagined it into being.

'There you are.' Libby rushes towards her. A moment's hesitation as she tries to read the look on Jessica's face before smothering her in a hug. 'We've been waiting hours for you.'

Jessica catches Jacques' eye over Libby's shoulder.

'I've been calling,' he says, claws of exhaustion under his eyes.

'I was working. I turned my phone off.' Aware that she is swaying in the middle of the room as Libby moves away, Jessica adds, 'I went for a few drinks afterwards.'

Jacques gives her a flat look, but how can she tell him the truth in front of Libby without giving away Matthew's anniversary surprise? She needs Libby to leave. Immediately.

'So how come you're here, Libby?' Her tone more accusing than she'd intended. In the corner of her eye, Jacques is shaking his head in disgust.

'I'm going to bed.' He skirts around her outstretched hand and she notices for the first time that he is wearing slim, navy trousers.

It means nothing because the umbrella in the hallway is red, not pale blue.

'Matthew's gone AWOL,' Libby chirps. 'I thought he might be here, getting drunk with Jacques.'

Jessica presses her lips together. Matthew will have to make his own excuses. Her earlier clarity has vanished. She is sinking beneath a rolling surface of vodka, where nothing makes sense.

All she can see is Jacques and Libby on the sofa. With a single, kaleidoscope turn, it has become the two of them together with her on the outside.

Layers and lies.

16

The sea-dragon box has brought with it forgotten dreams like stowaways. Every night she is a child again, searching for her dad or pulling splintered wood from the mouth of a monstrous sea. At the core of even the most surreal nightmare lies a forgotten nugget of memory, which persists into daylight. One morning she catches herself wondering which churchyard her father lies buried in. She punishes the thought under an icy shower.

The dreams, unwelcome as they are, still infect her with a longing to revisit old haunts; the secret bays and ragged clifftops. Thomas's chapel. She needs time and space – the freedom – to remember Thomas properly.

That's when she thinks of Nathan.

Thomas's older brother by five years, he was already a grown-up when she first met him. Or so it seemed to her thirteen-year-old self. Tall, sporty and clean-shaven. She'd been instantly drawn to his expression of perpetual amusement as if he couldn't quite get over the antics of the human race. He loved his brother as fiercely as she did. Apart from Hannah, he was the only other person who had known about her and Thomas's friendship.

She needs to show him the red notebook.

Jessica tells Jacques she is going to visit her mum, to see how Birdie has settled into the new caravan. He takes her to Paddington Station and as they wait for the train, she turns to him.

'Do you think I should have gone last year?'

'To where?'

Jessica scans the departures board. 'The funeral.'

It takes him a moment, then he pulls her into a fierce hug. 'No, Christ no, sweetie.'

She pushes back so she can see his face. 'You seem so certain.'

'Honey, think back. As soon as you opened that damn card your reaction was so . . . strong that I – we – can trust you made the decision that was right for you.'

She presses her forehead to his jumper again, unwilling to read in his face the memory of the days that followed. First, how the anger had made her shake so violently and persistently that for a whole day she dropped and broke everything she touched. The next day, as if a giant hand had swatted her down, she lay in bed; couldn't eat, couldn't sleep and wouldn't talk.

'Is this why you're going down there?'

Now Jessica looks him in the eye. 'No. Absolutely not.'

As the train pulls out of Paddington, she pictures his

open, trusting face – *Go do the dutiful daughter thing*. When she's ready, she will show him the counsellor's notebook and tell him about Thomas. Just not yet.

Settling back into her seat with Ms Callum's notes, she whiles away the hours with Thomas's voice in her head.

After a six-hour train journey, she catches a bus to Morley-on-Sea – the nearest village to Nathan's old house – and disembarks at the Pit-Stop Café. It hasn't changed; the same red and white chequered tablecloths and the promise of an all-day brekkie chalked onto an A-frame board on the pavement.

The three of them used to come here all the time – she, Thomas and Nathan – sitting at the back, drinking stewed tea and eating buttered toast.

Sitting down with a tuna melt and a tea she has added too much sugar to, she wipes a spyhole in the window's condensation. The flat seafront features a plait of cropped, ornamental bushes and a merry-go-round covered in dirty, transparent tarpaulin. Paint curls off the frozen horses.

Everything needs fixing in this place, she once remarked to Thomas.

Everything and everyone, he'd answered, and she thought he was talking about the hurt her dad caused by abandoning her. It had made her feel cherished, like Thomas was going to put her back together.

Now, remembering what was to come, she knows he was talking about himself.

The door opens. A thin man with dirty-blond

dreadlocks walks in. He stares at Jessica, who returns to her spyhole.

'Jessica?'

She frowns up at the man as he approaches her table.

'Little Jessie. All grown up.'

His voice is familiar. 'Did we go to school together?'

'It's Nathan.' He waves a hand over his head. 'With a little more hair.'

And then she sees him, the clean-shaven Nathan she'd known, now with dreadlocks and a short beard.

'It *is* you.' She stands up. They face each other, unsure what to do next, until Nathan holds out his hand and they laugh over their awkward handshake. 'The hair suits you, even the facial stuff.'

Nathan beams.

Spliffy, Thomas used to say, rolling his eyes at his older brother. *That stupid ganja grin.* Libby's comment about the local underage market comes back to her.

'Visiting your mum?'

'Actually,' Jessica pushes a chair out for him, 'I came to find you.'

Nathan nods because nothing ever seems to surprise him.

'Let me just grab a tea.' As he places his order, he inclines his head towards the waitress in a way that stings Jessica with familiarity. She'd never noticed how similar the brothers' movements were. A pressure like a threatened migraine throbs in her head; she presses the heels of her hands to her eye sockets.

'Are you OK?'

'You looked like Thomas just now.' Then she wishes

148

she hadn't said his name, unsure how Nathan will react, but he just nods, grins.

He hadn't been smiling the last time she saw him. The memory is sharp like she's turned a page in a magazine and found it there. A bright morning on top of Hasleborne Hill where a group of people are huddled together in their dark Sunday best, making black holes against the white sky. Jessica had stared at the marble plaque with its gilt words.

Beloved Son and Brother.

The pastor – with a perpetual sniff that kept making her lift her head, thinking he was about to cry – spoke intimately about a boy he'd never met. Nathan insisted she come, holding her hand throughout, she remembers. He was the only one who had wept openly. Jessica had been too angry for tears. Thomas had been gone for less than three months and there was nothing but mud and worms beneath that fancy headstone; they were giving up on him. Thomas's memorial sat on the ground like a shrug: *We tried.*

'So. You were looking for me?' Nathan smooths the fine hair of his moustache past the corners of his mouth. It is an unconscious gesture that strikes her as a measure of the time that has passed since she last saw him; long enough for new tics to develop.

'Are you still at Frotherton West Farm?'

'I run the shop now.' He sips his tea, strokes the sides of his mouth again. 'Still do the odds-and-sods stuff as well.'

Jessica's heart skips. 'Do you remember someone called Albertine Callum?'

'Bertie.'

'You knew her?'

'She was a good friend once.'

Jessica sits back in her chair. 'Did you know she was giving Thomas counselling at school?'

'That's how we got to know her, yes.' Nathan studies her like she's a circuit of wires that he's trying to connect.

'I found her notebook with transcripts from every session. I wondered if you might want to have a look at it.'

'That's OK,' he says, shaking his head. 'I already read it.'

'It was you, then. You put it through my mother's letter box.'

'A long time ago now.' Nathan fiddles with a twist of hair. 'Bertie gave it to me before she moved to Spain. I thought you might want it.'

Jessica looks at her forgotten sandwich, the paper wrapper sticking to the cheese as it cools plastically. 'It's shaken me. Because they're not *my* memories, it feels like he's stepped out of the past. A new him.' She can't tell if Nathan is following what she is struggling to explain. How she has reclaimed a piece of Thomas.

He says, 'I'm guessing there's no one you can really talk to about Thomas these days.'

She'd forgotten his talent for plucking out small truths the way some people always find coins on the ground. Jessica nods.

Nathan hesitates. 'I found some of his stuff the other day when I was having a clear-out.'

'Like what?'

'A few photos. That tatty blue jumper of his.'

That tatty blue jumper. Whenever she thinks of Thomas, he's in that jumper, the roll neck fraying against the stubble of his chin. She wants to see it, to clench it in her hands so badly it makes her stomach ache.

17

Nathan's open-back Land Rover is parked behind the Pit-Stop. She's surprised by how clean it is, and catches herself looking for signs of a woman – there's not so much as a sticker on the windscreen.

He drives more carefully than he ever rode his scrambler. There's something about the deliberate way his hands move as he changes gear, like he's reading the things he touches. Thomas's hands had that same expressiveness. Jessica turns her head to the passing countryside instead.

Everywhere seems to hold a memory of her and Thomas, their friendship rooted in marram dunes and pine forests. Snippets of his voice are caught like balloons in trees.

. . . if anyone ever hurts you, I'll find them and hurt them worse.

Has anyone ever kissed you, Jellybird?

Nathan turns off the B312 onto a forested path which opens into a gravel yard, fringed by overgrown leylandii. It takes her a moment to recognise his house. She and

Thomas would sometimes wind up here on one of their nightly wanderings but they never stayed long; Nathan was rarely on his own. On a quiet night, a body or two might be sprawled on his sofas; closer to the weekend there'd be huddles of people puffing bongs made of plastic lemonade bottles and empty biro cylinders. She hated coming here, never knowing what to do with herself in front of all those strangers intent on getting stoned. She wonders if Libby had been among them – the same age as her but more sophisticated, blending easily.

'Do you know anyone called Libby? Elizabeth Hargreaves?'

Nathan shrugs. 'Should I?'

'She used to come here, years ago.'

'Ah,' Nathan says, and nothing more. He slows for a hobbling turkey and parks beside the crooked makeshift shed that once housed the home-made wine he sold for two pounds a bottle. 'Welcome to Nathan Country.'

He takes her on a tour. The Moonshine Shed, as everyone used to call it, now houses tomato plants. He points out fastidious rows of vegetables, an apothecary of herbs growing in a rusted bath and his hen coops – three mismatched cabinets whose doors have been replaced with chicken wire.

'Total self-sufficiency,' he says, indicating solar panels on the roof.

As they return to the front of the house, Jessica listens for voices and music from within but it is dark and silent. Nathan pushes the front door open and steps aside for her.

'Still don't lock your door, then?'

'No one comes here,' he says, as she wonders what happened to all those casual drop-ins, the impromptu parties.

Jessica chews on a desiccated segment of tangerine while Nathan runs upstairs to get the photographs of Thomas. The bowl of citrus fruit offers a tiny relief of colour against the sitting room's hand-me-down furniture and bland seascape paintings. She'd had to look away as he hunched over the small hearth, fiddling with damp matches, the sight suddenly filling her with loneliness. Self-sufficiency, he'd called it.

Nathan bounds into the room and places two photographs face down beside the fruit bowl. He flips one over like a magician's trick. Jessica's hand falters in mid-air.

'I never saw the two of them together.'

It must have been one of the last photos of Thomas; she recognises his jeans with the ripped-out knees. His father is leaning on a walking stick, an arm about his son's shoulders. Support or embrace, she can't tell; Thomas's wiry frame bending like a green twig under his father's weight. The fingers gripping the walking stick have long, rounded nails like a lion's claw. Neither son nor father is smiling.

'It's me,' she says, surprised, picking up the second picture. She can't remember the moment but recognises the sea wall overlooking Selcombe Harbour where she and Thomas used to watch fishermen mending nets. She studies her teenage self.

'I had hair like a witch.'

'Thomas said you were the colour of autumn with your red hair and green eyes.' Nathan strokes the peel off a tangerine with his nimble fingers. 'I ragged him about that, obviously. Getting all poetic.'

Jessica hugs her knees, staring into the fire. 'Who took the photo?'

'Must have been Thomas.'

Something about the way she is gazing straight at the photographer – at Thomas – with such fierceness of feeling, full of laughter and challenge, makes her agree. She's missed that feeling, can almost feel a hole in her body where it used to be. She wonders if it was still there when she first met Jacques. Perhaps it's what drew him to her.

She gets up. 'I need to make a quick call.'

Outside, the clearing has grown long shadows and the first stars are out. An owl is calling from the invisible branches of a tree. It doesn't sound real, like someone whistling in imitation. Her mobile has no signal and she can't call home. She experiences a pang of guilt, imagining Jacques' face if he saw her now, in the house of a stranger. She tries one last time without success.

'Can I see his jumper?' she asks, going back inside.

'I left it in the kitchen.'

Before he can move, she rushes across the room. 'Don't get up. I'll grab it.'

The jumper is lying in a heap on the kitchen counter. Her arms feel lead-weighted as she reaches for it, hands shaking. Turning her back to the sitting-room door she pushes her face into it, breathing in, then drops her arms in disgust. The wool has a greasy texture as though it's been damp for so long it has started to melt. It gives off a powerful fungal smell. Forcing it back to her nose, she inhales deeply, trying to get beyond the stench to catch a trace of Thomas. Finds none.

It is a piece of dead material.

'Where are you staying?' Nathan's voice in the doorway makes her jump. She drops the jumper by the sink, ghastly with embarrassment.

'My mother's. I think.'

'You could stay here, if you like. We haven't really talked about Thomas yet, have we?'

She considers this. 'If you're sure?'

She accepts an offer of tea, fishing about in her rucksack for Ms Callum's notebook as he pours her a cup. They both stare at it as she lays it on the table.

'Not a light holiday read, is it?'

'I haven't finished it yet.' She needs to break it up into manageable snippets or risk being overwhelmed by the resurfacing loss of him. 'Some of the sections aren't clear. It's like they're talking in code.'

'Yeah, there's a lot of stuff referring to conversations outside of the sessions. They became friends.'

Jessica nips the inside of her lower lip. Those unrecorded moments in which the roots of a friendship spread and took hold, fed by words and looks and physical presence. Safely lost in history where they can never be held up to the light.

'Does this bit mean anything to you?' She flicks

156

through the notebook and her fingers feel their way to the right page. 'Callum asks if he's afraid of anything and he says, *I bet you never knew a whisper could scare you to death.*'

The perpetual smile at the corner of Nathan's eyes is gone. 'My father.'

She wipes her palms on her trousers, finding them slippery with dread. 'Sometimes his face would be bruised and bloody but he wouldn't talk about it.'

Nathan sighs, shifting his feet apart, stooping over his knees as he peels another tangerine. A Thomas posture.

'That wasn't my father. That was Thomas.'

'What do you mean?'

'He used to hang around pubs at closing time and say something stupid to the biggest lad he could find. He'd let the guy really punch the shit out of him before he even raised his fists. Once he started to fight back, it was hard for him to stop.'

Jessica is shaking her head. 'If I was hearing this from anyone else I'd call them a liar. I know it was your father . . . doing that to him.'

Thomas with his face and hands swollen and newly scabbed. *Did your father do this?* He'd deny it every time; sometimes wearily, often with a sour laugh. *He wouldn't dare.* She'd taken it for bravado and found his courage devastating.

Nathan is staring straight ahead. 'The marks my dad left on Thomas couldn't be seen on the outside.'

'Is that the whispering?'

Nathan blinks like he's trying to clear the film of his

157

eye. 'It started when Thomas was little, being too loud or lively. My dad would bend his head right down next to Thomas's and speak in his ear. Thomas's face would go blank like the life had been sucked out of him.'

'What was he saying?'

'I don't know. I knew not to cross him. Thomas never had that kind of survival instinct.'

They sit quietly for a moment, listening to the hiss of the fire.

'I can still see him. This little, wild four-year-old climbing out of the attic skylight. Whooping with excitement until my dad came into the yard. Then he went quiet. I swear he was working out if he could jump down and crush the old man. I think my dad saw it too.'

Jessica doesn't say anything. She wants to take the little boy Thomas in her arms and wrap him up tight and safe.

'The thing about my dad is you never see his anger, only its actions. He can do the most awful things, calm as you like.'

Jessica shudders, remembering Ms Callum's comment after Thomas's first session. *The lack of visible anger.* 'Why didn't you try to protect him from your dad?' She tries for a neutral tone, to strip it of any accusation.

Nathan sighs, rubbing his forehead. 'By the time Thomas turned fourteen he was taller than my father and believe me, the old man had started giving him a wide berth.'

Jessica gets up, all of a sudden wanting nothing more than to press herself into Jacques' warm, welcoming body. Her comfortable home, her safe life in London seems overwhelmingly far away.

'I might have an early night, if you don't mind.'

Nathan doesn't move. 'I guess it was too late by then. My father had whispered all his fury into Thomas. You can see why he went looking for trouble.' Then he stands up, his slow smile weighted with acceptance. 'At least he had us. He knew we loved him, Jessie.'

She nods for his sake and looks away. 'Perhaps I could have done more though. He needed someone to help him.'

'He had Bertie.'

'Yes,' Jessica says. 'Of course.'

Nathan takes her upstairs to a box room with a curtainless window and flocked wallpaper. A thin mattress with yellow stains like spilled tea fills most of the floor. He leaves her in the doorway and returns with a roll of bedding under his arm and a lit candle in a glass pot. It leaves a thin trail of Christmassy scent. 'The room hasn't been used in a while.'

As he sets the candle on the windowsill, she gives his arm a quick squeeze. 'It's good to see you, Nathan.'

'I see you're wearing a wedding ring,' he says softly.

She stretches out her fingers and they both study the ring.

'It's good.' As Nathan plumes the sheet through the air, black specks like peppercorns scatter from the musty folds. Jessica squats down on the pretext of tucking the sheet under the mattress and finds further mouse-droppings clinging to the cotton.

'Your life has moved on,' Nathan is saying.

'I haven't forgotten Thomas.'

He straightens, his fingers scrunching the dreadlocks at the base of his skull as though trying to free a troublesome thought lodged there.

'Don't spend too much time on Bertie's book.'

Under a stage-light moon, the trees in Nathan's front yard are so sharply delineated they resemble theatre cut-outs. Jessica turns from the window. Folding her coat into a pillow, she lies on the edge of the mattress as far from the mouse-droppings as possible. She keeps her shoes on, soles dangling over the edge. Pulling her sleeves over her hands, she tucks them between her thighs, skin itching with the thought of the dirty sheet.

Not a trace of summer warmth has been caught between the walls of the room. Within minutes she is shivering. There is still no mobile signal to call a taxi, and she can't throw Nathan's hospitality back in his face by asking him to drive her to the station. Not only is she trapped for the night, but she has learned nothing.

Being here and witnessing how far Nathan's life has moved on from those early days has only made Thomas seem even further removed. A lifetime away.

A scratching noise from behind the skirting board makes Jessica abandon the idea of sleep. The only option left is to read. Taking the red notebook from her rucksack and lifting the cinnamon candle down to the floor, she opens the book.

It takes her half an hour to read it from cover to cover.

'Well.' It's her mother's word; the one she uses when there is simply too much to express and too few ready words.

It's him and it's not him. She'd never realised before how utterly lost he was, and it shames her now. Silly, self-centred child that she was.

Pushing the notebook up onto the windowsill, she lies back and closes her eyes, exhausted suddenly. Too tired to care about mice and dirt. She is almost asleep when a noise startles her. Jumping up, she searches for the origin of the crash, unnerved to find the room unchanged.

Then she sees it – the notebook lying face down beneath the window, the stiff leather cover at an odd angle, like the wing of a pigeon flattened on the road. The paper lining has torn away, revealing a corner of turquoise card. She prises it out with thumb and finger-nail.

A picture postcard. She can hardly bring herself to touch it.

On the front is a photograph of a modern office block with a pointed roof, the sun glinting off glass walls, like a giant crystal shafting out of the earth. *The Iceberg at Stollingworth* reads the caption beneath.

She turns the postcard, her heart going over with it. The handwriting is very different from Bertie's crisp script. Odd words stand out, ploughed into the card with such force that it shows through the Iceberg tower in mirror image. One of the words is *FREE*.

Dear Bertie
Yesterday I drowned but today I am FREE.
Luv from Tom

At the bottom of the postcard, the same pen has drawn a tiny fishing boat, its prow pointing skyward as it sinks into angry waves. On the billowing sail it says *The Bad Ship Thomas*.

Jessica's hands start to shake. Pressing the card flat on her lap, she reads it again.

It is postmarked 27 December. Eight days after Thomas disappeared.

TQ: No, he never loses his rag.

AC: In which case, your father must have amazing self-control.

TQ: When something makes him angry, he does something about it.

AC: Like what?

TQ: I don't know. I guess like the time Midge snapped at him . . .

AC: Your dog?

TQ: One of them. We keep ridgebacks for security and stuff. They're big dogs but if you train them well, they're softies.

AC: What happened when Midge snapped at your father?

TQ: It was because of her paw. She'd hurt it and it was making her grouchy. Otherwise she'd never have done it.

AC: What did your father do?

TQ: He hugged her and made her calm.

AC: That sounds kind.

TQ: . . . and then he wrapped a long chain around her neck. Over and over until she was making this coughing noise. Coughing all the air out of her lungs.

AC: He killed the dog?

TQ: You can't let your dog snap at you.

~ 18 ~

April 1995, Selcombe

Thomas came to see her every night.

At dinner, she shovelled her food in silence while Hannah tried to provoke and Lisa nagged and their mother looked out of the window. Plate scraped clean, she went upstairs and waited for the scuffle of sandy pebbles against her window. When it came, she climbed out of the window and followed him through forests, secluded coves and abandoned tin mines; sometimes to Nathan's. Their world the empty night.

Then one evening he wanted to make a plan.

Meet me tomorrow at the Tree, six thirty.

Can't it be later? We don't eat dinner until seven.

Six thirty or don't bother. Excuses are for cowards.

So the next evening, Jessica told Birdie she was going over to Lucy's. The lie was foolproof. Her mum and Mrs Trelawney would never meet by chance. She tried to imagine Lucy's mother in Seasalt Holiday Park, floating in her summer dress and gardening hat through beige rows of caravans. Her skin still crawled with embarrassment remembering how her mother had introduced herself to Lucy's mum last summer at Speech Day. Birdie small, dark and plump with her sharp eyes and sparky movements – the way she'd launched herself forward, arm out like a jousting pole to shake Mrs Trelawney's limply offered hand. A fizzy Coca-Cola beside a cool glass of milk. Only now her mother wasn't fizzy any more, she was flat.

Her mood lifted as she closed the front door, stepping into a pollen-dusty evening, the air full of melting tarmac and wild lilac. She took the cliff road down into the valley. When she reached a field of brilliant yellow flowers with a grove of beech trees in the middle, she climbed over the stile and onto a rutted path.

The beech-tree copse had become one of their favourite places now that the weather had turned warm. In its centre was a long-dead oak that made a perfect viewing tower. In its bare branches they were hidden from view. They spied on dog-walkers, couples holding hands and deer that Thomas potted, his arm stretched out under the length of an invisible hunting rifle.

When she reached the oak, Thomas was already there, swinging his bare feet, his trainers lying among the roots like fallen fruit. He didn't acknowledge her until she eased herself onto his branch. Then he turned to regard her through a pair of battered green binoculars.

'I was about to give up on you.'

'It's laundry day. I had to help Birdie. Where did you get those from?'

'Birthday present from my dad.'

'Your birthday? So you're seventeen now?' Seventeen. Just a few years between them but somehow it was an age that sounded far away, as though he was leaving her behind. 'I'll be fourteen soon.'

Thomas pulled a silver hip flask from his pocket, screwed off the top and took an audible gulp. He held it out to her. She sniffed the contents. The smell was sweet, catching the back of her throat like cough medicine.

'Is this also from your dad?'

Thomas fixed her in the binocular sights again. 'Do you know where he got these from?' He let them thud back against his chest. 'A box in the shed. Where they've been rotting since my uncle died. They were his.' He took the flask out of her hand. '*This* was my present to myself.'

'Looks really expensive.'

'Did I say I bought it?' Thomas gave her a grin that was more a baring of teeth, and Jessica felt her stomach knot. She didn't like it when he was in this mood. It could go anywhere.

He raised the binoculars again, leaning forward to rest his elbows on his knees, teetering as he adjusted his balance.

'Here we go.'

Jessica heard voices. Two people were picking their way towards the trees through the undulating rapeseed.

The woman walked with her face tilted to the evening sun; she was pretty with freckles and high cheekbones. Behind her, the man moved more cautiously, his head down. All she could see was his hat. Jessica sucked in her breath, her fingers scrabbling for a hold in the bark as her horizon tilted. Her father's hat, his old panama, the one he used to plonk on her head as he walked in through the front door, making the same joke about her head shrinking as it slipped down her brow. She could see his thick curls gathered under its brim and knew when he took off his hat the hair beneath would be flattened, sticking to his head.

'What's he doing here?' she choked through a dry throat.

Thomas shushed her, not listening. Jessica pulled her legs into a shaky crouch, gripping twigs for support as she turned to climb down.

'What are you doing?' Thomas held her arm. At that moment the man raised his face and she saw she was wrong. Those weren't her father's eyes – the laughter lines were missing – and the nose was too small, the mouth wide and thin. It wasn't him after all. It wasn't him.

'What's wrong?'

'Nothing.' The wind picked up, rattling through sun-parched leaves like spilling shingle. It whipped away the brief exchanges between the couple as the man stamped a space in the plants and the woman flapped out a blanket, pinning the corners with two bottles of cider.

'What are we doing here?'

'Time for you to grow up a little.' Thomas smiled, that same wolfish grimace. Jessica stayed in her crouch. Her mouth was still dry with residue shock; she wanted to go home. Below them the couple slugged from a bottle, the man's murmurs making the woman snicker. She flicked off his hat. Instead of matted curls there was a bald spot, round and shiny as a china saucer.

They finished the cider and as the empty bottle arced into the field, the man reared up on his knees and tipped the woman back onto the rug. Thomas put the binoculars in her hand, looping the cord about her neck and pushing her down into a seated position. 'Don't look so scared, little rabbit.'

The man hooked up the woman's skirt with a broken rape stalk and peered under the tented material. The wind stilled long enough to catch his words.

'Val, Val, Val. Does Marcus know you go out like that?'

Val sprawled her arms over the spread of her pale hair. The stalk flicked the skirt to her waist and poked her knees apart. Thomas placed his fingers beneath Jessica's wrist and raised the binoculars to her face. The man sat back on his heels, head to one side, regarding Val's naked triangle of curls like he was savouring his Sunday roast. Then he lowered himself with slow deliberation upon her. They kissed. Small, chaste kisses that grew deeper until they gasped and snorted for air like they were fighting over a single bubble of oxygen. The ugliness of it all fascinated

Jessica. Thomas straddled the branch, facing her with a grin, something amusing him in her face. Her neck began to ache in its rigid posture. The woman threw her face up to the sky so the man could peck at her neck. Jessica lowered the binoculars. Thomas moved closer, clasping his hands over hers so that she was caught between his arms as he lifted the lenses back to her face. Val's throat glistened with saliva snail-trails. Her lover moved his hand downwards, making it into a play gun and pushing his fingers deep inside her as she fiddled with his zip.

'Look,' Thomas whispered. 'He's wearing a wedding ring but she isn't.'

Jessica pulled a hand free and tried to tear his grip off the binoculars so the cage of his arms would open. 'We can't watch this.'

Thomas's breath was on her face. 'This is what it's all about.'

'Why are you doing this?' Jessica hissed. Furious tears blurred the writhing, moaning form beneath her.

His voice grew gentle. 'I'm the only one who will never hurt you.'

He brought his face closer. He smelled like sea air and wet grass. Not like the boys at the school disco with their sickly aftershave and fruity hair gel. If she turned her head, their lips would touch. She wanted to run away, leaving her body behind so she could watch, from a safe distance, what might happen next.

'Jellybird,' he mouthed against her cheek and she thought, *I'm going to turn my face.*

'Oh, you sweet bitch,' the man grunted below.

Jessica pushed Thomas away and scrambled down the tree.

AC: So, did you have a look at Wisborough College?

TQ: There wasn't time. My dad needed some help.

AC: But you mentioned the Open Day to him?

TQ: No.

AC: You were worried about his reaction?

TQ: Not really.

AC: Then what is it, Thomas? I can tell there's something on your mind.

TQ: The course is two years. Another two years stuck in that house with him.

AC: Ah, I see.

TQ: I plan to leave all the time but somehow I never do it. I'm stuck. I'm in prison.

AC: You can get away from him. You could even stay here if you needed to. Perhaps, Thomas, the prison is inside of you?

TQ: What do you mean?

AC: You've grown up listening to people telling you how hopeless you are, how incapable and antisocial. I think you believe them.

TQ: The prison is my blood. You can't escape your blood.

AC: Why do you say that?

TQ: Because I'm like my dad. I see him in my face when I look in the mirror. Fuck's sake, I even smell like him.

171

AC: You are not your—

TQ: What's the point of leaving? You can't run away from yourself.

19

A few days after the incident at the Tree, Jessica found herself alone in the house. Birdie was taking Grannie Mim to the midweek evening service at the Catholic church in Grantham. Han and Lisa were out somewhere.

All alone. The realisation filled her with a sense of prickly adventure. She went hunting for secrets. She walked past her mother's door – some things she simply didn't want to know – and into Lisa's room. Her search revealed nothing. Neatly stacked schoolbooks on her desk and clothes hanging in the wardrobe – no diary or secret notes squirrelled away. The bedside-table drawer was crammed with supermarket receipts. Lisa had taken it upon herself to make a note of all household expenses since Birdie had become so distant and careless. Prices had been underlined on some of the receipts, her sister's disapproval scrawled in stars and exclamation marks. Lisa's self-important red pen made Jessica furious. She grabbed two handfuls of crumpled papers and threw them in the air so they floated about the room like bleached autumn leaves. Something small and silver fell to the floor.

'No way.' A single condom still in its wrapper. A quick search through the remaining drawers revealed it was the only one. She tried to picture her sister having sex. Moaning and making those open-mouth faces she'd seen on late-night movies. She mock-gagged. 'No. Way.'

Putting the condom in her pocket, she was about to leave the room when the sight of her own reflection in Lisa's full-length mirror stopped her. Her jeans were too short, showing her ankles, and her jumper – pink with a huge strawberry on the front – was ridiculous. She looked like a baby. The condom was thrown back in the drawer.

You're still just a kid.

Thomas's words from two nights ago came back full of nasty little teeth.

He'd been late. She'd almost given up and gone to bed when he appeared in the back garden, whistling. Looking pleased with himself. For some reason, his good humour had soured her mood. It only got worse as he explained why he was late.

I was with a friend. She's helping me sort myself out.
She? She who?
Bertie. The school counsellor. If it's any of your business.

Jessica threw off her jumper. The sight of her white vest, straps drooping off her shoulders, made her even angrier. This, too, was flung on the floor. She stepped up to the mirror, glaring at her naked torso. Bones. Just bloody bones. Her ribs stuck out and her collarbones looked as if she'd swallowed a coat-hanger.

You're late because you've been hanging out with some old, do-gooding hag?

As it happens, Jealous Jelly, she is only six years older than me.

She put her hands over her breasts; what little she'd managed to grow since her nipples softened and popped out last summer. They were small but comforting with a slight weight she hadn't noticed before. She wondered if the school counsellor had large or small breasts.

A feeling caught hold of her, like a draught moving through a room. She unbuttoned her trousers, pushing them down until her hip bones poked out, and discovered that her waist now dipped in above her hips. Crossing her arms in front of her, she put her hands on her waist, closed her eyes and imagined they belonged to a stranger. Thomas's hands.

Then she slipped her trousers below her bottom, her panties with them. The hair down there was fine but enough that she no longer looked like a little girl. Lucy's big brother once asked if her pubes were red like the hair on her head, and she'd hit him. Now, in daylight, there was definitely a reddish tint but she couldn't decide if this was good or bad.

She pushed a tentative finger through the hair until it touched skin. The cool pad of her fingertip, gently pressing. Some of the girls talked about using their fingers, even a hairbrush – though everyone agreed that was gross.

Suddenly self-conscious before her own reflection,

she covered herself up and left Lisa's room feeling irritable and somehow crooked in her own skin. She flung herself on her bed. Lay there remembering how Thomas had looked at her later that same night when they were sitting on the beach, as though he was shocked to find himself so close to her. He had jumped up, grabbing a fistful of stones and skipping them across the flat sea. He always moved away.

She'd asked him, *How come you can't sit still? What's so good about sitting still?*

She wanted to reply, *That's when you kiss.* Instead she just glared at him and he looked away, shaking his head.

You're still just a kid, he'd said as if reading her thoughts.

Perhaps he was comparing her to his twenty-three-year-old counsellor now.

Putting her pillow over her head, she willed herself to grow. In biology they'd watched a speeded-up film of a sprouting seed. Jessica pictured her body filling out in the same way, her bones sinking behind swelling curves.

A loud crack made her jump. Another stone hit the window and she leaped up, hauling open the sash and shouting, 'You're going to break the glass, you idiot.'

Thomas made as if to throw another, laughing as she flinched back.

'Hurry up.' Then he rushed towards the house, full speed, leaping up and trying to climb the side of the wall with his feet before dropping back down.

'Stop that. Are you mad? You'll leave footmarks up the wall.'

He made another rush at the wall. 'If you don't get a move on, I'll come and get you. We've got work to do.'

'What work?'

He wouldn't say.

It was only once they'd reached the main road that she saw there was something wrong with his hand. He carried it at his waist as if suspended by an invisible sling. Two of his fingers stuck straight out, the knuckles swallowed up, the swollen flesh like a layer of putty. She stopped under the full beam of a streetlight.

'What's wrong with your hand?'

Thomas regarded it with mild interest as though it were something incidental lying on the pavement. 'I smacked against something.'

'What?' She moved around him, trying to catch a better look at the left side of his face, which looked odd and lumpy. His eye was beginning to puff out of shape.

'Nothing with an IQ of any sorts.' Thomas side-stepped her, leaving the orange circle of light. 'Come on, no time to dilly-dally, Jelly-jelly.'

'Can't you stand still for a second?' She reached for his arm but he evaded her, leaving her hand scratching air. 'Who did this to you?'

'Getting bor-ed.'

This time when she dived forward she caught a handful of t-shirt. 'Your dad did this. Admit it.'

Thomas contemplated her fist for a moment, then lifted his blank eyes. With a single explosive movement, he wrenched her hand off and spun away.

'Don't you ever grab at me again.' His tone so low

and snarling that the skin on her arms goosebumped. She had never heard that voice before.

'I . . .' She swallowed. 'I hate seeing you hurt.'

'Stop talking as if you know anything.' Now shouting, the cords of his neck pushing out. Anger distorted his features. Made him ugly, a stranger.

Jessica covered her mouth with her hand and bit her lip against the wobble in her chin.

Then his rage drained away like a punctured bag of rice. Eyes widening, he took a couple of quick steps towards her, hand out. She thought he was going to pull her into a hug but then his arm dropped away and he never reached her. 'I just don't want you to talk about my dad.' Conciliatory now, plaintive with an apology he couldn't voice. His manic energy returned, feet jiggling against the pavement. 'Come on, let's go.'

'Go where?'

He answered with a grin, his temper forgotten. 'Don't be frightened, Little Scaredybird.'

By the time they'd finished, the sun had set and the forest behind Thomas's house was full of creaking, shifting darkness. His left eye had swollen into something obscene and clam-like. Jessica tried not to look at it.

The thing stood a foot higher than Thomas, a piece of sacking for a head, stuffed with grass and leaves and forced down over the prongs of a rake. It had no face but as shadows formed across its lumps and folds, sinister features developed, shifting as she circled it. From its broom-handle arms hung a sheet of mud-splattered tarpaulin that moved with the wind; one minute sucked flat against its crucifix body, the next billowing out, rustling and hissing at her.

Thomas stood back to regard their handiwork. 'One last touch.'

'Where are you going?' Jessica asked as he turned to leave the clearing.

He grinned. 'Is Mr Scarecrow doing a good job?'

'I'm not scared, if that's what you mean.' She tried to force conviction into her voice. He stooped down behind a tree and picked up something large and dark in his good hand. It swung, boneless, from his grip.

'God, what is that?'

Black eyes and feathers. A wing opened and she nearly screamed. Thomas glanced about, raising one stiff, damaged finger to his lips.

'You're going to ruin everything if you can't be quiet.'

As he laid the monstrous, feathery thing on the ground it took shape and became two dead crows.

'Ugh. Where did you get them from?'

'Roadkill.' But they didn't look like they'd been squashed under a car wheel. With his right hand and the clumsy use of his left thumb and little finger, Thomas tied string around their necks and dangled them off the scarecrow's arms. His breathing hissed and caught with pained effort, spit flying through his teeth. 'What do you think?'

'It's horrible. Tell me why we're doing this?'

'To teach someone a lesson.'

'Who?'

But Thomas, intent on stringing the birds' wings open in a posture of attack, didn't answer.

Jessica started to shiver. The temperature had dropped with the last of the sunlight. 'Can we go now?'

He was about to say something when they heard it. A man singing, the sound heading in their direction.

'Bingo,' Thomas whispered, taking her wrist. He led her from the clearing to a thicket of brambles. 'Can you see?'

'See what?' Tension made her shiver harder.

Thomas shushed her. The singing had stopped but they could hear the crunch of approaching footsteps along the path leading from Thomas's house. Jessica gasped, clapping a hand over her mouth, as the figure of a man appeared barely a metre from where they were hiding. He stumbled over his own feet and shouted a strange word into the night sky.

'Bloody Russian,' Jessica mouthed.

'Revenge,' Thomas whispered. 'For scaring you at the bus stop.'

At that moment, Bloody Russian saw the scarecrow. He screamed, a high, constant thread of noise that kept on going as he fell to his knees. Thomas snorted with amusement. The tramp held out his crucifix, trying to ward the thing off, crying and babbling in his own language. Thomas was now clutching himself with laughter. Jessica stood up.

'It's only a scarecrow,' she shouted.

Bloody Russian fell backwards as he spun in the direction of her voice.

'What are you doing?' Thomas tried to drag her back

down but it was too late. The Russian had stopped weeping and praying. He stood up, the crucifix still held out before him, and shouted something short and rough.

'It's not real,' she added.

He couldn't see her properly; she could tell from the way he was craning his head in her direction. He began fumbling through his pockets and suddenly her eyes stung with harsh light. With the torch on her face, their roles were reversed and it was now Jessica who was exposed, the man hidden behind the glare of light.

'Is Freckles.' Bloody Russian started to laugh.

Thomas was on his feet, tearing straight through the hawthorn bush. He grabbed the torch and held it against the man's eye.

'Don't speak to her.' His voice was odd – detached and utterly calm. The tramp dropped his head and let Thomas shove past him. As he was walking away, he stopped, spun round and delivered a sharp kick to the back of the Russian's knees, and he crumpled to the ground. The man didn't make a noise or attempt to move.

Jessica felt sick as they left Bloody Russian in the clearing.

Thomas walked her home without a word. As they reached her garden wall, she stopped.

'You've started a war with him now, you know.'

'He got what he deserved.' His voice was still tight and toneless. She realised he was furious once more; his enormous effort of control like a dog straining at the leash.

You shouldn't have kicked him, she wanted to say but couldn't, for fear of a casual dismissal. She'd witnessed two men in a vocal but half-hearted scuffle at a country fair once and a fight at school with shirt-ripping and cat scratches; but she'd never seen a violent act delivered with so little emotion.

'You didn't have to take his torch.' Jessica hugged her arms.

'It's mine.' Thomas showed her the initials TQ scratched into the rubber. 'He's always nicking our stuff.'

AC: *What makes you happy?*

TQ: *Jellybird.*

AC: *What's Jellybird?*

TQ: *Jessica. Her sister called her Jelly when she was little because she couldn't say her name properly. It's just a nickname.*

AC: *The two of you are very close, aren't you?*

TQ: *You don't like it, do you? You think she's too young. Well I don't like her in that way, even if she does act older than most girls my age. I'm not sick in the head, you know. She's a friend.*

AC: *I'm not being critical. Remember, we're trying to focus on positive feelings.*

TQ: *Right.*

AC: *In fact, today you walked in looking the happiest I've ever seen you.*

TQ: *It's her birthday. I made her a bracelet out of beach stones. Ones with holes and quartz crystals inside.*

AC: *Did she like it?*

TQ: *She was surprised you could make something beautiful out of everyday stuff.*

20

May 1995

Jessica's fourteenth birthday was on a Saturday. She could tell by her mum's busy air that something was being planned. For the first time in ages, Birdie was humming. Jessica pretended to write her history project on the Great War, all the while keeping an eye on her mother's activities.

By lunch, all the furniture in the living room had been pushed to one side, stacked up against the wall. Making space for something. As her mother scrubbed the newly exposed floor, Jessica dared imagine it might be for a party.

A surprise birthday party.

Lisa and Hannah didn't help but they didn't leave the house either, mooching around pretending not to notice what was going on. They even sat down together for what Birdie used to call a Saturday pic 'n' mix lunch, finishing off the week's leftovers. Jessica couldn't remember the last time they'd all been home at the weekend.

They were pretending to have forgotten her birthday, and that's how Jessica knew for certain that something big was being planned.

After lunch she took out every item of clothing she owned and tried to put together something grown-up, something for dancing in. She wondered who was coming. The girls at school had kept it quiet. No one had even mentioned her birthday all week, which had made her feel a bit down. Until now. As she was tying a knot in a long white t-shirt to show off her stomach, Hannah walked in. She lifted the corner of her mattress by the wall and took out her Jim Beam bottle. It was full of dark red liquid.

'What are you doing?' She'd caught Hannah's surreptitious sips at night but never during the daytime.

'I'm bored.' Her sister yawned. 'Can't watch telly with all that spring-cleaning going on downstairs.'

'What's Mum doing?' Jessica couldn't resist testing Hannah's reaction.

Her sister shrugged. 'Turning into a lunatic, that's what.' Then, noticing Jessica's knotted t-shirt and tight jeans, she added, 'Hello, what's going on here? You about to scurry out the window to meet that pikey?'

'Come on, tell me why Mum's clearing a space in the sitting room.'

Hannah shrugged, shaking her head. 'She's also cleared her bedroom and the dining room. No idea why. Don't want to know.'

Jessica sat on the spread of clothes across her bed. 'It's not for my birthday then?'

'Birthday?'

Jessica saw her sister try to bite back the word, the little wave of surprise it rushed out on. She turned her head away but it was too late; Hannah had seen the tears spring in her eyes.

'Oh, Jessie. Oh shit. Are you sure it's today?' Hannah jumped up, tried to put an awkward arm about Jessica's shoulders. Her breath smelled sweetly stale. She must have been drinking the stuff during the night as well.

'It doesn't matter.' She shrugged Hannah's arm away. Fourteen. Time to grow up. Rubbing her face with the unravelled hem of her t-shirt, she went to find Birdie.

Her mum was stacking chairs by the kitchen door, singing and smiling to herself.

'What are you doing, Mum?' Her voice sounded angry when she'd intended it to be uninterested but at least the tears were gone.

'It's May, Jessica my love. What do people do in May?'

Celebrate my birthday, she nearly said. 'Don't know.'

'Spring clean. We're going to have the biggest bugger of a bonfire tonight.'

Jessica looked around the kitchen, which was bare except for the stone island which Birdie had once tiled with little blue and white schooners on rough seas. The Aga and fridge also remained. Through the open doorway, she could see the dining-room furniture precariously stacked.

'What are we burning?' Jessica already knew.

'The past,' her mother said.

Back upstairs in their bedroom, Hannah was crying noiselessly, her face wet and screwed up. She didn't seem to care that her lips were stringy with slime from her nose.

'I just want things to feel normal,' she kept saying as Jessica climbed out of the window.

She found Thomas fishing on the beach. He looked up at her but didn't speak. There were purple smudges of fatigue under his eyes and a fading bruise on his temple. The stillness around him was solid. The grin of pleasure as he gave her the bracelet that morning felt like something she'd imagined.

She sat down beside him. 'It's just you and me, Thomas. Everyone else is shit.'

She waited for him to tease her but he didn't react; she took it as silent agreement. There was nothing shameful in being sad together. When it got dark, she left Thomas on the beach.

By the time she came home, all their furniture had been piled at the bottom of the garden like the actions of an orderly hurricane. From the garden gate, she watched Hannah drag the rug that used to sit under the coffee table.

'Weh-hey,' her sister called, unsteady on her feet. 'We're having a bonfire.'

Next came Birdie and Lisa, their arms full of awkward shapes – vases and picture frames. Lisa had a beer bottle sticking out of her jacket pocket. 'We're finishing off Dad's – Daniel's – beer.'

They were each given a box of matches and told to go and play with fire.

'Do it like this.' Hannah showed her how to hold the match-head against the gritty side of the box and flick it off, making a tiny, mute firework.

'Careful you don't set your breath on fire,' Jessica muttered.

She stood to one side for a few minutes before deciding to join in. Fuck it. This is how she'd celebrate her birthday; by setting fire to her childhood. In her pocket was Thomas's bracelet. She pulled it out stone by stone, careful not to snap the string, and slipped it over her wrist. Then she pinged a lit match at Hannah, who did a hilarious, hand-flapping dance as it hit her chest.

So the fun began. The sisters flicked matches at each other, at the sky, the piled furniture. Hannah lit a cigarette and tried to set fire to the armchair with the red and green stripes. *No one sits in the telly-throne but me*, her dad used to boom in a pretend giant's voice, and then they'd all try to pile in the chair, banishing him with their socked feet.

'It's got the bubonic plague,' Lisa laughed as Hannah covered the chair in smouldering pocks. Jessica waited to see what their mother would say about the cigarette but Birdie was busy throwing match after match at her king-size mattress.

Jessica took the opportunity to burn the red jumper her mother had made for her last Christmas; the patchwork dog on the front had recently started bulging out over her breasts so that people always seemed to be staring at the lumpy dog on her chest. The pink and burgundy floral runner from the stairs smothered the fire before the flames burst through with a magician's finger-snap, and the girls cheered. Jessica coughed on burning rubber and acrid melting plastic. She wished Thomas would come to the house and see what they were doing. He would laugh and that would make it seem ordinary. The beer in her empty stomach started frothing up her neck.

She touched Birdie's fingers. 'I don't feel well, Mum.'

Her mother nodded into the fire. Jessica hugged her mother's arm to her chest, resting her head on Birdie's shoulder.

'Stop being silly.' Her mother didn't move, leaving Jessica to unwind her arms and move away from the contact.

'Hey, don't forget this.' Hannah was carrying a black leather case, big and formless as a carpet bag. It was the vet's case their dad kept for emergencies. *You never know when you'll need a spare. My friend Mike lost his case under a cow.* Jessica still remembered her dad laughing as he told her the story.

Her mother said, 'Fling it on, Han. Big sweeping arm.'

Jessica grabbed Hannah's arm, hissing under her breath 'Don't.'

'Why not?' Her sister shook her off.

'He might need it.'

Hannah laughed, the sound of Chinese burns and telling tales.

'He won't be back for it, you idiot.'

As she swung the bag back, Jessica pushed her to the ground. Birdie rounded on them, snatching the case out of Hannah's grasp, hurling it at the fire like a hand grenade. She walked to the other side of the bonfire without a word or glance. Jessica braced herself for Hannah's onslaught but her sister squashed herself into the dining-chair swing and rocked, staring at the flames. Jessica's raised fists looked stupid. She wanted to throw herself down on her bed, except it was burning in front of her.

For weeks afterwards, the sea breeze blew ashes towards the house, leaving smuts in odd places – streaked across a clean plate, or on their cheeks.

21

June 2012, Nathan's House

Nathan doesn't say a thing. Pinching the postcard by its edges as though it might be lined with poison. Jessica grips her arms so hard her nails dig in. She can't look at him – sitting on the top step in his baggy pyjama bottoms with his concave chest and small pudding-bowl belly resting on the elasticated waistband.

He makes a noise as if to speak, then turns his head to the window instead.

'Look at . . .' Her voice is tremulous. Clearing her throat, she tries again. 'See the postmark?'

Then she has to sit down, her legs deboned. 'What does it mean?'

Still he doesn't speak, staring out of the window at the theatrical, constructed night. A sense of the unreal settles on Jessica, calming her. They have stepped off the world's slow-moving rotor into a nocturnal dimension. A place where Thomas might walk through

Nathan's front door once again. Jessica holds her head, palms damp against her cheeks.

It startles her when Nathan stands up and hands the postcard back to her.

'It doesn't mean anything.'

'How can you say that?' She scrambles to her feet, following him into his bedroom. He pulls a jumper over his head, stands for a moment with his hands on his hips, regarding his feet.

'What do you think it means?' His voice is soft.

'That he.' To dare to say it. 'That Thomas is alive.'

Back in Nathan's sparse guest room, Jessica props Thomas's postcard against the folded blanket and lies down, staring hard at it as though it might speak to her.

Somewhere in the forest outside his house, Nathan is walking, having refused to comment further on the postcard. *Give me an hour to sort my head*, he'd begged, and she had understood that need.

Somehow, without sensing its approach, she falls asleep.

An early sun on her face wakes her. Even as she's stirring, her hand reaches for the postcard. Bolting upright as she discovers it is gone.

'No.' She could weep as she flings away the blankets, rips the sheet from the mattress, empties her rucksack; vertiginous with the horror of having dreamed up the postcard.

Throwing open the door, she shouts for Nathan, her voice echoing in the empty house. At her feet lies the postcard – and beside it a local newspaper with a note scrawled across it in thick black pen.

Come to the farm shop. We'll talk then.

Adrenalin branches through her as she tries to leave the house. Rushing about, tripping blind, around the room. Her shoes, her coat. Leaving the house, door gaping. Racing back to close it. Stopping, steadying herself, hot face against the splintery wood of the door. Just breathe.

In her hand the postcard, clutched so tight it curls to the shape of her closed fist.

Then she starts to run, following the path Nathan took through the leylandii as he walked out in the middle of the night. It takes her into open fields. A nagging in her head says she doesn't know the way and she stops. Early-morning air scrapes through her. Birdsong is whipped from the hedgerows and away into a huge, white sky.

A stillness, like something celestial descending. When she starts to walk again, her footsteps are wide and earthed, pulling their roots out of the ground with every step. She knows these open planes and their boundary of sighing woods.

This world once belonged to her and Thomas.

By the time Jessica reaches Frotherton West Farm, she has walked off the delirious edge of adrenalin. Climbing the gentle elevation to the farm shop, she feels the delicious crunch of chalky stone beneath her feet, relishes the blood flow to the muscles of her thighs and the wind lifting away her hair.

This is strength. This is joy. This is how it feels when life shifts towards a new path.

The farm has changed since she last saw it. The outbuildings are now cornflower blue with wide windows and a cobbled courtyard. Light bounces off the glass and she heads for a dark opening in the corner. As her eyes adjust to the farm shop's muted interior, her mobile vibrates in her bag. A text from Libby, which she tells herself not to check – and does anyway.

Hurry home. If you leave your nest for too long a cuckoo will lay her eggs in it. Libs xxx

Sent at one in the morning, the signal on her phone only recovering enough to receive it now.

Jessica replies, *Perhaps I'll make an omelette. Back soon.*

And of course she hasn't called Jacques yet.

Nathan is behind a deli counter, serving a young couple with a baby in a sling. His dreadlocks are tied back with a piece of red and purple cloth, making his face look young and tanned.

She rushes to the counter, forcing the young couple to shuffle sideways. 'I got your note.'

Nathan's eyes flick to the disgruntled face of the man holding the baby. 'I'll be with you in just a tick, Jessie.'

With an iron-weighted effort of restraint, Jessica walks through the shop to pass the minutes, her head reeling with Thomas. Wandering along aisles of rough wooden shelving, tiny details spring out. Delicate, gold-edged labels; pungent twists of loose tea leaf; the salty, sexual smell of cured meat. She picks up marzipan fruits for Jacques, drawn by their chemical colours.

Back at Nathan's counter, he refuses to let her pay for them.

'Come on,' he says, giving her a double glance as though his sharp eyes have caught something in her face. 'It's quiet today.'

She follows him through a doorway behind the meat counter, into a windowless room. Cardboard boxes tower over a narrow desk with a computer and a fake tomato plant. They sit on upturned mushroom crates and he offers her tea, which she refuses. Can't think about eating or drinking.

'What do you think of the shop?' he asks.

'I've never seen pink Himalayan rock salt before.' Now that she has reigned herself in, she will take her time, an exquisite agony of self-control. 'How do you find all these amazing things?'

'Got a nose for it.' Nathan winks. 'I'm a natural-born shopper.'

'I can only imagine how popular that makes you with the ladies.'

Nathan rubs his nose. Still shy. 'I'm too scruffy for female company.'

Then she can't wait any longer. 'You sealed the postcard into the back of the notebook, didn't you?'

He shakes his head. 'That must have been Bertie.'

'But why?'

When his fingers start twisting a dreadlock behind his ear instead of answering, a flare of frustration sends her to her feet. 'And why aren't you surprised? Why hasn't this floored you?'

He looks up at her, his world-indulgent smile returning. 'I've always had a gut feeling that he was still alive.'

'But you sobbed at his memorial service, Nathan.'

He nods but makes no comment.

Jessica pulls off her jumper. The box towers are closing in, the room a sealed vacuum. Dizziness. She can't breathe.

'Also, I think I saw him.'

'Oh.' The sound is punched out of her. She steps back, heel colliding with the door. Grabs the handle so roughly, two of her fingernails bend backwards. 'When?'

'A few days after he smashed my boat on the rocks. I couldn't sleep. I was upstairs in the room you slept in last night . . . Are you OK?'

Jessica slides down onto the floor, focusing on the red crescent of blood gathering under one fingernail. She manages to nod.

'I saw a man standing under the trees in the yard. I think it was him.'

'You think so.'

'It was snowing, no moon. He was in the shadows.'

'What then?'

'Then he was gone again.'

'Didn't you call after him?' Jessica's voice cracks, she coughs. 'Chase him?'

'No,' Nathan says, as though it's the simplest truth in the world. 'That's not what he wanted.'

Yanking at the handle, she tears a blind path through

the shop until she finds a door. Once outside, she focuses on slow, steadying breaths; in through her nose, out through her mouth. Nathan stands beside her, smoothing his moustache along the sides of his mouth.

'Sorry. I feel odd. Like I can't find my balance.'

'Yeah,' he says quietly. 'Yeah.'

She stands on the hill with the world falling away from her. With each deep breath she pulls it back until the scrub, the distant trees and the blue horizon of water crystallise. With the sharpened focus comes a resolution.

She turns to Nathan. 'What was the name of the police officer?'

A blank look. 'Police?'

'Who investigated Thomas's disappearance.'

'That old bugger.' Nathan grimaces. 'Nilson was his name.'

'I'm going to speak to him.' Her heart begins to thud under her ribs.

'Don't.' Nathan stands back from her as if the suggestion bears a repugnant smell. 'From what I remember, he wasn't much interested at the time.'

'A young boy goes missing and he's not interested?'

'They had a bit of history, Nilson and Thomas. He'd done Thomas for a few minor things. Thought he was a troublemaker.'

'Thomas got in trouble with the police?'

Nathan shrugs.

'What kind of trouble?'

'Jessie, I loved that boy but there was no helping

him.' The strings holding his features snap, his face sagging.

'But don't you see? Nilson might remember something.'

He hasn't looked directly at her since she showed him the postcard. Now he faces her, arms sticking out from his sides, asking a question with his whole body. 'What difference would that make?'

'I've got to start my search somewhere.'

Nathan grabs her hand. His fingers are cold, bloodless, and there's a tremor running up his arm. So the postcard has affected him, she thinks.

'Listen to me very carefully, Jessica. He does not want to be found.'

She tries to protest but he leans closer, his fingers pressing into her palm. 'After all this time, that much is certain.'

22

Nathan asks her again not to track down the investigating officer. But his reasoning makes no sense; she doesn't understand how the length of missing years is excuse enough not to look for his little brother. She asks to borrow his car to visit her mother at Seasalt.

Leaning through the window of the driver's seat, pointing out various buttons and levers, he says, 'Take comfort in the fact that he survived the accident. He got away. Be happy for him, Jessica, and close that particular door.'

She nods and tries to mould her face into a convincing expression of acceptance. Then she turns the car towards Selcombe and the police station in the centre, silently apologising for her duplicity.

Rogue memories line the route. The posh lawn tennis club where she and Thomas once hid by the high hedge, pocketing balls that strayed over. Underage pints of cider at the Ship on the seafront. The pier, in whose dank shadows she and boys whose names she has forgotten drank dry martini straight from the bottle, long after Thomas had disappeared.

She whispers another apology to Nathan as she parks by Selcombe police station. The red-brick Victorian building is easy to locate, rising two storeys higher than the fishermen's mews houses on either side. Noting its darkened windows, she worries that perhaps rural police stations close for lunch.

But her real hesitation is fear; of trying to find Thomas and failing.

Of finding him.

If you think you can or you can't, you're right. Her dad's favourite phrase persuades her to climb the steps to the front door and press the intercom button.

'Can I help?' The voice, electronic through the receiver, sounds polite but vaguely suspicious.

'I was hoping to speak to Sergeant Nilson, if he still works there.'

Smart footsteps approach along a stone floor behind the door. A middle-aged lady in a loose-fitting policeman's shirt and trousers ushers her in.

Jessica explains how Sergeant Nilson investigated the disappearance of a friend of hers, a teenager called Thomas Quennell, seventeen years earlier. The officer makes no comment and Jessica is left alone in a square entrance hall with worn black and white floor tiles. One wall is papered with photocopies of cats and grainy, unsmiling faces, the word MISSING leaping out of the posters.

To her surprise, the woman returns a moment later

and shows Jessica into an L-shaped office that smells overwhelmingly male – stale laundry, unaired rooms and black coffee. There are three desks, each flanked by a wilting banana plant. Two of the officers in the room are on telephone calls. The third – an angular man with long, thinning hair slicked back from a high forehead – leans back in his chair, feet on the windowsill, tapping an unlit cigarette in time to a lively jazz tune from the radio on his desk.

'Sergeant Nilson?'

'Detective Inspector.' He indicates the chair opposite with a jut of his chin, palming back a string of blond hair that has shaken loose from his temple. 'So. A friend of a missing Thomas Quennell. Name rings a bell.'

'His father is Finn Quennell. He had a garage of sorts.'

Nilson swings his legs off the windowsill. Taps his cigarette on his chin. 'I know who you mean. Nasty piece of work, he was. Didn't he drown, or some such thing?'

'He disappeared in a boat accident. His brother says it was your case.'

Nilson's nodding, staring blankly at her the way people do when they are unpicking a ball of thoughts. 'It was.'

'I found something – new evidence – to suggest he didn't drown after all.' Her words trapeze into empty space without a response to catch hold of them.

His nervy fingers roll the battered cigarette back and

forth on the tabletop. 'Let me show you something,' he says. 'If you would follow me outside.'

Nilson leads her out of the police station and into the car park, where he lights his cigarette. He takes deep, panicky drags like he's sucking an asthmatic's inhaler. They are standing beside Nathan's car. Nilson rests a shoulder against the Land Rover's open-back frame and Jessica wonders if he's deliberately leaning on the car she just arrived in; a provocation of sorts.

She waits for him to speak, watching the seagulls overhead, their cawing reminder of the nearby sea.

'What do you see between the bakery and the chippie?' He points his cigarette at the row of shops on the other side of the road.

'Bins?'

'The sea.' With a glance at her wedding ring. 'Mrs . . . ?'

'Larsson. Though I normally go by my unmarried name, Jessica Byrne, the name of my jewellery brand.' *Funny*, she thinks, *this desire for utter transparency just because he's a cop.*

'Jessica Byrne.' He draws out her name like he's holding it up to the light. 'Another ringing bell.'

'You were saying something about the sea.' It's all an act, she figures, pretending to remember a case he has forgotten. He doesn't know her name because it wasn't linked to Thomas's disappearance.

Nilson squints at the narrow glimpse of water between the shops. 'Do you know how many missing boys I've had to deal with over my excruciatingly long career in the police force?'

She shakes her head.

'Young men are always drowning. They can't help themselves.'

'But he didn't drown.' She turns to face him, demanding his attention, the way Libby might have done. 'I was hoping you might reopen the case.'

'Like the telly programme?' Nilson grins, his teeth yellow-streaked between shapeless lips. '*Cold Case*, that's the one. I'm afraid that's not my department. You need the Missing Persons Unit.'

Jessica feels for the car keys in her pocket. This is a waste of time.

Nilson flicks the cigarette butt away, holding his fingers under his nose and sniffing. 'There are few things I love so much as a decent smoke.'

He bounds up the steps to the front door of the station and holds it open for her. 'Let's have a look at this new evidence of yours. Seeing as you've made the effort.'

Jessica follows him inside but doesn't sit down, handing the postcard across his desk. He studies it, a hand running his hair back from his face. 'And you're sure that this is postmarked *after* the accident?'

'I will never forget the date he disappeared.'

'Hah,' Nilson says under his breath. 'That little shit.'

His weary indifference has vanished. She holds her hand out for the postcard.

'I'll keep this,' he says. 'Fingerprints, and all that.'

'But I've only just found it.' Horrified, she stares at the postcard, feeling eight years old again, leaping in the air to grab her toy back from Hannah. 'I thought I needed to speak to Missing Persons?'

'I'll make sure it gets there.' There's something about his emphatic response that unsettles her; the grin on his ugly mouth. Nilson opens the grey cabinet beside his desk and drops Thomas's postcard into an empty sleeve.

Jessica stands up, her fingertips on his desk. 'You'll keep me informed?'

'Of course, Ms Byrne.' Nilson turns his attention to the computer, giving the mouse a shake; dismissing her.

'Shall I write my number down?' Jessica asks through her teeth.

'Leave it with Nikki on Reception.'

He doesn't look at her again, and Jessica walks out.

Nathan meets her at Gomeldon Station on his push-bike, which he shoves into the back of his car.

'How was your mother?'

'My mother's always the same.' Jessica can't muster the energy for another lie. 'Thank you for the car and for letting me stay.'

Hands in his pockets, Nathan stares at the ground, shifting his weight from foot to foot. Jessica waits for whatever it is he needs to say. When he doesn't speak, she tries to offer him a starting point. 'I'm sorry if the postcard has upset you.'

He nods, squeezes her hand before walking back to his car. Jessica is left with the sense of having fumbled the ball. There is something about the postcard he isn't telling her.

For the duration of the train journey home, the wild possibility of Thomas still alive flips over in her head like a coin spinning through thin air.

The train arrives in London just before one in the morning. She has been gone since yesterday morning without speaking to Jacques. She calls home.

'Where are you?' he asks evenly. His voice doesn't belong to someone newly woken; he's been waiting up for her call.

In the face of his level-headedness, an effusive apology seems unnecessary. She has, after all, only been visiting her mother.

Twenty minutes later, she hears the boisterous whine of his metallic green moped – the Green Beast – as he rounds the corner, her helmet dangling from one of the handles. He looks tired but there is nothing in his manner to suggest that her absence has worried him. As she thanks him for collecting her, she finds herself perversely irritated by his unquestioning trust. It lasts a matter of minutes, then she clings to him with arms and thighs as the moped's tin-can engine sounds rudely through the empty streets.

At home, he loses his fists in her hair, licks her spine, ties her in knots like a cat's cradle.

It's almost three in the morning by the time they are lying with their legs linked, heads together. Both drifting, neither allowing the other to sleep. Just to keep them there a little longer.

'Take a day off work tomorrow,' she whispers in his ear.

'Sure,' he says, but she knows he won't.

23

July 2012, London

A week after she discovered the postcard, Jessica wakes to the sound of the phone ringing. She doesn't answer, distracted by the sight of Jacques' untouched pillow, smooth as a bar of soap. Recently he has started sleeping on the sofa after a late night, so as not to disturb her. Once again she has slept alone.

The ringing persists and she lifts the receiver to find DI Nilson on the end of the line. Her stomach skips. The hope of finding Thomas has been dimming and flaring inside her chest like the rotating beam of a lighthouse.

Nilson launches into a long preamble; though he couldn't reopen the case himself he'd been putting out some feelers, doing a bit of research on his own time to assist the overworked boys in Missing Persons.

'Have you found him?' Jessica cuts in. She had meant to say *anything* not *him*.

'You've stolen my thunder,' Nilson says. 'Now whatever I say will sound lame.'

'But you've found something?' Jessica swings her legs out of bed and stands up. 'Tell me.'

'What we know is this. The boat smashed against the Lady's Fingers. Rough bit of sea, that, with an unusual current due to the shape of the bay. So says the coastguard.'

'OK.' Her fingers are cramped around the material of her t-shirt. She releases it, smoothing out the creases against her thigh. 'Go on.'

'Every splinter of that boat washed up. You could have rebuilt it. But no body.' Nilson's voice is jovial, as though they're discussing the weather.

Through the open doorway, Jessica can hear the floorboards creaking in the sitting room. Jacques is still at home.

'The interesting thing is, he couldn't have done it alone.'

'Sorry?'

Nilson chuckles, enjoying himself. 'Again, just the coastguard's opinion, but he says it takes some effort to scupper a boat as opposed to merely disabling it. The extent of the wreckage suggests it was deliberate. You pretty much have to go down with it.'

'So what does that mean?' Her heart is beating so hard, the fine cotton of her t-shirt shivers over her left breast.

'There's no way he swam out of those waters that night. The waves were three metres high in the dead of winter. Someone was waiting for him in a boat.'

'Who?'

'I was hoping you might have an idea.'

'No.' Jessica takes a deep breath, needs to calm herself in case Jacques walks in. 'How come you didn't find this out before?'

'No one was that bothered, if I'm honest. I did what I could with the little help I was given. But his family weren't interested.'

She thinks of Nathan and his lack of response over the postcard. How he begged her not to look for Thomas. Now she is certain he was hiding something.

'I'm grateful that you are taking the time to find him.'

'This isn't just about a missing boy, Mizz Byrne.' Nilson's voice has lost its false note of gaiety. 'This is an unsolved murder case.'

'Murder?' She almost laughs. 'How can it be? Everything suggests he's alive.'

'I have something you need to see.'

He refuses to elucidate. Before the call ends, she agrees to meet him on Wednesday at William Mansion's just before closing time. Replacing the receiver, she stretches out in the empty bed and stares up at the crumbling ceiling rose.

The call has unsettled her. Nilson's insinuating tone, his deliberate air of mystery making her feel somehow implicated in something she doesn't understand. The fact that he is travelling up to meet her on his day off to discuss a case that is no longer his.

An unsolved murder.

Can't say too much at this point, he'd said before

hanging up, and she'd wanted to smash the receiver against the side-table until its wire entrails hung out.

Jessica closes her eyes. Then she hears Jacques' voice, like the hum of an untuned radio from somewhere in the flat.

Talking to someone on his mobile.

When he laughs, it's a tamped-down version of his usual laughter and she wonders whom he's speaking to. Holding her breath, she gets out of bed. Walks across the room on legs like broken flower stalks. In the doorway, she catches her reflection in the hallway mirror.

And sees her mother. Pressed against the door frame, listening with the whole of her body. The image so vivid she can see the pink rosebuds and curling lace hem of Birdie's nightie.

Who were you talking to? Pouncing on Jessica's father, her fingers digging white into his shoulder and his look of disgust that somehow seemed to include Jessica, standing a few steps behind.

There's silence in the flat as his call finishes. Jessica pulls her t-shirt over her head, flings it at the mirror, kicks off her panties.

'You're pathetic,' she hisses at her reflection.

On her way to the shower, something cuts into the pad of her foot. Skipping back in pain, she finds an earring squashed into the carpet. She hobbles into the bathroom and holds the piece of jewellery up for inspection.

It's one of Libby's. She remembers its jangling ugliness – an art deco design with sharp angles and clashing yellow and pink stones. Before she can question why it is lying outside the bedroom, Jessica throws it into the toilet and flushes it away. Foot still throbbing, she turns on the shower and meets the bracing freeze of the water face on.

By the time she gets out of the shower, she's shaking so hard she has to hold on to the towel rail to step out of the bath. But her head is clear.

Nilson is playing games; he'll explain himself in two days' time.

And the earring could have fallen off during any of Libby's frequent visits. Perhaps even yesterday when she dropped round for coffee.

'Hey, you're awake.' Jacques walks into the bathroom as she is brushing her hair. He puts his arms about her waist. 'Christ, you're ice cold.'

Putting his lips to her neck, his hot breath fans across her skin and Jessica clenches her jaw against the shivering. It makes her mouth look thin and mean.

Who did you call on your mobile? She could ask him, and he would tell her. The question wouldn't anger him. But, unlike her mother, she would never chase a cheap piece of reassurance.

'I slept through the alarm,' she says.

'Don't be mad, but I turned it off. I thought we might take a duvet day. I just spoke to the shop and my office and made terrible, flimsy excuses for us both.'

This was another thing her mother had never understood. The explanation would come in its own time; it took nerves to wait for it. Taking his face in her hands, she touches her lips to the delicate skin of his eyelids. 'I forgive you.'

He gives a big, settling sigh like he's sinking into bed. 'Hey, I heard the phone ringing earlier. Did you get it?'

'It was a wrong number.' She rakes her fingers through the hair at the nape of his neck, making him shiver. 'I fancy one of your famous cheese toasties.'

Jacques grins. 'Let's eat them in bed and roll around in crumbs all day.'

Wrapping her hair in a towel, Jessica goes back to bed and watches Jacques drag the television into the bedroom, fuss with the curtains. She waits for his light mood to lift hers, but Nilson's words have made her afraid of what she doesn't know. Then there's the earring. The irrational dread of its discovery lingers like the pain of stepping on a sharp stone but it will pass. She needs five minutes alone to make a phone call.

'You OK, hon?' Jacques puts a mug of tea and two Rich Tea biscuits on her bedside table.

'I might get a little more sleep.' She sinks down into the bed, the spine of the counsellor's notebook under her pillow running a hard ridge along her cheek. 'Why don't you go for a run? Otherwise you'll be bouncing off the walls by mid-morning.'

'Sure. I'll get the papers.'

With her eyes closed, Jessica tracks the sound of Jacques' progress; his t-shirt drawer scraping open, a slight shuffle as he grabs his trainers from among the bonfire-pile of her shoes at the bottom of the cupboard.

As soon as the front door closes she dials Nathan's number, using the telephone in the sitting room where she can keep an eye out for Jacques. Across the road in Cavendish Square Gardens, office workers are sitting on their spread jackets, basking in the petrol-scented sunshine. A man with blond, tousled hair is walking on the pavement beneath. As if sensing her gaze, he glances up and Jessica jumps back from the window. When she looks again, he's gone.

Nathan doesn't answer, and she hangs up. Covering her breasts with her arm, she leans her head on the glass. Her eyes are drawn to every light-haired man down in the street, some tantalisingly similar to her childhood love. But they are never quite him. She keeps looking, because Thomas is no longer to be found in the pages of an old notebook; he is out there, somewhere.

She calls Libby's shop next, the earring put to the back of her mind because she has to speak to someone. Libby understands about Thomas. 'I need to tell you something before my chest explodes.'

'I hope it's filthy. I love filth.'

Jessica laughs, sounding breathless. 'Remember we talked about Nathan, Thomas's older brother? Well, I went to see him and while I was there, I found something.'

'You went to see his brother?'

'I found a postcard sealed into the back of that red notebook. Thomas sent it a week after he was supposed to have drowned. When I showed Nathan, he wasn't surprised. Do you see what that means?'

Libby sucks in her breath. 'Oh, Jessica. Is this what you've been up to?'

'You're not listening.' Jessica's voice rises with frustration. 'Thomas didn't drown.'

'You told Jacques and I you were visiting your mother.'

She sits down on the arm of the sofa. 'I can't explain this to Jacques until I know exactly what it is.'

'Don't think your absence hasn't been noticed. Even when you're here, your head's somewhere else.'

Jessica sees the earring crushed into the hallway carpet. 'What do you mean?'

'You're chasing ghosts when you should be taking better care of the living.'

'Thomas is alive.'

'Listen to me, darling.' Libby's voice takes on the low, melodious quality of someone trying to coax a cat from a tree. 'I understand why Thomas seems so important. He was your first love, your big adolescent passion.'

'This is not about a childhood crush, this—'

'Let me continue. We all had that first love and got over it. But because of what happened, your feelings never had the opportunity to take their natural course. They didn't get to fade and wilt like they're supposed to as you grow up.'

'I hear what you're saying, but—'

Again Libby interrupts. Jessica lets her arm drop to her side, so all she can hear is an electronic pitch through the earpiece. Sighing, she puts the receiver to her ear again. 'Libs, I know you're concerned but there's no need. I've got to go. Let's speak later.'

There's silence on the end of the line. Jessica wonders if Libby has hung up.

Then she says, 'Call work and say you'll be a bit late. I'm coming over.'

Before Jessica can protest, Libby is gone. When Jacques comes home, she'll suggest an early brunch at Fernando's. With any luck, they'll have left the flat before her friend arrives. There is a danger that Libby, in one of her impulsive moments, might mention Thomas in front of Jacques and in that way force Jessica to end the search before it has even started.

Twenty minutes later, the entrance buzzer sounds. Jessica ignores it. There's a moment of silence in which she breathes easily again.

Then Jacques' key is in the door.

'Look who I found loitering outside,' he says, and Libby steps around him into hallway. She fixes Jessica with an angry smile which Jacques misses, taking off his trainers.

'You can't go chasing men from your past.' Libby kicks the sitting-room door shut so that Jacques, going to making cheese toasties in the kitchen, can't hear.

Jessica sighs, sitting down on the arm of the sofa. 'You have a knack for making things sound seedy, you know.'

'You're going to jeopardise everything we have here.'

There's a pause, the length of an intake of breath.

'We?' Jessica asks softly, and watches a play of expressions – dismay to composure – move across Libby's face like the shifting of a theatre set.

'Yes, we.' She juts out her chin to bear the weight of conviction. 'It won't be the same if you and Jacques split up.'

Because then you can't see Jacques. The thought catches Jessica by surprise, a malicious voice whispering in her ear. 'Split up? A bit extreme, isn't it?'

Libby crosses the room, sitting down and resting her head on Jessica's arm.

'I love the four of us together. You and me and the boys. I can't bear it to change.'

Jessica nudges her gently away so she can meet Libby's eyes. 'I will tell Jacques everything when the time is right.'

'And when will that be?'

'When I know exactly what happened and why.'

Libby nods but says nothing.

'In the meantime, Libs, you're the only person I can speak to about this.'

'And you must.' Her hot fingers circle Jessica's wrist, eyes wide with sudden energy. 'Promise me you will?'

Before Jessica can reply, Jacques comes in with a tray. Helping herself to a toastie, Libby prowls the room while Jessica chooses one of the many black and white murder mysteries she records on Sky Plus but never watches.

'When was this taken?' Libby picks up a small framed photo from the mantelpiece. 'You both look so young and awkward.'

Jacques studies the picture with Libby, heads close together, causing Jessica a pang of discomfort with the easy proximity between them. He looks back at Jessica, smiling. 'I mortified Jessie by asking the sour waitress to take our picture.'

'I didn't know whether to be charmed or disturbed.' Jessica smiles, the memory swelling and lifting the atmosphere in the room. 'That he'd brought his camera to our first date.'

'Honey, it was to take pictures of the Longhaven Pavilion for my dissertation, if you recall.'

'Ever the keen student.' Jessica grins at him, and they settle together on the sofa, plates on laps.

Libby looks away, directing her attention to a cuckoo clock in the centre of the mantelpiece. She picks it up to read the scroll above its face. *'You'll find love in Longhaven Bay.'*

'I bought it for Jessica as a joke.' Jacques gets up. Taking the clock out of Libby's hands, he replaces it between the photographs. 'It made us laugh.'

'You'll find love in Longhaven but no working toilets,' Jessica says.

'You'll find love but no sunshine in Longhaven.'

'Or friendly waitresses.'

Libby's gaze shifts between them.

Those ravenous eyes of hers.

24

Jessica replaces the telephone receiver and drops her head in her hands. She shouldn't have called Nathan but nerves got the better of her. Instead of dismissing Nilson's reference to the murder with one of his lazy chuckles, his voice had tightened.

Don't speak to Nilson again, Jess.

Why not?

I should have warned you what he was like. He used to hound Thomas.

What for?

Scrapping. Petty stuff.

But he's coming to see me this afternoon.

Cancel it. Don't see him. The man's a nutter.

But it's too late. And she needs to know.

A muted bell sounds in the shop floor below and Jessica leaves her desk to check her reflection in the gilt mirror on the mantelpiece. Her eyes look wide and dazed with panic. She's tempted to slap her own face.

Marni's voice calls up from the shop. 'Jessica. There's a Detective Inspector Nilson here to see you.' The shop assistant's voice lowers as she directs the policeman up the stairs to the staffroom.

Nilson appears with an A4 envelope tucked under his arm. 'Watchsmiths and Jewellers by Royal Appointment,' he says. 'How genteel.'

Glancing around, his lip curls with disdain. Damaged candelabra, awaiting renovation, sprout from the floor like stunted silver trees. A lightning-shaped crack in the window has been repaired with brown tape. Jessica offers him her hand but instead he catches hold of her elbow. The contact is light – she lifts her arm easily out of his grasp – but its imposition sends an angry shiver through her. He throws up his hands with a backtracking smile, his eyes hard and brilliant.

'You'll want to take a very good look,' he says with his mirthless smile. 'Just in case you ever find him.'

Jessica takes the envelope to the oak table that serves as her desk.

'So what's the big mystery?' She is smiling to soften her words, to seem friendly, likeable. It occurs to her that she is afraid of Nilson. He stands over her as she opens the envelope. Three photographs slide onto the table, colours jumping out at her. Browns and charcoal-blacks and dirty, naked whites.

The body of a man lies in the mud, his arms and legs crooked and angled out like a flung marionette. His shirt is ripped open to expose a long belly, the blue-white flesh like the smooth skin of a mushroom pushing through a mulch of rotten leaves and mud.

'Look closely,' Nilson urges and against her will, she does.

There is a large gash across his chest, the ragged lips of the wound packed with grit. Worse, so much worse, the blackly pooled liquid which has set in one eye socket. There is something wrong with the lower half of the man's face – the mouth a huge and bloody hole, the jaw lying slack on his neck. Tufts of grey hair are visible through a thick plaster of debris and gore. Jessica swallows on a dry throat. Nilson leans in, smothering her in stale nicotine.

'The victim was Nikolai Oleg Galitzine. That's a Russian name, by the way.' Dread waterfalls across Jessica's scalp.

'Bloody Russian. Isn't that what you kids used to call him? He was found dead at the bottom of an unused slate quarry.'

Jessica nods, remembering Hannah rushing into their bedroom, the *Mercury* held above her head like a trophy. *Bloody Russian's gone and smashed his own head in.*

Nilson's finger runs a circle around the beaten head. 'This is what's worrying me. The way his jawbone's snapped. It's quite common to fracture your jaw in a fall, but this is different. It takes leverage. According to the forensic report there was evidence of trauma inside the mouth. Cuts and scratches. So what are we supposed to make of that?'

Jessica hikes her shoulders and looks away.

'Perhaps he was screaming and fell on some twigs. Could account for the lost eye, I guess, but my feeling is it would take a weapon, a knife perhaps, driven deep into his throat, to rip such a hole in a man's face.'

Jessica presses the back of her hand to her mouth, closing her eyes. 'I can't see this.'

'But you must.' Nilson lifts the photographs closer to her face. 'It's our mutual friend's handiwork.'

'Not possible.' Shaking her head, disbelief and anger burning off the nausea. 'This was . . . was an accident.'

'And yet Thomas was seen running away, covered in blood.'

'I don't believe you.' Jessica staggers out of the chair. Putting space between herself and the hideous images. 'Who saw him?'

'A credible witness.'

'Thomas was troubled; he made enemies. I'm sure there were plenty of people with a petty gripe willing to step forward.'

Nilson watches her carefully, tapping a finger on a close-up of the man's broken head. 'Including his own family?'

Jessica slumps onto the sofa by the door. 'His father . . . ?'

'Obviously I can't share that information, but we have no reason to doubt the witness statement.'

Shaking her head, she whispers, 'It's a mistake.'

'Only one person can answer that, and it seems he has miraculously risen from the dead.'

A rush of hatred sweeps through her as Nilson tucks the envelope carefully inside his jacket, protecting his nightmarish pictures. He smiles, head to one side. 'Honestly, Ms Byrne. Did you never make the connection? Your boyfriend vanishes, and then this particular man turns up dead not far from his father's land.'

'So speak to the father about it.' Her lips are stiff and untrustworthy, distorting her words. She hugs her arms about herself. 'Thomas didn't have that kind of violence in him.'

'He became quite the hero, didn't he?' Nilson shakes a cigarette from a packet of Marlboro Red and slides it behind his ear. 'Just like that, an entire community forgot what a little shit he was. Suddenly he was everyone's son. *One of our own lost at sea.*' Nilson's voice lifts in a creaking falsetto. 'Made me want to spew.'

Smoothing loose strands of hair off his forehead, he continues in a calmer voice. 'What was your first thought when you heard about the Russian's death?'

Jessica licks her lips. 'I thought . . . a bad man had met with a bad end.'

And she had fought the urge to open her bedroom window and shout, damning Bloody Russian to hell. But God and the universe were always listening, and they might punish her by keeping Thomas hidden and never give him back. So she had read the short article in Hannah's hand and shrugged. *Stupid bugger.*

'Quite a season for accidents, wasn't it, Ms Byrne?'

'It doesn't make sense. Bloody . . . the Russian died long after Thomas had disappeared.'

'A dog-walker found the body three weeks after Thomas disappeared. Perhaps it felt longer, what with Christmas and New Year and all that guff but it ties in with the autopsy findings. It'd been there a good while.'

Jessica shifts position, her body rigid against the sofa's slouching comfort. Exhaustion hums in her head, somehow not reaching her limbs. She gets up and stands in the doorway but Nilson shows no sign of following her.

'No one made the connection between a local boy drowning and an old drunk falling down a hole. Not until your postcard turned up. Then I saw the boating accident for what it was. A great neon sign saying *Look at me, I'm dead.* And I thought, why?'

'It wasn't Thomas.'

'How can you be so sure?'

'He was desperate to start a new life.' The conviction in her voice strengthens her. It comes from her heart, from the dark space where Thomas has lived all these years. She unfolds her arms. 'I'll see you out.'

Her hand bumps over trapped bubbles in the crusty wallpaper as she steadies herself on the stairs. Nilson's tread is light and quick behind her. She finds Marni by the glass display counter, holding an emerald chandelier earring to the light for the benefit of a stooped lady. She catches Jessica's eye, a question in her raised eyebrows.

Nilson slows as he steps into the room, studying the black-lacquered panelling, the glass cabinets with mantel clocks and candelabra, the dazzle of polished metals and satiny woods. 'So much shiny stuff.' He gives a mock shudder. 'Some people are no better than magpies.'

Jessica opens the door and follows him out. 'Why are you doing this ?'

Nilson's smile hitches over his gums and she thinks, *God, he's full of hate.*

'I found something interesting the other day. Something that seemed totally irrelevant until you showed up with your postcard.'

He pauses, waiting for a reaction, which she denies him.

'A police report, Ms Byrne. With your name in it.'

Jessica starts to close the door, forcing Nilson to step backwards into the street.

'What's fair and not fair. That's all anyone gives a toss about.' Nilson raises his voice. 'And getting away with murder is most definitely not fair.'

AC: *You're upset about something today, Thomas.*

TQ: *Nothing I can't handle.*

AC: *You don't have to put on a front with me. We're friends, aren't we?*

TQ: *Doesn't mean you get to know everything.*

AC: *You're right. But if you need to talk, I am here to listen and never judge.*

TQ: *It's Bloody Russian. That filthy sod who works for my dad.*

AC: *The one you and Jessica played a trick on? Thomas . . . what's wrong?*

TQ: *He did something to her. It's my fault.*

AC: *What do you mean, he did something?*

TQ: *He waited for her outside school.*

AC: *What did he do, Thomas?*

TQ: *The scarecrow was my idea. If she hadn't been there, he wouldn't have taken any notice of her.*

AC: *Thomas, listen very carefully. Is this something Jessica needs to tell an adult about?*

TQ: *I'm going to kill him.*

AC: *You have a right to that anger. In fact, I'm encouraged to see it but you must get Jessica to speak to someone she trusts.*

TQ: *There's no one. Just me. And I'm going to kill him.*

25

June 1995, Selcombe

As soon as she reached the school gates, she saw him hanging upside down from the branch of a tree on the other side of the road. His funny-shaped crucifix – rounded edges with a double bar and tiny rubies – dangled over his face, hiding his left eye, like the gold coins laid on dead people in the olden days. His jumper was rucked up, showing a white stomach with long black hairs and a pokey-out belly button. Black scabs crusted his chin. Bloody Russian was watching her with one eye.

Jessica stopped and waited for Micky, despite having rushed out of school moments earlier to escape her – Micky had been particularly irritating during biology, squealing and causing a scene as Ms Drew had dissected a rat. But there was no way Jessica was going to walk past the homeless man on her own. Since the scarecrow trick, he had started singling her out with his drunken babbling.

As they walked through the gates, Micky giggled into her palm, eyes popping. 'What's he doing?'

'Trying to get our attention.'

'Did you see him last week when he lay on his face pretending to be dead?' Jessica nodded. 'Until Jemima went up and asked if he was all right. She's so stupid, that girl.' Bloody Russian had leaped up, roaring like an ogre, and Jemima had stood rooted to the spot, hiding her face in her hands and bawling like a baby.

Both girls walked a little faster at the memory. In the tree, Bloody Russian started to chuckle. From the corner of her eye, Jessica saw him swing off the branch, landing neatly like a circus acrobat. Usually he staggered about, drunk and unbalanced, but today he was fast and light on his feet. Keeping to his side of the lane, Bloody Russian began walking in time with her and Micky. He had taken off his huge crucifix and was swinging it like a hypnotist's pendulum.

'Look at his cross,' Micky said in a high-pitched voice. 'It's got jewels and everything. He used to be one of them Russian kings, a Tsar or whatever.'

'Stop staring.' But Jessica couldn't help looking, either. Bloody Russian dropped his head back and dipped the crucifix into his open mouth.

'Eww,' squealed Micky, and he started laughing; a horrible, rumbling sound like something wet and slimy was coming up out of his chest.

The sound infected Micky, who started to giggle again.

Jessica shook her arm. 'Stop it.'

But it only made the girl laugh harder until she was bent over, no longer walking.

'Don't just stand there.' Jessica looped an arm through Micky's but the stupid girl couldn't catch her breath, let alone walk.

The tramp stopped walking and Jessica started to feel sick. They'd reached the end of the school lane and there was no longer anyone around. He was still waving his crucifix.

'You like?' His accent made it sound as if he was licking his words. 'Pretty jewel for pretty girls.'

He started across the road then sprang back as a red Volkswagen Golf rounded the corner, cutting him off from the girls. Jessica's legs were wobbly with relief. The woman in the driver's seat opened the passenger door and Micky, still wiping tears from her face, got in.

'Hi, Mum,' she said, chucking her school bag in the back. And to Jessica, 'See ya tomorrow.'

Jessica caught the car door as Micky tried to shut it.

'What's up, Jess?' In the safety of her car, the tramp was already forgotten.

'Say your goodbyes, girls.' Micky's mum gave Jessica a smile so quick it barely reached her upper lip. 'I've got nothing in for tea yet.'

On the other side of the road, the tramp had vanished. Micky peered past her mother to where Bloody Russian had been standing moments earlier. 'See, he's gone. He's just a bit of a laugh anyway.'

They drove away. And Bloody Russian rose from behind a bush, weaving like a snake from a basket. He stepped out onto the road.

She couldn't meet his eyes. Stared at his shoes instead. They were like her dad's best brown brogues except they were stained and the sole was coming away from the leather in places. He wasn't wearing socks, and the hems of his trousers were ragged and matted with mud. The shoes started doing a shuffling dance towards her, two steps to the right, two to the left.

Her legs ached to break into a sprint but if she ran, he might chase her and then they'd be in agreement that something bad was happening. She started walking again, her feet like awkward blocks of cement.

'Freckles.'

Bloody Russian was close enough for her to hear his breathing. Her back prickled. Any moment now, he would grab her. Tears started to run down her face; she bit her lip hard to stop from making a noise because she knew, she just knew, the sound of her crying was the cue he was waiting for.

At the end of the road she faced a choice; the longer but busier main road, or the cliff path – home in ten minutes via woods and empty fields.

As it turned out, Bloody Russian made the decision for her.

TQ: I went round to see if she wanted to go out in
Nathan's boat.

AC: You don't have to talk about it unless you want to,
Thomas.

TQ: I was throwing stones at her window but then I saw
something moving in the bushes. I thought it was a
dog. But it was her.

AC: And what did you do, Thomas?

TQ: I laughed. I thought she was playing a trick. Going to
jump out at me. But then she wouldn't come out or let
me take her hand. I had to climb in the bushes and
pull her out. Then I saw her face, her legs . . .

AC: It's OK. She's safe now. Do you realise, Thomas, that
what you are doing now is probably the hardest thing
you've ever done? Voicing something so traumatic,
after years of distancing yourself from your own
emotions. You're actually allowing yourself to feel it.

TQ: How can you sit there and say this is great, I'm doing
great, when I caused this?

AC: I can't comment on what happened to Jessica because
I don't know, but your reaction to it shows me how
much progress you have made.

TQ: Yeah? Well I'm going to kill him. How's that for
progress?

26

Stick close to people and passing cars.

Jessica took the ring road and was about to pass the cliff path when, with a quick shuffle of grit, Bloody Russian was standing in front of her. She veered away, crossing the road to avoid his outstretched arms. But there he was again, this time managing to catch a strand of her hair, letting it glide through his fingers. She ducked away but he kept blocking her path, hemming her in.

Herding her off the road into empty scrubland.

A car passed. She threw a silent plea in its direction but the driver didn't glance at her. Not even when Bloody Russian grabbed a whole fist of hair. She shrieked and he let go. Dropping her bag, she raced into the wasteland between the road and the woods. She could outrun him. Run all the way home.

As she glanced over her shoulder, her shoe caught a rock embedded in the path. A moment of startling flight before she collided, chin and knee first on the ground. The earth and sky swapped places and she struggled to get up, head spinning. Looking wildly about, she brushed grit and loose stones from her clothes, her knee and palms scraped and bleeding. Bloody Russian was nowhere to be seen. Feeling nauseous and shaky, she hobbled as fast as her injured knee would allow. There was still no sign of him. He'd been trying to scare her; punishment for the scarecrow.

If she could just get through the woods, she could cut across to the road leading up to her house. She'd be safe there. But a noise stopped her halfway through the forest. Keeping very still, she turned to face the track behind her, scouring the trees and bushes for the slightest movement.

She didn't hear him coming. The shock of arms padlocking her waist pushed all the air out of her chest. She couldn't even scream. An arm like an iron belt gripped her stomach while his other hand pushed through her hair and clutched hard, yanking her head up to the sky. Then he sniffed her neck like a dog. He stank of dried sweat and shit.

Awkward sobs forced out of her constricted neck. There was a wet, unsticking noise as he opened his mouth. Until that moment, she'd been cowering under an animal impulse to hunker down until the danger passed but the feel of his tongue on her face brought her to life. She smashed her head backwards. He gave a muffled sound as his jaw clamped down on his tongue. For a dizzying second, his hold on her fell away and she bolted forward, only to slam down onto the path, her feet locked inside his tackling grip. He pinned her legs to the ground.

'Get off,' she screamed, twisting round. There was fresh blood in the corners of his mouth. She'd done that. But he was laughing. Lowering his chest on her thrashing calves, snaking his way up her body.

Rage burned up her tears. She stopped trying to scrabble out from under him and swung her fists over her shoulder, blindly aiming for his head. Catching hold of her wrists, he crushed them together. His other hand smacked her head down onto the path. Pain and shock made her suck dust deep into her chest. He pressed harder; the raw scrape of stones against her cheekbone, her nose squashed into the path. Couldn't get any air. Suffocating. She scraped her head sideways, just enough to free a nostril. Coughing and retching on a gritty breath.

Something hard with a heat of its own throbbed against her buttocks, jabbing her through thin layers of material. She started to sob again, tears and mucus further choking her.

The fingers in her hair loosened. The relief of being able to lift her head from the road and breathe in fully. Then she felt him fumbling with his trousers.

With all her might, she started to shriek, 'Help me.'

Her screams forced his fingers away from his clothing, his hand returning to stifle her voice against the road. He sank on top of her, rubbing and thrusting with such force that her pelvis was a raw bone sanded down against the gravel. He was growling in rhythm. Crushing her chest, eyes filling with blood, ready to burst.

She was going to die. Going.

The sound of violent, shuddering breaths brought

her back. The weight was gone. The noise, her own breathing. Rolling over, she found him standing over her. The front of his trousers had a dark, irregular stain and her hand, moving of its own accord, found wetness on the back of her skirt. She gagged once, staggering to her feet. Her face was burning with pain, dirt ground into her teeth.

When he stepped towards her, she lost her balance but he slipped a hand behind her head, making her whimper, and lifted the cross to her mouth.

'You kiss,' he said, and touched the cool metal to her ragged lips.

27

July 2012, London

Jessica sits alone with a vodka tonic. Fingers fretted together, still shaking an hour after Nilson's visit to the shop.

Bloody Russian's death. The girls at school had discussed it in low voices – *He fell down dead. Dead drunk, he was* – and their laughter boasted their daring and irreverence. Jessica could imagine it all too clearly, the vagrant staggering around his campsite in a mindless stupor on a black, rain-slashed December night. No moon, no stars, no streetlights. Blindly stepping out over the lip of the quarry, his foot finding nothing but air. She shivers, finishes her drink and orders another.

Looking around the restaurant, Jessica tries to empty her head of those hideous photographs by focusing on her surroundings; the mundane and everyday. The place reminds her of Selcombe village hall, with dusty evening light falling through the windows onto a scuffed parquet floor. In the corner, a man in a three-piece suit plays the piano.

Libby breezes in – twenty minutes late – and stops to admire her reflection in the entrance mirror. Her dark hair, having grown out of its bob, is serpentine and glossy but it doesn't detract from the circles under her eyes or her unsmiling mouth.

'Now, what's the big drama, darling?' She bends to kiss her, reaching for Jessica's vodka at the same time.

'I've done something stupid.'

'Tell me.' She strokes Jessica's fingers, a contrived and distracting gesture. Under the guise of taking a drink, Jessica removes her hand.

'I want you to listen. Then count to ten and respond like you're on my side.'

Libby waves the waitress over and orders a grapefruit juice. 'I know how I am, Jessica.' She folds her hands into her lap. 'I can be tricky and difficult. I chase attention like other people chase their tails. But if you're ever in trouble, I'm the one to turn to.'

She bends and shapes words like balloon animals, Jessica thinks.

'Half of me wants to tell you, and the other half is warning me not to.'

Libby nods as if this is to be expected. 'Everyone loves my flamboyance and naughtiness. The party starts with me, you could say . . . But I don't think they trust me.' She fiddles with the edge of her napkin. 'That includes Matthew.'

It's an act, Jessica thinks. *More drama*. But when

Libby lifts her head, there are tears in her eyes. It throws her.

'The thing is—' Voice trembling, she dabs at her eyes with a napkin. A credible performance. 'I would really like us to be close.'

Jessica tries to bolster herself with a dozen images of Jacques and Libby together; the earring outside her bedroom; Matthew admitting to his wife's affairs.

'You can trust me,' Libby adds.

'Can I?' Despite herself, Jessica is relenting. It is always the same. Every time they're alone together, Libby wins her over.

The waitress slips Libby's drink onto the table and retreats. After three audible gulps, Libby shakes her hair back from her face and smiles through smudged make-up. 'Do you realise I never, ever cry?'

'Things would be much easier if you were less troublesome,' Jessica says. Then Bloody Russian's lifeless, gaping mouth fills her vision; she sways, light-headed and sick.

'Easier but duller.' From far away, Libby is laughing. She stops abruptly, catching sight of Jessica's face. 'What's wrong?'

'I saw the police officer who investigated Thomas's disappearance.'

'What did he say?'

The waitress comes to take their order, and Jessica is grateful for a moment in which to sieve through her thoughts; what she should and shouldn't tell Libby.

'He's convinced Thomas committed a crime before he disappeared.'

'What crime?'

'It doesn't matter.' Jessica grinds the knuckle of her thumb into the table's rough undersurface. 'Because he didn't do it. I know it in my bones.'

'But he must be basing his assumption on some kind of evidence?'

Jessica leans forward, her voice low. 'The point is, Nilson's suddenly interested in the case because I showed him Thomas's postcard. And there's a file.' She shakes her head, chewing the inside of her cheek. 'On me.'

Libby sits back in shock. 'What does it say?'

'I don't know. But I think I can guess. I just don't understand where it came from.'

'I swear I'm on your side.' This time, when Libby reaches for Jessica's hand, it feels honest. Her palm is damp but Jessica leaves her fingers there. 'What happened to you, Jessica?'

But Jessica can't bring herself to tell Libby about Bloody Russian.

The pianist beats out 'New York, New York', his fingers racing along the keys, flinging notes through the air where they catch in the back of Jessica's head like ringing saucepans. She drinks a third vodka tonic while Libby inspects her ruined make-up in a gilt compact.

Oversized bowls of Caesar salad arrive. Jessica chews and chews on a mouthful of lettuce and crouton, unable to swallow until she sluices it down with a mouthful of vodka.

Libby doesn't touch her food either. 'Do you think this secrecy is fair on Jacques?'

She says it so gently that Jessica bites back her angry response. In that moment of restraint, Libby's words sink in. How, caught up in the fear of his betrayal, she is guilty of betraying him in turn. She worries the inside of her lip with her teeth. The secrecy would hurt him. She can't think what to say.

'Whatever is going on with this policeman and Thomas, you need to keep us involved. You can't do this alone.'

Jessica is nodding. Looking at Libby, she finds only candid concern. Perhaps her suspicions are nothing more than her mother's voice grafted into her head. The earring could have fallen out at any time, and the red umbrella in the hallway had shamed her for imagining that Jacques had been visiting Libby in secret. 'Thank you, Libs.'

Libby winks, flips her palms to the ceiling. 'So, bring on the past.'

A bubble of excitement rises in Jessica's chest. Bring on the past. Nibbling a piece of chicken, she finds she is hungry after all.

'Did you just give me your blessing?'

They share a complicit grin and her anxiety over Nilson slips a notch like the loosening of a belt.

Jessica arrives home to an empty flat. She drops her bag, followed by her coat, onto the floor. Fumbles in her pocket for her mobile. Jacques' phone goes straight to voicemail. Next she checks the answering machine in the sitting room, and finds the red light blinking.

A man speaks, his words shaped with precision.

'A message for Mr Jacques Larsson from Paul Norsworthy at Mason and Dunthorpe's. We are delighted to inform you that your suit will be ready for collection on Thursday. Also, I believe you left your blue umbrella here at your last fitting, should you be wondering where it is. Wishing you a pleasant day.'

28

The sun shines out of a Greek island sky, filling the square with garish fairground light. All around her, people are laughing and lolling on the pub's benches, weekend weather on a workday evening making them punch-drunk. A hot, fried-onion breeze tickles her neck as Jessica pony-tails her hair away. It offers no relief from the heat.

Jacques has dived through the late-afternoon crowd into the black mouth of the Kingfisher's doorway to get the next round. When Matthew walks away from the busy tables to smoke a cigarette, Libby shifts along the pub bench. She frowns at him, then turns to Jessica. 'He looks unhappy, don't you think? I don't make him happy.'

Before Jessica can say something comforting, Libby's voice adopts a conspiratorial tone. 'Now, any news on the Thomas thing?'

'None. I need to go back and see Nathan face to face.

And perhaps Thomas's father as well.' The thought fills her with dread but if she confronts Finn Quennell – now surely harmless with age – he might let something slip and exonerate Thomas.

'Good plan.' Libby is nodding. 'When are you off?'

Jessica hesitates. 'I'm not sure.'

'You still haven't told Jacques, have you?' Libby is about to say more when Matthew rejoins them. She stands up.

'I'm going to give Jacques a hand.'

The thought of the two of them, concealed behind the walls of the crowded pub, safe from her eyes, makes Jessica's mouth dry. It is the reason she can't leave London to go in search of Thomas.

Matthew takes Libby's place on the bench, raising his face to the sun, his forehead already a raw pink. 'I've been meaning to ask about the progress of Libby's necklace.' He tilts his sunglasses to squint at her. 'Sorry, is it OK to ask, or does that constitute unhelpful pressure?'

'I've almost finished the outer casing.' Jessica shifts, sips her flat Corona which tastes like the cigarette smoke from the group of middle-aged women further along the bench. 'Remind me again when your anniversary is?'

'Twenty-third of September.'

'Still a few weeks away.' Her insides constrict with anxiety. Everything is slipping. A hundred times a day, she wonders whether Jacques' blue golf umbrella proves it was him visiting Libby that morning – surely there must be a million blue umbrellas in London. In this way, her thoughts tip back and forth like unbalanced scales, no conclusion to be reached. To distract herself, she thinks about Thomas but those thoughts drag with them the body of the dead Russian.

'Jessica?'

'I'm sorry, were you saying something?'

'I was wondering if I should go and help our other halves. They've been gone ages.' Matthew squints at the dark, crowded doorway.

Just then Jacques and Libby emerge, a drink in each hand. Sour-faced, they walk side by side like strangers, without a word or a glance.

'Cheer up, you two. You made it out alive.' Matthew pushes his sunglasses onto his head so that his hair tufts out behind the lenses, haloing his sunburned forehead.

'Now, where's the beer?'

Jessica wonders if Matthew has also noticed the tension between Jacques and Libby recently. They had become friendly, easy in each other's company after the weekend at Pear Tree Cottage. Now they are barely speaking.

Jacques gives a smile that doesn't reach his eyes, clapping Matthew on the shoulder and pushing a fresh Corona into his hand. Libby hands Jessica a large glass of white wine, treacle-yellow in the sunlight. 'Quite the little Texas whorehouse going on in there. Hands everywhere, and it's barely six o'clock.' Libby raises her glass to Jacques. 'Mr Larsson had to scold a man for pinching my bottom.'

Across the square, the sun has turned the large floor-to-ceiling windows of an ad agency into searing orange rectangles that burn their shape onto Jessica's retina. A sport's huddle of men in rolled-up shirtsleeves occupies a narrow shelf of blue shadow in the lee of the pub. Jessica touches her fingers to her damp hairline, feeling for droplets of sweat. Meanwhile Libby and Jacques are yet to sit down. Libby is asking Jacques about his latest project and he, in return, asks about the wedding season. Neither seems much interested; a conversation like a curtain pulled across a broken window.

Jessica closes her eyes against the tangerine glare and finds Bloody Russian's dead body waiting for her. What happened that night? She pictures Thomas the last time she saw him. Dirty and unkempt, his mood like an overblown balloon that could burst at the lightest touch. Her frightened fourteen-year-old self had been convinced he was covered in blood; something in later years she'd dismissed as teenage hysteria. Now she wonders.

Libby's laughter cracks open her thoughts. Jessica looks up in time to catch it. A smile passing between her friend and Jacques; stale, weary, but an acknowledgement nonetheless. Of what, though? Matthew notes their silent communication with a fleeting glance. Nothing registers in his face. He drinks his beer, equanimous as ever.

'How do you know Libby has affairs?'

He doesn't react, and she is relieved he hasn't heard. She doesn't really want the details. Taking his wallet out of his back pocket, Matthew leafs through notes and receipts. What he fishes out is an earring. Its pink and yellow gems glitter in the afternoon sun.

'Because she is careless. Deliberately so.'

The heat smacks the top of Jessica's head; she feels herself swaying. 'That's one of hers, isn't it?'

He tucks the earring away again with a surreptitious glance at Libby and Jacques. 'She left it on her bedside table.'

'Perhaps the other one fell down the side of the bed?'

His gentle smile makes Jessica look away. She cannot bring herself to tell him that she found its sister crushed into her hallway carpet.

'She likes to leave me clues. I think she longs for me to fly into a jealous rage.'

Jessica barely registers Jacques approaching.

'You look pale, honey.' Bending over her, he cups her face in his hands, kisses the tip of her nose. 'The heat is making you ill.'

When they get home, she begs some time alone.

'Go for a run, Jacques. I need a long, cool shower.'

He knows there's something wrong; she can read it in his searching eyes as she closes the bathroom door. The floorboards in the hallway creak with his indecision. Then he's gone.

Jessica crouches on the floor, hunched over her stomach. Bites down hard on the knuckle of her thumb but the pain is too blunt. Then she spots the smooth, white pebble, big as a seagull's egg, sitting on the windowsill. It sits so sweetly in her hand. She doesn't have to use much force – the stone's weight does the damage. The mirror shatters into slivers and triangles.

She sweeps up a handful of glass and grinds it

between her hands. The jagged points spike her palms and the soft skin between her fingers, random and shocking as bee stings. Bloodied glass rains into the sink but the pain is elevating. She hasn't realised the weight she's been carrying until – like a wall of sand sliding from a dune – it starts to slip away.

'Jesus Christ.' A shout behind her. Hands gripping. Jessica ducks out of the grasp, shoving her injured hands into her armpits. Her high crashes, shame flooding its place.

Jacques wrenches her hands free, holding them for inspection in his shaking grasp. He pales with horror. Puckered ridges of broken skin, welling blood. The sight sickens her as she sees it through his eyes.

'What have you done?' He grasps her face. 'What the hell is happening to you?'

'Leave me alone.' Turning away, she tries to wash out the sink but the glass splinters block the plughole. The water on her fingers has an acid bite, no longer cleansing.

His voice is pleading, hands slipping off her back as she shrugs him away.

'Jessie, please. Let me help.'

'Get out,' she screams. 'Get out. Get out.'

Later, when she has cleared the mess – walking back and forth past Jacques slumped on the floor, head in hands – she wraps long ribbons of toilet paper around her palms and then crouches beside him. 'I'm sorry.'

He doesn't react.

'It was an accident. I tripped holding a cup of tea and then . . .'

'Just stop.' His eyes are red as he lifts his head. 'I thought we left all that behind in Threepenny Row.'

So he'd known about the piece of brown glass all along. She straightens. 'This was a one-off . . . accident.'

'What the fuck is going on in your head?' The curse so much more ugly coming from him, who never swears. He apologises, goes to take her hand and then stops. Holds her wrist in a gentle grip. 'It's my fault.'

She holds her breath.

'I haven't made the time to sit down and discuss your father passing away and . . . well, I think you are struggling to come to terms with things that happened a long time ago.'

'I need to show you something.' She takes him into the bedroom and unearths her rucksack in which the red notebook is hidden. Beneath it is the Tesco bag. She hesitates, then pushes the rucksack to one side and extracts the supermarket bag instead.

Flaps her father's tweed coat out on the bed.

Jacques shakes his head. 'What is this?'

'My dad's old charity coat. Birdie gave it to me when I went down to collect my stuff.'

She sees it register, moving over his features like a clown's trick. *Hand goes up, smile, hand goes down, sad.*

'You remember the note she found in the breast pocket? Well, it's still there.'

Nodding, he snatches it up, rolls it into a ball and

shoves it back into the bag. 'This is your parents' history, not yours. Forget it.'

'My dad claimed the note was in the coat when we bought it, but who knows? My mum certainly didn't believe him.'

Jacques knots the bag handles together. 'Tomorrow we'll donate the coat to a charity shop. End of story.'

'Why do you think Birdie gave it to me? That note ended their marriage.'

Jacques rubs his face. 'God only knows with that woman. Hey, what's this?' The folded newspaper with the article on her first exhibition is lying on the bed, having fallen out of the bag. 'Look, Jessie. Do you remember this?'

The frown lines on his forehead vanish. She looks away as his face softens at the memory of those early, uncomplicated years. The lacerations on her hands throb with shame.

'Look how far you've come, baby.'

Jessica moves to his shoulder but before she can study the photograph, Jacques steps away. With a frown, he cranes his face closer to the photograph.

'What is it, Jacques?'

Shaking his head, he holds the newspaper clenched to his side. 'Enough nostalgia. I have something *you* need to see.'

He leaves the room, newspaper still in hand, and returns without it. Placing a glossy *Canada Travels* brochure on her lap, he says, 'I'm taking you away.'

Jessica fans through it. 'A holiday?'

'To start with.'

248

Canada. Pine forests, glassy shallows and kayaks gliding out over violet depths. The pictures make her thirsty with longing.

'I've been making a plan,' Jacques says. 'When I finish the Arden Group project next March, I'm handing in my notice. We'll spend the first month getting to grips with our kayak on the Connecticut River and catching up with my folks.'

She's nodding, wide-eyed as a child.

To leave everything behind.

'Then we head off to Desolation Sound in British Columbia.' He points to a wide, blue expanse dotted with rocky islands. She imagines touching the unbroken silk of water with her open palm, feeling the cool suck of the surface as it draws her in.

'I have a picture of you in my head.' He smiles; an imitation of his usual lazy grin. She has ruined his smile. 'Sitting by the campfire, your hair wet from swimming, freckles on your shoulders. Just you and me.'

There is such longing in his voice. It overrides the gnawing pain of her suspicion and she can believe – for one brief moment – that he is the same good, trustworthy person she married.

'You said to start with?'

'The plan was to spend a few months away.' He cups her injured hands. 'Now I'm not sure we should come back at all.'

TQ: *He's back.*

AC: *Who, Thomas?*

TQ: *Bloody Russian. Turned up out of nowhere, knocking on the door last night. My father took the fucker back.*

AC: *Avoid him. Don't let him undo all the progress we made over the summer. You're so different from our first session – communicative, more connected to your own emotions, happy. Thomas, you've been happy recently.*

TQ: *Because he disappeared, that's why. No one's seen him in months. I can't believe he's stupid enough to show his face around here again. Now I have to kill him.*

AC: *Macho rubbish, Thomas. You're more intelligent than that.*

TQ: *It's genetics, not intelligence. When my dad gets angry, he sorts it. That's all I know.*

AC: *Fight it. Break the pattern.*

TQ: *What, turn the other cheek?*

AC: *No. Do the right thing. Behave like the functional, intelligent member of society that you are. What would I do, in your position?*

TQ: *You would . . . go to the cops.*

AC: *Exactly. Don't wait for your temper to get the better of you. Take control of the situation and do exactly the opposite of what your father would do.*

29

August 1995, Selcombe

'My dad once killed a man.'
Jessica had been drifting off, her head resting on the outboard's rubber side, face in the sun, listening to the *slap slap* of waves against the hull.

Now she squinted up at Thomas. 'He killed a man?'

'In a bare-knuckle fight in some East End sweatshop. He used to make a lot of cash doing it.'

She sat up. 'How could he get away with that?'

'The man he killed wasn't supposed to be in this country. An illegal.'

Thomas cut the engine, letting the boat rock with the surf. Jessica lay back down, shading her face with her hand.

'Didn't he feel bad?'

'Could just as easily have been him.'

Jessica didn't say anything. Half an hour earlier, she'd been watching him bail rainwater from his brother's red tender, slopping it over his trainers; grinning through his curses. She'd laughed so hard her ribs hurt.

Until the man in a neighbouring skiff had complained that his six-year-old didn't want to hear such foul language. She saw his face change, emptying of all emotion. With a single bound, Thomas was on the man's boat. The little boy slipped his hand into his father's, blinking at Thomas. When the father stood up, his full height fell an inch short of Thomas's, and Jessica watched the man's Adam's apple dipping in and out of his beard, his grip making his son squirm. Jessica tried to say something but her mouth had gone dry. She had stared at Thomas's back as he silently shifted his weight between his wide-planted legs, making the skiff rock. Telling herself she knew him. There was nothing to be frightened of; and yet an adult's fear was contagious. It cracked open the ground.

Having said not a word, Thomas had leaped back onto the tender, whistling as he finished slopping out the bilge water. Jessica told herself it was a show of bravado. The man and his son quietly left.

Thomas then guided the tender out of the harbour, past seagulls bobbing like fishing floats on the still water. She'd lain down on the narrow bench, feet and head on the tender's rubber sides with the sun and perhaps – she imagined – his eyes on her face. Trying to regain some of the happiness she'd felt before Thomas frightened the man and his little boy.

And now he wanted to talk about his father beating someone to death.

'Sounds like bullshit to me.'

'You wouldn't say that if you knew him, Jells.' Thomas stood up, spread his feet and started rocking the boat from side to side. She closed her eyes, seeing the man stagger slightly as Thomas had rocked his boat. 'My dad was the same age as I am now.'

His voice gave nothing away. She couldn't tell if he was impressed or ashamed. He gave the start-cord a mighty yank and the noise of the engine tumbled the seagulls away.

'Look,' he shouted over the noise. 'Buffer Bay.'

Jessica knelt up on the slat bench and caught sight of a white fingernail of sand surrounded by flint cliffs. Her dad had promised to take her on one of the big catamaran tours – even though he loathed anything touristy – to spot seals. Instead, he'd left. This was better anyway. Just she and Thomas in their own boat. The kind of outing she'd pictured, gazing over the sports fields from the locked window of a stuffy classroom, counting down the last days of term.

Somehow that perfect summer couldn't quite get started. Thomas would run off, or fail to show up, or his face and hands would bear such an ugly stamp of violence that after a while she would leave, weary with the pretence of not noticing.

'Can you see any seals?' he asked as if they hadn't just had a conversation about his dad killing a man.

She shook her head. Thomas steered the tender through a narrow gap between the boulders guarding the bay. Behind it, the water was tropical blue.

'Isn't that your chapel?' Jessica pointed at the stone

building balanced on a slab of crumbling rock, halfway up the cliff.

'This is the only way to reach it now. They've got guard dogs on the land behind it.'

Jessica screwed up her eyes in the brilliant light. 'Thought we were looking for seals?'

'I'll take you to Harbinger Bay sometime. There are loads there.'

He let the boat run up onto the beach then grabbed his fishing rod, clambering along the rocks to a flat boulder where he cast off. Jessica lay on her stomach, pressing the shape of her body into the sand. The bruises on her hips were long gone but she was no longer comfortable lying on her front. Sitting up, she crossed her legs and tilted her head back. Somewhere under the same summer sky was her father, perhaps driving or eating a sandwich. He might even be looking up and wondering where she was.

When her neck began to ache, she got up to hunt for sea glass, filling her pockets with green, blue and white pieces like scuffed gemstones.

'What've you found?' Thomas called over to her.

'Treasure,' she said, then wished she hadn't. Sometimes he rolled his eyes when she said babyish things. She climbed over to Thomas's boulder.

'Coming to show me your treasure?' His elbow made a nudging motion without reaching her. Thomas seemed to keep himself just out of reach, shifting with the dexterity of a boxer to avoid a touch. Which was ironic, Jessica thought, given the only human contact he found acceptable was delivered with a fist.

She ignored his tease. 'Yesterday in Selcombe High Street, a car drove really slowly past me. Then it speeded up before I could see the driver properly.'

'So what?'

'I thought maybe . . . it might have been my dad.'

Thomas flicked his line out into the sea again. 'What kind of car was it?'

Jessica shrugged. 'It was silver. Quite big. The kind of car he likes. He left the old one with us, so he must have bought a new one. To do his rounds.'

'It wasn't your dad.'

'How do you know?'

'It was just some old perv.' Then he added through gritted teeth, 'Sorry.'

Jessica pretended the mention of some old perv hadn't sent a sick shiver through her. Thomas wound in his line with rough haste; tensing, reeling himself in. The thing with Bloody Russian was always there, the two of them stepping around it like roadkill.

'Why shouldn't it have been my dad?' she demanded.

'Because your dad has a white Ford Fiesta.'

'You've seen him.' Jessica scrambled up, bare feet slipping on the rock. 'Where? When?'

'I can't remember.' Thomas scowled at the water. 'Why does it matter?'

'Why? What do you mean, why?'

'I can't remember.' It came out as a shout as Thomas sprang to his feet. Flinging down his rod, he started to climb back to the beach.

Jessica squeezed her fistful of sea glass. With all her strength, she pelted them at his back.

'That bloody hurt.' He chased her as she jumped onto the sand, his face suddenly blank. With a shriek, she evaded him but he dived and caught her foot, dropping her face down. She kicked out hard, a brief spasm of panic.

'Get off.' Her voice was squeaky, her heart like a trapped bird in her chest.

'You're dead, Jellybird.'

Scrabbling to her feet, the pressed white light that always seemed to be lurking at the back of her head descended. Through a blind haze she ran for the shallow steps carved into the cliff-face.

'Stop running.' His voice reached her from far away but it was too late to reign the terror in. Her body locked into a forward plough, feet slipping on steps treacherous with salt and sand. Thomas came chopping up behind her. He caught her at the top of the stairs, grabbing her wrist.

'It's me, Jellybird.' Holding his face close to hers, trying to catch her eyes. 'It's only me.'

With shuddery breaths, Jessica's head began to clear. 'I thought I saw Bloody Russian yesterday. Near the caravan park.'

Thomas released her arm. 'You saw him near your house?'

'But it can't have been him.' Jessica dropped down onto the long grass. 'No one's seen him since . . . you know.'

'Next time you see him, come and find me. OK?'

The blood drained from her face, chilling her as though a cloud had crossed the sun. 'He's back?'

'Come on, let's go to the chapel.'

She let Thomas take her hand – docile as a whipped dog and full of shame because he'd seen how damaged she was. And Bloody Russian was back.

He led her along a path, tightrope-narrow, which hugged the cliff. Seagrass knotted between her toes as she shuffled forward, a sheer plunge, inches to her left, trying to tug her over the edge. She was empty now, too drained to experience a new fear.

When they reached open ground, Thomas swung her into a fireman's hold.

'We made it, we made it,' he sang and Jessica broke into hysterical giggles, head and arms lolling as he ran to the chapel. She was still bent over, convulsed with laughter as he opened the wooden doors and pushed her inside the dark cave of the chapel.

Damp and dust filled her nose. There was a story she'd heard about a girl who breathed in poisonous fungi spores and died. A great flapping noise made her jump. Thomas was shaking out a blanket and laying it in a corner. Beams of light shone through gaps in the roof and walls. One of them fell on an alcove with candle stubs and photographs. Ignoring the grit sticking to the soles of her feet, she crossed the floor to look at them, afraid they might be pictures of another girl. Instead they were of a woman reading in a garden deckchair; looking out of a window; chasing two boys in a hallway, laughing. She was pretty and sad at the same time.

'My ma,' Thomas said from the corner. He'd pulled a

sleeping bag out of a crate in a cupboard and was laying it on top of the blanket. 'Do you think I look like her?'

The woman was slight, her legs as thin as a child's. Her hair was long and very straight. Thomas, in comparison, was tall and broad, his hair falling in thick, unruly waves.

'You have her eyes.'

'And her hands.' Thomas stretched out his fingers. 'Look at her hands.'

Jessica nodded, but his mother's hands looked small and fluttery as bird's wings, where his were wide and powerful. There were deep, red cuts on his fingers. More like the hands of a bare-knuckle fighter.

'Sit down with me.'

She perched on the edge of the sleeping bag, which suddenly seemed too small. Thomas started fidgeting, a hand under his t-shirt as if he were trying to reach an itch on his back. Then he grinned and held out his hand. Three pieces of sea glass sat on his palm.

Jessica picked up the blue piece. 'When my dad first left and I used to think about him all the time, it was like holding broken glass.'

'And now?'

'Now I've rubbed it smooth with all my thinking.'

'That's how it feels to grow up.' He looked straight at her in a way that made her face grow hot. Then his eyes drifted down to the scar on her chin and his face went blank.

She needed to distract him. 'What made you follow me, you know, before we knew each other?'

'I saw you on the edge of all those dumb, giggling girls and I thought, *She's like me. She does her own thing.*'

Jessica shrugged. 'So what?'

'And I thought you were pretty.' With a sigh, he dropped back onto the sleeping bag. 'I sleep here sometimes.'

'It feels lonely.'

'Lie down.' He crossed his arms awkwardly over his stomach and she lay back, head on the sleeping bag, body on the filthy floor. The light-haired saint stared at her from his sea of silver fish, his face full of sorrow as he searched for drowned sailors.

Thomas squinted at her. 'Don't be silly. You can't sleep like that.' Slipping his fingers inside the waistband of her trousers, he jiggled her towards him. He can't have meant to, but his fingers hooked beneath her underwear so his knuckles were against her naked hip.

Mortified, she pushed his hand away. 'Sto-op.'

Even so, she shifted closer until their sides were touching. Her breathing was all wrong, too loud and fast.

'I'll take better care of you from now on, Jellybird.' Reaching out, he stroked the rough scar running along the bottom of her chin. 'I promise.'

She watched the muscles in his jaw jumping. 'It wasn't your fault.'

'I told my dad about that fucking bastard.' Thomas was speaking through his teeth, caught up in the memory. 'He didn't care. He said cheap labour had more value than a useless son.'

Her skin was beginning to feel tender under the

pressure of his thumb. She lifted her chin away. 'It doesn't matter.'

With a growl of anger, he pushed his fists into his eyes. 'Then he said you'd stop making stuff up to get my attention if I . . .'

'What?' Jessica sat up.

Thomas grabbed her hand. Rolling onto his side, he pulled her arm around him, tucking her hand between his ribs and the floor.

'Who cares what that stinking old git thinks. You and me. That's all that matters.'

With her body pressed against the length of his, she could feel the hard wrap of muscle over bone and the subdued heat of his skin through his T-shirt. What shocked her was how slight he seemed, how easy it was to circle him in her arms.

Jessica lay very still, his heartbeat in her palm.

30

Jessica sits, eyes closed, in a column of drowsy sunlight from the skylight above, eating a home-made tuna sandwich. The desk fan ripples the pages of her sketch-book as it paddles currents of stuffy air around the quiet studio. When the phone rings, she can barely muster the energy to answer it.

'You're going to a party,' Libby trills. 'You'll love it.'

But Jessica loves going home to the leather-shoe smell of the sitting room as the carpet heats in the sun-light. She has made a collage of aquamarine water, pebbled shorelines and seals, blue-tacked to the wall. Jacques comes home early these days and checks the collage for new additions. Holding on to their escape plan as keenly as she is.

'Come dressed in purple or gold.' There's a forced note of confidence in Libby's voice. Soon, Jessica thinks, she can release the dragging remains of this friendship for good. Until they board the aeroplane, she will keep Libby close, where she can watch her.

'I don't have anything purple to wear. Let alone gold.'

'You're a goldsmith, for God's sake, drape yourself in your work. Six thirty at mine, please.'

Her drama no longer intrigues Jessica; it has a staged, needy quality now. Libby can feel her pulling away. It's why she keeps coming round, as if she's afraid that one day, Jessica will simply drop out of contact. Or perhaps it is an excuse to bump into Jacques. She wonders if Libby has told him about this purple-and-gold party of hers.

'Live a little, darling.'

Jessica rips the page out of her sketchbook. Her concentration is shot. She can't risk Jacques going without her.

At six thirty, Jessica arrives at a four-storey Victorian terrace, its scrolled portico pillars twined with climbing roses. Libby greets her on the doorstep in an evening dress the colour of antique gold, a purple fur stole around her shoulders. She takes in Jessica's studio jeans and the red polishing dust caked under her fingernails.

'Luckily I've thought of everything. As always.'

In the guest room, a purple wrap dress with a deep V hangs from the cupboard door. When Jessica puts it on, the top sags open showing the ridges of her breastbone. She presses her fingers to the fine skin, feeling her ribs.

'I look like a chicken carcass.'

'That's the spirit.' Libby drapes a heavy gold coil around Jessica's neck and hands her a pair of black velvet stilettos that tie at the ankle with a bow.

'You could seduce the Pope in those shoes. There, beautiful again.'

A brief pang of guilt over the nasty thoughts she's been cultivating in the dark glasshouse of her head. The guilt doesn't last long.

She manages to say, 'What would I do without you, Libs?'

'Die of boredom.' And Libby drops a light kiss on her bare shoulder. 'Taxi'll be here in fifteen.'

The minicab drops them at Bartholomew Lanes.

Jessica frowns. 'We're going to your shop?'

Libby smiles, linking her arm through Jessica's. A small group of people wearing purple and gold stand outside the florist's. Libby stops before she reaches them, pointing up at an old-fashioned shop sign with gold lettering and a purple, droop-headed flower.

'I've had the whole place rebranded. E.H. Flowers is now . . .' She waits for Jessica to read the sign aloud.

'Belladonna.'

'Deadly nightshade. Beautiful on the outside, poisonous on the inside.'

Libby sends her off to inspect the newly decorated shop while she catches up with her PR agency. 'Remember to think nice thoughts if you speak to a journo.'

The shop is crowded. Waitresses with golden paper flowers in their hair serve purple cocktails, which Jessica avoids, accepting a glass of champagne instead. She hardly recognises the interior. Gone are the dusty, whitewashed shelves and black plastic buckets; in their place stand pedestals of exotic flowers in gold, wide-mouthed vases. A chandelier above the new marble counter casts triangles of confettied light across the crowd.

Her first visit to the shop had been in February; over half a year ago. She remembers the smell of pollen and wet soil, and how the orange street light was sliced into tiger stripes as it fell through the plants. Libby had charmed her. She'd come home to Jacques and declared that her new friend was unlike anyone she'd ever met. Libby had a way of making her feel chosen. The flower shop became their regular haunt, a place for a quiet drink once the shop closed, with leaves tickling their legs and the air-conditioning grizzling in the corner.

Jenny – one of Libby's shop assistants – waves across the room at her. Jessica returns her smile but keeps wandering. A hand-tied bouquet by the counter catches her eye. She's never seen black tulips before, their petals so lustrous they look as though they'd leave a velvet smudge if touched. There's a note among the flowers. It's the handwriting that makes her stop, squat down and hold the message in fingers like crumbling leaves.

Black is for the days I cannot see you.

Written in Jacques' steady hand. Pushing the note back into the bouquet, she steps back. The door is sealed by a tight wall of bodies, and she bites back a panicky urge to hurtle through them.

Libby appears at her side, cheeks flushed. 'Un-recognisable, right?'

Jessica can't look at her. The bouquet has been left where she might find it. *Deliberately careless*, Matthew had said.

'I'm so glad you're here.' Libby squeezes her hand. 'I was expecting another excuse.'

'Work's been busy.'

Libby nods, working her mouth the way she does when something is bothering her. 'You're up to something, Jessica. I know it.'

Her voice is so flat, it breaks their light pretence. 'You're just feeling left out.'

'I'm not the only one.'

'You mean Jacques.' Jessica's voice is bitter with accusation; she hears her mother.

'He's a friend. We talk.'

Jessica slips her hand inside her bag and finds the hard cover of the counsellor's notebook. It gives her strength. Thomas is alive, and she will find him. This moment shrinks until she can step outside it.

A bald man with a purple flower behind his ear steps between them, speaking in a low, melodic voice that excludes Jessica from the conversation. As she places her glass on the counter, a lock of her hair curls forward. Libby reaches past her companion and tucks it behind her ear. 'You're not leaving?'

'I'm not in the mood for a party.'

Libby follows her to the door, the man with the purple flower trailing behind. 'I know what you're doing.' Stepping closer, her voice lowers to a hiss. 'You're running away.'

Libby's companion pretends not to listen.

Jessica wants only to be gone. 'Let's not ruin your big night.'

'Mysterious Jessica with all her secrets. Does Jacques even know you?'

'What about you? Smiling at my face, winking at my husband behind my back.'

Libby dismisses her words with a furious snap of her wrist. 'I had to tell Jacques, you know.'

She starts to feels dizzy. 'Tell him what?'

'About your quest to find your long-lost lover boy.'

Taking a step back, Jessica's heel catches the back of a man's leg, who curses, scowling at her as he rubs his calf.

'You told Jacques about Thomas?'

'He's beside himself with worry. He knows something's going on.' Libby's voice rips a hole in the polite conversation around them. People stare, their collective interest like a tightening noose.

'Sometimes a true friend has to put herself on the line,' Libby adds.

'Friend?' For one giddy moment Jessica allows herself to say the most awful thing she can think of. 'I don't trust you any more than this bunch of sycophants. You're absolutely correct, Libby. No one wants to risk a friendship with you.'

'Why are you being so awful, Jessica?' Libby lifts her chin. 'Is it because I mentioned Jacques?'

'You just can't help yourself.' Jessica turns away, upsetting a flower pot which lolls on the floor, spilling water and white lilies. 'Don't call me, don't turn up at my house and you can tell Matthew I will no longer be making your anniversary present.'

Libby crouches to pick up the lilies. The petals shake as she places each flower back in the pot, the water soaking into the hem of her dress. There's a light, dizzy feeling in Jessica's head, something close to a deep, clean cut.

'Did I mention that Jacques and I are moving to Canada?'

'Your precious Jacques.' Libby doesn't move, hunched over the spilled vase. 'Ask him the truth about me, Jessica. I dare you.'

'Nothing you say touches me.' Her limbs loose and awkward as a broken doll, Jessica stumbles towards the door. Following the street lamps like beacons, she makes it to the end of the row of shops before staggering down a side alley, retching and miserable.

When she feels utterly and painfully empty, she straightens. Rummages through her bag until her fingers touch something cold, metallic. A penknife with a flame pattern of reds and oranges. It had been a present from Jacques, years ago, after she left Three-penny Row to move in with him. *To sharpen your charcoals with*, he'd said, but what he was really saying was *I trust you*.

It fits beautifully inside her hand. She presses the tip into her palm until the skin puckers without breaking. Saliva floods her mouth, anticipating a spear of clarifying pain.

With a tremendous effort of will, she snaps the knife

shut. Pictures instead how she will remove every scrap of her Escape Plan collage from the wall and burn it.

Her father used to say, *As one door closes, another always opens.*

She is now free to search for Thomas.

31

Jessica walks all the way to Shaftesbury Avenue before the pain in her feet becomes excruciating. Untying the bows of Libby's stilettos, she places them neatly on the pavement and continues barefoot to a McDonald's on Tottenham Court Road. She buys a milkshake for her empty stomach and finds a corner to hide in, blankly observing the throng of youngsters. There's an occasional glance at her elegant party dress and filthy, naked feet; nothing more than a passing flare of curiosity. When custom thins enough for her to become self-conscious, she walks home. Even at this late hour, the day's heat – hard and manufactured – radiates from the buildings. Her back is damp, Libby's dress clinging to it by the time she reaches her front door.

The foyer is stuffy with dust-trodden wood and lemon cleaner. Its familiarity drops her onto the first step. A space of sweet, domestic memories: her and Jacques struggling up the stairs with supermarket bags; the two of them coming home late, their erratic footsteps thudding upwards, arms about each other; and the time he pressed her up against the wall on the first-floor landing, hand between her legs, the stairwell like a sail swelling with the sound of their breathing.

She climbs the stairs, looking back. Noticing for the first time how cramped and dingy it is. Nothing is the same. She's already leaving it behind.

It is past one o'clock in the morning and the flat is unlit, dead.

'You're back.' Jacques appears in the doorway of the sitting room.

Jessica jumps, hand on chest. 'You scared me.'

'I was about to go looking for you.' He's wearing a coat over his tracksuit bottoms.

'When exactly did you become my keeper?'

And it hurts, hurting him. It has a different resonance, this pain, so different from that of a metal blade or an edge of glass.

He can't speak, holding out his hands as if to catch the first drops of rain.

'I was at Libby's shop opening. I left a message on the answering machine.'

'Libby got home two hours ago.' He's taking in her bare feet and gaping dress.

'Libby.' She puts the name between them like a cat dropping a dead mouse on the carpet. She can't bring herself to say more than that; the dread of his confession more than she can bear at this moment.

Jacques is squinting as if he can't quite bring her into focus. 'What about her?'

The caution in his voice shoots a feverish prickle along her spine.

'Forget it.' Walking past him, she tenses against the grasp of his hand but it doesn't come. She wishes it would. The relief of fingers digging bruises into her arms, the burn of dragged skin and scratching nails. Wishes just once he would hurt her and break the water skin they are skating across. She stops by the doorway. 'You've always been so unquestioning. I always took it as proof of trust and love.'

'I *trust*, Jessica, that when you are ready to talk to me, you will.' In his anger, he sounds like a stranger, his accent always more pronounced under stress.

'Nice pat on the head, Jacques. The truth is, you let me keep my secrets so you could keep your own.'

She sees it then. A calculation in his eyes. Wondering what she knows.

'You're right. There's too much unspoken crap between us.' He looks so pained, his eyes blacked out with fatigue that she pinches the soft underside of her arm, punishing the urge to cradle his head.

'Tomorrow we'll sit down and talk.' Softly, he adds, 'You can tell me anything, you know.'

It's too late, she thinks.

In the darkness of the bedroom, she spills Libby's dress in a heap, the gold necklace coiling on top like a possessive snake. The airing-cupboard door creaks as Jacques makes himself a bed on the sofa.

AC: *A police officer, Sergeant Nilson, came here yesterday asking about you.*

TQ: *Yeah?*

AC: *He said you've been starting fights in public.*

TQ: *He doesn't like me, that's all. His youngest brother Mike tried to take my lunch money at school so I broke his nose. Nilson's had it in for me since then.*

AC: *But Thomas, I can see from the state of your face you've been involved in some kind of violence.*

TQ: *It's nothing.*

AC: *What does your father say when he sees you like this?*

TQ: *Nothing. He wouldn't fucking dare.*

AC: *You're looking for an outlet for your anger and frustration, but it's harmful. Not just physically but also in terms of your mental and emotional health. Focus on something you long for instead. There must be something.*

TQ: *To drown.*

AC: *I'm sorry?*

TQ: *Somewhere on the bottom of the English Channel there is a mountain of iron railings.*

AC: *Iron railings?*

TQ: *My grandad said the government asked people to donate iron as part of the war effort. So they cut down the railings around their houses. It turns out it wasn't needed so it was dumped out at sea.*

AC: *What a terrible waste.*

TQ: *I can see it. Like rusty bones deep in the water. I think about swimming through the railings and getting tangled up. At first I struggle, then I just let go. Drowning's peaceful, like falling asleep.*

32

October 1995, Selcombe

Micky, Lucy and Jessica were sitting on the cemetery wall in the shadow of an oak tree when
the cars started to arrive. Jessica was glad of the distraction, fed up with Lucy's endless talk of who fancied
her. It wasn't enough to check out her face and skinny
figure in every shop window or parked car; now she
was obsessed with how she appeared to other people
– specifically boys.

'Look – they're all wearing black. It must be a
funeral.' This for some reason made Micky giggle and
Jessica sighed, throwing back her head to look up
through red and amber leaves. Snatches of sunlight
dazzled her eyes as the wind stirred the branches.

'Let's gatecrash it.'

Both Micky and Jessica stared at Lucy.

'It's not a village disco, sicko.' Jessica slid off the wall.
She wondered where Thomas was.

'Yes, but look.' Lucy had also jumped off the wall.

Despite the chill in the air, she was determined to show off her fading tan in a denim skirt that flared above her knees. She stepped out of the tree's shadows, hands in her jacket pockets, pretending to study the church rather than the group of young men hunched together in ill-fitting black suits, their hair slicked and shining.

'Lucy's got a point.' Micky said. 'Funerals are normally full of wrinklies.'

'Maybe the person who died was young.' Jessica shivered and leaned against the wall, hoping to catch some warmth from the stone.

Micky gasped, eyes wide over her cupped palm. 'I know who it is.'

Her squeal turned heads among the mourners. Lucy pointed the toe of her trainer into the grass, swinging her knee in a lazy arc to make her calf flex.

'This boy drowned trying to swim the Lady's Fingers. My mum read it in the papers.'

'What boy?'

'I don't know.'

'What was his name?' Jessica grabbed Micky's arm.

'There's no need to pinch me.' Micky rubbed her arm, her voice shrill as ever. 'My mum said he was seventeen years old and a local boy, that's all.'

Jessica spun away. She pressed her stomach to the church wall, feeling dizzy and sick. Lucy came to stand beside her, pressing her side against Jessica's, her head leaning conspiratorially close. 'What's wrong?'

Not trusting her voice, Jessica shook her head.

'It's not your boyfriend, is it?'

Swallowing, she managed to say, 'He's not my boyfriend.'

Lucy's eyes widened. She snapped her fingers at Micky, beckoning her over with a panicky flap of her hand. 'Micky, you idiot. We think it might be Jessica's boyfriend.'

Hemmed in by the sudden thrill of their excitement, Jessica fought the urge to scramble over the wall and run away. Instead she turned back to the church. The last of the mourners had gone in.

Of course it wasn't him.

Lucy pushed her arm through hers, the silver petals of her ring scratching Jessica's side. 'When did you last see him?'

'Ages ago.' Jessica chewed her lip. Their cloying concern was making it hard for her to breathe, to concentrate. When had she last seen him?

She thought back to the summer holidays. They had made so many plans; camping – with fried gull eggs for breakfast; seal-spotting, swimming in Selcombe Bay. None of it happened. Not once Bloody Russian reappeared. After that, Thomas lost interest in everything. In her. Minutes into a walk he'd lose interest, his mood swerving from blank distraction to manic energy. Then he'd rush off, leaving her behind.

Looking back to the day they had lain down together on the chapel floor, Jessica could see it was a goodbye of sorts. The Thomas she knew had slipped away.

'I told you, he's not my boyfriend,' she muttered. 'I bumped into him a few weeks ago.' Wearing stained trousers, his hair splitting into ragged, unwashed locks.

At the corner of his mouth a livid, crusty sore that his tongue kept poking at. She'd wanted to ask what was happening to him but couldn't think how.

'Did he say he was going to try and swim the Fingers?' Micky wanted to know, picking moss off the stone wall, already bored.

'Of course not.' Instead they'd spoken about her father.

He was at my house. He bought his car from my dad's garage.

Are you sure it was him?

Yes, because he spoke to me.

What did he say?

Tell Jessica I will always watch over her. I'll be her guardian angel.

And she'd laughed in anger. *Great job he's done so far,* she'd shouted. She shouldn't have run off. She should have calmed down and stayed with Thomas and behaved like a proper friend.

Jessica took a few steps forward. 'I'm going to find out whose funeral it is.'

Lucy was at her side again. 'Good idea.'

'Alone. They'll notice if three of us try to sneak in.'

'Come on.' Micky yawned, plucking at Lucy's sleeve. 'Let's go to the shops.'

No one spoke inside the church. Their clothes and service sheets rustled as they moved carefully through the pews, hunched over a collective stomach ache. The air was choked with flowers, a queue of wreaths lining the aisle.

At the altar stood a white coffin on a black velvet plinth. Blue and purple flowers fountained from its lid, framing the picture of a young man. Jessica gripped the back of the first pew, staring without blinking at the photograph until her eyes watered and she was certain it wasn't him.

It wasn't Thomas.

AC: How are you, Thomas? I haven't seen much of you recently.

TQ: I'm all right.

AC: You don't look all right. I'm worried about you.

TQ: OK, I'm angry.

AC: Has something happened?

TQ: No. It's just how I feel all the time.

AC: It's OK to be angry. It's progress to admit it.

TQ: You keep saying that but when my father lost his temper, he killed a man.

AC: You're not your father, Thomas.

TQ: You'll see.

AC: I'm going to say something, and it's going to sound unprofessional, but I truly believe you should break all contact with your father.

TQ: I barely go home as it is.

AC: Then move away from this area, Thomas. Find somewhere new to live.

TQ: Just like that?

AC: In fact, I'm going to help you. I'm going to give you some money.

TQ: I can't take your money.

AC: Two hundred pounds in exchange for your promise that you'll get as far from this place as you can.

TQ: You make it sound easy.

AC: Just go, Thomas.

33

Another three weeks had passed without sight of Thomas. At night Jessica couldn't sleep until she had recreated the photograph of the young man in her head and reassured herself it was not Thomas lying in the coffin.

She criss-crossed the inside of her thighs with the brown glass shard as she waited for the sound of pebbles against her window.

He'd needed her – but all she'd done was go on about her father.

She found new, untouched parts of her body for her piece of glass. Armpits, the soles of her feet and once, inside her mouth, where cheek met gum.

Then one evening, there was a thud against the bedroom window, a noise her heart echoed in sudden hope. Pulling the curtains open, she found a round, oily imprint, circled in feathers. A bird had flown into the window. Resting her head on the pane, she looked down into the garden. She could just make out the feathery mound of a wood pigeon on the grass below.

'Stupid bird,' she said through her teeth. 'Stupid, dead bird.'

Then a figure rose from the dark lee of the garden wall. Fumbling with the rusty window catches, she heaved open the sash. Would have called out his name, if Thomas hadn't put a warning finger to his lips.

'Where've you been?'

With his face in shadow, she couldn't read his mood.

'Hurry up. You want your mum to catch me here?' he called up in a voice she hadn't heard in a long time – light, excited. The way he was in the days when every evening brought them adventure.

She skinned her knees in a hasty, downward slide, the thin rubber of her plimsolls hitting the frozen ground with jolting force. Without a coat, the cold was shocking.

'Poor little thing.' She stepped over the dead bird. 'Did you see it hit my window?'

'Yeah.' Thomas chuckled. 'Because I threw it.'

Jessica gaped at him. 'What's wrong with pebbles?'

Thomas lunged, gripping her about the waist and swinging her round and round, legs flying out as though she were a small child. He released her, laughing.

'You've gone crazy.' She gave him a tentative smile, wanting to trust this happy, larking Thomas.

'I have a plan.' Grabbing her hand, he broke into a run, stopping only once they reached the huddle of pine trees by the cliff path. 'You and me are going to run away.'

'You what?'

'I can't be here any more. I can't . . .' Thomas ran a

hand through his hair, his breath pluming in the air. 'Be near that bastard any more.'

'Your dad?' She knew he meant Bloody Russian.

'Him too.' Thomas stepped closer, his grin rising and dipping across his face. 'We'll leave them all behind.'

She and Thomas. Far away. She saw them sitting on a train, or maybe a ferry crossing misty water. 'When?'

'Really soon. First I have to sort someone out.'

'Sort them out how?'

'There's nothing to worry about. You'll see.' He was hugging his hands in his armpits, nodding to some internal voice. Wearing less than she was, in a T-shirt and jeans ripped at the knees. Noticing her shiver, he took her hand and led her through the trees.

He heard the sound before she did, standing very still, a finger to his lips.

A snarling squeal, metal-shrill, followed by vigorous rustling.

'What's that?' The horror on her face made him grin. Motioning her forward, he crept towards the noise. Where the forest opened onto a gorse field, two foxes were snapping at each other.

'Look, the smaller one has something in its mouth,' Thomas whispered. As they watched, the larger fox with scabbed tufts of fur attacked, digging its teeth into its opponent's neck and wrenching hard.

Jessica looked away but Thomas was transfixed. 'Shit. It's still alive.'

'The little fox?'

'No, the rabbit they're fighting over. It moved when the fox dropped it.'

In spite of herself, she looked up and saw the hunched rabbit, eyes liquid bright in the moonlight. The foxes tumbled over and around it.

'Why doesn't it run away?'

'It's done for, Jells. There's no point trying to escape.'

Jessica jumped up and ran into the clearing, waving her arms and shouting. The scrapping animals froze; one lolloped away, the other scrutinising her before trotting off. The rabbit still didn't move and she couldn't bring herself to go near it.

'I'm cold,' she told Thomas, who was laughing, shaking his head. 'I'm going home.'

His shoulders dropped. With huge strides he covered the empty ground until he reached the cliff edge. Didn't even look round to see if she was following.

'I went swimming last night,' he said as she caught up. 'To see how far I could go.'

'Are you mad? Don't you know someone drowned a few weeks ago trying to swim the Lady's Fingers?' She pinched his arm but he was too absorbed with the sea crashing against the boulders to notice.

'The water was so black I couldn't even see my arms.'

'Liar.'

'I almost kept going, you know.' His voice was wistful, weary.

She didn't like the way he was staring, mesmerised, at the sea, as though it was singing in his head. Urging him over the edge.

'I couldn't see the beach.' His hand slipped up her arm, his eyes leaving the water to follow its progress. 'The water pulled me under.' His palm weighed down on her shoulder, fingers curling into a grip when she tried to shake it off.

'You're just trying to scare me.'

'It was peaceful. One day I'll keep going.'

This was the real Thomas now, she thought. Sad and lost. Jessica pulled her sleeves over her cold hands, wrapped her arms about herself. Sea-foam fell like snow in their hair.

'You said you had a plan.'

His grip loosened, fingers slipping from her shoulder, bumping lightly over the small pinnacle of her breast. She had his attention now.

'I do.' She could see him trying to shake off the dragging weight of the sea. 'First, I'm going to sort out that Russian bastard, and then—'

'Don't,' Jessica interrupted. 'Every time you go near him, you make it worse for me.'

Eyes widening, his hand shot into the space between them. Arresting it before it could strike her or fend off her words, she couldn't tell which. His breath hissed through his teeth. 'This time I'm going to do it properly.'

'No, please, don't.' She tugged his sleeve but his expression was set, reminding her perversely of her father; how he used to watch her, patiently confident that she would eventually understand his point.

'After tomorrow he will never, ever come near you again.'

Jessica scuffed the toe of her trainer in the loose grit and thought about the injured rabbit, frozen in defeat while the foxes fought over it. She understood then the sense of submitting to forces stronger than yourself. 'And then?'

'I will tell my father exactly how it feels to be his son.'

She followed him back to the clearing, watching him bend low, sweeping aside the long grass. When he found the rabbit, he held it up for her to see. It struggled once, feebly. Then sat in his hands, its side palpitating with the rapid burst of its heartbeat. Thomas jacked his knee up, bringing the rabbit down hard against it; the thin snap as its neck broke.

He didn't seem to hear Jessica's cry. Sitting down on the frozen ground, Thomas pulled his knees to his chest and tucked the dead rabbit in the space between, wrapping his thin arms around his legs. 'All better now,' he murmured, keeping his eyes on the horizon's black water.

A crowd had gathered in the playground. Mrs Arlbrook and the new chemistry teacher everyone called Beanpole were manning the closed gates. They weren't letting anyone leave the school. Jessica pressed her head against the first-floor window, craning for a better view. A police car was parked in front of the gates, its blue lights silently round-housing. A man in uniform walked over to the head teacher and spoke so quietly that Mrs Arlbrook leaned towards him, a hand cupped about her ear.

Jessica's first thought was that a girl had been run over – there were frequent notices sent home asking parents to reduce their speed on the school lane. Mrs Arlbrook nodded at the policeman and scanned the bobbing heads before her. Opening the gate a fraction, she let the girls leave one by one. They all twisted their heads to get a better look at the police car. Some of them stopped further down the lane and pointed, ducking their heads like grazing animals as they whispered to each other. Jessica could see the outline of a person in the back seat, face obscured by the cold, crystalline sky mirrored in the window.

She made her way downstairs, and was about to walk into the tarmacked forecourt when she heard her name. Raising her voice, Mrs Arlbrook addressed the waiting girls.

'Has anyone seen Jessica Byrne from Three F?'

The group stirred and shuffled, her name tossed from girl to girl like a ball. Shaking heads and shrugs.

Jessica flung herself back behind the door, heart like a runaway train.

'Jessica Byrne, are you there?' Mrs Arlbrook had her trumpety voice on; the one that announced the shit was going to hit the fan for someone.

Jessica bolted up the stairs to the third floor, tearing past the empty science labs until she reached the long, spiral steps leading to the sports field behind the school. Sheltering in the doorway, she caught her breath, checking the fields and shingle pathways were empty. Then she ran a straight diagonal across the hockey pitch and into the trees that concealed the outdoor pool from the road. The stone wall behind the changing rooms was low enough to climb over, though it scraped a hole in her tights. She took a moment to calm down before slinging her bag over her shoulder and starting the walk home.

Having escaped, she needed to figure out what was going on. The police were looking for her. Something bad had happened. Isn't that what you saw on TV? The police officer at someone's door, all sorry-eyed, and a woman fainting away.

Perhaps she shouldn't have run away.

The police car was beside her before she even heard it. Her feet, of their own accord, planted themselves in the pavement but the vehicle didn't stop. In the back seat, Bloody Russian pushed his face to the window. His head swivelling like an owl, keeping her in his sight.

34

September 2012, London

Jessica leaves the flat just before six a.m. She doesn't write Jacques a note on the blackboard because she doesn't know what to say.

Ask him the truth about me, Jessica. I dare you.

She takes the Volvo and drives for five hours without a break. Directing all attention to the road and other traffic, she keeps her thoughts reigned in.

Thomas's childhood home is as she remembers it. An austere, two-storey building with oversized chimneys and windows, its white face marbled with cracks. The windows are plastered over with newspaper.

His father's probably dead, she thinks, following the gravel path to the house. Truck innards are still taking root in the front garden and behind it the vast, open-sided barn where Thomas's father and Bloody Russian used to fix buses and lorries.

The doorbell gives a shrill ring. She imagines it blasting through cobwebs, stirring up dust. The silence, as she strains to catch the sound of approaching foot-steps, swells in her ears.

A crunch on the gravel makes her jump. A short, plump woman with feathery grey hair and smart tailored trousers has stopped halfway along the path, scowling at the toe of her shiny, patent-leather Mary Jane. She stamps up to the door, peering at her shoes over the cardboard box in her arms.

'Every time I come here,' she says. 'Blasted scuff marks.'

From inside the house, Jessica thinks she hears a scrape. A shoe shuffling over gritty floorboards.

'Family, are you?' The woman eyes Jessica's short skirt and favourite leather flip-flops, loose string and gaps where the turquoise beading has torn away. As if her clothes link her to the neglected house.

'No, I'm making an enquiry.'

'You wouldn't mind taking this in, would you?' The woman holds out the box. 'If I'm honest, the old man gives me the creeps.'

The cardboard box says *Meals On Wheels*.

'I don't think there's anyone in,' Jessica says.

'Mr Q never leaves the house. The food'll need a good hour in the Rayburn.'

It occurs to Jessica it might be easier this way; playing a role. She takes the box.

'You won't get much out of him.' The Meals On Wheels woman rubs the scratch on her shoe and straightens, tugging the hem of her red jacket as it threatens to lift up over her belly.

'Why not?'

'You know how old men get.'

'Does he ever mention any family?'

The woman shakes her head, leaning past Jessica to rap the door knocker. 'Mr Q,' she bellows. 'Your lunch is here.'

Lowering her voice, she adds, 'I went to the pictures with him once. But I was a silly thing in my twenties. Looking for a bit of danger.'

The shuffling sound comes from behind the door this time. 'Danger?'

'They're an old family, the Quennells. Been in this area for ever, and always had a reputation.'

'For what?'

'They're just not right. Like a bad gene, or something.'

Jessica's hands are clammy against the side of the box. When she turns back to the door, she sees it has opened a couple of inches. Someone is standing there, watching her. A dark shape on an even darker background.

Holding up the food box, she says, 'Your lunch.'

'You're not Betty. Where's Betty?' His voice is deep and smooth. It has strength and melody where she was expecting the tremulous reed of old age.

'I'm Jessica.' She steps into a hallway so dark it's like dropping into the sea at night. Her foot slides on loose dirt. Mr Quennell towers over her before standing aside and pointing at a doorway to her left. As she heads towards it, his walking stick raps out a surprisingly quick rhythm behind her.

A powerful farmyard smell swamps her as she enters

a large, sparsely furnished sitting room. Ring marks in the navy carpet and the outline of missing paintings on the faded floral wallpaper leave a ghostly imprint of the home it once was. It reminds her of her own house after the bonfire, and the semblance shakes her.

We come from the same place, you and I, Thomas.

Thomas's father lowers himself awkwardly into a single armchair, one leg stiff and unbending. In the light of a large sash window – the only one not plastered in newspaper – his face has aged like an orange rotting from the inside, collapsing in on itself. The back of his bald head puckers as he leans forward to pick a *National Geographic* off a stack of yellow-spined magazines. She stares at the hand clutching a mahogany dog-head cane. Ridges of bone push up through the skin, the knuckles no longer aligned where old fractures have gnarled together.

The hands of a street fighter. A man who killed another with his naked fists.

Her heart is beating too fast. She clears her throat and tries to play her role.

'My father used to collect *National Geographic* as well.' Her voice infuriates her, thin and stuttering as a dripping tap.

Quennell sniffs and points his cane towards another doorway. 'The kitchen.'

To reach it, she has to step over a mattress with two badly folded rugs and a pair of blue, overwashed pyjamas. Trying not to look at the stains on the bottom sheet like the outline of orange flowers.

The kitchen is even cooler than the sitting room, the

heatwave unable to shift the stubborn cold ingrained in the building's thick walls. She can see why Thomas and Nathan were happier outdoors.

A draught whips away any heat which might have been coming off the red Rayburn. She shivers, looking for an open window, and finds instead that the door leading onto the backyard has rotted away, leaving a foot-long gap above the floor.

Pushing a cluster of used mugs to one side, Jessica places the Meals On Wheels box on the solid kitchen table. As she opens the packaging, she tries to gather herself. There's a danger she will lose her nerve, dish up his meal and leave, having never said a word.

This is the man who poisoned his son with whispers.

She takes a foil container out of the cardboard box. Someone has written *Shepherds Pie* in red biro across the lid. Opening a door in the Rayburn, she pushes the meal onto a black-crusted shelf. A weak heat touches her face.

The cupboards, she discovers as she hunts for a plate, are unexpectedly full of crockery, jugs and vases but their dust coating suggests they haven't been touched in years. Spiders trickle out of sight every time she opens a door.

Thomas as a little boy in this house. The thought makes her shudder.

'It'll be about sixty minutes,' she says, walking back into the sitting room. Mr Quennell doesn't look up. Jessica sits opposite him, on a green leather sofa stretch-marked with age.

'Do you have much family locally?'

He sniffs again, closes a magazine on his lap and looks at her. With the light behind him, she can't tell the colour of his eyes but she feels their sudden focus, gun-dog alert.

'Who are you?'

'I brought your lunch.'

'You've made the mistake,' he taps a finger to his temple, 'of assuming the brain is as decrepit as the body.'

'I'm sorry?'

'I watched you and Betty before she drove off in her little white van. So who are you?'

'I knew Thomas.' For a tiny beat his searching, probing energy recoils. 'I want to know the truth about his disappearance.'

Suddenly he's moving, rocking once, twice to hoist his weight out of the chair and onto his bad leg. Stabbing his stick across the floor, bearing down on her with the force of a collapsing wall. He drops onto the sofa, twists his torso to face her, chest heaving. Gripping his stiff leg, his breath hisses out like a leaking gas tap.

'The truth?' His voice, strangled with pain, has lost its melody.

She forces herself to remain seated. 'About the boating accident.'

Quennell's face shows no expression as he stares at her. Jessica shifts further into the arm of the sofa. 'You have red hair.'

The man has lost his mind, she thinks.

Wagging a thick twig of a finger, he adds, 'I know exactly who you are.'

Jessica shakes her head. 'We've never met.'

The heavy paw of his hand comes to rest on her wrist, his thumb stroking her bare skin. 'Ah, but I knew your dad.'

'I doubt that.' She tries to inch her hand away but the caressing thumb tightens against the tendons of her wrist.

'Daniel Byrne. The red-headed ladies' man.' His face is so close she thinks he might plant his red, watery lips on her mouth. The urge to burst out from under the weight of his proximity is overwhelming. *But if you run, they follow.* That's when it hits her – the acute memory of Bloody Russian grabbing her hair on a busy main road. A buried fear snakes into her head like lava through a fissure. The skin on her arms stipples into painful goosebumps. She wrenches free of the old man's grasp but his legs are stretched out, blocking her in and she baulks at the necessity of straddling them to escape. 'How did you know my father?'

Quennell is nodding his bald head. 'Was a time when he used to pop round for a chat. Keeping tabs on his wayward daughter and my wayward son. Ah, the trials and tribulations of parenthood.'

'I need to check the—' She gets up, awkwardly butting his legs with her shin. With a tiny pincer motion – perhaps an accident – he manages to trap the heel of her flip-flop between his shoes as she steps over his feet. She staggers forward and Quennell hooks a hand into her armpit, steadying her. His strength shocks her.

'Clumsy.' Quennell's voice has regained its low thrum. 'But such confidence. To come here on your own.'

Jessica tugs at the hem of her denim skirt and stalks to the kitchen. Leaning over the sink, she sucks deep, slow breaths into her lungs. Focuses on the metal rim of the sink, pressing her hips hard against it until its solidity steadies her.

She tries the rotting kitchen door which leads onto the yard. It is locked and unexpectedly sturdy in its frame. The windows have been painted shut.

Finn Quennell is an old, incapacitated man, she tells herself. She is permitting this intimidation. Shame marches her back into the room. 'I have a postcard from Thomas. I know he's still alive.'

'A postcard?' This time he rocks to his feet with such force it almost pitches him to his knees. Staggering, he prods the carpet with his cane, feeling out his balance. A sudden rage takes him in a strangling hold, voice strained, his face and bald head suffused with blood. 'You've been snooping through my things.'

'Pardon?'

Quennell lunges forward and Jessica backs up against the sofa. He knocks her shoulder as he brushes past. When he is out of sight, his footsteps slow to leaden thuds, sandwiched by grunts of exertion.

She can't bring herself to follow him into the unlit confines of the hall. Peering through the doorway, she sees Quennell halfway up the staircase, leaning against the bare plastered wall.

Adrenalin hobbles her movements. She trips towards the front door, numb fingers fumbling with the handle. Locked. Through the dim light of panic she can't locate the catch. His head cocks to one side at the sound of the rattling handle.

'The key is in my pocket,' he grunts through laboured breath. 'You'll have to ask me nicely.'

He starts to lower his bad leg onto the step behind him, feet slipping in the dust. His cane falls as he grips the banister with both hands.

'My cane,' he shouts, thrusting his hand behind his back and waggling his fingers.

She hesitates, then, afraid of his worsening temper, places the dog-head handle into his open palm. His grip snaps shut like a trap.

'You've been upstairs.' Spittle flecks his chin as he reaches the floor. 'Rifling through my possessions.'

'How could I? You only just let me in.'

Muttering to himself, he limps back to the sitting room. Jessica glances at the stairs. Wonders what he is hiding.

'Is there something you wanted to show me upstairs?' She returns to the living room, where Quennell is sitting on the cracked sofa leaning on his cane, which wobbles like a single pole supporting a tent.

He turns his head away, jaw working. An old man chewing his gums. Missing the monster of his own youth, she thinks. Trapped in the collapsing cage of his body.

He wipes his mouth. 'It's your fault.'

'What is?'

'It ate away at him until he couldn't control himself any more.' In one swift movement, he drops back from his cane and swings it through the air. Jessica leaps away. 'You pushed him to do it.'

'Do what?'

'Monster or not, I loved that boy. I did what any other father would do.' This time when he rises to his feet, it is a more fluid movement; his feebleness perhaps nothing more than an act.

Nilson's photographs rising like flood water before her eyes. It's not true. It's not possible. She glances towards the kitchen. Something heavy, a pot perhaps, anything to smash the window and escape. 'Thomas wasn't a monster.'

'He beat that Rusky pig and then he shoved his fancy crucifix all the way down his throat.' Quennell's voice rumbles through her. He takes a step closer and she backs away, unable to stand her ground.

'Tell me where he is.' Her voice thin as a vapour trail.

His laughter shocks her, roaring like a gale through a cave, never touching his features. 'You think you're brave enough? To witness what you've done to his life?'

'Why do you keep saying it's my fault?'

With shuffling footsteps, Quennell crosses the space between them. Jessica retreats until her head and heel bump against the wall.

'I don't know what you think you're . . .'

So close she can smell the decay on his breath. His

eyes are fixed on her mouth as he encases her little finger in his bone-mangled fist.

'Get back. Don't . . .' Her protests break against him like brittle sticks.

'My son told me what Nikolai did to you.'

Tries to stop breathing so hard, knowing it is feeding his interest. She can't speak.

'Disgusting.' The word sizzles over his tongue.

'Enough.'

It comes out as a shout just as Quennell is stepping away, shaking his head. 'I'm too old for such fun and games.' He waves over his shoulder as he heads for the kitchen. 'I'll get my own lunch, shall I?'

Jessica watches him leave the room before running into the hall. This time she notices the deadbolt pulled shut. It slides back without resistance and the door swings open. Quennell had lied about the key.

Hearing his muffled voice singing in the kitchen, she hesitates. The door is open, her escape route clear. She stares up at the stairs disappearing into the blacked-out recess of the first floor.

There is something up there he didn't want her to see.

Clenching her fists, she bounds up the stairs on feet as light as dust. The darkness on the landing blinds her, ears straining for the sound of Quennell moving below. Teeth clenched, panicky breaths skimming thin air, she grasps the nearest door handle. It doesn't budge. The next one, also locked. Forgetting to be silent, she throws her weight against the last door as she slams the handle down. It bounces open onto a bedroom of rotting carpet and dead moths. Yellowed newspaper blocks most of the light but she can make out a four-poster bed, two bedside tables and a dresser cluttered with bottles and pots.

Above one of the side-tables, a small dark rectangle is nailed to the wall.

A postcard.

Snatching it, she tears downstairs. Quennell is waiting for her in the hall. A barrier between her and the door. 'Caught you,' he whispers.

'Is this from him?' Terror makes her voice high and breathy as a child's. She tries to scan the words but there's not enough light. 'Tell me what it says and I won't take it.'

'You think I'd let you leave with it?'

The sound of her breathing fills the hall, her palm slippery against the banister. 'My husband knows I'm here. He's waiting—'

'No one knows you're here. That's why you're shak-ing.' He raps his cane against the floorboards and Jessica springs backwards, stumbling up two steps, deeper into the house. Further from the door. He chuckles.

'Keep the postcard if you want it that badly.' He doesn't move, his bulk sealing her only route of escape. She takes a deep breath, gathering herself to leap down the stairs, to pit her speed against his size.

Then Quennell steps aside and a blissful rush of light and warm air reaches her from the open doorway. Jessica races past him with the same skittery terror that used to propel her from floor to mattress every night as a little girl; the unspeakable fear of grabbing hands from under the bed.

'You saw him that night.'

Jessica stops halfway along the garden path. She turns to face Quennell. He is framed in the shadow of his house. Nothing he can say will make her go back inside. 'What did you say?'

Thomas's father emerges from the concealing darkness of his porch and blinks furiously in the sunlight. He points his cane at her.

'You hid him in one of your mobile homes. You and I helped him get away with murder.'

35

Jessica drives for ten reckless minutes to distance herself from Thomas's father. Pulling into a lay-by beside a wheat field, she staggers out of the car and drops cross-legged on the ground, grabbing fistfuls of straggly verge grass. Breathing in baked earth and lemon-scented leaves. When she is calm, she takes the postcard out of her pocket. The photograph is an aerial shot of a fish market – a great industrial box of a building – on the edge of a quay. The water is flat and solid under a cold dawn.

Stollingworth Fish Market – Nothing Beats Fresh Fish.
She turns it over.

Got a job at the market and somewhere to sleep.
You and me are done now.

The postcard was sent on 19 January. A month after he disappeared. Jessica presses the card to her chest. A place of work – somewhere concrete to start her search.

He would have moved on, of course, after seventeen years, but someone might just remember him.

Jessica delays the drive back to London with a late lunch at the Pit-Stop Café. Each time the bell above the door sounds, she glances up, hoping Nathan might walk in. She heaps sugar into a cup of dishwater tea and forces down a few mouthfuls of plain omelette. The grey-haired woman behind the counter has an air of brisk and cheery efficiency, and despite the sluggish tide of customers, enquires twice whether there was something else she could get for Jessica – a verbal nudge towards freeing up the table. Jessica pays the bill, unable to procrastinate any longer.

Turning out of Morley-on-Sea, she stops beside a road she doesn't recognise. The gravel path that once led to the empty land behind Thomas's chapel has been tarmacked and named. Sandringham Avenue – a lonely stretch of road cutting through the scrub to a huddle of new housing. An inconspicuous metal sign points from a lamp post towards the sand-brick buildings. *17th Century Chapel.* Thomas's chapel. Jessica turns into the road.

The houses are spacious and double-fronted, with the soulless uniformity of new builds. Between two carpets of turfed lawn, a chalk path leads to the cliffs and the unruly sea beyond.

The barbed-wire fencing she and Thomas used to leap over is gone. A metal rail protects visitors from the cliff edge, and prevents them from using the stone steps carved into the cliff face to reach the chapel on the plateau below. In compensation, a concrete viewing point struts out over the lip of rock. Jessica hesitates before stepping onto the platform, afraid of what she will see.

For years after he disappeared she imagined Thomas living there, in St Francis of Paola's abandoned chapel. Closed her eyes and willed him to swim up from the broken bones of Nathan's crabber and onto the beach. Once, in the middle of the night, she became so convinced of the possibility, she climbed out of her bedroom window and walked all the way there. She'd faced the guard dogs by the fence and shouted his name over their rabid barking and the sea's rolling thunder.

To her surprise, the chapel is still standing, though its walls hunch together like pinched shoulders and most of the roof has caved in. One of the double doors hangs at an angle, wedged open with a gap just wide enough for a person to squeeze through. Jessica swings her legs over the railing. Shuffling sideways, she slides her hands along the metal bar behind her back and concentrates on placing each foot on firm ground. The steps are brittle with salt corrosion; she takes them one at a time, shoulder pressed to the rock.

At the bottom, she looks up at the viewing platform's solid block of cement. The earth beneath her feet feels loose and porous as though it might give way at any moment. Vertigo sends shooting pains through her legs. With a skipping rush, she covers the ground

303

between the steps and the chapel. Her palms slip against the door, the wood seeping with rot and sea spray, as she pushes through the gap, body first.

Jessica stands in a pocket of shadow beneath the remains of the roof. The sun shines through a thin layer of cloud, filling the chapel with smoky light. The pews are covered in rubble and broken tiles. Fat-stemmed plants poke through cracks in the walls and flagstone floor, their thick, vegetative scent mixing with dust and airborne grit.

Somehow his mosaics have survived, veiled beneath a green, fungal coating. With the sleeve of her cotton top, she scrubs away at a picture she has never seen; one that Thomas must have cleaned on a solitary night many years ago.

Its beauty takes her breath away. The young face of the saint stares at her with pale eyes, his golden hair haloing and rippling in the water as he stands on the bed of the sea. He is holding out his hands as if to take Jessica's in his. Tiny, silvered fish hover by his fingers. A small tile has come loose in its setting and Jessica picks it out. It bears a scrap of silver and the black bead of a fish's eye. She puts it in her pocket.

Turning back to the door, she finds the panels with their list of missing sons and fathers still intact.

Vandals have carved jagged, angry words into the weather-softened grain and as she passes, Jessica refuses to read their mindless obscenity. But the words catch her like a familiar face in a crowd. She stops with a sharp intake of breath and traces the scored letters with her finger, catching splinters.

One last entry – a final plea to the Patron Saint of Souls Lost at Sea.

Thomas Quennell   *19th December 1995*

By the time she finds a resident's parking space near her apartment block, it is almost ten o'clock at night and fatigue is making her eyes blur. Before she unlocks the main entrance, she looks up. There are no lights on in her flat.

In the hall, she kicks off her flip-flops, moving on bare feet, praying he's asleep. Before the night of Libby's shop relaunch, Jessica would have crawled into bed and pressed her face to Jacques' warm, sleeping back.

'Where have you been?' Jacques' voice is thick with alcohol. 'I thought we were going to talk.'

He's filling the entire doorway as if the drink has loosened the tight bands of his body.

'I went to see Birdie.' The lie comes from her mouth like the lines of a play.

'I don't believe you.'

With cotton-wool fingers, she undoes the buttons on her cardigan. 'In that case, I can't tell you where I've been.'

He turns, wheeling into the kitchen, where he tilts the last dregs of a bottle of cheap, supermarket Beaujolais into his glass. She follows him, catching the bedroom door before he can close it behind him. A stratum of coaly smoke hangs in the room, making them both cough. Weak flames flicker in the black grate opposite their unmade bed. Something crinkles under her foot as Jessica goes to open a window. She looks down in horror. The newspaper clippings from her sea-dragon box have been laid out like a mosaic on the floor.

'What are you doing with my things?'

'I'm helping you say goodbye to the past.'

'Have you been burning them?' Her voice rises.

'I thought about it, Jessica, I really did.'

Bertie's notebook is lying on the bed. 'You went through my rucksack.'

She scrambles up handfuls of paper until Jacques rests a single finger on her shoulder.

'It's for you to burn, not me.'

'You're putting the blame on me?' She shakes off his touch. 'It's nothing to do with me or my past.'

'Tell me then.'

But she can't. Not even for the satisfaction of seeing his bravado fall, of catching the guilt that must seethe under the calm surface of his face. That kind of satisfaction would kill her. Her hands seem small and distant as she gathers up the newspaper articles.

Jacques kicks the sea-dragon box. It hits the far wall, drops to the floor with the lid hanging off a single hinge. She tries to move past him to get her box, but he stops her, lifting her chin so she has to meet his eyes. She's never seen him so angry.

'Burn them.'

'No.'

'I knew you were running away from something when I met you, and I accepted it.' The wine is sour on his breath. 'I knew about that piece of glass you hid in the back of the drawer. I let you give me your excuses, cat scratches and whatever. But do you know how hard it was for me to sit back in the hope that one day you'd open up to me, love me back?'

He grasps her face in his hot palms, her hair caught over her left eye making her feel blinkered and trapped. 'But I have loved you, Jacques.'

'Not enough. You kept part of yourself separate.' He releases her, grabbing the red notebook off the bed and shaking it at her. 'So that one day you could run away again.'

With Thomas's postcard in her pocket, there is nothing she can say.

'Running away is in your blood,' he adds.

Shock loosens her fingers. A few papers slip from her grasp and before she can stop him, he throws them into the fireplace.

'Black,' she says, 'is for the days I can't see you.'

'What?'

'That's what your note said on the flowers. Libby left it where I would find it, you know.'

Jacques frowns, shrugging. 'Didn't she give them to you?'

'To me?'

He closes his eyes, tries to pull her to him. 'Who else?'

She bites her lip against the urge to cry. She got so close to confronting him about Libby and now this small, brief reprieve has tripped her. He lets her gather the scattered newspaper clippings. Among them is the article her mother left for her in the Tesco bag and Jessica stares at her young, rabbit-eyed face. All that hope and expectation. And Jacques, his handsome face in profile, arm reaching for her even as he glances away. Then she draws in a sharp breath. Rushes into the hallway where the light is brighter.

'What is it?' Jacques slurs.

With the tip of her nail she traces Jacques' captured gaze. To Libby.

Shorter hair, rounder face but no mistaking her. There is her proof. Jacques and Libby gazing at each other, all those years ago while she fretted, naive and blind, about her first exhibition.

Jacques is flat out on the bed. She drops the paper on his chest and removes the red notebook from his hand. He glances at the newspaper.

'This is what we need to talk about, Jessie.'

'It's too late.'

'Just what,' he struggles to his elbows, 'am I being punished for?'

'Your secrets,' she whispers and he doesn't respond, perhaps not having heard. Lying down beside him, the notebook hugged to her chest, she wishes she could cry but the tears won't come. He tries to wrap his body around her but she is as stiff and unyielding as a felled tree.

After a while, he gets up. Collects every scrap of newspaper and presses them into the dying embers until there's nothing left but ash.

'And what about *your* secrets, Jessica?'

But Jessica is picturing a bloodied and desperate boy adding his name to a list of lost sons. Declaring himself dead.

~ 36 ~

Jessica wakes up to the smell of ash. Beside her, Jacques has his eyes open. He doesn't move as she pulls on jeans and a white cotton shirt that she remembers, too late, used to belong to him. *It looks cuter on you, honey.*

The day outside is grey with the first taste of autumn. An ashen day. Brushing out her hair, she shouts at Jacques in her head. All the things she can't bring herself to say aloud for fear of him validating them and begging forgiveness.

From under the bed, she pulls a battered brown suitcase which hasn't been used in years. She opens the cupboard, some drawers, grabbing random handfuls of socks, T-shirts, an old scarf. Terrified he's going to stop her, or worse, that he won't.

Straightening, Jessica searches the room for the red notebook and finds it on his bedside table. He's been reading it, she is certain, while she slept. She flicks through it, but of course the pages offer no proof of readership. At the back of the book where the postcard was concealed, she notices something – the final page has been ripped out, the remaining stub so tight to the seam she hasn't noticed it before.

'Did you tear a page out?'

Jacques barely glances over; he gives a mute shake of the head.

She runs her thumb along the torn edge before putting the notebook inside the case and zipping it shut.

Which brings her to this moment – the same threshold of departure her dad must have experienced. Of stepping from one world into the next.

Jacques is still staring at the ceiling. 'You're going to find him, aren't you?'

'Yes.'

'Are you coming back?'

She doesn't answer. The way to inflict the most pain is to walk out of someone's life.

The dialling tone sounds for almost a minute before Nathan answers. 'Frotherton West Farm Shop.'

Her mobile is slippery in a sweaty palm, and no matter where she moves to on the bustling concourse, someone intrudes on her space. 'It's me, Jessica.'

He doesn't sound happy to hear her voice, so she stalls with meaningless chatter to keep him on the line; asks how he is, how the shop is doing, and then cuts him off as he starts to talk about a new range of English wines. 'I need to ask you a question.'

'What now?' His voice is barbed with wariness.

'The last page in Bertie's notebook has been ripped out. Do you know anything about it?'

A moment of silence. 'It was a note for me from Bertie. I'm sure I was supposed to find the postcard as well.'

'But why did . . .' Jessica swallows, knows she should stop before he hangs up on her, 'you rip the letter out?'

'It was private. Look, I'd better—'

'I'm on my way to Stollingworth,' Jessica interrupts. 'At St Pancras now, in fact.'

'Is that supposed to mean something to me?' The bluntness so unlike Nathan. He knows what's coming.

'I went to your dad's place and he . . . gave me another postcard from Thomas.'

'You have no idea what you're doing. You're going to ruin lives.'

Jacques, rolling away from her, a glitter of tears in his eyes as he burned the newspaper clippings.

'He didn't do it, Nathan.' She hears him suck air as though struck, then is silent. 'I'm going to find him and prove it.'

'I saw him, Jessica.'

'I know, you said. In the snow.' A tannoy announcement forces her further from the platforms into an arched side-entrance.

'Not then. I made that up. I hoped you'd take comfort in knowing he was still alive, but also consider the fact that he never got back in touch with us.'

'So when did you see him?'

'Are you listening? He wants to be left alone.' He mutters something, a whispered curse of frustration before his voice returns to her ear. 'I saw something on the night he took my boat.'

'What?' Her back prickles with nervous heat.

'My dad and Thomas were arguing outside my dad's house. Thomas looked wild, terrified. There was blood on his hands and clothes.'

The letters on the departure board flip and shuffle sideways and she realises the Stollingworth train is leaving in three minutes. Rushing back onto the concourse, she bumps blindly through oncoming passengers, their curses washing over her. The ticket in her hand shivers violently as she tries to slot it into the barrier. 'It was you, wasn't it? You're the witness.'

His silence provides the answer.

She sinks onto a platform bench opposite the open door of the train. 'How could you call the police on your own brother?'

'You don't know the full story, Jessica. You need to leave this alone.'

She watches the train doors shut. 'How could you believe he did it?'

'Because of what the Russian did to you, Jessica.'

She closes her eyes and waits for the click and tone of a dead line but Nathan carries on. 'Bertie reacted like you are now. She wouldn't believe it either. When the Russian's body was found, she got scared that the transcripts and postcard would implicate Thomas and possibly herself. That's what her letter said – the one I ripped out of the notebook. She handed it all over to me before she moved to Madrid. She trusted I would keep it secret.'

And Jessica reads the accusation in his tone. *If only you'd done the same.*

Just as the guard raises his whistle, Jessica pounds the door release and leaps onto the train. Dropping into the nearest seat, she opens her suitcase and scrabbles the counsellor's notebook from its trappings of t-shirts and socks.

Wrong. They are all wrong. Thomas did not kill Bloody Russian.

She tries to recall what Bertie looked like – long brown hair and curves accentuated by hippy skirts and blouses; a woman whose advantage of age and maturity had added a sheen of sophistication in Jessica's young eyes. She'd hated Bertie for it. Now the picture shifts and she sees how young the counsellor had been; how out of her depth. But her confidence in Thomas had never wavered.

At that moment – with the train pulling out of the station, extracting her from her life, from Jacques – it makes Jessica feel less alone.

Bertie never doubted Thomas's innocence, and nor will she.

TQ: The police let him go.

AC: What happened?

TQ: They picked him up outside Jessica's school last week. Then my dad got him out.

AC: Your father bailed him?

TQ: He hadn't been arrested, only brought in for questioning. My dad went mad. He wasn't about to lose his cheap labour.

AC: Have you told your dad what that man did?

TQ: I tried, but he wasn't listening. Maybe he just doesn't care.

AC: What about Jessica in all this?

TQ: I haven't seen much of her. I think maybe I scare her.

AC: Has she said so?

TQ: No. It's just the way she looks at me. I thought if Bloody Russian was locked up, things would go back to being how they used to be with her and me.

AC: You've done all you can, Thomas. It's up to her now.

37

December 1995, Selcombe

On the last day of school before the Christmas holidays, Jessica and Hannah arrived home and kicked their satchels into the cupboard under the stairs. They had just opened the packet of Toffee Pops that Hannah had shoved under her coat at the newsagent's, when the doorbell rang.

Thomas stood in the doorway, clothes slicked with mud, his hair – wet with sweat – steaming in the icy air. She smelled him as soon as the door swung back; sharp and meaty, like the stewing beef Birdie sometimes forgot in the back of the fridge.

'What have you been doing?' Jessica covered her nose.

'I need to see you.' He sounded like he'd been running, taking short, light breaths as he swayed in the doorway. Leaves and black grit were twisted in his damp hair.

'What's happened?'

Thomas grabbed her sleeve, twisting the material in his fist as though she might run away. His hands were crusted with muddy streaks, their stench overpowering. 'I tried to do the right thing, you know.'

She bit her lip, afraid to ask what that might be. 'You have to come back later. My mum's on her way home.'

Tugging free of his grip, she saw that his fingers had left deep red smudges on the white cotton. She flung her arm away from herself, staring at her school shirt in horror. 'What is that?'

Thomas raised a filthy finger to quieten her, eyes pleading. The crusted muck on his fingers rose up his wrist and onto his jacket cuff, where it glistened like drying ink. Stains splashed the length of both his arms, shifting from earthy blacks and browns to red wine where it thinned and feathered outwards. Dotted among the streaks were splashes of liquid matter so thick and viscous it had pocked the material as it dried.

'Fu-ucking hell.' Hannah's voice made Jessica start. 'What happened to him?'

Thomas tried to grab her hand. 'Come with me.'

She recoiled. 'I can't.'

'You shouldn't be out in public looking like that.' Hannah mock-gagged.

His shoulders had started to twitch and spasm, eyes wide, mouthing something that might have been *Please, Jellybird.*

'Don't let him in,' Hannah was saying in her ear. Jessica turned to her, light-headed with horror, while Thomas sank to the floor, his back against the door frame. 'Get him out of here.'

Thomas's fingertips were feeling through his hair as though searching out bits of glass. Hannah elbowed Jessica out of the house, slamming the front door with such force it bounced Thomas's head forward. The porch window opened and Jessica's denim jacket and wellington boots came flying out.

'You two better run,' Hannah shouted.

Thomas wouldn't go near the road, which suited Jessica as she scanned the crest of the hill for her mother's headlights. Despite the stinging wind, she suggested the beach but Thomas shook his head. Pushing his hand into a gap in the caravan park hedgerow, he peered in.

'What about one of the caravans?' He was shaking so hard his words stuttered out.

'No way.' She took a few determined strides onto the bay path but he wouldn't move, still staring into the park. She saw how he might appear to someone who didn't know him. A tramp. A criminal. She'd be in so much trouble if her mother caught her with him.

'I need to lie down for a bit, Jells.'

Jessica pictured the caravans' pristine, ironed sheets; was about to shake her head when she caught the sound of an approaching car. 'Fine. Quick. Follow me.'

A gust of wind hit them sideways on as if a giant door had opened to let the weather in. Brittle leaves and road grit tornadoed around them as they skirted Seasalt Park's perimeter. Opposite the derelict council gardens a narrow door, oily with rot, was half submerged in the pine hedge. It was locked but Jessica knew if she barged it with her shoulder enough times, the catch would give.

The winter light had sunk into twilight. Jessica's eyes took a moment to adjust in the shadow of the hedge. She led Thomas to Caravan Nineteen, which only got bookings in peak season due to its view of the shower block. Jessica made him hide behind the mobile home as she groped for the spare key under the top step. When she turned to beckon him, he was bent over his knees as though dizzy. Muttering under his breath.

'I can't hear what you're saying,' she called above the pitched whine of the storm. 'Come on.'

He shook his head, his fingers worrying at his scalp again. Receding deep into himself; something she'd never seen before.

'Is that blood on your hands?' Her raised voice brought him back.

'There's no blood.' A violent shake of his head made him stagger, losing his balance. 'Oh, Jellybird.' He ground his palms into his eyes, a scabbed flake catching in his lashes. 'Why didn't you speak to the police about Bloody Russian?'

'How do you know about that?'

'The whole bloody county knows.'

Panic zipped through her. Hannah had sworn on her life to tell no one. That's it. She was going to tell Birdie about the bottle under Hannah's mattress.

'The stupid pigs picked him up outside your school. Of course everyone knows about it,' Thomas added, arms waving in erratic, angry circles.

She couldn't understand what he was getting so upset

about. 'The police came to my house the next day. Did you know that, too?'

'No.' He stopped moving. 'And?'

'I sent them away.'

Hid, crying upstairs, begging Hannah to tell them she was never, ever going to speak to them.

'Why?' Tendons lifted on his neck, his anger rising.

She pictured Hannah sitting on the bed after she'd sent the policewoman away, clutching her secret bottle, twisting the screw top – on, off, on, off – as though it were a magic lamp that could make everything better. She'd been angry as well. *Why do the police want to talk to you, Jessie? Is it to do with Bloody Russian getting arrested?*

'Because I want to forget it.'

Thomas covered his face, keening, *Why oh why oh why?*

The wind funnelled through the park, lifting off the ground in an inverse wave and snapping a branch off the beech tree above Thomas's head. It landed at his feet, cutting dead his rant. Jessica unlocked the door and ushered him in.

It was colder inside Caravan Nineteen than out. Jessica plugged in the small electric heater from the cupboard under the kitchen sink, keeping Thomas in the corner of her eye. He'd crouched into a tight ball beneath the window, shuffled sideways and wedged himself beneath the breakfast bar. Every time a fresh blast of wind boomed against the side of the caravan, he jumped. She knelt beside him, clenching her jaw against

320

a reflex gag as his smell wrapped around her. 'Thomas? Are you all right?'

He shook his head, rubbing his fingers together as if testing fabric. Without a word, he lurched past her towards the narrow cubicle between the kitchen and bedroom. The taps went on full, water spattering, and Jessica worried about the mess he was making.

He came out wringing his hands on the small towel that would have been folded into a neat triangle and stacked with three bars of soap on the sink. 'Can I stay here for a few hours?'

She nodded, staring at the towel he'd dropped and stepped on.

'Will you wait with me?'

'I can't. My mum . . .'

She didn't finish because he was nodding, blank distraction falling across his face, fingers picking through his hair again. 'Sometimes I feel like I'm looking through a window at myself. I get confused about stuff that I should know without thinking.'

'You just need some sleep.' It's what her mum used to say when she was wrestling with homework or grumpy with Hannah.

'People say I'm not a good person.'

'That's not true, Thomas.' Jessica took his damp fingers and led him to the sofa. Changed her mind about sitting on it and pulled him to the floor instead. Biting back her revulsion at the filth on his clothing, she pressed her side to his. Like pieces of Lego, she thought, holding each other up.

'I can't say if they're right or wrong. I don't know any more.'

Jessica lowered his hand from his scalp and worked her fingers through his. 'But I know.'

His face was expressionless. 'My dad kept shouting, *Look what you did, look what you did*. He was trying to make me believe it.'

Jessica swallowed. 'What did he mean?'

Thomas pushed himself upright with unexpected energy, slamming his hand with its filthy cuff down onto Birdie's spotless sofa. Whirling round and tapping the side of his head harder than seemed necessary. 'But I'm not confused tonight.'

Jessica stared at the dark smudge he'd left on the seat, like a storm cloud with a solid, brooding centre and wispy edges.

She climbed into the corner of the sofa, squeezing a cushion to her chest and wishing she was at home. Even with Hannah shouting, Lisa scolding and her mother slipping between them, a silent ghost. She knew how to deal with all that.

'You see, Jells, all these years he's been trying to turn me into him.' He stared out of the window at the rolling clouds. 'I'm going to go swimming.'

'How's that going to help?'

'I'll swim until I'm clean again.'

She looked at him. Trying to see through the dirt on his clothes and the spatters on his trainers that, no matter how she squinted at them, could only be blood. The real Thomas was lost in his own nightmares. He was never going to find his way out.

Tears rose through her vision. 'Shall I get you something to eat?'

He shook his head. 'Whatever people say, I was the one who did the right thing.'

'What did you do?'

'Remember that.'

An urge to lie down crept over her; to pull the covers over her head and wake up as an adult. *That's how the rabbit felt as the foxes fought over it*, she thinks. *Just waiting for the scary stuff to pass.*

He said something so quietly she missed it. When she asked him to repeat it, his fingers tightened on his coat sleeves, knuckles whitening.

'Will you kiss me? Just once.'

She'd forgotten those dreams; the countless different scenarios she'd conjured in her head, mapping out every detail until it seemed so plausible it was just a matter of time.

He didn't wait for an answer, pressing the broken frill of his lips to her closed mouth.

20 December 1995

Thomas was supposed to move in yesterday. We agreed on the last day of school but I've heard nothing from him. I don't believe it's because he's changed his mind. When I offered him the room, I saw the gratitude on his face.

I am prepared to face the inevitable questions of propriety because this boy is in desperate need of help and no one else seems to feel responsible for him. If – by offering him a clean, safe place to stay over Christmas and New Year – I offend the small people of this community, then so be it. I will put him on that train myself, having made sure he is clean and fed and ready to start a new life far from here.

Something is preventing him from coming to me as planned, so I shall have to find him.

I went to see Finn Quennell this morning. When I asked after Thomas, he flew into a frightening rage and chased me out of the gate. He kept shouting that he hadn't seen his son. He blamed me. He said I'd messed with Thomas's head so that he wasn't right any more.

I went to Nathan's afterwards, but he wasn't home. His boat is not in the harbour, either. I found Thomas's friend Jessica there. She denied having seen Thomas but she wouldn't look me in the eye.

I can't stop thinking about Mr Quennell's reaction when I asked after Thomas. I'm beginning to think something has happened. I feel sick with dread.

38

Jessica woke the next morning on top of her bed-covers, still dressed. She could hear her family eating breakfast – the muffled chink of cutlery against plates where once it was voices laughing, talking over each other. Without bothering to change, she climbed out of the window.

The caravan was stifling, the heater still on.

'Thomas?' She opened the bedroom door and found the bed empty, its sheets in messy ripples. On the floor beside the bed lay a small plastic-handled chopping knife from the cutlery drawer, its blade twisted, the tip bent in on itself. Unable to make any sense of it, she kicked it under the bed.

He was gone.

Though it smelled like something dredged off the ocean floor, Jessica crawled into the bed where Thomas had been lying just hours before. The sheets were gritty, dirt trickling like squashed ants into the bedding's folds as she moved.

A brilliant drop of red stood out against the dirty

snow of the sheets. She inspected it under the bathroom's strip light and discovered it was a gemstone, the shape and colour of a globule of blood. She held it up to the mirror, entranced.

And found his message written in soap across the glass.

Gone swimming it said, in crumbly white letters.

But of course he wouldn't. Not when he reached the water and felt the icy spray like acid across his cheeks. She lay down on the bed and watched the trees bending under the weight of the gale, heavy and slow as though everything were underwater. Rolling away from the window, she stared at her shoes on the floor, pictured herself springing out of bed and running off into the storm. He could be anywhere by now. She'd never find him. In any case, he wouldn't be so stupid. Jessica closed her eyes.

She must have fallen asleep because the sound of footsteps brought her bolt upright, dizzy and disorientated.

'Thomas?' she tried to say but her throat was dry. The silhouette in the doorway was the wrong shape.

'Did you sleep here last night?' her mother asked.

Jessica nodded and an idea bloomed. 'I don't want to share with Hannah any more.'

'Why's that?' Birdie was frowning about the room, her eyes returning to the filthy sheets. Perhaps her mother's instinct, long dormant, was stirring.

Jessica cleared her throat. Without looking at Birdie, she said, 'You need to look under Hannah's mattress.'

Her mother didn't ask why. She stared at Jessica for a

long, uncomfortable moment and then sighed. 'We're out of milk and bread. Would you mind getting some from the shop?'

It had been so long since Birdie had bothered about such things that Jessica got up without protest and started putting on her shoes. 'OK.'

'Wear an extra layer,' her mother added. 'It's been blowing a gale since last night.'

She couldn't remember the last time her mother had noticed what she was wearing. She walked to Selcombe with the hope of things getting better.

Outside the newsagent's a tall, bony-faced boy was wrestling with the shop awning which had ripped free from its steel arm and was flapping violently in the wind. Ian, his name was, an ex-boyfriend of Lisa's who used to think he was being hilarious by waving Jessica away with his hands and saying *shoo little fly* whenever she walked in on them snogging on the sofa.

'Woah, woah,' he was shouting, as if the awning could be tamed like a bucking horse. As Jessica approached, he flapped limp fingers at her. 'Stay back.'

Her collar around her ears, she rocked with the gale blasts, waiting for him to wind the awning in. When he finally let her into the shop, Jessica grabbed a pint of milk and a sliced white loaf.

'How's your sister?' he asked when she brought her groceries to the counter.

'Hannah?' She busied herself counting out coins so he wouldn't see her grin.

'Lisa.'

'She's fine. In love again.'

Ian's mouth twitched down at corners. 'Who's the unlucky fellow?'

'A sailor. He's twenty-five and has his own car,' Jessica said, making up a story.

'Let's hope he doesn't get himself drowned in this weather.'

Jessica grabbed her shopping and opened the door, which caught in the wind, nearly ripping out of her hand.

Gone swimming, Thomas's message had said. She ran across the road to the harbour, her head dizzy with Ian's comment.

A chewy winter swell was butting the sailing boats by the pontoon against each other, their rubber buoys squealing. Nathan's crabber had a berth at the end of the jetty. Before she even reached it she could see the gap where it should have been, startling and unnatural among the jostling vessels like a missing tooth. The red tender was still there. Whoever had taken the crabber out wasn't intending to reach dry land.

Seawater washed over the surface of the jetty, almost sweeping her off her feet. With a stumbling jig, Jessica steadied herself and scanned the horizon. Not a single boat was braving the monstrous bulge and trough of the ocean. With the wind shrieking through the masts, she didn't hear someone walking up behind her. There was a light touch on her shoulder.

'Are you Jessica, by any chance?'

It took her a moment to register who the woman was. The wind was making a wild mess of her hair, but with her blouse tucked neatly into the waist of a long blue skirt she looked like a teacher. She had that kind of voice. Jessica went cold.

'Yes.' She hugged her arms about her waist, the milk bottle knocking against her hip. And though she knew full well, she added, 'Who are you?'

The woman held out a hand which Jessica pretended not to see, turning her face back to the empty mooring.

'Albertine Callum. A friend of Thomas's.'

Jessica chewed the inside of her cheek. 'He's never mentioned you.'

The woman didn't answer but when Jessica risked a sideways glance, Bertie's expression was thoughtful, kind rather than offended.

Together they stared at the space where Nathan's boat should have been. 'Have you seen Thomas today?'

Jessica shook her head.

'Do you remember when you last saw him?'

'Why are you asking?' Jessica kept her face turned away from the counsellor.

'I'm worried about him.' Bertie leaned in, searching Jessica's face as if secrets were like tears that might leak out unexpectedly and give you away. 'And I think you are too. That's why you're here.'

'I was looking for Nathan, actually.'

Bertie drew back, craning her head at the swollen sea beyond the harbour wall. Her eyes were red-rimmed, gory in her pale face. 'The thing is, Nate would never take his boat out in this.'

Nate. Like she, Thomas and Nathan were all best

mates. Jessica hunched her arms tighter about herself. She would say nothing more.

Another wave swelled over the pontoon lip, the water swallowing up her ankles so that for one giddy moment, she appeared to be stranded in the middle of the sea with its black depths and the colliding boats. The bag of groceries dropped from her fingers and Bertie caught her arm as she reached for it, the receding wave already sucking it out.

'We can't stand here any longer.'

Jessica shrugged her away. 'I'm fine where I am.'

'I think it's been hard on you, hasn't it?' The gentle tone in Bertie's voice made Jessica glance round, despite herself.

'What has?'

'You've been such a good friend to Thomas. I can only imagine it has been tough and made you feel sad. And perhaps a bit frightened.'

Jessica's eyes filled with tears. She didn't need to blink them back because the rain would hide them.

'I think you've been trying to help him as best you can.' The counsellor slipped her arm through Jessica's and started to lead her away from the jetty's edge. 'Did Thomas say anything about taking Nathan's boat out?'

She shook her head, the wind hiding her face in her hair. The urge to tell Bertie about Thomas and the mess he was in last night was overwhelming; the relief of handing it all over to a grown-up to make it better. She stopped walking.

Bertie whipped round to face her, grabbing Jessica's

hand. Her fingers were cold and thin and squeezed too hard. 'It's down to you and me, Jessica, to save him.'

Jessica nodded, licked her lips, tasting salt. She was just thinking where to begin, how far back she needed to go to explain how lost Thomas had become, when Bertie added, 'We just need to find him and everything will be fine. Thomas and I have made a plan.'

Thomas and I have made a plan. Said with a nod and a smile of teacherly confidence. *Thomas and I . . .* As though he belonged to her, not to Jessica.

Freeing her hand from Bertie's grip, Jessica stepped back and raised her chin. 'I don't know where he is.'

She started to walk away.

'Are you sure?' The counsellor's voice was shrill above the wind. 'Because he was planning to see you. To say goodbye.'

Jessica started to run.

39

The journey to Stollingworth takes almost five hours. Unwilling to use their joint account, Jessica allows herself nothing more than a cup of scalding peppermint tea and a cheese sandwich. For the time being, she'll rely on her sole account – tidal at the best of times – swelling with sales, depleting with the purchase of raw materials. Her hunger pleases her, a symptom of recovered independence.

Just after five o'clock, she steps off the train and books into the Midway Hotel, a modest Victorian terrace with a view of Stollingworth Station and a communal playground. The air smells foreign: chimney smoke and industrial metals.

Reception is tucked beneath the stairs, half hidden by a dusty yucca plant on a plastic pedestal. Behind it, Jessica can just make out of the head of a man in his early twenties. He doesn't look up until she dings the countertop bell.

'Can I help you?' He peers out of an overgrown fringe resting in his eyes. She pictures him spending an age in front of the mirror combing it into place with both hands.

On the registration form, she provides her mother's address.

'I like your look.'

Jessica glances up from the form. 'Sorry?'

'I only meant in an aesthetic sense.' He shapes invisible tumbling curls with his hands. 'Very Titian.'

Jessica signs the form and pushes it back to him.

'I'm doing an Open University course in Art Appreciation. That's the Titian link.' He gives a slanty grin. 'On holiday?'

'No, my boyfriend's been offered a job here. I'm helping him move in. Place is a dump at the moment, so here I am.' Out it popped. The same lie she had told to the overfamiliar landlord of Threepenny Row before Jacques came along and made everything better. She clears her throat. 'Is there Wi-Fi in the room?'

'What do you reckon?' The boy rolls his eyes at Reception. He hands her the keys but as she reaches the stairs, adds: 'Actually, the manager's not in. You can use the computer out back.'

Johnny Boyzie – as the receptionist introduces himself – lifts the counter flap and shows her into a cupboard-sized room behind the front desk. He settles himself on the edge of a table that takes up most of the space while Jessica googles Stollingworth on the ancient Mac. Then he takes out a half-empty bottle of Jägermeister from the drawer, along with a mug for Jessica and a shot glass for himself. 'Crazy juice. Against the boredom.'

She takes in his narrow chin with its splash of pimples, his wide-set blue eyes and the diamond stud in his ear. Smiles to herself as she takes a sip from her mug. The brown liquid tastes like cough syrup, warming her all the way up from her stomach, giving a little zing as it hits her head. 'I see what you mean.'

'So, does anyone actually buy the boyfriend job story?'

She laughs. 'Not since I was seventeen.'

Her internet search reveals little about the town Thomas escaped to. The only photos she finds are of a power station and the Iceberg Tower – in sunlight, at night, viewed from a plane or from the ground up.

'How far are we from the sea?' she asks.

'Dunno.' Johnny Boyzie shrugs. 'There's a canal in the old part of town. Must start somewhere.'

He goes to top up her drink but Jessica holds up her hand. 'Are you trying to get me drunk?'

'Yes.' Another crooked grin.

Jessica smiles, shaking her head. 'Go pick on someone your own age.'

'I've dated most of my big sister's friends.'

'Now there's a CV.'

Boyzie laughs, leaning forward to top up her mug, but Jessica's attention is distracted by a website – a single page only – for Stollingworth Fish Market. It offers little more than the opening times and a list of wholesalers and their produce. She thanks the receptionist, who offers to show her to the room.

'I can find number five all by myself, thank you.'

Room five is at the top of the second flight of stairs. Switching on the bedside lamp, she finds a small, sparse room with a tiny television set and fake tulips in a cut-glass vase on the desk. She gives her surroundings a moment to settle upon her, anticipating their depressive pull. Instead, she feels energised. All those months wondering where Thomas was, the slow rake of time like fingernails across her skin as she waited for the right moment, and finally it is here. She strips, throwing her clothes on the green poplin armchair, and climbs under sheets that smell of lavender and laundry powder. She falls asleep following a brick-lined canal to the sea.

In the morning, she switches on her mobile and messages flood in. She deletes them without checking and rings Birdie.

'Jacques has been calling.' Her mother's angry tone surprises her, a shiver dropping through her like a slot-machine coin, landing in her stomach.

'What did you tell him?'

'What could I say? I don't know where you are.'

'I can't explain yet.'

'Running away doesn't fix anything.' Birdie sniffs. 'It's how you ended up in that God-awful squat all those years ago. And it's what your father did.'

Jessica's throat dries. She replaces the receiver as quietly as she can. Birdie could voice her hoarded-up bitterness to a dead line.

After a long shower, she heads down to breakfast and

336

overfills her plate from the buffet. She's not hungry, but as it's included in the price she can no longer afford the luxury of leaving it. She manages a coffee and a few mouthfuls of egg.

After breakfast, she picks up a local map and asks Boyzie for directions to the fish market. As the receptionist draws a route in blue biro to the bus station, she is still raging at her mother in her head. *When will you stop punishing me for being my father's daughter?*

Jessica folds the map. Sunlight shines through the frosted glass of the front door. 'I don't suppose I could have another slug of that stuff? For energy?'

His face breaking into a huge grin, Boyzie glances about the empty reception area before retrieving the bottle of Jägermeister. 'Jägi before eleven. I'm loving it.'

Jessica drinks straight from the bottle.

40

The bus outside the hotel takes her to a large terminus in the centre of Stollingworth. Buses roar and belch around a concrete roundabout with a wooden bench where Jessica sits down to wait for the number thirty-two, as instructed by a chatty female bus driver.

Beside the seat is a signpost with arrow-shaped place names pointing in the direction of their location. According to the London arrow, she has put two hundred and thirty-eight miles between her and Jacques. The distance between one life and the next.

She wonders if Thomas sat on the same bench, bus fumes smoking the sea air out of his chest as he wondered what to do next.

The number thirty-two attracts a small group of people bound for the fish market; a father with young twins, three elderly ladies and a sallow-faced, middle-aged man who barely lifts his head from his guidebook. Jessica sits at the back, as far from them as possible, too anxious for small talk.

It takes fifteen minutes to leave the grey-faced city behind and reach flat, heavily farmed countryside. As the bus swings, bottom-heavy, through twisting lanes, Jessica catches an occasional glimpse of the canal, glittering opaquely in a low autumn sun. The bus follows a tarmacked road through the metal grille gates of an industrial estate, which ends abruptly with the ugliest view of the sea Jessica has ever seen – a wide, soiled expanse of water full of oil tankers. A fleet of large fishing vessels are docked alongside the pontoon. The market itself is a huge industrial block, windowless and besieged by diving seagulls. Men in white overcoats mill in and out of the market entrance with trolley-loads of crated fish. Jessica's heart is beating so hard she barely hears the bus driver announcing their final destination.

'This is it, young lady. The famous Stollingworth Fish Market.' He peers round from his seat. When she doesn't respond, he adds, 'I have to turn back in five mins, just so you know.'

Jessica thinks she nods but she's not sure. Suddenly she's afraid to get off. Every time a porter walks out of the huge building, her pulse explodes in her head. Then the driver's standing over her, his frown a mix of concern and irritation. 'A bit of fresh air, perhaps?'

As soon as she leaves the bus, the air clears her head. It's a smell she recognises; fish – fresh and rotting – and the sea itself. She slips past her fellow passengers, who are grouped around a man in a straw boater, and in through the market's cavernous doorway. The main hall is brilliant under a neon glare; it bounces off floors, shimmery with water and fish slime, catching the opalescent scales of the day's catch. The light makes her feel exposed, spotlit. There's a constant criss-cross of male banter and laughter between the merchants and porters. The assault on her senses is so vivid she almost scurries back outside. Then she notices the row of white plastic tables and chairs at the back of the hall and heads for the café.

Calm yourself, she thinks. He is not here.

The man behind the counter at the small café gives her such a beaming smile that she relaxes. 'What'll it be, love?'

His face is plump and stubbled with fair hair, the skin around his eyes puckered with humour.

'Just a black coffee, please.'

The man gives a theatrical double take. 'You're in a fish market, love, not Costa Coffee. How about a little smoked salmon? No? Some potted shrimp?'

Jessica shakes her head. 'Think I'd better line my stomach first.'

'Fair enough.' He pours tarry coffee from a thermos into a flimsy plastic cup which scalds her fingers.

'How long have you worked here?'

'Couple of years now. Used to be a postman but that was the loneliest job in the world, let me tell you. Stolly Market's best place I've ever worked, with the camaraderie and all that.'

She pays for the coffee and sits facing the hall. Feeling more at ease, she can take it all in. The displayed seafood is glossy with freshness, in hues of visceral pinks and reds, pulpy whites and intestinal browns. She takes small, fast sips of her coffee, hoping the caffeine will burn away her slight nausea.

'Is it a job you're after, love?' The man behind the counter asks.

'I'm looking for someone, actually.'

'Ah, the plot thickens.' He comes out from behind the counter and squashes himself into a chair opposite. 'You obviously weren't here for the fish.'

'Thomas Quennell. He was a porter here about seventeen years ago.'

The man sits back. 'Well before my time, but ask Greg at Mikkelson and Sons. He knows everyone. Worked here since the dawn of time.'

As she finishes her coffee, she watches porters disappearing through a curtain of thick plastic strips and returning with stacked polystyrene boxes brimming with fish. Young men with dark pony-tailed hair and the pale, fine features of Eastern Europeans. She studies their faces as they throw crumbs of broken English into the general banter.

Glances reach her, quick and curious as butterfly kisses, but nothing lingering. Except for one man in the opposite corner, hosing a section of floor. With a stocky build and blond, unstyled hair, he stands out from the other porters. His constant gaze makes her shift in her chair. She glances over. He doesn't seem to notice the water from his hose gushing over his rubber boots. Simple but harmless, she decides, and heads over to Mikkelson and Sons.

Greg is a tall man with a single grey plait under his stallholder's hat. He is discussing sea bream with a customer. A single, arachnid claw waves from a box of spider crabs. As the customer leaves, Jessica introduces herself.

'I was told you've worked here the longest, and know everyone.'

'Aye.' He's clearly pegged her as a non-sale.

'I'm looking for a boy, a man, I mean, who used to work here as a porter.' A movement behind Greg's shoulder catches her eye. The light-haired man is now standing by the doorway. The sun has broken through the grey sky and slants through the curtain strips. It catches his hair, and the gleaming fish scales in the polystyrene crates surrounding him, and ripples along the newly hosed floor. A wavering flux of brilliance like sunlight viewed from the seabed.

He is still watching her.

'Who is that?' Jessica points past Greg's shoulder. But she doesn't hear the answer as her pulse fills her ears, blood rushing to the surface of her skin. Before her head can catch up, her body has recognised him.

Thomas. Her lips shape his name, and she sees a matching certainty snap into place. Now he knows her too.

Thomas, grown into a man. His body and face thickened with years. She would have passed him by on the street. Nearly walked out of the market, dismissing him.

Greg looks around and addresses him sharply. Thomas stares back with the bemused eyes of someone waking from a deep sleep. Then something quickens in his face, but he doesn't move.

She picks her way carefully past the close-packed displays and across the slippery floor, never taking her eyes off him. Expecting him to bolt through the doorway and disappear once more. He doesn't move, frozen in the light.

Face to face, she suffers another moment of hesitation. Thomas, and yet not Thomas. She finds him in his eyes again.

'It's me. Jessica.'

His head drops, forehead almost touching her shoulder. For a moment they catch their breath.

'I found you.' Her words come out in spasms, her whole frame shaking violently.

He reaches for a lock of her hair, lifting it free from beneath the collar of her jacket and rubbing it lightly between his fingers. A tattoo like mermaid's hair runs between his thumb and forefinger down to his wrist. 'You found me.'

She closes her eyes because his voice – unchanged – brings the seventeen-year-old Thomas back. Her Thomas.

41

They don't speak as they follow the canal towards his home. Jessica lifts out of herself, following the two of them like a kite in the air. They walk like strangers, the woman with her arms wrapped about herself, the man's gait tight, reined in. A steady arm's length of space maintained; silence like a bag of stones between them.

Jessica studies the canal in minute relief. Grass sprouting through brickwork, clotted algae on the brown water, an empty crisp packet on the path with a mouthful of rainwater. Thomas stops suddenly, squatting down. He rubs his eyes, his face, brings a hand over his cropped hair. When he looks up, he's grinning.

'Jellybird,' he says, shaking his head. 'Jellybird.'

And she smiles back. One of them starts to laugh, the other joining in. She makes herself stop because her mouth starts to tremble, loose and untrustworthy. When they walk on, his hand finds hers and Jessica knows, with perfect clarity, that this moment will never be bettered.

Thomas's house is the last in a terrace of red-brick bungalows, facing a patch of stubbled grass with a bench. Beside it lies a child's tricycle, but other than that the place feels deserted.

He searches in his white coat for a single key and unlocks his door.

Thomas's home, Jessica thinks, and is overwhelmed once again by the enormity of having found him. When he walks through the door, she doesn't recognise the broadened shape of his back, or his head without its blond straggles.

She has to relearn him.

He doesn't invite her in, falling into a routined sequence of homecoming; boots placed on the porch step, coat removed, squashed into a ball and thrown into a washing machine inside the hallway cupboard. She follows him into a narrow kitchen, where he dispenses an egg-sized dollop of liquid soap into his palm from an industrial bottle, scrubbing his hands under steaming water until they are red and raw. The smell of fish reeking off his clothes catches the back of her throat in the confined space. Wiping his hands on a kitchen towel, she sees tiny filaments of blood where his over-washed skin splits with the bend of his fingers.

It's only after he's filled the kettle and switched it on that he looks at her.

'Tea?'

'Yes. Please.'

He takes two blue-striped mugs and a bag of sugar

from a kitchen cabinet. 'I can't remember how you have it.'

'Milk.' She wishes there were some background noise to relieve the self-conscious clink of cups, the sound of her swallowing and his breathing. 'And three sugars please.'

He dips his head in acknowledgement and she can't tell if he is remembering how he and Nathan used to tease her. *Want a little tea with your sugar?* He keeps his eyes on the kettle, which starts to rumble and whine. Jessica steps out of the kitchen. The house is unheated. She keeps her coat on, taking a seat on the brown suede sofa in the living room. Trying to take it all in, to find something typically Thomas which might bridge the time gap. By her feet, and scattered across a small table by the window, lie neatly scissored pictures of deer, owls and wild boar. The shelves on either side of the electric fire are stacked with magazines whose pages hang out in lacerated strips.

Thomas hands her a mug of tea and again she is assaulted by the smell of discarded scales and dis-embowelled viscera that have adhered to the fibres of his jeans and blue sweater.

He collects his animal pictures and piles them on the desk. She wants to ask about them, but there's some-thing protective about the careful way he stacks them to prevent any crumpling. Sipping her tea, she glances between the brown, leafy pattern of the carpet and Thomas; trying to unwrap the years that have coarsened his features and find the boy she knew.

'Gabbler,' Thomas says between gulps of tea. 'My nickname at the market.'

'Your nickname?'

His eyes flick away as soon as she meets their pale stare. 'It's a joke because I don't say much.'

'I don't have a nickname any more.' *Not since you left*, she almost adds.

He nods, still looking everywhere but at her. 'I fell out of the habit of talking.'

'Why did you leave?' She regrets her words immediately. They are too sharp for the fragile veil of connection that hangs between them. 'Sorry. Don't answer that yet.'

'Let's go out for a walk,' Thomas says, getting up. Still happier outside than in. It makes her smile. Some things remain true.

The further they walk, the easier they become in each other's company.

'Like the old days,' Jessica comments, and is then embarrassed by his silence.

They cross open parkland of yellow grass and lone oaks. Mottled red and brown leaves blow about their feet, and Jessica has the odd sense of having lost time. When she left London it was late summer; here, autumn is already giving way to winter.

Thomas stops walking and points into the bare branches of a towering oak. 'See the little blue bird? A nuthatch. Only woodland bird that can climb head first down trees.'

Jessica smiles. 'I know. You told me.'

For a moment he looks bewildered. 'When?'

'When you and me used to do this.' She sweeps her arms at the countryside.

'You remember about nuthatches?'

She notices for the first time the frown lines like the mark of a two-pronged fork between his eyebrows.

'I remember everything, Thomas.' *I remember you and your beautiful grey eyes*, she thinks.

'You were just a girl.'

'And?' It occurs to her that he's afraid. It makes her less so.

'And . . .' Shaking his head, he lets his eyes move over her face, her hair. She sees them catch, a moment-ary stalling, on her breasts, and heat floods the pit of her stomach. Then he turns away, scouring the oak branches again.

'You look different,' he says. 'I don't know you.'

She finds herself digging her nails into her palms. Takes a deep breath, eyes closed, feeling the wind sweep off the ground and move through her hair. 'You don't know the details of my life, Thomas. But you know *me*.'

'Details?'

'Like baubles on a Christmas tree. They don't change the tree.'

Jacques, London, her jewellery. Baubles on a fallen tree.

Thomas starts walking again. 'There's a pond near here, full of Canadian geese.'

The rusty *chuck chuck* of a pheasant catches his atten-tion as a brown-feathered flurry bursts from the under-growth. He stretches his arm out like a rifle and follows its flight through the air, squinting along a pointed finger.

'Shall I fill you in on my life? Just the bare bones?' Jessica asks.

'The bare baubles, don't you mean?'

She smiles but he doesn't respond, studying her expression with the same sober intensity with which he fixed the tiny nuthatch.

When they reach the lake, he lays his sweater on the ground between the long reeds at the water's edge. The cotton of his t-shirt is almost transparent with wear beneath his armpits, but unlike the last time she saw him, it's clean and he had insisted on showering before they left the house. A tattoo of barbed wire snakes up both his forearms. Another change.

They sit on his jumper; protected from the wind by the long grass, their sides almost touching, a cocoon of warmth surrounding them. Jessica rolls up her sleeve and clinks her pebble bracelet at him. Thomas raises his eyebrows, acknowledges it with a huff of air through his nose.

'Want to know what I do for a living?' she asks.

Chewing on a stem of grass, he nods. So she tells him a story. All about a girl called Jessica who studied design in London and landed a part-time job in a prestigious jeweller's, which is helping fund her growing jewellery-design business. The tale is full of her successes and achievements – first sales, exhibitions, glowing reviews – but she never mentions Jacques. Without him, her story is so obviously pared down, its missing facts like new holes cut into paper snowflakes, obscuring the original shape.

His unquestioning acceptance of her story surprises her. Then she catches him considering her wedding ring. Until that moment, she hadn't thought of it. It was simply part of her finger. She can't bring herself to remove it.

'It's good,' he eventually says. 'Your life sounds full.'

'How about you?' she asks, as his silence settles on them again.

'It goes along as it should.'

'What about all the little clippings in your front room?'

As soon as the question's out, she regrets it, afraid it might be a symptom of some peculiarity that has developed in the passing years.

'I make collage packs for kids and sell them at local fairs and school fetes. Parents buy them in the hope their kids will make pretty pictures of animals or beaches instead of playing on their DSes.'

Hugging her legs, Jessica says, 'I wouldn't really know about kids.'

A breeze flattens the grass around them and he rubs his arms. Jessica traces a fingertip along his forearm, following the barbed-wire tattoo. Wanted to touch him to see what would happen. He doesn't move away but his eyes are sharp on her face.

'What do they symbolise?'

'Nothing.'

A fine rain forces them to their feet. Thomas stays two steps ahead, his head darting to catch movement in the undergrowth and skies. Trailing behind his unfamiliar frame, Jessica has never felt so lost.

Thomas goes out to get pizzas. Having no car, it will take forty minutes on his pushbike. Jessica puts the oven on to reheat the pizzas and hunts through his kitchen for plates and glasses. She finds his cupboards crammed with tinned soups, vegetables and pies and packets of pasta, biscuits and cereals; as though in anticipation of a natural disaster which might render him the last man on earth. It makes her smile; how typical of Thomas to be so self-sufficient and separate. The corroboration pleases her, until the rows of neatly positioned tins overwhelm her with loneliness.

She turns on the television in the sitting room and sees Jacques' favourite sports quiz – in front of which the two of them have often shared a takeaway pizza. Switching the set off again, she lets the silence wrap around her as the alien strangeness of the situation, and their attempts to dress it in everyday life, hit her. Perhaps it's the chill in the house, but she starts to shiver and once started, it won't stop.

In the bathroom, she inspects the avocado-coloured tub and finds it clean. Hesitates before turning on the taps, worrying about its appropriateness and the fact that the door has no key. Then the temptation of a hot, cleansing bath is too much. She barricades the door with her rucksack and boots, filling up the tub. Sinking beneath the surface with only her face above water, the shaking eases.

When she hears him come home, she sits up, arms crossed over her breasts, watching the bathroom door.

'Jessica?' His voice muffles as he walks into the kitchen. 'Are you here?'

She catches the slight rise of his voice, and reads it as a sudden fear that she has gone.

'I'm in the bath.'

Silence. 'I'll put your pizza in the oven,' he says after a pause.

As she washes her hair with his lime shampoo, she wonders if he's listening to the sound of water against her naked skin in his quiet, quiet house.

By the time she is dressed, he has turned the electric heater on and cleared his cuttings out of sight. They eat pepperoni pizza and drink Heineken straight from the bottle. She can feel his eyes on her. When she meets them, he doesn't look away but wears a frown of concentration as though he's puzzling out a mystery. They don't speak, the noise of the television providing a layer of lagging to fill their silence.

'Pizza and beer. All that's missing is the Friday-night video.' An inane, clumsy effort to interrupt the stillness emanating from Thomas.

'I don't have a DVD player,' he answers, and there is not a trace of humour in his face.

When the pizza box is empty he disappears into his room at the rear of the house, returning with a pillow and duvet. Again, that sweet-salty whiff of fish. She suspects they are his own covers and tries to refuse.

'I'm afraid there's only one room.' He makes a bed for her on the sofa, and suddenly she is so tired the room tilts. After a brisk goodnight, he closes his bedroom door with quiet, almost surreptitious effort.

Within minutes, she is asleep.

42

Sometime in the night Jessica wakes up. She tries to roll over and back into sleep but she is wide awake. An orange moon, as bright and low as a street lamp, is framed in the window, its light poking her eyes open.

Thomas's bedroom door is pushed to but no longer shut. She takes a few cautious steps into the hall, curious for the sound of him in his sleep. Silence. Perhaps the moon has woken him, too.

She taps on his door with two knuckles. It glides open enough for her to see the foot of a bed. There's still no noise from within. Pushing the door a little wider, it is almost a shock to see him sprawled on the mattress, no covers or pillow, wearing a pair of grey jogging bottoms.

Heart thudding, she moves a little closer, knowing she should leave; but there he lies in moonlit relief for her finally to study him. Face relaxed in sleep, he bears a stronger resemblance to his younger self. An exaggerated version of the boy she knew. Stronger chin, wider face, the same brow. Perhaps if she asks him, he'll grow his hair again.

His body is a different matter. A stranger's chest and shoulders shaped by tough, physical work. His fingers look too long and delicate for his muscled forearms. She searches his face again for the Thomas she knew. The harder she looks for him, the more he disappears. A temporary image sunburned onto the retina, always fading.

She doesn't recognise this sleeping stranger. Her Thomas is never coming back.

Out of nowhere the tears come. Those golden days are gone, when the world was as intimate as the branch of an oak tree, peopled only by her and Thomas. She clamps down on her jaw but she can't stop. She finds herself crying for everything she's ever lost. Her father, who effectively took her mother with him. Thomas, the friend she clung to like a lifebelt. Her life in London, the promise of babies like future Christmas presents.

Jacques. Letting her walk away.

She buries her head in the basket of her bent elbows, hands in her hair. Takes a deep breath and wipes her face. Looks up to find him still lying there, eyes now open. Turning away, she manages three steps before he's on his feet. He stops short of touching her.

'It's OK,' he mumbles, groggy with sleep.

Faces him. It's not OK at all. 'How could you have done it?'

The blank look on his face infuriates her. 'You let me think you'd drowned.' Her words spitting out like bitter seeds. 'Did you never think what that would do to me?'

'Hey.' He steps closer, palms outwards as if fending her off. There's a look in his eyes – a look she saw only once, outside Caravan Nineteen when he shouted at her for not talking to the police. 'Stop.'

She slaps his hands away, heart catapulting as his arms slowly drop. His eyes recede as though he's stepping back into himself, a cat settling on poised haunches. A curl of fear in her stomach. She has no idea who this man really is.

The sound of their breathing seems to reach them simultaneously, untwisting the air between them.

'You were the one who kept me going when my dad left. I still remember the love I felt for you. If I close my eyes and picture you on the beach, I can still feel it.'

Thomas sits down, leaning his elbows on his knees and holding his head. 'There's no going back once you leave a place,' he says. 'Same with people.'

'You say that because you're scared.'

'It was a different life, Jessica. It happened to different people.'

Without knowing she was going to do it, she drops to her knees in front of him, plants herself in the safe haven between his legs, as she has done so often in her dreams, and raises her face. 'Look at me properly.'

He gazes down at her for a moment before closing his eyes. His fingers lift to her face, gently tracing her cheeks, her jawline and brow. Her lips. Before his hands can drop away, she snakes her fingers behind his neck and brings his mouth down to hers. He freezes – a single, blank moment – then his arms come up and he's pressing his full force against her lips. Hands in her

356

hair, he moans into her mouth as their lips open and his tongue slips along hers. Then the tension returns to his body.

'No,' he mumbles against her lips. She falls onto her heels, the back of her hand to her mouth. He shakes his head in a short, rapid motion, a shiver more than a gesture. 'There's something you need to see.'

Outside, she fills her lungs with sharp, wintry air. It smells of smoke and damp bracken. With the moon now behind cloud, they follow the canal towpath through an unseen landscape. A tree materialises in her path, shocking Jessica with its unexpected size and bulk. Thomas seems unaffected by the poor visibility, his feet tracking the canal edge.

He grabs her hand to quicken the pace, and his urgency makes her nervous. She begins to drag her footsteps. 'Where are you taking me?'

'I can't explain. You'll see.'

Leaving the towpath, they cross open fields. Jessica stumbles over frozen knuckles of earth. The moon is out again and she can see a forest silhouetted against the sky. They reach a signpost for Bishopshigh at the side of a road leading under a canopy of laced tree branches. Beneath it, the darkness is solid. Jessica shuffles forward swinging her arm like a machete. After a few minutes, without warning, Thomas scrambles up a bank of roots and into the woods. Jessica remains on the road.

'We're going into the woods?'

Thomas's voice comes from a little way above her on the bank. 'Yes.'

She licks her lips, finds her mouth has gone dry. 'Surely it's too dark to see anything?'

'It'll start getting light soon.'

She hears him moving away, leaving her alone with no idea of where she is.

'Shit,' she mutters, and follows the crashing sound of his progress through the undergrowth. When he appears at her side, she almost screams. He grabs her wrist to pull her along. If he left her now, she would never find her way back. Gripping his hand, she stumbles, feet catching stumps and fallen branches camouflaged in the black slurry of shadow lining the forest floor. Thomas twists around trees, pushes his way through straggling bushes, never hesitating.

'Are you sure you know where we are?' A nagging suspicion. This can't be a route; he is deliberately getting them lost.

'It's not far,' is all he'll say.

She digs her heels in, wraps her arm around a damp branch and anchors herself.

'What is it now?'

This snapping impatience is not something she recognises. Here, in the dark, Thomas is a complete stranger.

'It's too dark and cold. I . . . I want to go back now.'

'It's just through those trees. In the clearing.' He tries to take her hand again but she shrinks out of his reach, still clinging to the branch. Thomas steps back, regarding her in silence. Then he walks on without her, pushing his way through a tangle of thicket and leafless bush. His head ducks down on the other side and disappears. She listens for a clue as to what he is doing. Rustling. Trees cracking and sighing in the wind. It is much worse not to see him. She moves forward and finds Thomas squatting down to muck out twigs and mud from what looks to be the entrance of a badger's set beneath the exposed roots of a beech tree. With his head and shoulder close to the ground, he pushes an arm deep inside, gropes about and then pulls something out.

Despite herself, Jessica moves closer. He holds up a dirt-crusted casket of plain wood with a simple catch, like a jewellery box. As he balances it on his out-stretched palm, his hand is shaking.

'What is it?'

'You open it.' His voice sounds rusty, as though he hasn't spoken for a long time.

A feeling of dread comes over her. 'What's inside?'

'You'll know when you see it.'

She takes it from him, the wood slippery with mud so she has to crouch down and rest it on her knees.

'You have to know this, Jellybird,' she hears him say through a humming in her head. Holding her breath, she flicks the catch open and drops back the lid. Some-thing gold gleams dully in the dusk. It makes no sense; her panicky brain can't decipher it so she picks it up.

In her hand is a heavy golden crucifix embedded with rubies. Dry-slicked with black matter. With a gasp, she drops it.

'No, Thomas, no,' she cries.

The cross lies half buried in fallen leaves. He fingers it out of the mulch and loops it over his head. Drops down onto the ground as if floored by the weight of it. Jessica staggers back, trying to distance herself from Bloody Russian's crucifix.

'My cross to bear.'

She stumbles onto a fallen log at the edge of the clearing and covers her face with her hands, too dizzy and numb to arrange thoughts into words. What horrifies her almost as much as the sight of the cross is that her instinct has been so skewed. She had never once doubted his innocence.

And if she was so badly mistaken about this, how can she trust her judgement in anything else? What else has she misunderstood?

Her hands drop to her lap. With her thumbnail she scrapes at the mud smeared in her palm from handling the box. Thomas is speaking, his words aimed at the crucifix dangling from his neck, and she has to push aside the noise in her head to concentrate.

'. . . still alive when I found him.'

'What did you say?'

Thomas won't lift his head. 'Though it could just have been when . . . I . . .' He makes a strangled noise, halfway between a cough and a choke. 'When I pulled it out of his mouth.'

'Pulled what?' Jessica approaches Thomas on unsteady legs, bends over him, straining to catch his words.

He is still gazing down at the soiled cross on his chest. 'His cross had been shoved deep into his throat. Blood was coming out of his mouth. I heard it gurgling up his throat.'

Bloody Russian's broken, jack-levered jaw. Jessica feels sick, hears herself moan in protest. Oblivious to the mud and waterlogged leaves, she slumps to the forest floor beside Thomas. 'You found him like that?'

He dips his head and relief like a hot, narcotic bloom flushes through her. She throws her arms around his neck, clasping hard, the cross embedded between them. He rests his face against her neck, heavy in her arms. This is the silence in him, a deep well that has swallowed him up.

Into his hair, she whispers, 'I knew it wasn't you.'

It is Thomas who stands up first, helping Jessica to her feet. As they walk, he starts to speak, his voice more tangible in the darkness than his body. She listens with her whole being, the forest receding, her feet finding their own path through the matted undergrowth. His story comes out in halting sentences, and she realises he has never told it before.

'When Bloody Russian disappeared I thought that was the end of him. Then one day there he was, in the garage with my dad. I wanted to kill him – you have no idea – but instead I did what was right. I went to the police.'

The knowledge startles her. She had never questioned how the police found out about Bloody Russian's attack.

'You told them what he did to me . . .' So here is the origin of the police file with her name on it.

'They couldn't charge him though because you wouldn't . . .'

Jessica worries the inside of her lip with her teeth. 'I'm so sorry.'

'But why, Jessica?' The fact still haunts him after all these years. She owes him an explanation.

'When the police picked him up outside my school, that's all anyone could talk about. One of the Year Sevens had a cousin or a boyfriend in the police and it all came out. Exaggerated, of course. What they said he'd done. I couldn't bear them to know it was me.'

She stops speaking, the memory returning in vivid, sensory waves – the cloying steam of breath and wet coats as girls funnelled through the corridors after break. Screeching like starlings about Bloody Russian.

'Then someone remembered I'd come in looking all beaten up a few months earlier.' Girls sidling up in small groups, pecking at her with questions, their eyes communicating conclusions above her head. *What happened to your face, again? Summer term, wasn't it? Fell off your bike? Really? You must have been going a hundred miles an hour.*

A twig catches her coat sleeve. Thomas waits as she tugs her arm free, careless of the material. Her hand brushes bark slick with damp, the cold bulk of the trunk looming over her. She shifts closer to Thomas, hoping to catch a trace of warmth. 'OK,' she says but he doesn't move.

'I went to confront my dad that day. I had packed a bag and was going to leave that evening.'

Without me? A forlorn echo of her lost, fourteen-year-old self.

'When I got to his house, the front door was open

but he wasn't in. I knew he wouldn't be far, so I went looking for him.'

She slips her hand in his but he doesn't seem to notice.

'In the woods I saw something lying on the ground. I laughed, you know. I thought—' His hand withdraws, the outline of his arm grey against a break in the trees. He rubs his eyes as if he could scrape away the memory. 'I couldn't understand what I was seeing. It was like he'd had some stupid accident, tripped up and landed on his own cross. Then I got closer.'

The Russian's broken-jawed, gore-streaked body joins them in the forest. Thomas grabs her wrist and they start to run.

They don't stop until they have scrambled on heels and hands down the embankment and reached the open stretch of road. Catching a dull glint at his chest, she realises he is still wearing the crucifix. The weapon.

She doesn't wait for their breath to catch up. 'Who did it, Thomas?'

'My dad.' His reply punch quick.

She swallows, nods. The old man had been trying to frighten her off Thomas's trail, knowing his murderous deed would be exposed if she ever found his son.

'I was trying to get Bloody Russian to sit up when suddenly my dad was there, shouting and swinging his cane at me. *What have you done, you monster? What have you done?*'

Jessica flinches at his sudden roar. 'Why would he say that?'

Thomas taps the side of his head. 'Because he's a crafty old bugger. I told him again and again it wasn't me. Then he said, so what? Everyone will think you did it.'

They face each other, fighting over a single rag of breath. His fingers tremble, forgotten, at his temple. She takes hold of his hand, presses it between her own; can't bear to witness the horror that has lived inside him all these years. 'And he was right, Jessica. I had a motive. My fingerprints were on him. I was fucked-up, sleeping rough and getting into fights. It didn't really matter who'd done it, they would blame me.'

'What happened then?'

'My father said my only chance was to make a run for it. He said he'd help me, but first I had to help him drag the body to the quarry.'

They start to walk slowly back along the lane, and Jessica is suddenly glad of the darkness.

'What makes you so certain it was your dad?'

Thomas's laugh is hard and bitter. 'It's the only time he ever went out of his way to help me.'

She hesitates, afraid her questions will rile him but the shock of seeing Thomas loop the soiled cross about his neck still lingers. She needs everything to slot into place, like sequencing the notes of a tune. 'But why would he do it?'

'It took me a while to work it out. He didn't care what that Russian bastard did to you, so it wasn't that. Then I remembered we'd caught him stealing tools.' Thomas nods to himself. 'It wasn't about missing hammers and screwdrivers, though. It was the fact that

364

Bloody Russian had taken advantage of him. After he'd bailed him out, and everything. Like how my dad killed one of our dogs for snapping at him. It was the same thing.'

'Why did you take the cross, Thomas?'

'Insurance. My father's fingerprints must be all over it.'

Nilson, she thinks. How does she tell him about Nilson?

When they reach his house, she holds back, reluctant to leave the blanketing darkness of the open fields to face each other under stark light. Thomas struggles with his boots in the hallway. Giving up, he trails mud into his bedroom. She finds him sprawled on the bed.

'Tell me about the boat.' She would rather close her eyes and sleep but this subject will never be discussed again after tonight.

'It's his feet that bother me,' Thomas says. 'Bloody Russian's shoes had come off, and his feet were white and smooth like a child's.'

Jessica's arms goosebump. 'Did your father come up with the boat idea?'

'Yeah.' In the dragging silence, she thinks he's fallen asleep, but then he continues. The plan had been simple. Thomas was to hide out until night fell. They were to meet at the harbour at one in the morning. Together they would sail to the Lady's Fingers, drill a hole in the hull and take his dad's old outboard back to shore, leaving the waves to carry and smash the boat against the pillars of rock.

'The storm nearly got us. We made it out of the harbour without being seen, but the waves . . .' Thomas shudders. 'I still don't know how we got out of Nathan's boat and into the outboard. My dad wouldn't have stood a chance with his bad leg if he'd fallen in the water.' In the unlit room, his eyes are black, opaque marbles. 'Part of me wanted that murdering bastard to sink beneath the waves.'

'Why did you agree to it?'

Thomas rises unsteadily off the bed, surprising her as his cold hands slip behind her neck. 'It was my chance to die and start over. A new me.'

'Did it work?' Her voice a whisper.

His smile brings tears to her eyes. She stops the slow shake of his head with her lips against his, and sorrow swells into a different wave.

Dizzy with him. With the rough skin of his hands along her back, his lips and breath on her neck; he twists and presses her into his bed like he's creating a mould of her body in the mattress. The smell of his skin is overwhelming, it's the deep ocean floor and beneath it the scent she knows; Marmite and toast. She licks the bare skin within reach of her mouth – a shoulder, a clavicle, a nipple.

Thomas. She has found Thomas after all these years.

With a rough movement, he draws away from her. Tugs off her trousers, his stubby nails scratching her skin, making her grind her teeth with delight. Together – his hands, her feet – they pull off his sweatpants and

366

boots and he's lifting her legs high and wide, pushing deeply, endlessly into her.

Afterwards, she doesn't know if she's crying or laughing.

'Ssshhh, Jellybird,' he says, 'ssshhh.'

When he finally tells his story, it is brief, as simple as a two-dimensional stick drawing. At first she thinks he's hiding things. When she realises he isn't, it makes her sadder still.

They are lying on his bed, sharing the single pillow and duvet recovered from the sofa. Through the curtainless French doors which lead onto the back garden, Jessica watches the horizon crack open in purple velvet. She glances at her watch: almost six o'clock in the morning. A new day.

Six a.m. in London. The deep, nesting sleep before the alarm. And when it sounds today in less than an hour, will Jacques leap out of bed to turn on the coffee machine for her morning cup? Then stop, catching himself, as he sees the bed empty beside him?

She and Thomas. It had seemed right, overdue, a natural progression from the point where they had been torn apart. Now, blood and skin cooling, the grounding, itchy trickle of wetness, of hairs on sheets, he seems strange to her again. The blond hair of his leg is tickling her thigh. She shifts so abruptly he opens his eyes and continues with his story.

'I took the first train as far as it would go, then jumped on another,' he's whispering into her ear. Her left arm goosebumps with his feathery words. Reaching over the side of the bed, she retrieves her jumper, her nakedness shaming her. What has she done? A new day – in a different world, with a stranger, when yesterday it was Jacques. She has tumbled by mistake into someone else's life.

'Hunger stopped me at Stollingworth.'

Trying to focus on what he is saying as a rigid wall of panic builds about her chest. 'So you found a job at the fish market, and . . .'

He nods, says nothing but she can fill in the silence. A job at the market and this – an empty house surrounded by endless fields like a moat keeping him safe. Cutting him off from the rest of the world.

His hand slips under her jumper, fingertips drifting along her stomach. She rolls onto her front.

'And women?' She grins, to lighten her mood as much as his but he doesn't smile back. Years ago, back in Selcombe, he hadn't smiled much either though she could often sense the humour beneath the surface.

'Some.' He looks away. This Thomas has no joy left in him.

'And love?' Love. She is here, and Jacques is in London with Libby and their secrets. Love cannot hold a life together any more than a cloud can catch a falling stone.

'There was a girl who hung around for a few years, but I just . . .' He trails off, closing his eyes as though falling asleep.

A shrill ringing cuts through the house and they both start, glancing at each other in bewilderment before Thomas leaps out of bed. 'That's my phone.'

The call lasts minutes, Thomas's voice contributing little. When he returns, he pulls on his trousers, sits on the mattress with his back to her.

'Is something wrong?'

He doesn't look round. 'Who knows you're here?'

'No one.' But even as she speaks, it occurs to her that she bought her ticket with her card. She pictures police officers at the train station asking questions at the ticket office – her red hair makes her stand out – and the receptionist at the Midway who shared his bottle of Jägermeister with her. She has left tracks. 'Only . . .' Jessica turns cold, pulling the covers to her shoulders. 'Your father. He gave me a postcard. That's how I found you.'

'Who else?'

Her mouth has gone dry. 'I'm sorry, Thomas.' She tries to touch his shoulder but he springs up and away towards the glass doors, face averted. 'I went to the police officer who—'

'Nilson.'

The dry click in her throat as she swallows. 'I never connected your accident with Bloody Russian's death. I thought you were dead. Nothing else mattered. The papers were full of you – a local boy – going missing. When they found the Russian's body a month later, it barely got any coverage. A not-so-tragic accident, was the general feeling.'

'Nilson's here.' Thomas drops his head in his hands. 'He was asking questions about me at the fish market yesterday afternoon.'

Is it possible she has led Nilson straight to Thomas?

369

'What will you do? You can't go back to the market.'

Thomas shrugs with a resigned sigh. 'No one knows my name. I'm Gabbler, remember?'

'But your employment records?'

'Tom Byrne.'

Despite the severity of the situation, she is flattered that he used her name. 'But how did you get away with that?'

'Someone down the market knew someone who got me fake National Insurance, bank account, the works.'

'He'll recognise you.'

Thomas shakes his head. 'Not after all this time.'

'I did.'

'You weren't looking for a monster.'

'He'll recognise *me*.' Jessica's thoughts are still chasing trails like spilled coins. 'You have to leave.'

Thomas falls back on the bed, running a hand along the sheet, looking for her. Snakes his cold fingers along the base of her spine. She draws away.

'Are you listening, Thomas? You have to go before he finds you.'

'I didn't do it, remember?'

'As far as he's concerned, you did. Case closed.'

'There's the cross.'

'With *your* fingerprints on it, Thomas.'

'Why are you here?'

The question throws her. 'Because I had to see you again.'

'What about your great life in London, your jewellery and all that?'

Jessica hugs her knees to her chest. 'My great life fell

to pieces. Everything I trusted was built on lies. Then I found out you were alive, and—'

'You thought it would be the two of us, like before. Thomas and Jellybird.'

'Maybe,' she whispers, staring at the blotched light above the fields.

Thomas hauls open the sliding glass door. Icy air sweeps through the room like a hungry dog. 'So you have nothing to go back to, and I have nothing here.'

His face, for the first time since she found him, is animated, his eyes fixed with longing on the horizon.

I have nothing here either, she thinks.

He turns to her. 'Are you going to come with me?'

His question betrays nothing of his wishes. She can't even tell if he has a preference for which way she might answer.

Jessica looks into his eyes, pale as the weather-bleached bones of a lost boy, and shakes her head.

'I'm not Jellybird any more.' It is time to stop running.

43

Jessica sits on the floor in the hallway, unable to watch Thomas picking through the minutiae of his life; the weary process of judging which item has meaning and which does not. There's something in his shuttered practicality that reminds her of herself, barely three days ago. Fleeing rather than confronting the situation.

'All done.' He walks into the hall, tucking a few loose photographs into the inner pocket of his coat. Jessica bites her lip. The fact that he is calm, that her refusal to go with him did not devastate him, only proves it is the right choice.

Glancing about the hall, taking in the aluminium-framed mirror by the door and the otherwise bare walls, he almost looks bored. 'I always knew I'd have to move on.'

'This is my fault.'

He shakes his head, helping her to her feet. 'Thank you for finding me, Jessica.' Cupping her face in his hands, he presses his lips to her forehead. 'It's enough to last me a lifetime.'

'Will you be all right?' She reaches for his hand, which slips through her grasp. Can't bear him just to walk out. 'Where will you go?'

He smiles for the first time. 'That's a secret.'

Jessica wanders through Thomas's empty house. Finds his unfinished collage packs in a neat stack on the table as though someone might take up his work where he left off. Apart from that, she can't find a trace of him, as though he had existed only in her imagination these last seventeen years.

She wishes she could cry to ease the pressure inside her chest. It is not so much a loss as a realigning of herself, as if her body had grown up and around the memory of Thomas in the same way a sapling can grow to incorporate the fence it leans against. She leaves the bedroom till last, knowing she will allow herself to lie on the sheets and breathe him in one final time.

When she reaches the bed, she finds Bloody Russian's crucifix lying in its centre.

Will you be back?

Jacques' question had startled her. In the heady, livid rush to leave the flat, to hurt him by walking out, Jessica hadn't been thinking of long-term consequences.

The train is an hour out of Stollingworth before she finally dares to turn on her mobile. It has been switched off since finding Thomas. Texts and voicemail messages arrive in a procession of electronic beeps. Not as many as she'd anticipated. Three messages from Libby, begging to know where she is. One from William

Mansion's saying she'd left them with no choice but to terminate her contract. Her mother, then Hannah. In her impatience, she cuts the messages off before they're finished. Scrolls through her texts and finds nothing. Jacques has not tried once to contact her. She bitterly regrets deleting her unheard messages when she arrived at the Midway Hotel.

The train stops at a station with a single platform. A young mother expertly tilts her baby's buggy over the gap and into the carriage. As the train rocks into motion, she takes her time removing layers of blanket, a glow of anticipation on her face as though she were unwrapping a present. She picks up a pink-swaddled baby, who stretches its little fists in the air, bottom out, tiny legs tucked under. The mother irons out the little body against her shoulder, resting her cheek against the fine down of hair. Jessica can almost feel the warmth of the baby's head against her own face and with a jolt – something close to panic – she remembers how she struggled with the idea of having her own baby. Fending it off as a pleasant but distant notion.

She checks her mobile again, knowing there are no messages.

Jacques, she remembers, had abandoned his mission to clear the box room, sensing her uninterest. Jessica sits up in her seat. When she gets home, she will pick up where he left off. She'll empty the crates of outgrown furniture and clothing, paint the walls a buttery yellow and stencil patterns, the colours of boiled sweets, across them. A way of saying sorry for running away, for giving up on their marriage. They would thrash out the issue with Libby. They would get over it.

A few seats away, the mother settles the baby into the crook of her elbow and Jessica has to look away, a curious, empty ache in her own arms; a feeling she has never before been conscious of. That foolish, selfish fear of sharing Jacques' love with her own baby has vanished under the turmoil of the last year. Now she can't think of anything more blessed.

The remainder of the journey passes in a blur of suspended anticipation. She can't think about what is waiting for her at home, or what she will say to Jacques when she sees him but even with her mind blank, her homecoming reels her in, an ever-tightening rope. When the buffet cart stops by her seat, she struggles with the notion of food.

'Who's the lucky fella, then?' asks the slight girl manhandling the cumbersome metal cart through the aisle.

'What do you mean?'

Flipping long, thin hair over her shoulder, the girl leans in. 'I can tell from the way you hummed and ha'ed over the Kit Kat. Us women only hesitate over chocolate when it's about a man.'

'I'm going home. To my husband.'

'Good for you,' she says, handing Jessica the Kit Kat. 'Glad there's still a few of us out there who believe in marriage.'

Jessica pays, feeling like a fraud.

When she is alone once more in the carriage, she

places Bertie's notebook on the seat beside her and the bloodied cross – now sealed in a plastic sandwich bag she found in Thomas's kitchen – on the fold-down table. Black crusts of dried blood litter the bottom of the bag. She notices an empty, round eyelet in the centre where a ruby is missing and all of a sudden remembers the gem she found in the bed of Caravan Nineteen on the day Thomas disappeared. It explains the twisted knife used to lever the stone from its setting. She wishes she could ask him why he left her the stone seventeen years ago, and why he has now left her the cross. Unable to divine his intention, she shoves it deep into her bag once more and turns her attention to the notebook, flicking through the pages out of habit.

Something drifts to her lap. A photograph. Picking it up, she is confronted with herself and Jacques, sitting in the Longhaven Bay Café grinning awkwardly for the unfriendly waitress. Or rather she was, because Jacques was looking at her. The camera had caught him smiling both at her and to himself. As if it had just struck him that he might love her.

At some point in those last awful days in London, Jacques had taken the picture out of its frame and placed it in the pages of the red notebook.

By the time the train pulls into St Pancras, a sense of urgency fizzes through her. The taxi queue is long, a domino trail of businessmen heading home. She imagines giving the man in front a shove and seeing them all topple over so she can reach an empty cab. The wait drags on for ten minutes until she's ready to scream with frustration. Once in a black cab, she distracts herself by ticking off old, familiar sights. The Planetarium's domed roof on Euston Road; an alien glimpse of the BT tower rocketing through the skyline; the aquatics shop on Great Portland Street where sometimes she ducks out to lose herself in the languid motion of fantailed fish; the circular green of Cavendish Square; the Phoenix pub on the corner of John Prince's Street, her road. Home.

She gets out and has to be reminded by an irate driver to pay her fare.

Inside the hall, she notices a stack of letters bound by a rubber band on top of their postbox where the postman couldn't cram any more in. She sprints up the stairs and struggles to get the key in the lock.

The apartment is dark, and the smell is wrong. Cleaning fluids and unstirred air. Not a trace of cooking or coffee grounds. Dropping her bag, Jessica heads straight to the kitchen. Without turning on the lights, she opens the fridge door. A waft of bleach hits her, the shelves empty and gleaming as new.

Her legs buckle, the floor tilting up to meet her.

44

October 2012, Seasalt Holiday Park, Selcombe

In pyjama bottoms and a vest, Jessica inspects the bruises on her shoulder in the long mirror tacked to the back of her bedroom door. The discoloration has mellowed into jaundiced yellows. She tries to count back on her fingers how long she has been there, but winter days in the park pass by in bland hibernation. The fading bruises are her only way of marking the passage of time.

When the door opens and Grannie Mim appears, she scrambles for a jumper. 'How about knocking?'

Mim's hand on her arm is surprisingly forceful. She frowns at the bruises. 'Is this why you left London?'

'No. How can you think that? You know Jacques.'

'People are damn good at hiding their ugly bits, let me tell you.'

'I fainted, that's all. Hunger, exhaustion.' Pulling on her jumper gives her an excuse to hide her face.

The refrigerator cleaned out with such finality. Jacques gone.

Suddenly she's too tired, too raw to hide anything. 'Actually, I think it was shock.'

'I can read it in your face.' Grannie Mim's nodding. 'You, my girl, need to start talking. Come and help me with my chores.'

Jessica looks at the snow falling in sleety clumps. 'Birdie makes you do chores?'

'I set my own, thank you very much. Today I'm clearing litter from the gardens across the road.'

'Can't we wait until the weather's a bit better?'

Mim slides Jessica's boots across the floor. 'City's made you soft.'

As they walk through the park, Jessica tells her about finding the flat empty and how, once she came round, she hadn't the will to get up. Lay on the floor, drifting in and out of sleep, never changing position even when her shoulder became a piece of dead meat. She doesn't mention the vague memory of warm liquid trickling over her thigh as her bladder emptied itself.

'It felt like I was dying.' Jessica tucks her hair inside her collar to stop the wind whipping it in her face.

Her neighbour double-blinks. 'Possible, I guess.'

'I let everything go. I felt my body giving up.'

She stops talking. Afraid to tell Mim how detached she felt, experiencing the agony of recovering circulation from far away. She has cloudy memories of showering and packing a bag. Of rushing back to the sitting room as she was about to leave her home.

Taking the cuckoo clock off the mantelpiece, she had removed her wedding ring and left it in its place.

'I am feeling better here, though.' Which is true. Bit by bit, she feels herself coming back together.

'You're still rake-thin.' Mim's eyes wander back to Jessica's shoulder. 'Why *did* you run away?'

They are approaching Birdie's caravan, so Jessica doesn't answer. Her mother is gouging clumps of leaf and moss from the roof guttering with Joss, the gardener, steadying her ladder. Though he keeps to himself, it is clear he's now a daily visitor to the park. Jessica and Grannie Mim wave as they pass. Her mother nods back; Joss, too, giving them a quick bob of his head.

'Are you going to tell Birdie what I say?'

'Nope. That's your business.'

She looks over and catches a glint in the old woman's eye. It reminds her of Grannie Mim leaning out of her caravan door with a glass jar of hundreds and thousands, saying *Hold out your hand but don't tell your mother.*

'You used to give me sweets.'

Grannie Mim shrugs, trying not to look pleased. 'You were always poking sticks in rabbit-holes and hiding under the caravans, getting wet and filthy. I had to bribe you out of the cold. Little wild thing, you were.'

They walk through the main gates of the park and cross the road into the council gardens. Jessica grimaces as she looks about. 'It's a miserable place now.'

They find a dead seagull half submerged in the lido's

shallow water, its feet cramped into scaly fists as if it clutched at the sky as it fell.

'We used to play here, me and the caravan kids,' Jessica says, and she sees herself, the leader of a ragtag band of children, devising games and avoiding her chores. Then she remembers Libby had been one of those children, and that they had probably played together. Biting the inside of her cheek, she waits for the swell of anger to subside.

Grannie Mim tosses the seagull behind a tree, tutting at a burned-out tyre surrounded by empty beer cans. She takes a bin liner from her coat pocket and starts feeding them into the bag. 'Back to your story. We were just getting to the good bit, I believe.'

'Do you remember the boy who used to hang around my house? Tall with messy blond hair and light-grey eyes.'

Mim considers it before nodding. 'One of Finn Quennell's boys.'

Jessica picks up a scrap of soggy newspaper between her finger and thumb and drops it into Mim's bag. 'Well, I went looking for him.'

Grannie Mim glares at her. 'Why on earth did you do that?'

'Jacques and my friend, Libby . . .' Her voice trails off. She doesn't want to explain about them but then from the look on Grannie Mim's face, she doesn't need to. 'I couldn't face it, so I went looking for Thomas instead.'

The bin bag makes a tin clatter against the ground as Mim lets her arm drop. 'That was your solution?'

'I wanted desperately to believe it was.' She starts hunting about for litter, suddenly too angry to look at Mimosa. 'The situation was making me ill. I kept catching them whispering together. She was always in my house, always knew what was going on with me before I told her.'

'What did Jacques say in his defence?' Mim holds open the bag for the single beer can she's collected.

'Nothing. I didn't give him a chance to.'

She senses Grannie Mim biting down on her response. They wander towards the boarded-up pavilion, eyes on the ground as they search for rubbish and avoid looking at each other. Jessica sits on a peeling step leading to the pavilion's porch.

'It felt like I'd lost Jacques and was being offered Thomas in return. It made a terrible sort of sense. I persuaded myself it had been Thomas all along.'

'Did you find him?' Grannie Mim joins her on the step with a grunt.

Jessica starts to nod, then stops. 'No.'

Because she hadn't found the boy she'd known, just a stranger with his likeness.

'So you didn't find what you were looking for, and decided to go back to Jacques?'

Jessica shakes her head. 'Actually it helped me find what I needed. It turned out to be Jacques all along.'

Grannie Mim takes her hand between hers, which are somehow warm and dry. 'You know what you must do then?'

'He's gone. I don't know where . . .' Catching the plaintive note in her own voice, she stops.

Mim gets up, straightening with minor jerks as her arthritic joints pop into place. 'Birdie knows. He left a number.'

Closing the door, she heads for the bedroom and strips down to her t-shirt, pants and socks. Climbs into bed. The urge for numbing sleep is never far away. Having drifted off, she hears a knock and thinks it's a dream. Until her mother walks in with an expression so grave, her desire for sleep vanishes.

Nilson, she thinks. It was only a matter of time before the policeman tracked her down. She is unprepared; hasn't even found a hiding place for the crucifix yet.

'What is it?'

'I didn't mention it before because, well, I didn't feel it was my business.' Birdie has her hands pushed deep into her skirt pockets. 'But Jacques was here.'

'When?' The word rushes out.

'About ten days ago.'

She scrambles her legs out of the sheets as though preparing to run. 'Ten days?'

'Well, I can check the register for the exact date but he came here the day you disappeared.'

'I didn't disappear. I called you.'

'As far as your husband knows, you disappeared.' Birdie's voice rises – a glimpse of the determined woman she once was. 'He stayed here. In this caravan.'

The question she is both desperate to ask and terrified to have answered is singing in her head. 'Where is he now?'

'He was going back to America. To his folks, I believe.'

Jessica mutters a thank you, lies back down and pulls the covers up to her ears. The sound of the closing door as Birdie leaves spurs Jessica into action. All at once, she's rattling between the walls of her mobile home like a bluebottle. Spreads her fingers, touching and smoothing sofa seats, countertops and handles, searching for evidence of Jacques as though his presence might be written in Braille across the surfaces of the caravan. She hauls the sheets off the bed, pushing her face into the denuded pillows and duvet desperate to catch a scent of him. Scours the bare mattress for a single dark hair, a hollow in the shape of his body. She finds stray hairs, possibly his or not, dust-bunnies, a pound coin. Jacques is gone. Jacques has gone over the seas to the other side of the world; so far away he will soon become unreal. Like Thomas.

The caravan stifles her. She tugs her clothes on again. Flinging back the door, she takes the steps in a leap. Jessica runs to her mother's caravan, lit from the inside against the grey afternoon. Without knocking, she opens the door so hard it bounces off the wall and the place shivers. Her mother freezes in an awkward position, head turned back, body intent on continuing forward.

'I don't know what I'm doing,' Jessica says in a quiet voice. 'I'm lost.'

Her mother lowers her head for a moment, then closes the door.

'Now you come in and sit down.' Her fingers are cold

as she takes a light hold of Jessica's wrist, leading her to the foldaway table. She opens the drawer under the sofa and lifts out a bundle of material that keeps on coming like a magician's trick. 'It's just as well you're here, you know.'

Jessica can only swallow, her voice untrustworthy.

'Sewing night,' Birdie continues. From another secret drawer comes a battered tin with pictures of the Royal Danish biscuits it once contained. Jessica remembers it from her childhood, how she used to poke among the shiny spools of thread for hatpins and silver needle-threaders.

'You'll have to mend the seat covers because your hand is neater than mine, and people always look before they sit.'

Her mother disappears into her bedroom, returning with a black bin bag full of damaged cushions. The first one has a hole like a puncture wound. Jessica looks through Birdie's tin for matching thread. This is the mother she remembers. As if she'd been hiding in the sewing box all along. The way she would take a distressed daughter and give her a task, something for her hands, talking at her in that bossy, no-nonsense tone until the woes of the world started to look fanciful beside the practical necessities of mending, chopping, cooking.

Jessica threads a needle, finds a blue and gold porcelain thimble and starts to mend the hole while her mother flaps out a curtain, clucking her tongue.

'The damage people do. Nice people, as well.'

Jessica lets her mother talk. It doesn't make the storm

inside her go away – she's not five any more – but it grows calm, sitting heavy and still like a bowl of water.

'Thank you, Mum.'

She is surprised when Birdie reaches out and touches her face. Sitting over their sewing, Jessica thinks that perhaps there's a different quality to the silence between them. Less saturated with their lost years.

45

December 2012

They spend the morning twisting multicoloured Christmas lights through the perimeter hedges. A winter sun shines from a cut-glass sky. Through the open window of the office, carols are playing on the radio.

By lunchtime, Jessica's arms and shoulders are aching. 'Remind me again why we are doing this?'

'Because it looks pretty,' Birdie replies. Which is exactly what she used to say as she attached lace edging to caravan cushions which would only be ripped and stained by the end of the season, and stayed up late icing cupcakes for the school fete.

'Mum, I just want to say that . . .' Jessica pauses. She wants to find the right words to explain that this is exactly where she needs to be. That being with Birdie is – against all previous expectations – making her feel better.

Her mother gives a good-natured tut. 'Just because it's Christmas doesn't mean we have to get all silly.'

For the first time in weeks, Jessica feels hungry. 'Why don't we go for lunch? We could try that new café on the promenade by Whitehead.'

She anticipates an excuse but then Birdie nods. 'A walk would be good on a day like this. It does a nice panini, I hear.'

Jessica raises her eyebrows. 'Next you'll be ordering a skinny mocha latte.'

As her mother goes back into the office to lock up, the telephone rings. The call is short but when Birdie rejoins her, she is quiet.

They walk without speaking, and Jessica tries to empty her head; to walk along and be part of the present, watching tiny birds dart in the gorse and tracking fox prints in the narrow strips of snow that line the cliff path. But as their walk continues, her mother's silence becomes a stiff finger in her side.

'What's on your mind, Mum?'

As they reach the steps leading to Selcombe Bay, her mother stops and gives Jessica a searching look. It unnerves her; she catches herself trying to think what she has spilled or broken.

'Why would the police want to speak to you, Jessica?'

'The police?' The blood drains from her face.

Her mother's sharp eyes widen. 'What have you got yourself mixed up in?'

'I haven't done anything wrong.' She tries to sound indignant but her mother's anxious expression waters down the conviction in Jessica's voice. 'Was that the phone call you just took?'

'From an Inspector Nilson, yes.' Birdie's frown deepens.

'He's looking for a friend of mine.' She needs to get her story straight. Is suddenly afraid of returning to Seasalt in case Nilson's waiting for her.

'Your friend from up North?'

Grannie Mim. Jessica bites down on the sore spot inside her cheek. If her mother can make these assumptions, then Thomas doesn't stand a chance against Nilson and his obsessive hunt. He only has to open her rucksack sitting inside the bedroom cupboard to find the murdered man's cross with its telltale forensics.

'Did the policeman ask to speak to me?'

'I told him you were out,' Birdie says. 'Come on, we'll miss lunch at this rate.'

Her mother continues past the bay steps, keeping to the narrow path which curls steeply towards the broad shoreline of Whitehead Beach. Jessica is grateful they are forced to walk in single file so that Birdie's observant eyes aren't on her. She needs to plan what she will tell Nilson.

Thomas believes the cross will exonerate him, even though his own fingerprints smudge those of his father's. Finn Quennell will fabricate a plausible reason for his marks being on the crucifix but Thomas – still running – can't defend himself. With a sick realisation, Jessica understands that this alone is all the evidence Nilson requires. And of course there is the question of her role. What will happen to her if she comes forward with a crucial piece of evidence?

There is only one person she can discuss the crucifix with. As soon as they return from lunch, she will make a phone call. In the meantime, she has lost her appetite.

As they reach the promenade, Jessica eyes the crowded tables through the café's misted windows. 'I'm not really hungry.'

'Well, let's breathe in a bit of sea air before we head back.'

They sit on the beach, the sand cold but dry. Jessica lets the crash and roll of the surf distract her. She'll think about Nilson later.

'Oh, lord,' Birdie says after a while, sounding amused. 'Would you look at the inappropriate foot-wear.'

A figure is stumbling across the beach, high-heeled boots sinking into the sand and catching dry ropes of seaweed.

'Someone's had too many white wines over lunch,' Jessica says. Then her mouth goes dry. She gets up. 'Let's go.'

'What's the matter?'

The figure calls out and Birdie stops. 'That woman just called your name.'

'Can we just walk?' Jessica tries to keep going but her mother stops her, squinting at the approaching figure.

'That's the woman who was asking after you the other day.'

Jessica shrugs off her hand. 'I have nothing to say to her.'

'Please wait,' Libby shouts.

'Be brave.' Birdie reaches again for Jessica's arm, her fingers snatching uselessly at her coat sleeve. 'You used to be my fearless child.'

Jessica works her jaw, watching Libby curse and lurch across the sand.

'Thank God you didn't run away. I'd have broken a leg.' She's breathless by the time she reaches them, touching the back of her hand to her brow. A smudge of mascara underlines one eye. 'Where the hell have you been hiding? Jacques went looking—'

'Don't say his name.' The volume of her voice makes both Birdie and Libby straighten.

Libby drops her head, still gasping for breath. 'That's why I'm here. You never let me explain about Jacques and I.'

Birdie suddenly steps forward, placing herself between the two younger women.

'I know who you are.'

So Jacques had spoken to her mother. Had told her about Libby. Jessica's head is starting to throb. 'Mum, it doesn't matter.'

'I know exactly who you are,' her mother repeats, voice shaking.

Despite the urge to cover her ears and walk away, there is something about the way her mother has caught Libby in her glare that also holds Jessica.

'You look just like her,' Birdie says.

Libby nods. 'I know.'

'Does Jessica know who you are?'

'Not yet.'

Jessica grabs her mother's hand. 'What's going on?'

Her mother sighs. 'I don't know how you got to know each other but she' – Birdie jabs a finger in Libby's direction – 'is going to tell you exactly who she is.'

Nilson, Libby, Jacques. Weariness, like a familiar craving, sweeps over her; she could simply lie down on the sand, close her eyes and sleep.

Libby's voice is barely more than a whisper. 'He was desperate to see her. He hoped you might relent when he got ill.'

'Selfish to the last.' The words snap from Birdie's jaw.

'Stop!' Jessica shouts. 'Stop talking over me.'

'This is what I have tried to protect you from.' Birdie takes her hand, which further unnerves her. But worse, so much more frightening, are the tears in her mother's eyes. 'From the day your father left us.'

46

They watch her walk away, Jessica's thoughts like a
sandstorm and Libby still catching her breath.
Birdie's ankles kink over the uneven surface of the
beach. It pains Jessica to recognise her mother's age-
ing; she doesn't want Libby to see it too.

'What's going on?'

Libby, trying to steady herself on sinking heels, says,
'Here. I have something of yours.'

She rummages in her bag. Her hands are shaking
as she places something pink and sparkly in Jessica's
hand.

A plastic brooch that spells TRUE LOVE.

'What is this?' Jessica knows it but can't place it.

'You left it at my home.'

The brooch winks in the pale sunlight. Jessica closes
her fingers over it. She sees it now – the jewelled bower
where a beautiful woman lived like a bird of paradise.
Her mother, Daniel's plain brown robin, hadn't stood a
chance.

She has the oddest sensation of time stretching away like a length of elastic connecting her teenage self – young and naive, letting a stranger play with her hair – to her present self, standing on a wind-torn beach, legs weak with shock. As though she has spent her life running away from this moment only to be caught and snapped back.

'Jessica, I'm your sister.'

'Don't be ridiculous.' She needs to sit down. Turns on her heel and staggers towards the bench with the sound of Libby's heels clipping the pavement behind her. 'How can you be? You're the same age as me, for God's sake.'

'I know.' Libby says it with such gentleness that Jessica falters.

Then out of nowhere, anger blasts through her. She has to grip her elbows, digging her nails in to stop herself from grabbing Libby's shoulders and shaking her.

'What kind of sick game are you and your mother playing? She steals my father, you steal my husband.'

'Is that what you think?'

Jessica slaps Libby's proffered hand away. 'Don't touch me.' Her words start to pour out, stumbling over each other in the rush. 'Sister or not, it means nothing to me. You just couldn't let Jacques be. You had to have him. All those times I walked in on the two of you.'

'Doing what, exactly?'

'Talking. Whispering.'

'About you.' Libby glares back from her perch at the

far end of the bench. 'Your erratic behaviour. Your secretive trips away. We were worried.'

Shaking her head, Jessica says, 'My first exhibition. You were there. You and Jacques already knew each other.'

'No. We didn't.' Libby pauses for an elderly couple to shamble by with their portly Labrador. 'I didn't have the courage to say who I was. I pretended I was an interested customer and asked him a few questions about you. I wanted something to take home to Dad.'

'Dad.' Jessica spits the word, tears popping up in her eyes. She turns her face away, staring at the far horizon so she doesn't blink and let them fall.

'I'm sorry.' Libby's voice wavers. 'Do you want me to carry on?'

All Jessica can do is shrug. She will not cry in front of Libby. Her sister, her father's hidden daughter.

Libby clears her throat. 'Dad kept trying to get in touch with you. Your mother wouldn't let him. She threatened to sell the caravan park and move away with you and your sisters if he tried to contact any of you behind her back.'

Jessica closes her eyes. She sees herself at fourteen, cocooned in a lost place with Thomas while secret conversations and decisions circled and passed her over like currents in the air.

'And then one day I came home and told him something I'd heard about you from a girl I knew at your school.'

'What?'

'That you were hanging around with a boy, a trouble-maker.'

'Thomas.'

Libby takes in a long breath. 'Of course. Your Thomas.'

'So you were going home with playground gossip.' Jessica wipes her eyes. Anger is good. It makes her strong.

'At first. Then we realised between the two of us we could find out all sorts of things. How you were doing at school – he just called your school office, actually. We nearly lost you when you ran off to Bridge. Then it turned out one of my friends had got to know your sister Hannah through hockey, and it was easy to get information. She liked talking about her tearaway sister.'

'Good old Hannah.' Jessica can't sit still any longer. Getting up, she starts to walk back towards the cliff path leading to Seasalt Park. The sun is already low in the sky and the wind rises off the beach, skimming sand into the air. She thinks about her father befriending Finn Quennell. Telling Thomas he was going to watch over her; a guardian angel.

'This still doesn't explain how you ended up being my friend.'

'Jessica, I'm trying, I really am but I can't talk to your back.'

She stops walking. 'Go on then.'

Libby's face is pink with cold, her eyes watering in the stinging breeze; far removed from her usual, polished self. 'I built a fantasy life around you. You were my lost sister, my missing twin. I wanted to meet you.'

Jessica thinks back to the night at the shop, Belladonna, with Libby crouched over the spilled lilies daring her to ask Jacques for the truth. 'Jacques knows who you are, doesn't he?'

Libby nods. 'I was desperate for you to come to the funeral. The fury of your reply . . .' She breaks off, shaking her head. 'Someone had to let you know that your father never intended to walk out of your life.'

At this point, Jessica is unsure how she is feeling. There's anger at her core, but layers of emotion have started to smother it like tree rings – bemusement, curiosity, disbelief. 'So you contacted Jacques?'

'I googled him and turned up at his office two days before the funeral.'

'He should have told me.'

Libby reaches out and touches her arm. 'He said the notice of the funeral made you sick. That you lay in bed for days afterwards. You'd made your decision, and there was no way he was going to persuade you to go. He was afraid of how you'd cope if you learned about me.' Libby sighs, running her hands through her hair, and Jessica feels the tension in her chest giving, stitch by stitch. There follows a post-race silence, both of them recouping, gathering themselves.

'Then you bought my jewellery.'

'I couldn't help myself.' Libby bites her lip over an apologetic smile. 'I can't tell you how furious Jacques was at the flower market that day.'

Jessica sighs, rubbing her forehead. 'I felt something between the two of you. It ate away at me.'

'I guess you picked up on the tension between Jacques and me. It was an ongoing discussion between us – whether or not to tell you who I was.'

Jessica shivers as a shoulder of sea wind hits her. The café has finished its lunchtime trade and the staff are upending chairs on tables. 'I'm going to go home.'

'I have the car here.' Libby goes to hug Jessica, then stops herself. 'You could come back with me now.'

'I meant back to the park.'

Jessica takes wide steps up the steep shale path, relieved not to hear the sound of following footsteps. The sun is reaching the white-whipped sea, its settling reds and oranges spreading over the beach. It's only now, having returned, that she is realising how beautiful the place is.

'Jessica,' Libby calls after her. 'Have you spoken to Jacques?'

Lying in her unlit caravan, Jessica tries to unpick the threads of Libby's story.

When the birds start to sing, her mum brings her a cup of tea. From the shadows on her face, it is clear she hasn't slept either. Placing the tea on the windowsill, she fusses about the room, refusing eye contact. The Birdie of Jessica's grown-up life, struggling to connect. But still, she is there.

Jessica sits up, bunching the covers around her knees. 'Mum, why don't you sit down?'

'It's laundry day, and there's more snow on the way.'

She tugs at a corner of rumpled sheet, tucking it under the mattress.

'Birdie. I need to know something.'

Her mother stops moving. She stands still, hands folded like a penitent child. 'Ask me, then.'

'Did Dad try to stay in contact with me?'

Birdie doesn't answer at once, her chin trembling. Then she lifts her head and faces Jessica, eyes glittering but steady. A glimpse of the old Birdie, full of spark and bluster. 'Yes. He begged me. For years. Until you moved away, in fact.'

Jessica scrambles to her feet, hands clenched. She opens her mouth to rail against her mother but suddenly she can't find any anger. Her shoulders slump. 'Why?'

But she knows. She can see the grey ghost of her mother all those years ago. Silenced by the truths she was protecting her children from.

The strength it took had sucked the life out of her.

Before Birdie can answer, Jessica throws her arms around her mother's neck. 'Oh, Birdie. My poor mum.'

Her mother hugs her back; the same fierce embrace with which she used to scoop up an unaware child, eliciting shrieks of laughter and protest. Always followed by a moment of surrendering to the comfort of each other's arms.

'I still think it was the right thing to do,' Birdie says as they sit together on the bed. She dabs her eyes with a thumb knuckle. 'But I have wondered over the years if I should have tried to stop your father from leaving.'

'How? He just vanished,' Jessica manages to say.

She's shocked at how casually her mum mentions her father, after a childhood with his unacknowledged shadow in every corner of the house.

'He didn't vanish. He only moved as far as Rormonton.'

Jessica looks away. Wonders if he lived out the rest of his life in the house furnished like a theatre dressing room.

'I could have fought a bit harder to keep him.' She raises her eyebrows. 'Do you understand what I'm saying?'

'It's too late to fight for Jacques.' Jessica flops back onto her mattress and closes her eyes. Finds sleep waiting for her.

'He left his number.'

Jessica shakes her head. 'I was so sure he'd let me down that I didn't consider my own behaviour. In the light of what I thought he'd done, my own actions seemed . . .'

'Justified?' Birdie offers.

'Irrelevant.' Jessica lifts her head. 'I've destroyed everything.'

'It's a very human talent to distort things to fit your own perspective.' Her mother's voice grows even quieter. 'Your father mastered that particular skill.'

'If I can't forgive myself, how can Jacques?'

Birdie gives a long sigh, sinking down onto her elbows then tipping her head backwards onto the bed. Her mother, who even in her years of silent misery never stopped moving and doing. Jessica curls up beside her and Birdie reaches out to cup her cheek in her hand.

As they lie there, her mother fumbles a folded yellow Post-it note from her skirt pocket and hands it to Jessica. 'Just in case.'

47

Nathan looks tired. The scraping light through the caravan window pools in the deep sockets of his eyes, his skin stretched thin over the pebble of his cheekbones. His usual smile has been put to rest.

'So. Here I am. Having called in sick for the first time ever.'

Jessica pulls up another stool and faces him across the breakfast bar. 'I found Thomas.'

The coffee mug in his hand slops brown liquid over the countertop. 'You saw him?'

She nods and stares hard at the hedge through the window as tears rise in Nathan's eyes. Pulling off his red bandana, he wipes his face with it, blows his nose. 'Shit. Sorry. I just didn't expect that.'

She tells him how she found his younger brother, fills her story with every detail she can, stalling the inevitable subject of the crucifix. His tears keep rising, along with a watered-down version of his smile. He shakes his head, incredulous.

'A born survivor, that boy.'

Then she reaches the point at which they walk into the woods and stops.

Nathan's face sobers. 'Everything. I need to know everything.'

'Wait here.'

When she returns from her bedroom with the crucifix and lays it between them on the table, Nathan shifts in his seat.

'What's this?'

'Thomas pulled it out of Bloody Russian's mouth when he found him in the woods behind your dad's house.'

Nathan squints at her. 'Found him?'

'He told me what happened that night, Nathan. He didn't do it.'

'But who, then?' He swallows, his body sagging.

'Your father. That's why Thomas took the crucifix and left it with me, I think. Because Finn's fingerprints are all over it.'

A pause, followed by a vigorous shake of the head. 'Not possible.'

It takes Jessica considerable effort to keep the frustration out of her voice. 'How could you so readily believe it was your brother but not your father? With his history of violence?'

Nathan mops the coffee spill with his bandana, then his sleeve. 'Because for the first time in my life, I saw my dad cry.'

'When?'

'A couple of days after Thomas disappeared.' He lifts the mug to his mouth but replaces it untouched. 'The old man broke down and sobbed, saying Thomas had killed the Russian.' Nathan raises his fist to his mouth, his face sickly white. 'And that he'd helped hide the body and then taken the boat out with Thomas. I hadn't even realised it was gone. With the storm and all.'

He looks ragged with despair but Jessica can't bring herself to comfort him with a touch.

'You never questioned your father's story? You just went straight to the police and told them your brother was a murderer?'

Nathan shakes his head. 'No, no. I'd already *been* to the police by then. To file a missing person report. I told them about Thomas and my dad's violent row and how he'd not been seen since. I knew my dad was hiding something. I thought he'd finally lost it and hurt my brother.'

'What did the police do?'

'They went round to question my dad. I was there, panicking, having just learned what really – what my dad said – had happened. Knowing if they searched the area they'd find a man beaten to death. I meant to save my brother but instead I'd ruined his life.'

'Your father did that, not you.'

He doesn't reply, staring out of the window as his fingers knead the stained bandana.

'I take it the police didn't search the place then?' Jessica prompts him.

Nathan sighs. 'I apologised for wasting their time; said I'd been drunk and overreacted to the row I saw. Then we told them about my missing boat.'

'And your father got away with murder.'

Nathan folds his arms on the table, resting his forehead against them. 'Finn Quennell. Grand puppetmaster.'

'Thomas thinks he got in a rage over the Russian stealing tools and—'

'It doesn't matter now,' he interrupts, his voice still muffled by his arms. 'Lives have been lived, Jessica.'

Jessica walks Nathan to his car on the boundary road. Waits until it has disappeared over the dip of the hill and the sound of his engine has thinned into silence.

Back in Caravan Nineteen, she shoves the cross into her rucksack and runs through the pleasure gardens and all the way down the slippery beach steps. When she has checked once, twice to ensure she is alone, she rips the sandwich bag open and hurls the crucifix far over the open water.

Afterwards, she scrubs her hands with sand and icy seawater.

48

Later that day, Jessica borrows Birdie's car and drives into Bridge. She is surprised to find the art supplies shop she used to visit after her lunchtime shifts at the Tea Chest, whiling away the hours until Jacques left the library or finished a tutorial.

Except for the staff, it is unchanged. She spirals up the metal staircase to the paints section on the mezzanine and finds a small pot of Liquid Sunshine.

The rest of the afternoon is spent dipping eggshells in golden lacquer, hoping her mother won't notice one of her collection jars is missing. The varnish preserves every hairline crack and chipped fragment, emphasising its fragility while lessening it. Transforming it into something a foot couldn't so easily crush beneath it.

Jessica is lining the birds' eggs up to dry on the windowsill facing the hedge – so Birdie doesn't spot them – when there's a knock on her door. It's not Birdie because her mother no longer knocks. All the same, she shouts, 'Stop. Don't come in.'

'It's me again.' Nathan's voice is muffled through the

crackle-glass of the caravan's front door. 'Sorry to bother you. Is this an inconvenient time?'

His formality alarms her. She can just make out the shape of a man standing behind him on the porch. 'Is it important, Nathan?'

She sees him shuffle round to look at his companion. Strains to catch their voices, but they exchange a look rather than words.

'I guess so.' The sudden weariness in his voice gives him away. He is here against his will or better judgement. Then he knocks more urgently on the door, pressing his face to it so that she receives a distorted vision of an eye and nose.

With a vicious yank, she flings back the door to find Nathan and his dad. A painful smile of apology tweaks Nathan's features while his father glowers at his feet, cane stabbing the ground as though squashing a beetle.

'Why is he here?'

'He insisted on—'

'You saw my boy.' Quennell bares his teeth as he swings his injured leg up each step, shouldering his son aside.

She tries to remain in the doorway but the sheer collapsing bulk of the man forces her back.

'Well?' Quennell plants himself round his cane in the middle of the room. 'I want to know what happened.'

'Thomas told me the truth.' She slips behind the breakfast bar, a flimsy barrier between herself and Thomas's father.

'Come on, Dad. Let's have a cup of tea first.'

'Don't want tea. I want to know if she apologised for ruining my son's life.'

'Dad, please. We can be civil about this.' Nathan slips between Jessica and his father. It's the acrid smell of acute discomfort rising off Nathan that makes Jessica slam her open palm against the countertop. His shoulders hiccough at the sound. The old man doesn't even flinch.

'Just how exactly did I ruin his life?'

She catches a glint like the flash of fish scales beneath the watery surface of his eyes. Relishing a fight. But she's sick of being afraid of an old man, of the truth. Afraid to voice the things circling endlessly in her head. She pushes Nathan gently to one side as she steps forward. 'Because I'm pretty sure he said *you* were responsible for that.'

Nathan groans as he turns away.

The old man takes a step forward. 'You riled him about Nikolai. Incitement to murder, that's what it was.'

'Do you remember the Russian's cross?'

'Jessica, wait.' Nathan rouses himself, tries to defuse their battle stance by encouraging his father towards the sofa. The old man backs towards it, holding out an arm for his son's assistance. She barely recognises the solemn, hunch-shouldered man who hesitates for a moment before lowering his father onto the cushion. Aware of her scrutiny, Nathan refuses to meet her eyes. 'My dad just wants to know how Thomas is doing.'

With a disdainful flick of his cane, Quennell silences his son. 'What cross?'

'Bloody Russian's. Huge thing, it was. You can't tell me you never noticed it.'

Quennell's jaw works away, chewing over his thoughts. 'What about it?'

She has his attention now. He must have wondered what happened to the crucifix.

'Thomas pulled it out of the man's broken jaw as he was trying to save him.'

'Save him?' Quennell flaps a scarred hand in the air. 'He beat that man to death. For you.'

'He took the cross to protect you.'

She looks across at Nathan, white-faced on the edge of the sofa, an unwilling spectator having removed himself from the event. 'Isn't that so, Nathan?'

His father doesn't even glance in his direction, so Nathan merely gazes helplessly back at her.

'That crucifix is covered in your murdering finger-prints.'

Quennell flails his cane in the air, his face turning deep red. Still, his voice doesn't rise a decibel. 'As much as it kills me to admit it, my son is a murderer. I have protected him and I have lived with that knowledge.'

Jessica smiles and notes with gratification how it unsettles the old man. An odd calm fills her. Joining them on the sofa, she takes Quennell's hand. She can feel him resisting the urge to pull his hand away. Grips harder.

'If he'd left it there, you'd have been jailed for murder.'

As she speaks, the truth of it hits her. Whether or not

Thomas admitted it to himself, part of him had been protecting his father.

'Preposterous lies.' Quennell makes a half-hearted attempt to stand before slumping back onto the cushions, breathing hard. 'I had nothing to do with it.'

'Personally I don't understand his loyalty to you. He knew the boating accident was to save yourself, not him.' Jessica leans over Quennell. 'That's how badly he wanted to escape you.'

Nathan's breath hisses out in the silence. His father is frowning at his hands resting on the dog-head cane, his face caving in on itself as he shakes his head, once, twice.

'I saved Thomas.'

'No. He saved you.'

Quennell's eyes bulge. 'I didn't do it.'

'You condemned your son to a life of running.' Jessica's words are soft as a mother crooning to her baby.

'Well?' Some of the bullish strength returns to Quennell's jaw as he snaps his head in Nathan's direction. 'I don't hear you saying anything.'

'Jessica's right, Dad.' Nathan can't meet his father's eyes, but he continues in a stronger voice. 'Thomas was taking the blame for you.'

'He still is.' The image of Thomas packing his few meaningful possessions brings tears to her eyes. 'He lives alone, separate from everything and everyone because he's afraid of being found.'

Quennell shoots his arm out, staggering as Nathan

helps him to his feet. He regains his balance before stalking to the front door. Where he stops.

'I heard Daniel Byrne died last year. Apparently he was desperate to see his girls before it was too late. Only one of his daughters even went to the funeral.'

'That's enough.' Nathan picks his father's crabbed hand off his arm.

'The one he had behind your mother's back, I believe.' Quennell shakes his head. 'Ah, the pain of a father's love.'

Jessica stares straight into his rheumy eyes. 'What would you know about a father's love?'

The old man juts his chin and yanks open the door. Nathan looks back at her, nods and blinks once like the shutter of a camera, and she understands he is saying goodbye.

49

The next morning Grannie Mim, Birdie and Jessica are having coffee and toast in Caravan Nineteen when there is a knock on the door. Through the frosted glass Jessica can see a tall, slim figure with light hair. When she makes no move to get up, Birdie opens the door.

'Ms Byrne.' Nilson ducks his head as he walks through the doorway. 'There you are.'

Jessica replaces her mug on the table with steady hands. She is prepared, having decided to tell as much of the truth as possible, giving him enough material to build a conceivable story in the hope that he will not notice the single missing brick – Bloody Russian's crucifix.

Then she'll pray Thomas has run far enough never to be found.

'What a funny coincidence, I was planning to visit you today.'

Flanked by the two older women, Jessica feels strong and certain. Her mother indicates the stool at the breakfast bar and Nilson sizes it up, taking in its height. 'If you ladies don't mind me towering over you all.'

Once seated, he reminds Jessica of a daddy longlegs, all awkward limbs and sharp joints. She is no longer afraid of him.

'I have some good news, Ms Byrne.'

Jessica nods and smiles but her mouth has gone dry. Grannie Mim's eyes flit between Nilson and Jessica like a robin pecking at crumbs. Birdie stares into her coffee.

'We've had a confession for the murder of Nikolai Galitzine.'

She closes her eyes. It is too late. They've found Thomas.

'Nicky who?' Mim's voice is shrill.

'Nikolai Galitzine. Bloody Russian to the locals. He was beaten to death seventeen years ago. Horrible case, it was. Unsolved until now.'

Jessica has opened her eyes enough to see her hands clenched into a ball of white knuckles under the table. The room is rolling on waves and she's afraid to look up in case she blacks out.

'I don't know what the relevance is of this murdered Russian.' Birdie straightens, pulling back her shoulders. 'Say your piece and kindly leave us to our breakfast.'

'Fair enough.' Nilson jumps off the stool, which wobbles and tilts but remains upright. He walks up to the table. 'Jessica, do you remember Finn Quennell, Thomas's old man?'

Jessica glances up, the blood leaving her face. 'Yes.'

'He came to the station this morning and gave a

written statement. Apparently Nikolai had assaulted one of his son's friends. A young girl. He was outraged and when the Russian taunted him with it, he lost control. I don't have to go into further details; you'll recall the photographs, of course.'

'Finn Quennell, a murderer,' Grannie Mim exclaims. 'They were always a troublesome lot.'

Jessica stares at Mim, then back to Nilson, feeling as though she's running through sand. '*Finn* Quennell?'

'You seem surprised?' Nilson smirks at her but his eyes are unsmiling. It's the anger in them that persuades her to trust what she is hearing. Thomas's father has taken the blame. After all these years, he has finally saved his son.

'I'll see you out,' she tells Nilson. She follows the DI outside, closing the door behind her. 'I trust I never have to see you again.'

Nilson leans forward, his voice dropping into a tone of confidentiality. 'There was one small detail in Finn's confession that interested me.'

'Really?' Let him have his say; he can't touch her or Thomas now.

'Thomas's little friend, the one Nikolai attacked, had red hair, so Finn said.'

Through the thin caravan walls, she can hear the scrape of chairs moving and the clink of crockery as Mim and her mother clear the breakfast away. But their voices are indistinct. If she can't hear them, they can't have heard what Nilson said.

'There are lots of us redheads around.'

Nilson taps a Marlboro Red out of his cigarette packet. Runs it under his nose. 'Did you find him?'

Jessica smiles. 'It doesn't matter now, does it?'

50

Two days before Christmas, Jessica is walking through fresh snow, frost crystals glittering under a sky of blue glaze, when she hears Jacques' voice.

Nothing sweeter than a bluebird day.

The longing to speak to him halts her footsteps, damp towel in her arms, the points of her wet hair stiffening with ice.

'You not feeling well, dearie?' She turns to see Grannie Mim approaching.

'A headache, that's all.'

'Why don't you call him?'

Jessica gapes at her.

'Yes. I can read your mind.' Grannie Mim laughs. 'Nothing to do with the misery on your face.'

'He'll hang up. He might not even be there.'

'All true.' Grannie Mim nods, shrugs. 'Life's shit.'

She waves over her shoulder as she walks off. 'Remember the time difference.'

Later, in Caravan Nineteen, after she has taken a walk, picked at a turkey and cranberry panini in the

Whitehead café and helped Birdie scrape moss off Caravan Three, Jessica is cursing Grannie Mim for planting the seed in her head. Just call him. So simple and terrifying, it takes her breath away. But it's taken hold and grown into a jungle of possible conversations in her head.

Just to hear his voice.

She looks at her watch. It is barely eleven in the morning and Connecticut is five hours behind. She makes herself a promise. Come two o'clock she will call Jacques. By then he will have woken, had his run and be back for breakfast.

Two o'clock arrives, and she lets it pass. Then Libby is knocking at her door, Birdie like a ferocious terrier behind her, muttering warnings.

'Please let me in.' Today she has dressed for the countryside. Shiny leather Dubarrys and jeans. She's never seen Libby in walking boots before. 'Just for a minute.'

Jessica nods. It will distract her from her broken promise.

To her credit, Libby waits to be offered a seat, in contrast to her proprietary behaviour in Jacques and Jessica's home. She doesn't say a word as Jessica makes tea. They sit on the sofa, the foldaway table between them with the remains of last night's dinner − a plate with two lamb-chop bones, her wine glass, dirty cutlery. Jessica pushes it all to one side.

'Why are you here?'

'I want us to stay friends, Jessica.' Libby spoons sugar into her tea, stirring in slow, deliberate circles.

'But our friendship was something you engineered.' Not so much an accusation as a testing of the notion now that the landscape around her has shifted into something unrecognisable. 'It wasn't real.'

'Don't you feel a bond between us? If you're honest.' Libby taps a nail against her mug. Thinking. 'How do you take your tea?'

Jessica gives a small shrug of frustration. 'What's that got to do with anything?'

'Three sugars, right? Just like me.' Libby gives a self-conscious smile; all drama set aside. 'Not that you ever noticed.'

'So, we like sweet tea. What does that prove?'

'Did you ever make Dad a cup of tea?'

Jessica starts to shake her head then, like a switched channel: she sees her mother in the kitchen dropping sugar cubes, one at a time, into her father's favourite mug. Laughing about the extra hours she'd have to put in at the park to satisfy her man's sweet tooth.

'That's our bond?'

'Of course not.' Libby sips her tea. 'But you thought I was chasing your husband, and I thought you were suddenly and inexplicably cold towards me . . . and still we stayed friends. That means something, I'm sure of it.'

Jessica gives a short, unconvinced *hum*. A cold draught of adrenalin sweeps over her as she prepares to ask a question that has been hibernating in the back of her head. 'Is there anything he wanted to say to me . . . at the end?'

Libby presses her lips together, tears rising. She shakes her head, breathing loudly through her nose. When she is ready to speak, she says, 'There was nothing new to add.'

Jessica stands abruptly, her chair scraping against the floor. She empties her cooling tea in the sink and washes the mug. A task for her hands.

'But I promised him I would speak to you. So you'd know how much he suffered in losing you.' Libby joins her at the sink. She slips her hand under the running water, prising the mug away and taking hold of Jessica's cold, soap-coated fingers.

'He said, maybe you'll be friends.'

After Libby leaves, Jessica stands in the shower until her fingers welt with wrinkles and the water runs cold. She allows herself to cry for him. For the man she adored as a little girl, and the stranger he'd become. Her father and Thomas; caught in the receding tide of years, drawn further and further away until they were lost.

The same thing would happen to Jacques, if she let it.

The sound of pebbles against her window wakes her from a dream. Pushing the curtains aside, she sees only caravan shadows broken into squares and rectangles by a full moon.

It is two in the morning. Nine o'clock at night in Connecticut. With just a jumper over the shorts she was sleeping in, she runs through Seasalt Park, her naked feet breaking the frozen skin of snow.

'Mum,' she calls, knocking softly on the office door. 'Can I use your phone?'

It's Joss who answers, shocking Jessica with his bare, white-haired chest and sleep-electric hair. 'Birdie's asleep.'

Jessica apologises, backing away.

'Use the phone, love,' he says. 'Just let yourself out when you're done.'

She unfolds the Post-it note Birdie has given her. Recognises the number of his parents' home. The first Christmas after they met, he went back to see them and she worked extra shifts at the Tea Chest – the ones no one else wanted on Christmas Eve and Boxing Day – so she could afford to call him every day. He never complained when she forgot the time difference, jumping out of bed to answer the phone before it had rung three times.

In the second bedroom, which her mother has converted into an office, she sits in the swivel chair by the desk and dials the number. A long tone sounds, like that of a broken line, then it falls into regular rings which she counts. On nine, he answers.

His voice trickles through her like warm milk. She can't speak.

'Jessica?'

'Yes.' Suddenly she's afraid he'll slip away in the silence so she adds, 'How are you? How's Ma Larsson?'

'All fine.' His voice, in contrast to hers, is slow. Reluctant.

'I'm staying at Seasalt. With Birdie.' The thawing pain of her feet burns up her calves. She hitches her knees, pulling the jumper over them. 'It's funny because I'm staying in Caravan Nineteen. Which is where you stayed, isn't it?'

'I don't recall.' The line crackles and sighs as though they're communicating across outer space.

'How are you?' she asks again.

'I bought a kayak. For springtime.'

'Have you tried it out?'

A long pause. She can feel him wrestling with the urge to hang up. 'It's a little cold. Took a walk up to Cornish, though, following the river by Mount Ascutney.'

Cornish, Mount Ascutney. Those distant, alien places delivered in his thickened accent take him even further from her. She sees the two-dimensional brochure pictures still taped to her sitting-room wall, glorious but unreal.

'Sounds like a long walk.'

Again the silence. She has to keep him speaking. 'You and your dad used to kayak along the Connecticut River when you were a boy, didn't you?'

'I should go now,' Jacques says.

'I know.'

The next night, again at two in the morning, she finds a note from Birdie on the office door.

No need to knock. Just go in, Mum.

The blessed relief as he answers. 'Jessica?'

'Did you go out again today?'

'Sure did.' Tonight the line is clearer. She hears him swallow, a clink of ice against glass. The fact that he has poured himself a drink fills her with hope. Perhaps he was waiting for her call.

'Where did you go?'

'I drove to the Quechee Gorge to see the frozen falls.'

'It sounds beautiful.'

'It's pretty peaceful. I caught sight of a peregrine falcon.'

She's not sure what it looks like but she pictures a bird with golden-brown feathers catching the sun as it lifts above the pines.

I have a picture of you in my head, he'd said in another life. *Sitting by the campfire, your hair wet from swimming, freckles on your shoulders. Just you and me.*

She buys a map of Connecticut and calls him every night, trailing his excursions with her finger along the blue artery of water. He tells her about snow blizzards, ice glittering in the air, an old grizzly at the water's edge. She listens intently and with a new kind of freedom, now that all the inner noise is gone. A few days into the new year, she buys an open-return ticket to the States from the travel agency in Barnestow. When she calls Jacques that night, she holds it in her hand for courage.

'I have something I need to tell you,' she says. 'It's about a boy called Thomas.'

And Jacques says, 'I'm listening.'

Acknowledgments

I am hugely grateful to everyone at Orion, especially my editor Kate Mills. I still remember being bowled over by her warm and uplifting response to *Jellybird* and I cannot thank her and her team enough. A special thank you to Louisa Macpherson and Gaby Young.

To my agent Rowan Lawton, a big thank you for brilliant advice, for always having the time for yet another 'quick question', and above all for her boundless enthusiasm and energy.

I am also grateful to Helen Corner and Kathryn Price at Cornerstones; the first people to read the book cover to cover and respond with such encouragement that I forged on rather than shoving it to the back of the drawer (as I had promised myself).

My thanks also to Anne Aylor, friend and tutor, whose creative writing workshops I have returned to over the years for her singular insight and inspiration. Without Anne I would never have had that 'light-bulb' moment.

My husband Mark, for his love, support and belief,

and for the many impromptu excursions with our children so I could scribble in peace for a few hours. A heartfelt thank you.

Never forgetting my mum, Elizabeth Maltarp, for being as excited as I am about the publication of my book, for always having the time to listen to my short stories and never failing to love everything I've written.

Finally, but never least, a thank you to my friends for their support, for very necessary coffees when I was missing human contact and for never forgetting to ask how the book was coming along.

Lincolnshire
COUNTY COUNCIL

discover libraries

**This book should be returned on or before
the due date.**

NAZ

NC2 11·17		NAZ
NA1 a/ia		
1 6 AUG 2023		

WITHDRAWN FOR SALE

To renew or order library books please telephone 01522 782010
or visit https://lincolnshire.spydus.co.uk
You will require a Personal Identification Number.
Ask any member of staff for this.

The above does not apply to Reader's Group Collection Stock.

05166178

UNTOLD

UNTOLD:

THE DANIEL MORGAN MURDER EXPOSED

ALASTAIR MORGAN & PETER JUKES

BLINK

bringing you closer

Published by Blink Publishing
3.08, The Plaza,
535 Kings Road,
Chelsea Harbour,
London, SW10 0SZ

www.blinkpublishing.co.uk

facebook.com/blinkpublishing
twitter.com/blinkpublishing

Hardback – 978-1-911274-60-5
Trade Paperback – 978-1-911274-61-2
Ebook – 978-1-911274-62-9

A CIP catalogue of this book is available from the British Library.

Typeset by seagulls.net
Printed and bound by Clays Ltd, St. Ives Plc

1 3 5 7 9 10 8 6 4 2

Blink Publishing is an imprint of the Bonnier Publishing Group
www.bonnierpublishing.com

To Dan, who lost everything but is still shining a light on corruption

One story about the media has already been told – the tale of phone hacking. Another equally sinister chapter – involving a raft of unanswered allegations about impersonation and even email hacking, and interference with the process of justice – has yet to be told. Alastair Morgan and Peter Jukes' book is an important contribution to that story.

Gordon Brown, April 2017

Contents

Contents

Foreword by Alastair Morgan

I've carried this story inside me for over thirty years. Most of this huge chunk of my adult life has been spent challenging the actions of the police, lobbying politicians and badgering journalists to bring the case of my brother's murder to the public's attention. From the earliest days of the first investigation into Daniel's murder, I knew something was going very badly wrong. That instinct still drives me today.

Daniel's murder has had a profound effect on policing and the media in Britain. Most people are still unaware of this but it was not for nothing that Nick Davies dubbed Southern Investigations 'the cradle of the dark arts' in his book *Hack Attack*.

At the time of writing, so much in this country hangs in the balance. The campaign for a much needed Leveson II continues, Ofcom is scrutinising the Murdoch bid to take over Sky and a Panel of Inquiry ordered by the now Prime Minister Theresa May will soon be in its fifth year of scrutinising the activities of the police and the media in relation to Daniel's brutal killing. We expect the panel to report early in 2018. We hope to produce an updated version of this book after the panel has reported.

My family and others close to us have fought for thirty years to get to the truth about Daniel's murder. This book, we believe, goes a very long way towards achieving this end. For this, I owe an enormous debt of gratitude to Peter Jukes and Deeivya Meir for conceiving the idea of the @UntoldMurder podcast and bringing the story of Daniel's murder to millions. It was this podcast that created the appetite for this book.

Peter Jukes' vast knowledge of the Murdoch media and his detailed research into the police have been an outstanding complement to my family's years of relentless toil in seeking justice for Daniel and holding our police to account. We hope that our work will inspire and inform our readers; firstly in the fight for honest and accountable policing, but perhaps even more importantly, for a press that serves the interests of the British people rather than those of a small but immensely powerful group of press barons.

Part One | Potter

Part One	Police

KEY CHARACTERS, 1987–1990

The Morgan Family
Daniel Morgan – Private detective
Alastair Morgan – Daniel's brother
Isobel Hulsmann – Daniel's mother
Iris Morgan – Daniel's wife
Jane McCarthy – Daniel's sister

The Rees/Vian Families
Jonathan Rees – Private detective
Sharon Ann Rees – Jonathan's wife
Garry Vian – Sharon's brother
Glenn Vian – Sharon's brother
Paul Goodridge – Uncle of Glenn Vian's wife, Kim

Southern Investigations
Kevin Lennon – Company bookkeeper
Peter Newby – Office manager
David Bray – Company courier

South-east London Police
Sidney Fillery – Detective Sergeant
Duncan Hanrahan – Detective Constable, Norbury
Derek Haslam – Police Constable, Addington
Alan Holmes – Detective Constable, Serious Crimes
Laurie Bucknole – Former Detective Inspector, Croydon

Murder Investigators
Douglas Campbell – Detective Superintendent, first investigation
Alan Jones – Detective Inspector, first investigation
Malcolm Davidson – Detective Sergeant, first investigation
Alan Wheeler – Detective Superintendent, second investigation
Paul Blaker – Detective Chief Inspector, second investigation

Media
Alex Marunchak – *News of the World*

<table>
<tr><td>**CHAPTER 1**</td><td>The Call</td></tr>
</table>

11th March 1987, 6:30am

ALASTAIR MORGAN: That telephone call changed my life. Thirty years on, I'm still trying to answer it.

I sat up on the camp bed in the sitting room of my grandmother's small flat, peered at my watch and wondered who would telephone an 84-year-old woman at six-thirty in the morning.

I opened the door to the small hallway, picked up the phone and heard my mother's voice.

'Al, sorry to ring so early. I've got some bad news. You'd better brace yourself. This is really bad ...' Her voice was almost a whisper. 'Dan's dead.'

'*Dead?*'

My question sounded as if someone else had spoken it.

'What's happened?'

'I don't know. I got a call from the Metropolitan Police a couple of hours ago. The officer who rang would only tell me "Your son is dead."'

'But didn't he say how? Was it a car accident, or what?'

'I don't know!' she continued. 'I asked him again and again. He just said he didn't have any more information. And that was that.'

My brother Dan was a healthy 37-year-old with no history of illness. As a private investigator, he'd been threatened occasionally and even attacked in the course of his work but for him that was par for the course. He used to shrug it off with a laugh. Had somebody harmed him? The question of murder entered my mind like a worm.

'Al,' my mum continued. 'I need you to get up to London as quickly as possible to be with Iris and the children.'

Iris was Dan's wife. They had met about ten years earlier, before my brother first started out as a private investigator. By now they were bringing up two young children in south London. Sarah was aged five and Daniel, who was only three, called me 'Uncle Wallister'. I'd stayed with them only a month before while Dan was away on business. Mum said she'd be leaving Wales very soon – she lived near Crickhowell in the Brecon Beacons. Her journey would take about five hours.

'Just get there as quickly as you can. I've got to ring Jane now to tell her …' she told me.

She sounded apprehensive. My younger sister Jane lived in Herford, Germany with her husband, Justin. She adored Daniel. I knew the news would hit her hard.

'I'll get up there as quick as I can, Mum. I promise. I'll see you in London.'

I went to the bathroom, gulped down some cold water and splashed my face. Having returned from Sweden two years earlier after living there for seven years, I was still rebuilding my life in Britain with a series of casual jobs. I was staying with my gran because of a delay in a letting contract on a new flat. Now I had to get a taxi to London. But first I needed to ring Daniel's office to find out what had happened – I needed to prepare myself mentally for what lay ahead.

* * *

My first instinct was to talk to Daniel's business partner, Jonathan Rees. They had known each other for seven years when they both worked together in a large south London detective agency, Madagans. Four years ago, in 1983, Dan had decided to form a company of his own – and a year later business was so good, he formed a partnership with Rees and renamed the company South-ern Investigations. Business was thriving but there had been tensions in the previous year.

I didn't want my gran to hear this conversation with Jonathan Rees and I had to wait till Dan's office in Thornton Heath was open so I told her I needed to go up to London to be with Iris and the children. I dressed quickly and left her flat. It was a grey, windy morning. I was too scared to call Daniel's wife yet. I felt a strong craving for a cigarette and bought a pack in a newsagent's then rang the door of a friend who lived on the high street. I'd spent the previous evening with him and other friends playing Trivial Pursuit. We spoke at some length about my mother's phone call and my fears as I drank tea and waited for Daniel's office to open.

At 9am I made the call.

Dan's office manager Peter Newby answered. He handed the phone straight to Jon Rees.

'Alastair ...'

Though he had a Welsh surname, Jonathan Rees had been brought up in Rotherham and had a strong south Yorkshire accent.

'Jon! What's happened?'

'Daniel and I had a business meeting arranged last night in a pub in Sydenham. Do you know Sydenham?'

'No.' My heart sank; this didn't sound like some kind of accident.

'It's a rough sort of place, lots of druggies and that sort of thing.'

That was it; that was the moment I knew for sure that Dan had been murdered.

'What happened, Jon?'

'We'd arranged to meet a third party...'

Third party? What did this mean? I was in a state of hypervigilance, and hanging onto every word.

'A third party who didn't show up,' Rees continued. 'My car was parked in front of the pub, in the street. Daniel had parked in the car park behind the pub. I left Daniel finishing his drink and drove home. The police came to my house around midnight. They told me Daniel had been mugged ... fatally mugged. Alastair, I'm absolutely gutted.'

'What happened, Jon? What did they do to him? Did they shoot him? Was he knifed? What did they do to him?' My words came tumbling out.

I could tell by the pause that Rees was weighing his words very carefully. What was he trying to protect me from?

'I think he was battered to death,' Rees finally admitted.

Somehow I already knew that fragment of information would be important.

'Look, Jon, I'm coming up to London immediately. I have to see Iris and the children. I'll see you later,' I told him.

* * *

I looked at my friend. It had just dawned on me that while we'd been laughing and playing Trivial Pursuit together the previous evening somebody had taken my brother's life. I broke down ... He walked with me to the bank and then the taxi rank at Petersfield station. I hired a cab for the two-hour drive to London, and watched the traffic float by.

I felt disorientated, detached, like I was outside myself, just a spectator of the life passing by outside.

I'd had the same feeling 20 years earlier when my father died suddenly after an operation. I'd been in a taxi that time too; I was going to fetch my mother. Everything felt suddenly real and significant – but nobody seemed to notice. And now I was trying to think the unthinkable: the brother I'd shared a room with for 15 years, the guy who'd been there for me through thick and thin, was gone. I'd never again pick up a phone and call him, argue with him, share a joke …

There were clumps of daffodils on the verges of the A3 road to London, but I was back 30 years earlier, when Dan and I were kids. I pictured him in a pair of khaki shorts, with his thin right leg and different sized sandals – he'd been born with a club foot. His hands were dirty from messing around with a car battery. He rubbed his nose with the back of one hand and left a smear. We were standing at the top of the steps outside our house in Llanfrechfa, Cwmbran. I broke down again.

'Ere, mate …'

The taxi driver took out a box of tissues from his glove compartment and handed them to me in the back seat. He'd been watching me in his rear-view mirror.

'Sorry …' I spoke to the back of the driver's head. 'My brother was murdered last night.'

'I'm sorry,' he muttered. 'That's terrible.'

I blew my nose and stuffed the tissue into my pocket. We'd soon be in London and I needed to keep my wits about me.

Rees had told me my brother had been 'fatally mugged' but already I didn't trust him. The unnerving talk of a third party made me think this must have been something more than a random street robbery. What had happened recently that could have got my brother killed?

And then my mind went back to the call I'd made to Dan from a public phone box in the market square in Petersfield, a year earlier, when he told me Jonathan Rees had been robbed of £18,000 the previous evening – in cash.

YOU'VE READ THE BOOK, NOW LISTEN TO THE PODCAST.

audio**Boom**.com

AudioBoom is home to some of the best and biggest true crime podcasts including the no.1 hit podcast **UNTOLD: The Daniel Morgan Murder.**

Check out AudioBoom's other great true crime podcasts including:

Up and Vanished (US)
They Walk Among Us (UK)
Felon True Crime Podcast (AU)

Subscribe to them all on iTunes, Google Play and wherever else podcasts are heard.

KEY CHARACTERS

Sid Fillery, former Detective Sergeant.

Jonathan Rees, Private Detective.

Detective Constable
Duncan Hanrahan.

The Vian brothers.

THE PRESS

Alex Marunchak, ex-executive editor at the *News of the World*.

Andy Coulson, ex-editor at the *News of the World*.

Rebekah Brooks, ex-editor at the *News of the World*, and now CEO of News UK, also owned by Rupert Murdoch.

THE POLICE

John Yates, Assistant Commissioner for the Met.

Metropolitan Police Commissioner, Lord John Stevens.

Metropolitan Police Commissioner, Lord Ian Blair.

Dave Cook, Detective Chief Superintendent for the fourth and fifth investigations.

Jacqui Hames, TV presenter and detective.

I knew then, after all our interactions with the police, that we ought to have a solicitor with us when we met the Commissioner. Kirsteen and I had little money and up to this point, taking on a solicitor had been out of the question but we'd found out to our cost that the police can be very stubborn and slippery. The case of the Guildford Four had been handled by Birnberg & Co. so I decided to see if they could help.

I rang and told them about Dan's murder and my planned visit to Paul Condon with Chris Smith. I mentioned in passing that I believed that Hampshire Police had tried to 'fit up' an innocent man. The person taking my call brought the conversation to an abrupt halt.

'We're representing a party in this case, so there could be a conflict of interests. I'll talk to one of my colleagues and get back to you.'

This gave me one hell of a shock. Were they representing Jonathan Rees or Sid Fillery?

An hour later, a solicitor named Russell Miller called. To my great relief, he said he represented celebrity minder Paul Goodridge. Miller was cautious. I assured him my call to Birnberg was a coincidence – I didn't know that Goodridge was active in the case. All I wanted was advice and back-up for my meeting with Condon.

A couple of days later I was sitting in Birnberg's offices in Southwark. Russell Miller led me up several flights of narrow stairs to a small office and introduced me to his colleague, Raju Bhatt. My description of the first two inquiries into Daniel's murder dispelled any doubts they had about my motives. They told me Paul Goodridge was suing Hampshire Police for malicious prosecution.

Russell informed me that in the middle of the Hampshire investigation a meeting had taken place at Scotland Yard. It was attended by the Chief Constable of Hampshire, John Hoddinott. Miller had learned about this from an affidavit sworn by Alan Wheeler. In the affidavit, Wheeler stated that the inquiry's terms of reference had been changed at the meeting. Instead of investigating Fillery and others, it was decided that they would pursue Rees, Paul Goodridge and Jean Wisden.

This was news to me. The Hampshire Inquiry was meant to be an investigation into the way the Met had handled the original investigation. Now it appears they'd only looked at civilians and that the question of police involvement had been swept aside.

Paul Goodridge's case against Hampshire was to be heard the following year. I told him I would do what I could to assist. The meeting ended well. I left feeling more certain than ever that I should keep on pushing for the truth. At the end of the meeting, Russell asked if I would like to meet Paul Goodridge.

* * *

'Hello, Alastair,' Paul Goodridge said in his deep south London voice.

The man charged with axing my brother to death stood up as I entered the room and stretched out his hand. Goodridge was impressively powerful, almost as broad as he was tall. He was certainly physically capable of wielding a fatal blow, but for years I'd doubted the police's version of events. But I was very uncomfortable and not at all sure I was doing the right thing.

Goodridge was nervous too. He'd spent the last decade under a cloud of suspicion and he clearly wanted me to believe he had nothing to do with murdering my brother.

Paul Goodridge had been a friend of Jonathan Rees and his niece Kim was married to Glenn Vian. At the inquest Rees had said Goodridge was meant to be at the Golden Lion on the night Dan was killed. According to Rees, Goodridge was going to lend them the £10,000 they needed to fight the civil action with Belmont Car Auctions, but he hadn't shown up at the pub.

It had never made sense to me that Rees, who apparently wanted Dan dead, had tried to borrow money from a man whom the police suspected of carrying out the murder.

In 1989 Goodridge had been charged with murder by Hampshire Police. Now he was telling me that he'd felt that the Met had wanted to frame him from the outset. He said that he and his then girlfriend, Jean Wisden, had attended the police station unrepresented to answer questions.

'If I'd had anything to hide, I would have taken a solicitor, wouldn't I? It was horrible. Jean came out that first interview in tears,' he told me.

Goodridge then described the morning in February 1989 when Hampshire Police had arrested him. His phone had rung early in the morning. A man had asked to speak to him and then hung up immediately. He tried to make a call and found that his phone had been cut off. Feeling that he was about to be arrested, he'd dressed and drove to a newsagent to buy cigarettes. When he returned home, his garden was filled with policemen. He was placed under arrest and driven to Fareham. On the way, the police had stopped at a café to relieve themselves. They'd allowed him to walk to the gents alone.

'They were inviting me to do a runner,' said Paul. 'Only I didn't oblige them.'

At Fareham, he was questioned and eventually charged by an officer from the Metropolitan Police. He said that after this Alan Wheeler, the leader of the Hampshire team, had come into his cell and spoken to him.

'We don't want you for this, Paul. If you give us a statement on Rees, you can be out of here within 24 hours,' he was told.

Goodridge said he knew they had no real evidence against him and that if he'd falsely incriminated Rees, he'd have been ripped to shreds in a trial. And so he refused. He told me he'd been able to raise £50,000 in bail and within a week he was released.

He told me that when he'd been arrested he owned his own house outright, along with a Bentley. Why would he risk a life sentence for a few thousand quid? I'd read that he'd once been a bodyguard for Richard Harris and Elizabeth Taylor. He told me that all this had a big effect on his livelihood. Famous people don't like being associated with suspected murderers.

Then he talked about Dan: 'I had nothing against Daniel,' he said. 'With Daniel, what you saw was what you got.'

But he didn't appear to feel the same about Jonathan Rees and Sidney Fillery. 'I used to meet up with Rees socially quite a bit,' he explained. 'But the more I saw of him, the more he got on my nerves. My father couldn't stand him. When he asked to borrow money, I didn't want to turn him down to his face, but I had no intention of giving him the money. I knew I'd get ripped off if Fillery was involved, so I just spun him along.'

It was strange talking to someone whose life had also been dramatically altered by the murder. I'd spent many long hours talking to my mother, Jane and Kirsteen, speculating about whether this man had anything to do with my brother's killing. Was he fitted up by the police? Had he told them everything he knew?

Perhaps I was being naïve, but I'd thought for years that he just didn't fit the bill as a suspect and that Hampshire Police had thought, *Okay, you'll do.*

* * *

By this time Kirsteen had been offered a place on a one-year course in radio journalism in Hamilton, near Glasgow. We decided to move to Glasgow for the year as my translating work could be done anywhere with a telephone and an email connection. In September 1997 Kirsteen began her course in Hamilton.

I was really pleased. Finally, I could do something to repay her for all of the support she'd given me. I could pay the rent and bills and make a home for us while she studied.

About three weeks before the scheduled meeting with Sir Paul Condon that autumn, I was in Manchester Town Hall interpreting for a group of officials from a Swedish trade union. At around eleven o'clock our hosts, the GMB Union, took us to a sumptuously wood-panelled room on the first floor for coffee. I scanned a rack of newspapers on the wall as I entered.

The headline of *The Guardian* leapt out at me: 'MET CHIEF: CRIMINALS IN MY FORCE'. According to the article, Sir Paul Condon had been booed by members of the Police Federation when he'd talked about corruption in his force. Unlike the Federation, I was delighted by his admission. Police corruption had finally made the front page.

Back in Glasgow, it was time to get ready for our visit to Condon. I spent most of that week stoking up media interest in the story, determined to get as much coverage as possible: the Met needed to know it was being watched. We picked Mum up at Paddington the day before the meeting. I was tense about the following day; we'd worked for a decade to achieve it. Would we be taken seriously, or would we be brushed aside as we had been on every other occasion?

Kirsteen and I had agreed that her media invisibility would have to end. We'd argued many times about her being left out of meetings. She'd been through some dark years with me, reluctantly missing out on meetings but coming again and again with me to Chris Smith's surgeries.

I can't say I was totally comfortable with it, but it would have been wrong to exclude her from the meeting. After all, she was training to be a journalist and the chance to meet the country's number one cop doesn't come around that often.

* * *

That Friday, just before seven in the evening, Mum and her MP, Richard Livsey, Kirsteen and I pulled up in a taxi outside New Scotland Yard. My efforts to alert journalists had paid off and the media was there in force.

There were three TV camera crews, a couple of radio journalists, a reporter from the Press Association and several photographers. I wanted the Met to squirm. We walked into reception and waited for Chris Smith, who soon arrived in a ministerial Mercedes.

The Met weren't aware that Kirsteen would be with me. I insisted that she was my partner and if she wasn't allowed in, I would refuse to go. I think they believed she was a media plant. Chris intervened and said he'd vouch for Kirsteen. But they wanted to know her profession. She simply told them she was a student – it didn't seem a good idea to mention journalism.

We were escorted up to the eighth floor where Sir Paul Condon was stood in civilian clothes, waiting to show us into his suite. He was huge, about six foot six tall. Chris made the introductions and Condon showed us into a conference room where another police officer was waiting, seated at the far end of the table with a notepad. He introduced him as Deputy Assistant Commissioner Roy Clark.

A woman appeared with a tray and served tea. Chris Smith began by thanking the Commissioner for seeing us. 'There's a stink about this case, Commissioner,' said Chris before giving a short account of what had happened over the three years that he'd been my MP.

Condon nodded gravely: 'I had a lot of honourable officers working on that case.'

I wanted to say that I didn't see any of them but decided to hold back. Instead I told him there'd been police perjury at the inquest and that Hampshire Police had failed to investigate an attempt by DS Fillery to get me out of London.

Condon didn't respond. He looked across the table at Chris Smith.

'It's not helpful to have all this media,' interjected Roy Clark.

'It's always the same,' Mum continued. 'Every time we raise the question of Fillery, no one ever wants to answer us. This case has been crooked from day one because of that man!'

I too went on the offensive. 'And I'd also like to say that if you've got a corruption problem in your force, Sir Paul, then you only have to look at the way this case was handled to understand why.'

I could see Roy Clark making notes as I spoke.

Sir Paul again declined to respond, and looked straight ahead of him at Chris Smith. Richard Livsey, who'd been silent up to this point, began to chastise Condon over the role of Fillery.

'The man's taken over his business, for goodness sake, right under the noses of the Metropolitan Police,' he told Condon: 'It's disgraceful!'

Condon hadn't reacted to my comment, but Richard's passionate tirade clearly embarrassed him. He was nodding and swallowed hard.

Condon finally responded by saying that he would order some of his senior officers to review the case. I was very disappointed – we'd already had a review by CIB 2 and a flat refusal to reopen the case from Bill Griffiths. What good would another review do?

I said nothing. No good would come of losing my cool in the Commissioner of Police's office. We thanked him unenthusiastically and made our way back down to the lobby. The media posse was outside looking in through the glass. As we stopped to consider what to say, Chris Smith was looking impatient and glancing at his watch.

'You are going to say something to the media for us, Chris?' I asked him.

He looked harassed.

'Err … actually I'm in a hurry at the moment, I have to get somewhere very quickly so I'm afraid I have to go.' He shook my hand and strode off in the direction of the door.

At that moment his car pulled up just outside. Cameramen and journalists moved aside. Chris quickly opened the door, ignoring the questions fired at him. Within seconds he was gone, smoothly accelerating into the night.

I heard Richard Livsey's voice to my left.

'Right, let's face the media,' he said.

'Who's first?' I asked.

'You and Isobel, of course!' he replied.

We walked out through the main door into a barrage of flash photography. Mum and I gave a couple of short interviews to the radio and television people. We said we were disappointed, but undeterred.

Chris's lack of enthusiasm for the media did raise questions in my mind. The government had recently announced that a public inquiry would be held into Stephen Lawrence's murder. I found it hard to believe that Chris would not have discussed Daniel's case with Jack Straw, given that both murders raised serious questions about police integrity and both took place within a few miles of each other in south-east London.

What was going on in the Cabinet in relation to the police? I'd already asked Chris whether the Home Secretary would consider holding a public inquiry into Dan's murder. To me, his case was just as important, for different reasons. I couldn't understand why any home secretary couldn't see that too. Chris told me that the Home Secretary would always believe the Commissioner before me.

* * *

In April 1998 Paul Goodridge's civil action came up in court. We travelled down from Glasgow to Winchester, mainly to get some publicity for our campaign.

We'd already been told that Goodridge had failed in his attempt to show that Hampshire Police had arrested him out of malice, but Russell Miller had forced them to admit that he'd been arrested and charged 'without probable cause'.

Goodridge was pleased with the result. 'For the past ten years everyone's been thinking, "There goes that man that killed Daniel Morgan and got away with it,"' he said. 'It's because of the way I look. I look like a villain, so everyone thinks I'm guilty.'

He wanted a photograph of us standing together.

'It's just for me, I promise you it's not for the press. It's just personal.'

I could see it meant a lot to him to be able to show a photo of himself standing beside the murdered man's brother. Many people must have assumed that he really had killed Dan and I'd never met anyone that looked more like a stereotypical hard man.

I was happy that he had been cleared. For years I'd believed that he was innocent and that the charges against him had stood in the way of our efforts to get the case reopened. This barrier had now been removed and an untruth exposed.

As we drove home to Glasgow, I rang all my media contacts and told them just what I thought of Hampshire's behaviour.

The next day, Duncan Campbell quoted me in *The Guardian* saying that the police 'hadn't heard the last' of this matter. I also did an interview for the *Petersfield Herald* in which I called for the Chief Constable, John Hoddinott, to resign. The following week, it carried the headline 'FORMER LISS MAN CALLS ON CHIEF CONSTABLE TO RESIGN' across the front page.

A few days after the *Herald* article, I was walking up the hill to our flat in Glasgow when I noticed two tall, smartly dressed men standing on the corner of our street. There was something out of place about them as they stood there chatting, but I thought no more about it that evening.

The following afternoon I walked down the short hill to Byers Road to buy something for dinner. I was halfway home again when I noticed two men of the same description standing in the exact same place – I think they must have sensed my unease. As I walked up the path to my door, I could see from the corner of my eye that they were still standing there. Something unusual was going on.

I picked up the phone to my mother. 'I think we're being watched,' I said.

Mum had a similar story to tell. The day before, she'd been out with her dog for a walk. Her flat in Hay-on-Wye is separated from the road by a pavement and a small garden about four metres wide. Mum said that she was walking along her garden path searching for her keys in her pocket when she heard a clicking sound behind her.

She turned and saw a woman at her front gate taking photos of her. Behind her was a saloon car with a male driver, its engine running. The woman then turned, stepped into the car and was driven off at speed. A wall obscured the number plate so my mother couldn't see it.

And it didn't end there. Mum had immediately rung Jane, 600 miles away in Germany. She had a similar story.

That same day, Jane had driven from her house to the local supermarket. The houses in her area are well spaced out and separated by fields and fences. She'd turned from her drive onto the country road and noticed a small Honda van oddly parked at the roadside, 50 metres ahead. As she approached it, she was surprised to see a man lying in the ditch next to the van with a telescopic camera in his hands. The camera was pointing at her house.

This scared me. I had no doubt that we were all being watched, but I didn't know who was doing this or why. Whoever it was, they'd gone to considerable effort. These events took place in Wales, Scotland and Germany, separated by hundreds of miles.

I tried to persuade Mum to go to a hotel immediately. She refused point-blank. We argued but she wouldn't budge. I reported the incidents to Dyfed Powys Police and asked them to keep an eye on her flat. I even rang the German police and explained the situation to a German police officer. He said he would note this and keep his eyes and ears open.

I also had to think about Kirsteen and me. I decided we had to leave the flat in Glasgow for the night. Kirsteen was ill at the time with bronchitis and a fever. She thought I was mad and was furious that I was going to drag her out of bed and spend money on a hotel. I insisted and we drove to Helensburgh, about 20 miles outside Glasgow, and booked into a hotel on the shores of the Firth of Clyde. I was sure someone was trying to intimidate us.

Maybe Hampshire Police were angry about me calling for their chief constable to resign. It could also have been Rees or the other suspects. Paul Goodridge's successful civil action marked a new era in the case. Cracks were beginning to show in the previous inquiries. I was anxious and tried to explain my reasoning to Kirsteen over a meal in the hotel. She wasn't well, and was angry that I'd dragged her away from home.

The following morning I telephoned the Home Office. I'd taken a copy of a Home Office letter to Richard Livsey with me to Helensburgh. It was from the Minister for Policing, Alun Michael, and gave a direct line to his private office.

I explained what had happened to an official who clearly thought I was barking mad. Things didn't improve when I received a call from Richard Livsey. Alun Michael had obviously rung him to complain. Richard was annoyed that I'd embarrassed him by using a phone number from a private letter to him; I had to apologise to him. But I was certain that we had been placed under surveillance and equally sure this had been done to scare us.

I wanted to stay another night at the hotel, but Kirsteen was adamant that this was a waste of time and money. We went over the arguments of the night before. She seemed to think it was all a peculiar coincidence. But she was right that we couldn't afford to stay away forever. She also looked ill and needed to get home and rest.

Years later, this surveillance took on a significance that we could never have imagined at the time.

Kirsteen's cough didn't clear up for weeks. Just before Christmas she'd heard that she was going to become a BBC trainee. The Disability Programmes Unit in London offered two traineeships a year. Traineeships at the BBC are like gold dust and usually go to the cream of Oxford and Cambridge graduates. Kirsteen counted herself extremely lucky to be able to apply for this placement. It would give her two years' paid employment and some very professional training. We returned to London excited about her new prospects.

I didn't know it then, but things were about to dramatically shift gear in my brother's case.

| CHAPTER 24 | Nigeria |

1998

A common behavioural pattern within the network of former police officers, private investigators and journalists around Southern Investigations was the number of times the various players would fall out: Hanrahan fell out with Rees, Fillery and Leighton. Leighton would later fall out with Rees; Southern Investigations would fall out with the *News of the World*.

Despite the antipathies, a joint interest soon reconciled them: money and fear of exposure, whitemail and blackmail.

As Derek Haslam reported back to CIB 3 throughout 1998, an internal progress report concluded: 'Rees and Fillery have for a number of years been involved in the long-term penetration of police intelligence sources,' the report said. 'They have ensured that they have live sources within the Metropolitan Police Service and have sought to recruit sources within other police forces. Their thirst for knowledge is driven by profit to be accrued from the media ...'

The money was certainly coming in. As Haslam told his handler, DCS David Wood, both Rees and Fillery had a share of a boat with Leighton. Rees was about to lease a new Mercedes car.

For most of the 1990s, Southern Investigations had boomed because of 'commercial' clients, sometimes lawyers, councils and, often, organised crime. Their 'confidential inquiries' had helped to spawn a remarkable and uniquely British media sub-industry of the dark arts, which involved surveillance, covert videos, bribing cops and other officials, burgling, bugging, blagging and illegal access to criminal, medical and financial databases.

Rees and Fillery's main media employer was still the *News of the World* and in 1997 they even helped set up a Vodka import-export company for editors Alex Marunchak and Greg Miskiw.[1] But by the end of the year the volume of cash disappearing down the south-east London plughole was attracting the attention of the *News of the World*'s managing editor, Stuart Kuttner.

Kuttner refused to pay some of the invoices. In retaliation Rees and Fillery launched a civil action in Croydon County Court against the Sunday tabloid in December 1997, which eventually Alex Marunchak was brought in to reconcile. Daniel Taylor, acting on behalf of News Group Newspapers, the holding company for *The Sun* and the *News of the World*, capitulated in the face of the civil claim in early 1998 and paid out £18,216.

Nevertheless, the management of the Sunday tabloid soon began to look for cheaper options than the private eyes who had been arrested for the Daniel Morgan murder.

The solo phone hacker Glenn Mulcaire, a semi-professional footballer, was a contact of Greg Miskiw's, and would soon become the main source of 'confidential inquiries', though his retainer for £150,000 was not much less than Southern Investigations had charged.

Perhaps there were other reasons the *News of the World* had a sense that things couldn't continue like this forever.

* * *

In the spring of 1998 Derek Haslam, now a more frequent visitor to London, reported meeting Bryan Madagan, Daniel's former boss, who told him Dan had 'been offered £20,000 by the *News of the World* for details of a cocaine importation that was being overseen by Senior Police Officers'.

Back in 1987, Madagan had told police about Daniel's claim a few months before his murder that he had 'hit the jackpot' with a story of police corruption he was selling to the press. This was the first time he had detailed – or been asked – which newspaper.

Haslam also noted how Jonathan Rees was concerned that the Ghost Squad's anti-corruption investigation was beginning to close around him. Rees was 'very agitated', Haslam told his handlers, about news reports on London Weekend Television and Sky News which suggested 'pending arrests of up to 20 Police Officers' for corruption, which featured a photo of Rees.[2]

CIB 3 were under no illusions how tricky it would be to catch Rees and Fillery in any kind of hard evidence that could result in a prosecution.

'They are alert, cunning and devious individuals who have current knowledge of investigative methods and techniques which may be used against them,' another internal report warned. 'Such is their level of access to individuals within the police, through professional and social contacts, that the threat of compromise to any conventional investigation against them is constant and very real.'

Rees had already spotted a woman he assumed was a CIB 3 officer inspecting the rubbish from the back of the offices. Nevertheless, Haslam noted that Southern Investigations security measures weren't great. An alarm with a Passive Infrared detector was rarely activated and a back-office extension wasn't alarmed.

As part of the preliminary work to set up a covert listening device in the office, Haslam's handlers suggested to him he should steal the office keys. Haslam pointed out that if they went missing, Rees and Fillery would immediately change the locks. Instead, they agreed he should take imprints of the keys in clay so the covert entry team could use copies to install their bugs.

In March 1998 Derek Haslam was handed half a dozen clunky metal boxes, which he somehow had to smuggle into Southern Investigations. It was a warm spring day. He was wearing a light shirt and chinos and secreted the bulky boxes in a carrier bag.

Without being noticed by Rees or Fillery, Haslam managed to take three ADA security keys from the offices during a moment of distraction and retired to the lavatory, where he carefully pressed each into clay until he had the full set. Haslam then returned the office keys without Rees or Fillery noticing. He still hadn't managed to get an impression of the main joint front door, but kept an extra key press back for another occasion.

After an offer to join Sid Fillery, Jonathan Rees and Alec Leighton for a cruise of the Norfolk Broads in the last week of April 1998, Derek Haslam asked his handlers to keep an eye on the two boats to check that he returned from the week-long cruise safely and that his cover had not been blown.

By May the Met's anti-corruption command's lifestyle surveillance operations, Hallmark and Landmark, had provided enough information for CIB 3 to plan placing a covert listening device into the Thornton Heath offices of Southern Investigations.

Though the operation was supervised by DCS David Wood, the written authorisation for the intrusive probe was authorised initially by Assistant Commissioner David Veness, though subsequent monthly authorisations were signed by a rising star in the Met, Deputy Assistant Commissioner John Stevens.

* * *

John Stevens had first risen through the ranks of the Metropolitan Police and was transferred to the Hampshire Constabulary around the time of their investigation into Daniel's murder and allegations of police corruption. In the late 1990s he was spending part of his time in Northern Ireland investigating allegations of RUC collusion with extremist loyalist groups. For all his high-level responsibilities, as he explains in his autobiography, *Not for the Faint-Hearted: My Life Fighting Crime*, Stevens took operational control of what happened next at the south London detective agency.

The walls to the back extension were 'built like a bunker, and it took six months to drill – very slowly – through walls of steel reinforced concrete,' he wrote. 'That surveillance exercise triggered Operation Two Bridges.'[3]

This was in effect the third Daniel Morgan murder inquiry. But why did the operation change its name from Operation Nigeria?

More perplexing is John Stevens' two-page account of Operation Two Bridges. Not only is his hands-on control of such an investigation unusual for a deputy commissioner – it was well below his pay grade – but he fails to mention the Daniel Morgan murder at all in his book, written six years later.

* * *

While the CIB 3 technical team slowly drilled through the thick walls of the bunker in the night, the anti-corruption unit was targeting other corrupt police officers in Rees' and Fillery's circle through a new investigation called Operation Russia.

DC Tom Kingston was a close colleague from SERCS and known as 'Fat Tom' to Rees and Fillery, who were hardly waifs themselves. Kingston was also close to Ray Adams. Although Adams had left the force to become an important security advisor to Rupert Murdoch, Kingston would still perform PNC checks for the former commander, according to contemporaries.

In 1998, Kingston was caught doing one of his illegal checks and then named as a corrupt officer who stole drugs when on police raids. While on suspension pending an investigation, he was employed by Southern Investigations. He would soon get caught up in other illegal activities.[4]

The next arrest from the SERCS circle was Detective Constable Neil Putnam. He'd been one of the people Rees had called on his car phone in the December before Daniel's murder and saw the private detective only two weeks before he was killed. Based at the South Norwood CID office, he contributed several statements to the first murder inquiry: 'The last time I saw Daniel Morgan alive was on 24th February 1987 at the George Public House,' Putnam told murder investigators a few weeks after the murder. 'Again Mr Morgan was drunk and on this occasion was aggressive towards other people in the bar. His remarks were on occasion vindictive and sneering.'

Apart from creating an impression that Daniel deserved to be killed, Putnam also told the first inquiry that Dan had complained of 'threatening phone calls'. Later, he suggested these threats were connected with some investigation Rees and Daniel were doing in the Surrey Docks area, which may or may not have been tied up with a Flying Squad case. No actions came of these tip-offs.

Putnam remained part of the circle of corrupt cops associated with Rees and Fillery, and according to intelligence reports collected the payments from Rees to Duncan Hanrahan for illegal use of the Police National Computer.

Ten years later, DC Neil Putnam was caught up in Operation Russia, an anti-corruption investigation into the SERCS office at East Dulwich which had begun in April 1998 following intelligence offered by Eve Fleckney, a registered informant who detailed a catalogue of corruption among the Dulwich officers.

In July Putnam was arrested for corruption and, like Hanrahan the previous year, he became a resident informant or 'supergrass' with a mass of evidence against other regional crime squad officers, including his fellow detective DC Tom Kingston, who was arrested with two other SERCS detectives for stealing two kilos of amphetamine from a drug dealer during a raid.

Astonishingly, Southern Investigations knew of Neil Putnam's arrest 30 minutes before it happened. Jonathan Rees revealed to Derek Haslam that he had heard of a visit to Putnam's wife, during which DCS Chris Jarrett (who was by then Haslam's handler) tried to persuade her to get her husband to do the 'right thing' and turn Queen's evidence and inform on other corrupt officers.

For all the secrecy and subterfuge of the Ghost Squad, Rees seemed to breach its security with ease. No wonder Haslam wanted backup during their trip to the Norfolk Broads.

Organising the debrief of Putnam was another rising star in the Met, Detective Superintendent John Yates, who – as a deputy assistant commissioner – would play an important part in further Daniel Morgan inquiries. At this point, Yates was interested in Putnam's evidence of corruption against two other SERCS officers, unconnected to Southern Investigations.

In April 2000, Putnam was convicted of conspiracy to supply cannabis and amphetamines, theft, accepting a bribe, perverting the course of justice, conspiracy to commit theft and handling stolen goods, and was given a reduced four-year sentence for cooperating with the anti-corruption team – even though the trial of the two other SERCS officers eventually collapsed.

The story didn't end there. Six years later, on the BBC1's flagship current affairs programme, *Panorama*, Putnam made allegations of corruption around the Stephen Lawrence murder.

Interviewed by Mark Daly in 'The Boys Who Killed Stephen Lawrence', broadcast on July 2006, Putnam alleged that he told his de-brief officers in 1998 that DS John 'OJ' Davidson, who had important roles in the early days of investigating the black teenager's murder, had admitted to being in the pay of Clifford Norris, father of one of the Lawrence murder suspects.

Putnam, who worked with Davidson at SERCS, said Davidson 'looked after the interest' of Clifford Norris' son David during the initial murder investigation, and remarked, 'He's a good little earner'.

Davidson has denied this and no contemporary record from the debrief records this claim. Putnam also alleged that Davidson had been involved in thieving goods after a lorry hijacking in 1994, and involved in a cocaine deal. Davidson was arrested in 1999, but was never charged.

Though the Davidson allegations went nowhere, Putnam did help convict two other South Dulwich SERCS officers from the Southern Investigations circle of corrupt police officers, Detective Constables Tom Reynolds and Tom Kingston. They would eventually be sentenced to 42 months each for stealing two kilograms of speed, 'skimmed off' during a raid in Clapham, south London, in 1995.

* * *

Beyond touching on the same circle of police officers, nothing in Putnam's confession added much to the Daniel Morgan story. But Duncan Hanrahan's arrest did produce an important new lead.

Stephen Warner, the drug dealer involved in the Chiswick ecstasy tablet raid with Duncan Hanrahan, was targeted by an undercover officer who sold him a kilo of cocaine. Warner explained he had another request – a hit job on an associate who was threatening his life. The first undercover officer then recommended a second undercover officer, who took a down payment for the assassination, and then a Browning pistol provided by Warner.

The man Warner wanted killed was none other than Southern Investigations specialist repo-man, Jimmy Cook.

Stephen Warner was arrested on 17th September 1998 and charged with supplying Class A drugs and possession of a firearm with intent to kill. The day after, at Croydon Magistrates Court, he told the police he was willing to assist them on 'a number of matters' including serious criminality and police corruption. He agreed to provide evidence to the Crown in return for a reduction of his prison sentence.

Warner's debriefing began on 30th September 1998, and he would give 12 taped interviews and sign 11 statements, mainly focused on the multiple allegations of corruption around Duncan Hanrahan. But a tape recorded on 1st October 1998 had special significance for the Daniel Morgan murder.

Stephen Warner explained his reason for wanting Jimmy Cook dead: it was to protect himself against Cook and Glenn Vian, who had revealed their role in the axe killing a decade before.

Warner was in prison when Daniel was murdered, and first met Jimmy Cook on his release. A well-known 'face' among the criminal fraternity, Cook was a bouncer on the door of the Cricketer's pub in Sutton, and was also reputed to be working for a private investigation firm in Thornton Heath, which involved repossessing cars and collecting debts. According to Warner, 'this firm was run by ex-police officers by the name of Jon Rees, Duncan Hanrahan and a fat bloke called Sid'. Warner agreed to sell stolen tax discs for Cook.

In 1989 or 1990, Jimmy Cook confided in Stephen Warner about his role in a murder, and claimed that both he and Glenn Vian had been paid by Jon Rees to kill someone.

According to Warner, Cook had told him 'the man who was murdered was either a serving or ex-policeman and had been a partner in the private investigation firm in Thornton Heath'. After an argument with his partners the assassination was planned. Jimmy Cook was paid to drive Glenn Vian to the scene, where the victim would be killed by 'striking him on the head with an axe'.

After the murder, the getaway car was said to have been driven by Cook to a garage in Cheam, south-west London, owned by his friend and fellow co-worker at Southern Investigations, Barry Nash. There it was stored, covered by a tarpaulin. 'Jimmy Cook told me that when things had died down, they had collected the car and destroyed it,' Warner said.

Though Warner did not know the identity of the murder victim, or precisely where he was killed, much of his information fitted with the known facts. He had heard Glenn Vian and Jonathan Rees were arrested for the murder, and 'walked away from it'. Warner described Vian as an 'unsavoury character' and claimed not only had he turned up to Daniel's funeral, but that his kids had been playing with Daniel's kids at a barbecue shortly before the killing.

'Cook told me to show how callous Vines [sic] was,' said Warner. 'One day he could be playing with the victim's kids and then the next day he had stuck an axe in the victim's head.'

Warner would soon wish he had never heard these admissions.

Not long after the confession, Jimmy Cook approached Warner and told him 'that if I ever said anything, Glenn Vines [sic] would kill me, my children and my family.'

The threats apparently escalated a few years later when it became clear Barry 'The Fish' Nash also knew too much.

Sometime in 1994 or 1995, Stephen Warner was sitting in a café when he was spotted by Jimmy Cook, who asked him to come outside for a 'word'. There, Cook grabbed Warner and pushed him up against the café window, angry about the fact that Barry Nash had discovered the car stored in his garage had been used in Daniel's murder.

'Cook gave me fourteen days to kill Barry Nash or he said I would be killed,' Warner told the police. 'I took the threat very seriously, but I told him that I wouldn't kill Barry Nash and said [to Cook]: "You'll have to do what you've got to do then."'

The threats continued. Six months or so later, both Jimmy Cook and Glenn Vian turned up outside Warner's house in Sutton. As Warner got in the back of their car, they repeated the threat: 'They told me that if I ever repeated anything to anyone about the murder, then they would kill me.'

Warner discussed these threats with both Duncan Hanrahan and Barry Nash, who appeared disgusted by the confession, and shocked it had gone this far. It was for this reason he had contracted the undercover officer to kill Jimmy Cook.

Though his evidence was mainly hearsay it still provided key intelligence on a hitherto unknown suspect: Jimmy Cook.[5]

There was contemporaneous evidence to back Warner up. Overlooked until then, mobile phone records obtained during the first murder investigation proved that Jonathan Rees had called Jimmy Cook on his car phone only two days before Daniel was killed.

Warner's confession thus provided a new impetus for the third Daniel Morgan murder investigation.

By 26th January 1999 the bug was working. In a test phase in February the eavesdropping team recorded Rees and Fillery preparing written statements for a civil case against Hampshire Police for his second arrest. They were also overheard discussing how to get Lennon to change his evidence, and sharing intelligence on the debrief of Neil Putnam, and wondering what he knew of the Daniel Morgan murder.

Rees also talked of a notorious enforcer for the north London Adams crime family, who had been arrested for slicing off someone's nose and ear. It was clear Rees was planning to help him in his forthcoming trial, using 'Old Bill' to 'sort things out'.

| In the Dark

January to March 1999

ALASTAIR: Back in London I made one of my regular calls to Roy Clark's office, who had been put in charge of the review promised by Sir Paul Condon. My aim was to pressure the Met into starting a new inquiry.

Calls to Clark reached him via his secretary, June. I'd spoken to her many times in the past. She told me he was in a meeting and that she'd tell him I wanted to speak to him. In the next breath, she revealed a surprise.

'Oh … the Minister is coming to New Scotland Yard over your brother's case,' June said.

'Which minister is that?' I asked, taken aback. 'Is it Alun Michael?' As Minister for Policing he seemed to me the most likely candidate.

I sensed June was clamming up and guessed that she wasn't supposed to tell me this. I tried to extract more information, without success.

Most of that day was spent trying to get in contact with Alun Michael. I knew he'd been made aware of the case through Richard Livsey. After several hours, I got through to someone important enough to pass on a message and was told that 'the Minister' would call me shortly.

I waited for about three hours before Alun Michael finally rang. I explained what I'd heard from Roy Clark's office. To my surprise, he said that he wasn't going to visit Scotland Yard.

'Can you tell me which minister is going to Scotland Yard?' I wondered.

'Talk to your MP about it,' he replied curtly.

'Well, Mr Michael, even if you aren't going to Scotland Yard, I can tell you that after 11 years I'm extremely happy to speak to the minister in charge of policing about police involvement in the murder of my brother.'

'Talk to your MP about it.'

'But Mr Michael, it's been 11 years and this—'

'Talk to your MP about it.'

'Thank you, Mr Michael.'

I put down the phone in no doubt that the Minister for Policing had no desire to talk to me about Dan's murder.

* * *

Half a day had passed since I'd first heard about 'the minister' and I still didn't know who he was. I rang Chris Smith's office. Half an hour later his assistant got back to me and said that Chris *was* the minister in question.

'Do you mean to say he arranged this meeting without telling me?'

'Listen, Alastair, I'm not quite sure how all this happened,' said the assistant defensively, 'but I believe that Chris was invited by the Deputy Commissioner, John Stevens, and Roy Clark to a private briefing on the case.'

'Private briefing?'

'Maybe Chris thought that Stevens and Clark would tell him more if you weren't there. You'll have to talk to Chris about this,' the assistant said.

He couldn't explain why I hadn't been invited or even told about the meeting. I felt sidelined and patronised.

Some days later, Chris wrote to me about the meeting. He explained that he'd been offered the chance of a meeting with John Stevens and Roy Clark on his own, simply to be updated on progress, and he'd decided to accept the offer. He promised he'd write to me immediately after the meeting.

A couple of weeks later the familiar yellow envelope from the House of Commons dropped through our letterbox. Chris seemed to be convinced that Roy Clark was making a determined effort to investigate the murder. He ended the letter by saying: 'They did tell me there were a number of hopeful leads they were pursuing, although they were unable to give me details or (of course) any guarantee of success. But I have to say that I felt able to accept their *bona fides*.'

I thought Chris was being naïve and that John Stevens and Roy Clark were just trying to pacify him. I had no idea at all at the time what was really going on behind the scenes and it took many months before I had any inkling of what the Met were up to.

After this letter, I dismissed the meeting at the Yard as an attempt to flannel my MP and thought little more about it.

* * *

In the meantime there had been an important development. One of the police officers who gave evidence at the inquest had been convicted of several serious corruption offences. Former Detective Constable Duncan Hanrahan was to be sentenced at the Old Bailey.

Hanrahan had been used by the police in the first investigation into Dan's murder as a 'double agent', but it had always been difficult to tell which side he was really on. He'd been friendly with Rees before the murder and had carried on the relationship afterwards. Hanrahan was also the officer on duty on the night in 1986 when Rees was supposedly robbed of the takings from Belmont Car Auctions. His evidence at the inquest indicated that he doubted Rees' story.

Duncan Hanrahan had left the police some years after Dan's murder. In 1994 he'd started a private investigations company. It finally became clear that he was definitely on the dark side when he was arrested after openly trying to corrupt a CIB officer in 1997. His clients were a pair of criminals who were hoping he could sabotage their prosecutions for fraud and GBH.

I decided to visit the Old Bailey to watch Hanrahan being sent down on 9th March 1999. His sentencing was to take place in one of the older courts and I climbed the flights of steps up to the public gallery.

The proceedings were very short. The judge read out the crimes Hanrahan had been convicted of. As well as attempting to pervert the course of justice by bribing a police officer, he was also convicted of the theft and sale of 40,000 ecstasy tablets. The judge, Mr Justice Blofeld, said: 'The offences strike at the very roots of justice. If society is to have a future, the police force must be above corruption.'

Hanrahan received eight years and four months' jail. I was surprised at the leniency of the sentence. Hanrahan didn't exactly look happy, but then he didn't look too upset either. He'd spent a long time on remand, so with good behaviour he'd probably be out in two or three years. I left the court feeling that Hanrahan knew much more about Dan's murder than he was saying.

* * *

'I'll represent you, Alastair,' Raju Bhatt told me on the day I engaged him as my solicitor, 'but don't expect justice.'

We'd needed the support of a London lawyer for some time, but I hadn't managed to find one in time for our meeting with the commissioner. My income was small, £15k at the most, so I wondered if there was any kind of legal aid available. I doubted it, but I'd decided to approach a lawyer to find out.

The first man that sprang to mind was Raju Bhatt, whom I'd met when I saw Paul Goodridge at Birnberg & Co. I rang Birnberg and asked to speak to him. The receptionist told me that Raju had just started his own firm, Bhatt Murphy.

Raju's offices were in what used to be an old shop premises in Pitfield Street, near Shoreditch. The walls were stacked from floor to ceiling with files.

The name Shiji Lapite jumped out at me. I'd read about his death in custody. He'd been stopped by a police officer on 16th December 1994 for 'acting suspiciously'. A struggle followed. Lapite was put in the back of a police van and was dead within minutes. The cause of death was asphyxia. At the inquest, officers admitted kicking Mr Lapite in the head, biting him and placing him in a neck-hold. The inquest jury returned a unanimous verdict of unlawful killing. Four years had passed and still no action had been taken against the police.

I'd been impressed by Raju when I met him at Birnbergs. He had a clear, meticulous mind and a way of explaining complicated things in an easy manner. Seeing the kind of cases he worked on had convinced me that he was the man I wanted to represent my family. But how could I afford his fees?

Raju offered me a chair and cleared a space among the papers on his desk. Unlike most solicitors, he was informally dressed in a casual shirt and tie with his top button undone; his sleeves were rolled up. Raju was already familiar with Daniel's story from his knowledge of the Paul Goodridge case. He asked how things had developed since we'd last met.

I told him about our meeting with Condon, the promise of a review and the meeting between Chris Smith, John Stevens and Roy Clark. Raju sat back in his chair and rolled an Old Holborn cigarette from a leather pouch as he listened.

I knew I had to broach the question of money as soon as possible.

'Before we go any further, Raju, I need to be honest with you about money. My earnings are small.'

Raju interrupted me. He explained that most of his clients were inner-city families who could no more afford lawyers' fees than I could. He told me that he received public funding for most of the work that he carried out. Then he confirmed my suspicion that there was no legal aid for people in my position.

'I'll act for you pro-bono,' he said. 'It's such an amazing story.'

'I can't do that,' I replied. 'You can't work for me for nothing. Just let me pay you as much as I can afford.'

We agreed. I was elated at finding a solicitor whom I instinctively trusted, and relieved that we'd come to a financial arrangement that was feasible.

Then he told me not to expect justice.

'What do you mean?' I asked him, suddenly perplexed. 'I mean, that's why I'm here. That's why I've been fighting so long!'

Raju paused. 'Alastair, most of the work I do involves trying to get the truth out of the state. I want you to be aware from the outset that the odds are heavily stacked against you. I'll do the best I can to help you, but I can never make any promises,' he told me.

'Of course, I understand that,' I said. 'I know you can't suddenly make everything right. It's a battle, I know. But we're up for it.'

'You must feel that you can walk away from this at any point,' he continued. 'You can't let "the case" stop you living your lives. These boxes,' he added, pointing at the shelves to his right, 'are full of stories of good families whose lives have been taken over battling with the police, the prison service, mental health institutions and so on. In the end, many feel that they have to walk away.

'It's not a reflection of the depth of injustice they've suffered or of how much they cared about the person they lost,' Raju explained. 'It's about being realistic over how difficult it can be to get satisfactory answers out of the establishment.'

Getting Raju's assistance was one of the luckiest things that ever happened to us. The anger I felt towards the police was often overwhelming. Raju is measured and cool. He speaks calmly and I've never heard him raise his voice. In fact, the more scathingly he speaks about something, the softer his speech. In short, he is the complete opposite of me.

Raju didn't start out studying law. He completed a degree at the London School of Oriental and African Studies in 1981. While he was a student, south London was a tinderbox of racial tension.

In April 1979, Margaret Thatcher was on the brink of being elected. People had just lived through the Labour government's Winter of Discontent and the Conservatives were proposing radical economic reforms. The National Front used this to advance its case to get Black and Asian people 'sent back to where they came from'. They vowed to raze Southall to the ground and to preserve it as a typical English village. On St George's Day they staged an election meeting at the Southall Town Hall.

The fact that councillors didn't cancel the meeting caused outrage and a protest was staged. New Zealander Blair Peach, a 25-year-old campaigner against the far right, joined the rally. The protest turned violent. Peach was knocked unconscious and died in hospital the next day. Fourteen witnesses said they saw a police officer strike him but no one was charged. Blair Peach's killing may have gone unpunished but 700 protesters were arrested for various offences and 350 of them were charged.

Raju worked as volunteer helping those who had been arrested in Southall and in other racial conflicts that erupted across the country that summer. He went on to study law and qualified in 1988. He then worked at Birnberg & Co. for ten years before setting up Bhatt Murphy with Fiona Murphy in 1998. His help and support for our cause would turn out to be a lifesaver.

CHAPTER 26	InfoWars

April to September 1999

The evidential stage of the probe into Southern Investigations began on 15th April 1999. Over the next five months, under the supervision of the Deputy Commissioner, John Stevens, CIB 3 recorded conversations from the suspects, and gathered evidence of 46 potential crimes, most of them involving British journalists. In other words, Rees and Fillery were caught committing a crime every other working day, and even this is probably an underestimate.

Derek Haslam told his CIB 3 handlers that the surveillance team would have been better advised placing a bug in the Victory pub rather than the Grange Road offices, as Jonathan Rees and Sid Fillery conducted most of their business there after lunchtime. It's certainly clear from intelligence reports that the public house was a clearing house for corrupt cops wanting to sell information.

The *News of the World*'s chief investigations reporter Mazher Mahmood was spotted there by an informant in 1998 trying to buy a story from a plainclothes detective about a dowry in the form of livestock.

As the first day of the recordings proved, Mahmood, the *News of the World*'s chief investigative reporter and a close friend of Rebekah Brooks, was still working with Rees and Fillery regularly. At this point in April, Southern Investigations were providing bodyguards for John Alford's trial at Snaresbrook Crown Court, where the Fake Sheikh was due to give evidence.

If the connections between Rupert Murdoch's best-selling newspaper and the crime and corruption of Southern Investigations weren't already disturbing enough, Garry Vian and Jimmy Cook were initially suggested as Mahmood's personal protection team; three murder suspects working directly for the Fake Sheikh.

In the end Garry Vian was backed up by another local hard man, ferrying Mazher Mahmood between the News International headquarters at Wapping and Snaresbrook Crown Court.

John Alford, the young actor who decided to conduct his own defence, recalls being faced with constant death threats throughout the trial. Two similar heavy-set bodyguards were also remarked upon by the judge at the trial of another one of Mahmood victims – Lord Hardwicke.[1]

Throughout the duration of the probe into Southern Investigations, Rees remained relaxed about his criminality, openly bragging about his ability to subvert the criminal justice system.

'I've worked with solicitors,' he boasted to a client on the phone in those first few days. 'I've got QCs, I've got judges, I've got people I can pick up the phone to any time of the day and say "Can you do something for me, please?" and it's done.'

The same day Rees could be heard explaining how easy it was to obtain Land Registry details, mobile and landline billing, and personal bank accounts. Three days later he confirmed the pricing: two to three months of phone data costs £375, or for an express job 'in four days, it's £500'.

Though still working with Mahmood and the *News of the World*, Rees and Fillery had by now established another major source of press income.

Alex's Marunchak's successor as chief crime reporter, Gary Jones, had now followed Piers Morgan over to *The Daily Mirror*, where they were also eager to use his dark arts.

On the phone to Jones, Rees did nothing to hide his status as a criminal suspect. Indeed, he celebrated it, telling him they were being monitored by CIB 3, 'but they didn't catch us'. Just as during the first Morgan murder investigation, Rees was using his friends in the press to discredit the lead investigators, in this case the Commissioner himself. Rees explained that he planned to retaliate by releasing 'all the information on Condon'.

Rees was, even 12 years after Daniel's murder, still revelling about the way he had used the media to undermine police officers in the first inquiry. Now he and Fillery were actively trying to work out what was in the confessions of supergrasses Putnam and Hanrahan, and checking there were no leaks from associates like Barry The Fish or the repo man, Jimmy Cook.

And just as in 1987, Rees was planning his own legal moves against the police, launching his own civil action against them, this time for wrongful arrest during the Hampshire Inquiry, ten years previously.

Then, on the morning of Thursday, 9th January, a 38-year-old man called Simon James arrived at the Thornton Heath office. A wealthy jeweller, James was estranged from his wife, Kim, and was seeking custody of their young son – which was unlikely given his criminal record. Rees immediately arranged surveillance on the woman using his former SERCS contacts.

The next day Rees was checking on the movements of Kim James and describing openly how, as well as corrupt police officers, he had Customs and Excise officers in his pocket. 'It's very, very rare you come across a bent customs officer,' he explained to another client. 'We have got a couple in there that will take a drink to give information and they are both ex Met Police.'

On Friday, 14th May 1999, it suddenly became clear that the Southern Investigations surveillance of mother Kim James was a preparation for something much more sinister. Since his wife seemed to be living a blameless life, Rees suggested to Simon James there could be another way to get custody of his son.

'I just wondered ... We can do things,' Rees told the jeweller.

'I'm not being funny,' James replied, sounding confused, 'I'd rather you talk to me straight.'

'I just wondered if it might be worthwhile, going in and planting some gear,' Rees continued. 'Now, having said that it's done, it's available, but it costs.'

'I'm not averse to doing anything,' James replied.

'What we are doing is fraught,' Rees warned him. 'Me and you could end up doing porridge as well, if we get caught out.'

'Yeah, I mean, you're professionals,' James agreed. 'That's why I have come here ...'

'All right, I'll have a chat to our people today.'

As well as a conspiracy to break into a young mother's apartment and 'plant' something, other random crimes were caught on tape that month – Rees advising someone of how to handle stolen goods, another how to launder Scottish money through bureau de change outlets. It soon became apparent to the CIB 3 surveillance team that Rees and Fillery themselves were engaged in money laundering for the underworld.

One of their key contacts at the time was the manager of a local Barclays bank who they aptly nicknamed 'Rob the Bank'. The bug picked up a conspiracy to elude UK drug trafficking legislation.

On 18th May 1999, Sid Fillery and suspended detective Tom Kingston deposited £140,000 in cash in the private detective agency's Barclays bank account. This was then transferred to the account of the wife of a friend of his former brother-in-law, Garry Vian.

Jackie Ward was married to a major drugs importer, James Ward, and she claimed to deal in arts and antiquities. Two months later, another £182,000 went through the same route, this time purportedly for the sale of a David Hockney painting. The money laundering was investigated by the police, but no charges were ever brought against Jackie Ward.

* * *

For the rest of May 1999 Rees was working out how to set up Simon James' estranged wife.[2] To guarantee that she went to prison and her husband got custody of their 15-month-old child, Kim James would have to be fitted up with enough Class A drugs to convict her for 'intent to supply'.

The price of the job was rising steeply. Early the next month Rees would take £4,000 in cash to 'bury' Kim James –it would rise to £18,000 in total. But as Rees reminded the jeweller, 'The ultimate goal is she goes away for ever and the only time she gets access is when she's supervised.'

After a discussion with Tom Kingston about burgling Kim James' flat, Sid Fillery suggested an easier route: plant drugs in her car instead.

The same day, news came in that Duncan Hanrahan had done his deal with CIB 3, and was 'happy' with an eight-year sentence. Rees was also relieved Hanrahan's debrief appeared to be over. 'He's the one we thought they were using to try and nick me for the murder,' Rees mocked. 'He'll come out with a little bit of bollocks, but I will be able to pick the truth out of it.'

* * *

Though they never discovered the bug, Rees and Fillery were suspicious they were being investigated, and conducted regular counter-surveillance sweeps of their homes and offices.

Rees was then caught by the probe telling ex-SERCS officer, Alec Leighton, who ran Mayfare Associates that the police were 'massively after us' and they would all need to be 'super surveillance conscious'.

Despite the caution, Rees was back in business with his main clients – the British press. One of the stories based on information Rees had illegally obtained from Prince Michael of Kent's bank account had now attracted a legal suit. Piers Morgan's lieutenant, Gary Jones, was in contact with Rees, asking him to meet *The Daily Mirror*'s legal team.

Just as at the *News of the World*, Mirror Group Newspapers were dealing with a murder suspect at a very high management level. Both Derek Haslam's intelligence and the covert listening device caught Rees claiming he sold stories to both *The Daily Express* and *The Daily Mail*.

Rees was also working with another newspaper, *The Sunday Mirror*. To one of its journalists, who was a regular visitor that summer of 1999, Douglas Kempster, Rees displayed his skills as a computer hacker, accessing the database of *The Sunday Times* for info.

Kempster, a former employee of the *News of the World*, also wanted Rees to provide details from the bank accounts of Sophie Rhys-Jones, wife of Prince Edward, to see if she had been paid off by *Hello!* magazine.

After the shooting of BBC TV and *Crimewatch* presenter Jill Dando in the spring of 1999, Rees was in the race to get leaks from the murder inquiry. 'There's big stories,' he was recorded as saying, 'nearly every day with good information on the Jill Dando murder. We found out one of our bestest friends is also on that fucking murder squad, but he ain't told us nothing.'

Rees was also still close to Alex Marunchak, meeting him and a couple of Irish Garda police officers visiting the UK for the classic annual horse race – the Derby. Rees wanted Marunchak to sign an affidavit to support his civil claim against Hampshire Police. Fillery was compiling similar affidavits for Gary Jones and Douglas Kempster to sign.

The evidence of extensive criminal activity was mounting up, and yet the police had done nothing about the Daniel Morgan invesitgation. And now the Kim James' project was ready to go.

Through an intermediary, a former cop called Nigel Grayston, Rees and Fillery had found another corrupt police officer to help with the fit-up. DC Austin Warnes boosted his income, like so many cops in the Southern Investigations circle, by stealing drugs during police raids. Like Rees and Fillery, he provided information about ongoing investigations to professional criminals.

'He would be able to tell you what statements the police had obtained,' one underworld figure called 'Mick' told Tony Thomson at *The Observer*, 'who they had interviewed, which properties were under surveillance, which phones were being tapped – the lot. You would pay between £5,000 and £10,000 a time, but it was well worth it.'

Based at Bexleyheath, Warnes' other speciality was the 'fake informant' scam, where rivals were targeted, rewards claimed and information gleaned through registering a member of the underworld as a confidential human intelligence source.

One of Warnes' most important fake informants was David Courtney, a celebrity gangster who had organised the funeral of Ronnie Kray and faced ten court appearances from 1985 to 1999, and been found not guilty every time. Courtney's best-selling autobiography, *Stop the Ride, I Want to Get Off*, was inspiration for Vinny Jones's character in the 1998 film *Lock, Stock and Two Smoking Barrels*.

Warnes used Courtney's code name Tommy Mack and entered intelligence that Kim James was a suspected drug dealer on the criminal intelligence system, CRIMINT. The intelligence was then sent on to the local Wimbledon Police Station for action.

That weekend, Rees initiated the next part of the set-up, calling his repossession expert, Jimmy Cook, to plant the drugs. Late the same night, Cook arrived in his BMW at Kim James' Mitcham address. A CIB 3 team filmed him wearing gloves, using a tool to gain access to James' Fiat Punto, opening the driver's door and then the rear door, before wiping the car down and driving off.

According to Deputy Commissioner John Stevens, it was his decision to remove Kim James' Fiat Punto to a secure location so that it could be checked for Class A drugs. Secreted inside the car, CIB 3 found a small box marked 'Pfizer' containing 15 paper packages of white powder which tested positive for cocaine (18% or 8.6g in total). The officers replaced the wraps with bicarbonate and returned the car to its parking place.

As expected, DC Warnes then passed on urgent information to the Wimbledon Tactical Support Group leader that a very reliable informant had told him that Kim James was hiding up to 30 or 40 wraps, well concealed within her car.

A few hours later, Wimbledon Police knocked on James' door with a search warrant. The young mother fainted with shock. After a search of her vehicle a plastic bag with seven wraps was found in an air vent. James exclaimed, 'He's trying to take my child, I know he is!'

The following week Simon James returned to the Southern Investigations office for the final pay-off, during which Rees explained how, instead of planting drugs in the flat, they'd decided on Kim James' car. The jeweller now sought immediate custody of their 15-month-old son through his barrister.

* * *

On Sunday, 20th June, Simon James absconded with his son. On the Monday, Rees warned James that police wanted to interview him over his ex-wife's allegations he was behind the drug bust. Rees urged his client not to cooperate.

By the Tuesday, Kim James had secured a 'Seek and Find' order from the High Court and two days later her husband was tracked down to Newport in South Wales, where he surrendered their son to the authorities. Kim was reunited with her son that morning.

Meanwhile, CIB 3 had bugged Warnes' car and were putting pressure on the Detective Constable through his bosses, who now wanted confirmation of the tip-off from Jimmy Mack. Warnes set up a meeting with David Courtney to explain the tricky situation. An anti-corruption command surveillance team followed him to the Old Mill Public House in Plumstead the next day, where Courtney arrived on a Harley-Davidson.

Clearly suspicious he was being set up, Courtney moved the meeting to Plumstead Common, and returned with his wife on the back of his motorbike. The CIB team noted that she was photographing her husband and Warnes together and noticed that Courtney was 'unhappy with Warnes' and was 'poking him in the chest with his finger'.

Reluctantly, Courtney agreed to confirm to Warnes' boss that he was the source of the Kim James' tip-off. The subsequent meeting was recorded both by the bug in Warnes' car and the senior officer.

When he returned home, Warnes checked the underside of his BMW to find a hidden tracking device.

Back at Southern Investigations, Jonathan Rees was beginning to sense something was wrong. The police didn't seem to have analysed the 15 wraps found in Kim James' car yet. Meanwhile, her allegation that her husband planted the drugs had changed the focus of the investigation.

Panic was beginning to set in. The other ex-police officer in on the scam, Nigel Grayston, feared he could lose his job and get arrested.

As Simon James arrived for a crisis summit, Fillery astutely observed that the informant might be the weak link. Rees was convinced the anti-corruption investigation was behind their misfortune and blamed the Met Commissioner: 'Condon needs to be topped, all he's done is hurt the people who don't deserve to be hurt.'

The following week, with the Kim James' investigation unaccountably stalled, the man who planted the drugs, Jimmy Cook, had more bad news for Rees and Fillery. Visiting the bugged-up offices, Cook told them that he'd been randomly stopped while driving a month ago, and days before a neighbour had warned him Scotland Yard wanted to use their house as an observation post.

Cook reiterated that he had placed 15 sachets of drugs in Kim James' car. Rees confirmed the police found them. 'If so, what's the problem?' Cook demanded. Rees reassured him it was just Warnes' boss wanting to interview the informant and promised to check on the police computers to see if either of them were 'of interest' to any new investigation.

Their main conclusion was that the police activity was due to the contract Steven Warner had put on Jimmy Cook's life. Barry Nash was suspected of having supplied a photo of Cook for the killing. Rees clearly knew Warner's plot was in retaliation for threats to the lives of Warner and Nash. 'You said you and Glenn were doing something but it never happened,' Rees noted.

As he left the office, Jimmy Cook reassured Jonathan Rees: 'What we've done, that's between you and me.'

* * *

Ten weeks into the evidential part of the Southern Investigations probe, there was sufficient evidence to arrest Rees and Fillery for a number of offences, from perverting the course of justice to money laundering. But it was only in early July that the Two Bridges team decided to activate the other main part of their investigation, the third Daniel Morgan murder inquiry.

With the surveillance in place, DCS David Wood activated a 'prompt' or trigger event to excite comments that would be caught by the bug in the offices. That prompt was an article, partly inspired by Stephen Warner's admissions about the getaway car, in *The Daily Telegraph* on 2nd July 1999.

July to August 1999

ALASTAIR: In early July 1999 my phone rang rather earlier than usual. Kirsteen's father, Malcolm, was on the line.

'Hi Alastair. I just thought I'd tell you that there's an article in today's *Telegraph* about your brother's murder.'

'What? What does it say?'

'Apparently, the police have obtained some sort of intelligence about the murder,' Malcolm said. 'It seems they know the identity of the getaway driver and the type of car used.'

I was completely taken aback. 'That's the first I've heard about that,' I told him. 'They haven't said a word to us about this.' Though the news excited me, it also made me angry that the police had told *The Telegraph* before telling us. 'I'll run down to the newsagent's now and buy a copy.'

By the time I returned home, I'd already read the short article. It was just as Malcolm had said: a source at Scotland Yard had informed *The Telegraph* that the Met knew the identity of the getaway driver, the make and colour of the car that was used, and how it had been disposed of. But why hadn't they told us? How had they come by this information? I rang my solicitor Raju Bhatt and told him. He said he'd call Roy Clark for an explanation. It was good to have a solicitor asking questions for me for a change.

I waited for half an hour before Raju called back.

'Roy Clark said that he would come around to my offices in two weeks to explain, Alastair,' he told me.

'Two weeks! But Raju, they've left us stewing for years and now they've got something important to tell us, they are making us wait for two weeks!'

'I know, Alastair. But that's what he said.'

'They've got form on this kind of thing. Both the Met and Hampshire. Why should we find out *after* the media?'

'I did point out to him that the family were very upset that *The Telegraph* had been informed before they were,' Raju said. 'Clark was apologetic, but he said the earliest he could come was two weeks from today.'

The following days were agonising as we waited to find out what the police knew. Who had given them this information? Who was the getaway driver, and what about the car? The phone was busy all week as I discussed this new information with Mum and others.

In the event, Raju rang me after only one week to tell me that Roy Clark had shown up totally unexpected, saying he'd made a mistake with his diary. I didn't own a mobile phone at the time and Raju hadn't been able to contact me. To my relief, Raju had decided to hear Clark's account of events in my absence.

Clark told him that they not only knew who drove the getaway car but had also identified the man who wielded the axe. For years, we thought we'd known about Rees' and Fillery's roles but we were never sure who had actually dealt the fatal blow.

'Clark's going to return in one week so that he can speak to you personally,' Raju added.

I don't know how we managed to hold on for another week before we got to meet Clark. Mum made the trip up to London and Kirsteen managed to get off work early so that she could attend the meeting in Raju's office.

I was a ball of nervous energy. We were finally going to hear who killed my brother. After the introductions, Roy Clark impressed on us the need for absolute confidentiality. Investigations were at a delicate stage, he emphasised, and what he was about to tell us could be shared with no one. We all agreed to that.

Clark explained that they had planted a listening device in Southern Investigations' offices. He believed they now had a true picture of what happened on the night of the murder. As Daniel left the pub, associates of Rees were waiting in the car park. Glenn Vian then struck Daniel with an axe. He left the scene in a getaway car driven by another man. The getaway car was hidden in a garage and later destroyed.

The getaway driver was a man we'd never heard of – someone called Jimmy Cook. Clark would not name the person who hid the car. We agreed to refer to him as 'garage-man'. However, I did know the man Roy Clark had just named as my brother's killer: Glenn Vian was one of Rees' brothers-in-law. I'd met him with his brother Garry at Dan's office, where they were doing some building work. The Vian brothers were also Rees' bodyguards on the night of the Belmont robbery.

The meeting then turned in a different direction. There were going to be arrests … but not for the murder. Clark said they now had good evidence that Rees and others were guilty of serious unrelated criminal offences. He said he was not able to tell us about these.

Mum interrupted him with a question: 'Mr Clark, is Fillery one of the people who's going to be arrested?'

'No, Mrs Hulsmann, we don't think Fillery is involved in this unrelated offence,' he replied. 'Nor do we have any indication that he was involved in the murder.'

I could see Mum's anger as Clark continued, saying he was keeping an open mind about police involvement.

Meanwhile, Jimmy Cook, the man named as the getaway driver, would be arrested with Rees. There was a possibility that 'garage-man' would be arrested too. This would give the police an opportunity to try to get someone to talk about the murder.

We'd learnt more about the murder in half an hour than we had in the past ten years. I think we must have been shell-shocked during the meeting. It was only afterwards that we realised there were so many questions we should have asked.

Just who was this Jimmy Cook, believed to be the getaway driver? And what was this serious, unrelated offence?

July to September 1999

The impact of the *Telegraph* article on the Southern Investigations office was immediate.

Fillery was the first to be tipped off. Around 10am on the morning of 2nd July 1999, he told Rees to pull up page nine of *The Daily Telegraph* on the computer. Together, they read out the section about the disposal of the getaway car – 'whatever getaway means'.

To Fillery, none of this directly implicated Rees because the mobile phone records located him firmly in his BMW for the two hours around the murder. 'I suppose that is good because everybody knows where you were, you know,' he reassured his business partner. 'Nobody is disputing where you were following the murder so you can't be driving any getaway cars.' However, the former detective sergeant added the warning: 'You'll have to be on guard about telephone calls obviously,' he told Rees. They both noted that the *Telegraph* article mentioned a 'strong suspect' and a possible 'management committee behind this murder'.

Rees was immediately onto Jimmy Cook.

At 11.01am Rees left a message on his mobile: 'Hello Jimmy, It's J.R. here, give me a call ...' He then slammed down the phone, cursing: 'Fuck!'

Soon he was leaving urgent messages for Jimmy Cook's family and cross-checking with his media contacts.

'Hello Jim, there's a funny old story in *The Telegraph* today,' Rees said, reading out passages from the article. 'I've phoned the reporter ... I'm in the office over the weekend if you're about ...'

Alec Leighton was next to be informed. The former SERCS detective-turned-private-investigator agreed the getaway car couldn't be his BMW: 'So, they think it is someone else,' Rees agreed, speculating the police would not arrest or interview him. 'Fucking wankers!' he continued. 'No witnesses, no forensic evidence.'

The rest of the day, apparently reassured he didn't face immediate arrest, Rees continued with his media contacts, trying to pitch a story 'involving Noye, prostitutes, drugs and MPs and all that type of thing' which required .videos and pictures to 'shop around' for the highest price. He carried on making inquiries for Douglas Kempster on *The Sunday Mirror* and the husband of a journalist doing a story for *The Daily Mail.*

It wasn't until nearly 3pm that Rees finally got hold of Jimmy Cook and took him through the contents of the article, even though Cook had never been mentioned.

* * *

Through the rest of July, Rees was still working on his civil claim against the Hampshire Constabulary, paying particular attention to the bookkeeper who provided key evidence.

'The coup that the Met had was to get Kev Lennon on their side,' Rees told an unknown caller, wondering if they could get him to say he was lying.

Suspended SERCS detective Tom Kingston was soon back in the office to discuss with Fillery his problem: the 'official drugs jobs' that he and OJ Davidson had been arrested for. He also wanted to know about the new intelligence in the Daniel Morgan murder.

'We read this fucking article in *The Telegraph*, didn't we?' Fillery told Kingston. 'Well, what that means, who knows? I'd say it was good news because nobody's ever alleged that Jon was driving the getaway vehicle.'

Fillery also told Kingston that Southern Investigations was being helped by their major client, a senior executive by now at the *News of the World.* 'We've obviously … we've read all the statements,' Fillery told him, 'and Marunchak has said he's right on top of it. He'd know more about it, and he said he'd never heard of a getaway vehicle. Nobody's mentioned it until now.'

The suspended cop, former detective and private eye were then joined by Doug Kempster. The four men pored over photographs of the Morgan murder, discussed Daniel's injuries, the torn trousers and the two bags of Golden Wonder crisps he apparently left on the cold tarmac of the darkened car park.

Ten days later, a call into Rees from Mazher Mahmood confirmed that, despite mounting investigations and the arrests of their associates, both partners in Southern Investigations were still working for Rupert Murdoch's star journalist.

The Daily Mirror seemed sanguine about the new allegations too: Rees and Fillery were soon celebrating placing a story about the former Conservative Minister Jonathan Aitken in Piers Morgan's paper. But the private detectives were sufficiently concerned to consider changing the name of the company yet again. And there was still the unresolved situation with Simon James.

When the jeweller arrived at the offices to see what was happening with his estranged wife's criminal investigation, Rees lied to him that the drugs in her car tested positive and advised him to contact social services as his ex would receive a custodial sentence for the drugs found in her possession. But Rees was still sufficiently suspicious of the whole affair to ask James to get phone-billing records of the calls Kim had made to ensure she wasn't in contact with CIB officers.

But what of the other alleged conspirators in Daniel's murder?

Simon James' visit was followed by that of Rees' former brother-in-law, Glenn Vian, and his wife, Kim. They were told by Rees that he checked his own name, and Fillery and the Vian brothers, on the sensitive police 'Box' INFOS system to make sure there were no police investigations into them. That month Glenn and Jimmy Cook had been flagged up, but no one at Southern Investigations.

Having warned Glenn to keep his 'phone clean and be careful where you go', Rees expressed relief that his name was not on the 'Box' police computer – 'Makes a change, them not chasing me'. (Rees charged his former brother-in-law £100 for this information.)

'I reckon it's most likely to be over that Warner thing,' Rees reassured Glenn, referring to the planned hit job Stephen Warner had been arrested for in response to death threats from Jimmy Cook and Glenn.

'Yeah, that's going back years when we did that,' Glenn mused.

* * *

Throughout late July and the rest of August, Rees and Fillery continued their regular criminal activities as if they were somehow immune. Rees joked to one caller about selling illegally procured police documents: 'I've got two-thirds of the Met trying to lock me up and the other third are trying to nick me for murder.'

While Fillery was talking to a journalist called Sylvia, Rees was in regular contact with Gary Jones, the senior *Daily Mirror* journalist to whom he was trying to sell a story of a Special Escort Group VIP protection officer.

Paul Valentine had been allegedly caught by a CIB 2 sting in a gym for steroid abuse and 'shagging Palace staff' while on duty. Rees was offering an exclusive for *The Mirror*, with a kiss and tell from the officer under investigation, who could be a future source of great stories as the Special Escort Group also looked after the Prime Minister and Deputy Prime Minister.

'I've just tried to say to him, I said we will blame the bird for it,' Rees said of the sexual allegations, 'our man is a senior man, you know. At the moment, he is running around with Tony,' Rees told Jones excitedly. 'Tony Blair ... Mr Tony Blair.' Rees claimed that Valentine had overheard the Prime Minister say on the phone 'that fucking bastard John Prescott is getting on my fucking nerves'. The PM then apologised for his bad language.

The Special Escort cop was also 'very close' to Tom Kingston, Rees told Jones. 'He is the one that got that magazine I faxed.'

Though the reference was to the confidential intelligence publication that detailed ongoing investigations and secret high-level operations, *The Police Gazette*, which Kingston had procured despite being on suspension pending a criminal investigation, the Mirror Group obviously shared this resource across various titles because journalist Douglas Kempster was a major purchaser of *Police Gazettes* from Rees and Fillery.

But then Kempster had a problem with the confidential publications. He rang Rees in a panic to tell him that his editor had lost a copy: 'I can't believe it – he's fucking thrown it out – the fucking wanker. Why did he take it home?'

Kingston, who was in the office, warned Rees that Kempster had to get it back: 'or else he won't get any more'.

'Fucking hell,' Rees was heard exclaiming to Kempster when he turned up at the office. 'I'm having heart attacks over these fucking things.' The *Sunday Mirror* journalist agreed: 'I know, it's terrible, innit? I daren't let the bloody thing out of my sight.'

Kempster agreed to pay £200 to make up for the lost edition of *The Police Gazette*.

For all the lucrative press work, the ongoing CIB 3 investigations were never far from the private detective's mind. Rees spent much of the summer ranting about Neil Putnam 'grassing' up all of his 'decent colleagues'.

'They're just fucking riding roughshod all over the fucking legal process,' protested Rees, hoping a series of related trials would collapse because of problems in Putnam's evidence. 'I hope that fucking wanker gets fucking cancer,' he went on. 'Do the decent thing and fucking hang himself in a cell!'

At the end of July, Sid Fillery was away in France, working on a story about illegal immigrants with Mazher Mahmood. He would charge the *News of the World* £1,488.72 for that work – one of the largest single invoices the firm raised in that year.[1]

With Fillery away, Rees was busy going through the costs of extracting billing data from the Orange Mobile network and explaining the economics of the dark arts in the British press. *The Sunday Mirror, Daily Mirror* and *The Express* 'don't spend fortunes researching and they don't get involved in in-depth investigations,' Rees told a caller. Whereas they received £550 for a half-page story in *The Sunday Mirror*, the *News of the World* would have paid £1,500.

In these few months alone the agency sent 66 invoices to Murdoch's Sunday tabloid to a total value of £13,000 – all but one of them addressed to Alex Marunchak.

'There's no one pays like the *News of the World* do,' Rees marvelled.

Two days later, while talking about selling another story to Alex Marunchak, Rees admitted he made a lot of them up.

'I can tell fucking brilliant lies,' Rees laughed to one caller. 'I like telling lies. It's good, it's fun, telling lies … Sometimes I tell lies for no reason at all … This fucking bollocks coming out of my mouth is all lies.'

* * *

With Fillery back from his trip to France with the Fake Sheikh, somehow he had procured a witness statement from the supergrass Neil Putnam case and began to pull it apart.

Rees meanwhile was busy procuring confidential details about potential targets using Marunchak's connections at the Passport Office. (Marunchak billed Southern Investigations regularly for these 'consultancy' services, which included vehicle checks.)

Then there was the money laundering. Rees was caught on tape boasting about helping the wife of James Ward, a drug dealer associated with Garry Vian, to hide their illicit earnings. 'They got these other accounts with loads of money in it which they hadn't declared to the Old Bill,' Rees explained. 'So, we give our old bank man a fucking good drink for it and he just kept the accounts away from the Old Bill.'

As if the stench of corruption and criminality wasn't already overpowering, Rees was also boasting about 'sorting things out' for the Adams, the north London crime family, whose prime enforcer had badly mutilated a victim: 'We got our man off,' Rees bragged, 'the chopping the bloke's ear and nose off.'

That August, Mazher Mahmood's story about illegal immigration was published, along with another by Marunchak based on a confidential Special Branch bulletin sourced from the Special Escort Group source. And though the roaring trade with the *News of the World* continued, Rees and Fillery were acutely aware their stories could be stolen.

A tip-off from a former police driver that New Labour's foreign secretary, Robin Cook, was having an extramarital affair had been handed over to the Sunday tabloid's in-house journalists. 'Alex took us off it and put some other people on the surveillance,' Rees rued to Gary Jones. 'Yeah, pissed us off ... It was that "Brad" ... You know, the new firm "Brad"?' he continued, referring to Mazher Mahmood's new dedicated in-house photographer, Bradley Page.

The next day, even *The Mirror* was causing problems when their accounts department started querying some of Southern Investigations' invoices. Though the newspaper had already paid out £16,981 that year, there was still £23,381 outstanding on invoices to Mark Thomas and Gary Jones.

In a long and angry follow-up conversation about the details of invoices with *The Daily Mirror*'s Gary Jones, Rees began to lose it. 'This is tiresome, fucking tiresome,' he complained. 'Well, because we are not going to put the numbers in there, because what we are doing is illegal, isn't it? You know I don't want people coming in and nicking us for criminal offence, you know,' he told the *Mirror* journalist.

Perhaps the *News of the World* were also now aware that Southern Investigations was no longer as above the law as it seemed. According to Fillery, Marunchak was beginning to resent the sale of information to the rival Mirror

Group newspapers and was hinting, ominously, that Southern Investigations could get raided.

But Rees was ready to retaliate. He told his partner that if that happened, the *News of the World* management 'will get fucking tipped off about who gets backhanders'.

* * *

Though the surveillance permits for Operation Two Bridges had been authorised by Deputy Commissioner John Stevens as part of a third Daniel Morgan murder investigation, there hadn't been that many incriminating conversations about Daniel's murder in the six weeks since the *Telegraph* trigger.

However, on 13th August Glenn Vian visited Southern Investigations for the second time and his conversation about the reported getaway vehicle used in the murder was caught on tape.

'What, what happened to the car?' Rees asked, referring to his repossession expert Jimmy Cook. 'I mean, did he have the car at one time was that …?'

'He did, yeah,' Glenn interrupted. 'But he's got to rope someone else in.' He suggested that Jimmy Cook would be unlikely to confess to police because of incriminating others. 'Someone else has said, well, I think he's got too much to lose. To go right the other way. It'd be involving too many people,' Glenn told Rees.

'I mean they haven't got a hope to reach that car,' he continued. 'That car's not there anymore. There's no proof. It's all hearsay, all hearsay, innit? One person's hearsay.'

* * *

Five days later, ex-Detective Sergeant Alec Leighton visited the offices, purportedly to discuss Rees' affidavit for his civil case, but their conversation soon turned to Kevin Lennon's evidence from a decade ago.

The evidence of Southern Investigations' former bookkeeper Kevin Lennon, detailing Rees' plans to have Daniel Morgan murdered during the year before it happened, was a major plank in Hampshire's criminal case against Rees, and neutralising it was a key part of his civil claim against them. Leighton planned to visit Lennon to see if he could be induced with a few thousand pounds to change his story and blame police 'duress' for implicating Rees in Daniel's murder.

But Rees warned Leighton to use subterfuge to approach the former Southern Investigations bookkeeper. Lennon couldn't be trusted, Rees told Leighton, and could go to the police, which would just land them up in a prison cell together.

The next day, Leighton confirmed he'd visited Lennon and made a very subtle offer of a bribe. He'd told Lennon that Rees might be in for a substantial payment in compensation in a civil suit against Hampshire Police if he changed his story. Rees was confident they had won Lennon over.

For the rest of September, it was business as usual. Rees was marvelling at the front pages in the tabloids he had contributed to, spinning phone numbers into home addresses, and addresses into phone numbers, hacking the *Sunday Times'* computer and discussing new stories with Mazher Mahmood and Gary Jones.

| CHAPTER 29 | Sideshow |

Autumn 1999

ALASTAIR: On 24th September 1999 more than a dozen people were arrested, including Jonathan Rees and Sid Fillery.

Over the following months we slowly got the answers to some of our questions. Fillery had been arrested on suspicion of money-laundering, nothing to do with the murder. As for the 'unrelated offence' the police had mentioned, this was yet another sordid story that clearly illustrated Rees' character.

A man called Simon James had gone to Southern Investigations looking for help in a custody battle with his wife over their 15-month-old son. James' problem was that he had a criminal record and it was unlikely a judge would award him custody. His wife Kim, a former page-three girl who now worked as a fitness instructor and part-time model, had a clean record. Rees came up with a plan to change that. For £11,000, he would have Kim James fitted up on drugs charges that would see her sent to jail. Simon James would then automatically gain custody of his son.

Jimmy Cook, the man named as the getaway driver in Daniel's murder, had allegedly planted the drugs. He obtained 15 wraps of cocaine and placed them in Kim's car. Three crooked cops were also involved. Tom Kingston, who was suspended and charged with drugs trafficking, helped set up the scam. Former DC Nigel Grayston, forced out of the police in 1997 for illegal PNC checks, acted as a go-between. Detective Constable Austin Warnes, a serving officer, played a crucial role in getting Kim James arrested.

Of course, Rees, Simon James and the bent cops were nicked, but there were others that we'd never heard of. Among them was another dodgy private investigator who had worked for Southern Investigations and was accused of carrying out illegal phone taps. The list also included a cop who was accused of selling sensitive information from police papers to the media. The journalist who allegedly received the documents was also arrested.

I couldn't help wondering how many scams the police would have uncovered or stopped had they been watching Southern Investigations more closely over the 12 years since Daniel's murder. We were all glad that Rees was going to jail but saw these arrests as a stepping stone on the way to getting justice for Daniel.

Two of the men arrested could give information about Dan's murder. Rees was highly unlikely to do so. He was too deeply involved and it would mean grassing on his brother-in-law, Glenn Vian. Our hopes were pinned on Jimmy Cook.

Everyone agreed he was the weakest link. Roy Clark assured us the case against Cook was overwhelming. He had been caught on film planting drugs and was subsequently charged with drugs offences and perverting the course of justice. The police assured us that judges take this very seriously and that he could go down for up to 15 years.

If Cook gave credible evidence about Dan's murder, a judge could substantially reduce his sentence.

What nobody knew was whether Jimmy Cook was aware that my brother was going to be killed that night in the Golden Lion car park. Roy Clark had told us that he could have been 'the innocent driver or a full participant'. Obviously, if Cook gave evidence against the others, this would make a big difference to the sentence a judge might hand down.

For months, we all speculated about the likelihood of Cook turning. If he did, he could end our family's 12-year battle in an instant. As the getaway driver, he could evidence against Glenn, the man who allegedly wielded the axe. He must have known about Fillery's role too.

We were told by Roy Clark that we weren't the only ones who thought Cook was the weakest link. According to the surveillance tapes, so did all the other suspects!

Whenever we met the police or I spoke to Clark on the phone, I tried to find out what he thought our chances were. In one meeting he told us that the investigation team had asked Jimmy Cook about the murder and warned him he might be in danger. But Cook had refused to cooperate. Clark thought that Cook would say nothing until he'd seen the prosecution's cards on the table. Even then, Jimmy could decide 'to take what's coming as a better option, even if that's ten years inside'.

Clark thought they might have more success with 'garage-man'. He had simply stored the getaway car and it seemed unlikely that he'd played a major part in arranging the killing.

And we hadn't forgotten about Fillery. It didn't look like the Met had enough evidence to prosecute him for money-laundering, and he was never charged. Everyone who had investigated Dan's murder had brushed aside Fillery's role. The Met's original investigation, the Hampshire Inquiry and the Police Complaints Authority all refused to even contemplate the idea that a police officer could have been involved in setting up a murder.

All we could do in this situation was to wait and see how the prosecution panned out in court.

Spring 2000

ALASTAIR: It was at this point that I met two journalists who had a considerable influence on me and who would gradually become my friends.

One day in March 2000, while we were waiting for the drugs-planting case to get to court, I came upon an article in *The Guardian* about the Met's anti-corruption squad. The authors, Laurie Flynn and Michael Gillard, were critical of the Yard's anti-corruption operation. I rang them up to find out more.

'We'd very much like to talk to you too,' said Laurie Flynn.

An hour later I met Laurie and Michael in a café in Exmouth Market, a stone's throw from *The Guardian*'s offices in Farringdon Road.

Over coffee I gave them an account of what had happened to date. They told me they had a contract with *The Guardian* as investigative journalists with a brief to investigate whatever they wanted. They'd decided on police corruption. It looked like we'd have a lot to talk about.

Like me, Laurie and Michael thought police corruption was a major problem and that the Met had been 'managing' it for a very long time. I mentioned that Roy Clark was conducting a review of the case. Michael raised an eyebrow when I mentioned his name.

'Have you heard of Operation Jackpot?' he asked me.

'Wasn't that the investigation into corruption at Stoke Newington Police Station a few years ago?' I said.

'Did you know that Roy Clark was the station superintendent at Stoke Newington when all of that stuff was going on?' Michael said.

This came as a shock to me. 'And now he's head of anti-corruption?'

'Our information is that Roy Clark has been "scoping" corruption at the Yard since 1993,' said Laurie.

'Bloody hell! I would have thought that the Daniel Morgan murder would be top of his list in that case,' I said. 'He was with Condon when we met him in November 1997. He didn't say much at the meeting except that he didn't think the media attention was very helpful.'

The two men laughed. 'I bet he didn't,' said Michael.

They told me that they would look at Rees and Fillery very closely and we agreed to stay in touch and keep each other informed of developments.

* * *

So, was Roy Clark good cop or bad cop? I wasn't sure. I'd always had doubts about him and this inquiry, particularly because they hadn't told us that there was an investigation going on. But my doubts had only grown since meeting Laurie Flynn and Michael Gillard.

Since Paul Condon announced that he had a corruption problem in 1997, the newspapers had been full of anti-corruption stories, but success in bringing bent cops to justice seemed elusive and very hard-won. It seemed to me that the police had created this problem by ignoring or covering it up for years.

I had a lot of contact with Laurie Flynn after this first meeting. He and Michael Gillard seemed to be the only people outside my family who were really concerned about police corruption. They were writing articles about the failures of the supergrass system and they were particularly interested when the supergrass was a bent copper.

Duncan Hanrahan was one of the biggest supergrasses the Met had ever dealt with. Hanrahan had been arrested after attempting to bribe an officer from CIB, the anti-corruption squad. After his arrest, he had confessed to some crimes, but kept quiet about others. While in custody, he'd admitted crimes to a fellow prisoner that he hadn't told the police about. His cellmate then passed this onto the police.

When CIB later tried to use Hanrahan as a witness against other officers, the case collapsed because Hanrahan was a proven self-serving liar whose evidence could not be relied upon, even if he was telling the truth.

All this was very difficult for me to hear. After all, our main hope lay in getting Jimmy Cook or garage-man to confess.

Feelings of distrust tortured me constantly and made me difficult to live with. Kirsteen was coming to the end of her traineeship and was on a placement with Children's BBC. She couldn't understand how my feelings could swing so wildly; she never knew what she was going to face when she got home at night. Sometimes I'd be full of praise for the work Clark was doing; if I'd been out for a few drinks with Laurie or Michael, Kirsteen was guaranteed to get it in the ear when she got home.

My moods always got worse in the run-up to a big meeting. It had been the best part of a year since the police had revealed who killed my brother as we approached the next meeting in April 2000.

* * *

'The problem here is that we don't know Mr Fillery's role in all this,' said Detective Chief Superintendent Bob Quick, the new head of CIB, as we sat round a table in Scotland Yard.

We'd barely been in the meeting ten minutes when suddenly my sister Jane stood up. 'I'm sorry, I'm not going to sit here and listen to this nonsense!'

Roy Clark's staff officer, Elaine Casey, stood up.

'Let her leave, Inspector,' I said.

I knew that visitors to the Yard weren't allowed to move around unaccompanied, but it would be futile to try and stop my sister now.

'See you in the lobby, Jane,' I called as Casey followed her out.

I turned back to Bob Quick and Roy Clark. 'I'm sorry, my sister's upset.'

'Don't apologise, Alastair! Jane's done nothing to apologise for,' said Raju Bhatt, our lawyer.

'We've got to clear up the past, Roy,' I insisted. 'We keep on hearing from senior officers that everything was squeaky clean, and we think that's rubbish. I think the Hampshire Inquiry was carried out under the Old Pals Act.'

Both officers shook their heads dismissively.

'Okay, well then, prove it. I want to see the Hampshire Report.'

For a second, Roy Clark looked genuinely shocked.

'One way or another, we're going to have that report,' I persisted.

Clark composed himself. 'I'd have to consult with Hampshire Police, just as a matter of courtesy,' he said.

Raju pointed out that the report was the property of the Metropolitan Police and that he didn't need Hampshire's consent. Clark agreed, but thought that courtesy should nevertheless be observed.

'And so the final decision will be yours,' said Raju, to underline the position.

Clark agreed.

I turned to Mum, saying, 'I think we've just about covered everything then. What do you think?'

'Well, thank you, Mr Quick and Mr Clark,' said Mum, rising to her feet. 'I think we need to go down to the lobby and see if my daughter is all right.'

As we left the room Raju assured Roy Clark that he wouldn't use our access to the report as any kind of legal precedent. 'We should look at this as a trust-building exercise,' he suggested.

When we arrived in the lobby, Jane was standing staring up at a plaque. She was holding her umbrella upright in front of her; she seemed distracted.

'What are you looking at, Jane?' I asked.

'It's the Met's mission statement, Al,' she said scornfully. 'Do you know, when I saw it, I was that close to smashing it with my umbrella.' She held up her thumb and forefinger, a centimetre apart in front of the sign.

'I understand why, Jane. But I'm bloody glad you didn't! They'd have arrested you on the spot for doing that!'

The Macpherson Report into the Stephen Lawrence murder had just been published. It recommended that complainants should be allowed access to Police Complaints Authority reports. Dan's case had persuaded me that the public interest immunity covering these reports was a crooks' charter.

About three weeks after this meeting Roy Clark called, saying he had some good news for us: Hampshire Police had agreed to release the report. I was delighted. He went on to explain that they had imposed one condition.

'And what's that then?' I asked him.

'They want you to indemnify them against any future civil action before reading it.'

I sat down. Had I heard him correctly?

'Do you mean to say they want me to sign a waiver guaranteeing that I won't take civil action against them?'

'That's right.'

'Before I even read the report?' I laughed. 'You can't be serious, Roy!

'Apart from anything else it makes me wonder what's in that report that could make them went to impose a condition like that,' I continued. 'This was supposed to be a trust-building exercise, if you recall.'

'I'm bending over backwards to try and help you, Alastair,' he said.

'I'm sorry, Roy, it's completely unacceptable. I'm going to take advice and get back to you.'

I rang Raju Bhatt and told him the news.

'It's repugnant,' said Raju. 'Leave it with me, Alastair, and I'll think about how to respond.'

This marked the beginning of a long exchange of correspondence between Raju, Roy Clark and the Met's Legal Affairs until they agreed access to the 83-page report.

Despite its length, it was proposed that Clark read the report to us, without allowing us to take notes or make any record. We would also be forbidden from discussing its contents with anyone other than Raju.

We rejected this proposal out of hand – it seemed litigation was the only route open to us.

CHAPTER 31	Untouched

1999-2000

The arrest of Rees and Fillery and the effective lockdown on the powerhouse of the dark arts, Southern Investigations, sent shockwaves through the offices of Britain's tabloid press.

The Mirror Group was first in the frame. Doug Kempster was arrested while staying at his parents' house, where a page from a confidential *Police Gazette* was found. The *Sunday Mirror* reporter made no comment, but during the search of his own home, the postman helpfully delivered 'a letter in a large brown envelope addressed to Douglas Kempster ... containing a short letter from JR [Jonathan Rees] ... also containing an original issue of the copy of *The Police Gazette*.'

When Rees was arrested, he protested that the bug in Southern Investigations violated his human rights, but a police search found another two copies of *The Police Gazette*, one in his home and the other in this Thornton Heath office.

Detective Constable Tom Kingston read out a prepared statement when he was collared. Paul Valentine from the Special Escort Group made no comment in response to the allegations of corruption.

To the anti-corruption command, this strand of Operation Nigeria/Two Bridges promised to put a stop to a raft of 'media crimes' and collusion between corrupt police officers and the British press.

Their advice file to the Crown Prosecution Service concluded that 'sensitive police documents have been obtained without authority and passed to journalists for a financial consideration by Rees and Kingston'. The police asked for the CPS to prosecute Rees, the two serving police officers and the *Sunday Mirror* journalist, for offences under the Prevention of Corruption Act. However, like the money-laundering suspicions that led to Fillery's arrest, the Crown Prosecution Service decided there was insufficient evidence to bring charges.

Part of the problem was the vague state of the law over police relationships with journalists at the time. Twelve years later, when dozens of journalists – mainly from Rupert Murdoch's *The Sun* and the *News of the World* – were arrested under Operation Elveden for payments to public officials, they and their sources were prosecuted under the obscure common law offence of misconduct in public office – which would prove equally fraught.

Most juries didn't consider journalists to be public officials, so acquitted them for buying stories, meanwhile convicting over 30 public servants, many of them police officers, for abusing their positions by selling them. All these offences predated the more explicit Bribery Act, which only came into force in 2013.

Yet what of the *News of the World* – the main client of Southern Investigations for at least 13 years?

Commander Bob Quick, whom the Morgan family had met in his role as Commander of CIB,[1] compiled a report in the spring of 2000 which he sent to the head of the Department of Professional Standards (DPS) – the new name for the CIB internal investigations branch of the Met.[2]

'As a result of intelligence from Operation Nigeria,' Quick wrote a short report for his superiors, 'highlighting the role of journalists in promoting corrupt relationships with, and making corrupt payments to, officers for stories about famous people and high-profile investigations in the MPS.' It was one of the first MPS reports to highlight what Quick would later describe as 'media crime'.[3]

This report was sent to the new head of the DPS, Deputy Assistant Commissioner Andy Hayman.

In this report Quick recommended a police investigation into three senior figures: Alex Marunchak, news executive at the *News of the World*, Gary Jones from *The Daily Mirror* and Mazher Mahmood, chief investigative reporter for the *News of the World*.

In further discussions with Hayman, Quick argued that normal journalistic protection did not apply to these crimes. Hayman said he would 'visit a particular editor or newspaper and confront them with this intelligence.'[4] Quick also had the impression that Hayman 'referred this matter further up the command chain' – in other words, to Sir John Stevens, the new Met Commissioner who replaced Paul Condon on 1st January 2000.

So, what happened to this damning report that documented dozens of crimes involving journalists, and named three senior figures from the tabloid press? The report has since disappeared according to Quick's Leveson evidence.

It is not known whether Andy Hayman spoke to any editors at the Mirror Group or News International, but the Met Commissioner, John Stevens, did meet the incoming editor of the *News of the World* around the time of this report.

Originally Commissioner Stevens had been scheduled to meet Phil Hall on 23rd March 2003.[5] But by then Hall had been replaced by Rebekah Brooks, who had returned to her Fleet Street roots after spending the previous two years as deputy editor of *The Sun*.

There can be little doubt Brooks would have heard of the scandal around Southern Investigations. She'd spent most of her professional life since 1989 working for the *News of the World*, which coincided with the heydays of Rees' and Fillery's work with Alex Marunchak and her friend Mazher Mahmood.

After his arrest, Jonathan Rees met Tom Crone, the head lawyer of the Sunday tabloid. The fallout from the arrests was being dealt with at the highest management levels of the newspaper.

So how did Brooks react to the allegation her senior editor, Alex Marunchak, was named at the top of a list for urgent investigation?

Extraordinarily, Alex Marunchak was also invited along to meet the new Commissioner, according to Dick Fedorcio, the Met's chief communications officer present at the meeting.[6]

Contemporaries at the *News of the World* suggest that Marunchak might have even been the person who set the meeting up. Though he was spending most of his time as an associate editor of the Irish edition of the newspaper, Marunchak wanted to make himself 'indispensable' and made 'extra efforts to cement his already-strong relationships with senior officers'. Marunchak 'made it known he was the link between the Yard and *News of the World*'.[7]

Whatever was said between John Stevens, Rebekah Brooks and the newspaper executive who was top of the anti-corruption command's list of targets for urgent investigation, Marunchak wasn't reprimanded or sacked. Indeed, he was promoted to a senior executive role a few months later. Brooks, meanwhile, would continue to wine and dine the Met Commissioner for the next four years of his tenure.

There can be little doubt Rebekah Brooks knew about some of the background to the Daniel Morgan murder. Soon after this meeting with Marunchak, Fedorcio and Commissioner Stevens, the newspaper she edited ran the only other story about Morgan.

On 16th April 2000, the *News of the World* published a two-page spread by Greg Miskiw about the alleged victims of the gangster Kenneth Noye. Top of the list was DC Alan 'Taffy' Holmes. The article claimed Holmes' death was a murder – not the suicide decided by the inquest – but presented no evidence to support this and erroneously stated Taffy died of gunshot wounds to the head.

Second on the *News of the World*'s list was Daniel Morgan. They claimed: 'Police believe he was killed because he was on the verge of exposing corruption within the police force that would have implicated Noye and senior officers at the time.'

Though Marunchak does not appear on the byline of this second only ever mention of Daniel Morgan, he was still busy as a crime expert. A week later, he co-wrote a crime story with reporter Robert Kellaway, quoting a 'flying squad commander' who thanked the *News of the World* 'for their assistance'.

Given that Quick's report had proposed a criminal investigation into Alex Marunchak and his colleague Mazher Mahmood, Marunchak still seemed to have exceptional access to senior ranks in Scotland Yard. By this point he was also partially employed by them as a translator from Ukrainian.

Whether prompted by that meeting with the new Met Commissioner or not, Rebekah Brooks quickly embarked on a radical revamp of the *News of the World*'s news gathering soon after. In June that year she recalled Greg Miskiw from New York (where he'd set up an office for the paper) to head up a 'Special Investigations Unit'.

Neville Thurlbeck was made chief reporter in the new unit alongside Greg Miskiw. Thurlbeck already had a track record in problematic payments to police, and that August had been acquitted of corrupting an officer at the headquarters of the National Criminal Intelligence Service (NCIS), a liaison body between the Special Branch and MI5, by obtaining information from the Police National Computer.[8] He was also a registered police informant.[9]

In some of the few surviving emails of that first year of her editorship of the *News of the World*, Rebekah Brooks was recorded fighting for a pay rise and promotion for Thurlbeck, telling her finance director Colin Milner they 'must do this' because Thurlbeck had 'battled through a trial'. Twelve days later, Brooks wrote to her deputy, Andy Coulson, and veteran managing editor, Stuart Kuttner: 'I want Neville to have that promotion ASAP.'[10]

By October, Brooks' friend Mazher Mahmood, according to his byline, was part of the new investigations unit, presumably joined with his specialist surveillance expert Conrad Brown, and photographer Bradley Page.

Finally, Glenn Mulcaire was joined to the unit by Greg Miskiw, replacing much of the intelligence gathering lost by the arrest of Rees and Fillery. At this point 'Greg's Man', a former semi-professional footballer, was regularly invoicing Miskiw over £10,000 a month, but his company, Euro Research, didn't go on to an annual contract until February 2001. Mulcaire was even named as part of the 'Investigations Unit' in a football article by Geoffrey Sweet a year later.

Mulcaire specialised in tracing people and blagging personal information. He cloned the identities of bank staff, telecommunications officers and other professionals to access an array of private data. He had also developed a systematic way of intercepting voicemail messages across all the major mobile phone networks.

Over the next six years, Mulcaire would target thousands of people, including most of the New Labour cabinet and their special assistants, the Royal family, the senior ranks of the Metropolitan Police, and any member of the public who happened to be caught up in a newsworthy story. Mulcaire was regularly tasked at this point by Thurlbeck, Miskiw and (through Miskiw) by Mazher Mahmood.

The extent of Mulcaire's phone hacking, and the cover-up around it, would cause an international scandal a decade later, and lead to the resignations of a Met commissioner and deputy commissioner, the arrests of Rebekah Brooks and Andy Coulson, and dozens of other News International executives and journalists. But in the historical context of the dark arts of Southern Investigations, this illegal story gathering looks relatively benign.

Unlike Rees and Fillery, Mulcaire did not associate with a circle of corrupt police officers and members of the underworld. A clean skin with no criminal record, he worked from his own office on a technical and remote form of surveillance. Apart from his meticulous notes, he was also eminently deniable by *News of the World* executives.

Even Mulcaire's remuneration, which, at over £150,000 per annum well exceeded the £50K limit that editors had to refer to News Group Newspapers' managing board, was organised in small weekly payments that were never declared for tax and remained hidden from financial controllers.

For all the attempts to find a less obvious and odious source of confidential information and intelligence, the legacy of Rees and Fillery would not disappear so quickly. They would be back – Marunchak would see to that. And traces of police corruption were still lying around in plain sight.

When the *News of the World*'s Royal editor, Clive Goodman, was arrested with Mulcaire in 2006, police found 13 copies of the confidential Royal phone directories in his house, some going back as far as 1992.

* * *

Though the Met appeared to turn a blind eye to the *News of the World*'s multiple connections with the Daniel Morgan suspects and a network of corrupt police, other journalists weren't so fortunate.

Laurie Flynn and Mike Gillard had started investigating allegations of corruption around the Stephen Lawrence murder in 1999 for a series of articles they planned to write for *The Guardian*. It didn't take them long to realise there was a complex web of corruption that led back to the brutal murder in the Golden Lion car park.

They began to approach key figures associated with Southern Investigations. Derek Haslam knew nothing about the arrests of Sid Fillery and Jonathan Rees until he heard on holiday via a text message. He soon discovered Rees was released on £100,000 bail, using £63,000 of his compensation from the Solicitors Indemnity Fund as collateral, and was checking the NCIS site to see if he was still under surveillance.

In October 1999, Haslam passed on to his handlers a letter from Gillard and Flynn, saying they were investigating 'Condon's so-called corruption crusade and CIB's activities' and wanted to meet. Rees told Haslam that Alec Leighton was the contact for the *Guardian* journalists.

Though a 'little cagey' on the phone, Leighton confirmed to Derek that he'd met Flynn and Gillard four times already, and they were interested in information on Commander Quick at CIB. Leighton told Haslam that he thought Rees was caught 'bang to rights' by the police, and his only hope of avoiding conviction was technical – on the legality of the probes and the admissibility of the eavesdropping evidence.

Having been warned about not acting as an agent provocateur, Derek Haslam met Mike Gillard at lunchtime on 10th November to discuss 'the methods of CIB 3 and the possible innocence of their targets'.

In late November 1999 Rees explained his reasons for encouraging contact with Gillard and Flynn. He told Haslam he was convinced the Kim James' case would be 'thrown out' on technicalities, especially if CIB 3's methods were highlighted. Problems in another anti-corruption case in February 2000 gave him hope that the judge might rule against one of the chief investigating officers, Haslam's handler DSU Chris Jarrett.

The intelligence reports about Rees' legal manoeuvres were clearly causing some consternation in Scotland Yard. To ensure Haslam was not breaking legal privilege, strict rules had to be applied to make sure no information from the legal documents Rees kept sending him made it back to his handlers.

The Met's reaction to the investigations of Flynn and Gillard was more aggressive. Years later, Bob Quick told the Leveson Inquiry that 'Hayman and I did take some action in relation to these journalists that resulted in them no longer being employed by the *Guardian* newspaper.'

On 12th August 2000 Andy Hayman wrote to the editor, Alan Rusbridger, stating that Gillard and Flynn were 'at risk, perhaps unwittingly, of assisting Rees in unethically or unlawfully seeking his acquittal'.

Rusbridger said he never saw the letter and denies being influenced in any way by Hayman,[11] while his deputy editor, Paul Johnson, has stated he put it in a drawer and ignored it.[12] Hayman was promoted to Chief Constable of Norfolk. However, from then on, Flynn and Gillard claimed most of the stories about CIB 3 and police corruption they had planned for *The Guardian* were spiked. They left the paper in disgust and went on to write *Untouchables*, published three years later, which remains a bible for anyone interested in police corruption in this era, and the problematic progress of the anti-corruption command.

Whatever the reasons for the fallout, there is no doubt the Met had at least tried to mute the *Guardian* reporting on Rees and Fillery, while the *News of the World*, the main beneficiary of their criminality, was allowed to carry on its activities without any obvious interference.

The explanation for this apparent impunity is probably best explained in the third part of this book, which follows the Daniel Morgan murder story to the highest levels of government, the police hierarchy and corporate management.

| Part Three | Government |

KEY CHARACTERS, 2000–2013

The Morgan Family
Alastair Morgan – Daniel Morgan's brother
Isobel Hulsmann – Daniel's mother
Jane McCarthy – Daniel's sister
Kirsteen Knight – Alastair's partner
Raju Bhatt – The family's lawyer

The Rees/Vian Family
Jonathan Rees – Private detective
Garry Vian – Former brother-in-law of Rees
Glenn Vian – Garry's brother
Kim Vian – Glenn's wife
Sharon Vian – Garry's wife
Dean Vian – Sharon's son
Andrew Docherty – Former partner of Patricia Vian, mother of Glenn and Garry

Southern Investigations
Richard Zdrojewski – Inquiries
Jimmy Cook – Car repossessions
Barry Nash – Car repossessions
Gary Eaton – Occasional debt collecting

Met Police Officers
John Stephens – Met Commissioner
Ian Blair – Met Commissioner
John Yates – Deputy Assistant Commissioner
Andy Hayman – Deputy Assistant Commissioner
Dave Zinzan – Detective Chief Inspector, fourth investigation
Dave Cook – Detective Chief Superintendent, fourth and fifth investigations
Noel Bestwick – Detective Chief Inspector, fifth murder investigation

Media	**Rebekah Brooks** – Editor, *News of the World* and *The Sun*
	Andy Coulson – Deputy and then editor, *News of the World*
	Piers Morgan – Editor, *News of the World* and *The Daily Mirror*
	Laurie Flynn – Freelance journalist
	Mike Gillard – Freelance and Times Group journalist
	Paddy French – TV documentary maker
Politicians	**Jennette Arnold** – member London assembly
	Len Duvall – chair of Metropolitan Police Authority
	Hazel Blears – Minister of State for Policing
	David Blunkett – Labour Home Secretary
	Tom Watson – Labour member of parliament
	David Cameron – Prime Minister
	Theresa May – Conservative Home Secretary

2000-2002

ALASTAIR: The trial of Jonathan Rees, Simon James, Austin Warnes, Jimmy Cook and Dave Courtney started in November 2000.

The police told us not to attend as this might alert the suspects to further investigations. My nephew Daniel attended the sentencing in the public gallery – we knew no one would recognise him. He was only four years old when his father was murdered.

Jonathan Rees and Simon James were sentenced to six years' jail. The bent cop, Austin Warnes, was given four years. True to form, Dave Courtney appeared in court in a jester's outfit, which I'm sure did not go down well with the judge, but convinced the jury he was innocent. Amazingly, Jimmy Cook was also acquitted in spite of the video evidence. We were left suspecting the jury had been nobbled, nothing else made sense.

Both defence and prosecution appealed against the sentences and the criminals ended up getting an extra year in jail as their reward. Rees was behind bars and one bent cop had been nailed. Over Christmas 2000 we had the pleasure of seeing Rees spend the festive season in jail. But without any leverage on Cook, nobody spilled the beans on Daniel's murder.

A golden opportunity to solve the murder had been sabotaged, it seemed, by the discovery of another crime involving yet more corrupt policing. The suspects now knew all about the secret surveillance they had been under. In future, they would be even more guarded about what they said. So when, once the trial was over, the Met told us they were about to launch another investigation using the same methods we were highly sceptical.

The seed of a new inquiry grew from a unit called the Murder Review Group. This body looks at cold cases to see if there are any new or old leads that can be followed in light of new forensic developments, police tactics, or if potential witnesses have changed their allegiances over the years.

The Murder Review Group had started looking at Daniel's case in June 2000. In October that year, they came up with 83 recommendations. These recommendations formed the basis of Operation Morgan 2.

The new investigation was to be led by a different team. Roy Clark was retiring. After the way he had dealt with our request to see the Hampshire Report we weren't sorry to see him go. His replacement as head of the DPS, Deputy Assistant Commissioner Andy Hayman, agreed with our lawyer, Raju Bhatt, that he would reconsider Clark's refusal to disclose the Hampshire Report.

Meanwhile, the new murder inquiry, Operation Abelard, would be run by Detective Superintendent David Zinzan. And for the first time in 13 years we were allocated a family liaison officer, Detective Sergeant Dick Oliver. Dick's job was to keep us up-to-date with the investigation.

* * *

In the first few months of 2000, the police plan was presented to us. The new murder inquiry was to have two 'arms'. The first was a covert arm called Operation Abelard that would bug and secretly record the suspects. This would be followed by Operation Morgan 2, the overt arm.

This squad would conduct all the standard work of a normal murder investigation, such as interviewing witnesses and dealing with the press. It would be their job to go public with the fact an investigation was underway once all the bugs were put in place.

The intention was to bring about 'trigger events' that would get the suspects talking and record them incriminating themselves on tape. The key targets were Jonathan Rees, Glenn Vian, the man thought to have wielded the axe, Jimmy Cook, allegedly the getaway driver and the 'garage-man' as we called him.

David Zinzan told us that they needed comprehensive profiling of the suspects and surveillance before attempting to place the bugs. They also needed complete profiles of the suspects' families. Who did they live with? Where did they work, if at all? And when did they leave their houses? The officers planting the bugs would need to know when properties would be empty.

We knew that Rees was still in contact with Sid Fillery because Sid was still running Southern Investigations. But did Rees still talk to Jimmy Cook or Glenn Vian and were any of them in contact with garage-man? Rees couldn't be put under formal surveillance as he was still serving time for the Kim James' conspiracy, but the police told us they had 'eyes and ears' in the prison.

They also needed to think what sort of 'trigger events' would stimulate the suspects and get them talking to each other. The murder weapon had recently been sent for forensic tests, as had Daniel's clothing. If they got positive results, David Zinzan thought that announcing new DNA evidence could be the sort of thing that would panic the suspects into speaking to each other.

(In the end the DNA evidence from the axe turned out to be inconclusive. All that was left after the fingerprinting was hair under the plaster. The surviving mitochondrial DNA linked back to Kim Vian, and her uncle, Paul Goodridge.)

The investigating squad now considered garage-man to be the weakest link and the most likely to turn on the others. They named him for the first time as Barry Nash or 'Barry The Fish', the nickname they gave him because he'd once worked as a fishmonger.

Zinzan described Nash as a small-time crook in his mid-forties who may have been unwittingly used by the others to store the car. If the triggers worked, it was possible that the suspects could pay garage-man a visit to keep him quiet. So getting a bug into Nash's home was a key priority.

All the information about Glenn Vian, Jimmy Cook and garage-man was based on the evidence of a criminal called Stephen Warner. In 1999 Warner had been arrested for attempting to arrange the contract murder of Jimmy Cook. It was his testimony that had formed the basis of the *Telegraph* article that first mentioned a getaway car. But given that Warner was a convicted criminal, who wanted to kill Cook, could we really trust what he was saying?

The probe evidence from the third investigation suggested we could. On the day of the *Daily Telegraph* 'trigger', Rees had telephoned Jimmy Cook immediately after reading the article. Also, a panicky Glenn Vian had paid a visit to the offices of Southern Investigations. This persuaded the police that Warner's intelligence was reliable.

We were impressed with David Zinzan. His attitude was totally different to any cop we'd encountered. He gave us an undertaking that we would always hear of any developments before the media. He was careful not to lead us on and continually stressed how difficult it was to get bugs into homes or cars.

I appreciated his honesty when he admitted that this was the most difficult investigation he'd ever been involved in. The fact that Zinzan didn't wince when we spoke about Fillery's role gave us hope that this investigation really was different. But at the same time, the Met's senior management still hadn't given us the Hampshire Report.

We were beginning to trust David Zinzan, but the top brass at the Yard were still being secretive and defensive about the past. We'd waited a very long time for justice and although it seemed that serious steps were being taken, we still wanted to know *why* it had taken so long. That's why we wanted the Hampshire Report and were prepared to fight for it.

'It's like dealing with a two-faced monster, a Janus,' I told Raju Bhatt. 'One face is open and communicative, the other's sly and secretive. It's driving me mad!'

* * *

The day I got the letter from Andy Hayman refusing us the Hampshire Report I went berserk.

Rather than ear-bash Kirsteen at work I thought 'I'll direct this anger where it belongs', dialled Hayman's number on the Met letterhead and got through to a staff officer.

'I've just had a letter from your boss telling me that he's not going to let me see the Hampshire Report.'

He seemed unaware of this.

'Well, you can tell Mr Hayman from me,' I told the staff officer, 'that I think his decision is a bloody disgrace after everything my family has been through! Will you do that for me?'

'Er ...?'

'I want you to quote me verbatim. In fact,' I continued, 'you can tell Deputy Assistant Commissioner Hayman from me Rees and Fillery were like a bloody great billboard advertising corruption all around south London for a decade. It was only my family's pressure that stopped that scandal getting even worse. And look what happened!'

There was nervous laughter. I hung up.

Hayman later wrote back to tell us we were not to see the report under any conditions and added that if we continued to insist on seeing it, he would stop communication with us concerning the current inquiry.

* * *

Despite Hayman's antics, the investigation plans were impressive. The police had decided to use a BBC *Crimewatch* broadcast as the first trigger with an announcement in the local and national press of a £50,000 reward. This should rouse the suspects into contacting each other and talking about the murder.

But the process of getting the bugs into the suspects' homes was agonisingly slow and difficult.

Getting a bug into Glenn Vian's house was crucial, but it was almost never empty. Glenn didn't work – he was a couch potato who only went out to drive his daughter to school and his wife to work. So the team were very excited when they learned that he had booked a holiday. This could give them the chance to get the bug into his house. Unfortunately, Glenn had a very sophisticated security alarm and two dogs. But what really scuppered the police was the fact that his two daughters weren't going on holiday with their parents.

They had managed to train a video camera on Barry The Fish's home and had established that he worked fairly long hours and didn't go out much. He seemed relatively normal, with a stable home that he shared with his partner and her two children. The police were hoping, if they could create the right situation, that he was the person most likely to give evidence against the others.

Jimmy Cook was a different kettle of fish. At one of our meetings, Detective Chief Superintendent Bob Quick had described him as a 'very dangerous man'.

Cook was 46 years old and lived a totally different lifestyle to the others. It was strange that the police had ever thought of him as a weak link. We were now told he was 'a heavy' and had worked on the doors in pubs and clubs. He also had serious criminal connections. Although Jimmy Cook lived with his wife, the police thought he had a girlfriend as well.

Getting a bug into Cook's house was proving difficult, mainly because it was large and difficult to access. And there was always someone at home. He too had security alarms and dogs, but there was one domestic detail that caused surprising difficulty: Jimmy had a gravel drive. This meant anyone trying to approach the house was likely to be heard.

In the end, they decided that bugging Jimmy Cook's house was just too difficult so they decided to target his car instead. We thought this was a risky strategy as he had several cars and could use any one of them after the trigger. But the police were confident that he would use his Mercedes. They said it was his favourite; in fact, he treasured it and would sometimes go out and wash it in the middle of the night.

As always, the point would come where Mum or I would ask 'What about Fillery?'

On one of these occasions, David Zinzan infuriated us by saying current intelligence didn't merit bugging Sid Fillery. He was keeping his distance from Rees and knew all about surveillance techniques. David told me Fillery considered himself to be on the police's 'most wanted list' and thought he was constantly being monitored.

'We know that he has knowledge of anti-surveillance techniques,' David told us. 'He's used this knowledge while under surveillance and he's no doubt regularly advised on new anti-surveillance methods through his known corrupt police contacts.'

Although it was maddening that Fillery still wasn't at the centre of the investigation, we were heartened when Zinzan told us that he believed he had a role in Dan's murder, or the events that followed it, but what he couldn't say is what part he thought Sid had played, nor rule out that he wasn't involved at all.

* * *

Sometimes it felt as if my whole life revolved around dealing with what had happened in 1987. The endless waiting was tortuous. Nothing could happen until the police got the bugs in place. I didn't trust Andy Hayman, the man in charge, because of his decision not to let us see the Hampshire Report.

Our solicitor Raju Bhatt was exploring the possibility of going to the courts to force the Met to disclose the report. But there was no way we could issue legal proceedings without legal aid. Even my meagre £15k a year disqualified us from this, so the application was made in Mum's name as she only received the basic state pension and some disability benefits.

I continued to meet Chris Smith to urge him to lobby the Home Office on our behalf. He wrote to the Home Secretary, David Blunkett, saying he would be grateful 'if Mr Morgan is given sight of the report'. The Minister John Denham replied a month later, saying 'any report is the property of the chief officer of the force under investigation' and that 'Ministers cannot intervene in this decision'.

At a meeting in January 2002 we learned that the squad had finally succeeded in getting a bug into Glenn Vian's house. Raju asked whether the *Crimewatch* trigger would go ahead in the summer.

Barry Nash was still our greatest hope. Everything the police had told us painted a picture of a man who'd been a crook in the past but was now keeping clean and getting on with family life. If the police could assure him that Rees,

Cook and the Vian brothers would be in prison and no longer able to harm him, there might be a chance he would talk. Nash's role was so minor that any judge would be lenient on him if he came forward with information.

Sid Fillery would never confess or grass on the others. As an ex-cop, he would have a very hard time in prison. David Zinzan told us there was no longer any communication between the suspects, apart from Rees and Fillery. He added that it would strengthen the evidence against them if, after *Crimewatch*, they suddenly started communicating again.

In April, we were told that everything was ready. *Crimewatch* was set to go on air on 26th June. Bugs were in place in Barry Nash's house and Jimmy Cook's car, along with the one at Glenn Vian's house. Three video cameras were also trained on Barry Nash's house. The police were worried about his safety.

There was no bug on Fillery. The police had planned to get one in, but a chance event had thwarted their efforts and the opportunity never came again. But there were two cameras filming his property. Another was in place outside Southern Investigations.

2002-2003

ALASTAIR: *Crimewatch* was to be fronted by an officer we didn't know, Detective Chief Superintendent David Cook from the Met's serious crime group.

The first time we met Dave Cook we weren't sure what to make of him. A Scotsman from Ayrshire, he was direct, and even blunt. I rather liked him. He wasn't patronising and seemed to have no interest in spinning the party line on corruption. He was only brought in to be the face of *Crimewatch*.

Although none of us knew it then, David Cook was to have a massive impact on the case.

The police arranged for us to meet representatives from *Crimewatch* at White City. Kirsteen came down from her office upstairs in order to attend. The meeting was tense. A stony-faced producer sat and listened to Mum as she reiterated our grievances over the first programme.

On the night of the broadcast I was in a bad mental state. I was apprehensive about how Dan was going to be portrayed and still furious with Andy Hayman. This poisonous cocktail of emotions proved too much for me and I began drinking a couple of hours before the broadcast. Kirsteen was angry with me as she knew it would end badly.

Nine o'clock finally arrived and Nick Ross announced an appeal for witnesses in the Daniel Morgan murder. He commented on the arrests of the three officers in the aftermath of the murder, pointing out that two (Foley and Purvis) had received an apology and damages from the Met.

Dave Cook said that the identity of those behind Daniel's murder was 'the worst-kept secret in south London'. He told viewers that the Met had received new intelligence and wanted to encourage new witnesses to come forward. They now knew the identity of the man who wielded the axe and of the getaway driver, the make of the getaway car and where it had been stored overnight, he added.

Then some of the old clips showing a reconstruction of Daniel's murder were broadcast, including the shots of a man looking at the silhouette of a woman behind a net curtain. I cringed as I watched it.

The discussion then moved on to Dan's personality. Dave Cook said that he was 'definitely not a criminal, although he "might have cut a few corners"'. By this time, I was inflamed with alcohol, anger and suspicion and this perfectly reasonable description of my brother sent me right over the edge.

I almost missed the *Crimewatch* update at 10:35. Dave Cook was on again. 'I am pleased with the response,' he told Nick Ross. 'We've had a number of calls in [and] the same person has been mentioned. And the good thing is people have given contact numbers for us to get back to them, so a possibility of some witnesses there.'

'We've received a particularly good piece of information about the car that was possibly involved in this and what happened to it,' he added. 'It's put a big smile on my face.'

By this point, I was too emotionally drained for anything to put a smile on *my* face. But when I woke up the next morning, ashamed of my behaviour, I realised how carefully Cook had chosen his words.

* * *

I'd barely drunk my first cup of tea before Dick Oliver was back on the phone, reporting how the suspects had reacted.

The squad had put a lot of effort into ensuring that they all watched it. They'd visited Rees' ex-wife, Sharon, before the broadcast. Since their divorce she had moved to Devon with her children. The police told me she hated Rees because he showed no interest in his own kids but as Glenn Vian's sister, she'd given them nothing about the murder.

The night before the broadcast, Glenn was recorded in his house saying, 'I know I would get life or 20 years. D'ya know what I'm saying?'

The bug in Jimmy Cook's car had also caught him responding to the threat of an informant. 'They have to fucking stand in the dock and fucking point the finger, ain't they?' said Cook on the phone. 'They can't do us by just a little bit of verbal, they've got to go sit in the dock.'

On the night of the broadcast, Glenn Vian's wife Kim was recorded telling her husband over the phone, 'It's on now!'

Immediately after the programme, Jimmy Cook had gone out to his car and made another phone call, exclaiming about the reward money: 'Fifty grand! One was a copper who works there now. They're going to need proper evidence.'

This seemed like strong evidence to me. It showed that Jimmy knew about the murder and that Fillery was involved. Unbelievably, the officers monitoring Jimmy Cook's bug that night had failed to press the record button and had only officers' notes of what Cook had said.

But it was still early days, the suspects were reacting and things were really happening.

We'd been sworn to secrecy again, but journalists were ringing us all the time. I'd be on my landline and Kirsteen would be taking messages for me on her mobile. For years I'd been pestering them, but now all we could say was that the police had reopened the inquiry.

I was worried that this would sound suspicious. I'd been in contact with many of these journalists for years. If I was too tight-lipped, they would know something else was going on. Dave Cook suggested that we should project an aura of scepticism as this had been our position for many years.

Dick Oliver would ring me twice, even three times a day, telling me what they were picking up on the bugs. We were overwhelmed by this new openness. The day after *Crimewatch*, Jimmy Cook was heard saying: 'Many problems at the moment, but, er, yeah, big problems. It's been going on for a long while, it's been on the telly and everything ... but, it's a naughty one.'

The same day there was a three-way conference call between Sid Fillery, Glenn Vian and Jonathan Rees in Ford Prison. The police saw this as very significant – they were looking for changes in their behaviour that could infer guilt.

In the next few weeks Fillery and Margaret Harrison visited Rees in prison. They'd visited him together before so perhaps this wasn't so useful. More significantly, Glenn Vian and his wife Kim went to see Rees. The police had prison records dating back to August 2001 – they showed that Glenn had never visited Rees in all that time.

Although there was no bug on Fillery, the police had been watching him closely. Surveillance was later withdrawn after Fillery thought he was being followed.

Five days after *Crimewatch*, the squad deployed their second trigger. For months, David Zinzan had been excited about a 'legally audacious' plan to fool

Jimmy Cook and had been in contact with the CPS about it to make sure they kept on the right side of the law.

A female police officer rang Jimmy Cook incognito and told him she knew he was involved in the murder. She said she would go to the police and claim the £50k reward unless Jimmy paid her the same amount of money. She gave him a number for a BT telephone box and told him to ring her in two days' time.

David Zinzan was hoping that this threat to Jimmy Cook would force him to contact the others and give them a chance to capture incriminating conversations. But Jimmy Cook just rang his solicitor, who advised him there was nothing he could do apart from make notes of what had taken place. He never called back.

The police told us they had a mass of tapes to review and needed a pause in the investigation to look at these and decide what to do next. The bugs were turned off, but would be up and running for Phase 2 in a couple of months.

* * *

It had been thrilling to see the suspects react when the police prodded them. Without Dick Oliver's daily updates, life felt suddenly flat. However, there was a dramatic change in Jane's life: my sister decided to move back to the UK.

Over the years her marriage to Justin had deteriorated to the point where they were virtually living separate lives. For a long time she had long been talking about divorce and moving back to the UK, but she felt she couldn't leave her animals. When her horse was ill early in 2002, Jane was devastated that it had to be put down but she also knew it was her chance to make the break. Her dogs had already died. Justin would take care of the goat and one of her neighbours was happy to take her cat.

After living in Germany for 20 years, returning to Britain was a big step but Mum was delighted. Jane stayed on the sofa in Mum's flat for several weeks before she found a small terraced cottage to rent. I think they spent their first week together talking non-stop.

* * *

Operation Abelard had broken new ground with its innovative methods. The sound quality of the bug in Glenn Vian's house was poor because of background noise. For Phase 2 of Abelard they procured a new piece of kit that they hoped would give them sound studio quality. The squad now planned to arrest key individuals in a very public manner, to get the suspects talking.

We'd been highly sceptical about how much they really wanted Fillery bugged. But they had assured us that they really were trying. Now they explained why it was so hard to bug the former detective sergeant. He had a video recorder in his car that would film anyone trying to plant anything; he also had experts sweep his house for bugs. The police were so determined to get electronic surveillance on him that they planned to ask the Security Services for help and advice.

The most dramatic news was that the list of individuals to be bugged now included Duncan Hanrahan. We were fascinated to hear that Hanrahan was suddenly back in the frame and that he'd been released from jail in 2001.

After the *Crimewatch* programme, police had received a number of anonymous calls from a man they later discovered was a serving officer in Sussex Police, who also happened to be Hanrahan's best friend. He'd tried to feed police misinformation about the murder and attempted to find out what was happening with the investigation. When questioned he had said that Hanrahan had provided a false alibi for Fillery.

The police told us they'd been given permission to bug Hanrahan's house and car. We knew that Hanrahan had also known Barry 'The Fish' Nash very well because they were involved in a drugs issue when they had worked at Southern Investigations.

Police conceded that if people like Fillery and Hanrahan – serving police officers in 1987 – were involved in the murder, then it would make sense that the original investigation was 'subverted'. They conceded that Dan's death was steeped in police corruption and that this corruption was deep-seated in south London in the 1980s.

Every time a senior officer made an admission of corruption this felt like a major victory for us.

The police kept their word and did eventually manage to get a bug into Sid Fillery's car. They picked him up for drink-driving and fitted the device while his car was in their possession.

* * *

The first major trigger event in Phase 2 was the arrest of Barry Nash at the beginning of October 2002.

The operation behind the arrest was enormous. Forty-eight officers were carrying out round-the-clock surveillance on the five targets. The team needed to be extremely careful because they were worried that Nash might be harmed.

Nash was arrested at his home address at 6:25 in the morning and taken to Croydon Police Station. The police deliberately took him to a station where they knew the suspects had police contacts because they wanted news of his arrest to leak back to them.

When interviewed, Nash denied any involvement in the murder but said that in 1987 he occasionally looked after vehicles for Jimmy Cook. Between interviews and off the record, he said the vehicle used on the night of the murder was a green Volkswagen Polo.

Nash also gave police some completely new information. He told them he was visited by Jimmy Cook on the night of the murder and that he'd said he had stood over Dan's body while the axe was embedded in his face and his body was 'gurgling'.

The last blow to Dan's head had been so violent that it had severed his brain-stem. I always hoped he'd lost consciousness instantly but I often wondered whether he saw the men who had come to kill him.

Nash's new information, though gruesome and upsetting, was important. At this point he was refusing to repeat it in a formal police interview. The police visited him months later and got him to confirm what he'd said about Jimmy Cook standing over the body. This time Nash added that when he met him after the murder, Cook had looked terrible.

The arrest was also having the desired effect on the others. Fillery and Glenn Vian had made a conference call at midday with Rees in prison.

Later, Glenn and his wife spoke of the arrest of Barry Nash. 'They got him,' Kim said. 'They know that he knows something and that he ain't saying nothing.'

In the same conversation, Glenn said, 'They'll wipe my arse if I crack.'

The newspapers reported the arrest but didn't name Nash. Detective Chief Superintendent David Cook, who was still leading the overt arm of the inquiry, was quoted as saying the arrest was a 'significant development' that helped him 'complete the picture of what happened to Daniel Morgan'. In one newspaper, *The Western Mail*, he said 'the case is solvable'.

* * *

Nash's arrest caused a great deal of alarm, so much so that Jimmy Cook felt the need to concoct an alibi for the night of the murder.

Just 15 and a half hours after Nash was picked up, Cook was seen collecting a couple in their sixties from their home in Carshalton and taking them to a restaurant.

Gwen and John Sturm had known Jimmy Cook for 35 years. Their son Colin had been his schoolfriend and they had kept in regular contact for years. From the bug in Jimmy Cook's car, it was clear they were rehearsing an alibi for him for the night of the murder, though the couple were struggling to get their heads round the concocted story.

'All we know is that you was round our house one night, many nights,' said Gwen. 'But one particular night, why I remember it, was because you came round the day after and said, "I'm glad I was over here last night." Why? "Cause last night a friend of a friend got killed, and I remember him telling me."'

Gwen's husband John butted in to challenge the absurdity of her alibi. 'But you ain't got to say "I'm glad I was round here,"' he mocked, 'because why would he say that?'

It was almost comic and the team were delighted. The new development was hard evidence that Jimmy Cook was looking to place himself elsewhere on the night of the murder.

Now information was coming in thick and fast. Dick Oliver was on the phone to me every day and I would pass the news on to Mum, Jane and Kirsteen. It was impossible to carry on with normal life. Thank goodness, as a freelancer, I could move my work around.

The day after the arrest, one sentence was caught on Glenn's bug that had the potential to implicate Fillery in the planning of the murder.

'I remember Garry told me once Sid bought walkie-talkies,' Glenn said.

The police couldn't be sure what the phrase walkie-talkies related to, but said it could mean that two-way radios were used on the night of the murder to ensure the area was clear of witnesses or to provide a signal to the killer.

This led the police to tell us it's 'not possible to preclude Fillery from the planning of the murder'.

* * *

The next big trigger event was Jimmy Cook's arrest. David Zinzan had told us they were going to stage-manage the proceedings. They deliberately went to the house 'mob-handed' when they knew he would be out. The police spoke to his wife, Jackie, and said, 'Oh dear, we've missed our man.' The idea was to give Jimmy the impression the police were about to arrest him.

As intended, Jimmy's wife fed back the information and on 7th October 2002, Cook attended Wandsworth Police Station by appointment and was arrested in connection with the murder. He gave a no-comment interview on the advice of his solicitor. The detectives interviewing him were very careful not to ask him anything that might reveal the existence of a bug in his car.

Again, the police did not reveal the name of the person arrested to the media. The papers described him as an ex-employee of Southern Investigations just as they had Barry Nash.

To stir things up even more, the team then visited Glenn and Garry's mother, Patricia Vian. She was asked about Dan's murder and questioned about her previous relationship with a career criminal called Andrew Docherty.

Docherty had recently started a 15-year jail sentence for killing someone during an aggravated burglary. In 1987, he was living with Patricia Vian and was a close associate of Sid Fillery. He'd also worked part-time for Southern Investigations. The visit triggered a discussion by Patricia Vian's two sons, as Garry went to see Glenn. Andrew Docherty was in poor health. Garry seemed worried about what he might do

'Even though he's got like 15 [years], he's dying,' Garry said of Docherty. 'He don't want to die in there. You never know what he's coming up with, you know, a deal eh?'

Garry said the police had told his mother that they'd received a lot of information, but thought they were bluffing. Both brothers believed the police would come and knock on their doors but that the investigation had gone as far as it could.

Once Garry had left, Glenn carried on talking with his wife. He referred to Docherty as the 'sweaty sock' and said he'd told his mother that her ex-partner was a waste of space. Later in the conversation, Glenn's wife Kim agreed Docherty was a problem. 'If someone told him he only had 12 months to live, he might confess,' Kim Vian suggested. 'You never know with him.'

A couple of days later, one of Glenn's daughters was caught on the bug reading out a detailed article from *The Croydon Advertiser*. It announced that both the men arrested had been released.

'I'm interested in what's happening with me ex fucking brother-in-law,' said Glenn in response to the article, 'and I know everybody that's involved.'

He was referring to Paul Goodridge, who had been married to his aunt's sister. It wasn't the first time Glenn had been recorded talking about Goodridge.

'They've gone to see him,' Glenn said of Goodridge on another occasion, 'or he's gone to see them, which is more likely, to give his story – £50,000.'

'If he comes round,' Glenn said of Goodridge, 'knocks on that fucking door, I'll tell him to fuck off. Fuck off before I fuck you off!'

* * *

The police continued to apply pressure on the Vians. On 16th October they left David Cook's business card at Kim Vian's brother-in-law. The next day he was visited at work and questioned about the murder and his association with Glenn and Garry Vian, and mentioned a green Volkswagen Golf and Jimmy Cook.

These visits provoked a lot of conversation. Kim relayed to Glenn what the police had said.

'You're both going away for a long, long time,' she said in despair.

'They can't …' Glenn mocked. 'You fucking idiot, that will never happen.'

But shortly afterwards Kim asked Glenn why he was shaking. He wouldn't reply. But she observed: 'Yeah, it's getting a bit too close to home now, innit?'

On Saturday, 19th October, there was an alarming development at Glenn Vian's house as Garry visited his brother. Officers monitoring the address could hear the dry firing of a firearm.

Only days before, Glenn had met two men in a pub and discussed buying guns, stun grenades and phosphorous bombs. They also had good reason to believe there was a gun in Glenn's house. The bug recorded him instructing Garry on how to use it. Glenn explained that it was difficult to cock such a weapon in the back of a vehicle and that it was better to use a different weapon, a handgun.

'All you have to do is walk up and go "bosh" in the back of the head, and it's all over,' Glenn told Garry. 'It doesn't make a lot of noise and by the time he's hit the ground you're ten feet away, walking in the opposite direction.'

As Garry left the house, the police believed that he might have been carrying the gun. Extremely concerned about the safety of those they'd approached as potential witnesses, they decided to arrest Garry.

Dick Oliver described him as 'a real handful'. He had resisted when arrested by armed officers and had even taken a swing at a dog-handler. The dog responded by biting Garry's backside. I laughed, but this was a serious matter. From their conversation, it was apparent that the brothers had access to a pump-action shotgun and possibly even bombs.

I was very anxious about their intended target. Dick assured me this wasn't related to Dan's murder. He said it involved the brothers' 'ongoing criminality', adding that Garry Vian was 'very well connected' with some heavy London criminals.

No weapon was found on Garry that night but in order to protect the presence of the probe, the police had to pretend they were arresting him over Dan's murder.

Glenn was so convinced it would soon be his turn to be arrested he'd even packed a bag. He was right, but that was partly because the following day the police overheard a conversation where he appeared to be telling Kim about an imminent plan to kidnap and torture someone. As a result, it was decided to mount round-the-clock armed surveillance on Glenn Vian.

They let him sweat for a few days and then arrested him on Thursday, 24th October. Like his brother, he gave a no-comment interview. A search of his house was conducted, but no gun was found.

My sister Jane was now experiencing the drama and frustration at close quarters, but was finding some of the day-to-day details difficult to deal with. Dick Oliver and I used to laugh at the way the suspects spoke to their families; Jane felt that it was like staring into a sewer. When I rang to tell her about Glenn's suspected scheme to silence witnesses she was shocked.

'I get angry because Daniel knew these people.' she told me. 'I have angry conversations with him in my head sometimes. Why did you leave us with this terrible mess to sort out? Why did you associate with such low and foul people?'

'I can't answer that, Jane,' was all I could say.

'Danny's brought us into contact with this cesspit,' she continued. 'I know it sounds insane but we're just not that sort of people.'

'Neither was Dan,' I said.

'But why didn't he have a sense of foreboding about what was happening?' Jane went on. 'Why couldn't he see that Rees isn't a decent person? I blame him for his lack of character judgement. I blame him for not telling you what was going on. I do, I honestly don't think Daniel was a good judge of character and that's what lead to his death and where we are now.'

* * *

The bugging operation for Phase 2 was suspended at this point so that the police could review the information they had gathered. Phase 3 started in December 2002. The plan was to make arrests again to provoke conversation.

This time, four people were arrested on one day. Jonathan Rees was the first.

On 16th December, Rees was arrested in prison and interviewed under caution. He was questioned about recorded conversations that he'd had during the third inquiry, Operation Two Bridges. He declined to make any comment, except to say that his experience of the Two Bridges trial had taught him that much of what was recorded in police transcripts was incorrect.

Jimmy Cook was arrested on suspicion of conspiring to pervert the course of justice. This related to his concocting a false alibi. He was also confronted by what Barry Nash had said about him standing over Dan's body with the axe in his head. Cook made no comment in response to any of the questions.

The Sturms were arrested for the same offence. Gwen Sturm gave a no-comment interview. John Sturm was 65 and had a number of previous convictions, including robbery and possession of explosives. He was shown a transcript of his conversation with his wife and Jimmy Cook.

Sturm denied that they were rehearsing Cook's alibi. 'We haven't really said anything,' Sturm said. 'I can't see how we said anything really spectacular in any way.'

The arrests did generate some conversation, but not nearly as much as in the first and second phases. But the police did get new evidence on Sid Fillery, which took them by surprise.

The surveillance squad had noticed Fillery often left the Southern Investigations' offices and drove to a nearby public lavatory. Here, he would spend a considerable time before returning to work. They guessed that he was cottaging.

On 17th December the police searched Fillery's home, boat and Southern Investigations. They were looking for the missing Belmont Car Auctions file and other material relating to the murder. Two computers and correspondence were seized. When the computers were examined, the hard drive taken from Fillery's desk contained indecent images of children.

Sidney Fillery was arrested for possession of indecent images of children in January 2003. He was also arrested for misconduct in a public office for failing to deal appropriately with the Belmont Car Auctions file.

Fillery's arrest put the final nail in Southern Investigations' coffin as a going concern. Nobody would associate with him publicly any more. This was the end of the company that had evolved from the business my brother created in the early 1980s. It had taken 15 years of pressure from us to get to this point. I still wonder how many other crimes they committed while the police were looking the other way.

* * *

On 10th March 2003, the sixteenth anniversary of Dan's murder, the file from the Cook/Zinzan inquiry was sent to the Crown Prosecution Service. The police were of the firm belief that there was sufficient evidence to charge Jonathan Rees, Glenn Vian and Jimmy Cook with conspiracy to murder Daniel Morgan, and Jimmy Cook and the Sturms with conspiracy to pervert the course of justice.

Of course, we wanted Fillery to be in the line-up, but the police thought the only way they would get him was if one of the others gave evidence against him. I thought that this seemed possible. Once it looked like they were going down for murder, surely one of them would want to squeal that a police officer was involved? After all, Glenn had been heard saying he wasn't going to go down alone.

So far, the police couldn't persuade Barry Nash to give evidence. We hoped that this would change once the suspects were charged. In all probability, they would be refused bail and Nash might feel safer once they were behind bars.

I was very hopeful that there would be a trial. David Zinzan had said, 'The individual details may not be significant on their own, but when they are all put together, it could be quite a compelling case.'

For the fourth time we waited to see whether anyone would be charged and stand trial for Daniel's murder.

CHAPTER 34	Watching the Detectives

2000-2003

Although Operation Abelard involved some of the most advanced surveillance techniques available to the police at the time, neither Dave Cook nor the Morgan family had any idea of the extensive counter-espionage measures deployed against them by the *News of the World* under the editorship of Rebekah Brooks.

The fourth murder investigation was top-secret for two years, and it wasn't until May 2002 that Detective Chief Superintendent Dave Cook was approached to become the frontman for the BBC *Crimewatch* appeal going out on 26th June. But the murder suspects were the first to find out about his role, and react.

DCS Dave Cook seemed like the ideal choice to front Morgan 2, the overt arm of the Abelard inquiry, because he had held a senior position within the Murder Commands and had no association with previous investigations or the south London detective circle of the late 1980s. He was 'happy to volunteer' at the time having been told he would only be needed for a couple of weeks. Had he known what was about to happen, he would never have become involved.

Cook's wife, Jacqui Hames, had been a police officer presenter on BBC's *Crimewatch* since 1990. She had also been a close friend of Jill Dando, the main presenter and TV personality shot dead on the doorstep of her flat in Fulham in April 1999.

Jacqui was pregnant with her second child at the time of Dando's murder. Though she'd dealt with many murders and violent crimes in the past, this was the first time an unexpected death had been so close to home. She spent considerable time consoling the traumatised *Crimewatch* team and briefing them on the police inquiry to track Dando's killer, a crime that still hasn't been solved.

Extra security was installed at the Cook-Hames household in Surrey, with a covert camera to identify visitors, though this did not prevent the house being burgled and ransacked in September 2000. The burglars were arrested, but confessed they knew about Dave Cook's role as a senior officer, and Jacqui Hames as TV presenter and police officer. A panic alarm was then installed at their house.

By the time Dave was preparing to launch Morgan 2, Jacqui was on a career break from the police, spending most of her time at home with two very young children. Her husband had appeared on *Crimewatch* before, but they never worked together on cases or shared confidential details.

Five days before the show aired, and a day before information about the reward and the new inquiry was published in the local and national press, intelligence reports suggested that Dave Cook was a target of Fillery.

Sid Fillery was still running Southern Investigations while Jonathan Rees sojourned in prison. On 21st June 2002, intercepts on his phone calls revealed that he knew Dave Cook was to lead the fourth Daniel Morgan murder inquiry and was already making inquiries about him. One of these intercepted calls was to the *News of the World* editor Alex Marunchak, who was in regular phone contact with Fillery and visited Rees in prison. The content of that call caused alarm to senior management at the DPS.

Just before the *Crimewatch* show went live on the evening of 26th June, Dave Cook was warned that Fillery was trying to 'sort him out'. At the time, Cook didn't know how he would be targeted or by whom. After the programme, he warned his team to be extra-vigilant.

Jacqui Hames was the first to experience what this 'sorting out' could mean. An anonymous email was sent to the BBC claiming she was having an affair. Though embarrassing, Hames dismissed the false allegation. But the couple had been trying to sell their house and were sufficiently concerned to instruct their estate agent to stop marketing the property in case someone viewing could plant something to discredit them or check for vulnerabilities in their security.

Soon afterwards, Dave Cook was told by Surrey Police, where he had worked from 1996 to 2001, that someone purporting to be from the Inland Revenue was attempting to blag his personal details by asking for Cook's home address so that they could send him a tax rebate.

Even Derek Haslam, still working undercover he believed, posing as a friend to Rees and Fillery to investigate the violent deaths of Daniel Morgan and Taffy Holmes, was tasked by Rees to target Dave Cook and chase up black intelligence on his background.

Meanwhile, Alex Marunchak was swinging into action. He contacted the assistant editor of the *News of the World*, Greg Miskiw, to put surveillance on Cook and Hames.

'The following week, Marunchak approached me and asked me to authorise surveillance on Cook and Hames,' Miskiw recalled, 'because one of them was having an affair.'

Miskiw's suspicions were aroused. In the competitive ethos of the Sunday tabloid it was 'very unlike Alex to give away a story to the news department,' he said. Miskiw knew that Marunchak 'had a close relationship with a private detective agency, Southern Investigations, who performed his dark arts.' Miskiw had met Rees and Fillery 'several times' but 'always at the behest of Alex and always in his company'.

Over the 16 years they'd both worked at the *News of the World*, Miskiw and Marunchak had been dubbed the Rottweiler Twins because of their common Ukrainian ancestry. Though they briefly started a vodka company registered at Rees' and Fillery's address in Thornton Heath, the two were no longer close. A year earlier, Miskiw had also been the author of the only other article in the paper about Daniel Morgan.

'I knew Rees had been a suspect in the murder of his former partner at Southern, Daniel Morgan, who was found in a pub car park with an axe in his head in 1987,' Miskiw admitted. 'It was suggested he was killed because he was about to expose corruption in the Met Police south of the river.'

Miskiw didn't believe Marunchak's pretext of the affair. 'At the time, it struck me – why didn't he use his team at Southern Investigations? Then it dawned on me. Cook is leading the Morgan murder inquiry; the boss of Southern Investigations was the prime suspect. It would have looked bad if Southern were found to be watching Cook and Hames.'

Nevertheless, though he felt 'conned', Miskiw tasked Glenn Mulcaire to find out everything about Cook and Hames.

Mulcaire's notes from 14th July 2002 contain a wealth of details. He'd managed to find Dave Cook's home address, his Met payroll number, his date of birth, and the monthly figure the couple were paying for their mortgage.

Mulcaire had also procured Jacqui Hames' payroll number, warrant card number, the name of the police section house she had briefly lived in when she joined in 1977, home and work telephone numbers, mobile phone numbers, and information from the couple's joint bank accounts. A lot of this information came from Hames' confidential police files and was not even known by friends or family members.

Mulcaire's notes also contained Hames' mobile phone number and the password for her mobile phone account. Both husband and wife's voicemails were hacked.

Reviewing his notes in 2016, Mulcaire dismissed the idea that he was tasked to look into some kind of affair, either between the couple, or with anyone else. 'No relationship features,' he observed. The information about Cook and Hames was entirely focused on their work and finances. Furthermore, the information about their joint bank account, two children and joint ownership of their house would have demolished the pretext for targeting them.

Cook and Hames knew nothing of Mulcaire's trawling of their private data until 2011, though the Met had these notes when Mulcaire was arrested in August 2006. And if the blagging and hacking wasn't bad enough, worse was to come for the senior investigating officer on the fourth Daniel Morgan murder inquiry.

* * *

Dave Cook knew that Southern Investigations had extensive connections with the violent criminal underworld in south London. After the killing of Jill Dando, it was obvious that nothing, not even national prominence, could guarantee their safety.

With the unspecified threat emanating from Fillery and Rees in the summer of 2002, the Met's Witness Protection Unit upgraded security at the home of Dave Cook and Jacqui Hames, adding a new 'panic' alarm and a second covert camera to the rear of the house.

However, a few days later Dave Cook was walking his dog in the park opposite his Surrey home when he spotted a van with a male occupant parked near his house. The next morning the van was still in position, but had been joined by another, this time with a female driver.

At first Cook was unsure if he was being watched or if there was an innocent explanation for the two vehicles. But as he drove his two-year-old son to a nearby nursery at 8am that morning, he noticed both vehicles had followed him to the nursery. They followed him back to his house, and then again as he dropped his 5-year-old daughter off at a local school.

Using his counter-surveillance training, Cook managed to lose the two vans as he drove away from his daughter's school. Rather than cause his wife too much concern, he didn't tell her about the surveillance, but planned to intercept the vehicles if he saw them again. This was a decision he later regretted.

The following morning the two vehicles returned and 'plotted up' the family home for more surveillance. Anticipating this, Cook had organised a full counter-surveillance team. He had noticed the previous day that one of the vans had a defective tail light. As Cook drove off to work in London and both vehicles followed him, he planned to have them stopped by uniformed officers on the pretext of the tail light.

On the motorway into London, everything went to plan. The vans were flagged down by uniformed officers. The counter-surveillance teams were ready to tackle close associates of Fillery and Rees, but when the driver of one of the vans was confronted, he explained he was a journalist on legitimate business. The blue Vauxhall combo subsequently turned out to be leased to Bradley Page, Mazher Mahmood's photographer. The police let both vans go.

Undeterred, the photographer and journalist returned to monitor the family home.

Oblivious to all this, Jacqui Hames was washing up at the kitchen sink when she saw the van parked near the rear of her home. In slow motion, she watched as the occupant wound down the window and poked a metallic barrel towards her.

Hames ducked and cowered on the floor. Though it was only a telephoto lens pointed in her direction, she was momentarily terrified. The trauma of her friend Jill Dando's murder three years earlier returned in full force. Hames pulled herself together and called Witness Protection, but the sense she would never be safe on her own doorstep, or able to take her kids to school without fearing someone was watching them, was impossible to repress.

The following week Cook discovered that someone had been asking questions about him around the village. A credit card bill had been opened before being delivered to his house.

Jacqui Hames and Dave Cook's peace of mind was not the only thing to be shattered that summer. Within a few years, the combination of Hames' trauma and Cook's guilt that he had brought the dangers of his work home would wreck their marriage.

* * *

At this time Dave Cook had not seen all the material from Operation Nigeria/ Two Bridges and was unaware of the close relationship between the *News of the World* and Southern Investigations. As soon as he discovered he was being targeted by Rupert Murdoch's newspaper, Cook informed his superiors and demanded an investigation.

The Met's Director of Public Affairs, Dick Fedorcio, decided to make an informal approach to the editor of the *News of the World* – Rebekah Brooks – instead. He reported back that Brooks received 'an unsatisfactory answer' from the photographer and journalist about the surveillance. Mention was made of an allegation of an 'affair' between the murder detective and the BBC *Crimewatch* presenter, even though Cook and Hames had been a couple for 11 years.

Dissatisfied with Brooks' response, which he characterised as 'complete rubbish', Cook went back through the evidence of the first two murder inquiries. In August 2002, his murder team obtained new statements from Daniel Morgan's ex-employer, Bryan Madagan, and Southern Investigations' bookkeeper, Marjorie Williams.

For the first time in an official police statement, Madagan confirmed that the man to whom Daniel Morgan was selling his story of police corruption in the weeks before his murder was Alex Marunchak.

Marjorie Williams set down further details of the *News of the World* closeness to Southern Investigations in the three years after Daniel's killing, and how Alex Marunchak was Rees' and Fillery's main client, providing a huge volume of cash payments.

On 27th August 2002 Dave Cook's deputy, Neil Hibberd, sent an urgent request to the head of the DPS, Andy Hayman, to investigate the financial relationship between Marunchak and Southern Investigations. At the time, Marunchak was in Soham, Cambridge, investigating the murders of two young girls and according to intelligence sources, paying police officers for information and pictures.

Deputy Assistant Commissioner Andy Hayman never responded to the request but the following evening, Rebekah Brooks met up with the Met Commissioner Sir John Stevens at the upmarket Ivy Club for a three-hour dinner. It seems implausible that the subject of her paper's surveillance of a highly sensitive murder inquiry didn't feature in the conversation, nor at a second dinner at the Ivy two weeks later, on 12th September 2002.[1]

Rebekah Brooks could not have missed the storm gathering about her newspaper's long collaboration with Rees and Fillery.

A week later, on Saturday, 21st September 2002, Graeme McLagan wrote two major articles in *The Guardian* about the *News of the World* and its connections with Rees and Fillery: 'Journalists caught on tape in police bugging' and 'Fraudster Squad'.[2]

In over 3,000 words based on material gathered during Operation Nigeria, McLagan described how Rees was caught on tape digging up confidential information on the Stephen Lawrence Murder Inquiry, the London Nail bomber David Copeland and the murder of Jill Dando. The articles explained how Rees could be heard trying to sell information to the press about the murderers Kenneth Noye and Peter Sutcliffe, and the arrest of Chilean dictator Gustavo Pinochet, offering to check on vehicles, obtain credit details, even forging a warrant card.

The extent of illegal news gathering couldn't have been more obvious. More importantly for Brooks and the management of News International, one of her senior executives was named and approached for comment.

'Asked to comment on the transcripts, Mr Marunchak said: "Are you recording this call?" Asked if he disputed that he bought material from Rees, he said: "You haven't heard me admit it".'

* * *

As Rees and Fillery reacted to the carefully orchestrated trigger events throughout the summer of 2002, Dave Cook's initial two-week stint as the frontman for the third murder inquiry developed into a full-time role.

Cook believed that Rees and Fillery, through their 'corrupt relationship with the *News of the World*', would deploy whatever material they had gathered from surveillance or other measures if charges were brought.

At home, it was difficult to keep the secret of the surveillance from neighbours in the small Surrey village. Cook would secure the rubbish bags particularly carefully each night and check they hadn't been interfered with in the morning. The staff at their daughter's school and son's nursery had to be apprised of extra security measures. The Witness Protection Unit assessed that Jacqui Hames was suffering from acute stress and required intensive treatment.

As the overt face of the inquiry, Dave Cook was regularly mentioned in the papers when arrests were made but soon he would find it hard to share with his wife some of the dangers of his work.

As part of the investigation, Cook wanted to speak to Paul Goodridge, who had been arrested after apparently providing an alibi for Rees in 1989. But Goodridge would only meet Cook alone in his own house. Cook agreed.

During the course of the meeting in October 2002 Paul Goodridge told Cook he 'had something for him'. He went into a cupboard and pulled out a shotgun, which he pointed directly at the senior investigating officer. Cook just stared down the gun barrel. Then Goodridge handed him the gun with a deactivation certificate, which proved it didn't work.

When Cook told his wife about this, her anxiety and sense of imminent danger only increased further.

That same week, on 19th October, when the surveillance team overheard on a probe what sounded like the dry firing of a weapon and a plot to murder, Cook had to make the split-second decision to arrest Garry and Glenn Vian. Sharing these developments with Jacqui became impossible, and the mistrust and silence between the couple grew.

* * *

For all his efforts on the fourth murder inquiry, DCS Dave Cook was not being fully supported by his senior officers, especially in the DPS. The vast bulk of the material that linked Southern Investigations to the *News of the World* was withheld from him. Meanwhile, Sid Fillery's computer, seized by the DPS in mid-December 2002 but kept away from the murder investigation, contained more than indecent images of children.

Fillery's hard drive held a wealth of other incriminating information. Eight years later, searches of the hard drives revealed a continuing association with the *News of the World*. The paper came up with one of the greatest number of hits in searches – 106 – while the name of its senior executive, Alex Marunchak, appeared no fewer than 79 times.

In one document, Southern Investigations appeared to be reporting back to the *News of the World* executive on the results of a break-in – that Fillery or Rees 'or an associate at their behest, has gained unauthorised access into a private domestic premises with a view to gaining information on the resident'. In another, Fillery or Rees seemed to be asking Marunchak to track down the 'keeper details' for a car registration – a bizarre reversal of the normal process. But Southern Investigations had paid Marunchak for information from his contact at the Passport Office, so the trade in confidential information was two-way.

More extraordinary still was Fillery's continued access to high-level police intelligence. He seemed to have the 'duty states' of four CIB 3 officers involved in the Two Bridges Operation – including Bob Quick. There was also a letter from Rees to Fillery claiming he had received covert transcripts involving Hanrahan and Putnam, the two police officers close to Rees and Fillery arrested in the anti-corruption drive.

Nevertheless, armed with the new witness statements about the long relationship between Alex Marunchak and Rees and Fillery, DCS Dave Cook confronted the *News of the World* editor Rebekah Brooks at a meeting arranged by Dick Fedorcio, and sanctioned by the Commissioner, Sir John Stevens.

In the lift up to the sixth floor of New Scotland Yard on 9th January 2003, Cook recalled being told by another commander: 'Remember, she is very close to Sir John Stevens.'

'I took that as a warning,' Cook said.[3]

Dave Cook then briefed Rebekah Brooks on the surveillance of his family. He showed her witness statements detailing 15 years of dealings between Marunchak and Rees and Fillery, beginning in the late 1980s. He went on to explain that Southern Investigations appeared to have paid some of Alex Marunchak's credit-card bills and the school fees for one of his children.

According to Cook, Rebekah Brooks 'became very defensive about Marunchak, saying how since he'd moved to the Irish desk, sales there had gone up and he was doing such a great job'. Cook was stunned, but didn't press the matter further. Brooks, however, promised to make her own inquiries.[4]

The editor of the *News of the World* then left the room and went off to meet Commissioner Sir John Stevens for another drinks reception.

The next day, Friday, 10th January 2003, Brooks consulted her managing editor. Stuart Kuttner had been paying – and questioning – Southern Investigations' invoices for years, and he took notes of the meeting, which were later seized by police in the phone-hacking investigation in 2006.

Contemporaries suggest a third person attended that meeting: one other unidentified person. Either way, three senior officers of the company were present when Alex Marunchak's attempt to subvert a major murder investigation was discussed. But there is no indication that Marunchak was warned, punished or sacked. He would remain a senior executive editor of the newspaper for another four years.

Instead, it was Rebekah Brooks who was suddenly moved. That weekend she was told to clear her desk at the *News of the World* and on Monday, 12th January 2003, assume the editorship of *The Sun* newspaper. Andy Coulson replaced her as editor of the Sunday tabloid.

This move to Britain's best-selling daily was a promotion, certainly, for Brooks. She was the close friend of Rupert Murdoch's daughter Elisabeth, had met and impressed Murdoch himself, and was being groomed for high office. But why was Brooks suddenly moved out of the *News of the World* immediately after being confronted over the activities of Southern Investigations and their long association with her newspaper? Was the sewer of corruption that underpinned its news gathering in danger of overflowing and tainting her too?

CHAPTER 35	Between the Lines

2003-2004

ALASTAIR: A couple of weeks after the police had submitted their file to the Crown Prosecution Service I got a call from Dave Cook.

'Alastair, I've just come from a meeting with Treasury Counsel. Bad news, I'm afraid. They've said they're not going to prosecute.'

I was speechless.

'David Zinzan and I are going to meet them again soon. We're going to try to persuade them to change their minds. But don't hold your breath.'

'Jesus ...'

'I know. If it's any comfort to you, we feel the same.'

'No, you don't, Dave.'

'Alastair, we've argued and argued. But they won't have it. The problem was we don't have a witness who would give evidence about the role the suspects played on the night of the murder,' Dave Cook explained.

'So, that's it, then?'

I don't think I waited for a reply; I just hung up. Like a piece of meat from a deep freezer, I was frozen to the core. I think our systems are built like that for survival. It was a full ten minutes before I could carry out the simplest act.

Dick Oliver and David Zinzan drove down to Wales the following morning to tell Mum and Jane in person. Jane rang me as soon as they'd left.

'Why the bloody hell did they give us another 24 hours of agony?' she protested. 'They arrived at Mum's house all suited and booted. I don't think they'd sat down before David said he'd got bad news for us. I just hit the roof and screamed. Driving over, I wanted to crash the car into a brick wall or tree.'

When her anger subsided, Jane said to me, 'I believed in this investigation. They let our hopes get so high, I really thought they would do it this time.'

I spoke to Mum a few days later. She was also devastated by the fact there wasn't going to be a trial. She also knew that at the age of 76 there was little chance of her seeing Dan's killers brought to justice.

'I can still see him so vividly now, so clearly that I feel I can touch him,' Mum confided in me. 'I feel he's close and I talk to his photo by my bed. I say "We're getting there, Dan, we're trying to find out what happened to you."'

'It's like saying goodnight to someone,' she said of these late-night goodbyes to Daniel's photo. 'I will always remember him as a young man. It's too raw to think how old he would be now.'

We'd been so busy fighting that I don't think that any of us had ever properly mourned Daniel.

'Al, this has taken over my life so totally and utterly. Okay, so we aren't going to trial, but we have to do something,' she told me. 'Do you know what my last words to David Zinzan were when they left my flat?'

'No.'

'See you at the public inquiry, David.'

Though the CPS had ruled against us, Mum wasn't about to give up.

* * *

Soon after the CPS's initial decision, BBC correspondent Graeme McLagan rang me to say that his book, *Bent Coppers*, had just been published. I made my way up to Waterstones on Islington Green to buy a copy.

On the sleeve was an endorsement by the new Commissioner, John Stevens: 'This is a story that deserves to be told – warts and all'.

I quickly found the chapter entitled 'Murder at the Detective Agency'. The chapter explained how a police probe had been planted in Rees' and Fillery's offices late in 1998. Permission to use the probe had been given by the Home Secretary, Jack Straw, for the express purpose of investigating Daniel's murder. It seemed that the Met had a fully operational bug in Southern Investigations' offices for many months before the Kim James' conspiracy emerged.

Graeme's book described how the police had leaked information to *The Telegraph* in July 1999 as a trigger, after the evidence in the Kim James' case had been obtained. But what had the police done during that interval?

The book made it clear that, months before that, police believed Rees and Fillery and their associates were sabotaging police investigations and prosecutions on behalf of clients. Then I came to a paragraph quoting a monitoring report in April 1999 after Hanrahan's imprisonment: 'Fillery is particularly concerned at what Hanrahan might have told police about the association between them,' the report said, 'and whether Hanrahan has given information about the murder of Daniel Morgan. Clearly Fillery is concerned and feels more vulnerable around this issue'.

I went to my files and dug out the police notes of our meetings that had been disclosed in the process of our ongoing challenge for the Hampshire Report. I found the police notes from 15th July 1999 – the day Roy Clark had turned up unexpectedly at Raju Bhatt's offices.

In response to Raju's questions about police involvement in Dan's murder, the notes said that Roy Clark had replied: 'No police officers appear to have been involved in or on the fringes of this crime.'

But the obvious inference I drew from the monitoring report was that Fillery was scared that Hanrahan would grass on him over the murder. It was impossible to square this with what Roy Clark had told Raju.

This made me wonder why Stevens and Clark had kept me out of their meeting with Chris Smith in October 1998. This bugging operation was a golden opportunity to gather evidence on Rees and Fillery. Why had they waited until they had them for another crime before they tried to use the bug to gather evidence on the murder? After all, the murder was the very reason why the bugging permit had been granted. Was Fillery being protected by the police again?

A secret police report quoted by McLagan described Fillery and Rees' contacts with the police: 'Such is their level of access to individuals within the police, through professional and social contacts, that the threat of compromise to any conventional investigation against them is constant and very real.'

Yet another secret paper talked of Rees and Fillery being a 'crucial link' in police corruption and continued: 'Should we be able to successfully arrest and prosecute Rees and Fillery for corruption matters it would be seen within police circles as "untouchables" having been touched and will put off many who are currently engaged in malpractice, and indeed, those officers who may be contemplating committing crime.'

I didn't know whether to laugh or cry.

Sitting in a small pub in Clerkenwell with Laurie Flynn a few hours later I told him that bugs had been in Southern Investigations for more than six months before we were told, and that no effort appeared to have been made to stimulate conversation about the murder.

'I don't believe this was ever about your brother's murder, Alastair,' Laurie said. 'I think they used the murder as a pretext to bug Southern Investigations. They wanted the business closed down but they didn't want the embarrassment of admitting that police corruption played a role in Daniel's death.'

Laurie pointed out that Graeme's book had included an intelligence report showing that Rees and Fillery were involved in a smear campaign designed to shame senior officers on the anti-corruption squad. That, he thought, was the real reason for Operation Nigeria/Two Bridges.

Laurie was convinced that the Met had known for years that Southern Investigations was being used as a conduit between bent cops, organised crime and the media. The authorities seemed quite happy for the company to continue all the time that they were selling stories to the tabloids about Labour and Lib Dem sex scandals. That all changed, he explained, when Rees and Fillery started to take aim against the anti-corruption squad.

'You'd probably learn more,' he continued, 'about why your brother's murder was allowed to remain unsolved through a public inquiry than you would through a trial.'

I agreed, but there was something we had to do first: we had to get our hands on the Hampshire Report.

* * *

In order to get the Hampshire Report we had to go through the process of a judicial review of the Met's decision.

In his report on the Stephen Lawrence case, Lord Macpherson had recommended that all complainants should, in principle, be given access to reports by investigating officers. But there was a lot at stake. If the Met lost and the judge made a ruling in our favour, Scotland Yard would be swamped by lawsuits by disgruntled complainants wanting to see how their complaints were investigated.

Another major problem was money. None of us could afford the costs of such legal proceedings. Mum lived on a state pension and some benefits, so Raju Bhatt applied for legal aid funding for her as the litigant, and succeeded.

The first hearing took place at the Royal Courts of Justice in March 2003. Raju led us up to our courtroom and introduced us to our barrister, Rabinder

Singh QC, the only barrister in the British courts permitted to wear a white turban instead of a wig.

Counsel for the Met opened by arguing that our application was out of time. Rabinder countered by showing that this was because we wanted to negotiate and because Andy Hayman had threatened to stop communicating with us. The judge rejected the Met's out-of-time argument.

'This is a body blow to my clients, my lord,' said the Met's counsel, theatrically distraught that his first line of defence had crumbled.

Rabinder then outlined the history of Daniel's murder and the ridiculous terms of disclosure offered by the Met – no note taking, no copying, indemnity before access, etc. After half an hour of legal argument, the judge ruled that we'd won the right to judicial review.

Weeks later, on the morning before the full judicial review, Raju phoned to say that the Met had thrown in the towel. After 16 years, we'd forced the organisation to finally show us what we had a right to know: how Hampshire Police had investigated the matter of police involvement in Dan's murder.

All that remained was to agree the terms of disclosure. These were just as we'd expected: no publication, no discussion with third parties, etc. I arrived at the High Court just in time to see Mr Justice Silver announce that an agreement had been reached. I heard him make a pointed comment.

'Reading between the lines of the report,' he said, 'and there's clearly a lot more to read between the lines …'

The Met were ordered to disclose within 14 days and the report was to be delivered to Raju's new offices in Hoxton Square.

The deadline came and went, but no report was delivered. Raju contacted the Met's legal services department, who made feeble excuses and said the report couldn't be delivered until Monday. The Met couldn't even comply with the terms of a High Court order.

The following Monday, I rushed over to Hoxton Square and felt quite surprised when I saw the half-inch thick document with its matt blue cover and typewritten title.

For 14 long years, I'd been denied this information about my closest sibling's murder. Now it was lying in front of me on Raju's desk. Raju looked at me and grinned.

'There it is, Alastair. You've waited long enough for that, I'd say.'

'Thank you, Raju. Thanks for doing this for us.'

'It's been a privilege,' he said, putting it into a brown envelope. 'Now you can take it and read it at your leisure.'

I made my way to a café near my flat, where I ordered a coffee and read the report from cover to cover in just over an hour. I am still forbidden by law from saying anything about its contents.[1]

* * *

Getting a public inquiry, if it ever happened, would take years. Raju took advice from Keir Starmer QC, who advised him that the political climate wasn't right.

In September 2003, six months after the CPS had told us that there was to be no prosecution, the CPS notified us of this officially. They provided no reasons for their decision.

It made me want to leave Britain. I'd talk to Kirsteen about packing our bags and getting out. I dreamt of going to India, South America or just somewhere else in Europe. I could work anywhere if I could connect to the internet. But Kirsteen's job at the BBC meant a lot to her. And she always asked if I thought these countries were any better than here. I knew she wouldn't leave. By this time, we'd been through so much together I couldn't imagine life without her.

Frustration was eating me up inside and I was drinking too much. One Sunday I woke up to see the Commissioner John Stevens on the television news. He was out on the beat with his foot soldiers. Questioned about corruption, he said that the Met had 'taken its eye off the ball'.

At lunchtime, I decided to go to the local pub. It was empty apart from an elderly couple who were sat sipping their drinks. I ordered a pint and chatted to the barman. The bar television was on and the midday news re-ran the story I'd seen earlier of Sir John Stevens.

'He's talking bullshit,' I said loudly: 'They didn't take their eye off the ball at all. They were bloody covering it up!'

I turned to the elderly couple, who were oblivious to the television in the corner.

'It's the Commissioner of Police on the news. And he's lying to you. He's lying to the British public, too! What do you think about that?'

They looked at me, bewildered.

The barman was getting edgy.

'The lying bastards!' I growled, working myself up over Stevens, annoyed at being ignored.

'Alastair, would you mind leaving all that outside the pub?'

At this I exploded.

'Leave it outside? They killed my brother, the bastards! And for your information I've been coming here since you were in fucking short trousers!'

'Mind your language, Alastair, or I'll have to ask you to leave,' he replied firmly.

'You won't have to ask me, Anthony, because it will be a pleasure to leave,' I retorted, draining my pint and striding indignantly out through the door.

A couple of days later, I found the guts to apologise to the barman when I saw him in the street. But still I didn't go back to that pub for another year.

* * *

Raju thought the most useful thing we could do was to find out whether the police would support a public inquiry. Yet another meeting was arranged with David Cook and David Zinzan at Scotland Yard.

The police on this team had been more open and honest with us than any of their predecessors. Upset as we were, we couldn't fault them. At this meeting, Dave Cook went further than ever before in admitting what had gone wrong.

'The real mischief took place in the first Met investigation,' he admitted.

'Mischief' is a polite word used by the legal profession for misconduct or corruption.

Cook went on to say that the role of Sidney Fillery in the first investigation was at the heart of the mischief. He even conceded that, in his view, Fillery had been protected by other officers on the squad. This was the first time that any officer had been prepared to go so far. He described the first investigation as the 'worse mess I have ever seen'.

Action always made me feel better. We decided to hold a 'Counsel of War' with our supporters and arranged a meeting in Parliament. Mum's new MP, Roger Williams, had booked a room for us. Chris Smith attended, along with Raju and Michael Gillard. Everyone agreed that an inquiry was the way forward.

In February 2004 Raju finished his submission to Home Secretary David Blunkett. It was sent with a covering letter from our MPs asking for a meeting. The submission was based on Article 2 of the European Convention of Human Rights: the Right to Life.

On April Fool's Day 2004, the new Independent Police Complaints Commission replaced the long-discredited Police Complaints Authority. I'd learned that Roy Clark had been appointed Director of Investigations for the new body. I wrote to the IPCC's chairman expressing concern over Clark getting the job. I mentioned that he had carried out an inquiry behind our backs and his aversion to openness.

More than a year after their decision, we were still waiting for the CPS to give us their reasons for not prosecuting. Raju wrote accusing them of breaching their own policy on the care and treatment of victims.

It took another six weeks before we got the CPS advice on why they didn't prosecute the fourth murder investigation. The document told us nothing we didn't already know, i.e. that there was no eyewitness to the murder; no DNA; Rees was not the only person who could have had a motive for killing Daniel and the usual stuff about Lennon being a flawed witness. According to the CPS none of the bugged conversations unequivocally proved guilt.

Six weeks later, Chris wrote to the Minister for Policing, Hazel Blears, again complaining that three months had elapsed since we'd written to the Home Secretary. Blears replied, refusing to order a public inquiry, saying that she did not consider a public inquiry proportionate or useful. David Blunkett didn't even grant our MPs a meeting. All we could do was try to embarrass the government into changing their minds.

My mother's MP, Roger Williams, had set an adjournment debate under the parliamentary privilege, which meant nothing said there could be subject to libel action. The debate was a good news peg and I managed to generate a lot of media interest. It took place on 6th July 2004, more than two years after the failure of the fourth investigation.

Kirsteen spent days building up an email database of politicians and media outlets. For the remainder of the summer I kept prodding the press, trying to maintain a steady flow of articles such as 'Blunkett faces murder case writ' and 'Blunkett challenge over axe murder'.

Paddy French of ITV Wales *This Week* also approached me. ITV Wales had already made two documentaries about the murder. It was primarily a London story but no documentary on the case had ever been broadcast in the capital. Paddy had persuaded ITV London to make a parallel programme.

In September Roger Williams backed up his adjournment debate with an Early Day Motion calling for a public inquiry. I wrote hundreds of letters asking politicians to support our call. Eighty-three MPs signed and we managed to get a parallel motion in the Welsh Assembly. We even visited the Liberal Democrat and Labour party conferences in Bournemouth and Brighton to distribute leaflets to delegates.

Production of the two ITV documentaries began. Paddy French rang me saying that he'd had an interesting experience trying to interview Jonathan Rees. He'd door-stepped Rees at his address in Thornton Heath and had the door slammed in his face. A few minutes later, Paddy's film crew were approached by local police, who threatened them with arrest if they didn't stop trying to film him.

Rees still had friends in the south London police, it seemed.

* * *

In October 2004, we finally got our meeting with Hazel Blears. It was set for 7pm on a Thursday evening at the Home Office, very close to New Scotland Yard. We didn't arrange media coverage as it might appear confrontational. We waited outside the building in Queen Anne's Gate with Raju.

One by one our MPs arrived and were led into the ministerial sanctuary. Hazel Blears was sitting between two male civil servants, one with a yellow legal notepad. There were introductions and handshakes.

'It's taken us 17 and a half years to get inside this place!' I remarked as an opening salvo.

Chris Smith, our MP and her ministerial colleague, gave a brief outline of our grievances, stressing the concerns we had about information given to her by the police. I took this as my cue.

'You should be aware that senior management at Scotland Yard have been misleading ministers about this case for years.' I repeated to her what the Met had told Caroline Flint. The civil servant sitting on Blears' left scribbled energetically.

'Without doubt, there have been problems with corruption in the police,' Blears told us. 'I do know that the Metropolitan Police have been working very hard on trying to eliminate corruption.'

My frustration could contain itself no longer. 'I'm afraid I'm not going to stay here and listen to this nonsense,' I said, walking to the coat-stand near the door and picking out my raincoat. I heard Roger's voice behind me.

'Alastair! Don't leave, please.'

I returned to my seat, embarrassed and angry.

Hazel Blears repeated what she'd already written in her response to Raju. Hampshire had found 'no evidence whatsoever' of police involvement in the murder.

'But Minister,' I appealed to her, 'they didn't even bother to investigate an attempt by Fillery to get me out of London after I'd pointed to his close friend as a suspect. That's what I call interfering with a witness. And there was wholesale police perjury at the inquest. That's why we've been protesting for so long. My brother didn't have a chance of justice!'

Richard Livsey added that Fillery had left the murder squad and gone into partnership with Jonathan Rees, the prime suspect for the murder.

'This was all predicted at the inquest,' I continued. 'Kevin Lennon made a statement to that effect five months before it became a reality. Hampshire dismissed him simply because he was a fraudster. A fraudster with a crystal ball!'

'The Police Complaints Authority certified that they were satisfied with the Hampshire Inquiry,' Blears replied.

My heart sank. 'But Minister, what I'm trying to show you is that the whole system has failed us, the outside inquiry, the PCA. It simply doesn't work. That's why there should be a public inquiry.'

'Twenty minutes!' called a voice from behind the Minister. A blonde woman in a dark skirt was calling time on our visit and rescuing Blears from our uncomfortable presence.

'I promise that I will seriously and carefully reconsider my previous decision in the light of what has been said here this evening,' Blears said then smiled at us politely. Raju asked her to confirm that her decision was genuinely still open. She nodded. 'And could you give us a timeframe for your reconsideration?' Raju added, saying that our ordeal had already lasted a very long time. She promised to respond very quickly. The efficient blonde woman was hovering behind her. We stood up and offered lukewarm thanks.

'Don't take anything the police say about this case at face value,' Chris Smith urged her as he moved towards the door.

Outside the Home Office my MP, Chris Smith, had a few final words for me. 'Expect the usual Home Office apathy,' he said and walked off into the Westminster night.

That was the last time I saw him. He left parliament just before the 2005 election.

A couple of weeks later we received our reply from Hazel Blears. It was as expected: there was to be no public inquiry.

| Corporate Capture

2003-2005

Though the New Labour administration of Tony Blair had gone some way in challenging the Metropolitan Police over racism with the first public inquiry into the Stephen Lawrence murder, the Macpherson Report, they seemed very reluctant to tackle the allegations of corruption emanating from Daniel Morgan's murder.

What was the obstacle? Was it pressure from senior Scotland Yard figures? New Labour certainly followed a policy of 'tough on crime, tough on the causes of crime', which promised support for the police. But were other concerns hindering further investigations into the corrupt circle of cops around Southern Investigations?

One factor was the extent to which bent cops and dodgy private eyes had by then penetrated the media. The brief window of the probe into Southern Investigations revealed that Rees and Fillery had helped spawn a new industry, with numerous imitators and sub-contractors in the growing market for illicit information. Despite Rees' arrest, the industry kept expanding.

Glenn Mulcaire's phone-hacking operations, under the editorship of Andy Coulson, were ramping up. Individual journalists at the Mirror Group were by this time also routinely intercepting voicemails for stories. Meanwhile, when another private investigator, Steve Whittamore, was raided by the Information Commission in March 2003, they discovered that in the preceding years alone eight national daily newspapers and ten national Sundays had made 13,343 requests for confidential data 'certainly or very probably' obtained illegally.

Operation Motorman revealed that many senior Fleet Street journalists had made requests of 'Secret Steve' from 2000 to 2003, including Rebekah Brooks. It appeared as if Whittamore had picked up a lot of the business of paying for access to the Police National Computer that Rees had specialised in until his arrest.

Under a Met spin-off inquiry, Operation Glade, *News of the World* news editor Greg Miskiw was interviewed under caution with three other journalists on suspicion of paying cops for access to confidential information.

Whittamore was convicted for only a small sample of his offences and received the minimum possible sentence. No journalists were charged because, as a senior figure from the Information Commissioner's Office told Nick Davies, 'the newspapers would hire senior barristers who would fight every inch of the way and run up huge legal bills and simply bust their budget'.

The Whittamore raid took place only three days before the three leading editors of their generation, Piers Morgan, Rebekah Brooks and Andy Coulson, appeared before a Culture, Media and Sport select committee in Parliament.

From the books in which Whittamore recorded orders for confidential information, it emerged that 47 of the Mirror Group journalists had made 984 illegal requests. But the editor-in-chief of the newspapers, Piers Morgan, maintained that while the newspapers used to be 'lawless' they no longer were. 'I have worked in Fleet Street for 15 years,' he told the Parliamentary select committee. 'I have never known standards to be higher than they are today.'

Questioned about complaints from the public about privacy intrusion, Morgan said that *The Daily Mirror* followed up such allegations with 'massive inquests'. However, when a Conservative MP, Adrian Flook, asked: 'Can you give us an example of the last massive inquest?', Morgan had no answers.

Flook didn't know at the time, but a young *Mirror* journalist, Tom Newton Dunn, had requested a Police National Computer search on him. Because it was a criminal offence to search the PNC without proper authorisation, Whittamore charged newspapers £500 a time.

Piers Morgan's evidence was followed later that morning by Rebekah Brooks, who had just moved to *The Sun*, and Andy Coulson, who had taken over as editor of the *News of the World*. They were flanked by lawyers and advisors, along with Coulson's deputy, Neil Wallis.

As the session wound down, Labour MP Chris Bryant began to ask Brooks about the connection between private detectives and police officers selling on information to press. (A fellow MP had lost his wallet the previous evening and been called by *The Sun* about it before the police made contact.)

'Do either of your newspapers ever use private detectives, ever bug or pay the police?' Bryant asked *The Sun* and *News of the World* editors. When Rebekah

Brooks gave a vague reply, the Labour MP was blunter: 'And on the element of whether you ever pay the police for information?'

'We have paid the police for information in the past,' Brooks admitted.

'And will you do it in the future?' Bryant persisted.

Before she could answer, Andy Coulson interrupted, realising the clanger. 'We operate within the PPC [Press Complaints Commission] code and within the law,' he explained, 'and if there is a clear public interest, then we will.'

Stunned by the response, Bryant said, 'It's illegal for police officers to receive payments.'

'No. I just said, within the law,' Coulson repeated.

In his diary, *The Insider*, published three years later, Piers Morgan noted sarcastically that his good friend 'Rebekah excelled herself by virtually admitting she's been illegally paying policemen for information. I called to thank her for dropping the tabloid baton at the last minute.'

He needn't have worried about the police though.

Despite pleas to Andy Hayman, the Metropolitan Police did nothing. Instead of newspapers being investigated for admitting to breaking the law, the reverse happened: the lawmakers came under the spotlight.

Chris Bryant, like Adrian Flook before him, became a target of Brooks' and Coulson's employees for the next eight years, constantly being mocked and monstered in editorials, and in *The Sun*, and placed under surveillance and extensively hacked by the *News of the World*.

* * *

Like the reaction to the Parliamentary select committee, the response from Murdoch's newspapers to the media crimes exposed in the third Daniel Morgan murder investigation was not contrition or apology, but a counteroffensive.

Mulcaire's phone hacking was now directed to most of the senior members of the cabinet, including Tony Blair, his deputy, John Prescott, Chancellor Gordon Brown and Chief Spokesman Alastair Campbell. Twenty-one of the 29 politicians who settled phone-hacking claims were senior Labour Party figures.[1]

But there was also a striking focus on senior Metropolitan Police officers and the government department they answered to – the Home Office.

Commissioner Sir Ian Blair and Deputy Commissioner John Yates and Andy Hayman were among the many police targets, as well as Jacqui Hames and Dave Cook. Four successive home secretaries were targeted in the first six years of the millennium – Jack Straw, David Blunkett, Charles Clarke and John Reid.

This counter-offensive was dual-pronged – charm and blackmail. Rebekah Brooks, already regularly socialising with the Met Commissioner Sir John Stevens, became a particularly good friend of Home Secretary David Blunkett, socialising with him on many occasions. Blunkett's special advisor, Katherine Raymond, started dating and would soon marry Brooks' boss, CEO of News International, Les Hinton.

Meanwhile Blunkett was a prime target for the *News of the World*, who hacked the voicemails of those close to him, especially in 2004 around his relationship with a married woman. Andy Coulson, in constant contact at the time with his then lover, Rebekah Brooks, went to see Blunkett personally to tell him about the story on the Saturday before he was going to publish. Blunkett argued it wasn't in the public interest, but all Coulson would concede was not naming the woman in question. However, Brooks' paper named her as Kimberly Quinn the day after the *News of the World* splashed the affair.

Seven years later, when the *News of the World* was raided during the phone-hacking scandal, police officers found a dozen tapes with Blunkett's voicemails in the safe of the newspaper's lawyer, Tom Crone, and a copy of the birth certificate of Blunkett and Quinn's child.

When Blunkett was replaced by Charles Clarke in 2004, he was also extensively targeted by Mulcaire and their surveillance expert, former cop Derek Webb, on the orders of *News of the World* executives, who thought they'd discovered another home secretary was having an affair – he wasn't. But such was the hold the Sunday tabloid had over the politicians in charge of the police that Charles Clarke, who regularly socialised with deputy editor Neil Wallis, agreed to an unusual interview for the Sunday tabloid.

On 23rd March 2005, the Home Secretary was grilled by none other than 'Fake Sheikh' Mazher Mahmood, the dark arts master who had been trained by Southern Investigations.

Mahmood's interview with the man in charge of the Metropolitan Police was timely. Two years beforehand, after his story about a plot to kidnap Victoria Beckham fell apart, the Met launched Operation Canopus on the allegations of one of his associates, that Mahmood had committed various firearms and counterfeit crimes, and perverted the course of justice. These went nowhere.

Instead, like Alex Marunchak and Rebekah Brooks three years earlier, Mahmood and his editor Andy Coulson were invited for drinks with the Met Commissioner Sir John Stevens, according to Mahmood's own autobiography.

By 2005 Mahmood was not only grilling Charles Clarke, he was working with Scotland Yard, the CPS and the *News of the World* on another spurious splash, the 'Red Mercury – Dirty Bomb' plot. The case against the three men collapsed before it ever came to trial. But Mahmood was accused of more detailed crimes and a second investigation into him, Operation Canopus 2, was launched.

Mahmood was interviewed under caution in October 2005 and casually admitted his role in suborning police officers. 'I've got bent police officers that are witnesses, that are informants,' he told his interrogators, and later boasted, 'I've got some senior officers in Britain who are also my informants.' Nothing came of this inquiry; no investigation seems to have taken place into the identities of these bent cops and senior officers.

That November, John Ross, the former Met detective who had become Alex Marunchak's major police tipster, was acquitted after a trial for paying a police constable for information. He had been caught in an investigation into *The Sun* after actor and comedian Lenny Henry had complained the police had leaked details about racist threats to the tabloid.

Ross told the *Press Gazette* that the police dropped their investigation into *The Sun* because 'they didn't want to open that can of worms'. Once again, News International was like a Bermuda Triangle in which any potential investigation of media crimes disappeared without trace.

Part of this reluctance from the Met could have come from the close associations of senior police officers with senior press executives, especially around Murdoch's titles. Newspapers such as *The Sun* and the *News of the World* could make or break the careers of senior Metropolitan Police officers by favourable spin or adverse publicity.

News International also provided excellent work opportunities. When he retired in 2005, Sir John Stevens went on to write a weekly column called 'The Chief' for the *News of the World*, ghostwritten by the former *People* editor Neil Wallis. Meanwhile, Andy Hayman would soon leave the Met under a shadow to write a column for *The Times*.

But the corporate capture goes much wider than that: any senior officer could see that Brooks, Coulson, Wallis and Mahmood seemed to have access and control over very senior political figures, particularly in the Home Office. The prime minister, Tony Blair was godfather to Rupert Murdoch's two daughters with Wendy Deng. Who was to take on the powerful global media baron, the '24th member of the cabinet'[2] who had a tool more public and powerful than the security services – the dark arts – at his disposal?

* * *

The question remains, despite his weekly calls to *News of the World* editors, how much did the chair of News Corp, Rupert Murdoch, know about the dark arts, particularly Rees and Fillery and the SERCS circle of corruption?

Southern Investigations was certainly known to Murdoch's veteran managing editor, Stuart Kuttner, his in-house lawyer, Tom Crone, and of course his senior executive, Alex Marunchak.[3] But was the criminality underpinning Murdoch's first major newspaper in the UK in 1969 just an aberration? Was the penetration by bent cops and private detectives an accident of geography and history – the proximity of south-east London to Murdoch's new plant at Wapping, which required such a heavy police presence in its early days?

Marunchak's association with Rees and Fillery could be an accident; Mazher Mahmood's training by Southern Investigations could be a coincidence. But there are two more important points of contact between News International and associates of Fillery and Rees.

David Leppard, whom Alastair Morgan had approached in Wapping within months of Daniel's murder, was still the senior *Sunday Times* home affairs correspondent a decade later.

In 2000, according to Nick Davies, Leppard had been working for five years with a minor conman called Barry Beardall, who was using illicit means 'attempting to entrap various politicians'. In January of that year, Beardall conned an upmarket London law firm into handing over confidential material on Gordon Brown's finances. In May Beardall targeted a Labour candidate for the Mayor of London, Frank Dobson, posing as a property developer who wanted a deal in return for a £10,000 donation to the Dobson campaign.

However, by this point Barry Beardall had been arrested for conspiring to cheat HMRC out of £7m in VAT by importing 700,000 bottles of vodka without paying duty. In April 2001, Beardall's career at *The Sunday Times* came to an abrupt halt when he was convicted of fraud at Southampton Crown Court and gaoled for six and a half years.

While serving his sentence at the open prison, HMP Ford, Beardall soon hooked up with another inmate, Jonathan Rees. They shared information on their cases and attempts to overturn their convictions.[4] On their release from prison, Rees and Beardall would set up a company together, Pure Energy, with Alex Marunchak.

* * *

David Leppard was also familiar with the allegations around Commander Ray Adams, as he apparently called Derek Haslam for a response when Operation Russell led to Adams' exoneration in 1990.

In 1996 Raymond Adams had been recruited as European head of operation security for NDS, a satellite encryption service owned by News Corp, staffed by former police and intelligence officers.[5]

Given the high sensitivity of Adams' job, reporting directly to Rupert Murdoch, there is little doubt the Corporation did extensive background checks on Adams. It's also hard to believe that two of Murdoch's most senior reporters in London, Leppard and Marunchak, who knew all about the allegations surrounding Adams, didn't pass this on to their boss in New York.

By 2002, however, Raymond Adams was in trouble again in the first under-reported 'hacking scandal' involving a Murdoch company. The former Met commander was cited by plaintiffs in a billion-dollar piracy suit by rival smart-card manufacturer Nagrastar and its parent company, Echostar. They alleged NDS had hacked their access cards, and Canal Plus joined the suit for passing on the details and flooding the market with clones through a computer site for pirates, The House of Ill Compute (THOIC).

Lee Gibling was the main source of codes and software for manufacturing pirate access cards behind THOIC. He was caught hacking BSkyB cards by Ray Adams.

Adams vehemently denies the allegations that rather than prosecution, he offered Gibling employment and a budget of £60,000 a year to expand the site and distribute software and codes that could breach the encryption of BSkyB's rivals.[6] One of those rivals, ITV Digital, went bust in 2002 due to the piracy it was experiencing, losing $2bn for its investors and 1,500 jobs in the UK.

The Australian Financial Review would later allege that Australian Pay-TV companies had also been hacked. But Canal Plus dropped their civil suit against Murdoch when its Italian arm was bought by News Corp to create Sky Italia. In 2008, a Californian jury found in Echostar's favour and in 2012, the US Supreme Court upheld the judgement that NDS had violated anti-piracy laws.

A few days after a BBC *Panorama* programme exposed the extent of satellite card hacking, News Corp sold NDS to Cisco systems.

Raymond Adams left NDS in 2002 in the wake of the satellite smart card hacking allegations but alleged someone had stolen the hard drive to his computer from his car before he could hand it back to his employers. When the contents of that hard drive emerged a decade later, one email showed that NDS had paid Surrey Police £2,000 on a dedicated budget code account 880110, which provided for 'a contingency sum for police informants'.[7]

The former commander's charmed detective career didn't end there. By 2004, Adams had procured a travelling role with the UK National Crime Squad's high-tech crime unit.

| The Golden Thread

2004-2006

ALASTAIR: Early in November 2004 the ITV London documentary, *The London Programme*, on Dan's murder was broadcast. It occurred to me after the London programme that someone from the Metropolitan Police Authority might have seen it. This was a body set up by the Labour government to oversee the work of the Metropolitan Police. I wrote a letter to my local representative on the Authority, a woman called Jennette Arnold.

That December she came over to our flat and watched a recording of the ITV London documentary and I filled in some of the important details that the programme hadn't included. Jennette is a black woman and appeared to have few illusions about the British police. I wanted the support of the MPA in our call for a public inquiry. She promised she would take the matter up with Len Duvall, the new chairman of the MPA.

'There aren't many people in politics that I really trust,' she said. 'But Len is a man of integrity and I trust him completely. Give me some time and I promise I'll get back to you on this.'

I'd decided that in 2005 I would take our fight for a judicial inquiry to a new level. My job was to keep the media interested. By the end of February only two articles had been published. *Private Eye* had been following the story for years and Heather Mills wrote a piece. Another appeared in *The Pakistan Daily Times* – I've no idea why they picked up on the story.

We needed a more striking way of getting media coverage of our campaign. The eighteenth anniversary of Daniel's death was coming up. To my surprise, Mum said that she would visit the place where he was murdered.

In all the years since Dan died, Mum had never been to the Golden Lion – she said she couldn't bear it. The closest she'd come was looking at press cuttings from the time. One of them contained a picture of the car park with the spot where Dan was killed. The patch is easily identifiable because of a large dark stain on the tarmac made by Daniel's blood.

'I couldn't face it before, Al,' she told me, 'but I'm getting old. I'm getting more angina attacks and there may not be another chance to do this. I need to see the place. I need to be able to picture it. I want to put flowers there. The press and TV will surely be interested.'

It was a cold, grey day on 10th March 2005 but the media turnout was excellent. Sky and two ITV stations showed up with their reporters and crews. Kirsteen's father, Malcolm, took pictures for the new justice4daniel website that he was running.

The cameras followed Mum as she laid a fine bouquet on the spot where Dan died. I could see tears on her cheeks as she placed the flowers, but she didn't break down. I walked over to her and put my arm round her.

'What a horrible place to die!' she said to one of the reporters.

In the interview that followed we expressed our outrage at what had taken place and our determination to secure a public inquiry. As the cameras and journalists drifted away, we walked into the pub to get a drink with our supporters. Mum told me she was glad she'd done it.

'It's actually a relief to have finally seen the place. It's just an ordinary car park and seeing it was cathartic,' she said.

The TV coverage was broadcast as planned and the following day there was another flurry of stories in the press.

* * *

Labour won a third successive victory in April 2005. I didn't vote, I was so disillusioned with our democracy.

Two weeks later I met with Len Duvall from the Metropolitan Police Authority for the first time. Our band of MPs, Roger Williams, Jim Dowd and Emily Thornberry, who had taken over Chris Smith's seat and was now my MP, joined us at the MPA's offices. Jennette Arnold was also at the meeting.

Len Duvall was different from most politicians. A street-wise south Londoner, he took what I said at face value and quickly understood the gravity of the issues.

'Your family have been treated appallingly by the police,' he told me, 'and since you've told me about it, it's my duty to do something about it.'

I felt like hugging him. No one in authority had ever said that to us.

Len didn't have the power to order a public inquiry, but the MPA were only a stone's throw away from New Scotland Yard and the Met Police. 'I'll have to take legal advice to find out exactly what powers I have,' he told us. 'Give me a few weeks to think through this and I'll get back to you with a proposal.'

But he did make one immediate suggestion. He'd read our website and seen the exchange of letters over disclosure of the Hampshire Report. He asked if there were any police documents we wanted.

I felt like dancing in the street after my first meeting with Len. I compiled a wish list of documents I wanted to see, including anything written by DSU Campbell on the first investigation. I particularly wanted to see any material about Dan approaching the media and being offered '£250,000 for a story on police corruption'. I also wanted more recent paperwork like the un-redacted transcript of Duncan Hanrahan's bugged conversation in prison about Daniel's murder.

At our second meeting with Len Duvall, the usual MPs came along, and this time Kirsteen and our lawyer Raju Bhatt were also present. I thought the meeting would be about progress in getting the Met to hand over the documents, but Len had come up with a totally different idea.

'As you know, the MPA can't order a public inquiry,' he told us, 'but there are two things that we can do to move your brother's case forward. Under Section 22 (3) of the Police Act 1996, we can require the Commissioner to write a report on Daniel's murder and the subsequent investigations. The report will be made available to you.'

My heart sank. I had no faith in anything the police would say.

'I know how you feel, Alastair, because of your dealings with the police in the past. But this is a different process. It's not just you talking to the police, the MPA will be saying let's get to the bottom of this.'

Depending on our response to the report, Len could then decide to appoint an experienced QC – approved by us – to review all the case papers. This barrister would have the power to recommend a public inquiry. This option would require a vote by the full MPA.

* * *

In October 2005, the full monthly meeting of the MPA was due to consider Len's proposal. I'd been in regular contact with Jennette Arnold and she'd told me that Met Commissioner Ian Blair had been informed of the plan and that the Met had promised full cooperation.

It was a special day. We were met by Len's assistant, who told us that two rows of seats had been reserved for us in the meeting room. Several of the back seats were occupied by men we had never seen before. I quickly figured out that they were cops who'd been put there to prevent us expressing our feelings in unorthodox ways if we got upset.

Daniel Morgan was item 10 on the agenda. Ian Blair and around three of his senior colleagues were sitting in a row next to the table. I could only get a sideways view of them.

The MPA's Chief Executive Catherine Crawford opened proceedings by outlining the proposal that would be voted on. Sir Ian Blair, the Commissioner, would have to present a 'comprehensive and transparent report' by January 2006. At that point the Authority would be invited to consider appointing an independent barrister to carry out a review.

The Met's Assistant Commissioner Alan Brown then explained that the death of Daniel Morgan had been the subject of four investigations and that the last investigation had been considered by a QC and two barristers who'd said there was insufficient evidence to prosecute. He said the police were confident that they had done all they could to identify who committed the murder.

So far Alan Brown had said nothing unexpected. What he said next came like a bolt from the blue. 'The proposals you have in front of you would have a significant impact on resources,' Brown continued. 'It would be impossible to get the report here before next January. The second phase would be reinvestigated by a barrister. That will take longer than 12 months. We have an alternative suggestion.'

There was murmuring and fidgeting by the MPA members.

Brown then suggested that only the fourth inquiry should be re-examined by a barrister and that it might be appropriate to use one of the CPS barristers who'd already said there wasn't enough evidence to prosecute. His proposal was met by an embarrassing silence. The Commissioner shifted in his chair as he waited for the Authority's reaction. It was obvious that the whole Authority felt insulted and embarrassed by this last-minute move of the goalposts.

Jennette spoke first. She stressed how long the Met had known about the MPA proposals and that they had promised to cooperate fully. 'I'm therefore gutted that the service waits to this time for an alternative suggestion,' Jeanette protested. 'This is the sort of behaviour that people don't understand. We are here to hold the police to account on behalf of Londoners. The Service really needs to wake up and treat us with respect.'

Commissioner Ian Blair told the meeting, quite truthfully, that he knew a lot about the case as he'd been in overall charge of the fourth inquiry. He went on to say that the first inquiry was 'compromised', as if everybody already knew this. In fact, no commissioner had ever before admitted any failures in the original investigation. As he uttered the word, I knew we'd made a huge breakthrough. The Commissioner of Police was telling the truth about the first inquiry, at last!

Sir Ian continued that they would use a CPS barrister and to limit that role to looking at the fourth inquiry was 'professional'. 'I just don't know what you're going to find that the fourth investigation didn't,' he added.

The leader of the Conservative group on the MPA chimed in: 'Can I offer you some advice, Commissioner? When you're in a hole, stop digging!'

The matter was put to the vote and to our delight Len's proposal was approved unanimously. ITV Wales and ITV London were outside in the street with their cameras. For once we had something positive to tell them – and it felt fantastic!

* * *

The report should have been ready by Christmas 2005, but it wasn't. To our annoyance, the Met said it had been delayed for legal reasons. Late in January, I heard that it would be delivered to Len on Friday, 27th January. We waited impatiently to hear from him.

The following Monday I sent him a rambling email complaining about the delay. On the Thursday, I received an email from the Head of the Secretariat at the MPA, saying Len had read Commissioner Blair's report and decided that it was 'not adequate, for example in either reaching an understanding of past investigations or in acknowledging how possible misconduct by one or more officers may have affected the investigation of this murder'.

Len was going to tell the MPS the following day that he was 'not prepared to accept the report as it stood'.

Everything had changed. Suddenly it was as though we were calling the shots and the police were on the back foot. And all because a couple of people in authority had started listening to us! I banged out a press release and sent it out to the 600 or so journalists on our mailing list.

'Hallelujah! Justice for the little people!' I shouted down the phone to Kirsteen.

Len and I agreed that we would all meet on 10th February to discuss the report and the reasons why he had rejected it.

I was in for another surprise.

* * *

Len met us with David Riddle, the solicitor to the MPA. He told us that the police wanted to apologise to us for the first inquiry and had conceded that it had been significantly tainted by corruption.

'The Commissioner should be the one that apologises. I think it should be done formally. They can write to you or you can meet them, it's your choice.'

The Met were going to apologise, to us! We could hardly believe it! My head was still reeling from the idea that the top man at the Yard wanted to apologise to us when Len told us that Deputy Assistant Commissioner John Yates and DSU David Zinzan were there.

'I want you to meet them now, there's a new lead,' Len said.

We were in turmoil. What was happening? What about the report and the independent barrister? Len explained that it was his intention that the report should be finished. 'We will run our inquiry in parallel with the police investigation. I don't want to have stopped the MPA process in case the new lead doesn't come to anything.'

If the new lead did go somewhere the report couldn't be published but the family could still see it. Len said he usually liked things in the open but the MPA obviously didn't want to do anything that would prejudice an investigation.

'When does this become a red herring?' he continued. He could see I was still suspicious and echoed my thoughts saying he would request fortnightly reports on the police investigation.

The MPA's solicitor, David Riddle, interjected: 'We have some information about the new lead, but not everything. This is a fast-moving situation,' he said.

At that point DAC John Yates and David Zinzan entered the room. They sat down opposite us.

I'd never met John Yates, but I'd read about him in Michael Gillard and Laurie Flynn's book *Untouchables*. He'd been responsible for dealing with the police supergrass Neil Putnam.

'This has been one of the most deplorable episodes in the history of the Metropolitan Police,' Yates started saying. 'It was tainted by corruption. I'm prepared to apologise or the Commissioner will do this. Those entrusted with investigating homicide have to do it with commitment and that didn't happen. I can't prove some things but in my view, it's deplorable and we have to face up to it as an organisation.'

We were taken aback by his frankness.

'The fourth inquiry was a determined investigation,' Yates continued, referring to Operation Abelard. 'We nearly made it and the progress made in that inquiry helps us now. There's something that I want to discuss with you. It's so sensitive and technical and there are lots of difficulties. It has to be kept within a tight group of people. You're going to have to trust me on this. I know you trust David.'

David Zinzan took over. 'The new lead is potentially enormously productive. Orlando Pownall, barrister for the CPS, thought we were pretty close at the end of the fourth inquiry. Some of the witnesses are not perfect. Orlando Pownall says it just needs something to pull all this together. We're at the early stages but we may have that golden thread. It's complex, it will take some time to develop. We want to use triggers. We may want to use you, the family, to make these triggers happen.'

I looked at my mother's face. She was gazing intently at the two policemen. I knew that her hopes were being raised and I almost wanted to shake her to warn her.

John Yates must have read my mind. 'You have every right not to trust police, but this has very significant potential.'

David Zinzan backed him up. 'I wouldn't have come here if I didn't think there was a significant way forward. Dave Cook and I want to see this solved because we want to nail the bastards. This could give us an opportunity for a trial.'

Yates added that Cook has never really stopped investigating – 'he lives and breathes this case and is determined to bring this one home.' Because Zinzan was now working for Special Branch, David Cook would lead the new inquiry.

Everything was happening so fast, but they'd still told us nothing about the new lead.

'There's someone's life at stake and I have a duty of care around the way that sources are handled,' Yates said. 'I will give you a full and frank briefing after six to eight weeks.'

It was clear this was all they were going to tell us. Mum, I could see, was excited by the smallest chance that we might yet get Dan's killers to court. She pressed Yates about Sid Fillery's role and he didn't mince his words.

'Fillery is, and was, corrupt,' Yates told her. 'We know he was corrupt and he's a corrupter as well. He's a thoroughly bad lot. He's brought shame on himself and the police. Sir Ian is as disgusted as I am and knows it's brought shame on us. The MPS want to apologise to your family.'

* * *

Two decades of dealing with the Metropolitan Police had changed my relationship with the world forever. I trusted no one in authority. My temper was short; I suffered bouts of depression lasting days at a time. The sudden ups and downs on this brutal rollercoaster were hard to take. I don't know how Kirsteen put up with me. Once again, we were being asked to take a leap of faith and trust the organisation that had let us down so many times before.

When Mum and I told Jane what had happened with Yates and Zinzan she was quite clear. 'Just leave me out of this,' Jane would often say after these police briefings. 'The last time I believed a policeman was when Fillery told me to get Alastair out of London in 1987. I'm not going to let the Met peddle false hopes again. They're just trying to close the door on Len Duvall's plans.'

I had a lot of sympathy with her views. Of course we wanted Dan's killers convicted and maybe the new lead was a step in that direction but only a public inquiry could answer all our questions. A trial would simply determine whether the suspects were guilty – it wouldn't be concerned with what had gone wrong in the previous 19 years.

In my mind, two crimes had taken place. The first was the murder, the second was the cover-ups; I'd often talk to Kirsteen about this.

'A rat is a rat,' I'd say, referring to the people who had killed Daniel. 'And rats do what rats do. But a policeman's a policeman – he's there to detect criminals and bring them to justice.'

Jonathan Rees had betrayed us, but Sid Fillery's betrayal was much worse: he was a cop. Worse still was the fact he'd been protected by colleagues of every rank in the police service. We'd experienced layer upon layer of betrayal. I'd no intention of leaving the situation as it stood, even if the police finally got convictions.

Raju Bhatt understood what I was talking about. 'I know exactly what you mean, Alastair,' he would nod. 'I've dealt with many clients in similar situations. Often they feel that the cover-up is worse than the crime itself.'

'It's because they're the people we're taught to trust,' I said. 'That's what makes it so painful.'

But we had no choice; we had to go along with the new inquiry, however much we suspected the motivation behind it. And while this was going on, we were still waiting for the Commissioner's report.

Finally, on the afternoon of the very last day of their deadline, the Met delivered the report. They'd taken nearly six months to answer the eight questions the MPA had put to them.

When I read the report, I was disappointed. John Yates had told us the case was 'one of the most deplorable episodes in the history of the Metropolitan Police Service', so I was expecting something more dramatic.

Raju disagreed. 'The report is very significant,' he said, 'because it points out that the first investigation was flawed because of the corrupt involvement of Fillery.'

'So, that must undermine the grounds on which the Home Office refused a public inquiry,' I replied.

'Of course it does.'

'So, we've still got that card up our sleeve, then. Good!'

Raju had cheered me up. He'd read behind the bland language and could see what was really being admitted to.

We'd also learned several important things from the report. Firstly, that many of the exhibits from the investigation in 1987 had gone missing. The original exhibits officer in the case had been disciplined and another officer had leaked information to the media. The report also stated that none of the officers on the third, secret inquiry – Operation Nigeria/Two Bridges – were aware they were investigating a murder.

We'd joked about this privately as being the most secretive murder inquiry in history. We didn't know about it. And the investigators didn't even know what they were investigating!

We needed to speak to John Yates about the report, so a second meeting was arranged.

* * *

Mum was determined to come to London for that meeting on Thursday, 13th April 2006. Jane and I weren't keen on her travelling alone. Neither were the police after she'd had an angina attack on the tube a few years earlier after a particularly stressful meeting.

I sometimes think Mum's determination to see justice for Dan is what kept her alive. Jane did her best to dissuade her from coming, but I knew there was no point. When my sister told her that she couldn't come because of work commitments, Mum simply said, 'Oh well, you'll be able to look after the dog for me while I'm in London.'

A week before the scheduled meeting, Jane rang to tell me that Mum's heart problems had been getting worse. She'd been taken to hospital at two o'clock in the morning. She was discharged after some tests the following afternoon, but I now agreed with Jane that she had to be stopped from travelling alone. I rang Raju. He's very fond of Mum and she has great respect for him. I knew if anyone could talk sense into her it would be him. He got the MPA to set up a telephone conference. Not only could Mum avoid the journey, Jane could leave work an hour early and also 'be present' at the meeting.

At the meeting with John Yates and Dave Cook, who was heading up the fifth murder inquiry, we were finally told about the development that had started the fifth inquiry. As we'd suspected, it involved an informant.

'This person has indicated that he's had conversations with Glenn Vian,' Dave Cook informed us, 'that indicated he was involved in the murder. That's very significant.'

We were impatient to know how far they had got using this information.

'It's quite slow, but for good reason,' John Yates explained. 'Informants have to be cleansed so that they can become witnesses of truth. They have to confess to all of their past criminality. The whole aim of this is to seek collaborative evidence so that we don't have to use confessional evidence.'

'The focus of the investigation is on Glenn,' Dave Cook added. 'I believe we can link Glenn evidentially with Rees. And Rees, in turn, with Fillery. The fact is that despite the character flaws caused by being a convicted criminal, this person is saying he will give evidence against Glenn Vian as being responsible for the murder. We've never been able to do that before.'

Cook then quoted what the CPS had said when refusing to prosecute based on the evidence from the fourth murder inquiry. 'We'd got a lot, but not the glue to put it together,' he told us. 'I believe this could potentially glue the case together.'

I could hear the anxiety in Mum's voice. 'This is not going to drag on for months, is it?'

'I think it will,' replied Yates. 'It takes a long time to cleanse someone. We have got better at it though. There will be intense activity over several months.'

Jane asked the obvious question: 'What's in it for the informant?'

'People don't do this for nothing,' Dave Cook replied. 'He'll seek a reduction in a fairly lengthy prison sentence. I've done the first interview with him, but the rest will have to be carried out by a different team. We have a small team with firewalls so it's not contaminated.'

John Yates described the difficult process of getting people out of prison for interviews without raising suspicions: 'There are a lot of protection issues around the family. It's very delicate. His safety is paramount.'

CHAPTER 38	Trojan Horse

2004-2006

If attempts by the *News of the World* and the suspects to subvert the fourth Daniel Morgan murder inquiry weren't bad enough, the penetration of the fifth and final investigation, Abelard 2, was if anything, more comprehensive, and more disruptive.

The warnings sent to Rebekah Brooks and the Commissioner about the surveillance on David Cook and Jacqui Hames went unheeded, the perpetrators went unpunished, and so the moral was obvious: carry on as you were.

By now it was abundantly apparent to everyone involved that the corruption around Southern Investigations didn't just involve corrupt cops, unscrupulous private investigators and tabloid journalists willing to use any unethical or illegal means to get a scoop. The arrest and prosecution of Garry Vian and James Ward for drug trafficking in Operation Bedingham in 2004 only underlined the involvement of organised crime – something Daniel had been investigating many years before.

On 27th July 2005, Garry Vian was sentenced to 14 years' imprisonment for supplying Class A and Class C drugs, and James Ward was sentenced to 17 years. Five months later, Ward explained what he knew about the Daniel Morgan murder.

James Ward was in prison in 1987 during Daniel's murder, as part of the drugs syndicate run by Jimmy Holmes, the 'Eric Clapton lookalike' whom DC Alan 'Taffy' Holmes was monitoring before his death the same year.

When Ward came out of prison, he renewed his connection with Garry Vian, and went back to the drug-running business.

As a countermeasure to any police investigations, Ward asked Garry Vian to check the Police National Computer. Garry explained how he used his brother-in-law, Jon Rees, to do checks through his network of retired and serving officers. To make it clear he wasn't a police informant or grass, Vian told Ward: 'He owes me a favour as my brother has done a murder for him.'

When James Ward asked Garry whether he was directly involved in the killing, he replied: 'No, Glenn had killed him and a fella by the name of Jimmy Cook was driving the car.'

From then on for the next five years, James Ward said Garry Vian gave him 'snippets of information' about Daniel's killing. They sometimes referred to it as the 'Golden Wonder Murder' because of the two packets of crisps found by Daniel's left hand, which he had bought for his kids minutes before he was killed. At other times, Vian referred to it as the 'HP Murder' because it was done on 'hire purchase' for the price of around £20,000, to be collected at a later date.

Other contemporaries of Garry Vian recall him calling it the 'Hatchet in the Head murder' in 1987 and remember him saying Daniel Morgan was murdered because he 'knew too much' about 'Garry and others dealing drugs'.

In a later discussion with Garry's brother about getting rid of a difficult tenant, Ward says Glenn Vian also confessed to his role in the murder. They talked about assassinating the tenant, and Glenn told Ward he was 'too old to go rolling around the floor' with the target. Instead, Glenn suggested shooting him first, and then they could 'do him with an axe, the same as Morgan'. When asked how much the Morgan killing cost, Glenn Vian said £20,000 to £25,000.

* * *

While the Met were reviewing new evidence and writing the report demanded by the Metropolitan Police Authority, Jonathan Rees was preparing to leave prison and serve his parole period in Leeds.

Prison didn't deter Rees from his career of crime – quite the opposite. Derek Haslam, who visited him several times in Ford open prison, says that far from being crushed or repentant, Rees 'went into overdrive'. His considerable legal and police procedural knowledge were in great demand by other prisoners, such as Barry Beardall, to help appeal their cases and complain of police corruption. Rees also began to plan a scam involving green tax credits and grants by setting up a company called Pure Energy. Meanwhile, his other energies were still heavily focused on the press.

In one letter to Sidney Fillery on 23rd June 2002, which opened 'Dear Sarge', Jonathan Rees was asking his partner to sell a story to *The Mirror* sourced from a 'friendly prison officer' about a 'Dando suspect'. Rees also had extensive details about potential investigations into CIB 3 and the activities of Chris Jarratt, David Wood and Andy Hayman. He claimed that Mike Gillard was working with the *Sunday Times* insight team to pursue the story.

But it was Rees' ingenuity in looking for new illicit ways to source stories that would be most important in the future. In HMP Downview he had met two 'BT Chaps', who were now released. One of them was in Northern Ireland and had sold 20,000 copies of an illegal disk with ex-directory and barred BT numbers. The former offender had some other 'fabulous products', Rees told Fillery, including one which could access other people's emails.

'You merely send them an email and receive all theirs,' Rees raved. 'Of course, it's illegal – but not illegal to sell.' He went on to say these new tools of cyber espionage 'would have any newspaper journalist drooling over [them]'.

One journalist in particular would soon make rapid use of Rees' new computer hacking know-how.

* * *

Towards the end of his parole in December 2005, Jonathan Rees was – according to intelligence – absolutely certain he would be re-employed by the *News of the World* despite his criminal conviction and suspect status in the Daniel Morgan murder. He was planning to make an 'awful lot of money' from his 'insider' police stories sourced from the confidential *Police Gazette*.

Most important to Rees was his connection to Alex Marunchak, who – despite the complaints to his management about subverting the fourth murder inquiry – was still editing the Irish edition of the best-selling tabloid. According to Rees, Marunchak's protection went right to the top of News Corp, and he was 'still highly thought of by Murdoch and can do no wrong'.

Jonathan Rees is, by his own admission, a liar. But that didn't mean he never told the truth. Given the evidence from the correspondence between Bertie Ahern and Rupert Murdoch, and Alex Marunchak's continued senior executive role, Rees' claim is eminently plausible. That connection with Marunchak would soon pay dividends as the new Met Commissioner, Ian Blair, weighed up the new evidence over the Daniel Morgan murder.

It had already been agreed in March 2006 that the new evidence of 'resident informant' James Ward was insufficient in itself. So, for the first time in 20 years, material collected in the previous four investigations was amassed for review. The initial haul counted at least 250 large crates of documents, containing over 14,000 exhibits and some 2,900 items of covert audio recordings from various locations.

It wasn't until 4th April 2006, at a top-secret meeting of Commissioner Blair's management team in New Scotland Yard, that the Met finally decided to launch a fifth investigation into Daniel's murder. But this highly confidential and sensitive decision over one of the most notorious scandals in Scotland Yard's history was almost immediately leaked to Southern Investigations, giving them time to regroup, prepare for bugs and surveillance, and launch another counter-offensive.

In an intelligence report from 6th April, Jonathan Rees was caught boasting to others about how he had a link from the Commissioner's 'inner sanctum'. Rees claimed he'd manage to confirm the rumours of the new murder inquiry, thanks to Alex Marunchak at the *News of the World*, who had checked its veracity with the previous Met Commissioner, Sir John Stevens, who was by then a regular columnist for the *News of the World* – 'one of his many employers'.

There is no suggestion that Stevens was the source of the leak and that he confirmed it to Alex Marunchak has only Rees' word to support it. But know about Abelard 2 the suspects certainly did – and they did not waste much time.

* * *

Jonathan Rees was back in business with the *News of the World* despite all that had happened. Surviving News International invoices show Rees working on stories about prisoner Maxine Carr, footballer Gary Lineker, Deputy Prime Minister John Prescott, Princess Diana biographer Andrew Morton and Prince William's then girlfriend, Kate Middleton. According to *Hack Attack* author Nick Davies, Rees was back then earning £150,000 a year from Coulson's paper, despite a long prison sentence for perverting the course of justice.

There was no attempt to hide his identity in these few recovered invoices from 2006 when Andy Coulson was editor of the *News of the World*. From previous correspondence, managing editor Stuart Kuttner could not have failed to notice Rees was back. And once again he was breaking the law.

By the spring of 2006, Jonathan Rees and Alex Marunchak were deploying a more subtle and pervasive form of surveillance – email hacking. One of their first targets was a former army intelligence operative, Ian Hurst, who they suspected had regular contact with a former British double agent, Freddie Scappaticci, who had managed to penetrate the upper echelons of the Provisional IRA. Hurst had written a book about his story called *Stakeknife*.

Despite Scappaticci being high up on the IRA's list of targets, Marunchak wrote to his reporter, Martin Breen, on 2nd June 2006 that Rees had managed to track 'Scap' to Manchester through a police Special Branch source, who also revealed that Scappaticci's witness protection was of a low level. Marunchak also asked his staff at the Irish edition of the *News of the World* if they had Scappaticci's phone number. For £2,750 they could track the former spy down to a specific street or building from his mobile phone.

The *News of the World* had already procured the double agent's wife's phone records from Jonathan Rees in February 2006.[1] But Marunchak had another trick up his sleeve. In May, he tasked Rees and another former army intelligence officer called Philip Campbell Smith to initiate email hacking of Hurst.

Campbell Smith, who ironically had been arrested by Sir John Stevens in Northern Ireland in 1999, deployed a form of Trojan Horse. The software manufactured by SpectorSoft was called eBlaster, and it infected Hurst's home computer and two laptops owned by his family. The hidden programme was a key logger, which from May to October 2006 recorded everything typed on the computers, and relayed back confidential passwords and emails.

On 5th July 2006 Jonathan Rees passed on emails about Scappaticci that Campbell Smith had hacked from Hurst's computer, faxing them directly to Alex Marunchak at the *News of the World* Irish office in Dublin. None of this was known to Hurst until a *Panorama* programme in 2011, during which Hurst was shown the July 2006 faxes and got Philip Campbell Smith to admit to the email hacking on tape.

Operation Kalmyk, an investigation into this email hacking, was launched soon afterwards, and Rees and Marunchak were arrested in October 2012. But four years later, having told the police officers investigating that charges under the Computer Misuse Act were not out of time, despite going back to 2006, the CPS decided not to prosecute.[2]

News Group Newspapers, the holding company for the *News of the World*, have admitted liability for several other cases of email hacking, including Jane Winter of the Human Rights Watch, and celebrities like the actress

Sienna Miller. But the most disturbing element of this episode is that the Metropolitan Police did not inform the victims, including several in their own force.

There's no doubt the Met knew all about this new form of surveillance. Less than a year later in March 2007, the threat of key loggers like the eBlaster programme was the focus of the Serious Organised Crime Agency (SOCA) report, Project Riverside, a scoping exercise into the private investigative industry's unlawful use of private data. Project Riverside specifically mentioned Rees and Southern Investigations, as well as other inquiries into private detectives blagging confidential data from utilities such as British Telecom and British Gas.

The Met's reluctance to prosecute or tackle the *News of the World* over email hacking in the summer of 2006 was only underlined further when Glenn Mulcaire and Clive Goodman were arrested for phone hacking that August. Though Operation Caryatid seized thousands of Mulcaire's notes detailing hundreds of phone-hacking victims, they only informed a handful of victims, and neglected to tell Dave Cook or the Deputy Prime Minister. They also ignored the glaring evidence in the top left corner of most of Mulcaire's notes that he had been 'tasked' by half a dozen senior executives and reporters.

This limited Caryatid inquiry allowed Murdoch's best-selling newspaper to maintain its 'one rogue reporter' defence until 2011.

* * *

For the Abelard 2 team, the wariness of the police around Murdoch's operations could well have derailed the fifth Daniel Morgan murder inquiry.

The second prominent victim was the undercover informant Derek Haslam. To maintain his cover, Haslam had agreed to be a 'security consultant' to the company Jonathan Rees had set up on release from prison, Pure Energy, along with Alex Marunchak and Barry Beardall on the advisory board. But during one of their recurrent fallouts, Leighton had targeted them all with the eBlaster Trojan.

For six years, Derek Haslam had relayed back his confidential reports to his DPS handlers through dictating written notes, which they recorded under the codename 'Charles Little'. But in 2004, despite his reservations, his handlers began to require Haslam to file his confidential reports under the pseudonym 'Joe Poulton' on a floppy disk.

Thanks to the eBlaster software, Haslam's reports were discovered and his role as an informant revealed to Leighton and then Rees. His cover was finally fully blown by former *Mirror* journalist, Sylvia Jones, who had been sent some of Haslam's covert reports in the summer of 2006, and wrote to Kensington Police Station in June 2007 to complain about them.

By this point, Haslam had been pulled out and offered police protection. He still had no idea that his reports had been compromised and refused the offer of relocation. For nine years he'd worked undercover, passing on intelligence about Rees and Fillery for a total remuneration of about £23,000 in expenses.

Derek Haslam's investigation into the connection between Daniel's murder and the suspicious suicide of his old friend Alan Holmes was over. But email hacking may well have been much more widespread and damaging to the fifth murder inquiry.

Alastair Morgan had noted that his computer was running slowly and informed DCS Dave Cook, who took immediate steps to have the device reformatted. Since they were sharing information with the Morgan family at this point, it was a dangerous breach of security.

Then Dave Cook checked his own computer and found two key logger viruses on the hard drive, which would have compromised his emails. DCI Noel Beswick subsequently found another key logger on his computer in 2010. This was during extensive legal arguments in court, in which the defence always seemed to have the upper hand.

That summer further intelligence indicated that Alex Marunchak and his ex-Met pal, John Ross, were trying to hawk a story of Jacqui Hames' business interests around Fleet Street, in order to compromise her husband, Dave Cook, in charge of the fifth murder inquiry.

One afternoon the couple's children came home from school only to spot a man in a balaclava in the garden of their Surrey home. Once again, Cook and Hames had to step up their security protocols, and the new threat opened old wounds.

Even before the arrests of Glenn Mulcaire and Clive Goodman in August 2006, Andy Coulson and his deputy, Neil Wallis, did try to sideline Alex Marunchak in his executive role at the *News of the World*. He left the editorship of the Irish edition of the newspaper in June with an enhanced redundancy package, a pension signed off by Coulson, and a three-year pay formula. He still carried on working for the paper as an outside contributor.

In October 2006, intelligence reports state that Rees was trying to pump *Sun* crime reporter Mike Sullivan for the name of the police officer who had sourced the paper's story about finding Daniel's Austin Healey.

When Sullivan refused to divulge his Met source, Rees threatened to get hold of his 'call listings' to track down the police officer. The report indicated he was going to get the help of Alex Marunchak.

Marunchak and Rees seemed to be more permanent fixtures at the *News of the World* than any other editor or journalist. Andy Coulson resigned as editor in January 2007, when Goodman and Mulcaire were finally sentenced for their phone-hacking convictions. A few months later he was hired by the Conservative opposition leader, David Cameron, as his chief spokesman, on the recommendation of George Osborne and Rebekah Brooks.

Both Jonathan Rees and Alex Marunchak would continue working for the *News of the World* – Rees until November 2008, 21 years after Daniel Morgan's murder.

2006–2008

ALASTAIR: Dave Cook had warned me in June that he wanted to stimulate discussion among the suspects by getting an article published about DNA evidence. He'd chosen *The Sun* because of its circulation. 'These people don't read *The Guardian* and I want to make sure that they see this,' he told me.

The article that came out in July – 'COPS IN "KILL" PLOT' – was blunt and to the point.

'A secret police "ghost squad" has been set up to solve a private eye's murder,' the *Sun*'s crime correspondent Mike Sullivan wrote. 'The 20-man squad have spent two years working at a secret location and are waiting for the results of vital new DNA tests.'

Sullivan then quoted David Cook as saying: 'We'll bring the killers to justice even if it opens a can of worms.'

A few days later, Raju Bhatt rang me to say that John Yates had asked to see him alone in ten days' time. I was extremely agitated by this news – what could they possibly want to tell Raju that they couldn't tell us? I imagined that they were going to tell us they'd discovered that Daniel had a terrible secret life that none of us was aware of. I was fearful of slurs and fabrications by those that had murdered him.

Raju persuaded the police to reschedule the meeting and after a nervous couple of days, Raju, Kirsteen and I met David Cook. There wasn't enough time to arrange for Jane and Mum to come up.

Inside Tintagel House the atmosphere was tense.

'Well, where can I start?' Dave Cook looked uncomfortable. Then he saw Kirsteen opening her notebook.

'Can I ask you not to take notes, just this once?' Dave said. 'I'd like what I'm about to tell you to remain among ourselves.'

My heart sank: this was going to be bad.

'Garry has a stepson called Dean Vian,' said Dave. He coughed and then went on: 'Dean has been working for the Metropolitan Police for three years. John Yates was extremely embarrassed about this and that's why he wanted to see Raju alone.'

I was stunned. At the same time, I felt a surge of relief – but what did this mean?

'We've caught Dean on the probe at Glenn's house,' Dave explained, 'offering to do checks on the Police National Computer. He hasn't done any checks yet. We've tried to get him out on an assault charge, but he was found not guilty.'

'Does he know you're onto him?' I asked, still trying to grasp the implications of what I'd just heard.

'No, a different team is monitoring him, but they give the information to us. If I go in and arrest him, my cover is blown.'

I asked how Dean had managed to get through the Met's vetting system. Dave said he'd got in during a massive recruitment drive.

'I feel sure that Dean is not a danger to this case though, in fact we may be able to use him to our advantage at some point,' he added.

I don't know whether it was because Dave Cook was relieved to get the Dean Vian issue off his chest, or because Kirsteen wasn't scribbling down every word, but for the first time he named PW1 to us and explained how he had become a witness.

Protected Witness 1's real name was James Ward. Dave explained that James Ward and Garry Vian had been caught attempting to smuggle industrial quantities of cocaine into Britain inside a fake piano. Ward had been sentenced to 17 years' imprisonment in July 2005. When he was arrested he'd given Dave information about Daniel's murder but refused to provide a statement.

Dave had stayed in touch with Ward and on 22nd December 2005, while on a skiing holiday, he received a phone call from Ward saying he wanted to see him. When they met, Ward agreed to give evidence.

'He's in his fifties and he doesn't want to die in jail,' explained Dave, when we asked why he had grassed on Glenn. 'He'll get a considerable reduction in sentence for helping us with his evidence.'

Going back to the time when we were first told about the new lead, Dave Cook explained: 'I can see what the timing must have looked like … There you were, getting results with the MPA and all of sudden we walk back into your lives and say there's a new lead. But I can promise you, Alastair, there was nothing sinister. It's true that we did deliberately slow things down with Ward in January.'

'Why was that?' I asked.

Dave explained that they'd been forced to wait until the new Serious and Organised Crime and Police Act (SOCPA) came into force, governing how police dealt with supergrasses and informants. Previously, if a prisoner had helped to convict a criminal, the prosecution would have a word in the judge's ear and might get a reduction in sentence. But it was messy and led to a lot of suspicion that criminals would stitch each other up in return for a few years less in prison.

The new act formalised the supergrass system. Under the new SOCPA system before informants gave evidence they had to go through a debriefing process where they were 'cleansed'. This involved telling the debriefing team about every crime they'd ever committed and handing over all the money they'd made from crime. They then had to sign a formal written agreement with the Crown Prosecution Service.

'It must have looked sinister to you,' said Dave, 'but we really couldn't give you any details when we first told you about the new lead. Lives really were in danger and they still are. You mustn't tell anyone about this, not even Jane or Isobel. I don't want you to talk on the phone about it. I will go down to Wales next week and tell them what I've told you.'

As we left Tintagel House, I felt physically lighter. Not only was I relieved that nothing bad had happened in Dan's case, but it also meant a lot that Dave had told me about James Ward. The timing wasn't sinister, it was just a coincidence that the new lead had come at a time when the Met was being forced to confess to some awkward truths. I felt Jane would understand this too when Dave went to explain to her and Mum.

* * *

A couple of days later, Dave rang again with some very important information. He told me that after the *Sun* article they'd been approached by another person who wanted to talk – and this time the motive for Dan's murder was police corruption.

Once again, Dave could not divulge his identity for security reasons and we had to call him PW2 (Protected Witness Two) at the time, but his real name was Gary Eaton.

Over the next few months Eaton gave police a huge amount of information about the murder and his own criminal past. After his initial meeting with Dave Cook, he was handed over to a special debriefing team. This was made up of officers who had nothing to do with the investigation into Dan's murder. The reason for this was so that there was a 'sterile corridor' so these officers could not then be accused of 'coaching him' or inducing him to say anything that could taint the evidence that he was giving.

Gary Eaton told the debriefing team that he'd worked for Southern Investigations in 1986, mainly with the repo man Jimmy Cook. He'd met Jonathan Rees, Sidney Fillery and my brother. He told police that Cook and Fillery had known each other since 1982 when Fillery was a member of the No. 9 Regional Crime Squad (the precursor to SERCS).

At the time, Eaton said he was mainly working for Jimmy Cook as a courier, carrying weapons and drugs, mostly cocaine. In early 1987, Cook had asked him twice whether he would 'dispose' of Daniel for money. The sum of £50,000 was mentioned and it would be guaranteed because Sid Fillery was in charge.

Eaton said that he'd been asked to murder Dan some weeks before it happened. In fact, he said, Jimmy Cook had asked him to do it three times in one day. He'd refused every time, he said. The motive for Daniel's murder, he said, was that Daniel had discovered that Rees and Fillery were involved in drug dealing and money laundering.

At first Gary Eaton had said that was his only involvement in the conspiracy, but later on in his debrief he revealed he had seen my brother's body.

On the evening of the murder, Gary Eaton said he had been asked by Jimmy Cook to call in at the Golden Lion to discuss a lorry hijacking. While there, he had seen Rees by the bar with a woman. One of the Vian brothers then asked him to go out into the car park. There, Cook was waiting with another Vian brother in a car. The car pulled away to reveal Daniel lying on the tarmac behind.

Eaton thought he was being framed for the murder, and immediately got into his Daimler and drove off. The sight of Daniel lying there had haunted him for years afterwards.

Dave Cook said they weren't sure whether to believe this, but a statement by a witness in the bar supported some of what Eaton said.

Gary Eaton said he'd come forward partly because of Jimmy Cook's actions. After the murder, he'd moved away from London for many years. He'd recently returned with his girlfriend, who'd taken a job in a dry-cleaner's shop. One day, he said, Jimmy Cook had visited the shop with a couple of heavies in tow. He'd threatened the girlfriend that if Eaton talked to police, she would be killed.

This, Eaton said, had annoyed him to the point where he'd decided to grass Cook up. He also told police that sometime after the murder, he'd been approached by Sid Fillery in a pub, where Fillery had warned him that if he didn't keep his mouth shut then he would end up with an axe in his head, just like Daniel.

Eaton admitted to being involved in several armed robberies. During his debriefing, he also informed police about two other murders that his associates had been involved in.

'We've started to get a degree of corroboration,' Dave Cook told us. 'He's admitted to supplying firearms, drugs dealing, extortion and robbery. But he's actually walked in and said he wanted to talk. We still can't get our heads around this.'

'Under normal circumstances he'd get 20 years in jail for the crimes he's confessed to,' Dave continued. 'He says Jimmy Cook asked him to carry out the murder on a visit to Dartford in a white Peugeot 205. They were going to do a car deal. On the way back, Jimmy Cook told him that Fillery would guarantee the money for the murder. PW2 says he knew and liked Daniel, so he refused.'

Dave explained that the police had been taking to bits everything about Eaton's criminal past and what he'd been saying. They hadn't found anything that could undermine his position.

'He appears to be putting forward accurate stuff,' Dave continued. 'He's opening up more and more. I can't find anything to say he's lying. The first two weeks, we said, "Give us everything you've got." For the past four weeks, he's been giving much more detail. We're up to 1994 now and we've got a lot more to cover. He's painted a picture of the events and we've gone some way to corroborating what he's saying. He's talked to us about the context and that gives us comfort. He's told us that Jimmy Cook and Glenn were there, and that Garry was there with another car as a lookout.'

We were overwhelmed by all of this information: it seemed too good to be true.

'Maybe he was involved in the murder, Dave?' I suggested.

'But why come forward?' he replied. 'This man was never even on our radar. We'd never heard of him before he showed up, wanting to talk. He's even handed over £70,000 to us. This money is the proceeds of crime, he says. He's had it stashed in a secret account. We would never have found it if he hadn't handed it over. I've never ever seen a situation like this in the whole of my career.'

'Surely that's going to convince a jury,' I said. 'I mean, confessing to crimes is one thing, but voluntarily handing over a stack of money? Who would do that if they weren't genuine?'

'The defence could say that he's lost his marbles,' Dave replied. 'But we can show that a lot of what he's been telling us is true. He's told us about a farm that Jimmy Cook used for drug dealing. We took him down to the farm and it was clear that he knew where everything was.'

We were delighted by this development but the debriefing process seemed endless. Gary Eaton had so much to tell the police and they were faced with the job of corroborating as much as they possibly could. This was a huge task.

On top of this, we learned that Eaton was not in good health. He had emphysema and suspected bowel cancer and had to break off the debriefing sessions on several occasions because he needed medical care.

'What if he dies before this gets to trial?' I asked Dave.

'That won't really make a lot of difference. You see, the law's changed now. We can now use statements from deceased persons.'

* * *

In November 2006 BBC *Crimewatch* did a third update on the Daniel Morgan murder investigation. The update focused on the woman who had come forward after the first *Crimewatch* programme in 1987. She'd met with a female police officer at East Croydon railway station.

Since Dave Cook took over the investigation, we'd learnt a lot more about what she'd said at that time. She'd told the police officer that she'd overheard a conversation that took place at a pub in West Croydon before the murder. The pub was the Harp, the one that had sent the grotesque wreath that was placed on top of the hearse at Dan's funeral. The woman said that the people involved were very nasty types who were dealing in cocaine. She named one of them as Jonathan Rees.

Not long after Gary Eaton, Protected Witness Two, came on board, *The Sun* published another article about Dan's Austin Healey 3000. The police had found it. The article was about the rediscovery of his car.

Very soon after the *Sun* article was published, Dave Cook was contacted by another potential witness. The man in question lived in Cyprus, so we called him 'Cyprus man'. Cyprus man told police that Garry had told him he was present at the murder. He said he could also give information about corruption. Detective Chief Inspector Noel Beswick, Dave's second-in-command, flew over to Cyprus to interview the new witness. They found that what he had to say fitted exactly into a sequence of events that they could corroborate.

Cook told us how recent events had changed his perception of the case. 'Up until May this year, I still believed that Belmont Auctions and Margaret Harrison were the reasons why Daniel was killed,' he said. 'But there was no fact behind all of the rumours. Then all of a sudden we get PW2 and it makes so much sense and we can attach facts.'

The squad was also working on Andrew Docherty, the former boyfriend of the Vians' mother, Patricia. Docherty was in prison in Scotland serving a 15-year sentence for an aggravated burglary in May 2001, during which a person had been killed. He too agreed to give evidence. Now everything seemed to be going our way.

Docherty told police that after Daniel's murder he'd worked for Southern Investigations and one day, while he'd been at their offices, Glenn Vian had walked in. He was in a very angry mood. Docherty had asked him why he was there. Glenn had answered that he'd come to get £8,000 – the balance of his money for killing Daniel Morgan.

A few weeks later, Docherty said he saw Glenn Vian emerge with a large brown envelope from Jonathan Rees' office, and that Glenn had told him it was '£8,000 owing from Morgan's murder'.

As an aside, Docherty also described working with Sid Fillery while he was with Southern Investigations and dealing with 'Boris' Richard Zdrojewski, 'Drunken' Duncan Hanrahan and Alex Marunchak at the *News of the World*. It was his impression that Fillery was the 'heart of corruption' because of his influence among police and criminals and Freemasonry contact.

'All he had to do was lift the telephone and make a call,' Docherty said, 'to get them sorted out...'

* * *

Early in 2007 we knew we were approaching the twentieth anniversary of Daniel's murder, but still without justice. However, Dave Cook informed us things were moving fast and the police planned to arrest Jimmy Cook for money laundering.

Jimmy Cook had a large house in Tadworth, Surrey. He was making plans to demolish it and build a new £1,000,000 house on the site. In his latest tax return, he'd declared an annual income of only £10,000.

We were told that Cook was linked to a group of corrupt cops, some of whom were still serving. When he was arrested, the police planned to send out 116 letters to all of his associates, asking them for information about him. Dave told us that Jimmy Cook had many enemies. Lots of people hated him, but they were very scared. Police were hoping that more people would come forward when they realised that he was not untouchable.

Dave had also been contacted by the former wife of an officer who had been on the original squad that investigated the murder in 1987. She told him that after the murder he had changed beyond recognition. From a responsible husband and father, he'd turned into a drunk.

This was 'Boris', Sid Fillery's former driver, PC Richard Zdrojewski, who had been dismissed from the force in 1989 and had gone to work for ... Southern Investigations.

Dave Cook contacted Boris and he started talking. Early in 2007, Dave explained to us how Boris had told him about levels of corruption in the Catford crime squad that Dave described as 'obscene'. Boris had said that Sid Fillery was in charge of 'fit-ups', which involved planting drugs and stolen credit cards. Unfortunately, he couldn't, or wouldn't, give Dave any information about the murder.

Dave said he thought that there was a good case to take forward to the CPS, but stressed that they were still investigating. He believed it was quite possible that more people would come forward if the suspects were charged.

'We have two other people in the background who aren't prepared to give evidence at the moment,' Dave went on to explain. 'One of them is Jimmy

Cook's ex-girlfriend, Sallyanne Wood. She's unwilling to give us a statement, but I hope she will in the future. She says she was present when Jimmy Cook admitted to murder and had conversations about corrupt police officers.'

Then Dave told us the extraordinary lengths he was going to in an attempt to secure convictions this time round. He told us that the Met had bought the house next to Glenn Vian's place, but they didn't put anyone in it. They'd used it to bug Vian's house.

* * *

One month before the twentieth anniversary of my brother's murder we were told that Rees was to be arrested for mortgage fraud. After he'd left Ford Prison, he'd gone into partnership with a fraudster that he'd met there.

Rees and Barry Beardall had started up a company, Pure Energy, designed to extract government grants for clean energy. In the process they'd enlisted the support of a professor who was also a government advisor. I don't think the professor had any idea about the dark history of his business associates until Michael Gillard revealed this in an article in *The Sunday Times*.

By now Jonathan Rees and Margaret Harrison had bought a house in Weybridge. Dave Cook told me that Rees was practically bankrupt and that fraud was suspected in his mortgage application. Rees was arrested and questioned by the financial crimes unit.

A couple of days later, it was Jimmy Cook's turn. He and his wife were suspected of money laundering. Police seized several canisters of CS gas during the raid. The pair were detained under the Proceeds of Crime Act.

At around lunchtime on 10th March 2007, 20 years to the day since Daniel's murder, we drove down to the Golden Lion and were met by a posse of media. BBC London, Sky TV and ITV Wales were there with camera crews and reporters waiting to cover the event. I watched the camera operatives filming the pub from various angles and panning across the car park to the spot where Dan had breathed his last.

The reporters swooped on us as we arrived. Martin Brunt from Sky TV did a piece-to-camera explaining that the case had been 'mired in allegations of corruption' and that several new witnesses had come forward. He also explained that forensic technology was moving forward and new tests were being carried out on the exhibits that had been taken 20 years before. The whole thing was designed to stimulate alarm among the suspects.

I read from a prepared script. 'Twenty years ago today,' I said, 'my brother was viciously murdered on this spot, probably by a man who was paid to commit this crime. We believe that Daniel lost his life because he had innocently uncovered evidence of serious crime and police corruption. The men behind this cowardly act have never been brought to justice.

'For many years my family's relationship with the police has been characterised by distrust and hostility. In our opinion, the Met leadership's reaction to this situation was pitifully inadequate for many years. It was this that spurred our determination to keep on fighting through what has been a terrible ordeal for all of us. However, thanks to the outstanding work carried out by the team now investigating Daniel's murder, this situation has changed radically. We have total trust in this investigation.'

The reporters then interviewed my mother, who told them that even though progress had been made, we'd been through this so many times before that she hardly dared to hope.

* * *

In April, the debriefing of Eaton continued. We were told that he was haggling over the conditions and what was going to happen to him after prison. But it was vital for the credibility of his evidence that he was not seen to be benefitting from giving evidence.

The team were also interviewing a former girlfriend of Jimmy Cook. He'd been having an affair while he was married, they found out. Sallyanne Wood previously intimated that she had knowledge of the murder, but her current boyfriend was pressurising her not to say anything. But now we heard that she'd clammed up completely and had slammed the door in the faces of the police when they came to visit her.

On 13th June 2007, a file on the murder was finally sent to the CPS. We'd been informed that a CPS lawyer had been working for many months with the team advising them on case-building and disclosure issues in order to avoid any legal problems in the prosecution. I asked Dave Cook if he thought the CPS would prosecute.

'I can't speak for the CPS,' he said. 'But in my opinion if they don't prosecute then we need a whole new criminal justice system.'

A meeting was then arranged for mid-July at the MPA, which John Yates would attend. This was a big meeting, with Len, John Yates, Dave Cook, Noel

Beswick, the MPA solicitor David Riddle, our solicitor Raju Bhatt, my mother and me.

Raju began by asking about Met resources.

'We're going to see this through,' Len Duvall said. 'We're not going to pull the rug in terms of money.'

John Yates supported him. 'We're absolutely committed to this case. I've ring-fenced the resources. The only thing that could change that is a terrorist outrage.'

Dave Cook stressed that the investigation would continue right up to the trial. Raju raised the issue of the continued leadership of the inquiry.

'I don't want to embarrass you, David,' he told Cook, 'but the family has confidence in you. We know that your retirement date is soon and the family is worried.'

John Yates responded. 'It's a personal decision but I'm already in negotiations to split David's time, if he's offered a job in another part of the police. I understand your concerns. The planning has been going on for months.'

'I've had no firm offers as yet,' said Dave. 'And I've no desire to say goodbye. If we can come to an agreement that will suit me, but we'll have to wait and see.'

My mother felt very reassured. 'Do you know, Al,' she told me afterwards, 'I feel so different now when I travel home again. I used to come up to London before for meetings and travel home feeling really down and despondent.

'I used to think, "What was the point of all that, travelling all that way for nothing?" But now it's different. It feels as though we've achieved something.'

* * *

The debriefing of Gary Eaton continued and we were told to expect sentencing in September and that this would take place in court.

The police were taking the debriefing very seriously as it had to be very thorough. Crimes that Eaton confessed to had to be corroborated, as far as possible, and this was a painstaking process. The Crown Prosecution Service couldn't make any decision on charges for Daniel's murder until sentencing had taken place, so we just had to wait.

It was a long summer for us. In September, we heard that Eaton's lawyer was delaying the process and that sentencing would have to be postponed until January. I swore; I ranted – all of my reserves of patience and endurance had been spent, I felt. I was a piece of elastic that had been pulled and stretched until it was about to snap.

Mum had also heard about the delays around Eaton and she was so angry, she couldn't speak. Daniel's murder and its aftermath had been a black cloud over the last quarter of her life. Her anguish made me even more furious that we'd been put through such an ordeal. I would explode at the slightest hint of bad treatment or disrespect from anyone. The appearance of Hazel Blears or Caroline Flint on television would set me off on a rant – I needed a break from Britain.

Twenty years earlier, Kirsteen had travelled to Kerala in the south of India shortly after being diagnosed with MS. She'd wanted to go back and I'd never visited India at all so we booked a flight to Trivandrum, the state capital of Kerala.

In the middle of January Kirsteen and I returned from the sunshine of India to find Eaton's sentencing was to be delayed yet again. His hearing lawyer wanted the proceedings to be held in camera. The issue of his health was also brought up.

And so we waited. The family liaison officer visited Wales late in February and told Mum that the team had discovered probe evidence of Rees saying that he had obtained the money for Kevin Lennon's bail in 1987 from the IRA. Eaton had alleged that he'd worked for Sid Fillery and Jimmy Cook, running drugs and guns from the Irish Republic.

The connections with my brother's murder just spread and grew darker and darker, it seemed. By now Kirsteen and I had accumulated a whole office full of paperwork, and our computers were running slowly, probably clogged up with so many files.

The twenty-first anniversary of the murder came and went ... again. At the end of March my mother celebrated her eightieth birthday. She'd been 58 years old when Daniel was murdered and his killers were still walking the streets.

CHAPTER 40	The Glass Cage

2008-2010

ALASTAIR: Finally, in April 2008, 21 years, one month and 11 days after Daniel's murder, the day of the planned arrests arrived.

The previous evening, Jane and my mother had arrived from Wales and came round for breakfast at nine o'clock on the Monday morning. We waited for news from the police.

I knew that five of the suspects had been asked to present themselves at a London police station that morning. But I didn't know which police station and I deliberately hadn't asked. Dave Cook had told me that he planned to announce the arrests late in the afternoon.

At around 11:30, Dave Cook rang to tell me that Jimmy Cook, Jonathan Rees, Sid Fillery and Garry Vian had arrived as expected and that Glenn Vian was expected very soon. We were all on edge.

I emailed Kirsteen's father, Malcolm, and asked him to switch off the Justice-4Daniel website as I'd been advised by the police. We didn't want anything to prejudice future legal proceedings. Malcolm told me that the website had been busier than ever before he switched it off.

Sanchia Berg of the BBC Radio 4's morning *Today* programme emailed me a press release issued by the Met that day. After giving a short history of Dan's murder and the latest investigation, it mentioned the arrest of Garry Vian's stepson, Dean Vian, and the fact that the investigation was the first to use the SOCPA legislation through which people could turn Queen's evidence against co-conspirators and other criminals.

The press release included a quote from John Yates: 'The one consistent theme throughout has been the astonishing determination of the Morgan family to ensure that those responsible are brought to justice.'

Sanchia asked me if I would do an interview the following morning and I agreed.

The questioning of the suspects continued all day. We knew there would eventually be charges, but it was still nerve-racking. Emails came in by the dozen. My landline and all of our mobiles hardly stopped ringing all day.

* * *

Early the following morning, I did an interview for *Today* at BBC studios in Millbank. A feature writer for the *Standard* rang to ask if he could visit us to follow events at our flat the following day, to which we agreed. The questioning of the suspects continued all of the second day and the police put in an application to extend their period of arrest. This was granted.

Early the following day, we learned that two of the suspects had been charged. By the afternoon four had been charged with murder and Fillery with perverting the course of justice. John Yates rang to speak to my mother. We were all jubilant. Finally, after all the years of campaigning and all the disappointments, we were really getting somewhere.

On Thursday 24th, the suspects came up before the stipendiary magistrate at Horseferry Road Magistrates' Court, just a stone's throw from the House of Commons. The police sent a driver to pick us up so that we could watch the proceedings. As we neared the court, we could see a small army of TV cameras, reporters and photographers gathered outside. We made our way through the media throng and through the security checkpoint in the court. From there we took the lift up to another floor, where we waited for the proceedings to begin.

The hearing was scheduled for 10:30, but we were told there had been some delay in the custody transport, so we all sat down to wait for the business to begin. Then David Zinzan appeared from nowhere. He'd come specially to see us. We must have waited for an hour before we were shown into the courtroom.

As we sat there, the court dealt with a couple of minor cases involving fraud and petty theft. The defendants were ushered into a large glass cubicle in the rear corner of the court. The five men lumbered into the glass cage and took their seats.

I noticed that Sid Fillery was holding a thick paperback in his hands. The men sat in two rows, with Glenn Vian, Jonathan Rees and Sid Fillery at the front. Behind them sat Garry Vian and Jimmy Cook. The lawyers in the courtroom were busily preparing themselves, whispering to each other and leafing through their files. Glenn Vian leaned back and stared up at the ceiling as if in despair.

All of the defendants wanted bail and one by one, their lawyers argued that they should be granted this. While this was going on, Fillery sat reading his book as if totally unconcerned.

To our great relief, the magistrate finally decided that none of the defendants should be granted bail. One by one, they were told that they would be remanded in custody until further notice. They all filed out to the cells and we left the courtroom delighted by this result.

Our driver, a member of Dave Cook's murder squad, then drove us all back to my flat. We followed the prison vehicle, with police cars in front of and behind it, all the way along the Victoria Embankment to Blackfriars Bridge, where it turned south. I later learned that the defendants had been taken to Wandsworth. We asked our driver to drop us off at a pub close to my flat. We wanted to celebrate and we'd agreed to meet Laurie Flynn and Michael Gillard there for a drink.

At the end of July, there was a case management hearing. Kirsteen took a day's leave to attend it. I wasn't permitted because of my status as a possible witness in the trial.

No pleas were entered and we discovered that Fillery was going to apply for bail again the following week. Rees, it was said, was to enter an abuse of process defence. A trial date was set for 21st April 2009, but all of the defence barristers notified the court that they probably wouldn't be ready by then. Autumn 2009 seemed to be a more realistic start date for the trial.

CHAPTER 41	Pre-trials

October 2009–March 2011

KIRSTEEN: All the major players in the Morgan family have played different roles in the campaign. Alastair is chief agitator and investigator, ably assisted for many years by his mother. Jane supports Isobel. Iris' job was to bring up Daniel's small children and turn them into the two well-adjusted, kind and caring adults they are today. My role, apart from doing my best to keep Alastair on the right side of sanity, is writing notes.

Since 1997 I have written notes of every single meeting with the police and politicians. We knew that Alastair and Isobel couldn't attend the trial in case they had to give evidence. I took a three-month career break to cover the trial, hoping that Al and I could take a holiday when it was over. Little did I know that 18 months later I would still be taking notes.

It was to be one of the longest pre-trial hearings in British history.

On 12th October 2009 the hearing began in Court 8 of the Old Bailey before Mr Justice Maddison. The police explained that there would first be an abuse of process hearing where the defence would argue that the case couldn't proceed because the suspects couldn't get a fair trial. This was common in big cases, they told us, but nothing to worry about.

Real court proceedings aren't like the dramas you see on television. Huge amounts of time are spent leafing through paperwork after instructions like 'Turn to bundle six, tab four, paragraph 147'. There were five defence teams, each with leading and junior barristers and mountains of lever-arch files they brought with them every day.

Abuse of process can occur in many ways, but it's about showing that the police or CPS have done something so unfair and wrong that the prosecution should not go ahead. In this case, the defence teams were arguing that they had not been given the paperwork they needed, that witnesses had been handled so badly by the police that their evidence was worthless and that all sorts of other evidence was inadmissible.

Three days into the proceedings there was a development that was to affect me and Alastair personally. Prosecution barrister Nick Hilliard had warned me in the morning that the defence might try to stop me attending court because I'm a journalist and Alastair's partner. If that happened, no one from the family would have any eyes or ears in court.

Rees' barrister, Richard Christie QC, asked to raise a matter in chambers with the judge. All journalists and members of the public were asked to leave the court. My heart was pounding. The Press Association court reporter came to my aid.

'You are a proper journalist, aren't you?' she asked.

'Yes,' I replied.

'Are you a union member?'

'Yes, I'm in the NUJ,' I confirmed.

'Well then, you're one of us then and we will do everything we can to support you.'

The court reconvened and Justice Maddison gave a brief summary of what had happened. He explained that I was in court and that I was the partner of Alastair Morgan, a prosecution witness. He wanted to make it crystal clear that if it were to emerge that any information had been passed on to him, then almost certainly it would be drawn out when Alastair was cross-examined and the end result would simply be a damaging effect on his evidence.

I was so relieved! But this was to put a wall between my partner and me in the biggest issue in our lives.

The abuse of process argument resumed. It took me a while to realise this was a protracted but effective fishing exercise and the more the prosecution disclosed, the more the defence found further police failings. I was conflicted but even though it was often damaging to the Crown's case I knew it was the right thing to do.

The defence's main target was Dave Cook. They argued that Cook had put leading questions to supergrass James Ward during an interview in 2005. The interview transcript was read out in court.

'Tell me what you know. I'll give you a head start. It was Glenn with the axe. Garry was there and Jimmy with the car over at the car action.'

The prosecution pointed out that this was an intelligence interview and that Ward had made it clear he would not give evidence in court about Daniel's murder. But the defence were keen to point out that this was not the only time David Cook appeared to go further than he should in his questioning.

During Cook's first meeting with Eaton he said: 'Give me the names of them brothers' twice in quick succession. When this was first put to Eaton he seemed to know nothing about them. Months later, however, he described them being at the crime scene.

I knew this already. David Cook had always been open with us about problems with the witnesses' evidence, but hearing it in court was different. The defence made it sound like a sinister plot to fit up their clients. I knew that if Alastair had been in court he would have been worried sick. In one sense, it was a blessing that I couldn't talk to him about it. This may not make me sound like a very nice person but I've always had an ability to emotionally cut myself off. In court, I felt like a journalist. This was my job and somehow it didn't feel so intimately linked to my real life.

The defence's biggest complaint was the way the police handled Gary Eaton. They argued that officers knew from the outset that Eaton had serious psychiatric problems, but they didn't insist that an Appropriate Adult was with him during interviews.

The defence had instructed the head of forensic psychiatry at St George's Hospital to examine Eaton's psychiatric history. It was his view that Eaton had Personality Disorder and said in 'common parlance this means he is [a] psychopath.' He explained that lying and manipulation were a key part of the disorder and that a person with anti-social personality disorder may tell lies that are pointless purely because of their disorder.

The Crown's forensic expert refuted this and said Eaton had severe personality problems but didn't have either severe, borderline or anti-social personality disorder. He added the personality disorders are not permanent and often remit in middle age.

I didn't know what to believe.

* * *

Alastair was on tenterhooks at home waiting for the jury to be sworn in and for the trial itself to start. Days had been lost because the defence needed time to read the newly disclosed material and it was clear that the actual trial would not start on 26th October as planned.

In fact, that was the day the defence introduced a whole new argument.

Detective Sergeant Tony Moore was in charge of the debriefing of Gary Eaton. In October 2008 he'd sent the police a report in which he expressed concerns that Eaton had been contaminated by information communicated to him from outside the debriefing process. The defence were extremely excited because his report said: 'this will be viewed as a clear abuse of process'.

Gary Eaton was a supergrass, a criminal who gives evidence about other criminals he knows. There is a long history of supergrasses giving police false evidence in return for lower sentences and the whole system became discredited. As a result, SOCPA had come into force in 2005.

After his initial meeting with Cook and the Abelard team, Eaton was handed to the Witness Protection Unit, who arranged a safe house and looked after his welfare. There was a separate debriefing team who recorded Eaton's evidence. The murder squad was sent regular reports on what Eaton was telling the debriefing team, but was banned from any contact with him.

The defence argued that this sterile corridor had been broken and said they had unmasked a conspiracy to pervert the course of justice. This allegation became known as 'Mooregate'.

In 2007 Gary Eaton had told his debriefers that his father had died 14 months earlier. But in early July 2008, David Cook had received information suggesting that Eaton's father was still alive. On 8th July Eaton had told the Witness Protection Unit that his father was 'dead to him'. The crux of the issue was how did Eaton come to change his evidence in this way? Was he tipped off by police to say this so that it looked less of a lie?

I was finding it extremely difficult to follow exactly what was going on in court. I scribbled down verbatim shorthand notes in the hope things would make more sense when I typed them up in the evenings. Mr Justice Maddison was finding things difficult too.

'This is taking infinitely longer than I thought it would,' he told the assembled barristers. 'I have to say, the submissions and the number of them and their complexity are far greater than I thought they would be.'

The issues were so significant that on 3rd November 2009 the prosecution called for a voir dire – a sort of mini-trial within a trial without a jury present, with all the officers involved in 'Mooregate' called to give evidence on the witness stand. This was going to take weeks and Alastair was far from happy. He had no real idea of what was going on and felt totally excluded.

When I told friends that I didn't tell Alastair what was happening I don't think they believed me. But it was true: I took the judge's instruction very seriously. When I typed up my notes in the evening, I was wary in case he looked over my shoulder. I even gave my notes misleading titles so he wouldn't be able to find them on my computer.

At the same time, Al was really conscious of the stress I was under. One evening he started to give me a neck massage while I was at my computer. I snapped at him, thinking he was trying to read my notes. He wasn't, and I felt churlish. We were under a huge strain.

* * *

The voir dire called 12 officers to the witness stand and lasted a whole month. There was endless argument on who said what to whom on what day. Shockingly, many officers hadn't even taken notes of their actions, but even when they had, the evidence was sometimes contradictory.

What I did learn in the voir dire was much more about the extensive contact Dave Cook had with Eaton, again in breach of the sterile corridors. At first, Cook had only listed six days when he had been in touch with the witness. The voir dire had shown that there were actually 36. The defence went over these new dates meticulously, cross-referencing them with what was happening with Eaton at those times. Of course, they couldn't know what was said in those calls but they drew the obvious inference.

From the moment Eaton first came forward, Dave Cook had told us that he was a nightmare to deal with. Eaton frequently telephoned him inappropriately, he said. The supergrass had an extremely volatile relationship with his partner and Dave had assured us that all of these calls were about his welfare.

The defence had a much more sinister explanation.

There was also the change in Gary Eaton's evidence. When he first came forward, he named Jonathan Rees, James Cook and Sidney Fillery as being involved in the murder. He did not implicate the Vian brothers or put himself at the scene of the crime.

Glenn Vian's barrister drew attention to long calls from Cook to Eaton, far longer than their usual conversations, on 28th and 29th August 2006. On 1st September, for the first time Eaton alleged that he had been at the Golden Lion on the night of the murder. That evening, Cook spoke to Eaton for over half an hour and again the following morning for 12 minutes.

The defence had drawn blood and went for the kill. Glenn Vian's barrister asked: 'You told him what you wanted to hear.' Dave Cook was looking wobbly: 'No, he told us what he knew,' he replied. Cook was on the stand for seven days and the bashing he got was relentless.

The atmosphere in court was very difficult. Normally I chatted with the police and prosecution before we went into court, and even the defence barristers and solicitors. Now everyone had to be hyper-vigilant about what they said. The officers giving evidence were banned from talking to each other and the defence were very eager to catch them out.

Moorgate finished on 11th December. Justice Maddison responded that he would rule on 15th February whether to allow Eaton to give evidence. Raju Bhatt agreed this looked bad, but remained adamant that this was not enough to stop a trial.

On 15th February 2010 Justice Maddison ruled that Eaton could not give evidence. This meant that Fillery was free to go. I had to get out of the courtroom and call Alastair.

* * *

ALASTAIR: Kirsteen had already sacrificed five months of her life to be an unpaid observer in court. She'd been with me through 16 hard years and never once grumbled. My little woman had the heart of a lion.

She called me unexpectedly early from the Old Bailey.

'The case against Fillery has been stayed,' she said. 'Eaton's been excluded too!'

'Oh no! Oh no! Christ, he's going to walk!'

He's away, I thought. I pictured him in a light raincoat, hands thrust in his pockets, walking up the street from the Old Bailey to Newgate Street. In my mind's eye he looked back and saw me. Was that a swagger in his stride, or was it fear?

I was as angry as I'd ever been since Dan died. I even felt anger towards Daniel for not telling me about the danger he was facing.

I rang Jane. She'd been told the news by the police family liaison officer.

'I was driving into Hay, I was so angry,' she told me. 'It was pure rage. The road was empty and I put my foot down. I was thinking, right, do I go to Norfolk and shoot someone? I was accelerating along the road, going fast. Or shall I drive this car into an oak tree at 60mph?'

'Jesus, Jane…! Don't even think that!' I said.

'It was just the rage inside me. I wanted to put it somewhere, let it out. I wanted blood to be shed, blood for blood. At that moment I didn't care if it was *my* blood.'

* * *

KIRSTEEN: One witness was gone, but there was no let up in the battle. After 'Mooregate' they found a new cause: they called this one 'Crategate'.

On 20th November 2009, the Abelard team had found 18 new boxes of material, which would take them two months to review. But the defendants were due to have their custody time limits reviewed on 4th December. The prosecution had not disclosed this to the defence.

Crategate was very important for the defence. There are time limits about how long a suspect can be held on remand – the police and prosecution have to show due diligence and expedition. Had the defence known there were 18 new boxes of material during the custody time limits hearing in December, they could have argued lack of due diligence, and Rees, the Vian brothers and Jimmy Cook could have been released from prison before Christmas.

The defence portrayed it as another sinister conspiracy, but in reality it was a gigantic cock-up. The police had always believed there were more documents relating to the supergrasses' criminal history and had asked the DPS to check their stores repeatedly. In November, after long delays, these 18 crates were finally found by the DPS. Most of these documents had already been in their possession in 2007, but had been sent back to storage.

The prosecution argued that the material in the crates was either irrelevant or duplicated. But the defence found photographs of knives, bullets and knuckledusters in the crates that they'd never seen before.

On 3rd March 2010 Justice Maddison gave his ruling on custody time limits. My heart sank when the judge described the story of the 18 crates as a 'sorry tale'. He said that a 'clearer example of a lack of due diligence and expedition is difficult to imagine' and had he known in December he might have refused to extend the custody time limits.

'It follows,' Justice Maddison continued, 'that the limit which expires at the end of today will go no further.' In effect, the judge was ruling the suspects would be freed. 'I imagine that for practical reasons the defendants will be bailed at some stage during the course of the day.'

I rushed out of court with Noel Beswick – I was pretty sure I could see tears in his eyes. He kept saying 'I'm so sorry'. I wanted to hug him. Noel had the unenviable task of making sure all the other witnesses were warned they were potentially at risk and arranging protection.

I wasn't looking forward to going home. Living with Al for 16 years, I was used to coping with major setbacks. We'd got pretty good at it and I felt we could handle almost any bad news now – as long as we were on the same side. But this time we weren't.

Isobel being excluded from court had led to her speculating on why everything was going wrong. On bad days, she thought dark forces were acting behind the scenes to scupper the trial. Alastair usually set her straight. But hearing that the suspects were back on the streets, he joined in her in wild speculation.

* * *

ALASTAIR: For six months I'd been kept in a state of semi-ignorance about what had been going on in that court. Now the case seemed to be collapsing in front of me and all I could see was danger. Most of all, I was worried about our safety, particularly Kirsteen's – I knew I couldn't keep her away from court and this terrified me.

When she came home, we argued fiercely about everything. Jane was terrified on the telephone. It was an awful day and a horrible evening.

* * *

KIRSTEEN: Alastair woke up strangely calm and forgiving. He rang Dave Cook and told him to tell Noel Beswick he didn't blame him. He said he didn't want any individual police officers to be hurt or punished because they'd tried their best.

Raju told us we should prepare ourselves for the possibility that the trial wouldn't go ahead. But the prosecution barrister was in a surprisingly upbeat mood and said he was still confident there would be a trial.

After a while, the ability to hold two opposing forecasts of the future in your head at the same time becomes impossible. The provisional trial date had been put back so many times we'd lost count. Alastair and I entered a state of denial to survive. Nothing was happening in court.

So I just did all the things that I didn't usually get to do while working full-time. I went swimming most days, saw friends and I enjoyed lunches in the local café with Alastair.

* * *

ALASTAIR: Two months of relative normality ended when I got an astonishing call from Dave Cook. He told me that Sallyanne Wood was now implicating Jimmy Cook in about 20 other murders!

Like everything else, this had to be checked out by the police. In this case, it involved excavating parts of Epping Forest to look for dead bodies. The police started with four specific sites. No corpses were found.

Sallyanne was one of our best witnesses but suddenly her evidence seemed worthless. We knew the police had found much of her earlier evidence about Jimmy Cook to be solid. Why had she suddenly started making false allegations?

Cook was no longer on remand. In the event, we had to wait more than three months to find out that Sallyanne Wood's evidence had been ruled out and a further month to find out that this meant that Jimmy Cook would also walk free.

Soon after this, Jane and Kirsteen were sitting in our kitchen silently drinking tea when I told them what I had decided.

'I'm coming to court today.'

Kirsteen looked shocked. 'But what about …?'

'I don't bloody care!' I snapped before she finished. 'I'm coming to court and that's it. If Maddison kicks me out, so be it. But I'm coming to court!'

We'd already lost Fillery. Now we were going to lose the next defendant and I wanted to see it with my own eyes.

I arrived at court. Kirsteen drove us into the underground parking lot and guided us to Security. We were fast-tracked through and Kirsteen led us to Court 13 at the other end of the building. Outside the courtroom, I could see Dave Cook and Noel Beswick. They stopped talking as we approached.

'I'm not going to miss this. This is history being made before our eyes,' I said.

As we stood there, Jonathan Rees came up the middle of the hall. He'd put on a huge amount of weight over the past two decades. He began talking to his solicitor. Rees was soon followed by Glenn Vian, wearing a short, dark overcoat and with a shaven head. This was the first time I'd seen him since he'd given me the evil eye in my brother's office, 25 years earlier. Jimmy Cook, the only one of the defendants I'd never seen before, was nowhere to be seen.

They sat down in the dock, avoiding my eyes all the time.

Next in was Jimmy Cook. This was the first time I'd set eyes on the man alleged to have ordered Dan's murder. He was big, six feet plus, and muscular, with small cold blue eyes and a full head of hair. I remembered Bob Quick's words at the Yard, a decade earlier: 'Jimmy Cook is a very dangerous man'.

He looked it. Now he was going to walk. He sat down in the dock next to Glenn Vian and Rees. None of them spoke.

'All rise!'

Everyone stood up. Some rushed for their seats. The prosecution barrister got to his feet and told the judge that both Jane and I were in court and that nothing he would say that day would touch on my evidence. He then went on to the subject of Jimmy Cook. With the exclusion of Gary Eaton's evidence, and now of Sallyanne Wood (now she was speaking of in the order of 30 murders). All that remained against Jimmy Cook was a hostile witness, Stephen Warner, who claimed that a statement he had made against Cook in 1998 had been made under duress and later withdrawn.

'Accordingly, as we indicated to all concerned earlier this week, we offer no evidence against James Cook,' the prosecution told the judge.

Justice Maddison turned to Jimmy Cook and told him that the prosecution had withdrawn all the evidence against him. 'I therefore direct a verdict of not guilty in respect of Count 1 and you are now free to go,' he said.

As Jimmy moved towards the door he passed within an arm's length of Jane, who was sitting in front of me. 'Scum!' I heard her hiss at him as he walked through the door.

That was the last time I ever saw Jimmy Cook.

There was a short discussion between the defence and prosecution about whether I should remain in court during further submissions. Judge Maddison ruled that as long as 'nothing is going to be said that touches on his evidence, I can simply see no reason properly to exclude him.'

Then the prosecution went through defence requests for more disclosure. The Rees' team alone had submitted a list that extended to 300 pages, with more than 800 topics, requiring investigations into material which went way beyond what the Abelard team had, or was in the possession of law enforcement agencies.

I stood up and quietly left the court – I couldn't take any more. This prosecution was going nowhere.

I don't know how Jane sat through the rest of the day, but she did.

* * *

KIRSTEEN: We'd lost two witnesses and two defendants but the judge had ruled months ago that there would still be a trial. But as I headed towards my second Christmas not working, the defence wanted another voir dire – this time on an abuse of process argument about the first protected witness, James Ward, whose evidence about Garry Vian had launched the first murder investigation.

As ever, the defence got what they asked for. Raju was tearing his hair out: 'This judge is allowing the defence to run rings around him,' he said.

The voir dire started in January 2011. It had just begun when a bombshell came from nowhere. Raju, Alastair and I were called to meet the senior prosecution and police team. 'Ward can't be relied upon any more,' we were told. 'We're carrying on without him.'

I knew James Ward came with problems, but something had changed. Days earlier, we'd become aware that material had been found when an old police building was cleared out. This included two files with damaging information about him.

Although none of it related to Daniel's murder, it did contain evidence of criminality and inconsistencies that the prosecution hadn't been aware of, including what appeared to be an admission of soliciting a murder. Ward had failed to mention this small detail in his debrief!

It was also clear that there were still large amounts of material that couldn't be found. Keeping him a witness would be unfair to the defendants.

Despite the fact he was no longer going to be a witness, the voir dire about James Ward continued and defence portrayed this as deliberate police misbehaviour, which meant the trial should be stopped. They cited the way Dave Cook had questioned Ward in 2005, allegations that he'd paid a £50,000 bribe to a senior police officer, and that he only gave evidence on the murder because he was facing a 17-year prison sentence. They argued that the police had deliberately hidden the fact that Ward was a registered police informant.

I called Raju. We both agreed that from now on Isobel and the rest of the family should start attending the court. We were now in the death throes and Alastair was becoming convinced there wouldn't be a trial.

* * *

ALASTAIR: Mum's first day in court was 7th February 2011, almost a year and a half after the pre-trial began. After hours of listening to the defence barrister drone on about the failings of the prosecution, we left the court after the judge rose and I exclaimed: 'I'm losing the will to live, here!' Jane told me to shut up because one of the defence teams and their barrister were walking behind us. Later, she said she saw the barrister laughing about it, and she had to restrain me from going over and punching him.

The next day, while another defence barrister was cross-examining one of the police officers, Jane could take no more and stood up.

'My brother was butchered in a car park by these men,' she told the court, 'and I am sick, I am sick of listening to your offensive tone with hard-working police officers who are attempting to put them in prison.'

She then turned to Justice Maddison.

'Please call Security and have me evicted, my Lord,' she said. 'This is a pantomime. No way will we ever get to the part about who was in the car park at the Golden Lion on 10th March 1987. That's what's important, not little pieces of paper that aren't here 25 years later. Good day!'

Later, the judge's clerk approached Jane and told her that Justice Maddison wanted her to know that she was very welcome to return.

It was during one of those last, miserable days at the Old Bailey when I paid a visit to the gents' lavatory that I saw the man accused of physically axing my brother to death standing there.

It was a surreal moment. As I stood before the urinal I could see from the large mirror above, Glenn Vian washing his hands. There was another large mirror above the wash-basin so we watched each other's reflections in the mirrors the whole time in a tense stand-off. I felt deeply uncomfortable. But then again, so did he.

I was relieved when I saw his reflection walk out of the door behind me.

On the morning of 7th March, before we left for court, Dave Cook telephoned and told me they had discovered four more boxes of evidence.

I could take no more.

CHAPTER 42	Collapse

2011

ALASTAIR: It was a very, very bad couple of days. This ending to the prosecution had been on the cards for a long time and in one sense it was a relief, although saturated with exhaustion and sadness.

I'd been holding my emotions in check for what seemed an eternity. The dam finally broke when a TV interviewer asked me how I felt, in front of a camera. I broke down and wept. She said they wouldn't use the footage.

But I'd made two promises next to that crossing gate in Liss all those years before. I'd promised Daniel that I would get justice for him and expose the police corruption. I'd failed to fulfil the first part but this was not going to be the end of the story.

Next day, Iris and Daniel's daughter, Sarah (by now almost 30-years-old) came to court to watch the sorry ending of the trial that had never been.

We all sat and listened as Justice Maddison congratulated counsel for the defence on the quality of their advocacy, adding that the prosecution had also been of a very high standard. The bench and bar were engaging in a little love-in. Daniel's name had barely featured in 18 months of proceedings. And there was no mention that after a quarter of a century and five investigations there was no sign of justice for the people who killed Daniel Morgan.

After the final 'All rise', Mum walked over to Glenn Vian and handed him a note. On it, she'd written that we were going to campaign for a judicial inquiry. I watched him refuse it, shaking his head. Mum walked back through the crowded well of the court.

'He said he can't read,' she said, clutching the folded slip of paper.

I felt almost ill as I imagined the resistance that we were going to face in exposing the corruption. Would it take years of lobbying? How many phone calls? How many more meetings?

We walked together out of the Old Bailey. Superintendent Hamish Campbell was on the pavement in uniform surrounded by journalists and television crews.

The outcome of the trial was 'wholly regrettable' he began in his prepared statement. 'This current investigation has identified, ever more clearly, how the initial inquiry failed the family and wider public,' he continued. 'It is quite apparent that police corruption was a debilitating factor in that investigation. Significant changes have occurred since that time; nevertheless, there are important issues which we need to examine now in order to understand what led to today's decision.'

The word 'corruption' had been used publicly and officially for the first time in 24 years. I felt like stone – I'd been watching that corruption grow for all those years.

* * *

Over the weekend, *The Guardian* published a spread on Rees and his hacking activities. It described how he'd been earning £150,000 a year from the *News of the World*, peddling stolen information even after his seven-year sentence for perverting the course of justice.

On the Monday *Panorama* broadcast a documentary about Rees' involvement in email hacking an army security operative called Ian Hurst. Outside the Old Bailey after the prosecution had collapsed, presenter Vivian White asked Rees: 'What about the work you did accessing people's bank accounts?'

'What about the information that you've got?' Rees snapped back.

Rees's solicitor jumped in: 'How did *Panorama* get this information?'

'So, you don't deny that you've paid serving police officers for information?' White parried.

'Are you denying that you've paid serving police officers for information,' Rees spat back, 'because you've got information that could only come from police officers?'

On 25th March 2011 Justice Maddison handed down his judgment on the handling of Gary Eaton. It made excruciating reading, listing many instances of where Dave Cook made unauthorised phone calls to Eaton. Could we trust anything Eaton said? Justice Maddison said no. His judgement concluded that Eaton had a personality disorder that rendered him prone to telling lies, sometimes for no apparent reason. Maddison ruled that Eaton had been probably been prompted by Dave to implicate the defendants Glenn and Garry Vian.

I was shocked to the core when reading it. The judge's description of Dave Cook was not the man I knew and had grown to trust over almost a decade.

I'd heard that Eaton had been a nightmare for Dave to deal with, and I could understand a witness like him being extremely scared and distrustful. He was making serious allegations of murder against very dangerous criminals and corrupt police. Dave was the only officer he could rely on.

Besides, if Dave had 'coached' Eaton, he hadn't done a very good job. He got one of the brothers' names wrong and his description of the crime scene was wildly inaccurate.

Soon afterwards I met our lawyer Raju Bhatt with Kirsteen to survey the battlefield. He talked about the process of getting a judicial inquiry.

'I can promise you this, nobody will want to order a judicial inquiry,' Raju told us. 'That means the Home Office, the Met and the government.'

We were back in familiar territory – the failing state, desperately needing our help and flatly refusing it at the same time.

My mother had to decide over an outcome she might never see. 'Let's do it,' she said.

'I'll start preparing the submission at once,' Raju said.

We shook hands, said our goodbyes and left.

At the end of March 2011, the Met issued a public apology at City Hall. Acting Commissioner Tim Godwin spoke: 'I recognise how important it is to the family that the part played by corruption in the original investigation is acknowledged publicly. You are entitled to an apology not only for this failure but also for the repeated failure by the MPS over many years following Daniel's murder to accept that corruption had played such a part in failing to bring those responsible to justice.'

The MPA unanimously also supported our call for a judicial inquiry.

* * *

At around this time the issue of the 'dark arts' was beginning to feature in the media. I had very mixed feelings about this at first. Through the latter stages of the trial we were constantly called by journalists investigating *News of the World* and the phone-hacking scandal. They weren't interested in my brother's case. They just wanted to know when the prosecution was going to collapse so they could report details about Rees' history with the 'dark arts'.

But this story took a life of its own, and soon brought Daniel back into the news.

Clive Goodman, the *News of the World*'s Royal editor, had been convicted of hacking a Royal phone with the help of Glen Mulcaire. As the newspaper's editor-in-chief, Andy Coulson had taken responsibility and resigned, moving on to the job of director of communications for the Prime Minister, David Cameron, in July 2007 after unusually light vetting.

There were reports that Cameron had been warned about Coulson's history with Jonathan Rees but the PM said that he wanted to give him 'a second chance'.

Nick Davies had long been looking into phone hacking and was finding out that it was far more widespread than 'one rogue reporter', the line that News International was peddling. He wrote that Coulson must have been well aware of this. Questions were being asked about David Cameron's judgement.

There were also days of select committee hearings on the activities of the *News of the World*. The Culture, Media and Sport Committee questioned Rebekah Brooks about a meeting at New Scotland Yard in January 2003 in the aftermath of the *Crimewatch* appeal in June 2002. Brooks professed to have an entirely different recall of the meeting from that of David Cook, implying she was filling some kind of pastoral role.

In July, I was contacted by BBC Radio 4. Led by Adrian Goldberg from Birmingham, a trio of journalists came to visit me. They had interviewed Marjorie Williams, a bookkeeper for Southern Investigations after the murder. She identified Alex Marunchak as being one of Rees' big customers at an early stage.

And then, thanks to an article about the hacking of the murdered schoolgirl Milly Dowler by Nick Davies and Amelia Hill, first published online by *The Guardian* on 4th July 2011, the phone-hacking scandal went global.

At the time, though I felt for the Dowler family, I couldn't help but feel that there was an even closer connection between the Murdoch press and a murder victim than this. But the pace of events was phenomenal. Andy Coulson was arrested. The *News of the World* was closed. Senior police officers like John Yates and the current Commissioner, Paul Stephenson, were forced to resign because of their proximity to *News of the World* executives like former deputy editor Neil Wallis, who was employed by the Met as a PR consultant. The failure to properly investigate phone hacking in 2006 was part of the scandal.

Prime Minister David Cameron, on the run thanks to the intervention of Labour leader Ed Miliband and Tom Watson MP, who had campaigned for years about press intrusion, announced a public inquiry – the Leveson Inquiry into the culture, practices and ethics of the press.

The former Prime Minister Gordon Brown stood up in Parliament and made a ferocious speech about the criminality surrounding the *News of the World* and how it had been originally exposed in 2002, but ignored. He coined the memorable phrase the 'criminal-media nexus' to describe the toxic mix of bent cops, corrupt private investigators and complicit journalists that had now come to the public's attention.

I was reeling. This was another example of how my brother's unsolved murder and its cover-up had spread so rapidly through so many institutions. I had warned about the dangers of leaving the corruption around Southern Investigations to fester decades before, and now another symptom of the rot was playing out on the television screens of the nation.

* * *

In the midst of this uproar about corrupt relations between police, government and press, in August 2011 Raju sent a submission to Theresa May calling for a judicial inquiry.

The covering letter invited her to meet my family and was followed by letters from our MPs making the same request. I also spread the word with interviews with CNN, ABC and even *The South China Morning Post*. But getting the ear of the Home Secretary was a different proposition. Six weeks after sending in the submission, we learned that it had been sent to the Department of Justice by mistake.

In the background, and after the prosecution collapsed, the Met had decided to carry out a review of the failure of the last inquiry. We simply weren't interested in them marking their own homework and we knew there was far more to the case than this.

BBC Wales then made a documentary on the case in 2011. They filmed Jane and me outside the house in Llanfrechfa where we'd spent most of our childhood. Jane told a hilarious story of how Dan and I had idiotically set fire to the hedge in the front garden, reducing part of it to charred twigs. Amid all the gloom and sadness we could still find laughter remembering our brother.

The documentary also uncovered some very interesting information. The first murder investigator, Douglas Campbell, told the BBC producer Andy Maguire that he had asked line managers to hand over his inquiry to an outside force, telling them he couldn't trust the police in his own area. He was ordered to carry on with his inquiry.

Theresa May was still refusing to meet us because the Met and the CPS were taking forever to finish their review of the failed prosecution. We discussed the situation and Mum decided to write a letter to her and deliver it in person at the Home Office.

On the appointed day, I met Mum at Paddington and we took a cab to the Home Office in Marsham Street. To our relief, Channel 4 News and a Welsh television crew were already setting up outside. Jennette Arnold was also on the scene. Channel 4's soundman suggested fitting Mum with a mike so that we could pick up her conversation inside the building. The mike was placed on her winter coat and tested.

Filming began. Mum walked into the building, through Security, and produced a letter in front of the guard.

'This is for the Home Secretary and I want to deliver it in person. It's about my son's murder, 24 years ago,' I could hear her saying through the headphones.

Then she seemed to be surrounded by people. We lost the sound outside. We could see her arguing and pointing into the building. Finally, she handed over the letter to someone, turned and strode back to the cameras. She was angry, but raised a defiant fist.

CHAPTER 43	Darkness Visible

2011-2012

The key characteristic of any successful cover-up is that the heart of a criminal conspiracy remains unseen. When it comes to the murder of Daniel Morgan there are thousands of circumstantial details to be found in the million documents and exhibits that had accumulated by the time of the pre-trial hearings. But the killer facts – the credible untainted eyewitness, the substantial forensic trace, or the paperwork Daniel had apparently gathered about police corruption – all these were lost within a few days of the first inquiry, and have never been recovered since.

One of the favourite phrases of criminal lawyers facing holes in a case is that the 'absence of evidence is not evidence of absence'. You cannot infer, by something not being there, that it was removed for any nefarious reason. So too, with the first botched murder inquiry, the vanished fingerprint on Daniel's BMW, the missing Rolex, the failure to properly forensically test Rees, the non-appearance of witnesses at the inquest – all this could be incompetence or merely absence of evidence.

There's nothing there, because there's nothing there.

For the last 30 years the complexity of the Daniel Morgan murder and its cover-up has routinely been described as 'murky' by journalists and commentators as if this was a state of nature or some blurb for a fictional thriller. An air of fatalism has accompanied most accounts. The myriad links and threads and false leads make it hard to tell. But the murkiness is not accidental: the incompetence is organised. Confusion has been deliberately created in order to conceal something.

Following the timeline of the Daniel Morgan murder and its cover-up over three decades, some of the obscurity is becoming clearer. Just as sub-atomic particles cannot be directly observed, only negatively – by the gaps left when they are bombarded by smaller particles – there are some fairly solid conclusions to be drawn from the areas of darkness that remain.

Firstly, Daniel was the original true detective in this case. Half a dozen witnesses, from separate sources, say he was working on a story of police corruption in the months before his murder, to a standard of proof that he and others believed a major newspaper would publish it. That would most likely require documentation.

In this light, the bundle of beige folders Daniel carried under his arm on his way to the Golden Lion looks like a significant absence. So, too, could the documents the civilian scene of crimes officer saw detectives remove from Daniel's car shortly after the murder. And the removal of files from the offices of Southern Investigations by Sid Fillery all point to a definite hole in the jigsaw puzzle.

This black hole indicates the gravity of the matter. That Daniel was convinced the police corruption story was big enough to sell to a national newspaper suggests it must have been something more than the Belmont Car Auctions robbery, involving larger sums of money and more significant personnel.

One constant theme in all the various explanations for Daniel's murder is that it concerned police involvement in drugs importation. From what we now know of SERCS and other dedicated crime squads in the Met going back over the 30 years, there is an embarrassment of riches when it comes to potential conspirators.

Yet rather than one issue of police corruption, Daniel might have uncovered many of them. Rather than the crime itself, he might have focused on the conspirators and discovered a network of corrupt police officers.

The mention of a 'management committee' organising the murder and cover-up seems plausible. If there was a conspiracy to murder Daniel in the Golden Lion car park and then cover it up using police personnel, it would need to be carefully planned.

All the indications about the location and timing of the murder, the preparation of the weapon and complete absence of eyewitnesses suggest it was meticulously organised. The removal of incriminating evidence from all Daniel's belongings and the abortive media campaigns calling for more information suggest the conspiracy was in operation long after the murder too.

Subsequent cover-ups may have escalated to hide this initial conspiracy, long after those involved in the murder had gone. The desperate attempts of the Met to hide the corruption allegations around Alan Holmes could be in this vein. Two violent deaths in police circles in south-east London in four months may have been to damaging to the morale and reputation of Scotland Yard. And if the cover-up itself is crime, then there's a chain reaction that could threaten the whole institution. Perhaps this is what made the Hampshire Constabulary back off from investigating Fillery more fully in 1990.

With the revelation of a network of corrupt police, dozens of trials could have collapsed and convictions been rendered unsafe. Senior officers may have decided then that burying the true story around Daniel was the lesser of two evils. But, of course, the lesser evil just grew.

It's clear now that the only other true detective back in the 1980s was Alastair Morgan, whose pursuit of truth on behalf of his family probably triggered the arrests in 1987. Without the persistence of the Morgan family, the case would almost certainly have been forgotten.

When the new generation of the Untouchables began to pick away at the edges of the corruption in the mid-1990s, they targeted a dozen or so corrupt cops in Fillery and Rees' circle. But none of these were really high-ranking, and CIB 3 seemed extremely averse to going higher up to look for the controlling mind or central figure. They even withheld evidence from the historic Macpherson report into the Stephen Lawrence murder in 1997. Institutional racism was easier to accept, it seems, than prevalent corruption. The latter undermined the very function of the Met.

The problem with police corruption is not just the immediate psychological torment and emotional trauma experienced by victims such as the Morgan family. The corruption around the first murder inquiry destroyed the viability of further investigations, and not just evidentially. The perfect legal defence for any of those accused of involvement in Daniel Morgan's murder is that since the police were corrupt in the first investigation, they are probably corrupt now. (This abuse of process argument has been regularly abused, right up to 2017.)

From the damage limitation of the 1990s, it's clear that this corruption was so significant it must have been considered an existential threat to Britain's biggest police force. But by prioritising their own survival, the Met have helped to subvert the criminal justice system – and undermine the very reason for their existence.

* * *

The other great institutional failure revealed by Daniel's murder is the role of the media.

The only two people we know for sure who immediately benefitted from the removal of Daniel Morgan were his business partner, Jon Rees, and his replacement, Sidney Fillery. Over the next decades, they would profit from a roaring trade in illegal investigations financed by the press.

Journalism is supposed to be the most potent antidote to abuse of power. Alastair Morgan trained to become a journalist in the belief that investigative journalism was like an immune system, which would expose and attack the corruption he'd seen in his brother's murder. But if the immune system itself is infected, the body politic has no protection.

Rees and Fillery knew this instinctively and began their media campaign early. In the uniquely competitive and commercial 'chequebook journalism' culture of the UK, they quickly gravitated towards their natural home – the *News of the World* – where earning cash and cutting corners were encouraged.

With executives like Alex Marunchak, and journalists like Mazher Mahmood, the *News of the World* innovated in every aspect of the dark arts, and created a ruthless race to the bottom most tabloids felt forced to follow. As a result, for at least a quarter of a century, Rupert Murdoch's flagship tabloid hacked, bugged, blagged, burgled and bribed its way into prominence, earning the vast fortune which would fund his US TV network Fox and providing ample ammunition against any politician who tried to limit or regulate his empire.

At the bottom of this dark pit of media corruption lies the body of Daniel Morgan.

Perhaps the ranks of lawyers and advisors called in to manage the phone-hacking scandal from 2009–2011 knew this. Senior executives Simon Greenberg and Will Lewis first discussed closing the *News of the World* in April 2011 – four months before the Milly Dowler story broke. Part of their concern was no doubt to limit the damage to News Corp's bid for complete ownership of Britain's most lucrative broadcaster, BSkyB.

The second phone-hacking investigation, Operation Weeting, had started in January 2011 after civil cases kept on bringing more phone hacking to light.

News of the World chief reporter Neville Thurlbeck had been arrested on 14th March, partially as a result of the 'For Neville' email which contained transcriptions of voicemail messages.

But this was all predictable once the Met had reopened the case. News Corp had allegations from 2006 by Clive Goodman of the eight other journalists and executives who tasked Mulcaire or had other evidence proving they were phone hacking. Perhaps more salient in their minds was the collapse a few days earlier of the Daniel Morgan prosecution, which allowed BBC *Panorama* to broadcast its email hacking documentary, and Nick Davies to cover Jonathan Rees' 'Empire of Corruption'?

Around this time, according to court documents, the newspaper's senior lawyer Tom Crone met with Alex Marunchak (who had been retired from the paper five years previously) and – of all people – the former Met detective and close associate of Rees and Fillery's, Alec Leighton.

Certainly, Rebekah Brooks indicated there was something bigger than the voicemail interception of Milly Dowler when she addressed a town hall meeting of *News of the World* journalists after the decision was made to close the newspaper on 8th July 2011.

Brooks tried to explain to the angry staff now facing redundancy that senior management had 'visibility' of something far worse coming down the line.

'I think,' Brooks reassured them, 'in a year's time every single one of you in this room might come up and say, "Okay, well I see what you saw now."'

What did she see then? What was coming down the line? What could be worse than intercepting the voicemails of a murdered schoolgirl?

Rebekah Brooks was arrested by the Operation Weeting team as she arrived for interview at Lewisham Police Station on 17th July 2011. She was so shocked – she thought it would just be an interview under caution – that she brandished a copy of Sir John Stevens' autobiography and angrily slammed it down on the table of the interview room.

Three days later, on 20th July 2011, Brooks appeared in front of the Culture, Media and Sport select committee. She'd been rehearsing her answers with lawyers and advisors for most of the previous week. During questioning by the parliamentarians, Tom Watson MP asked her about a major figure in this story.

TOM WATSON: Did you ever have any contact directly or through others with Jonathan Rees?

REBEKAH BROOKS: No.

TOM WATSON: Do you know about Jonathan Rees?

REBEKAH BROOKS: I do. Again, I have heard a lot recently about Jonathan Rees. I watched the *Panorama* programme, as we all did. His wasn't a name familiar to me. I am told that he rejoined the *News of the World* in 2005 or 2006, and he worked with the *News of the World* and many other newspapers in the late 1990s. That is my information.

TOM WATSON: Do you find it peculiar that having served a sentence for a serious criminal offence, he was then rehired by the paper?

REBEKAH BROOKS: It does seem extraordinary.

The rehiring of Rees not only seems extraordinary, Brooks' claim she never heard of him until 2011 is incredible. She'd worked at the newspaper since 1989; she was friends with Mahmood. How could she not remember the private detective named in the double-page *Guardian* splashes about the newspaper she edited? How could she forget the same person had been named to her by Dave Cook when he challenged her about surveillance on him and his wife?

Earlier that day, in a more tumultuous appearance before the select committee, Tom Watson had quizzed Rupert Murdoch about another key figure in this story:

TOM WATSON: Finally, can I ask you, when did you first meet Mr Alex Marunchak?

RUPERT MURDOCH: Mister—?

TOM WATSON: Alex Marunchak. He worked for the company for 25 years.

RUPERT MURDOCH: I don't remember meeting him. I might have shaken hands walking through the office, but I don't have any memory of him.

Absence of evidence is not evidence of absence but carefully phrased amnesia is a powerful indication of danger and corporate risk. What could be worse than hacking the phone of a murdered schoolgirl? Perhaps betraying a source like Daniel Morgan, working with a suspected murderer, or helping to derail two investigations?

* * *

Another indication of how sensitive the Daniel Morgan murder was for News International was the way they dealt with two key witnesses who would have given important and shocking evidence at the Leveson Inquiry.

Derek Haslam was considering a civil suit against the Metropolitan Police for failure of duty of care and was put in touch with a lawyer who argued that, for the sake of his civil case, Haslam should not make any submission or attend the Leveson Inquiry, though what he had to say about press corruption would have been eye opening and germane.

More disturbing still is the way Haslam's evidence was held back from the officers investigating media crimes. As soon as the phone-hacking scandal erupted, Derek Haslam told his DPS handlers to pass on his details to Operation Weeting, and the related inquiry into corrupt payments to police, Operation Elveden. He had potentially useful information, he told his handlers on more than one occasion.

Having heard nothing, Haslam rang Operation Weeting directly. They were surprised – they'd been told by the DPS he wasn't willing to assist.

Both News International and the Metropolitan Police had very good reasons to limit the revelations of the Leveson Inquiry, and the one to suffer most from this joint censorship was former DCS Dave Cook.

In 2012, just as Cook was preparing to become a core participant in the Inquiry, News International delivered to Operation Elveden, completely to their surprise, thousands of emails and invoices that detailed payments to public officials – in the police, prison service, Treasury and Ministry of Defence. The police were swamped. Confidential sources were betrayed and over 100 people were arrested.

Among those emails was some innocuous correspondence between *Sun* journalist Mike Sullivan and Dave Cook, who was discussing with Sullivan a possible book collaboration on his Daniel Morgan murder investigations. No money changed hands or was suggested.

Nevertheless, on the eve of becoming a core participant at the Leveson Inquiry in early 2012, Dave Cook was arrested. Despite a 30-year career as a police officer, his lawyer advised him he could face prison time. He would not attend the Leveson Inquiry. Three more police investigations would mean he was effectively silenced for the next six years.

<table>
<tr><td>CHAPTER 44</td><td>Meeting May</td></tr>
</table>

2011-2013

ALASTAIR: My instincts about my mother's letter to the Home Office secretary proved correct. Next day Mum rang me from Wales: a letter had arrived from Theresa May by courier. She read me the letter over the phone.

'She'll meet us, but she wants no lawyer or MPs with us,' Mum told me.

We hit back immediately. Raju Bhatt wrote asking whether the Home Secretary thought it right to deprive an 83-year-old woman, denied justice for her son for 25 years, of her legal and democratic representation.

Embarrassment is a strong tool. A meeting was set for 6th December 2011 with Raju and our MPs present. The day before, Kirsteen and I held a meeting with Raju to prepare. I dreaded these meetings with officialdom. We had good cause to be apprehensive, given the abysmal history of the Home Office and the fact that we'd had to embarrass Theresa May into giving us a hearing.

The following day, the four of us arrived at the home office with Raju and our MPs, Roger Williams and Emily Thornberry. After a few minutes waiting in an ante-room, we were ushered into a large meeting room with a square of tables in the middle. After a round of introductions, we sat down and moved on to the real reason we were there: police corruption.

Raju pointed to Tim Godwin's apology and admissions to the MPA. I spoke briefly about the corruption that we'd actually seen. When I'd finished, Jane squeezed my hand under the table.

'You will have read the submission and that has all the detail,' Raju continued. 'For the best part of 20 years this family heard every level of authority saying there was nothing wrong with the first inquiry and that everything was dealt with by Hampshire Police,' he told the Home Secretary.

'Finally, in 2006 as a result of the MPA's actions, the police admitted it was corruption which crippled the first inquiry. It may be coincidence, but that admission was at the start of the last inquiry, which was five years of torture for the family. It was clear very quickly that the prosecution would fail, not because of SOCPA, but because it was weighed down by 20 years of corruption and the failure to address that corruption.

'The only way that the history of this case can have the scrutiny it deserves is through a judicial inquiry,' Raju concluded.

Theresa May then raised the issue of possible future prosecutions. Kirsteen stressed that it was clear that there would never be another prosecution.

'I accept it's unlikely there will be prosecutions,' May's advisor confirmed. 'What characterises this case is allegations of police corruption and that's what we need to investigate. A judicial inquiry wouldn't involve prosecutions.'

It was obvious that Theresa May had come to the meeting with the intention of pressing for further investigations and prosecutions for corruption. We didn't want the police anywhere near the case any longer. The discussion went back and forth, neither side willing to give way.

'You don't need to go further than the words of Tim Godwin when he said that the problem was not just corruption but a failure to confront it. That failure can't be prosecuted,' Raju argued.

I was becoming impatient and gathered my notes. Theresa May started to wind up the meeting.

'I hope that you will go away and think about an outside inquiry,' she said. 'I will wait to see what comes out of the Met/CPS report and I will reflect on what I have heard today.'

'My reaction is that this is a cop-out,' I responded flatly.

'It's not,' replied the Home Secretary.

'Will you undertake to look again?' asked Emily Thornberry.

'I haven't ruled anything out. I'll wait to see the review,' May replied.

'Isobel is getting on in age,' said Roger Williams.

'She doesn't have much time left,' I added and started to get up to leave. Raju stressed that we had no confidence in the Met's report.

'I hope you have confidence in the Home Secretary,' said one of her advisors.

'How can we have confidence if you won't go in a direction that will bring us closure?' Mum replied. 'The day the trial collapsed was one of the worst in my life. You have the power. Is it too much to ask after all these years?'

'I said that the purpose today was to hear directly from you,' said Theresa May. 'I will reflect on what I heard today, but as I said before, I won't look at the issue of a judicial inquiry while there is still a review.'

This was an empty argument. It was clear to anyone who had read the submission that the real problems arose many years before Operation Abelard 2 had started.

As I left the room I didn't say goodbye. I walked straight towards the lift, pressed the button, walked in and almost screamed with frustration. I could hear my mother pleading with May, then Jane's voice saying, 'Don't beg her, Mum.'

I waited in reception until we were all together then we walked out together to face the questions.

'We've had 25 years of dealing with the police,' I said to a microphone. 'We want nothing more to do with them. They've let us down on every single occasion.'

While we were regrouping, there was a shock in store for us.

David Cook was arrested.

* * *

Dave Cook had apparently sent some police papers to the *Sun*'s crime correspondent, Mike Sullivan. He'd been introduced to Sullivan, we later learned, by John Yates. Mike Sullivan had published an important story about Daniel's stolen Austin Healey. When News International surrendered its computers to the police after the hacking scandal, Cook's communications had been discovered and he'd been arrested.

Equally disturbingly, we learned that he was applying for core-participant status at the Leveson Inquiry at the time of his arrest.

Since the collapse of the trial, I'd got to know the Birmingham MP Tom Watson. Tom had been prominent in the news over phone hacking and other press criminality. He suggested an adjournment debate on Daniel's case. I met with him several times in his office, where I explained the background. On one occasion Derek Haslam was present and he told Tom how he'd become involved in the case and what had taken place while he was putting himself in harm's way, working undercover at Southern Investigations. Tom was preparing an adjournment debate in the Commons about Daniel's murder.

Still trying to duck the issue, Theresa May wrote to Roger Williams suggesting an investigation into the corruption that had been admitted by the Met in the first inquiry. We rejected her offer.

By this time, the Leveson Inquiry was gripping the nation with its revelations of sordid press intrusions, ugly entrapments and cosy relations between senior police officers and News International executives. The day before Tom's adjournment debate, the inquiry was to hear from former police officer and *Crimewatch* presenter, Jacqui Hames.

Her evidence centred on the way the *News of the World* had placed her family under surveillance in 2002, immediately after a *Crimewatch* appeal for witnesses in Daniel's murder. She recounted how her husband David had noticed a van parked unusually near their home and how he was followed by this van when he took their children to school and nursery. She told the inquiry about her sense of betrayal at how her personal details and service history had been accessed and passed on from inside the Met to the *News of the World*.

The Guardian reported on her evidence: 'When a senior detective re-opened a notorious murder inquiry, the suspects were able to intimidate his wife and family with the help of an executive at the *News of the World*, the Leveson Inquiry has been told.

'Making one of the gravest Leveson allegations so far, former *Crimewatch* presenter Jacqui Hames, the then wife of Detective Chief Superintendent Dave Cook, broke down in tears as she accused the paper's then editor Rebekah Brooks of covering up the real reason why her family were targeted.

'The intimidation was carried out after an offer of a £50,000 reward on Hames's *Crimewatch* programme for fresh information on the murder of Daniel Morgan, a partner in a private detective agency.

'Hames said: "These events left me distressed, anxious and needing counselling and contributed to the breakdown of my marriage."'

Leveson told her she did not have to continue. But having recovered her composure, Hames, a former detective herself, who said she had loved her job, told the inquiry: 'No one from any walk of life should have to put up with it. I would hate to think of anyone having to go through what we have had 10 years of.'

She alleged that former *News of the World* executive Alex Marunchak colluded with suspects who ran the *News of the World*'s private detective operations. They put the family under surveillance and targeted their phones for hacking. Brooks, as editor, failed to act when confronted with the evidence in 2003, Hames said, and Marunchak was even subsequently promoted.

After the broadcast, Dave Cook got official intelligence that the suspects planned 'to make life difficult for him', and the programme was sent an email suggesting Hames was having an affair with a senior detective. Two vans stationed outside their house were eventually traced back to the *News of the World*.

Police at Scotland Yard did little to protect the couple. Instead, the head of PR at the Met, Dick Fedoricio, spoke to Brooks, who made the 'absolutely pathetic' claim that the tabloid had targeted the couple because of the alleged affair. 'We had by then been married for four years, had been together for 11 years and had two children,' Hames said.

In a meeting with her husband she said Brooks 'repeated the unconvincing explanation that the *News of the World* believed we were having an affair'. Hames said: 'I believe that the real reason for the *News of the World* placing us under surveillance was that suspects in the Daniel Morgan murder inquiry were using their association with a powerful and well-resourced newspaper to try to intimidate us and so attempt to subvert the investigation.'

She told the Inquiry that it was impossible not to conclude that there had been 'collusion between people at the *News of the World* and people who were suspected of killing Daniel Morgan'.

The Met's press office swung into immediate and well-oiled action, releasing a story about an aged Met police horse that had been given to Rebekah Brooks and her husband Charlie. Most of the nation's hacks went haring off after this obvious diversion. I wondered how many of them had one eye on a nice job with the Murdoch press. A public allegation that journalists from the *Screws* attempted to wreck a highly sensitive and extremely important murder investigation held limited interest for most of the British media.

* * *

Early in March 2012 the former Commissioner of the Met, Lord Stevens, gave evidence to the Leveson Inquiry.

He was questioned about his relationship with the *News of the World* and about Operation Nigeria and whether he was aware that Operation Nigeria had uncovered corrupt links between police and journalists at Southern Investigations. He was also asked whether he was aware that the *News of the World* had put Dave Cook and his wife under surveillance. He answered no to both questions.

I was worried about Stevens' evidence. Operation Nigeria started after a contentious meeting between a cabinet minister and Stevens himself. Surely he would have paid close attention to what was going on in that investigation? Disappointingly, Stevens wasn't examined rigorously on these matters.

Next, it was the turn of Bob Quick. He told the inquiry that Operation Nigeria had uncovered corrupt links between police and journalists and that he saw this as a threat to the Metropolitan Police. He said he'd discussed this with Andy Hayman, who was opposed to prosecutions and wanted instead to discuss the matter with the various editors concerned. Remarkably, the Met had lost Quick's report.

Stevens and Hayman had later worked for Murdoch as columnists. Stevens was given his own column in the *News of the World*, under the title 'The Chief', and Hayman wrote for *The Times*.

* * *

In May, the police and the CPS finally completed their report on the collapse of the prosecution. The process had dragged on for more than a year. Kirsteen, Raju and I finally met them on 21st May 2012 at the CPS headquarters, where we were presented with three copies of the report. Strikingly, it contained nothing about the history of the case and the corruption that surrounded the murder.

'One of my assistants could have prepared this in three weeks,' Raju told Kirsteen and me. 'It basically recommends that the police and CPS do their jobs properly. The last three-quarters of the report is cut and pasted from transcripts. Shall I call them in?'

Assistant Commissioner Cressida Dick and DAC Simon Foy entered with two CPS officials and a note-taker. I refused to shake hands. Raju expressed his opinion about the report. I told them how we felt about the Metropolitan Police and its conduct over the preceding 25 years. They sat there, stony-faced.

The only reaction came in the lift as we left the building. The woman who had been taking notes during the meeting burst into tears. I was completely taken aback that she had been so upset by the saga of my brother and our long struggle for justice.

Theresa May was still ignoring our submission. By this time we were considering challenging her inertia in the courts. I kept on tweeting about the case and my small army of followers on Twitter was growing rapidly. It led to invitations to speak at University College London and the London School of Economics. Often I'd stay up tweeting into the early hours and was heartened that so many people seemed interested, and angry on our behalf.

* * *

September 2012 saw another bombshell event: the Hillsborough panel published its report into the disaster at Sheffield Wednesday's football ground in 1989.

David Cameron, the then Prime Minister, offered a public apology to the families of the 96 dead in Parliament. The panel finally established that there had been a sordid attempt by the police, supported by the Murdoch press, to smear the dead and the fans in order to rewrite history for their own benefit. Once again, we could see deeply worrying links between these two powerful organisations. Raju Bhatt, our solicitor, had been quietly working away as a member of the Hillsborough panel for two years. He'd never mentioned it to us.

In mid-October we received a letter from the former Commissioner, Lord Blair, saying that he had approached the Home Secretary privately, asking her to look favourably on our request for a judicial inquiry. He wrote that he was happy to repeat this publicly.

On 23rd November 2012 Raju wrote once more to the Home Office extending our deadline for a substantive response until 12th December. Nothing appeared to be moving inside Marsham Street.

This was about to change dramatically.

Acting under the orders of the Home Secretary, a senior civil servant telephoned Raju asking for a meeting. We agreed unhesitatingly.

On 25th November 2012, Raju met with a group of Home Office officials to discuss the setting up a panel of inquiry to look into Daniel's murder.

On 17th December 2012 we received a letter from the Home Office confirming agreement on the formation of the Daniel Morgan Independent Panel. It was formally announced publicly on 10th May 2013 with the remit: 'To shine a light on the circumstances of Daniel Morgan's murder, its background and the handling of the case over the whole period since March 1987'.

The panel promised to address any questions that arose, particularly those relating to: 'police involvement in the murder; the role played by police corruption in protecting those responsible for the murder from being brought to justice and the failure to confront that corruption; and the incidence of connections between private investigators, police officers and journalists at the *News of the World* and other parts of the media and alleged corruption involved in the linkages between them.'

After more than a quarter of a century, it looked as though light would finally be shed on the death of my little brother, Dan...

Acknowledgements

It is impossible in the space of a page to adequately acknowledge the support I've received from so many kind and talented people on this journey in pursuit of truth and justice. My family must come first, as they alone understand the pain of losing Daniel and living through five failed murder investigations. My mother, now 89 years old, deserves particular recognition for her unbelievable tenacity and courage throughout this ordeal. My sister Jane, although geographically removed from the drama for many years, has been my constant companion on this odyssey. As only siblings can, she shares treasured memories of growing up with Dan, with all the laughter and tears that these invoke. My son Ian, who remembers his uncle, has shared my pain and been a support throughout. My sister-in-law Iris has performed the astonishing feat, after the brutal murder of her husband, of raising Daniel's two children into the decent, well-adjusted and productive adults that they are today. This book is about a man they barely knew. I want it to be a concrete testimony for them of how much we all loved him.

I owe very special gratitude to the love of my life, my partner of twenty-three years, Kirsteen Knight. Without her this book would not have been written. Her assiduous note-taking in hundreds of meetings, coverage of the long pre-trial (that we were not allowed to attend), tireless research and fact-checking have provided indispensable support to Peter and me in the writing of this book.

We all owe huge thanks to our solicitor for the past eighteen years, Raju Bhatt. Without his wisdom, professionalism, patience, and kindness, our quest for truth and justice would have foundered long ago. He is an outstanding solicitor and a wonderful human being. Among many journalists I owe special thanks to Laurie Flynn, Michael Gillard and Paddy French. All of them have become my good friends over the years. When I felt I was confronting insurmountable odds, Laurie always had words of encouragement and Michael never stopped pushing me to write this book.

Among politicians I thank MPs Chris Smith, Tom Watson, Richard Livsey, Roger Williams and Emily Thornberry. Particular thanks go to Jennette

Arnold and Len Duvall of the then MPA, the first politicians in authority over the police to take our concerns seriously. Their help and support was absolutely crucial at an important stage of our campaign.

Among friends, we thank Andrea Bolitho, Chris Cummins and Peter and Alicia Taylor. Their friendship has been a light and a refuge in dark times.

Others who have provided vital help and support include Glyn Maddocks, June Tweedie, INQUEST, Duncan Campbell, Malcolm Knight, Hugh Grant, Neil Smith and Paul Murphy of GMB, Clare Hudson, Andy Davies, Glen Campbell, Sanchia Berg, Vikram Dodd, Eliot Higgins and Fred Hepburn.

Finally, I thank the hundreds of loyal followers on Twitter who helped fund the podcast, Untold – The Daniel Morgan Murder.

Sources: Complicity and Complexity

There are many reasons the Daniel Morgan story has been so hard to tell. And one of the more innocent reasons is sheer complexity.

Spanning thirty years and involving hundreds of related police investigations, the blizzard of names alone becomes blinding. And that's assuming you can remember the names.

There is no consistency in the public record for so many of the players, and even where there is, false duplicates confound. Jonathan Rees is variably spelled as John or Jon Reece. And there is another Jonathan Rees – a lawyer acting for the prosecution during the pre-trial.

The Vians are often described transcribed as the Vines. Garry and Glenn are often recorded as Gary and Glen. There are two Sharon Vians, depending on maiden or married name. One is related to Paul Goodridge, who isn't related to Michael Goodridge. There are three Holmes: the Met's detective software HOLMES, Alan Holmes and a Jimmy Holmes. There are too many Cooks – notably Jimmy Cook and Dave Cook. There is a Davidson and a Davison. There is (apparently) a David Wood and a David Woods. And Raymond Adams has absolutely no relation to the Adams Family.

Maintaining cohesion in this complex web of names and networks is a major hurdle to any historian, let alone a storyteller or reader. Apologies for any confusion. If errors persist, Alastair and I will correct them in a second edition.

Apart from the natural noise of time and error, there are more ominous reasons why the usually reliable sources for this book cannot be trusted or verified.

The police record of the Daniel Morgan murder is, by the Metropolitan Police's own admission, completely compromised. We will never know what, if any, portion of records from Southern Investigations before the murder still survive. Forensic evidence going back to 1987 has been botched. Important witness statements are missing. Others, it appears, have been doctored. The evidential links fade into obscurity and worse – a trail of misinformation has been laid that still befuddles investigators today.

This book was originally designed to be published after the Daniel Morgan Independent Panel reported. In the nine months it took to write and edit this book, the panel moved its publication date from the summer of 2016 to Spring 2017, and then to Autumn 2017, and as this book goes to press the panel report won't be published until early 2018 – five years since the panel was publicly announced by the then home secretary Theresa May.

Much of this delay is down to new disclosures from the Metropolitan Police. Back in 2011, the prosecution case against Jonathan Rees, Glenn and Garry Vian and Jimmy Cook collapsed because new boxes of evidence kept emerging. By that point there were already close to a million exhibits related to the murder. This number grows all the time.

Because of this unending and uncertain disclosure, this book can never be exhaustive. But the corruption of the original police record is telling in itself.

In these circumstances, print journalism and broadcast media are usually relied upon to set the record straight. In the case of Daniel Morgan the press, for various reasons, have failed to provide a fair and accurate account. The suspects were from the outset adept at public relations and suborning journalists to tell their side of the story. This charm offensive – or offensive charm – continues to this day.

Thirty years on, I've seen honourable documentary makers and experienced journalists seduced by it. Sometimes they're lured by the offer of some scoop or juicy inside information. Occasionally, they think they can extract a confession. Before long, they are the information, and their compromise is the thing to be traded on.

There is also a conspiracy of embarrassed silence for professional reasons. Throughout my five years working on this story I've heard Alastair be told by a senior investigative journalist that he would like to write Daniel's story but it's 'too political'. Another told me he didn't want to put his head 'above the parapet'. With half their potential employers also employers of Southern Investigations at some point, it would be career suicide for print journalists to go on about the Daniel Morgan murder.

Sins of omission and commission continue outside the time frame of this edition of the book. The 2013 media coverage of allegations of 'Blue Chip Hacking' for example, based on the Serious Organised Crime Agency's 2008 Riverside Report was highly tendentious and unusually convenient for Rebekah Brooks when she stood trial at the Old Bailey. Brooks often mentioned alleged hacking by law firms and large corporations to put press abuses in some kind of wider perspective. In reality the SOCA report, which came out of the discovery of email hacking at Southern Investigations, only mentions blue chip companies as victims.

Also, outside of the time frame of this edition of the book is the civil trial in 2017 in which Jonathan Rees, Sid Fillery, and Glenn and Garry Vian sued the Metropolitan Police Service for malicious prosecutions and misfeasance in office over their arrests in 2008 during Operation Abelard 2.

Justice Mitting threw out all the malicious prosecution charges in February 2017, but upheld one charge of misfeasance regarding Sid Fillery (and even this is still misreported as 'malfeasance'). Because of the problems around the handling of protected witness Gary Eaton the judge ruled that his evidence should have been inadmissible, and that Fillery shouldn't have been arrested for a second time. Fillery was awarded damages.

However, Justice Mitting ruled there was plenty of new admissible evidence to justify the arrests of Jonathan Rees, the Vian brothers and Jimmy Cook in 2008. And it wasn't until 13 months after the exclusion of Eaton and dismissing of the case against Fillery that the prosecution case collapsed in March 2011. This was mainly due to loss of witnesses and the impossibility of a fair trial without full and frank disclosure.

Though we hope this is thorough account of the five investigations into Daniel's murder, it is not yet complete. The story stops abruptly in 2013 when the Daniel Morgan Independent Panel was announced. Until the Daniel Morgan Independent Panel reports in 2018, the notes below are constrained in various ways. The Morgan family are bound to keep their discussions with the panel confidential and the new revelations in this book come from my original research or prior disclosures to the family. Many of these documents – such as the Hampshire Inquiry Report – cannot be cited yet in full for legal reasons, and are not included in the footnotes.

In the meantime, the main official sources of information for this book are the *Inquest into the Murder of Daniel Morgan, 1988*; *The Stephen Lawrence Independent Review, Mark Ellison QC, 2013*; *Operation Russell Report, 1990* (published partially redacted in an annex to the Ellison Review) and both the pleadings and judgement (17 February 2017) of *Rees, Vian, Fillery v. The*

Commissioner of the Police of the Metropolis, In The High Court Of Justice, Queens Bench Division, HQ14X01020.

To grasp the depth of police corruption around Daniel Morgan's story, two books are required reading: *Untouchables: Dirty Cops, Bent Justice and Racism in Scotland Yard* by Mike Gillard and Laurie Flynn (Cutting Edge Press, 2004 edition) and *Bent Coppers: The Inside Story of Scotland Yard's Battle Against Police Corruption*, by Graeme McLagan (Orion Books, 2004). On the parallel corruption of the media Nick Davies' *Flat Earth News: An Award-winning Reporter Exposes Falsehood, Distortion and Propaganda in the Global Media* (Chatto & Windus, 2008) and *Hack Attack: How the Truth Caught up with Rupert Murdoch* (Chatto & Windus 2014) cannot be equalled.

Peter Jukes – April 2017

Endnotes

Chapter 2

1 Daniel Morgan Inquest 1988, Day 6, page 53

2 BBC *Panorama*: Cops, Criminals, Corruption: The Inside Story, Friday 4 March 2015

3 Daniel Morgan Inquest 1988, Day 6, Page 49

4 Ibid, Day 6, Page 97

5 Ibid, Day 6, Page 37

6 Ibid, Day 1, Page 59

7 Ibid, Day 6, Page 43

8 Ibid, Day 1, Page 61

9 Ibid Day 4, Page 51

10 Ibid, Day 1, Page 62

11 Ibid, Day 3, Page 25

12 Ibid, Day 6, Page 101

13 Ibid, Day 6, Page 49

14 Ibid, Day 6, Page 68

15 Ibid, Day 6, Page 74

16 Interview with Jane Royds, February 2016

Chapter 3

1 Interview with Jane Royds, February 2016

2 Daniel Morgan Inquest 1988, Day 4, Page 19

3 Interview with Derek Haslam, April 2016

4 Interview with Alastair Morgan, December 2015

5 Daniel Morgan Inquest 1988, Day 3, Page 43

6 Ibid, Day 3, Page 9

7 Ibid, Day 3, Page 79

8 Ibid, Day 3, Page 70

9 Ibid, Day 4, Page 10

10 Ibid, Day 3, Page 30

11 Ibid, Day 1, Page 64

12 Ibid. Day 7, Page 44

13 Other examples of Daniel's reluctance to park in car parks from the Inquest: David Bray said Daniel's car was getting broken into every six months and he 'was getting into a right hump about it.' (Inquest Day 4, Page 8); 'That still got to me, because Daniel was the kind of person who would just bump his car up the kerb just leave it there'; he took such pride in his car his desk was littered with parking tickets, 'Daniel would leave his car anywhere normally than in a car park,' according to Newby (Inquest Day 3, Page 38).

14 Allegation by June Tweedie QC. Daniel Morgan Inquest 1988; Day 1, Page 46: Day 5, Page 60

Chapter 4

1 Daniel Morgan Inquest 1988, Day 3, Page 23

2 Ibid, Day 3, Page 8

3 Ibid, Day 3, Page 23, 43

4 Ibid, Day 3, Page 90

5 Ibid, Day 3, Page 26

6 Ibid, Day 3, Page 85

7 Ibid, Day 6, Page 107

8 Ibid, Day 4, Page 7

9 Ibid, Day 3, Page 83

10 Ibid, Day 5, Page 36

11 Ibid, Day 3, Page 10

12 Ibid, Day 7, Page 71

13 Ibid, Day 5, Page 89. In Fillery's inquest evidence he said he 'moaned with Jon about Daniel's argument the night before.'
14 Ibid, Day 6, Pages 105, 85
15 Ibid, Day 3, Page 28
16 Ibid, Day 3, Page 82
17 Ibid, Day 3, Page 71
18 Ibid, Day 2, Page 91
19 Ibid, Day 3, Page 37
20 Ibid Day 9, Page 15
21 Ibid, Day 3, Page 86
22 Ibid, Day 4, Page 24
23 Ibid Day 6, Page 6
24 Ibid, Day 6, Page 88
25 Ibid, Day 3, Page 36
26 Ibid, Day 6, Page 7
27 Ibid, Day 5, Page 69
28 Ibid, Day 6, Page 11

Chapter 6

1 At the Inquest in 1988 Alastair was convinced the second officer was Alan Jones though he denied it.

Chapter 7

1 Daniel Morgan Inquest 1988, Day 3, Page 74
2 DS Fillery, PS Barrett, PCs Crocket, Fentiman, Ferguson, Thompson, Thorogood and Zdrojewski
3 Daniel Morgan Inquest 1988, DSupt Campbell's Evidence, Day 4, Page 69
4 Metropolitan Police Authority Report, 5 April 2006. Refers to DI Jones' statement circa 2002
5 Alastair Morgan's recollection of a conversation with DI Jones
6 Daniel Morgan Inquest 1988, Day 5, Page 72
7 Interview with John Ross, *Untouchables: Dirty Cops, Bent Justice and Racism in Scotland Yard* by Mike Gillard and Laurie

Flynn (Cutting Edge Press, 2004 edition), Page 90

Chapter 9

1 Daniel Morgan Inquest 1988, DSU Campbell's Evidence, Day 5, Page 79
2 Ibid, Day 6, Page 73
3 Ibid, Day 4, Page 53
4 Ibid, Day 4, Page 54
5 Ibid, Day 4, Page 67
6 Ibid, Day 4, Page 57
7 Interview with Derek Haslam, March 2016
8 Daniel Morgan Inquest 1988, DSU Duncan Campbell Evidence, Day 5, Page 60

Chapter 11

1 Ibid, Kevin Lennon's Evidence, Day 1, Page 31
2 Ibid, Day 1, Page 15
3 Ibid, Day 1, Page 17
4 Ibid, Day 4, Page 5
5 Ibid, Day 1, Page 34
6 Ibid, Day 1, Page 28
7 Ibid, Day 1, Page 21
8 Ibid, Day 1, Page 28
9 Ibid, Day 1, Page 35
10 The unknown males appear to be called Tone, Keith, Eddy and Bernie.

Chapter 12

1 PC Derek Haslam contacted the Morgan 1 incident room on 11 March 1988 to report the encounter. He also informed the murder team that Rees claimed Daniel had met Taffy Holmes days before the murder.

Chapter 13

1 Daniel Morgan Inquest 1988, A C Pearce's Evidence, Day 3, Page 97

Chapter 14

1 The MPS explanation of what happened next: 'Following the inquest, concerns were expressed by the family of Daniel Morgan about possible police corruption. The complaint was voluntarily referred by the MPS to the Police Complaints Authority ("PCA").' Paragraph 51, Pleadings in the High Court of Justice, Queen's Bench Division, HQ14X01020

2 Lamper was investigating an official complaint by Rees in May 1988 into the handling of his arrest and forensic tests on his clothes. On 12 May 1989, through his solicitor Michael Goodridge, Rees launched a civil action for damages for malicious prosecution and unlawful imprisonment.

Chapter 15

1 This entailed transferring all the data from the Metropolitan Police's MICA system to the HOLMES system used by other constabularies.

2 Amended Defence by Commissioner of Police of the Metropolis: Rees, Vian, Fillery, In The High Court Of Justice, Queens Bench Division, HQ14X01020, Para 54

3 Ibid. Footnote: In a statement dated 16 August 2006, Mr Lennon was to disavow this information, saying that he had no recollection of meeting with anyone in an attempt to 'rip off' Rees.

4 Amended Defence by Commissioner of Police of the Metropolis: Rees, Vian, Fillery, In The High Court Of Justice, Queens Bench Division, HQ14X01020, Para 56

5 BBC Radio 4, The Report, with Adrian Goldberg, interview with Marjorie Williams, 18 August 2011

6 Daniel Morgan Inquest 1988, Day 5, Page 56

7 Ibid, Day 5, Page 38

8 Ibid, Day 6, Page 25

9 Ibid, Day 2, Page 80

10 Ibid, Day 5, Page 39

Chapter 17

1 It would later be renamed Law and Commercial but for continuity purposes will be called Southern Investigations throughout.

2 John Gunning, convicted of blagging information from private subscribers from British Telecoms database in 2006. Rees had known Gunning since November 1986 according to his car phone billing and was regularly calling him until the time of the murder.

3 Exaro Tapes, 2013. 'Rupert Murdoch vows to hit back over raid on Rebekah Brooks as he is caught on tape', by Hugo Dye, *Daily Mail* 4 July 2013. http://www.dailymail.co.uk/news/article-2355600/Rupert-Murdoch-caught-tape-branding-police-totally-incompetent.html

4 *News of the World*, 26 September 1986, 5 October 1986, 12 October 1986, 7 December 1986, 14 December 1986, 18 January 1987, 22 February 1987, 1 March 1987, 10 May 1987, 17 May 1987, 5 July 1987

5 'Scandal of Top Cop and Rent Boys' by Alex Marunchak, *News of the World*, 11 May 1986. The police officer in charge of the investigation, Brian August, could not recall which private investigators were involved in this allegation when approached in Spring 2016.

6 'Cop Killed Himself to Save Pals in the Masons', by Alex Marunchak and Gerry Brown, *News of the World*, 2 August 1987

7 A manual search of the British Library microfiche archives has failed to find any other mention. The *News of the World* online digital archive was deleted in 2011 when the paper was closed.

8 'Cover-Up Cops Axed My Partner to Death' by Alex Marunchak, *News of the World*, 14 May 1989

9 Apart from Haslam, Rees is the main contemporaneous witness who places Daniel Morgan and Alan Holmes together as close contacts. (Haslam later was shown some receipts by Rees which he claimed were Taffy's expenses paid for by Daniel, but there is no way of corroborating that to date.).

10 The authors have regularly tried to contact Alex Marunchak for comment, but he has consistently refused to respond.

11 BBC Radio 4, The Report, with Adrian Goldberg, interview with Marjorie Williams, 18 August 2011

12 Marunchak: Tom Watson allegations 'absolutely untrue', Dominic Ponsford, *Press Gazette*, March 1 2012

13 Which is also part of the tabloid business model see: 'The Sun Vault: the Death Star of British Journalism' by Peter Jukes, *Informm*, 23 March 2016

14 'Memoirs of A Minor Public Figure' by Des Wilson (Quartet, 2011) serialized in the *Daily Mail* 5 March 2011

15 *Untouchables: Dirty cops, bent justice and racism in Scotland Yard* by Mike Gillard and Laurie Flynn (Bloomsbury, 2012 Edition) Location 4506

16 *Confessions of a Fake Sheikh; 'The King of the Sting' Reveals All* by Mazher Mahmood (Harper Collins, 2008)

17 'Job descriptions that hid brutal life of a criminal' by David Connett, *The Independent* Saturday 31 October 1992

18 'An undercover operation led to the conviction of a highly prized police target', *The Independent*, David Connett, Saturday 31 October 1992

Chapter 19

1 The Stephen Lawrence Independent Review, Mark Ellison QC, Vol. I, 5.4, Page 104

2 Operation Russell Report, Vol. 32

3 Haslam's recollection of the conversation with Holmes about Daniel negotiating the story is very specific in time and place and there is contemporaneous corroboration that he informed Det Supt Campbell of the allegations with weeks of the murder. Haslam claims the hearsay allegation was made to him by DCS David Wood in late 1996.

4 Interview with Derek Haslam, 20 April 2016

5 The Detective Inspector later denied he had said any of this, though both Lunnis and Haslam stood by their story.

6 However, Davies would be subject to the subsequent investigation. Gray claimed to have seen him at the local Catford racetrack with underworld figures.

Chapter 20

1 The final report was released to parliament some 23 years later, in redacted form, after the Ellison Independent Review of the Stephen Lawrence Public Inquiry in 2013.

2 Gray had refused to back up the allegations on tape with a written statement when he was interviewed by Deputy Assistant Commissioner Peter Winship on 24 April 1987.

3 In an Operation Russell interview Adams says Jean Burgess worked for East London clothes manufacturer who

provided materials for Inga Adams'
boutique. Operation Russell, 1990
Report, Vol. 32, Para 631

4   Operation Russell, 1990 Report, Vol. 32,
Para 622

5   Gray had refused to back up the
allegations on tape with a written
statement when he was interviewed by
Deputy Assistant Commissioner Peter
Winship on 24 April 1987.

6   Interview with Derek Haslam, 20 April
2016

7   *Daily Express*, 3 August 1987, pp 1-2

8   *Daily Express*, 4 August 1987, Page 2

9   *News of the World*, 16 August 1987,
Page 13

10 'Yard Throw Party for Suicide Cop's
Lover' by Alex Marunchak, *News of the
World*, 16 August 1987

11 *News of the World*, 2 August 1987, Page 9

12 Russell Report, Vol. 8, Para 103

13 Ibid, Vol. 8, Para 8, Para 112

14 *Untouchables*: Location 1550

15 Ibid, Location 1708

16 Rees was still promulgating this theory
that Daniel was buying drugs for his
brother on his ChristianBraveheart
Twitter account as late as 2015.

17 *Untouchables*, Location 1680

18 In March 2014, the Ellison Review
acknowledged that Davidson had been
in a corrupt relationship with Clifford
Norris, the father of one the murderers
of Stephen Lawrence. Ellison concluded
that this relationship was suppressed when
the MacPherson Inquiry first investigated
persistent rumours of corruption in the
Lawrence murder investigation.

Chapter 22

1   *The Independent*, 'Corruption uncovered
at heart of the Met' by Marianne
MacDonald, 28 June 1996

2   *Untouchables* Location 3362

3   'Jonathan Rees: private investigator
who ran empire of tabloid corruption'
by Nick Davies, *The Guardian*,
11 March 2011. https://www.
theguardian.com/media/2011/mar/11/
jonathan-rees-private-investigator-tabloid

4   Leveson Inquiry Witness Statement,
Mazher Mahmood, 14 October 2011

5   *Bent Coppers: The Inside Story of Scotland
Yard's Battle Against Police Corruption*, by
Graeme McLagan, Orion Books 2004,
Page 289

Chapter 24

1   Companies House 363 Annual return,
Abbeycover Ltd, co. no. 03202067.
Return date is to 22 May 1997

2   LWT and Sky News reports, 26 March
1998

3   *Not for the Faint Hearted* by Sir John
Stevens (Phoenix 2006), Pages 308-310

4   Kingston was suspended in 1998 due
to the investigation of corruption and
serious malpractice whilst serving on
the South East Regional Crime Squad
(Operation Russia). In March 1999
Kinston was charged with 4 criminal
offences.

5   In return for his assistance to police,
Warner received a reduced 7-year
sentence in 1999 for a variety of charges.

Chapter 26

1   'The sheik unveiled', the *Guardian*, 4
October 1999. Alun Jones, QC for the
defence, quizzed Mazher on his two
heavies, and also about supplying as
well as buying cocaine. https://www.
theguardian.com/media/1999/oct/04/
newsoftheworld.mondaymediasection

2   Paddy French, in his essay the No. 1
Corrupt Detective Agency, suggests

it was the Simon James drug planting scam which initiated the new name – Operation Two Bridges.

Chapter 28

1 These documents revealed that in 1999 Rees and Fillery carried out 'confidential inquiries' into 'illegal immigration' after receiving a 'request' from 'Maz Mahmood'. https://pressganguk.wordpress.com/2014/11/10/mazher-mahmood/

Chapter 31

1 Appointed in Feb 2000 Commander of CIB, which included the Anti-Corruption Command' (formerly CIB 3) and Complaint's Investigation (formerly CIB 2)

2 Leveson Inquiry. Witness statement of Robert Quick, 12 February 2012. Name was changed in 1997. http://webarchive.nationalarchives.gov.uk/20140122145147/http:/www.levesoninquiry.org.uk/wp-content/uploads/2012/03/Witness-Statement-of-Bob-Quick.pdf

3 Ibid, Para 125

4 Ibid, Para 13

5 Leveson Inquiry: Compilation of diary entries involving contact with the media Diary of John STEVENS covering the period 1 January 2000 to 31 January 2005 whilst Commissioner.

6 According to Stevens, this was the one and only time he met Alex Marunchak.

7 Interview wth Greg Miskiw, 2 February 2017

8 'Court clears journalist and detective', BBC Website, 20 July 2000.

9 'NoW hacking suspect worked for the police as an "informer"', *Evening Standard*, 19 July 2011. Thurlbeck

admitted he was an unpaid informant for NCIS and Scotland Yard codenamed George and with an official police source number 281.

10 Peter Jukes, Live Coverage of the Phone Hacking Trial

11 Alan Rusbridger, Twitter, 26 June 2015 – 'of course we weren't nobbled'. https://twitter.com/arusbridger/status/614380384827113472

12 Paul Johnson, Twitter, 26 June 2015, 'Hayman letter – we didn't respond or act on it. Completely ignored.' https://twitter.com/paul__johnson/status/614381809648988160

Chapter 34

1 Leveson Inquiry. Compilation of diary entries involving contact with the media in the Diary of John STEVENS. http://webarchive.nationalarchives.gov.uk/20140122145147/http://www.levesoninquiry.org.uk/wp-content/uploads/2012/03/Exhibit-MPS-56-Lord-Stevens-meetings-with-the-Media.pdf

2 'Journalists Caught on Tape in Police Bugging' and 'Fraudster Squad' by Graeme McLagan, *The Guardian*, 21 September 2002. https://www.theguardian.com/uk/2002/sep/21/privacy

3 'Untangling Rebekah Brooks', by Suzanna Andrews, *Vanity Fair*, February 2012, http://www.vanityfair.com/news/business/2012/02/rebekah-brooks-201202

4 'Police confronted Rebekah Brooks with evidence of crime' by Nick Davies, *The Guardian*, July 6 2011

Chapter 35

1 However we can reveal some of the obvious errors of fact in the report. They

erroneously attributed Daniel's limp to polio not a club foot, thought Alastair was his younger brother, got the date of the inquests wrong and failed to explain why the Vian Brothers were not interviewed for this report.

Chapter 36

1 'Who was hacked? An investigation into phone hacking and its victims' Part I: News of the World, Martin More, *Media Standards Trust Report*. 7 March 2015. http://mediastandardstrust.org/wp-content/uploads/2015/07/Who-was-hacked-Report.pdf
2 Phrase coined by Lance Price, former communications chief for Tony Blair
3 Hansard, evidence to Culture, Media and Sport Committee, 6 September 2011
4 Rees also put Beardall in contact with Derek Haslam in August 2004, and through his solicitor, asked the undercover informant to undertake enquiries in support of his appeal. (Beardall's appeal was heard in February 2006 and dismissed.)
5 'TV piracy claims heap more pressure on Murdoch empire' by Georgina Prodhan and Sonali Paul, *Reuters*,

28 March 2012, http://www.reuters.com/article/us-newscorp-piracy-idUSBRE82R04720120328
6 'News Corp faces new rash of hacking allegations on a global scale' by Ed Pilkington, *The Guardain*, 28 March 2012, https://www.theguardian.com/media/2012/mar/28/news-corporation-nds-panorama-frontline
7 'Murdoch company in pay-TV piracy scandal "paid Surrey Police"' by Cahal Milmo, the *Independent*, 28 March 2012. http://www.independent.co.uk/news/uk/crime/murdoch-company-in-pay-tv-piracy-scandal-paid-surrey-police-7595084.html

Chapter 38

1 News International Supply, self billing invoice, 1 March 2006 £650 for Scappaticci search and investigation, 19 April £850, 21 April £750, 3 May £950, 23 June £450, 18 July £400, 11 August £400, 8 September £300.
2 'Any potential offending under s1 Computer Misuse Act could not be prosecuted as that offence was time barred due to the age of the allegation'.

<table>
<tr><td>CHAPTER 2</td><td># The Belmont Robbery</td></tr>
</table>

The Belmont Robbery

19th March 1986

Belmont Car Auctions was located on the southern shores of the river Thames after the massive loop around the Isle of Dogs on its way eastwards to the North Sea.

Back in the eighties, the peninsula upstream was still a wasteland of gas works and coal depots instead of the Millennium Dome entertainment complex that dominates it now. The vast docks on the northern shore had been abandoned, outdated by containerisation, but not yet redeveloped into the glass towers of the Docklands financial district.

A few miles upstream, in March 1986, police helicopters buzzed above media baron Rupert Murdoch's new headquarters at Wapping, filming nightly clashes between thousands of demonstrators and hundreds of police as trade unionists protested against the sacking of print workers. Downstream, between Greenwich and Woolwich, instead of the expensive riverside apartment blocks that line the river now were acres of grimy low-rise industrial units.

One of these warehouses, on Penhall Road, was the home of Belmont Car Auctions.

Unlike most the car lots south of the Thames, which had a reputation for dodgy dealings, Belmont was a new and respected enterprise with an open auction every Tuesday and Friday night. Dozens of vehicles would be displayed for inspection before bidding began. Deposits would be held as cheques or more frequently cash. This soon became a problem.

Belmont Auctions hired the national security firm Securicor to protect their takings but this didn't prevent an armed robbery in February 1986, during which the staff were threatened with shotguns and forced to lie on the floor at gunpoint while £17,000 in cash and nearly £3,000 worth of cheques was stolen.

The directors of Belmont Car Auctions were distraught. One of them, Michael Thorne, urgently contacted his cousin and close friend, a local police detective called Alan Purvis, saying, 'I need help straight away!'[1]

Purvis in turn called on his boss, Detective Sergeant Fillery, with whom he shared an office. Both men were Freemasons.

By 1986 Fillery was known to his fellow officers as 'The King of Catford' – the 'mentor' of the crime squad, someone all the junior constables aspired to be like.[2] Tall, heavy-set but avuncular, Fillery had by then been a police officer for over 20 years and was more influential than his rank of sergeant suggested. He had risen to acting detective inspector at Catford and transferred to the No. 9 regional crime squad before returning to head up the crime squad in 1985. Owing to his senior rank as Master of a Freemasonry Lodge, he was deemed to outrank the local detective chief inspector.

Fillery and Purvis had a solution for the owners of Belmont Auctions: they'd enlist a third police officer (and another fellow Freemason) Detective Constable Peter Foley. Meanwhile, Fillery knew a private company called Southern Investigations – a 'firm which deals with this kind of security'[3] – run by a good friend of his, Jonathan Rees.

Jonathan Rees was only 33 but had extensive connections with officers in the Metropolitan Police. He'd first met Fillery three years earlier in mid-1983 when introduced by a mutual friend, Detective Chief Inspector Laurie Bucknole, while investigating large-scale fraud and theft from lorries at the firm of Bowater Scott in the Grays, Essex area.

Thorne and his co-director Walter Penfold met Fillery and Purvis the next day (previously they'd met on social occasions[4]) at the Casablanca Wine Bar on Lee High Road in south London. They were joined by Jonathan Rees. The armed robbery had left the Belmont owner 'near to tears' Fillery recalled. 'How can I possibly have my car auctions on Friday? This could happen again, could it not?' Thorne complained. Rees reassured him he could provide security guards for the upcoming auctions.

That afternoon, with his former police inspector friend Bucknole, Rees visited the auction warehouse to draw up a site plan. The private detective proposed six non-uniformed guards would attend each Tuesday and Friday, and a smaller number on Saturdays when cash was also handled.

Three of these guards would be plainclothes police officers – Fillery, Purvis and Foley – who would make their presence felt during the auctions themselves.

Meanwhile, Rees would lead his own private security detail to guard the cash before it was deposited at a local bank.

For three weeks beginning 4th March, on Tuesday and Friday evenings, the six-man team worked effectively. The Catford detectives wandered around the busy auction house floor, making sure they were identified as police officers. Purvis would often join his cousin, Thorne, director of the company, drinking in the cafeteria. Foley had 'no specific duties' other than 'letting my presence be known'[5] as a deterrent.

Rees led his separate three-man team of civilians. This mainly comprised his brother-in-law, 27-year-old Garry Vian, and others employed on a 'one-off basis' from another pub, the Harp, on Handcroft Road in Croydon – one of Rees' other regular drinking venues.

One Harp regular, John Peacock, who worked as an occasional debt collector for Rees, attended Belmont Car Auctions five times with Garry Vian. He said they would stay on one side of the warehouse, away from the police officers.[6] This separation was perhaps understandable for Garry Vian, as he was under surveillance for suspected drug dealing at the time under a specialist drugs investigation, Operation Wimpey.

For the first five auctions, everything went to plan. Once bidding had closed and the customers departed, the police officers left together in one car while Rees and his team kept an eye on the money as it was counted and bagged up. The money was then handed over to an employee who would deposit it in the night safe of the local branch of the Midland Bank on Lee High Road, about two miles away.[7]

But on the night of Tuesday 18th March, Rees cancelled Peacock on the pretext that 'Belmont were unwilling to pay for the amount of men that we had down there'.[8] Instead, Rees asked his other brother-in-law, Glenn Vian, to join Garry in the private security team.

Glenn Vian was 29-years-old at the time and had convictions for assault, criminal damage, theft, going 'equipped' (with tools to break into premises), conspiracy to rob and possession with intent to supply cannabis.

That night Rees decided to deposit the cash at the bank himself as a 'favour' to the Belmont employees. The favour turned out disastrously.

On arrival at the Midland Bank with his brothers-in-law, Rees found the lock to the night safe had been blocked with Super Glue. He tried to call the

auction house on his car phone, he claimed, but nobody answered. Rees then resolved to take the cash home for safekeeping.

After dropping off the Vian brothers at their respective homes in Croydon, Rees claimed he had parked near his terraced house on a narrow residential street only to be jumped on by two unknown attackers six yards short of his front door, coshed on the head and sprayed with ammonia.

His assailants made away with the entire night's takings – £18,280.

Norwood police were informed and a female police officer, PC Carole West, came to visit Rees just before midnight to take a report of the robbery. She noted that Rees' demeanour did not fit that of someone who had just been robbed of thousands of pounds: 'He was vague and would only impart information in response to specific questions,' a later report said.

West also noticed the ambivalence of Sharon Ann, Rees' wife, who went to bed while the police officer was taking the statement, apparently 'unconcerned'. West noted that the ammonia only appeared to be sprayed on Rees' shirt and not his face, and wrote in her notebook that she doubted any robbery had taken place.

The calm demeanour of the alleged mugging victim was also noted by the casualty sister at the Mayday Hospital in Croydon later than night when Rees was taken for a medical check-up.

Another friend of Rees', Detective Constable Duncan Hanrahan, happened to be on night duty at his local CID office in Norbury. He visited Rees in hospital and confirmed that he had an irritant in his eyes and a small bump on his head. But in his official 'occurrence book', Hanrahan noted he was unhappy with Rees' version of events and 'considered it more than a straightforward robbery'.

To commit a random mugging and grab (what was initially thought to be) £30,000, Hanrahan thought, 'you would have to be the luckiest mugger in the world.' He concluded it was some kind of 'inside job'.[9]

The two Belmont directors, Thorne and Penfold, were even more sceptical when they visited Rees in hospital the following morning. Rees told the two he had been mugged by a 'young, blond boy' he'd seen at the auctions and coshed on the back of the head, though he could not point to any head injury. They noticed he was dabbing one slightly bloodshot eye, but otherwise the ammonia seemed to have left little trace.

Other elements of Rees' account didn't make sense. There was a police station only 'thirty paces' from the Midland Bank on Lee High Road. Rees

could have reported the tampered night safe there, and even stored the cash securely. And why didn't he just take the money back to Belmont? The auction house in Charlton was much closer to the bank than Rees' house in Croydon.[10]

David Chapman, the auctions manager who had stayed late at Belmont on the night of the robbery, said he never received a call from Rees. He thought the alleged robbery was a 'total farce' and the Belmont directors agreed. Thorne then went to see his relative, Alan Purvis, to tell him of his suspicions that the robbery was 'a sham'. Purvis was non-committal: 'Whatever course of action you have to take, you have to take,' the CID detective told his cousin.

On 1st April 1986, less than two weeks after the robbery, all three police officers involved – Fillery, Purvis and Foley – received a formal letter from the car auction company's lawyers identifying them as 'security officers' and notifying them of likely civil proceedings. 'We are writing to give you advance warning of the fact that if the proceedings are defended we may need to interview you ...' the letter stated.[11]

At Catford Police Station, Fillery dismissed the legal warning as 'scrap paper' and threw it away.[12] More concerned, Foley consulted his senior officer, who advised him that since the work was done off-duty, this kind of 'moonlighting' was 'not a criminal offence and you are not likely to get sacked'.[13]

Purvis was in a trickier position still with his cousin, Michael Thorne, who he knew wanted him to say that Rees was responsible for the loss of the money. But Purvis explained to Thorne he was 'not in a position to say that' and his former best man was left feeling 'very, very bitter'.[14] There was a 'rift in the family' and Thorne and Purvis fell out.[15]

By coincidence, Daniel Morgan's younger sister, Jane McCarthy, stayed with the Morgan family in South Norwood the day after the robbery. She was en route to Germany from Wales, where she was relocating with her husband, Justin, an officer in the British Army on the Rhine, when their horse trailer jackknifed on the M25 London Orbital motorway.

They were lucky not to have been killed, and had to chase after their bolting horse as it escaped down the motorway verges. The couple stayed with Daniel that night while their car and trailer were repaired. Daniel was concerned about the robbery of Rees, whom he'd visited in hospital, but let on very little. Jane and Justin resumed their trip to Germany the next day.

It was the last time she ever saw Daniel alive.[16]

| CHAPTER 3 | Maltese Rover |

July 1986 to February 1987

Though it caused massive friction, the Belmont car auction robbery or 'scam' was just one more sign of the growing rift between the two partners in Southern Investigations that was already widening well before 1986.

The tensions had always been there. Daniel Morgan and Jonathan Rees had first met while working at the large Croydon bailiff and private investigation company Madagan & Co. Daniel left after four years and set up on his own, taking some of his previous clients with him.

At first Daniel worked from a desk at home and 'bought an old banger' to replace the company car.[1] Before long he would be so successful he would own four cars: a brand-new BMW coupé with a car phone, a Daimler, an MGA sports car and a classic Austin Healey, which he was restoring.

Apart from practical handyman skills, Daniel had shown a phenomenal memory for facts. His ability as a child to recite statistics from *The Guinness Book of Records* continued in adult life with a capacity to store and recall the registration numbers of cars and home addresses. Such a methodical and fact-driven approach helped him track down civil litigants to serve writs, relocate missing vehicles, and sometimes reclaim children abducted in custody disputes.

Daniel worked 'incredibly hard', according to everyone who knew him at the time. Soon he had more work than he could cope with. When Rees was sacked by Bryan Madagan in early 1981 (for spending too much time in the pub), he approached Daniel, who, two years later, was persuaded to take him on as a partner.

Daniel and Rees had very different backgrounds. Born in Singapore in 1948, brought up in Wales and England, Daniel had studied at an agricultural college in Gwent before spending two years working in Denmark, where he learned the language. Five years younger, Rees had left school at 15 and spent

six and half years in the Merchant Navy before entering retail security and then bailiff work. Their skills seemed complementary, though.

More garrulous and sociable than Daniel, Rees' speciality was investigations, using undercover techniques and police contacts to detect fraud or trace missing people. If Daniel relied mainly on dogged evidence gathering, Rees was better at social engineering and play-acting. According to someone who worked with him in 1982, at Chancery Consultants Ltd., Rees would also fabricate evidence and lie a great deal.

Rees was 'a person who believes his own lies,' the colleague said. 'A person who would continue a lie even when it was blatantly obvious.' He was already employing his brothers-in-law, Glenn and Garry Vian, as 'heavies'.

* * *

In 1983 Daniel Morgan and Jonathan Rees formed Southern Investigations and another company, Morgan, Rees and Co., was later set up to cover their tasks as certificated bailiffs. Their work inevitably meant they had many contacts with local police officers, meeting in court and sharing intelligence in cases like commercial fraud. Both police and private detectives were often trying to trace the same people: an errant debtor needed for some defaulted payment might also be wanted for arrest for fraud. This could be entirely legitimate, but the trade in information gathering between private security and policing could cross over into a form of corruption: as when a police officer is paid by a private detective to pass over confidential details from the Police National Computer (PNC).

In the 1980s Rees and Daniel were both part of a growing twilight trade in information between cops and private detectives which was wholly unregulated at the time. But Rees' involvement with the local police was much more intense.

He was known as a 'police groupie'. To Malcolm Webb, who did process serving (officially delivering court documents) for the private detective duo, Rees was always 'playing policeman'.[2] His blue BMW was a frequent sight in the police car parks of south-east London.[3]

Above all, Rees liked to socialise with plainclothes detectives when they were 'out on enqs' – out on enquiries – shorthand for 'down the pub'. He was famed for buying rounds for police officers, and there was a plethora of pubs and a lot of socialising in south-east London in this era.

The extent of Rees' police connections can be seen from the brief snapshot around the car auction house robbery; it was a former Detective Chief Inspector (Bucknole) who helped scope out the security plan; three police officers assisted with the security detail (Fillery, Purvis and Foley) and the two officers investigating the robbery (Winter and Hanrahan) were all drinking pals of Rees'.

In an affidavit, Rees listed 16 serving officers of various ranks as good friends, mostly from Catford, south-east London. The police identified that he knew 17 of the 43 CID officers in the division.

Even before the Belmont robbery, Rees' dealings with police officers were beginning to grate on Daniel. 'Alastair, I've driven 40,000 miles this year,' his older brother recalled him saying, 'and Jon just props up the bar in the pub, drinking with his police mates.'[4]

Daniel's friend David Bray, who became a courier for Southern Investigations, remembers him complaining that Rees was 'just a certified bailiff, just sitting in the office answering phones' and recalled Daniel once telling Rees to his face: 'I think you should get off your fat arse and do some work, otherwise things are going to turn.'[5]

Rees would retaliate to Daniel's 'fat bastard' jibes by calling him a 'spastic' or a 'Welsh cripple' or worse.[6] Though Daniel could be argumentative over a point of principle, most of his colleagues attested that he rarely held a personal grudge and appeared to brush off most of these insults better than his business partner.

* * *

By the spring of 1986, however, two years into the formation of Southern Investigations, tensions were escalating. David Bray recalled hearing the business partners 'shouting at the top of their voices behind closed doors'.[7] Some of this discord was definitely over Rees' police connections.

By now, Daniel had several contacts in the press, having given Sally Deedes from *Private Eye* a story about a corrupt bailiff only weeks earlier. Around that time he had also spoken to Alastair Campbell, political editor of the *Daily Mirror*, though no one knows what about. Witnesses say he was in contact with two other *Mirror* journalists – Anton Antonowicz and Sylvia Jones.

In October 1986, five months before Daniel's murder, an aggressive man with an obviously fake Cockney accent arrived at the private detective agency

offices in Thornton Heath, looking for Daniel. Around the same time, Daniel complained to DC Hanrahan at Norbury CID of threatening phone calls late at night, and wondered if his phone number had been included in court records or police reports.

By Christmas 1986 it appears that a romantic rivalry was exacerbating the animosity between the two partners at Southern Investigations.

Rees had often complained to others about Daniel's philandering. According to David Bray, Daniel had one or two girlfriends over the previous two years and the boyfriend of one of them 'caused problems' in 1986. But at this point the only serious extra-marital relationship Daniel had was with a 39-year-old married woman with grown-up kids called Margaret Harrison, who worked at the estate agents over the road from Southern Investigations.

Daniel had first met 'Maggie' at a joint office party held by Furmston's estate agents in Thornton Heath for the Christmas of 1985.[8] In her late thirties, Harrison was attractive and vivacious. By all accounts the first liaison was casual, but Bray said Daniel and Margaret Harrison got back together for four months just before Christmas 1986.[9] Daniel told his office manager Peter Newby: 'If Margaret rings up, be discreet.'

Though he made no secret of this affair to Newby or his disapproving brother, Daniel tried to hide his relationship with Margaret Harrison from his business partner, Rees, who took the moral high ground over infidelity.[10] (Harrison, who still lives with Rees to this day, denied any sexual relationship with Rees at this point, though DC Duncan Hanrahan says Rees admitted to him that there was.)

By the end of 1986, the personal, professional and criminal pressures were all converging on Daniel. His wife Iris noted her husband was finding it hard to sleep.

In the New Year there was a reported confrontation between Daniel and the Vian brothers outside the Harp pub, during which Daniel accused Rees and his brothers-in-law of staging the Belmont robbery with the aid of the police. Rees' brothers-in-law were known to be violent. They were used as debt collectors and an anonymous source claimed that, on one occasion, they wielded hatchets during a disturbance outside the Harp.

Around the same time in January, Bray remembers Daniel coming into his office looking particularly upset, and telling him: 'We're going for a drive.' He

took Bray in his car from Crystal Palace down Sydenham Road to a pub he'd never been to before, the Golden Lion.

Described by police as a 'respectable public house that caters in the main for local businesses and residents', the Golden Lion was a family-run business known for its 'large Irish clientele'. It was not a regular haunt of the local police.[11] As Daniel waited with Bray outside the unfamiliar pub he would not explain what was worrying him; he simply said, 'I'm looking for Jon's car.'

After five minutes they drove to another pub on the Bromley Road.

Finally, Bray asked: 'Is Jon seeing a woman or something?' Daniel smiled enigmatically in a way that Bray interpreted as a 'yes'.

Bray got the impression the tension between the partners was now focused on a romantic rivalry over Margaret Harrison. Rees' mobile phone records show he made 67 phone calls to Harrison from October 1986 and March 1987.[12] He also paid for Harrison's daughter to attend a secretarial course and she worked for the company part-time.

In the first months of 1987, the threats to Daniel increased. Southern Investigations was broken into. Someone climbed on the flat roof to reach the first floor of the offices, broke a small window and took £50 in petty cash.

More worrying was a burglary at Daniel's family home in South Norwood. 'We slept right through it, all of us,' Daniel told his brother: 'All they took was the telly. But there must have been more than one of them to carry it.'

By now Daniel was so concerned he asked Alastair to look after his home and office while he made a week's trip to Malta at the beginning of February.

* * *

Lex Leasing was one of Daniel's most important clients. In the late 1980s they were targeted by a ring of sophisticated conmen who would hire one of their more expensive cars, usually a Jaguar or a Range Rover, and using false identity papers, steal the vehicle.

The cars were exported to the Middle East, usually the Lebanon, where they could be sold for a huge profit. By 1987 Daniel had discovered the stolen luxury vehicles were being smuggled out via Malta. His job was to track them down as they were stored prior to transit further east, and recover the stolen property.

While Daniel and David Bray flew from Gatwick to Malta on 1st February, Daniel's brother Alastair came up to London from Hampshire to keep

an eye on the family and business. During the daytime, he spent most of the next week indexing property companies at Southern Investigations but noted nothing untoward at the office. In the evenings, he would eat with Daniel's wife Iris and the children, Sarah and Daniel, and either watch TV or retire to the spare room with one of Daniel's books.

One night Alastair wanted to see a public speaker in Forest Hill, and parked Daniel's BMW in a church car park. He came back to find the rear windscreen shattered and the stereo system stolen – thefts from cars being one of the most prevalent crimes in the capital of the day. When he phoned to tell his brother at his hotel in Valletta, Daniel was annoyed at his brother's naivety: 'Don't you know that you should never ever park an expensive car in a dark car park in London.'[13]

Daniel arrived back on 10th February, happy because he had successfully traced a stolen Range Rover to the tiny island of Gozo, just to the north of Malta. He explained to Alastair how a Maltese cop gave him the location, but had told him to keep the source confidential or 'I'd be off the island before my feet could touch the ground'. Daniel also told his brother he had to bribe various people to get the car home, but he had authorised a bank transfer to cover these expenses.

In the next few days Daniel arranged to talk to two officers from the Fraud Section of West Yorkshire Police about the car theft ring. There were also reports that he wanted to talk to the CID in Sydenham.[14]

A colleague who worked at the estate agents with Margaret Harrison recalled seeing Daniel at a lunch club meeting at the Mythos restaurant shortly after he returned from Malta. She says Harrison confided in her later that Daniel was frightened about something and thought he was a 'marked man'.

| CHAPTER 4 | Lion's Den |

5th-11th March 1987

'There is good news and bad news,' Jonathan Rees told his office manager, Peter Newby, on Thursday, 5th March 1987, five days before Daniel's murder. Rees had just been attending the Royal Courts of Justice on London's Fleet Street with his brother-in-law Glenn Vian and police pal Sid Fillery, for a costs hearing about the Belmont Car Auctions robbery.

The good news was they hadn't lost yet. But the bad news was that the judge, Master Grant, had ruled that the private investigations company had to pay £10,000 to defend the claim.

Though the financial hit to the private investigations firm was not insuperable – Southern Investigations was by now turning over more than £150,000 a year – the Belmont legal case appears to have finally broken the ailing partnership between Daniel Morgan and Jonathan Rees.

In the aftermath of the robbery, Daniel had told his office manager, Peter Newby, he was 'upset' Rees had exceeded his authority as a partner as they 'had originally agreed not to carry cash'.[1]

Daniel's wife Iris was convinced the robbery was 'totally and utterly set up' by Rees. Daniel confided in his wife that he was going to terminate the partnership.

To his friend, David Bray, Daniel was more forthcoming: 'I just cannot believe that Jon took the money, went home and got mugged outside his house.'[2]

By March 1987, Daniel was thinking of dissolving the company and planned to 'lodge his own defence' against the suit.[3] Having been convinced by his solicitor this wouldn't work, he was raising his half of the liability through an overdraft and using the two company accounts to pay the rest.[4]

But Daniel's biggest concern seems to have been less about the financial penalty than the involvement of the Metropolitan Police. Above all he was 'most unhappy' the use of police officers would 'rebound' on the company in some way.[5]

* * *

That Thursday night, after the costs hearing, Daniel spoke to his neighbour, an elderly woman called Doris Wheeler, when he returned home.

'You'll never guess what I found out today, Doris,' she recalled him saying: 'All police are bastards!'

That same night Rees was meeting up with his close friend DS Sid Fillery at the Dolphin pub in Sydenham, just over the road from the Golden Lion, where the killing would take place. The head of Catford crime squad was in the area because he was now leading a 15-man team investigating the murder of a man, Leonard Clapton, who had been fatally stabbed the day before.

By the Friday, four days before his murder, Daniel had raised the money to meet the court order for the Belmont suit, but – according to Iris – had not told Rees because he wanted to make him sweat.[6]

On the Saturday Daniel spent most of the day at home, planning to watch a rugby match with some friends who never turned up. Meanwhile, Rees sought out Fillery at the Dolphin again for another drink.

On the Sunday before his murder, Daniel attended a rally at the Austin Healey Club in Hendon, north-west London. There he met Brian Crush, a garage owner and another classic car enthusiast, who had helped him find spare parts and restore his Austin Healey 3000.

Daniel told Crush that he now believed Rees and Fillery had set up the Belmont Auctions robbery and taken the money for themselves. He called Fillery a 'bent copper' and claimed one of his friends had been involved in the investigation into the robbery. When Crush asked why he hadn't done anything about it, the private detective replied: 'Who'd take my word against a policeman?'

To another attendee at the rally, Stephen Simmons, Daniel claimed he'd discovered 'massive police corruption'.

Some eyewitnesses say Daniel met up with Rees and the Vian brothers that Sunday night at their favourite haunt, the Harp pub.

Phone records from Jonathan Rees' car phone also show that he rang a part-time employee of the detective agency that Sunday, Jimmy Cook. Cook was an occasional car repossession man with underworld connections. The significance of this call would not be realised until nearly 20 years later.

* * *

On the day before Daniel's murder, on Monday, 9th March 1987, Sid Fillery's team arrested Barry Duffy as a suspect in the Leonard Clapton case.

'It was solved mainly because of the way I directed my men,' Fillery would later boast at the inquest.[7] After his squad had searched the suspect's house and 'booked him in' with murder charges, Fillery led 'half his troops' to the Golden Lion for a celebratory drink around 8:30pm. Fillery was now free for whatever the next case might be.

Daniel and Rees arrived an hour or so later, parking their green and blue BMWs separately on the main road. They joined Fillery and five other police officers at the Golden Lion around 9 or 9:30pm.

It was the first time Daniel and Rees had drunk together at the Golden Lion. Outside, it was a freezing cold night for March. Inside, it soon got heated.

One of Fillery's troops recalls Daniel talking to Rees, Fillery and another police sergeant about old cars. He described Daniel as 'loud and excitable' and as 'somebody it would be difficult to ignore in public'. There were reports of an argument between Daniel and the head of Catford crime squad, though Fillery later claimed it was a 'heated discussion' about the arming of police.

One customer, when interviewed later by police, recalled seeing an unknown male peering through the window of the saloon bar between 9 and 9:30pm.

One by one the police officers left, with Daniel, Rees and Fillery staying in the pub until closing time.

* * *

The next morning, 10th March, David Bray was woken by a 7:30am call from Daniel.

'David, I want you to come to the office urgently this morning,'[8] Daniel said, asking Bray to go to the family home, pick up his children, take them to school and then come to work as soon as possible. From his tone, Bray thought something important had come up.

However, by the time he got to Thornton Heath, Daniel was hoovering up the mess made by a carpenter the previous night. He'd put on a grey suit he'd collected from the dry cleaners to meet some potential new clients.[9] He was also talking to his office manager, Peter Newby, about 16 new jobs that had to be booked in for the company.

Daniel never did explain to Bray what he wanted to talk to him about so urgently a few hours before.

When Jonathan Rees arrived that morning, he made a point of complaining to the office manager about Daniel's behaviour in the Golden Lion. 'Daniel

did the usual thing in the pub last night, upsetting people,' he told Newby. He said that Fillery was so annoyed by Daniel he was furious that Rees had brought him to the pub: 'I got the finger treatment from Sid.'

Rees also mentioned they were returning to the Golden Lion that evening: 'I've got another meeting tonight. I don't really want to take Daniel, but I've got to.'

Around 11am, Paul Goodridge arrived at the private investigators' offices.[10] A local character and celebrity bodyguard, Goodridge was distantly related to Rees' wife, Sharon, and had done odd jobs for the agency, accompanying Rees collecting rent in Tulse Hill.[11] Rees had asked for Goodridge's help in raising the £10,000 for the Belmont case, but he had stalled.[12]

At 11:07am, as Daniel headed out to Slough to meet a property group for some bailiff work, Rees rang Fillery at Catford CID on his car phone.

This call came only minutes after Rees had arranged to return with Daniel to the Golden Lion.[13]

By now Fillery was free of any duties related to the Leonard Clapton murder. 'We are off this murder now,' the CID sergeant told Rees.[14]

Shortly after the call to Fillery, Rees met Margaret Harrison for lunch.

Arriving in Slough, Daniel had a lunch meeting with Mike Fairhurst at CWS property group and was 'very happy' with the new contracts they were offering, according to his companion, Tony Pearce.

Daniel called Rees twice from his car phone around 4pm as he drove back to London. Pearce remembered Daniel exclaiming, after one of the calls he made on that trip, almost to himself: 'Oh that reminds me, I must change my will.'

Daniel got back to the Southern Investigations office around 5:15pm.

By now one of the company's bailiffs, Malcolm Webb, had returned with £1,100 in cash he had collected from an industrial estate in Poole, Dorset. It was too late to bank it and the private detective company did not have a night safe. After the petty cash theft a few weeks previously, Daniel decided take the sum with him for safekeeping.

Peter Newby saw Daniel put the £1,100 in the left-hand breast pocket of his grey suit.[15]

On his way out around 6pm, Daniel popped his head round the corner of Rees' office and said: 'I'll see you later in the Golden Lion.'[16]

'Yes, OK,' Rees replied.

From the office Daniel went straight to Regan's Wine Bar to meet Margaret Harrison. They drank a bottle of wine.

The potential rival for her affections, Jonathan Rees, knew Margaret was drinking at that moment with Daniel – he told his solicitor and friend Michael Goodridge when they met at the the Victory public house around the same time. Rees was wearing a white raincoat, tweed suit, shirt and tie and brown brogues, the solicitor recalled, and left just after 7pm, telling Goodridge that he and Daniel were going to see someone about the £10,000 for the high court action. [17]

Brian Crush, the Austin Healey Club member, had arrived at Daniel's house and rang him on his car phone. They had arranged to meet that evening to pay for the next bit of work on restoring the car. But Daniel said he couldn't meet up: 'Oh no, I've got a very important business conference tonight and I'll be late.' He couldn't say whether he'd even be back by midnight.

The last sighting of Daniel Morgan before he arrived at the Golden Lion was around 7:15pm when he helped the manageress of Victoria Wine take her shop sign inside. She remembers that Daniel was carrying three or four beige files.

* * *

Jonathan Rees arrived at the Golden Lion first, at around 7:30pm. There were no traffic restrictions at that time in the evening and there was a free space on the main Sydenham road, so he parked outside the pub. Rees sat waiting at a table at the back of the saloon bar near the doors that led to the beer garden. Beyond that, out of sight behind a foliage-covered wall, was the secluded car park.

Daniel arrived around 15 minutes later in his green BMW coupé. Rees 'assumed he had parked in the rear car park' even though Daniel had entered through the front doors, which would have meant taking a tortuous route along the long narrow alleyway rather than entering through the beer garden and doors at the back into the saloon bar.

It was a busy night at the Golden Lion (police later interviewed 84 people who'd been there that evening). Among the drinkers were mourners from a memorial service held at a nearby church, while in the upstairs function room, 16 women from the Golden Lion darts team were playing their rivals, Charlton Valley.

Fifty-one people spent some time in the saloon bar between 7pm and 11pm. Several of them remembered seeing two smartly dressed men sitting at the table in a raised area by the door of the bar. Daniel had grown a beard to replace his moustache by this point, and there were only six men with beards in the pub at the time. Not many wore suits. Rees claimed Daniel drank rum or brandy while he drank lager.

Daniel's meeting in the Golden Lion was sufficiently important to have stopped him giving his process server Malcolm Webb instructions about a shop he was supposed to repossess at 6am the next day. It was unusual for him to leave a briefing so late, as he knew Webb had a pregnant wife and young kids.

When Daniel hadn't called by 8pm, Webb rang the family home. Daniel's wife answered. According to Webb, Iris was irate because her husband was never home.

No third party ever turned up inside the Golden Lion to meet the two directors of Southern Investigations according to everyone present.

Rees left the Golden Lion at around 9pm, a 'few seconds' ahead of Daniel.

One eyewitness, who thought both were policemen, heard Rees say: 'Goodnight, see you at work tomorrow.'[18]

Rees said Daniel 'was held a short while making notes on a piece of paper' – scribbling on a petrol receipt with his Parker stainless steel ballpoint pen. But no notes were ever found, no pen ever recovered.

Just as the previous evening when Daniel had argued with Sid Fillery, one eyewitness noticed a man peering through the window of the saloon bar three times between 9 and 9:20pm. Then again five to ten minutes later, soon after returning with a second man.

The barmaid said a man fitting Daniel's description bought two packets of Golden Wonder salted crisps from the saloon bar sometime around 9pm. She didn't see him leave but a few minutes later noticed he had gone.

* * *

Jonathan Rees was in his car by 9:04pm that night. The billing records for his car phone, which only recorded the phone numbers of outgoing calls, show an untraceable incoming call for 12 minutes beginning exactly then.

At 9:17pm, almost as soon as that long incoming call had ended, Rees called the 'third party' he said he had arranged to meet – the celebrity minder Paul Goodridge. His girlfriend Jean Wisden answered the phone.

At 9:19pm Rees made a short outgoing call to his wife Sharon. There was another untraceable incoming call at 9:21 for two minutes. After a brief call to Paul Goodridge's car phone, Rees arrived at the Beulah Spa pub around 9:30, where he would stay with Goodridge for the 90 minutes until closing time. All in all, there were 13 minutes of calls over 20 minutes.

By this point, Daniel's body was already cold.

A BBC sound producer, Thomas Terry, had left the BBC's Shepherd's Bush studios just after 9pm and pulled into the Golden Lion car park around 9:40pm. He saw what he thought was a 'dummy' lying in the beam of his headlights, with what he at first thought was one of those 'joke ties with wires in them, which make them stick up'. Terry parked his car and looked closer at the strange figure lying between a BMW and a blue Morris Marina estate.

It was Daniel, dressed in his grey striped suit, lying face up in a large pool of bright red arterial blood. The bizarre tie was an axe embedded in his face. Beside Daniel's left hand, there were two unopened packets of crisps and his car keys. The right side of his suit trousers was ripped from the pocket to just above the knee.

Terry rushed into the pub to alert the barman, Joseph O'Brien. They both went out to check the body. Terry touched the back of Daniel's left hand, which was cold. O'Brien called Catford Police Station.

PC Jeffrey Vaughan was the first officer on the scene with another uniformed officer around 9:50pm. He checked Daniel for signs of life, installed a crime scene cordon and called out the CID. In the confusion, most of the Golden Lion's customers were held on the premises, but not all.

A doctor, Angus Bain, arrived at 10:55pm to officially pronounce death.

Fifteen minutes later Detective Sergeant Malcolm Davidson, the office manager from the No. 3 Area Major Investigation Pool (AMIP) – a cross boundary major crime unit – was on the scene. The senior investigating officer, Detective Superintendent Douglas Campbell, arrived with his deputy, Detective Inspector Alan Jones, two minutes later, at 11:12pm.

Back at the Beulah Spa, a few miles away, Rees left the pub around 11:15pm and called his wife on his car phone to organise a takeaway. On his return, the couple sat watching TV and eating kebabs.

* * *

DS Graham Frost, a laboratory sergeant, had arrived at the Golden Lion crime scene. Assisted by a civilian scene-of-crime officer, Leonard Flint, together they began their forensic examination of the murder scene.

Twelve cars, including Daniel's, were parked in the rear car park. All the pub customers with cars were told to take taxis home – their vehicles would have to be fingerprinted. (In reality, no vehicle could be fingerprinted that night because a frost had created dew on their surfaces.)

A forensic photo taken that night by the Met photographer, Michael Rhodes, seems to show fingermarks on the right-hand driver's door of Daniel's car, which was still locked when the police got there. But by the time Malcolm Reynolds, a fingerprint expert of over 23 years, arrived to examine the BMW those marks had gone.

There were other disturbing anomalies too. The civilian scene-of-crime officer, Leonard Flint, watched DS Frost search Daniel's body and discover the large wad of bank notes – precisely £1,067.47 – in his left-hand pocket. Flint was alarmed to learn there was no police exhibits officer available. He also vaguely recalled seeing an expensive watch on Daniel's wrist.

Much more alarming was Flint's recollection that plainclothes officers opened the boot and doors to Daniel's BMW and removed a briefcase and paperwork. This caused him consternation because 'nobody appeared to be taking any notes and there was no exhibits officer to record it'.

A total of 21 police officers and forensic officers attended the scene that night.

The murder weapon, a 14-inch hand axe – marked as 'made in China' – was inspected in situ. Detectives noted that the axe appeared to be brand new, but that its wooden handle had been scored with a sharp object. There were two rings of Elastoplast wrapped around the handle.

The rip in Daniel's trousers was large. It spread across the waistband and right down the seam almost to the knee, consistent with it being pulled forcibly in some way. In Daniel's pockets, as well as his usual ID, the police found numerous bits of paper: business cards with notes, receipts from Gatwick Airport and several service stations; a piece of paper with 'Bank of Valletta' written on it; another with the phrase 'Fab Hands' or 'Fam Hams' scrawled on it. On the back of a 'Uno Plus' wine bar receipt dated 21st January 1987 Daniel had written the figures 250,000.000 and 1,800,000. This was another wine bar

in Norbury where Daniel and Margaret Harrison used to meet. But there was no pen or pencil.

Daniel's body was removed by undertakers just after 1am and taken to Lewisham Mortuary.

* * *

The first outsider informed of the murder was Jonathan Rees, the last person known to have seen Daniel alive at that point. The murder squad's second-in-command, Detective Inspector Alan Jones, arrived with Detective Constable Kinley Davies at Rees' home on Cresswell Road in South Norwood shortly after midnight.

DC Davies had a 'gut feeling that Rees was expecting them'. At the door they asked Rees if he knew Daniel Morgan and were ushered into the living room, where they informed Rees of Daniel's death. Davies recalled that Rees' wife Sharon didn't look up from the TV.

Rees was wearing a long-sleeved blue striped shirt, grey trousers, black socks and no shoes and confirmed those were the clothes he was wearing at the pub. DI Jones asked him to come to the police station with his clothes but Rees protested: 'Who do you think I am, the mad axeman of Catford?'

'It was not a reaction I expected,' said DI Jones, who gave Rees ten minutes to get dressed and come with them to avoid arrest. Rees put on a maroon tie, black brogue shoes, a blue blazer, red scarf and the short white mackintosh he'd worn earlier that evening.

At Catford Police Station, Rees was quizzed for over an hour and a half by Detective Superintendent Douglas Campbell about his business partner, the kind of investigations undertaken by the private detective company, and what enemies Daniel might have had. He was also asked more about the 'third party', Paul Goodridge, who never turned up.

DC Davies remembers Rees was constantly dropping the names of senior police officers and court officials he knew. DSU Campbell did not recall divulging to Rees any details about the axe, or any suggestion of a mugging or any connections to a drug deal.

Rees' clothes – his white mac, trousers and shoes – were given a visual inspection by forensic liaison officer DS Graham Frost, who could detect no visible signs of blood. The clothing was returned to Rees.

Meanwhile, another uniformed police officer, PC Laurence Hart, was told to call DS Sid Fillery, who said he was woken by the phone and told: 'Your mate's partner is dead.'

Fillery's wife recalls the event differently – she believes her husband was informed of Daniel's death by a call from Rees in the middle of the night.

Either way, as the senior figure from the Catford area where the incident happened – and now free from the Clapton murder – Fillery was assigned to the murder squad the next morning.

Around 2am, DSU Campbell asked Rees to accompany two police officers to inform Daniel's next of kin, his wife Iris. In an affidavit, Rees claimed he heard Iris Morgan exclaim on hearing the news: 'I knew they were going to hurt him, but I never thought they'd go this far!'

But the two officers present, PC Laurence Hart and DC Noel Cosgrave, had a completely different recollection – an expression of total shock and bewilderment: 'Why would anyone do such a thing?'

Other employees at Southern Investigations were the next to be informed.

Rees rang Peter Newby at 6:30 that morning, saying: 'Danny's been mugged and it's fatal.' He told the office manager about the 'third party' they were planning to meet at the Golden Lion, and that 'the person we were supposed to see didn't show'.

By then Rees appeared to know significant details about the murder scene, and how a motorist had discovered the body when parking out the back. But at this stage he was diverging from his 'mad axeman' line and saying Daniel had been killed by a 'blow to the neck with a knife'.[19]

Fifteen minutes later, Rees rang his solicitor, Michael Goodridge of Coffey, Whittey and Co., with whom he'd been drinking at the Victory the night before, and told him that Daniel had been 'fatally mugged'. Later that morning, Rees would suggest to his solicitor that Daniel might have caught someone breaking into his car.

By the time the process server Malcolm Webb arrived at the offices of Southern Investigations at 9am, Rees had told Peter Newby that his business partner had been killed by some kind of knife or machete at a pub in Sydenham. Webb asked if Daniel had had any money on him but Rees didn't have an answer to that.

It was at this point that Daniel's brother, Alastair Morgan, called from his friend's home in Hampshire and was told by Rees that Daniel had been 'fatally mugged'. After the conversation, Rees left the offices to talk to his solicitor.

As Rees went down the street, he bumped into Tony Pearce, who he told to talk to the office staff about an urgent matter.[20] It was left to Webb to break the bad news. 'Sit down, I have got something dreadful to tell you,' he told Pearce. 'Daniel has been axed to death.'[21] At this point Webb did not know that Pearce was Daniel's former stepfather.[22]

Sid Fillery arrived on duty in Catford around 9am to join the new murder squad and was about to make his way to the incident room at Sydenham Police Station when DS Malcolm Davidson diverted him.

Davidson told Fillery instead to go straight to the private detective agency at Thornton Heath and obtain a statement from Rees 'concerning Daniel Morgan and the workings of the company'.[23]

Around 9:30am Fillery arrived at Southern Investigations to clear Daniel's desk.[24] Rees handed over to Fillery and another crime squad officer, DC Stephen Thorogood, the 'Belmont Auction File' and another file on a long drawn-out divorce case. According to office manager Peter Newby, the two detectives left with a 'great big bag of files' in a black bin liner.[25] DC Thorogood later denied any Belmont Auction files had been removed.

No list of these seized files was ever given to Newby, though police in those days were not obliged to leave receipts except when requested.[26] The Belmont Car Auctions file never made it to the station.[27]

By this point the senior investigating officer, DSU Campbell, thought Fillery was the 'ideal man' to take a statement from the surviving director of Southern Investigations, so the Catford detective took Rees down to his local station for an interview.

In his first statement Rees emphasised the £10,000 owed to the court for the Belmont Car Auctions and the planned meeting with Paul Goodridge to help with surety.

Midway through taking the statement, Fillery received a call from Lewisham Public Mortuary informing him that the post-mortem on Daniel would soon be complete. He took Rees to formally identify Daniel's body, rather than a member of Morgan's family, which could then be included in Rees' statement.

* * *

The second-in-command of the Daniel Morgan murder squad, DI Alan Jones, had been at the mortuary all morning, attending the autopsy. Pathologist Dr Michael Heath had identified five lacerations on Daniel's head.

Four of those lacerations had deeply penetrated the skull. Three were to the back of the head, consistent with three rapid blows from behind with the sharp end of the axe. There was a fourth blunt trauma to the back of the scalp at the left, indicating either another blow with the blunt end of the axe, or Daniel's head hitting the ground. The first of these blows would have rendered Daniel unconscious almost immediately.

The fifth and last blow to the front of his head was the most devastating. Here, the axe had penetrated his right temple to a depth of four inches and had severed the brainstem, which would have led to immediate respiratory failure and cardiac arrest.

The pathologist estimated the pattern of the lacerations indicated a frenzied attack that would have been over in six or seven seconds. There were no signs of defence wounds and the attack could have been done by one person; first, stunning Daniel by striking him from behind.

Rees and Fillery arrived at the mortuary just after lunch and the detective sergeant left the private detective in the public area and entered the autopsy room, only to find the post-mortem wasn't over. So Fillery took Rees out for a beer and sandwiches at a local pub while the body was cleaned up for identification.

The tear in the pocket of the right seam of Daniel's trousers was already attracting the curiosity of the police and pathologist. Perhaps Daniel's hand had been in his pocket when he was struck, the force ripping it out of his pocket. But there was an alternative explanation: the blunt trauma to the back of his head could suggest he fell on his left side, leaving his right cheek exposed for the final blow. The torn pocket could have resulted from the body being moved onto its back after that.

There were hints and clues. The force of that final blow suggested the assailant was standing over Daniel's body. But as Dr Heath re-enacted the coup de grâce he used a backhand blow because it is stronger than a forehand one. If the assailant had been standing over Daniel's body, a backhand blow would suggest the wielder of the axe was left-handed.

As the autopsy required the skull cap to be sawn away and the brain exposed for removal and analysis, the axe had to be removed from Daniel's face.

By the time Rees returned to identify Daniel's body in the mid-afternoon, the brain had been returned, the incisions on the skull and abdomen sutured, the body cleaned up, washed and covered in a shroud before being moved from the post-mortem room to a viewing room.

When Rees saw Daniel's body there was no evidence of any injuries, let alone any sign of the murder weapon.[28]

After viewing the body, he and Fillery went for another drink and then drove back to Catford to finish the statement which would later be criticised as 'noticeable for its brevity and is inadequate for a murder investigation'.

Rees' first statement to Fillery failed to mention the Belmont Car Auctions job or the detective sergeant's role in brokering the deal and providing additional security at the auction house the year before. More glaring still, the statement failed to name the police officers – including Fillery – who had been in Daniel's company at the Golden Lion pub the night before he died.

Soon after Rees went back to the office to collect some money that he delivered to Daniel's widow, Iris. It was there he met Alastair.

CHAPTER 5

One True Detective

11 March 1987, 11:30am

ALASTAIR: As the taxi approached my brother's office in Thornton Heath, I was thinking about the last time I was there, a month before, keeping an eye on the family and the company before Dan went to Malta.

We were discussing what he wanted me to do when Rees came into Dan's office and asked to speak to him in private. About ten minutes later, Dan returned and walked over to the window and stood staring abstractedly at the view outside. I knew something was bothering him. My brother was biting his lower lip, a mannerism he had when he was anxious about something.

'What's up, Dan?' I asked.

Daniel turned to me and mentioned a name. Just an ordinary unmemorable English name. To this day, though I remember the ensuing conversation vividly, I can't recall the name. It wasn't anything like the name of other police officers I'd met or heard about from him, it was something nondescript, like John Smith.

'Who's he?' I asked.

'He's a bent copper, Alastair. They're all over the place down here!'

An hour later we were in a pub called the Victory, just round the corner from Daniel's office on Gillett Road. After buying a drink, Daniel and I went to sit at a table opposite the bar and Jon Rees came and joined us.

The conversation eventually came round to undercover work. A couple of years earlier, Dan had asked me to do an undercover job for his company. The client was a major supermarket chain. Senior management suspected that one of their branch managers was embezzling.

I was planted in the store as a trainee manager to keep an eye on him. After a whole month of watching him closely, I could find no evidence of wrong-doing. He seemed to me to be conscientious, doing his job to the best of his

ability. I wrote this in my final report to the company and concluded that the losses had some other cause that I couldn't establish.

'I really tried to get to the bottom of that business in East Anglia,' I told them.

Rees looked at me. 'If I hadn't found someone who was guilty, I would have fitted someone up,' he told me.

I glanced at Daniel's face. I could see he was uncomfortable and trying not to show it. How had he finished up in partnership with this man? Neither of us spoke. Rees stood up and moved off to the crowded bar.

I could see Dan didn't want to pursue the matter. He asked me about my situation in Petersfield and I told him that things weren't good. When I went back, I would be looking for a job.

I envied my brother. His life was established – he had his own home, a family of his own and his own business. But at the same time I knew I could never do the job that he did, or work with the people he had to work with.

* * *

A month later, here I was back on Thornton High Street, looking up at my brother's offices above an insurance broker. But Daniel would never be there again. Now all those conversations we had a few weeks earlier were echoing in my head with a sudden urgency. I knew there were clues there, something my dead brother was trying to tell me but could not.

I made my way back up to the stairs to a suite of rooms on the first floor. Inside Southern Investigations Peter Newby and Tony Pearce were waiting. The two men were just sitting there in stunned silence, but I didn't feel like commiserating with them or talking to them: it was Jonathan Rees I really wanted to see.

'Where's Jon?' I asked them.

'He's with the police,' said Peter. 'He's been with them all morning.'

'When will he be back?'

'I've no idea, Alastair. They could keep him there all day.'

By now I was in a state of high alert; I needed to know everything.

'Do you know what happened?'

All they could tell me was Dan had been 'fatally mugged'. Neither knew how he had been murdered.

'If you see Jon, tell him I want to talk to him,' I said as I left the office. 'I'll be over at Dan's house with Iris and the children.'

On the street I had a sense of dread at the thought of seeing Dan's wife and the children but there was no way out of it. I hailed a cab. Mum was also on her way and would arrive soon.

It was less than a mile to Dan's house. The cab dropped me outside.

There was the yellow-brick wall separating the patio from the drive, which Dan had recently built, having taken evening classes in bricklaying. Then there was the garage where he'd proudly shown me his restored Austin Healey 3000 the last time I was there.

I was choking back tears as I walked up to the front door.

As I reached for the doorbell, I lost my nerve and sat down and wept.

Daniel was so excited by his Austin Healey. He'd bought the car in a very poor state several years earlier for £600. I remembered seeing the rusting hulk on the forecourt outside their previous home in Howden Road, round the corner. Since then he'd stripped it down, dismantled and reconditioned the engine and cleaned and re-sprayed all of the bodywork that could be rescued.

We'd taken it for its first spin only a month ago on my last visit. Dan had put on a leather pilot's hat, a pair of goggles and a pair of leather gauntlets. I burst out laughing.

'Jesus, Dan, you look like Toad of Toad Hall!'

We got into the car and Dan revved the three-litre engine. It sounded like an aeroplane. 'I'm going to give it to Sarah as a present for her 21st birthday!' he shouted over the roar. 'With a crate of champagne in the boot!'

I wiped my eyes on my sleeve, stood up straight and rang the doorbell.

A man's voice with a Scottish accent called out from inside 'Who's there?' and a head appeared behind the stained-glass panel in the door.

'It's Alastair,' I called back.

A man in his thirties opened the door. I'd often heard about Iris's brother-in-law from Daniel, but I'd never met him. Joe Harty had flown down to London overnight with his wife Janet and Iris's parents, Ian and Nell. He showed me into the sitting room. Iris sat huddled on the sofa, her eyes red from tears. Her mother and sister Janet were in the room.

'Your voice sounded just like Daniel's ...' She looked up at me. 'I thought it was him!'

I sat down and put my arms around her.

'Where are the children?'

Janet told me Sarah and Dan were being looked after by a friend. I was deeply relieved, more for my own sake than for them. The thought of seeing Dan's children in this situation was more than I could bear.

The doorbell rang again. I heard Joe ask the caller's identity and then say, 'Go away, please!' A journalist from *The Sun* had shoved a note through the letterbox, offering money. Joe screwed it up in disgust and left for the kitchen to bin it.

I looked out of the window onto the street, watching for my mother's arrival. A man and a woman were hanging around on the corner, about 50 yards away. They looked like reporters.

Iris asked: 'How did you find out, Alastair?'

I told her about the call from my mother. 'Have you heard anything from Jon Rees?' I added.

'He was with the two policemen that came here last night to tell me about Daniel,' Iris replied. 'He said he'd come over today, but I don't know when.' There was an edge of anger in my sister-in-law's voice.

Fifteen minutes later, a grey saloon car pulled up outside and my mother stepped out onto the pavement. A man in his twenties got out of the driver's seat and opened the boot. A woman stepped out from the passenger side and joined him.

'My mother's here,' I said, rushing to the door. 'I've got to talk to her, she doesn't know what's happened.'

Mum was standing a few yards up the road, thanking the couple. I introduced myself, thanked them and they drove off, clearly not wanting to intrude. Mum began walking towards the front garden gate.

'Wait a minute, Mum. Don't go in yet, I need to talk to you.'

She turned to me, confused.

'Mum … Dan was murdered!'

It was as though I'd struck her. She froze, cried out, and rushed up the street away from the house.

I dropped her case, chased after her and put my arms around her.

'No! *No!*' she cried, pulling herself free and running back towards the house, crying out in disbelief. I caught up with her again and hugged her tightly to my chest.

'The children!' she exclaimed. 'What about the children? We can't tell them this. Oh no!'

'I know, Mum. It's horrible but I'm here. We'll deal with this, Mum. We have to.'

Together we walked into that house filled with traumatised people. Nobody knew what to say or do. Iris' parents, Ian and Nell, were quietly drinking tea in the kitchen. They offered their condolences. Janet came in with a bottle of brandy – I needed it.

* * *

About five minutes later Jonathan Rees appeared on the patio outside the kitchen door. I turned to my mother and Iris' parents to explain as he entered.

'This is Dan's partner, Jon Rees.'

'Hello dear,' Jon greeted my mother brusquely across the table. It was the first time he'd ever met her, there was no word of condolence. He nodded to the other relatives. Sensing that he hated having to see us, I moved towards the kettle to detain him.

'Tea or coffee, Jon?'

Joe and Iris came into the kitchen. While Joe was oblivious to the tension, Iris stood with her back to the wall, her eyes intently fixed on Rees.

'No thanks, Alastair,' said Rees. 'Things are hectic at the moment. I came to bring Iris some cash for expenses.' He pulled out an envelope from his pocket and handed it over. Iris took it without a word.

'I'll be off then,' said Rees, walking out onto the patio. Joe followed. I watched for a few seconds as Rees spoke to Joe then walked out to join them. Rees dug in a pocket for his car keys and moved in the direction of the drive.

'Wait a minute, Jon,' I said – I could feel his discomfort.

'I've got things to do, Alastair …'

'I want to talk to you, Jon. You were the last person to see my brother alive. I've got a lot of questions I need to ask you.'

'Okay, Alastair, but it's going to be nasty …'

'Of course it's going to be nasty, Jon!' I exclaimed. 'My brother's just been murdered. How could it be anything *but* nasty?'

'We'll have to go somewhere else.'

Rees' blue BMW was parked outside the house. I climbed into the back seat. Joe joined us and sat beside Rees. I could see Rees' eyes in the rear-view mirror as we drove off. We pulled up at a pub on a hill about half a mile away. We made our way up some steps into a quiet bar with only one or two

customers. Rees pointed to a table next to a window and bought three beers. He and Joe sat with their backs to the window.

As we sipped our drinks I waited for him to begin talking.

'I've just come from the morgue. It was still in his head ...'

'What was it, Jon? What did they kill him with?'

He hesitated.

'It was ... well ... Something between a machete and a cleaver ... Japanese.'

I was baffled. Earlier that morning, Rees had told me Dan had been battered to death. Now my brother had been murdered with some kind of oriental martial arts tool.

'I was in the office this morning and this woman rang up,' he continued. 'She told me she knew who'd killed Daniel.'

'*What*! She said she knew who had done it?'

'She said it was her son-in-law. She said her daughter was having an affair with Daniel.'

'Did you take her name and phone number?'

'Nah, she was some kind of nutter,' he scoffed. 'I handed the phone to Peter Newby.'

'So you don't know who she is?'

'Nah, she was just some nutter.'

At that moment, Dan's assistant, Dave Bray, walked in through the door. He spotted us immediately – he'd seen Rees' car outside the pub, he told us.

'I'm sorry, Alastair. I've just heard about Daniel,' he said, white-faced with shock.

'Thanks, Dave. It's horrible.'

'This is a private conversation.' Rees looked up at Dave, dismissively. 'Can you go somewhere else?'

At this I looked at Dave Bray and cringed. I knew he and Dan were close. Crestfallen, Dave walked to the bar to order a drink. But I knew I needed to keep Rees talking.

'Who's leading the inquiry, Jon?' I asked.

'Oh, some pisshead! I saw him last night after the police came to tell me about Daniel. I had to go over to Sydenham Police Station in the middle of the night. I was eating a takeaway with Sharon, watching telly. Two coppers came round at about midnight, said Daniel had been fatally mugged.

'One of them says, "Have you been wearing these clothes all evening?" I said, "yes". So he says, "Right, I want you to come over to the nick with me." So I said, "Who do you think I am, the mad axe-man of Catford or something?" There was another copper with him, one who knows me. And he says, "No, he's all right."'

'Is Sid Fillery on the squad?' I asked.

Rees nodded.

That was a relief, I'd met Fillery. Maybe he could help. I asked Rees to drive us back.

* * *

I'd been introduced to Fillery a year or so earlier on a visit to London. One afternoon, Daniel had asked me to accompany him while he served a writ on someone. When we got back to his car, Daniel suggested we drive to a nearby pub to meet Rees, who was with Sid Fillery.

Daniel explained he was a detective sergeant and a friend of Jon's. One of the reasons Dan took Rees on as a partner was his police contacts. In fact, he often described Rees as a 'frustrated copper'.

At a small, anonymous-looking pub nearby, Rees was standing at the bar, pint in hand, with three other men. Daniel introduced me to Fillery, a tallish man in his late thirties, clean-shaven and wearing a navy-blue blazer. I quickly discovered that the two other men were police officers too.

I didn't have much contact with Fillery during the visit to the pub, but I'd seen him at the office on another occasion when he'd disappeared into Rees' office.

* * *

Back at Dan's house, I told Joe I wanted to buy a paper and walked to the high street. On the way, I bought the early edition of the *Evening Standard*. I leafed through it.

At the top right-hand corner of a page was a small photo of Dan below a headline: 'PRIVATE EYE MURDERED'. Dan's eyes appeared half-closed, as if the camera had caught him blinking or looking at his shoes.

So this wasn't just a nightmare: my younger brother really had been murdered. Like a cold wave the awful reality washed over me again.

Then one of the details in the article struck me. A police spokesman was quoted describing the murder as 'savage beyond belief'. But the weapon was a 14-inch hand axe or hatchet, not a machete, nor a cleaver.

I found a call box and rang my friend John Xavier, who lived near me in Petersfield. I told him what had happened and that I needed to get to the incident room at Sydenham quickly, but I needed his help because I had no idea how to get there and I didn't have a car with me.

We met outside Norwood Junction station and on the way to Sydenham I told John the bare facts, but nothing about my suspicions. At the police station I told the uniformed officer on the reception desk I was Daniel Morgan's brother and asked to speak to someone from the murder squad.

Moments later, a dark-haired officer in plainclothes came to the front desk. After introducing himself as Detective Inspector Alan Jones he looked me up and down and gestured to a door in a passage behind the front desk. We left John sitting on a bench in the entrance hall. Jones ushered me into the room and we sat down at a table.

'I was hoping to see Sid Fillery,' I said. 'Is he here?'

'He's out on inquiries at the moment...' Jones told me. 'What do you do for a living then?'

I was unshaven; I hadn't brushed my teeth or combed my hair.

'I'm a window cleaner,' I replied.

'And what were you doing last night?' He eyed me with open suspicion.

Jones' question shocked me. I'd only taken up window cleaning as a stopgap while I rebuilt my life in England. Daniel had kindly given me £1,000 after his trip from Malta to help me to establish my own business. And now this police officer was treating me like trash.

'I don't like your tone, Inspector,' I said. 'I've come here less than 24 hours after my brother was murdered to help you catch whoever killed him. I've barely opened my mouth and you're treating me like a suspect!'

Jones looked put out by that. I suspect he didn't expect from my appearance that I had a university background. He fired off another question.

'What do you know about women in your brother's life?'

By now I was beginning to snap.

'As a matter of fact I do know about women in my brother's life. But I'm not going to tell you about it. When can I see Sid Fillery?'

'Come back tomorrow afternoon and you can see him, after four-thirty,' he said curtly.

I stood up and left the room. John was still sitting in the entrance hall. He looked puzzled – I'd barely been away two minutes. I was too angry to explain as we left the police station. It was already dark.

'I want to see where he was killed, John,' I told him.

* * *

As we drove to the Golden Lion everything was strange, as though we were part of a film – a disturbing feeling of unreality.

We found the pub at the bottom of the high street, next to a supermarket. It was a fairly large double-fronted Victorian built pub. A sign on the sidewall pointed to a rear car park. John drove down a narrow alleyway alongside the pub that seemed to go on for yards and yards. At the end was a brick outbuilding. We turned sharp left into a dark car park.

I was surprised to find that, less than 24 hours since my brother's murder there were no police cordons, forensic markings or signs that this was a crime scene.

I stood for a moment in the darkness, taking in the surroundings. The wall to the beer garden behind me was covered in ivy. On my right was a high windowless wall, the side of a supermarket. The two remaining sides of the car park were bordered by trees obscuring the view from any nearby houses. It looked like a very good place to carry out a murder.

One very dark spot on the right corner was overshadowed by the outbuilding. Though it was too dark to see any evidence of the crime, I had a very strong intuition it was here that Dan had been killed. From everything I saw, I was sure that this place had been chosen and that he had been set up.

We stood there for a couple of minutes, taking in the atmosphere.

'I could use a drink,' I said to John.

We entered the bar through the back door. It was empty except for a couple of solo drinkers – murder probably doesn't do a lot for trade. I ordered a beer, John wanted a Perrier, and we sat down in the corner. I told him what had happened since I'd heard about Dan's death that morning but deliberately avoided talking about my suspicions. The first thing he asked me about was Rees.

'Have you thought about the partner?'

Finally, I could tell him.

'I've thought about almost nothing else, John …'

<table>
<tr><td>CHAPTER 6</td><td>The Bait</td></tr>
</table>

11 March 1987, Night

ALASTAIR: The grilling by Alan Jones, and then his questions about my brother's love life had left me in a quandary. I remembered that last evening when Daniel had come back from Malta and the drink in the pub when Rees had suggested I should have fitted someone up for the supermarket's losses. Once Rees had gone, we sat in silence for a couple of minutes, watching the crowd at the bar. Daniel nodded in the direction of an attractive dark-haired woman in the same group as Jonathan Rees.

'That's my girlfriend over there.'

I was taken aback, embarrassed. We never spoke to each other about women or relationships so his confession had caught me off guard. I was also fond of Iris, who had always been good to me.

The next morning I left early for Hampshire and never had a chance to speak to Dan again

I told my friend John Xavier about the interview, and explained I wasn't going to discuss Daniel's private life with Alan Jones – I felt it probably had nothing to do with Dan's murder. Investigating Rees was much more important. I was protective of Iris too: Dan was dead, and Jones would probably have been very blunt.

Furthermore, I was almost certain Rees had suggested to the murder squad that Dan could have been killed because of an affair and that this lay behind Jones' question.

Then John came up with a way of testing my suspicions. He suggested that I ring Rees and tell him that I'd been to see the police and they'd asked me questions about Dan that I didn't want to answer – before talking to him. If he was involved, we reckoned he'd be very anxious to find out what this was about.

If we met, I'd then tell him that Jones had asked about women in Dan's life and that I'd refused to answer before asking him about this. If he encouraged

me to believe that Dan had been murdered by a jealous husband or boyfriend then I'd know for certain.

We left the pub and drove back to South Norwood. I'd decided to ring Rees from a call box ten minutes from the house. John warned me to be careful and began his journey back to Hampshire.

Rees' wife Sharon answered my call. I'd never met her.

'Is that Sharon? It's Alastair here, Daniel's brother.'

'Oh, hello Alastair! Yes, it's Sharon. Oh, I'm so sorry, Alastair. Isn't it awful! How could anyone do such a thing? Isn't it terrible what some people can do to each other?'

'Yes, it's horrific, Sharon. Can I talk to Jon?'

'He's out at the moment, I'm afraid,' she said.

I imagined him standing next to the phone.

'Can you give him a message when he gets in,' I went on, laying the bait. 'Could you tell him I've been to see the police tonight. They asked me some questions about Daniel's private life that I didn't want to answer before I'd spoken to Jon.'

'I'll tell him as soon as he gets in, Alastair.'

'I'll be back at Daniel's house in about ten minutes. He can contact me there … Thanks, Sharon.'

I hung up and walked the few hundred yards back to the house. Iris' father Ian was sitting alone in the kitchen. The others were talking quietly in the other rooms. I switched on the kettle and sat down. It had barely boiled before the phone rang and Joe Harty picked it up:

'It's for you, Alastair. It's Jon Rees.'

I walked into the hallway and picked up the phone.

'Alastair? It's Jon here. What's all this about?'

'I can't talk here, Jon,' I spoke softly into the receiver. 'Can we meet somewhere else?'

'I'll pick you up in five minutes.'

'I'll be out in the street.'

I got my coat, walked out and headed down the street in the direction of Rees' house. I'd barely covered a hundred yards before I saw his car approach.

He pulled up and opened the passenger door.

My heart was thumping. I didn't want to be alone in an enclosed space with this man, but there was no other way.

Once inside, I was relieved to see he was as agitated as I was.

'What's this about then …?'

He couldn't wait to engage first gear before quizzing me.

'Let's go somewhere we can sit down.'

He drove a few hundred yards to the South Norwood Sports Club. I bought him a lager and ordered a Guinness for myself. It would take time to draw; this would keep him simmering. Slowly I walked over to the table and handed him his drink.

'What's all this about then?' He was desperate. I took a long draught of my Guinness.

'I've been over at the incident room. There was a copper there who treated me like a suspect. He asked about women in Daniel's life. Is there any truth in that, Jon? Was he a womaniser?'

His relief was almost palpable: he'd feared something else, I was convinced.

'It was the only thing he thought about, Alastair. He was shaggin' half a dozen that I knew about. And there was probably another dozen that I didn't know about.'

'God, he must have been busy!' I half-laughed, knowing the idea Daniel was some kind of sexual athlete of this kind was ludicrous. I explained about the evening in the Victory when Daniel had pointed out a woman to me as his girlfriend. Rees seemed curious and asked me to describe her.

'Do you know her, Jon?'

'I'm not sure,' he said.

I felt he was lying. He asked about the copper at the incident room – he appeared to know who Jones was. Then he began grizzling about the problems Dan's death would cause for the business.

We finished our drinks. We were looking each other in the eye – they say they're the windows of the soul. By now we both knew that I thought he was involved. And that we'd been play-acting since the moment we met that day.

He drove me back to my brother's house. We didn't say much on the journey.

* * *

It took only seconds for the nightmare to return when I surfaced from sleep the following morning. I remembered the irritating, happy little kid brother with the club foot and the pet prize rabbit, the 15-year-old who built a kayak in our garage at Jerusalem Lane, Dan in an absurd leather flying helmet,

grinning while he revved up his Austin Healey in the street. And now he was gone.

I lit a cigarette and made a mug of tea in the kitchen. The disastrous interview with Alan Jones came back to me. I had to contact Sid Fillery, soon.

My mother had just woken when I came to see her and was sitting on the side of her bed holding a cup of coffee. I sat beside her, then stood up and paced the room.

'I think I know who killed Dan,' I said.

'You don't have to tell me, Al. I think I know too.'

I knew without asking that we were thinking about the same person. I felt a sudden pang that my sister Jane wasn't there with us.

'Have you spoken to Jane, Mum? When will she get here?'

Mum explained that she hadn't dared break the news to Jane when she was on her own. Jane's husband, Justin, was a major in the army and Mum knew he was away on military exercises in Bavaria. She'd managed to get hold of someone at the Ministry of Defence in London and told them about Dan's death – she didn't know then he'd been murdered. The MOD had contacted Justin's commanding officer in Germany, who had given him leave to return home to Jane.

Jane and Justin had just bought a small farm in Westphalia, about 50 kilometres from Düsseldorf, and when he arrived to tell her that her brother was dead, she was so shocked that she refused to believe it was one of her brothers, and kept on thinking it was one of his. She'd become hysterical and needed sedatives to calm her down. By the time Justin had found someone to look after their animals, he'd been up for more than 24 hours and he'd been working a nightshift while on exercise so was in no fit state to drive. Mum told me they wouldn't get to London until the following day.

* * *

Later that afternoon, having tried to speak to everyone who knew Dan to get more information, I returned to the incident room at Sydenham Police Station. I was shown into a small room by a uniformed officer. The furniture was a wooden bench, a chair and a table screwed to the floor. There was nothing movable except an ashtray. The window was heavily barred.

Sid Fillery and Alan Jones[1] entered and sat down opposite me. Fillery was the taller of the two men, over six feet tall. He was smartly dressed in a dark jacket with grey trousers.

'You wanted to see me,' he said.

'That's right, Sergeant Fillery. It's because you knew my brother and you know Jonathan Rees. You see, I'm sure that Rees is involved in this murder.'

Fillery looked quizzical.

'What makes you think that?'

I described the phone conversation with Rees and his talk of a 'third party', his account of the call from the 'nutter' saying she knew who'd killed Dan, and the trap John Xavier had devised, and finally how Rees had acted precisely according to expectations.

Both listened in silence. Neither man took any notes, which surprised me. I told them of my suspicions concerning the car auction robbery a year before and that this could be a motive for Dan's murder.

'What robbery was that then?' asked Fillery.

I was surprised that he didn't know about it and I didn't know the name of the auction company then – Belmont Auctions. Dan had only mentioned the robbery once in the intervening year. I urged them to look into it quickly. It would have been in their records.

'Have you any evidence of this?' asked Fillery.

'Evidence? Well, no, it's just suspicion. But it stinks.'

His attitude was beginning to upset me.

'So, it's just what you'd describe as a gut feeling?' said Fillery.

'Yes, a gut feeling, but a very strong gut feeling.'

'Your brother was a private investigator and there could be any number of people who might have held a grudge against him.'

'Sure, I understand that. But I'm sure Rees is involved …'

'We're pursuing a number of lines of inquiry. And I'm afraid, we can't go rushing off down what could turn out to be a blind alley … on your gut feeling.'

I felt sick. Jones stood up. He looked troubled by our conversation. He nodded to me and left the room. Fillery moved towards the window and turned to me.

'What do you know about David Bray?'

He was obviously suggesting that Dave was a suspect.

'No way!' I said, scornfully. 'I saw Dave yesterday and the poor kid looked like a ghost, he was so shocked – unlike Rees!'

He could see that I found his suggestion ridiculous. I stood up to leave.

'Listen,' Fillery said to me. 'If you've got any more concerns about this, just give me a ring. We can meet up and discuss them over a pint.'

I left Fillery looking out through the barred window. Something was wrong, but I couldn't put my finger on it. Nobody seemed to be treating my brother's murder seriously.

On the way back I stopped to put a few litres of petrol in the car I'd borrowed. I didn't realise until I'd lurched back, restarting the vehicle at every junction, that it ran on diesel.

Later that evening, I rang Alan Jones at the incident room to urge him to look into the auction robbery. He seemed conflicted and reserved. All I could get from him was an assurance that the police were pursuing a number of lines of inquiry. I slept very restlessly that night.

* * *

The following morning I studied the newspapers to see if anything else had come out. One of them reported that £1,000 in cash had been found in the inside pocket of Dan's jacket, but his Rolex watch had been stolen. This didn't fit in with a mugging.

Another report described the murder as having 'all the hallmarks of a professional hit'. The handle of the axe had apparently been taped with Elastoplast to avoid fingerprints. The murder had undoubtedly been planned.

That evening, as I was returning from the shops with my newspapers, I could see a group of people heading in my direction under the street lights. As I approached, I recognised my sister Jane and her husband Justin. They'd obviously just arrived from Germany. Mum was with them. All three seemed agitated.

'Al, we've been looking for you for ages!' Jane was visibly upset and anxious.

'What's going on?'

'We need to talk to you alone, Al. We didn't want to disturb Iris and all her relatives inside,' said Justin.

'The thing is, Al,' Jane took over the conversation, 'we need to get back to Wales with Mum.'

I couldn't understand this.

'You've only just got here, Jane. Why do you want to go to Wales?'

Mum spoke for her: 'It's me, Al. I need to be in my own home. I need peace and quiet, to make sense of what's happened.'

She didn't sound convinced herself, but then again she was staying with Iris' neighbours, people she didn't know.

'Okay, I understand. You can all go to Wales, but I'm staying here. I'm going nowhere …'

'We need you with us, Al. We need to be together as a family. Please come with us!' Jane pleaded with me.

'Leave it to the professionals, Alastair, they know what they're doing,' said Justin.

I lost my temper at this point.

'Professionals? You should see the people that I've been dealing with over at Sydenham … I mean they didn't even take notes when they interviewed me, for Christ's sake!'

They all looked at each other as if silently agreeing something.

Jane spoke first: 'Okay, if you must know, we've had a phone call from the police. They want you to go back to Hampshire. They say you're getting in the way of the inquiry.'

I was furious. 'That's complete crap! I've been trying to help them. I've been over to the incident room twice, trying to give them information.'

'Look, Allie,' Jane went on. 'They said they're way ahead of you and that you're getting in the way of the inquiry. They want you to go back to Hampshire.'

'Well they can piss off!'

I was so confused and angry. I couldn't explain to them what I'd seen and heard and what had been said in my meetings with the police. Also, I was hurt that they'd believed the police. How could they think I would do anything to hamper the investigation?

I turned away and crossed the road, leaving them standing under a street lamp, just as confused and bewildered as me. I'd never felt as lonely in my life.

* * *

Early the next day I decided to visit Sydenham Police Station one more time: I wanted to make a statement. I presented myself at the incident room. Reluctantly, they appointed a detective constable to take my statement. I went over what had happened since I'd heard about Dan's death.

The officer didn't seem at all interested and had great difficulty in writing coherently. In the end, it was a very poor statement, containing only fragments of what I wanted to say. As we were finishing this sorry process, DI Alan Jones entered the room.

'Are you a religious fanatic?' he asked me out of the blue.

I knew exactly where that question came from. Some years earlier I'd spent several months in a Buddhist monastery. I was interested in meditation. Having lived in Sweden for ten years and gone through an agonising divorce and separation from my little son, I'd just got back to the UK. The disciplined monastic lifestyle helped me back onto an even keel.

Rees knew all about this. I'd telephoned Dan while I was staying there. I'd even spoken to Rees on the phone.

'No, Inspector,' I told DI Jones, 'I'm not a religious fanatic.'

'I'm just wondering whether you might have got the wrath of God inside you and killed your brother.'

'I'll treat that remark with the contempt that it deserves,' I said, leaving the room in despair. Rees was clearly feeding them all sorts of baloney and they seemed to be taking it far more seriously than anything I had to say.

* * *

So far, I'd done all I could. And I was absolutely exhausted after running on adrenaline for three days. I'd barely eaten at all, slept only fitfully and I needed time to gather my wits and survive this horror. Jane and Justin were leaving for Wales with Mum, but before they went, I had to explain to my sister what I'd discovered since Dan's murder.

The two of us walked to a local pub. I told her I was convinced Rees was involved and how worried I was about the way the cops were handling the investigation.

'I'm sorry, Al, I had no idea of this. I thought Danny's dead, the situation can't get any worse. Then the police called and told us you're getting in the way. They said you were muddying the waters and getting in the way of the investigations. They said they were way ahead of you, Al.'

'Jane, if you'd seen the individuals that I've been dealing with over at Sydenham. It's crap, Jane, complete crap! I promise you, all I've done since the word go has been to try and help them.'

I could see she was struggling to take in what I was saying.

'I can't even get my head round Dan being dead, let alone murdered,' she said. 'He was just a normal guy. Why would someone murder an ordinary person?'

We were both weeping. Jane pulled some Kleenex from her handbag and we dried our tears. She told me about a dream she'd had the night before.

'Last night I dreamt the police told me a junkie had killed Dan,' she recalled. 'He thought Dan was Humpty Dumpty and smashed his head like an egg. When I woke up, I was strangely comforted by that dream because it was some sort of explanation.'

The idea that Daniel was killed by some random drug dealer had wormed its way into my sister's mind.

'We've just got to try and keep going and stay sane,' I said as we walked back in the direction of Dan's house.

* * *

That evening I returned to Petersfield. I walked from the station straight to my grandmother's flat – I hadn't rung her as I'd been too distracted by events in London. I gave her a short account of the situation, telling her only how Dan had been murdered and that the police were investigating. I told her nothing about the response I'd received from the Met.

On a practical level, I was in a difficult position. I was 38 years old, divorced and up until that point my own life had been a spectacular failure. I'd gained entry to two of Europe's most prestigious universities, University College London and Lund University in Sweden, and dropped out of both courses (English and German). I'd even applied to RADA, been invited to a second audition and failed to attend because I'd married and moved to Sweden – I didn't get the letter in time.

I'd returned to Britain in 1982 after a ten-year sojourn in Sweden. My exit had hardly been triumphant either. I'd spent the last three months in a drug rehabilitation unit in Malmö. I'd been prescribed a Swedish version of Valium during an agonising divorce involving my son Ian. After using the tablets for two years, I realised I was hooked. I knew if I didn't stop, this drug would ruin me, so I got myself into rehab. After several months, I was free of the drug and decided I'd return to Britain to rebuild my life.

Soon after returning to Chichester, where my mother was looking after a house owned by my sister, I got a job in Bognor Regis as a welder producing office furniture.

Socially, I felt completely adrift and through a series of chance meetings I came into contact with a quasi-religious cult called Lifewave. Its philosophy was a hotchpotch of Buddhism and Hinduism. After a couple of years of involvement, I found out that a couple of my friends were being manipulated

in a way that I found repugnant, so I pulled out. This left me virtually friend-less – and jobless too.

While in the cult, I'd started up a window- and carpet-cleaning business with a fellow member. When I left, this partnership broke up and I'd had to start again, but that was out of reach because I didn't have enough cash to buy a car.

I'd told Daniel about my straitened circumstances the last time I'd seen him before he was murdered, after he returned from his trip to Malta, and he'd rung the next day.

'Look, Al, I'll send you a grand, as a present, just to get you started.'

'Dan! That would be fantastic. It would really get me out of a hole. I know I can get customers straight away. In a few weeks I'll be up and running.'

The cheque arrived the next day.

I felt as though I'd been let out of a locked, darkened room. With the couple of hundred pounds that I had in reserve, Dan's gift of £1,000 would get me onto a flat of my own and leave enough to buy an old car, a roof-rack, a couple of ladders and the necessary tools. I could have kissed him.

A few weeks later he was dead, but I couldn't forget him, and I wouldn't give up. My immediate priority was work. I rang the estate agent and confirmed that my flat was ready for me to move in. Then I signed the lease and began transporting my few belongings in my battered blue, newly purchased Morris Marina to the village of Liss on the South Downs.

I unpacked my second-hand typewriter and bashed out a leaflet with my name, address and phone number. I had it photocopied and began tramping the streets, canvassing new customers for window cleaning.

| Morgan One

March to April 1987

Though it seemed fruitless from his point of view, Alastair Morgan's interview with DS Fillery and DI Jones – particularly his mention of the Belmont Car Auctions robbery – did mark a significant shift in the investigation.

Two days after the murder, Sid Fillery was asked to leave the incident room and spend the next three days at Southern Investigations gathering gossip and intelligence. 'All I want you to do is hang around the office for the next four days,' DSU Campbell told him on Thursday, 12th March 1987.

Extraordinarily, this allowed Fillery to make another clear-out of Southern Investigations files. For a second time, on this occasion with DC Micky Crofts, the Catford detective removed correspondence and files from the Thornton Heath office, which were deposited in the boot of his car.

Instead of logging them in with the murder squad as exhibits, Fillery went straight to the Prince of Wales public house in Thornton Heath for another rendezvous with Jonathan Rees. There, DC Crofts saw them joined by a third police officer, PC Derek Haslam, who would later on play a more significant role in this story.

That second tranche of files was never fully accounted for. Fillery's driver, PC Richard Zdrojewski, would later claim he helped clear out his sergeant's desk of a 'load of buff coloured files' marked CR and some police microfiches. He burnt most of them.

Apart from this document clear-out, Fillery was relatively idle during the murder investigation. He was tasked with only seven 'actions' out of hundreds, and these he mainly delegated to subordinates. In terms of notes or files he contributed little.

Fillery's only significant contribution to the inquiry after seeing Alastair Morgan was a message to the inquiry at 7pm that Thursday, 12th March with

information that Daniel Morgan had had an affair with a married woman in late 1982 or early 1983.

It appears that Fillery, like Rees, was pushing the irate husband or jealous partner explanation for the murder – while omitting any reference to Margaret Harrison.

According to the information Fillery passed on to the first murder investigation, Daniel had served an injunction and a child custody order on the estranged husband of a woman he was having an affair with. Fillery alleged Daniel had then embarked on an affair with the married woman's sister and 'may still be seeing her'. Daniel had called that woman on the day of the murder, Fillery added.

By now, however, these new leads from Fillery were having less traction, because Jones and Campbell had a better idea how closely Rees was embedded with local police.

Indeed, the private detective's familiarity with many members of the murder squad was hard to ignore. The night after the murder, Rees was seen drinking at the Victory with Peter Wilkins, a former police officer who worked for Southern Investigations.[1] Later that same evening he was spotted by DC Richard Davis in the Bricklayer's Arms on Willow Way, just around the corner from the incident room, carousing with members of the murder squad, including Fillery. Davis surmised Rees was being apprised of 'the relative aspects of the inquiry and how it was going'.

All in all, Rees knew at least eight people on the murder squad.[2]

DS Campbell put out a general telex to the entire Metropolitan Police district, covering the whole of the capital: 'Any officer who has had dealings with or has knowledge of Morgan is requested to contact the incident room. PS without delay.' Campbell would go on to interview 42 officers at Catford Police Station alone.[3]

As the inquiry focused on Rees, his close friendship and business connections with Fillery could not be hidden for long. For a start, Rees' statement to Fillery on the day after the murder was beginning to fall apart. The billing on his car mobile phone did not match up with Rees' statement of his movements. On 12th March murder squad detectives interviewed the 'third party' Rees had said Daniel had been waiting for on the night of the murder.

Though the celebrity minder Paul Goodridge confirmed that he had been asked by Rees to find someone who could loan him money for the legal proceedings over the Belmont Car Auctions case, he denied he had ever intended to meet Daniel and Rees at the Golden Lion that night. It was only when Rees called around 9:15 or 9:30pm that his girlfriend, Jean Wisden, told him that Rees wanted to meet at the Beulah Spa pub.

Four days after the murder it was impossible to ignore Rees as the prime suspect. After all, he was the last person to see Daniel alive. He had set the rendezvous on a pretext that was not corroborated by the 'third party'. His alibi for the time of the murder was falling apart. And there could be another motive beyond sexual jealousy or a random mugging – the strange robbery from the year before that Alastair Morgan had mentioned.

On Saturday, 14th March, four days after Daniel's killing, Fillery was asked to bring Rees to Sydenham Police Station so that officers could take his fingerprints and conduct a forensic examination of his BMW. According to a police officer present, he'd just had it cleaned.

While his car was checked, Fillery took Rees to the Crown pub on Bromley Common, where they both met Detectives Peter Foley and Alan Purvis – in effect, the three officers involved in the Belmont Car Auctions security detail that went so awry. For some reason, this meeting was so urgent that Purvis had to ring his commanding officer, DI Hughes, to ask to be excused from duty.

Suspicion was falling on Fillery too, now that he was known to be a close friend of Rees rather than just an acquaintance, and had been with Daniel and Rees at the murder scene the night before. DI Jones noted that after every briefing, Fillery went out to make calls.[4] After Rees made a visit to the police station, members of the murder squad noticed the private detective immediately call someone on his car phone. They rang Fillery's number, and it was engaged.[5] The detective sergeant was now asked to make his own statement to the inquiry team, which revealed a strange anomaly.

Fillery confirmed he had met Rees and Daniel Morgan at the Golden Lion the night before the murder, but bizarrely he put the start of the meeting at 9pm. Only four days before, he had taken Rees' statement which claimed they'd met at 7:30pm. A small matter, perhaps, but since Fillery had never disclosed he knew that first statement of Rees' was false, what else was he missing?

It would later emerge that the Catford crime squad head objected to becoming a person of interest, and even challenged the murder squad office manager, DS Malcolm Davidson, to show him the evidence against him.

By the following day, Fillery's role in a murder squad so disturbed Campbell that he asked the Catford detective sergeant to come before his normal 2pm shift. Instead of going to the incident room, they met at the Bricklayer's Arms. Campbell was accompanied by DI Jones, who had heard Alastair Morgan's allegation about the Belmont Car Auctions robbery.

Campbell told Fillery that he would have to leave the inquiry because: 'You are too close to Jon Rees.'

Fillery agreed, claiming he could see the problem coming, and added: 'I was going to ask you to come off anyway.'[6]

After this conversation Fillery went on annual leave and then sick leave from 20th March.

He'd never return to active duty again.

* * *

On 23rd March, nearly two weeks after the murder, the office manager Peter Newby was interviewed about the legal background to the Belmont Car Auctions dispute and the £10,000 Southern Investigations were ordered to lodge with the court in the week before Daniel Morgan's murder.

Employees at the car auction warehouse gave more details of the Belmont security job: how the three serving police officers – Fillery, Purvis and Foley – had been moonlighting as part of a security team that included Rees and his brothers-in-law, Garry and Glenn Vian.

DC Duncan Hanrahan was questioned about his investigation into the robbery of £18,000 from Rees outside his home. The Morgan murder squad then discovered the legal letters sent by Belmont Car Auctions' solicitors to the three police officers suggesting they should give evidence in their legal suit against Rees.

Two days later, detectives from the murder squad took a second statement from Peter Newby in which he recalled Fillery had attended the offices of Southern Investigations on the morning after the murder. He said Fillery had removed several files, including one about Belmont Car Auctions.

By now, with three Metropolitan officers under investigation, including a very senior detective on his own murder squad, Douglas Campbell was feeling

the strain. He consulted with senior officers, including Commanders Alan Fry and Ken Merton, and wondered if the murder investigation now needed to be taken over by an outside force.

* * *

Three weeks after Daniel Morgan was axed to death, on 2nd April 1987, the murder team sought warrants at Greenwich Magistrates' Court to arrest the six key figures thought to be involved in the Belmont robbery. But DSU Campbell was right to be worried his murder team could not cope with an investigation that also involved Metropolitan Police officers.

The night before the arrests one of the murder squad, Detective Constable Donald Leslie, invited a disgraced former police officer called John Ross into the incident room, which was a serious breach of protocol, especially given DC Leslie was a friend of Sidney Fillery, now one of the suspects.

And John Ross was no ordinary ex-police officer. By this point, he and his brother Michael, another Met detective, ran a wine bar called Briefs, near the Inner London Crown Court, close to Elephant and Castle. They'd bought the bar in 1980 from a South African defence lawyer, Michael Relton, who was later sentenced for 12 years for his part in the laundering of the Brink's-Mat bullion robbery.

At the time both Ross brothers were under investigation for allegations of fitting up two armed robbers and demanding money with menaces. Both were acquitted at an Old Bailey trial in 1982 but sacked from the police after an internal disciplinary hearing.

Five years on, the ex-detectives' wine bar had become a key meeting place for underworld figures and Scotland Yard detectives from SO8, the serious crimes unit, also known as the Flying Squad.

In John Ross' own words: 'The Flying Squad and the robbers used to drink together [in Briefs]. They did the same job. There were no problems because they all earned money out of bank robberies.'[7]

But while Ross made a living out of this exchange of information, there was a third core constituency for his trade – the press.

By the time he entered the Daniel Morgan murder incident room, John Ross was already well established as a tipster on Fleet Street, the go-to man for any information, legitimate or illicit, from the Met. One of his most import-ant contacts was Alex Marunchak, who was now the senior crime reporter at

Britain's best-selling paper, the Sunday tabloid *News of the World*, and about to be made deputy news editor.

Whatever Ross learned from visiting the Daniel Morgan incident room, it never made it to the pages of the newspaper. DC Leslie would be disciplined for the breach of security, but it was too late to stop the leak. Sylvia Jones at the *Daily Mirror*'s news desk was tipped off by a phone call from a Cambridge reporter that police officers were to be arrested over the murder. Southern Investigations' office manager Peter Newby stated that Rees knew of his impending arrest and asked him to warn his wife, Sharon.

April to July 1987

ALASTAIR: Three weeks later another bombshell exploded in our lives. At about eight o'clock one morning I got a call from a friend of John Xavier. 'They've arrested six people over your brother's murder, Alastair!'

'Six people! Who are they?'

'I don't know. I was in my car. I caught the end of a news bulletin on the radio. Your brother was a private investigator, right?'

'Yeah. And this was in London?'

'And your surname's Morgan?'

'It must be Dan. Thanks for ringing, I've got to go!'

I raced to the local newsagent's and bought a copy of every single national newspaper. *The Guardian* reported that three civilians and three police officers had been arrested. I was stunned.

A report in the *Daily Star* named all the men arrested. The civilians were Jonathan Rees and his two brothers-in-law, Glenn and Garry Vian. The report also named the three Met police officers. They'd all been arrested for questioning over their connections with a car auction company! Two of the names were unknown to me. The third was Detective Sergeant Sidney Fillery.

I grabbed the phone and rang Mum. She'd heard the news on television and had phoned the incident room.

'Tony rang me this morning,' Mum said, talking of her former husband, Tony Pearce, who also worked with Daniel and Rees. 'He was first to arrive and when he unlocked the offices, Fillery and this other cop took a black bin-liner and filled it with files and papers from the office. They even took Dan's desk diary.'

'Oh Christ!'

'But it gets worse, Al. I've just spoken to Jane. Do you remember how we were told by the police you were getting in the way of the inquiry? Jane says that the officer who told us to get you out of London was Fillery!'

It made sense. I'd caused real problems with my suspicions about Rees and the Belmont robbery. But before I could put it all together, Mum had more bad news.

'But you ought to know, Al. They've just released them all. All of them, without charge!'

'I'm going to ring Jane, Mum. I've got to speak to her.'

I hung up and rang my sister in Germany.

Jane repeated what she had been told by Iris' brother-in-law when he took the call at Daniel's house. Joe had said Fillery had introduced himself as a 'friend of Daniel' and that he 'was going to move heaven and earth to make sure that the killer was caught'.

Jane explained it was this message about me disrupting the inquiry that had led them to ask me to leave London when I met her and her husband Justin on the street. It had seemed so plausible at the time.

'Who are the Vian brothers, Al?' she asked me.

I explained to her I'd met the Vian brothers only once, soon after Dan and Jon Rees moved to Thornton Heath. Glenn and Garry were the brothers of Rees' wife, Sharon. As far as I knew at the time, they were builders. Dan had introduced them while they were doing some alterations to the offices. Garry barely said hello. Glenn shook my hand and looked as though he wanted to kill me. He looked psychotic and I was glad not to meet him or his brother again.

All I could do was to keep the media informed. I phoned Paul Keel of *The Guardian*, who had reported on the case. Two days later, we met in Petersfield. I told him about my interview with Fillery and his attempt to get me out of London.

'Do you think they'll cover this up, Paul?' I asked him.

'I honestly don't think they will,' he replied.

We were desperate for reassurance. In the space of three weeks, my view of the British police had been smashed to bits.

* * *

Every day I waited for news of progress, but nothing happened and I tried to distract myself with work. But I could think of almost nothing but Dan's murder.

After his arrest, Rees had no contact with us. A couple of weeks later I rang him just to hear his reaction. All he did was demand the £1,000 that Dan had given me shortly before he died to help me set up my window-cleaning business. He told me it was 'company money'. I refused, marvelling at his brazen attitude. He made no attempt to protest his innocence.

The Met were uncommunicative. We rang them constantly, desperate for updates. They gave us nothing that inspired hope.

'We are pursuing a number of lines of inquiry' was all we could get out of them.

At the end of April, police told us that the murder was to feature on the prime-time TV show *Crimewatch*. We waited to be contacted, but no one from the BBC approached us. The programme was scheduled for the middle of May.

I didn't want to watch the programme alone so I went round to a couple of friends to watch it in their company. TV presenter Nick Ross introduced the segment on Daniel.

'This case has been described by police as a "sticker,"' said Ross. He went on to describe the arrest of the three Met coppers, adding carefully that they'd all been released without charge.

Then began a dramatic reconstruction …

I was appalled by the programme's portrayal of my brother. *Crimewatch* used an actor whose only resemblance to Dan was a beard. He also characterised Dan as having a very pronounced limp. Daniel had a club foot, but unless you happened to notice that one of his shoes was smaller than the other, you certainly wouldn't have detected it. He'd even played scrum-half in the school rugby team. No one among the millions watching would recognise him from this reconstruction.

Part of the commentary was voiced-over footage of a shadowy man looking up at a window. Behind a net curtain was the silhouette of a semi-nude woman, suggesting Dan was some sort of Peeping Tom. I was infuriated by this seedy portrayal of Daniel as a man seduced by the glamour of being a private eye. In fact, he found his work anything but glamorous. He used to joke about carrying out surveillance from a cold van and having to pee in a bottle.

I knew straight away that this reconstruction had been designed to mislead the viewers. *Crimewatch* hadn't even spoken to any member of my family. Had the police kept them away from us?

Mum rang *Crimewatch* to complain. A producer replied that they were quite satisfied with their production.

Immediately afterwards, we were told that the programme had provided no significant leads.

* * *

After *Crimewatch*, nothing more seemed to happen. Weeks would go by without the Met contacting us on their own initiative, it was always up to us. We were told that the inquiry was progressing slowly and that there was 'light at the end of the tunnel'.

In July, I rang the murder squad again to express doubt about the integrity of the investigation and Sid Fillery's role. This time I was told that the Met had ordered an internal review of the case by a chief superintendent called Shrubshole. I contacted him and told him that Sid Fillery had tried to get me out of London after my visit to the incident room. He made no comment on this and said that everything was in order and he was satisfied that everything possible had been done to investigate the murder.

In South Norwood, Iris was struggling to bring up the two children, Daniel and Sarah. Fortunately, Dan had taken out life insurance, so they weren't suffering financial hardship.

Iris had told the children that their daddy had died in a car crash. They were still so young that they had no real comprehension of death, let alone murder. But Rees wouldn't even leave them alone in peace. As if she hadn't suffered enough, Iris was being dragged into a compensation claim made by Belmont Auctions.

Because he was Rees' partner, Dan shared Rees' liability for the Belmont Auctions fiasco. There was a civil action by the company and Iris ended up having to pay half of the loss and legal costs, amounting to nearly £20,000. And Dan had been against the Belmont job from the beginning.

But the harassment didn't end there. Dan had begun to store his renovated Austin Healey 3000 in a garage owned by a friend of the mother of the Vian brothers. Iris told me that sometime after the murder she'd rung her to get the car back. The woman had told her that she'd 'paid some gypsies £10 to clear out her garage' and that the car was no longer there.

Not content with making his widow liable for their activities, criminals from the Rees and Vian circle had also stolen Dan's car – worth at least £6,000 in its restored condition – and the twenty-first birthday present for his daughter. I felt sick with rage when Iris told me: Sarah would never get the car that her father had intended for her.

* * *

In the first few months after Daniel's death Jane told me she was glad she didn't have to work as she was crying all the time. But having only recently moved, she had few friends and was lonely.

After a few months, she managed to find herself a job with a coach company that travelled to Britain twice a week. She could speak enough German to explain to passengers where they should go on the ferry, serve the tea and coffee on the coach and interpret for the two drivers.

Every month there would be a trip to Wales and Jane would get paid £100 for the run. She would get into Cardiff about 2pm and take the train to Abergavenny, where Mum would pick her up. It meant they got to spend an afternoon and a night together.

Mum lived in a stone cottage attached to the grounds of the hotel that she and her husband Peter worked in. It was some time before she felt able to go back to work as a waitress and chambermaid. In those first months she was still getting a lot of calls from the media. Although she told me there were a few who were kind and treated her with respect, there were others who were pushy and aggressive, always wanting to know how she felt.

'How do they bloody well think I feel?' she said tersely.

Jane was worried about how Mum was coping. The coach trips to Cardiff were irregular and although it was exhausting, she made sure she bagged all the journeys she could.

On one trip, Mum told Jane about an incident that haunted her. She had been shopping and was on her way back to start a shift at the hotel, driving down the long bendy roads that lead to the hotel. The road is edged by a wall. As she turned a corner, she saw Dan sitting on the wall. But when she passed the place he was sitting, Dan was gone. It was then that she heard a voice saying, 'Don't go; wait, Mum.' She really believed she'd seen him.

These imagined sightings were becoming more frequent. Mum would often tell me when I rang that she'd thought she'd seen Dan in town. She would hurry after some man, only realising when she got closer that it couldn't be him because he had a bald patch or was too tall. I knew this often happened to people soon after losing someone; it had happened to me too. But Mum would have dreams where she could hear Dan talking and see him walking around with the axe in his head. Sometimes she would be awake and convinced she was with him. Other times she would be asleep and wake up screaming.

She had a recurring dream in which Daniel was in the morgue. Mum had once worked as a nursing assistant and part of her job was to take bodies up to the 'night parlour'. She knew how the bodies were numbered and stored in drawers. She hated this dream where she saw Dan in a drawer or being pushed around like a piece of meat.

None of the family had been allowed to see Daniel's body. We understood why we couldn't: his injuries were too horrific and his body had been in the morgue for four months by order of the coroner. Mum thought these hideous dreams and hallucinations might stop when his body was finally laid to rest, and so she kept ringing the coroner's office to find out what was happening.

In July 1987, the coroner's office finally told her that Daniel's body would be released.

Media Management

May to July 1987

The Morgan family were right to suspect that the BBC *Crimewatch* episode about Daniel Morgan's murder had been undermined. Apart from a standard briefing from the murder squad, the producers of the drama reconstruction had interviewed Daniel's former business partner, Jonathan Rees. The prime suspect in the murder had provided the characterisation of the victim.

The reconstruction also edited out from the dialogue Daniel's key parting words to Rees at the office: 'I'm off. See you at the Golden Lion at 7:30.'[1]

Meanwhile, released without charge, Fillery, Purvis and Foley met with Rees at a pub in Orpington the day after the BBC1 *Crimewatch* broadcast. All three police officers arrested on suspicion of involvement in the murder agreed the actor looked 'just like Rees' and the actor for Daniel 'looked just like him as well'.[2]

Despite its unrecognisable caricature of Daniel, the *Crimewatch* appeal did actually elicit some new information, which suggested a completely different motive.

A couple of weeks before the broadcast, an anonymous male had called the incident room claiming, 'It's 100% that Jon Rees is involved,' adding that Rees set it up with his brother-in-law, 'the big geezer with the ginger hair'. The anonymous tipster also talked about Daniel's missing Rolex. 'Rees done the business with the watch,' he continued. And what was the source of his information? 'I overheard it at the Harp.'

The Harp, after the Victory, was one of Rees' favourite pubs. It was close to the homes of his brothers-in-law, Garry and Glenn Vian, and a relative of theirs owned the house next door.

Another woman rang up soon after, claiming 'one or two nights before it happened' Rees was in the Harp pub in Croydon 'with two other people,

bragging about the fact he was going to fit up Danny'. The caller said she knew the people involved and Rees needed the firm to collect 'ten or 20 grand', which he owed someone. Asked if she was sure, the caller said, 'I'm positive' and then hung up. There's no paper trail to show police followed up these two tip-offs.

Seven weeks after the prime-time broadcast, on 10th June, a woman who would only be identified as 'Doreen' called the Morgan incident room at 8:20pm, saying she had information that 'Jon Rees is involved in heavy drugs and Morgan was going to tell and that's why he was killed'.

PC Karine Rowan was immediately dispatched to meet 'Doreen' at east Croydon railway station. Twenty minutes later, she encountered a woman with collar-length brown hair and they walked to the nearby Greyhound pub to talk.

Claiming to be a married mother of two teenage children, 'Doreen' said she worked in east Croydon and lived only 20 minutes away from Southern Investigations. Though she refused to reveal how she had come by the information, 'Doreen' claimed Rees was 'heavily involved' in trafficking drugs, mainly cocaine, and that he was dealing with some 'very heavy people', a 'drugs ring' that included a well-known south London gangster, Joey Pyle, a member of the infamous East End Kray crime family, and that the drugs importation involved Spain and America.

Though she didn't know who had wielded the axe, 'Doreen' repeated what she had said on the phone, that Daniel was killed because he was going to 'do something'. She promised to ring the next day after work with more information, but never called back.

* * *

Though the police failed to keep tabs on this potential informant, the suggestion of a drugs link should not have come as a surprise.

The implication Daniel was planning to expose something much bigger than an £18,000 scam was already being relayed to the murder team. A gangland driver with a connection to the Kray crime family had suggested to a friend of the solicitor Michael Goodridge that if Daniel 'didn't keep his nose out, he'd be topped' a week *before* the murder. But this was both hearsay, and hard to track back to contemporaneous evidence.

More reliable tip-offs came to the inquiry from two other police officers: Glasgow-born Detective John Davidson (known to his friends as 'OJ' – short

for 'Obnoxious Jock') and Detective Constable Alan Holmes (nicknamed 'Taffy' because of his Welsh origins), who lived in south London and were part of the extensive Freemason network among police officers.

Both detectives worked out of the serious crimes unit and task force based at Tottenham Court Road – SO7 and SO8. The squads had been investigating one of Britain's biggest-ever heists, the Brink's-Mat robbery in 1983, which had netted the armed robbers many millions in gold bullion. But they were also looking at a spate of international drugs deals.

Holmes and Davidson were then working on a project called the 'Collection Plan' involving a cross border investigation into drugs smuggling into the UK, mainly via Spain. Like the Drugs Enforcement Agency, Scotland Yard's serious crimes units were using tracking devices and Air Force Nimrod planes to follow shipments to the British coast.

Two of the investigations, Operation Concorde and Operation Wimpey, involved an 'Eric Clapton lookalike' called James 'Jimmy' Holmes (no relation to Alan 'Taffy' Holmes). Four years earlier, Jimmy Holmes had been arrested in possession of a substantial amount of cannabis but had been acquitted in a trial in 1984 with the help of evidence from Jonathan Rees' brothers-in-law, Garry and Glenn Vian.

In November 1986, surveillance for Operation Wimpey had noted vehicles going to Jimmy Holmes' house. These led directly back to Garry Vian, who, intelligence reports suggested, was trading in cocaine and heroin with Joseph 'Joey' Pyle – the south London gangster mentioned by 'Doreen', the *Crimewatch* witness.

Joey Pyle had more than one connection with Rees and Southern Investigations. Jimmy Cook, a scrap dealer with a HiAb crane lorry, which could remove vehicles, who helped the private investigators with car repossessions, was reported to be a close associate of his. Though it was not thought significant at the time, Rees had called Cook on the Sunday before Daniel's murder.

In the police argot of the time, Jimmy Holmes was still 'on the bell' – his phones were being tapped – and the Flying Squad officers urgently contacted the Morgan murder inquiry with information from a phone call between Jimmy Holmes and Garry Vian in which they discussed the murder of Daniel Morgan.

In their phone call, Vian and Holmes apparently talked about Joey Pyle, who had reportedly travelled to the US around the time of Daniel's murder

because he believed he was wanted as a suspect. Pyle was, they suggested, currently trying to check his status with his police 'contacts'.

* * *

Another line of investigation open to the murder inquiry was to try to turn some of Rees' many police pals against him. One of these operations gave the team a new insight into Rees' media-management techniques, and how he used his press contacts to attempt to derail the first murder investigation.

Detective Constable Duncan Hanrahan had known Jonathan Rees and Daniel Morgan for a couple of years. He was attached to Norbury CID, and had investigated the robbery of the Belmont Car Auctions cash from Rees outside his house. Hanrahan also said that Rees was also providing information into drug dealing before Daniel's death. (A year later, at the inquest, this investigation was not disclosed to the coroner's jury because there were 'still investigations going on'.[3])

By March 1987, Hanrahan had been moved to Kennington Police Station. He was told about Daniel's killing by Michael Goodridge, the solicitor who had introduced him to Rees, the morning after it happened when they met at Croydon Magistrates' Court.

On the day of Rees' arrest in April, Detective Superintendent Campbell approached Hanrahan as a known drinking partner of the private detective, since he'd been spotted in the Victory with Rees and another friendly local detective, Detective Sergeant Alec Leighton. They developed an 'understanding': Hanrahan was tasked to 'be friendly with Mr Rees and report back to Mr Campbell'.[4] In short, he became an undercover informant for the murder investigation.

Initially the team discussed putting a concealed tape recorder on Hanrahan, but Campbell rejected the idea because Rees was 'conversant with all methods of detection' and checking the Norbury detective for wires would be 'stock in trade' for him. Instead, Hanrahan's role as a double agent was to relay back verbal reports that soon revealed Rees was simmering with resentment.

By late May Rees was refusing to cooperate with the murder inquiry and openly stating that he didn't care who had killed Daniel. Rees had suggested various motives and suspects to the police, including a local drug dealer and even Iris Morgan, but for some reason the murder inquiry had not placed much value on his information. At a pub in South Norwood, Rees told Hanrahan how he planned to have his revenge on the two lead murder investigators.

Unaware his plans would be passed back to the murder squad, Rees told Hanrahan that Fillery could provide the 'dirt' on the lead investigator.[5] Rees planned to get a 'journalist friend' to write about Campbell and Jones, claiming they were both 'constantly drunk' and that Jones was having an extramarital affair.[6] (At the inquest Hanrahan did not reveal who this journalist friend was, but other witnesses attest Rees was already close to Alex Marunchak at the *News of the World* at this point and was in contact with the *Daily Mirror*.)

Nothing of this nature appeared in the papers, but Rees' desire for revenge increased when he was arrested for drink driving in August while ferrying around his mother-in-law Patricia Vian, her partner Andrew Docherty, and his friend, former Detective Chief Inspector Laurie Bucknole. He was fined £150 and disqualified from driving for a year.

Feeling persecuted, Rees planned to do something more serious than just harm the reputations of the two lead investigating officers. Hanrahan reported back that Rees was planning to actively destroy DI Alan Jones' career by having him 'fitted up' with drugs planted in his car.

Though Rees' plans for this particular drug fit-up never materialised, he did have some success with his media campaign. He spoke to both to the *London Evening News* on 13th August and the *Croydon Comet* on 20th August about the 'leads' the investigation weren't following up, and how they were harassing him instead.

Through his press contacts, Rees managed to persuade a local journalist to write a story about a drug dealer's minder whose house was raided, and a large axe discovered.

* * *

Within a week of the murder, another police officer, PC Derek Haslam, contacted the murder inquiry with information about a possible press story. Haslam knew both Daniel and Rees, and had worked with the senior investigating officer on the Morgan murder team before. Within a week of the axe killing, he went to DSU Campbell with information that Daniel might have been about to blow the whistle on a drugs importation and 'sell a story of high-level police corruption'.[7]

The source of this story was none other than DC Alan 'Taffy' Holmes, the detective involved in surveillance on a drug dealer connected to the Vians.

Six weeks before Daniel's death, early in 1987, Haslam claims he met Taffy Holmes at a curry house in Thornton Heath. During the meal, he recalled Holmes saying he had come across a potential conspiracy involving senior police officers, customs officials, and a multi-million pound drugs importation of cocaine from Miami, which he was going to sell to the press for £250,000.

Derek Haslam remembered doubting the wisdom of such a move, but Holmes explained: 'Daniel was doing the negotiations with a Sunday newspaper.' Haslam dismissed the figure as fanciful, and forgot about it until Daniel was murdered. Then he went to see the lead investigator on the first Morgan murder inquiry, DSU Campbell.

Though both Haslam and Campbell agreed the fee for the alleged corruption story was unlikely, the lead investigator did take the suggestion seriously enough to talk to the 'newspaper' in question – though he never explained to the inquest jury which newspaper that was.[8]

In the fog of a difficult murder investigation, one allegation about a huge press exposé of police corruption might have been ignored. But within a month of Haslam's tip-off, in May 1987, the inquiry team had independent corroboration.

Bryan Madagan, the owner of the Croydon-based detective agency where Daniel Morgan and Jonathan Rees had worked, made his own statement that chimed perfectly with Haslam's. Madagan said he'd met up with Daniel in December 1986 at the Cricketers pub in Southridge, where his former employee declared: 'I've just hit the jackpot!'

Daniel went on to say he was selling a story of police corruption for £¼m to a Sunday newspaper. (In later statements Madagan would specify which paper and which journalist Daniel claimed he was speaking to.)

The suggestion Daniel was hawking around Fleet Street some story of 'police officers engaged in illegal activities' was also backed up by the evidence from his former stepfather, Tony Pearce, and Peter Newby, his office manager.

Three detectives on the Morgan murder squad followed up these allegations of a major exposé of police corruption: DC Kinley Davies, DC Noel Cosgrave and DC Michael Crofts. They established that Daniel Morgan had been to '*Private Eye* and another paper' and expected to get £10,000 for his story. They also tried to contact one of Daniel's known media contacts, Anton Antonovicz at the *Daily Mirror*.

They then found a third witness to corroborate Haslam and Madagan. Peter 'Wilkie' Wilkins, the former cop who worked for Southern Investigations, also told the detectives that Daniel 'had a story of major police corruption and was going to sell it to the press'. Wilkins claimed that Daniel was in contact 'with an investigative journalist from a Fleet Street "Sunday"'. And Wilkins was in a position to know: his friend was a neighbour of the then assistant editor of the *Daily Mirror*, Nicholas Fullagar.

Interviewed by the murder team, Fullagar said that Rees had been introduced to him by Peter Wilkins, and sold him a couple of stories, but the assistant editor had only spoken to Daniel once, by accident, when he called Southern Investigations to speak to Rees, who was out. Fullagar said Daniel had 'ranted and raved' that Rees was trying to 'stitch him up'. Fullagar did claim, however, that Daniel had been in touch with another reporter at the paper, Sylvia Jones.

After the murder, Jonathan Rees called Nicholas Fullagar again, trying to sell him his version of the murder investigation, claiming it had ruined his business, but never expressed any 'regret, sorrow or concern' over his partner's death.

Armed with this new information, in June 1987 DCs Davies and Crofts suggested that the murder of Daniel Morgan was connected to a major story of police corruption involving Taffy Holmes, Ray Adams and the multi-million pound Brink's-Mat bullion robbery in 1983. A publican in Shirley, who knew both Crofts and Wilkins, recalled them talking about how Daniel was going to the newspapers and thought 'the murder was something to do with Kenneth Noye paying off policemen'.

The allegations were taken seriously enough by their senior officer, DSU Campbell, that they were told to circulate them on high-priority green forms.

Far from being rewarded for their diligence, that summer Cosgrave, Davies and Crofts were all dropped from the murder inquiry.

| The Broken Harp

August 1987

ALASTAIR: Our two families and some close friends waited nervously in the hallway of Dan and Iris' house for the hearse and cortège cars to take us to the South Norwood Methodist chapel.

It was a sweltering August day and I remember stepping outside the front door with my sister Jane to see if the hearse was approaching. My jaw dropped as I saw what appeared to be a lager advertisement on four wheels rolling sedately up the street. On its roof, the hearse carried a giant harp made of yellow and white daffodils. It was so huge and grotesque that I felt like crying. I heard Jane say: 'Oh God, please somebody take it off the roof! It looks like a bloody carnival float.' Then she laughed through her tears and said Dan would have seen the ridiculous side of it.

How had it got there? Later, we found out that it was donated by the patrons of a Croydon pub named the Harp: this place was to become very significant to the investigation in the future.

Dumbstruck by the garish display, we took our seats in the cars behind the hearse. Minutes later, we were standing on the pavement outside the chapel. Jane hated the idea of Daniel's coffin being borne by strangers – she wanted family members and friends to carry it into the chapel. The funeral director showed us how to shoulder the coffin.

As he was speaking, I caught sight of Jon Rees and another man about 20 yards down the street to my right. Rees looked edgy, puffing on a cigarette. It was obvious that this was the last place on earth that he wanted to be.

I turned my attention to the coffin as it slid smoothly out of the hearse. Jane's husband, Justin, my mother's husband Peter, me and two family friends shouldered the coffin and climbed the steps of the chapel.

I could smell Dan's corpse in the heat as I carried the cask. His body had been in a mortuary for the best part of six months. All I wanted to do was to

sit down and weep. I kept going long enough to carry the coffin to the front of the chapel.

We lowered the coffin onto two trestles and I took my seat in the front row next to my mother and sister. Mum handed me a handkerchief. The organ music stopped and the vicar began speaking.

'We're gathered here today to celebrate the life of Daniel John Morgan.'

I turned around discreetly and saw Rees sitting with another man right at the back of the congregation.

The vicar continued his funeral oration. He wasn't sombre or solemn, he spoke about Dan's life, his upbringing and family, his wife and two children and the things that he loved, like rugby, woodworking and classic cars, reminding us fleetingly of the happy things in Dan's existence. He then read a short Bible text and we sang 'The Lord is My Shepherd'.

When it was over, I noticed that Jonathan Rees had already left. I could see no sign of him as we walked out of the chapel, blinking in the hot summer sunlight.

'Did you see him?' I asked my mother.

'Who … Rees? *No!* Was he here? God, what a nerve!'

'He had to, Mum,' I replied. 'He's got to keep up the front of the grieving partner.'

The ordeal wasn't over: we still had to bury Dan. We drove through the large cemetery gates, a few miles from South Norwood, and along a broad tree-lined avenue. About 50 metres away was a neat pile of earth next to a newly dug grave. This time the professional bearers took over. They carried the oak coffin over the grass and placed it on two short planks. The vicar said the things that vicars say at burials about ashes and dust and hope and resurrection. The bearers then lowered the coffin slowly into the hole in the ground.

Jane and Mum had brought some white roses and threw them onto the coffin. Mum had written a little quote: 'Age shall not weary them, nor the years condemn' from Laurence Binyon's poem, 'For the Fallen'.

We stood there silently for what felt like an eternity. Then we turned away. When I looked back the gravediggers were already beginning to use their shovels.

We left Dan in that hole in the dark brown London earth. All I could think of was that my brother was lying in a polished oak box and that I would never see him again. Five months after his murder, the men who had cut short his life were still walking the streets of London.

| Double Cross

July to December 1987

While Daniel Morgan was buried in a reinforced coffin so that his body could be exhumed at a later date if needed, the investigation into his murder did make one crucial breakthrough in the summer of 1987.

The information came from Kevin Lennon, the Irish-born bookkeeper who helped found Southern Investigations. He had filed and signed the paperwork at Companies House when Daniel Morgan and Jonathan Rees set up their new partnership in 1983. Lennon looked after their company accounts for Southern Investigations for the next four years.

The 43-year-old bookkeeper was mainly Rees' friend and confidante, and thought Daniel was loud and boorish, and a bit of a liability to the private detective agency.[1] However, Lennon also said in three sworn statements that his friend Rees wanted to kill Daniel. It took several months and various covert recording devices to obtain these statements.

Lennon's first statement to the murder inquiry team, on 2nd April 1987, did not implicate anyone in the Daniel Morgan murder. At the time Lennon had been charged with involvement in a £500,000 tax fraud involving Tax Exemption Certificates. He'd been remanded in custody in early February 1987 pending trial, and only bailed the day before his first interview. (Rees had helped get hold of the £70,000 needed in sureties to get Lennon out of jail.) At that point he made a 'short non-committal witness statement'.

Four months later, Detective Superintendent Campbell and Detective Inspector Alan Jones were approached by Laurie Bucknole. The former DCI (who had introduced Rees to both Fillery and Lennon) had an extraordinary piece of intelligence about Rees from the bookkeeper.

Bucknole told the murder investigators that Lennon had revealed to him, over dinner at the Mythos restaurant in Thornton Heath in April 1986, that

Rees was actively trying to have Daniel assassinated. This was just after the Belmont robbery, and almost a year before the murder happened.

Because Lennon had not mentioned this in his statement, and would clearly be a reluctant witness, Bucknole agreed to wear a wire the next time he met the bookkeeper to see if he could extract the information and record it on tape.

The meeting took place on 28th July and Bucknole managed to get Lennon to repeat the allegation: Rees had been asking him to help in the assassination of Daniel Morgan a year before it happened.

Just over three weeks later, on 21st August, Campbell and Jones cornered Lennon. At first he denied implicating Rees in his conversations with Bucknole but when the police officers played back part of the taped conversation with Bucknole, Lennon capitulated.

In two statements on 4th and 15th September 1987, Lennon outlined a long-term plot to murder Daniel. According to Lennon, Rees' animosity towards Daniel had reached breaking point within two years of their partnership. By 1985, Lennon recalled Rees was planning to get Daniel arrested for drink driving. The loss of a driving licence would have been devastating for Daniel, who spent most of his time travelling and 'would have meant he could no longer perform as a partner'.[2]

Drinking on one occasion at the Victory, the small pub around the corner from Southern Investigations' office, Rees told Lennon he had arranged to take Daniel out of action with the help of his friends at Norbury Police Station that very night.

'When Danny drives away from here tonight, he'll be breathalysed,' said Rees. A broken tail light on Daniel's car, showing white rather than red, would give the police an excuse to stop him, test his alcohol levels and prosecute him for drink driving. For some reason, this never happened. But by early 1986, Lennon claimed, a far more permanent way of putting Daniel out of business was planned.

'Jon began to dislike Daniel more and more. This dislike turned to hatred,' Lennon recalled. Rees began to discuss ways of getting his business partner murdered on 'at least half a dozen occasions'.[3] Indeed, Lennon was so concerned about Rees' plot to kill his partner by this point that he finally told Laurie Bucknole about it at the Mythos restaurant in Croydon the April just after the Belmont robbery.[4]

Rees didn't give up on his plan. In August 1986, a well-known south London criminal whose car Daniel had repossessed called at the office and promised to break Daniel's legs. Rees was 'elated' about this, Lennon claimed, 'because the man could then be identified and connected with Daniel's death'.[5] There were 'a number of people who could be used in a similar fashion,' Lennon recalled Rees saying.[6]

A month later, in September, Rees had a change of heart. 'Forget about arranging his death,' he told Lennon 'I've the perfect solution for Daniel's murder. My mates at Catford nick are going to arrange it.' Either the local crime squad would kill Daniel or 'arrange for some other person over whom they had a criminal charge pending to carry out Daniel's murder and in return police proceedings would be dropped.'[7]

Rees said the murder would be carried out in the jurisdiction of Catford Police Station so local officers could 'suppress any information linking the murder with Jon Rees or themselves'.[8]

It was clear to Lennon that involving the Catford crime squad in the plot could be the beginning of an excellent business opportunity. Not only would it help Rees rid himself of his troublesome co-director, but also provide him 'with this new prospective partner who would be, in his opinion, a much greater asset to the business'.

The new plan was that Rees' great friend, Sidney Fillery, would 'take Morgan's place after his death'. Fillery would 'get an ill health pension or a medical discharge' before joining the private investigations company as his new partner.[9]

Lennon was left in no doubt that Rees was serious about his plan and happy to have police backup. He 'was so pleased with the situation which was now becoming resolved', Lennon observed, since 'the arrangements had been finalised with the officers from Catford'.

In one of his last admissions to police in 1987, Lennon also claimed that Rees had discussed his plan to have Morgan killed with his wife, Sharon.

* * *

Armed with this explosive witness statement by Lennon, the Daniel Morgan murder team decided to use the same covert recording technique that had entrapped Lennon to extract some kind of confession from Rees.

On Thursday, 26th November 1987, DI Jones broke the seal of a new tape that was then put in a tape recorder secreted under Lennon's shirt. The tape was turned on around 1:25pm to catch Lennon's conversation with Rees as he met him at the pub.

It was a cold November day. Lennon met Rees at a pub, ordering a pint of Guinness at the bar with several 'unidentified males'. The conversation revolved around TV shows like *Fawlty Towers* and *Coronation Street* and the perils of lighting Christmas puddings with brandy. One of those present appeared to be a police officer, regaling Rees and Lennon with tales of drunkenness and sexism among Croydon police officers.[10]

It was only after several hours of chat that Rees and Lennon finally drove back to the offices of Southern Investigations to discuss the murder. Over coffee, Lennon explained how a detective from internal affairs, CIB 2, wanted to interview the bookkeeper over his payments to serving officers for the Belmont Car Auctions work.

'Well, what they're saying is that me and the three officers that were locked up with me, plus Duncan Hanrahan ... and Alec Leighton,' Rees explained to Lennon. 'Six of us ... did the robbery. We stole the £18,000 ... Daniel found out about it and so we killed him,' was the theory internal affairs was pursing.

Rees dismissed this as a motive for the murder. The £18,000 from the robbery would be split six ways, which meant each of the three serving officers would only receive £3,000 each, while their annual salaries were around £20,000: 'So we're all gonna put our good name and careers and livelihood at risk for a lousy fucking three thousand pounds?' Rees mocked. 'It's a load of fucking shit and nonsense.'

However, Rees did admit to being in constant contact with Sid Fillery: 'Yeah, I keep in contact with him regular,' he told Lennon. 'It's me feeding them with the fucking information all the time.'

The theory that Rees had killed Daniel to 'protect Old Bill' was discussed at length. Rees said he was regularly approached by Met detectives offering to do Police National Computer or criminal record checks for Southern Investigations. Some of the officers were panicking, but Fillery was keeping them on side by telling them, 'we put our backs to him and fight the enemy coming on. Jon Rees is a fucking wall.'

Though hardly the words of a man with a clear conscience, there was no clear-cut self-incriminating statement from Rees, so Lennon was sent once again to covertly record Rees six days later – this time he went to the slightly quieter location of his family home.

Over cups of tea, Rees was less talkative. Though he probed the bookkeeper for the current state of the murder investigation (especially the police's interest in his many phone calls to Margaret Harrison), Rees gave away little except to advise Lennon to complain to his solicitor about police harassment before the inevitable trip to the pub.

Once tea had been replaced by Guinness, Rees became a little more expansive, admitting that he had had 'a little fling' with Margaret Harrison. Again, Rees boasted about his ability to undermine the lead murder investigators by planting material about their private lives to the press, and claimed he was in discussions with the *Sunday Times* to do a profile of himself.

Rees also admitted that by this time in December he had 'done the deal' with Sid Fillery, whose brother was already employed by Southern Investigations.

'Yeah, he's trying to work his ticket, isn't he?' Rees said of Fillery's sick leave for depression. 'Doing the mental bit, you know … If you go on sick, they stick an extra three years on top so they give him his full twenty-five … Gets £700 a month pension. Plus, you get a lump sum all the time.'

Ironically, Fillery was 'absolutely delighted' about the national press coverage of his arrest, Rees argued, since that gave him a perfect alibi to go on leave for depression and eventually leave the force entirely: 'very senior policemen… said to him, said to Sid, they've handed you a fucking open cheque'.

Though the secret recording confirms Fillery's long-term plan to join Rees as a business partner, Lennon could extract no repetition of their previous conversations at the Victory about having Daniel killed. Indeed, Rees dismissed the idea of a 'contract killing' as 'absolute bollocks'.

It appears Rees may have been tipped off about someone trying to 'tape him up' and was spotted weeping in the offices of Southern Investigations. Lennon believed he had been exposed by someone still working in the murder team.

Meanwhile, Sid Fillery, who had served as a police officer for nearly 23 years, and had been 'off-duty, certificated sick' for exactly a year, was finally discharged from the police force on 20th March 1988 suffering from depression.

CHAPTER 12

First Anniversary

November 1987 to March 1988

ALASTAIR: By November of the year my brother was murdered we were desperate. No progress had been made and we suspected a cover-up. I'd heard from Alan Jones on the telephone that CIB 2, the Met's Complaints Investigation Branch, was scrutinising the three officers who'd been arrested in April.

CIB 2 was based in Tintagel House on the south bank of the Thames, near Vauxhall Bridge. One day I decided to visit to see what I could find out.

Tintagel House was within walking distance of Waterloo station. Detective Chief Inspector Ernie Anderson came down to Reception to meet me. He led me to a lift and we rode up several floors to his office.

'Superintendent Campbell was here a few days ago,' he said in the lift. 'Mr Campbell's a very worried man.'

'Why's that then?' I asked, intrigued by his opening remark.

'Have you ever heard of double jeopardy?'

Anderson explained that if CIB 2 brought disciplinary charges against Fillery or the other two policemen, the murder squad wouldn't be able to charge them with a criminal offence.

'Campbell doesn't want that,' said Anderson. He added that CIB 2 were investigating discrepancies in the arrested officers' notebooks but he wasn't willing to elaborate. After about half an hour he suggested that we go up to the canteen. We ate with a spectacular view over the Thames. After lunch we continued talking. An hour or so later, he glanced at his watch and told me his shift had ended. Reaching under his desk, he pulled out a leather briefcase and produced a bottle of Famous Grouse whisky.

'One for the road?' he suggested.

I can't recall much of the conversation after beginning our drinks. I do remember Anderson suggesting that 'perhaps the good Lord didn't want the

case to be solved' and wondered whether 'the good Lord' was a reference to the police establishment. We drank a lot of whisky and I left Tintagel House somewhat the worse for wear.

A week or so later, I visited *The Sunday Times*. David Leppard from the *Insight* team met me at reception. I told him that I felt certain there was police involvement in Daniel's murder, thinking this was a sensational revelation. But David reacted phlegmatically, almost as if this was quite an ordinary occurrence. I was hoping that *The Sunday Times* would investigate the case and he said that he would see what he could do. Leppard seemed nervous, however, about being overheard and wanted to move when a cleaner started working nearby.

I thought his paranoia odd but I had no clue that, by this time, Rees and Fillery were doing a roaring trade with *The Sunday Times'* sister newspaper, the best-selling Sunday tabloid, the *News of the World*.

* * *

Soon after New Year, the Met informed us that the coroner was going to hold an inquest. We were worried as this suggested that the murder investigation had ground to a halt. In an attempt to reassure us, we were told that the inquest could provide valuable evidence as witnesses would be questioned under oath. Mum contacted a local solicitor, Glyn Maddox, to arrange legal representation. Glyn contacted the charity Inquest, who helped us fund this.

Later, Mum rang to say that she'd been in contact with a Tory MP called Roger Gail. She said he was sympathetic, so I telephoned him to discuss the case. He asked me to write a letter and send it to him. As a matter of protocol, he said he'd have to forward the letter to my own MP, Michael Mates.

In my letter, I'd described Fillery's attempt to get me out of London and the circumstances surrounding the murder. I expected a prompt reply but after a month I'd heard nothing at all. I wrote again to Michael Mates. He replied that my letter had been 'lost in the post' and that he'd sent it that day to the Commissioner. A month later I'd heard nothing so I wrote again to Mates. He wrote back, saying that he'd sent the Metropolitan Police Commissioner, Sir Peter Imbert, a reminder.

In February, I received a call from DI Alan Jones, telling me that Fillery had been interviewed again about the murder but that he'd used his right to silence and had refused to answer any questions.

In a way Fillery's silence incensed me more than Rees'. As a member of the murder squad I felt that Fillery should be obliged to explain his actions. But that was not how the law worked. The 'right to silence' had been raised by the home secretary of the time, Kenneth Clarke. It was a matter of public debate so I wrote a letter to *The Daily Telegraph* using Dan's case as an example.

Soon after this Alan Jones told me that Fillery had been discharged from the Met on medical grounds. I told him that this was exactly what I'd expected. Jones told me that this 'stuck in his craw too', but that there was nothing he or anyone else could do about it.

* * *

The first anniversary of Dan's murder was looming and Mum wanted to visit the grave with flowers. I hadn't been to the cemetery since the funeral, but Mum went whenever she was visiting her grandchildren in London and drew some comfort from it. But I didn't feel the same way. I was still fighting to find out what had happened – I wasn't ready to grieve yet.

We travelled up to stay with Iris on 9th March and visited the grave the following day. On the way back I picked up the *Evening Standard*. There was an article about Daniel. The headline read 'NEW BID TO SOLVE MURDER'.

The article said the police were to stage a reconstruction and appeal for witnesses at the Golden Lion that evening. It went on to say 'Morgan, 37, appeared to be a successful private detective with a profitable business. But the murder investigation has revealed he was a sexual braggart with dozens of enemies'.

I got straight on to the *Evening Standard* from a call box near South Norwood station. The receptionist put me through to the journalist who'd written the article. I told him politely that I thought the article was deeply offensive.

He said that he was sorry, but this description of Dan had been given to him by the police.

'By the police?'

'That's right.'

'You didn't get it from his partner?'

'No, I got that description from the police.'

'You mean the murder squad?'

'Yes.'

'Who in the murder squad?'

'I can't remember. It was just someone from the squad that I spoke to.'

I rang the incident room at once. Malcolm Davidson answered.

'Thanks for telling us about the reconstruction, Malcolm,' I said pointedly.

'Oh, haven't you been told?'

'No, we haven't been told.'

'Apologies for that. I thought you would have been told.'

'Well, we weren't. Just like when you made the arrests last year, we found out through the media. And there's one other thing. The article in the *Evening Standard* describes my brother as "a sexual braggart with dozens of enemies". The journalist who wrote it said that he'd got that quote from the murder squad. This is deeply prejudicial only weeks before an inquest. Can you explain this?'

'I can certainly say that the quote didn't come from us.'

'Really?' I didn't believe him.

'No, not from us.'

'Well, I'll be coming along to the reconstruction tonight. You can tell your colleagues, I'll be there.'

I had no doubt that the *Evening Standard* guy was telling me the truth about where they got the information. The info would certainly have come through the Met's press office.

It seemed odd, since the police were appealing for witnesses to come forward in Dan's murder, that he should be painted in such derogatory terms. It would hardly weigh on the conscience of someone who had seen something if they believed my brother was a scumbag. Did they really want to catch Dan's killers?

There were several police officers in the pub when I arrived at the Golden Lion. I recognised Alan Jones at once. He pointed out to me that Doug Campbell was also present.

This was the first time I'd ever seen the man in charge of the inquiry. I introduced myself, but he seemed distant and aloof. Journalists from the local media were also at the pub, including a woman from Capital Radio. I gave a couple of press interviews and one for broadcast on the radio.

Afterwards I sat and talked to Alan Jones. He told me that he'd just come back to work after being ordered by his doctor to take time off. He said my former stepfather, Tony Pearce, was drinking heavily and that Jonathan Rees was giving him a bottle of vodka a day to keep him drunk.

Tony was a troubled man. His marriage to my mother had ended ten years earlier because of his alcoholism, but they had remained on good terms. Daniel had recognised that he was an expert in some areas of law and gave him a responsible job and actively encouraged him to stay sober. Before Dan was killed, Tony had been sober for months. Alan Jones told me that Tony was now a complete wreck but still working for Rees. I was worried for his health and personal safety.

No witnesses had come forward and the evening was an anti-climax. I returned to Iris' house and listened to my interview on Capital Radio.

* * *

Next morning, I knew I had to try to find Tony Pearce. I couldn't phone him at the office – I didn't want Rees to know. But I expected Tony to visit a pub at lunchtime, so I took a seat in a local café from where I could watch the front door of Southern Investigations.

I drank coffee for the best part of an hour. Nobody entered or left the building so I decided to look inside the Victory pub just round the corner.

When I entered, there was Jonathan Rees chatting to a couple of drinkers at the bar. Everyone stopped talking in a general atmosphere of awkwardness.

Rees perked up and addressed me: 'Hello, Alastair, fancy a drink?'

I decided to play it cool and go along with him.

'I'll have a Carlsberg, Jon,' I said as I walked over to the bar.

'I've just come back from Yorkshire,' Rees continued. 'Had a couple of weeks away with the wife. You're looking pale, Alastair.'

I'd obviously blanched at the shock of seeing him. Rees nodded towards a man standing next to him. 'This is a mate of mine, Derek,' he said. 'Derek, this is Alastair.'

I shook hands with Derek, a man in his thirties with dark, curly hair. Rees turned back to me.

'I've just got to nip back to the office for five minutes,' he said. 'I've got some business I need to deal with.' He put down his glass and left the bar.

'So you're Daniel's brother?' said Derek.

'Yes, I am,' I replied. 'And if you don't mind me saying so, you're keeping bad company. The man who just walked out of here was involved in murdering him.'

Derek raised an eyebrow, apparently surprised at what I had said.

'What are you doing here with him?' I asked.

'He's lost his licence for drink driving and I've been driving him around today,' Derek told me.

I asked him when Rees had lost his licence. He told me this had happened a few months earlier. I found a scrap of paper, borrowed his pen and wrote down my telephone number.

'You spend quite a bit of time with Rees,' I said. 'If you see or hear anything that might be helpful, give me a ring.'

Derek tucked the piece of paper into his jacket pocket. Rees appeared again at the bar door.

'So, house prices are still rising in Hampshire?' Derek deftly switched the subject of conversation as Rees approached us.[1]

'Yes, they're going up like crazy.'

Rees joined us again at the bar.

'I'd like a word with you in private, Jon,' I told him.

'Okay,' he said. 'Let's go and sit down over there.' He pointed to a table at the other end of the bar.

'Look, Jon, I'm tired of play-acting with you. You know you're in deep shit?' I said as we sat down.

His friendly demeanour changed. 'You don't know anything, Alastair,' he protested. 'You don't know anything about the drugs from Italy. You don't know about the women. You don't know about …'

'You've had a whole year to tell me about this, Jon,' I interrupted him. 'You were arrested. You could have phoned me at any time to say that this or that was the reason for Daniel's murder. But you didn't say a thing. Now why was that?'

'Look, Alastair. Come back to the office with me now and I can show you things. You'll see what I mean. Come back to the office with me …' He was becoming very agitated.

'I'm not going anywhere with you, Jon.'

I stood up and walked out of the bar, nodding to Derek on the way. Outside I found a phone box by the station and rang the incident room.

DS Malcolm Davidson answered. I told him about meeting Rees and his invitation to return to the office with him. I suggested that they wire me up so I could go back and hear what Rees had to say. Davidson refused. I pressed him: 'He's such a blabbermouth, he's bound to say something incriminating,' I protested.

But Davidson was adamant. He asked me where I was and said they'd drive over immediately. Then he ordered me not to go to Rees' office under any circumstances. Without a wire, the visit would be pointless anyway.

Within minutes, Malcolm Davidson arrived with another officer. I was amazed at how quickly they'd showed up. In the car, I told them what had happened in the Victory. I was very disappointed that they wouldn't wire me up – they said they couldn't take the risk. Instead, they drove me back to Iris's place, where Davidson asked if he could use the phone. He telephoned Rees.

'Hello, Jon, Malcolm Davidson here. Looking forward to the inquest?'

I could hear Rees' voice at the other end. He was agitated and angry.

'Well, Jon, this is just to tell you that the inquest will only be round one,' Davidson said, and promptly hung up.

CHAPTER 13	Silent Witnesses

2nd–14th April 1988

ALASTAIR: On the first day of the inquest, Mum and I hailed a cab to take us the final mile or so to Southwark Coroner's Court. I was watching the pedestrians on the busy street when I recognised Sid Fillery walking in the same direction. He looked fatter and shabbier than the last time I'd seen him at Sydenham Police Station 13 months earlier.

We met up with our barrister, June Tweedie, in a café near the court. Over coffee she gave us a final briefing on what to expect.

Outside the court entrance were a couple of TV crews and some press photographers who snapped and filmed us as we walked in. By next morning, although we didn't know it then, details of the inquest would be all over every national newspaper.

DI Alan Jones approached me as we entered the court. 'I've got to tell you before this starts, that Fillery's now working with Rees, Alastair.'

'Do you mean he's working for Southern Investigations? I don't believe it!'

'It's true,' said Jones. 'We've been watching him and he's there virtually all the time. There's no other explanation.'[1]

My stomach churned as I pictured Fillery at Dan's desk. Had he really had the nerve to take over Daniel's position at Southern Investigations? I had to get this news to Mum and June as quickly as possible so I hurried through the crowd of barristers, clerks and policemen until I found a space on a bench a couple of seats away from Mum. I looked in Mum's direction and mouthed the words: 'Fillery's working with Rees!'

She looked at me quizzically so I repeated myself. I could see from the look of astonishment and then anger on her face that she'd understood me.

'All rise!'

Everyone stood up as Sir Montague Levine took his seat behind a large desk at the head of the court. The proceedings had begun.

* * *

The jury was sworn in and the coroner began by explaining the purpose of an inquest: 'A lot of people have the impression that an inquest is a trial,' he said. 'It is not. Nobody is charged here. It is a court of record, which is inquisitorial in nature and not adversarial.'

He went on to say that an inquest could only establish who the deceased was and how, when and where the deceased came by his or her death. This was followed by legal argument about which witnesses would be allowed to be present at the proceedings and the coroner decided that all of them should be allowed to stay. Alan Jones and Douglas Campbell were called; Jones because he'd supervised the identification of Daniel's body and Campbell because he oversaw the murder investigation.

The coroner then produced several photographs – the first set included pictures of the crime scene. He then produced a second set.

'The next set of photographs I have in my possession unfortunately show in horrific detail the injuries to the skull and face of Daniel Morgan. I am not sure at this stage whether you would wish to see them. If the members of the jury wish to see them at this stage you may have them. I would not dwell too much on them,' he warned.

June Tweedie was given a set – she deliberately kept them hidden from us.

I didn't want to see those pictures. I'm glad I never saw them. Had I done so the image of my brother with an axe buried inside his face would have been burnt into my memory till the day I die.

This gruesome business was dealt with so formally. The coroner even had pictures of Daniel's brain that had been dissected from his body.

The coroner spoke again: 'May we look at the axe that was actually used at the murder?'

A large plastic bag was produced.

'It is not to be taken out of the container. I do not think the members of the jury wish to look at the axe in detail. It is blood-stained and so forth ...'

DSU Douglas Campbell produced a replica axe that had been bought. The court was told that around 30,000 of them had been imported from China in the year of the murder. He went on to describe how the handle of the axe had

been bound with strips of Elastoplast and that this would aid the murderer's grip, as well as prevent fingerprinting.

Finally, it was time to call the first civilian witness. This was Kevin Lennon, the bookkeeper to Southern Investigations.

He was just as I remembered him when I met him one time before at Daniel's office, greying, slightly built and bearded. After he was sworn in, the coroner began to question him about his relationship with Daniel Morgan and Jonathan Rees and some statements that he had made to the police concerning this.

Lennon told the court that he'd been friendly with Jonathan Rees, who had asked him to keep the accounts for Southern Investigations. He spoke about his close relationship with Rees and described how that partnership had begun to sour over time. Rees, he said, considered his partner Daniel Morgan a womaniser and resented him for this. He also disliked Daniel's club foot, said Lennon, and used to call him a 'little Welsh cripple'. I turned my head to look at Rees, who was sitting several rows behind us in the court.

'You say that as time went by you realised that Jon Rees' dislike for Daniel had in fact turned to hatred,' confirmed the coroner.

Lennon explained that Rees had even tried to get Daniel breathalysed so that he would not be able to do his job in the partnership.

The court was silent as the coroner continued to question Lennon.

'You say that it was during the course of one of these by now regular conversations that you had with Jon Rees that he revealed to you his idea for having Daniel Morgan killed.'

The turmoil I was feeling was indescribable. I felt disgust that Rees could have planned such a thing. This was mixed with relief that our suspicions were being confirmed. I looked back at Rees to see his reaction to this. He seemed tense and angry; there was the hint of a sneer on his lips.

And Lennon's testimony just got worse. He described how Rees had repeatedly asked him to find someone who would kill Daniel.

The coroner continued to quiz him: 'I want you to think very carefully about the next statement I am going to put to you. This is what you have stated in the statement.'

The coroner proceeded to read: '"I formed the opinion that Jon Rees was determined to either kill Daniel Morgan or have him killed. When he spoke

to me about it, Jon Rees was quite calm and unemotional about planning Daniel's death …'"

Sir Montague Levine looked at Lennon: 'Are you quite sure about that?'

'Yes, I am sure.'

'And what do you say about that?'

'Jon had decided at this stage that he could no longer work with Daniel in the partnership,' Lennon replied. 'He had in his own mind found a replacement for Daniel. It was his objective to get rid of Daniel in order to replace him with this new prospective partner who would be, in Jon's opinion, a much greater asset to the business.'

'And who was this new partner who was going to take Daniel's place?'

Hushed, the court waited for Lennon's reply.

'At the time he was a serving police officer, Sergeant Sid Fillery.'

A murmur ran through the courtroom. Mum and I exchanged glances.

* * *

During cross-examination, the court found out how this evidence came into the hands of the police. Lennon, it emerged, was a fraudster. At the time he gave his first statement to the police Lennon was in jail on remand. Rees was busily trying to raise a large sum of money to bail him. When this had been achieved, Lennon was released.

Lennon was contacted by the police but Rees was keeping a close watch on him. The police even contacted Lennon through Southern Investigations. According to Lennon, Rees wanted his own solicitor, Michael Goodridge, to accompany Lennon to the interview.

The inference was clear: Rees knew what Lennon knew, because he'd told him. His efforts to get bail for him and monitor his contacts with the police were to prevent him from talking.

Rees had failed in this. Lennon had finally made his witness statements about the murder plot. The court heard that he'd received a very lenient sentence for his crime because he'd helped the police. This, of course, gave him a motive for lying. But there was a big problem in dismissing Kevin Lennon's evidence. Firstly, it was partly prescient. It was in September 1987 that he'd made the statement about the involvement of Catford crime squad and Rees' plan to recruit Fillery to the private detective firm. Fillery hadn't been pensioned off until February 1988 and we'd only just heard he'd joined Southern Investigations.

As the inquest progressed, more evidence emerged that supported Lennon's account. We learned that Fillery had taken Rees' statement on the day after the murder. This was obviously worrying. And something even more alarming emerged ...

Fillery and Rees had met Daniel at the Golden Lion on the evening before the murder. The police had told us nothing about this in the year before the inquest. It was alleged that Dan had argued with Fillery in the pub. Fillery had 'forgotten' to mention this meeting to the other members of the squad. We wondered whether this meeting was an innocent coincidence, or something more sinister.

* * *

The next day the inquest was all over the national papers. 'COPS IN MURDER PLOT' screamed *The Sun* on its front page. Other newspapers carried prominent articles about Lennon's testimony.

We read the papers on the bus on the way to the inquest. We could barely believe what was happening. From then on, we were bombarded with new information daily.

It was one of the most exhausting experiences of my life. Day after day, we had to be on full alert, listening carefully to everything that was said so that June Tweedie could question and challenge witnesses wherever necessary. We were also at a big disadvantage because the police had all the paperwork and we had none: the British state held all the cards.

Much of the earlier part of the proceedings was taken up with the Belmont Auctions robbery. Numerous witnesses were called, including the partners that owned Belmont and the police that investigated the robbery. Mysteriously, the Vian brothers weren't called as witnesses and didn't attend the inquest at all.

Mum went to the ladies' during one of the adjournments. We used to meet in the large garden at the back of the courthouse during the breaks. She came out looking angry. I asked her what had happened.

'Do you know that swine Rees tried to burn me with his cigarette as he walked past me.' She showed me a charred black mark on her beige coat. 'He stabbed his lighted cigarette at me as he walked past in the corridor!'

Later, we found out more about the woman Dan had pointed out in the Victory a month before his murder. She was Margaret Harrison and it became

clear she had a close relationship with Jonathan Rees ... so much so that Rees had made 60 calls to her workplace in the space of a month. Rees had even paid Harrison's daughter's £800 school fees after the murder according to Tony Pearce, who signed the cheque.

Remarkably, Harrison met Dan in the hours before his murder in a wine bar in Thornton Heath. They'd shared a bottle of wine before he drove off to his fate at the Golden Lion.

Harrison was a married woman with two daughters. Her husband was a chauffeur for a top executive in British Gas. She admitted that she'd had a brief sexual relationship with Dan. But the questioning was getting to her and she kept saying she 'couldn't remember'. The coroner even asked her whether she'd been got at.

The next day *The Telegraph* contained an article with the headline 'MURDER MISTRESS IN "GOT AT" DENIAL'. To us, she looked scared in the witness box. The coroner repeatedly asked her to speak louder so that the court could hear what she was saying.

Another woman who didn't wish to testify was Rees' wife Sharon.

According to Rees, she'd left home with the children and he didn't know where she was. We didn't believe this for a second. Rees' counsel, Julian Nutter, told the court that his relationship with Margaret Harrison was part of the reason for this. The next day the *Daily Mirror* showed a large photograph of Sharon out shopping under the headline 'RETURN OF THE MISSING WITNESS'. Her doctor later told the court that she was suicidal and was showing no interest in her children.

At one point June Tweedie challenged the coroner's decision not to adjourn until Sharon could give evidence but because of the medical evidence, there was nothing anyone could do to force her.

The court wanted to question her about a series of phone calls made and received by Rees after he left the Golden Lion. According to Rees, Sharon had rung him on his car phone when he left the pub and their conversation lasted 11 minutes. He said they'd discussed whether to have a takeaway! Interviewed by police, Sharon couldn't remember the call.

Rees' phone calls were a subject of great interest. He said that he had then rung Paul Goodridge, the celebrity bodyguard and occasional debt collector

for the private investigators, whom he alleged he and Dan wanted to meet at the Golden Lion.

Goodridge's doctor had certified that he was unfit to give evidence. Instead, his girlfriend, Jean Wisden, took the stand. Wisden testified that she had no knowledge that a meeting had been arranged with Paul. She told the court she had injured her back at work that day; that Paul had picked her up in his car and taken her home. They'd spent the evening watching television. She stated that Rees had later rung and told her that he wanted to meet Paul Goodridge at the Beulah Spa pub near his home.

Goodridge's statement was read out to the court. He denied knowledge of an arrangement to meet at the Golden Lion. He also stated that Rees had approached him for a loan relating to the Belmont Car Auctions case. He'd told Rees that he would try to get a loan from a friend, but he had no intention of doing this. He didn't like the sound of the proposition, but didn't want to refuse Rees outright.

I thought Jean Wisden was forthright and that she was telling the truth. Though concerned about Paul Goodridge's absence, I didn't feel that he was an obvious suspect. My main question was if Goodridge was a hired killer, why would he meet his employer in front of witnesses before the victim's body was cold? Advertising a link between them would have been idiotic.

During the proceedings, I often used to glance at Rees, who was sitting a couple of rows behind us in the courtroom. On a couple of occasions he was seated next to a dark-haired, thick-set man with a bushy drooping moustache. I'd never seen this man before, but many years later as more details of Rees' business relationships began to emerge, the memory of this moustachioed man began to take on a more sinister aura.

* * *

Over the following days the court heard from numerous witnesses, including several of the investigating team, and almost all of the staff who worked for Southern Investigations. Peter Newby told the court how Fillery had taken files and other material from the office. Malcolm Webb and Dave Bray told the court about the deteriorating relationship between Daniel and Rees. Tony Pearce testified about Daniel wanting to enter a separate defence in relation to the Belmont Car Auctions robbery.

All of them were cross-examined by both June Tweedie and Rees' counsel, Julian Nutter. Each lunchtime we would find a local restaurant to eat in and go over what was happening with Tweedie.

I wasn't on the witness list. We all thought that my meeting with Fillery, his reaction to what I had told him and his phone call to the family were highly relevant. But the police had showed no interest in it when it happened or later when we raised it with them in meetings. June Tweedie raised this in court and the coroner decided reluctantly that I should give evidence. I wanted desperately to tell the court what I'd seen and heard since Dan's murder.

The coroner cautioned me before June Tweedie began her questions.

'May I say this? If there are ladies or families that have been associated with your brother in the past I would wish you not to mention these names. I do not want this inquest to be responsible for the break-up of stable marital relationships. That is not the function of this court.'

I told him that I understood this.

As soon as June Tweedie rose to her feet, Rees' counsel, Julian Nutter, intervened. Rees clearly did not want me in the witness box.

'If you will hear me, all I have to say is this. In the ordinary course this gentleman would be expected to make a statement to your officer. Having made a statement to your officer, you will know what is relevant and you will examine this witness and then invite, if you choose to do so, all of us to cross-examine.'

The coroner told Nutter: 'This is my court. I have the prerogative as to how I question and what I do with regard to this witness.'

Tweedie insisted that I had new evidence. The jury returned and she began questioning me about tensions in the partnership between Dan and Rees and about Dan's confession to me that he was having an affair.

She then moved on to the Belmont Car Auctions robbery. I told the court about my suspicions, then about how I had heard of Dan's death. I then went on to speak about Rees' personality and things that he'd said that made me suspicious. I also spoke about the meetings I had with him on the day after the murder.

It was uncomfortable in the witness box. Tweedie had no statement on which to base her questions. The coroner had no idea what I was going to say and kept on interrupting. It was difficult to express a coherent narrative. When she finished, Julian Nutter began his cross-examination.

'In the past, Mr Morgan, is it correct to say that you have been addicted to certain drugs?'

Tweedie was on her feet immediately. There was an argument about relevance and the jury was asked to leave.

Nutter began again: 'In a nutshell it goes to this. The area of Sydenham is an area which is known to be one of the parts of Croydon where readily available drugs are sold on the streets and in pub car parks and behind this public house. My instructions are that this man has in the past been a drug addict as far as serious drugs are concerned. He was weaned off that and he was now occasionally and certainly during the lifetime of his brother, getting drugs off his brother and that might be a reason why Daniel Morgan was parked in that darkened car park on that night.'

Rees smirked as Nutter spoke to the coroner.

Dan hated drugs. I didn't have the opportunity to point out that the drug had been prescribed to me over a period of years during a painful divorce by Swedish doctors and that I sought help as soon as I realised my position. I denied Nutter's other allegations firmly. If I didn't already know it, I knew then that in Rees I was dealing with a human being devoid of any scruples.

Fillery and Rees were among the last to give evidence and I've never heard so many lies in such a short space of time. Virtually everything said by all the other witnesses was contradicted. Both denied any involvement in Dan's murder.

Fillery even called the allegation that he was working for Southern Investigations 'contemptible'. He was also questioned by the coroner about my meeting with him two days after the murder. He claimed he was accompanied by DS Malcolm Davidson and that the meeting 'lasted two or three minutes. That was it. We went back up to the meeting and I never saw Alastair Morgan from that day.'

In fact, I had first met Davidson in August 1987, five full months after the murder. Fillery was lying.

The coroner continued probing. 'During that conversation, call it an interview or what you will, mention of the Belmont Auctions was made,' he asked.

'If it had been made, I'm sure that Davidson would say "What's all this about the Belmont Auctions?"' Fillery replied. 'It was not mentioned.'

Sir Montague Levine then challenged him over my recollections.

'You told him "we can't go charging down there, Alastair, on gut instincts."'

'Nothing of that nature was said. It was a two-minute conversation with Alastair Morgan,' Fillery retorted, though he did not deny he might have invited me for a drink at the pub.

'I am not saying that I would not have said that,' said Fillery. 'I felt sorry for the man. His brother had been killed, he was in a sad state. I do not remember saying it, but I do not deny it.'

I felt nauseous.

At the end of the inquest, the coroner summed up. He began by praising the police investigation of the murder. He also made a pointed statement that Peter Foley and Alan Purvis were 'exonerated' of any involvement in the murder and that there had not been 'one single shred of evidence ... no blood, no fibres, no fingerprints, no odd objects found ... not one single forensic fact had turned up in these two weeks to link anyone who has given evidence in this court to the killing of Daniel Morgan'.

We sat there numbed, listening to his expression of satisfaction. He then went on to instruct the jury that their only real option was to reach a verdict of unlawful killing. The jury was sequestered to consider its verdict at 5:43pm. Only nine minutes later, they returned. The foreman, a woman, pronounced their verdict of unlawful killing.

The coroner thanked the barristers and the inquest was over.

May 1988 to January 1989

ALASTAIR: The vacuum after the inquest was frightening.[1] I'd never felt as exhausted physically and mentally as I did after those three weeks of hell. But what were we going to do next?

Only days after the inquest, I'd had a surprise phone call from Derek Haslam, the man I'd met in the Victory pub with Rees on the first anniversary of Dan's murder. Derek told me he was a Freemason and went on to say he believed that Dan's murder had something to do with the suicide of a cop called Taffy Holmes.

I'd read about the suicide of DC Alan Holmes the previous July but had never thought it was connected to Dan's murder in any way. The only common denominator was the south London location. Now Derek was saying that Dan knew Taffy. But I'd heard absolutely nothing to suggest that the murder and Holmes' suicide were linked.

Derek's call made me uneasy. I suspected he was one of Rees' stooges trying to tap me for information. I told him that I'd ring the murder squad and ask if they knew anything about this. He gave me a phone number to call him back on.

I rang DI Alan Jones. Jones said to me that they'd found nothing suggesting a link between the murder and the suicide. I gave him Haslam's phone number. A few minutes later he rang back to tell me that the phone number was incorrect. I dismissed Haslam's call as an irritation.

I was more concerned by Sid Fillery, who had now taken over Dan's role in the business. There was no communication from the Met – Sir Peter Imbert still hadn't replied to my letter. Mum wrote to him in the hope that he'd respond to a mother's plea.

'The horrendous manner that my son, who leaves a young widow and two small children, lost his life has, as you no doubt understand, caused the

utmost grief and we feel that no stone must be left unturned in the efforts to seek justice,' my mother wrote. 'I would ask you, Mr Imbert, to help us achieve this.'

A couple of weeks later I received a surprise call from DCI Ernie Anderson of CIB 2, the Met's complaints division. He asked how I was.

'Not happy, Ernie. I'm not at all happy with the situation.'

'Alastair, I've got an MP's complaint on my desk.'

'An MP's complaint?'

'Yes, I've got a copy of a letter from you that was forwarded to your MP, Michael Mates. It's being seen as a complaint.'

A few weeks later I received a letter from the Police Complaints Authority (PCA), informing me that the Commissioner of Police had tasked Hampshire Constabulary to 'investigate allegations that police were involved in the murder of Daniel Morgan and matters arising from this'.

Jubilant, I rang Mum and my sister Jane to tell them the news. I also rang our barrister, June Tweedie. Her reaction brought me down to earth with such a bump.

'Alastair,' she told me, 'never ever trust a policeman!'

'But June, they're an independent police force. And they'll be supervised by the Police Complaints Authority.'

She warned me to expect little, but I couldn't help feeling hopeful: my letter had brought about a second investigation.

The letter from the PCA explained that the inquiry would be supervised by the Deputy Chairman, Roland Moyle. I was asked to contact DCS Alan Wheeler of Hampshire Police and we agreed to meet the following day at their headquarters in Fareham. There, I was shown into a large office and introduced to Wheeler and his number two, Detective Chief Inspector Paul Blaker.

I sat with them for the best part of two hours, telling them everything I knew about the case. They didn't really ask many questions. Blaker took notes throughout. After I'd said what I had to, I asked if they wanted to take my statement.

'Not at this stage,' replied Blaker.

I was surprised but I didn't argue – I was sure they would do this later and didn't want an immediate confrontation with an investigation that was supposed to help us. I simply had to let them get on with it.

* * *

Early in August 1988, soon after the Hampshire Inquiry began, I took another unexpected call. This one was from a DS Dave Lloyd. He told me he was from SO1, which meant nothing to me. He said he was investigating a complaint from Jonathan Rees. It transpired Rees had accused the police of sending me to the Victory to wind him up.

When he came down to Liss to take my statement I gave DS Lloyd my account of looking for Tony Pearce and the chance meeting with Rees and Derek Haslam.

'That's strange,' said Lloyd. He looked through some papers in his briefcase. 'This is a report from the incident room from 11th March 1988. It says that a call was received from a PC Derek Haslam.'

I was baffled.

'Do you mean to say Derek is a copper?'

'It looks that way.'

Derek had never mentioned that he was a police officer. And why was he driving a murder suspect around during a murder inquiry?

'What does the report say?' I asked Lloyd.

'Haslam said you told him that Dan knew Taff Holmes and had drunk with him on several occasions at the Beulah Spa.'

'That's not true, Dave. I never mentioned Taff Holmes. I've no idea if Daniel even knew him. Why would he make that up?'

He seemed as bemused as I was.

'I sincerely hope you don't think we're all bent up in London,' he added, looking embarrassed.

I didn't know what to think. One suspect in the murder was now in partnership with one of the officers who'd investigated it and was being driven around by yet another policeman because he'd lost his licence through drink driving.

'I've got to talk to Hampshire about this, Dave.'

'Of course,' he said. 'But would you mind if we investigated him too?'

The case was becoming so tangled that I couldn't see the lines between police and criminals.

I informed Hampshire Police about my meeting with Dave Lloyd and what I had learned from it. A couple of weeks later, I rang Paul Blaker to find out what was happening about this and was told Haslam was off sick and couldn't be interviewed. I jumped on the next train to London.

I'd learned that Dave Lloyd's boss was Superintendent Dave Lamper,[2] the officer who attended the inquest as an observer. I made my way to New Scotland Yard and was shown up to his office on one of the upper floors of the building. There, I told Lamper about my recent discovery that Derek Haslam was a police officer. It baffled me completely that Haslam hadn't been sacked immediately when he was found driving Jonathan Rees around.

Lamper said he would recommend to his superiors 'at the very least' that Haslam should no longer be a police officer. He asked about the Hampshire Inquiry and I went into some detail about Fillery's role in the case.

I walked out and made for the nearest phone box. I rang Paul Blaker, who seemed very anxious about what I'd done. He asked me to come to Petersfield Police Station immediately.

When I arrived back in Hampshire, Alan Wheeler and Paul Blaker were waiting at Petersfield station. They asked what I'd said to Lamper and I went over my discussion with them in detail – they were clearly anxious to know exactly what I'd said and what Lamper had said to me.

* * *

I kept on ringing Hampshire Police to ask about progress, but they were very sparing with their information.

Early one evening in February 1989, I was watching the local TV news. To my astonishment, I heard that Hampshire Police had arrested two men and a woman in connection with Daniel's murder. The arrests had been carried out in London and the suspects were being held at Fareham Police Station. I phoned Mum immediately. Once again the police had made arrests without telling us. That evening I tried several times to get more information out of the police, without success. I was told that I'd be informed in due course and I had trouble sleeping that night.

Next morning, I finally got through again and found out that they'd arrested Jonathan Rees, Paul Goodridge and his girlfriend, Jean Wisden. I jumped into my battered car and headed for Fareham Police Station. DCS Wheeler came out to reception and we walked into the car park to discuss the situation.

'My mother's really annoyed that you didn't tell us about the arrests. That's the kind of thing the Met did,' I told him.

Wheeler apologised and explained that they were still questioning Rees, Goodridge and Wisden and that they were going for an extension, if necessary.

'There's one face that I don't see here,' I said to him.

Wheeler knew very well that I was talking about Sid Fillery.

'All in due course,' he replied.

I could get little more out of him so I drove home. The police applied for and got an extension to question the suspects.

Two days later, Paul Goodridge and Jonathan Rees were charged with murder and Jean Wisden with perverting the course of justice.

CHAPTER 15	The Hampshire Inquiry

1988-1989

The Hampshire Inquiry was in fact two investigations that came out of the allegations of a plot to kill Daniel involving Jonathan Rees and a member of the Metropolitan Police – DS Sid Fillery.

Scotland Yard passed this allegation of corruption in its own force to the Police Complaints Authority (PCA), the police watchdog of the time, who in turn approached an outside force – the Hampshire Constabulary – to investigate.

The lead investigator, Detective Chief Superintendent Alan Wheeler, agreed with the PCA that the corruption allegations could only be assessed in tandem with a reinvestigation of the murder.

On 28th June 1988 a team of six investigators and eight other staff began that task. Operation Drake was the name given to the police computer's HOLMES account for the second murder investigation.[1] The parallel inquiry into the allegations of corruption, under the auspices of the PCA, was called Operation Plymouth.

At the heart of both investigations was Kevin Lennon's allegation that Rees was planning the murder for a year before it happened, and eventually decided to work with Sid Fillery. Soon after the inquest, Lennon had received a suspended sentence for tax fraud, reduced in return for helping the first Morgan murder inquiry.

DCS Wheeler re-interviewed the bookkeeper on 1st September 1988, accompanied by his deputy, DCI Blaker. Lennon reiterated the same allegations he'd made under oath in April at the coroner's court and in his previous police statements but he added some telling detail.[2]

Lennon said that because of Rees' insistent pleas to find someone to kill Daniel, he had actually gone along with the plan to commission a hitman, but only with a view, he told the officers, to 'ripping off' Rees.[3]

Lennon admitted he had approached two men who would agree to the murder and take a £3,000 advance from Rees and yet do nothing. He'd planned to introduce them to Rees and secure the fee at a pub meeting. But Rees never attended. Then Rees told Lennon of a new plan to use the Catford Police to help carry out the murder.

In retrospect, this account makes sense of the prolonged and multiple discussions the bookkeeper had with Rees about killing Daniel. Why would the private detective have confided so much in Lennon unless they were working as allies in some way?

But to DCS Wheeler and DCI Blaker this new admission seemed to cause concern. They began to wonder about Lennon's 'credibility' and his 'demeanour'. The murder plot allegations, they decided, were 'totally dependent' on Lennon, by now a 'convicted fraudsman'. The Hampshire detectives found that they were 'unable to gain a shred of evidence that corroborates his statement'.

This was an odd assertion. The original source of the information, the former senior police officer DCI Bucknole, gained an admission from Lennon by wearing a wire. But by now Bucknole seemed to be backtracking. He refused to confirm or deny Lennon had told him of the murder plan – despite the evidence. The Hampshire Report would describe him as a 'disappointing witness'.

Whatever the incentives to eventually testify, Lennon's description of the suggested murder plot had three elements that could not be retroactively changed. In Bucknole's account they had predated Daniel's murder by a year; they had been recorded covertly by Bucknole before Lennon could be offered any kind of deal; and of course they anticipated Fillery taking Daniel's role at Southern Investigations by more than a year.

Perhaps it was the implications about Fillery, and the suggestion of major police corruption in a murder that deterred Hampshire from pursuing Lennon's evidence any further.

* * *

As part of their review of the remaining evidence, the Hampshire team re-examined the 'forensic aspect' of the Met's first murder investigation. A report on 19th January 1989 by Detective Chief Inspector Farley described the initial forensic effort by the police as 'pathetic'. 'Forensically the case was not handled at all professionally,' Farley wrote, 'and there was obvious neglect probably through either ignorance or incompetence and fragmented

involvement. There was an obvious lack of direction, co-ordination, management and supervision.'[4]

This accusation of incompetence related to both securing the crime scene, and the long delays in testing Rees' clothing. But Farley was careful not to see any patterns in this incompetence, or any possible ulterior motive. There was 'no apparent mishandling of exhibits, or omission of or delay in, the submission of such exhibits, likewise the examination of any particular item; which has or might have dramatically affected the progress of the original investigation'.

Though the Hampshire Inquiry did mention the civilian scene of crimes officer, Leonard Flint, who had witnessed plainclothes detectives moving paperwork and a briefcase from Daniel's BMW, they seem to have overlooked his alarming observations. In short, Hampshire concluded this was a cock-up rather than a conspiracy, even though the incompetence was so thorough it looked organised.

It was as if the detectives wanted to steer clear of any route that involved implicating the Metropolitan Police. They were conspicuously cautious about the former King of Catford, Sid Fillery.

Interviewed under caution on his first arrest in April 1987, Fillery denied ever having taken the Belmont Car Auctions files from the offices of Southern Investigations or destroying them, or indeed any involvement in Daniel's murder. He also protested there was no way he was ever going to benefit from Daniel's death, even though by 1989 he had retired and taken Daniel's place.

However, the Hampshire Inquiry did note the first murder investigation made no attempt at the time to establish what Fillery was doing at the time of Daniel's murder, or corroborate his alibi that he'd been at home with his wife and foster child on the night of 10th March. Neither Foley's nor Purvis' alibis were checked either. More astonishing still, given their involvement in the Belmont Car Auctions debacle, neither Garry nor Glenn Vian were re-examined, though their criminal associations were hard to ignore. In July 1988, Garry had been arrested with another man in possession of £125,000 in cash. Though no offences could be proved, and they were released without charge, Garry remained under surveillance.

Early on in their investigations, Hampshire Police had pretty much discounted the allegations made by DS Alec Leighton that some mafia connections with the recovery of stolen cars from Malta was a potential motive. Re-interviewed in June 1988, Leighton said any threats were confined

to his trip abroad, and not connected to any threats before he left, or when he came back.

Another unexplored but related avenue was the number of witnesses who had put forward a more significant motive for the murder: that Daniel was planning to sell a big story of police corruption to the press.

By 1989, there were five witnesses claiming Daniel had a huge exposé he was about to reveal through the papers: Haslam, Madagan, Newby, Pearce and Wilkins. Now they were joined by a sixth.

Marjorie Williams, who had started work at Southern Investigations within days of Daniel's death, told the Hampshire team that Rees had told her Daniel had obtained information from 'a Police Officer called Taffy Holmes regarding a Commander Adams' about the Brink's-Mat robbery and that he was going to sell this information to a newspaper. Rees had also relayed to her the information that two officers had been removed from the murder case when they passed on that information.[5]

* * *

In an effort to provoke a clear-eyed witness account of the night of the murder the Hampshire team reconstructed the scene at the Golden Lion in late 1988. They identified 110 customers from that night in the pub, and spoke to 11 staff. Another 19 people who were in the vicinity on 10th March were also identified and re-interviewed.

There were a few additional fleeting eyewitness accounts to confirm Daniel was seen with Rees on a raised dais in the saloon bar at the rear, but no one overheard their conversation.

The only person who could provide any motive for the visit to the pub, or what was discussed, was Daniel's business partner and prime suspect; 'This could be accepted if – and only if – it were established that Rees was a witness of truth,' the Hampshire detectives pointed out. 'He is not, the contrary having been proved.'

Rees was now the main focus of the Hampshire Inquiry, and they were fixated on the inconsistencies in his alibi. Wheeler and his team paid special attention to the car phone billing records and Rees' statements about his movements during the crucial 40 minutes after 9pm when Daniel was killed.

Interviewed under caution on his first arrest in April 1987, Rees claimed he'd been on the move for the duration of all the calls to his mobile during

that time. He said then it would take him up to 30 minutes to drive from the Golden Lion to his home if the roads were clear. But the investigation repeated that same journey every night for a week, and the drive time only ranged between 9 and 11 minutes.

The first untraceable incoming call – which most likely covered the minutes when Daniel was killed – lasted 12 minutes. Rees said this long call was from his wife.

But Sharon Rees had refused to corroborate this. Besides, 12 minutes was more than long enough to drive home for Rees – 'by the time he put the telephone down he would be outside the door'.[6] His next destination, the Beulah Spa, was even closer, less than halfway home.

The other incriminating element of Rees' testimony about the night of murder was his changing rationale for meeting Daniel at the Golden Lion.

Rees offered three motivations. Firstly, that Daniel wanted to return there because he 'fancied a barmaid he had chatted up the night before'.[7] However, the barmaid in question, a married woman called Deborah Armstrong, did not recall Daniel making any overtures to her.[8] She recalled another man 'with glasses' pointing to Daniel, saying, 'my mate wants to know your name', but was embarrassed by this as it was said in front of her husband.[9]

Rees' second flimsy explanation for the return to the unfamiliar pub was that Daniel wanted to meet the Catford detectives 'Sid and his crew'[10] even though there was no reason to believe this was a regular haunt of the squad.

Thirdly, and most importantly, Rees' repeated claim that it was to meet a third party to help with a loan for the Belmont case was denied by the person they were supposed to be meeting – Paul Goodridge.

Wheeler and his team noted that two of the people Rees was in communication with in the crucial hour – his wife Sharon and Paul Goodridge – did not attend the coroner's court in April 1988 because they were deemed 'medically unfit'. If they had attended 'and been subject to detailed examination,' Wheeler concluded, 'Rees' alibi would not have survived.'

This was the basis of an interim report that Wheeler provided to the Director of Public Prosecutions in December 1988.

By this time Rees was divorced from Sharon Vian, mainly due to the revelations about his affair with Margaret Harrison that had come out during the coroner's inquest. Harrison left her husband Leonard for the same reason – to live with Rees.

On 31st January 1989, almost two years after Daniel Morgan's murder, Wisden, Goodridge and Rees were arrested in the hope the first two would break and provide sufficient evidence to charge Rees. But the Hampshire Police found that in their interviews after arrest none of the three 'made any remark which could be construed as an admission'.

1989-1990

ALASTAIR: We were on tenterhooks yet again, as the legal process ground on after the second wave of arrests over my brother's murder. Once the legal papers were sent to the Crown Prosecution Service (CPS), Jean Wisden was released immediately on bail.

Over the course of the next three weeks, Rees and Goodridge were also released. It didn't look good, but we tried to remain hopeful. Then, at the end of April 1989, we were told that there was to be a hearing at Fareham Magistrates' Court, at which the Crown would offer 'no evidence'.

We were devastated. The hearing was a formality because after the arrests the CPS had decided that there was insufficient evidence to proceed. Mum told me that she'd rung Jane, who was equally distraught. Jane had packed hurriedly, grabbed her passport and was on her way to Liss as we spoke. She arrived just in time to get to Fareham for the hearing.

I was proud of my sister. A year before she'd been so depressed she was struggling to get out of bed in the morning. Now she was driving hundreds of miles across Europe to be with us.

Julian Bevan QC was at Fareham to represent the Crown. Jonathan Rees and Paul Goodridge were brought into the dock handcuffed to large policemen.

Bevan told the court there was insufficient evidence to support a prosecution and that the Crown had therefore decided to offer no evidence. One woman who was sitting behind us in the court said, 'That's disgusting.'

The magistrate then told Jonathan Rees and Paul Goodridge that they were free to go.

Outside, we were just in time to see Rees sweep out in his BMW and Goodridge in his red Mercedes.

And that was it! Two years of fighting, grief and fear, all for nothing. Our efforts had been totally in vain. Dan's murderers, whoever they were, were still walking the streets.

Jane spoke to DCS Alan Wheeler on the phone after the investigation. She was angry because they hadn't interviewed her about Fillery's call to the family.

'Don't tell me how to investigate a murder!' was Wheeler's response. He then hung up on her.

Wheeler and Paul Blaker travelled down to Crickhowell to see Mum and her husband Peter. I went to Wales to be there when they came. We sat there and listened to their account of what had taken place. They were obviously uncomfortable about the outcome. Paul Blaker described it as 'unsatisfactory', which was something of an understatement.

We kept on raising the question of Fillery's involvement. I remember Alan Wheeler describing him as an 'old-fashioned policeman' during our discussion. I wondered exactly what he meant by that. We still had a hope the Police Complaints Authority might expose some of the corruption around Dan's murder.

* * *

It was early 1990 before I had had any meaningful contact with the PCA. In the end, they sent us a letter, which I opened the minute it came through the door. It announced that the Hampshire Inquiry had found that the first inquiry was satisfactory and that there was 'no evidence whatsoever of police involvement' in Daniel's murder.

I'm not easily moved to tears, but this letter made me cry.

My father had fought as a front-line soldier in the Second World War. He'd taken a bullet, horrible shrapnel wounds, imprisonment and months of near starvation to protect our freedom. My grandfather had been blinded at the Battle of the Somme by a bullet to the head. My brother, I believed, had been butchered because he was about to blow the whistle on police corruption. And what did we get from the Crown? Feeble, corrupted policing, wilful blindness and sleazy denial!

I walked out of the flat and wandered over to the railway. A level crossing divided the road that went through the centre of the village. I didn't know what to do next. Then I thought of my brother: Dan as a kid in a go-kart, rolling down the Welsh mountains; as a man roaring around the streets of south

London in his Austin Healey, with his big moustache. I saw him so clearly, so full of life, and I said aloud: 'I won't give up, Dan. I promise. I won't let them get away with this. Whatever it takes, however long it takes, I won't give up.'

Part Two	Press

KEY CHARACTERS, 1990–2000

The Morgan Family
Alastair Morgan – Daniel Morgan's brother
Isobel Hulsmann – Daniel's mother
Iris Morgan – Daniel's wife
Jane McCarthy – Daniel's sister
Kirsteen Knight – Alastair's partner

Southern Investigations
Jonathan Rees – Private detective
Sid Fillery – Former Detective Sergeant
Margaret Harrison – Partner of Jonathan Rees

Police
Ray Adams – Commander
Alan Holmes – Detective Constable, Serious Crimes
Derek Haslam – Police Constable
Alec Leighton – Detective Sergeant, Norbury
Duncan Hanrahan – Detective Constable
John Davidson – Detective Sergeant
Tom Kingston – Detective Constable

Murder Investigators
David Wood – Detective Chief Superintendent, CIB 3
Chris Jarrett – Detective Superintendent, CIB 3
Roy Clarke – Deputy Assistant Commissioner

Media
Alex Marunchak – *News of the World*
Mazher Mahmood – News International journalist
Gary Jones – Mirror Group journalist
Piers Morgan – Editor of the *News of the World* and the *Daily Mirror*

Politicians
Chris Smith – Member of Parliament, Culture Secretary

| Getting Away with Murder

1990-1992

With Jonathan Rees arrested twice and Sid Fillery once on suspicion of murdering the co-founder of Southern Investigations, you might have expected the reputational damage to the private detective company would be so severe few police officers or members of the press would have much to do with it.

But precisely the reverse happened over the next decade. Southern Investigations went from strength to strength until it became the centre of the dark arts of illegal press intrusion, and a major brokering service for corrupt cops willing to sell information, often to Britain's national newspapers, but also to organised crime.

Even Hampshire's corruption probe, Operation Plymouth, concluding in July 1989 there was 'no evidence to implicate a police officer' in the murder of Daniel Morgan, couldn't help complimenting Sid Fillery as his replacement: 'Fillery ran the business with his strong personality and people say he reduced the debts,' the report concluded.

While Rees was on remand in prison in Yorkshire on murder charges in 1989, Fillery was working full-time at the private detective agency in Thornton Heath, which he briefly renamed 'S.A.F.E.' – after his initials (Sidney Alexander Fillery) and the final letter 'Enquiries'.

Fillery then recruited Richard Zdrojewski, a police officer who had been his driver at Catford crime squad but had left the force under a shadow of criminal charges.

Before he left the Met, Zdrojewski had known both Daniel and Rees on the south-east London cop pub circuit. He claims he was coached to give helpful evidence at Daniel's inquest about how often he drank at the Golden Lion. After his testimony Zdrojewski – nicknamed 'Boris' by his friends – went for the inevitable drink with 'Jon and Sid', who told him: 'You did well, Boris.'

In 1989 Zdrojewski was sacked from the Met for being in possession of marijuana, and he began work at the private detective agency. There he met Rees' brothers-in-law, the Vians, who he described as having 'a propensity for violence' and frequenting a 'rough pub' with Rees called the Harp. Observing the Vians, Zdrojewski thought that Rees had 'a hold over the brothers and they appeared influenced by him'.

The major part of Zdrojewski's work at the Thornton Heath offices was conducting telephone enquiries, process serving, and surveillance. He noted the unique and profitable business proposition Southern Investigations provided: illicit information gleaned, Zdrojewski said, mainly from 'corrupt officers working for them'.

At one point Fillery tried to rope Zdrojewski into illegally procuring intelligence from the Police National Computer 'by ringing up the local nick and trying it on by pretending to be a serving Police Officer, who required the details for legitimate purposes'.

However, Fillery's influence with the Met extended much further than just procuring illicit information: the ex-Met detective seemed to be able to intervene in court and legal processes at will. When Zdrojewski was later being sought by police for attacking someone with a baseball bat, Fillery managed to delay the arrest and provide a solicitor and barrister. Zdrojewski was given very lenient bail conditions, which his brother, a senior probation officer at the time, described as 'odd/bent'.

By mid-May 1989, with the murder charges against him dropped, Rees rejoined Fillery in London and they renamed the private detective agency Rees and Co.[1]

The revived agency now became a centre of innovation. With a growing network of police officers happy to sell on official secrets for a price, Southern Investigations set about devising ever more ingenious ways of satisfying the hunger for scoops from the press, pioneering the early days of cybercrime.

In the Thornton Heath offices, Zdrojewski noticed a secret log that recorded dozens of entries and payments for a computer hacker called 'John', who lived in a 'converted watermill in Downton, Wiltshire'.[2] 'He could find out virtually anything,' Zdrojewski said of the source they nicknamed 'Computer John'.

'Most of these enquiries,' Zdrojewski explained, 'originated from a reporter at the *News of the World*, who had a Polish or Croatian surname. I had actually met him and spoken to him on the phone but I can't remember his name.'

There was only one *News of the World* reporter with a Slavic name who had regular contact with Southern Investigations at that time – Alex Marunchak.

* * *

Despite his close connections with Southern Investigations and the various key players in south London policing, Alex Marunchak had written nothing about the Daniel Morgan case in the two years since the murder.

Soon after he joined the *News of the World* in 1981 after stints on local west London papers the *Slough Observer*, *Middlesex Chronicle* and then the *Evening Echo*, Marunchak had quickly established connections with senior officers at Scotland Yard. It was part of the paper's tradition.

Every Friday night the newspaper would buy drinks for police officers at the Albert pub on the corner of Victoria Street and Buckingham Gate. Murdoch himself was heard to admit that, when he took over the *News of the World* in 1969, he was told that the company safe was full of cash to pay off police officers on Saturdays before the paper went to press.[3] 'We're talking about payments for news tips from cops: that's been going on a hundred years, absolutely,' Murdoch told *Sun* journalists in 2013.

Against this background, Marunchak rapidly rose through the ranks of Britain's best-selling paper, graduating to chief crime reporter. By 1986 contemporaries recall him attending parties held by the CEO of News International, Bruce Matthews, at Eaton Square in the exclusive Belgravia district of London. He was often seen in the company of Commander Wyn Jones, the officer in charge of policing the tumultuous Wapping dispute after Murdoch defied the print unions and moved to a new plant in east London.

In the year of Daniel Morgan's murder, Marunchak's byline was prolific, with one or two stories in virtually every edition of the *News of the World*, and numerous front-page exclusives, nearly all these derived from police insiders.

Marunchak's 'sources' included senior officers in Surrey CID, Paddington Police, Sussex CID, Kent CID, instructors at the police training college in Hendon, Regional Crime Squad officers, the Suzy Lamplugh murder squad, Royal Palace protection officers, a 'Senior Scotland Yard detective', 'South London detectives', a 'cop protecting Maggie (Thatcher)', a 'Scotland Yard informer' and 'a man above the rank of Detective Chief Inspector'.[4]

Occasionally, Marunchak even wrote about the growing connection between private investigators and police. A *News of the World* story from May 1986

alleged that an anti-corruption investigation had uncovered a 'firm of private detectives' were providing 'sexual favours' for gay police officers in return for 'confidential information from the Police National Computer'.[5]

In the circumstances, the failure to mention the Daniel Morgan murder is a strange oversight.

In late July 1987, when DC Alan Taffy Holmes committed suicide, Marunchak covered the aftermath in graphic detail. The senior crime reporter claimed the detective had killed himself 'to protect fellow Masons over allegations of bribes paid by the now infamous Brink's-Mat gangster Kenny Noye' and a conspiracy around a '£1 million cocaine syndicate said to involve police officers'.[6]

Two weeks later Marunchak was all over Holmes' funeral, whom he nicknamed, like Rees but not other friends, 'Taff' rather than 'Taffy'.

Marunchak was so well regarded by senior Murdoch management he was promoted to deputy news editor of the *News of the World* in 1987. But he still made no mention of the Daniel Morgan murder the following year, even though by his own admission he attended the explosive 1988 inquest (possibly the 'moustachioed character' spotted by Alastair Morgan) and allegations of police involvement in the murder had made the front page of *The Sun* and featured in many other national newspapers.

For some reason, the *News of the World* did not cover the murder of Daniel Morgan until mid-May 1989. 'COVER-UP COPS AXED MY PARTNER TO DEATH' is Marunchak's one and only mention of Daniel Morgan – in fact, only one of two articles that ever mentioned the murdered private eye over a quarter of a century.[7]

The entire 1989 piece is a highly selective version of the murder from the point of view of the man twice arrested as the prime suspect: Jonathan Rees. Talking from his 'secret hideaway' three days after being discharged at Fareham Magistrates', Rees claimed that Daniel was killed over 'massive overtime fraud linked to the apparent suicide of Flying Squad cop Alan "Taff" Holmes'.

'Morgan and Holmes were great pals,' Rees told Marunchak. 'Both were Welsh and as thick as thieves. Taff was as bent as they come.'[8]

This was not the first time someone had suggested the two violent deaths of Taffy and Daniel in 1987 were connected. Derek Haslam had shocked Alastair Morgan by calling him after the inquest with the same proposition. Three

Morgan murder squad detectives had investigated the link only to be relieved of their roles.[9]

Oddly, the Marunchak and Rees' piece suggests three entirely different motives for Daniel's killing. The sidebar shows a picture of Daniel and one of the women, Carole Regan, with whom he was alleged to have had an affair. The 'irate husband' or 'jealous lover' theory is dangled before readers' eyes, yet there was no mention of Daniel's involvement with Margaret Harrison who, by this time, was living with Rees.

The second motive, suggested in the headline 'MASSIVE OVERTIME FRAUD', not only seems insufficient for murder, it is directly contradicted by the following paragraph with a suggestion of links to Taffy Holmes.

What was Marunchak's first and last piece in the *News of the World* about the murder of Daniel Morgan trying to achieve? Did it aspire to report the truth or was it just another dumping exercise, throwing more red herrings in an already overpopulated pond of theories and suspects? Or perhaps this article was a bit of both: a mixture of disinformation and information, some of it supposed to mislead, some of it meant to warn others that there was possibly more to come?[10]

* * *

Marunchak's motives for reporting just Rees' side of the story can only be imagined, but there is little doubt that the *News of the World*'s news editor had failed to declare an important interest.

According to Marjorie Williams, a part-time bookkeeper at Southern Investigations recruited within a week of Daniel's murder to set up new VAT accounts, Marunchak had already started a roaring trade in confidential inquiries with Rees and Fillery.

By the time Williams was interviewed by the police in 1989, the bailiff side of the company's work was in steep decline, but the enquiries side had stepped up. The *News of the World* had become Southern Investigations' main client, with up to 500 invoices a month for small cash amounts of around £50, for 'information on certain people that would ultimately result as a story in the paper'.

If those figures are at all accurate, that's a massive volume of cash payments of up to £25,000 a month. An annual total of £300,000 a year is twice as much as the documented payments Southern Investigations were receiving from the *News of the World* ten years later, so the figure seems to be inflated –

rather like the £250,000 Daniel was expecting for his story (even though this ranges down to £40,000 and £10,000 depending on the source and date of their statement).

On the other hand, Marjorie Williams suggests that a lot of this cash did not go directly to Rees and Fillery. She alleged this flood of smaller payments bypassed the normal accounting procedures, and were directly paid in cash by the news editor.[11] She'd also heard Rees claim he'd paid thousands off Marunchak's credit cards and the school fees for one of his children. Marunchak has denied this.[12]

Williams' description of the close relationship with the *News of the World*, however, is supported by other contemporaneous witnesses.

In the late 1980s, Richard Zdrojewski had met Alex Marunchak at the office. Andrew Docherty, a former partner of Patricia Vian, the mother of Garry and Glenn, often answered the phone when Marunchak called, mainly about some new celebrity scandal or salacious story for the Sunday's tabloid.

Docherty said he would also pass on requests to 'Computer John', who could access confidential billing records 'within an hour of being tasked'. If there wasn't a good story, Docherty claimed, Rees would often fabricate one – a fake news 'spoof' for the *News of the World*, which would get printed anyway with a cash payout.

This growing trade in illegal news gathering didn't stop with police bribes, computers or fake news, though. Soon a gamut of techniques would be combined to create one of the great innovations of the *News of the World* and Southern Investigations alliance: the tabloid sting.

* * *

The undercover sting began to be the modus operandi of Southern Investigations soon after Daniel's murder. These set-ups could not only be nice little earners, they could also be used to weaken or compromise perceived enemies.

Zdrojewski, Fillery's former police driver, remembered a chief inspector from the internal affairs department becoming a target of Rees and Fillery. The CIB 2 officer was lured to a meeting at a McDonald's in Bexleyheath on the pretext he would be given information about an armed robbery. A reporter and photographer from the *News of the World* were waiting.

As part of the set-up, Zdrojewski was told to serve the senior officer with legal papers in an envelope: 'He was photographed,' Zdrojewski recalled, 'and

his photo and a report appeared in the *News of the World* to look like he was taking a bribe.'

Within a year, the private investigators had graduated to what the Russian intelligence services call '*Kompromat*' – embarrassing or compromising information to be used against a target to either discredit, co-opt or blackmail.[13]

Zdrojewski secretly left London in the early 1990s to live on the Isle of Wight. Somehow Sid Fillery tracked him down and sent a taxi for him to meet at 'a posh hotel in Cowes' where Fillery was staying. They went to lunch and were sat next to the cabinet minister, Virginia Bottomley MP. To Zdrojewski the surprise lunch was obviously a pretext for Fillery 'to listen out for gossip or scandal to report back to the *News of the World*'.

The twilight world of corrupt cops and criminals was soon to make a direct intervention in national politics.

* * *

The year 1992 was an election year and it looked like the Conservative government would lose. Two years previously, Prime Minister Margaret Thatcher had been ousted by her Party in a bitter internecine war and her replacement as Party leader, John Major, was in a tricky position in the polls. The Labour leader Neil Kinnock was joined in parliamentary opposition to Major by a new dynamic leader of the Liberal Democrats – Paddy Ashdown.

Ashdown was a telegenic former Marine commando who seemed to lead a spotless personal life. He also looked likely to form an alliance with Labour to unseat the Conservatives after 13 years of uninterrupted power. Then the *News of the World* struck.

Ashdown's solicitor was Andrew Phillips (later Lord Phillips) who also advised the Liberal Democrat Party on legal matters. He'd kept a legal note in his safe of a conversation he'd had five years previously with Ashdown about a brief affair the politician had had with his secretary, Tricia Howard. But then Phillips' office was broken into and the solicitor's safe cracked.

The first Ashdown got to know of the illicitly gained personal information was when Tricia Howard called in January 1992, telling him that she'd been approached by the *News of the World* with an offer of £50,000 for a 'kiss and tell' story about their affair, five years previously. This was just months away from the general election.

To her credit, Howard turned down the *News of the World*'s generous cash offer but Ashdown soon realised the story was the gossip of Fleet Street and would eventually come out, potentially derailing the looming election campaign.[14] He held an emergency press conference with his wife, Jane, confessing to the affair five years previously. This led to the famous *Sun* headline 'PADDY PANTSDOWN'.

Whether or not Rees or Fillery were directly involved in the commission of the break-in into the solicitor's safe (there is evidence they commissioned another break-in), they were certainly brokering the stolen solicitor's letter and trying to negotiate a lucrative deal with the *News of the World*. But then two other police officers from the south-east London group of Freemasons intervened. DC Duncan Hanrahan was an old associate of Rees and Fillery from the time of the Belmont Car Auctions scam. He was also an informal go-between or 'bagman' for Commander Ray Adams, who attended his wedding to a female police officer.

By 1992 Hanrahan had left the Met with an ill health pension and had set up his own private detective agency, Hanrahan Associates Ltd., Security Consultants and Investigators. Following in the footsteps of Rees and Fillery, the ex-detective tried to get into the well-paid business of tipping off newspapers. One of Hanrahan's first ports of call was Alex Marunchak.

It didn't end well.

As Flynn and Gillard explain in their book *Untouchables*, Hanrahan discovered through a police source a story about a dominatrix that perfectly fitted the 'News of the Screws' formula of salacious scandal. So he passed it on to Marunchak. But when the story appeared in *The Mail on Sunday* instead, Hanrahan suspected Marunchak had sold the scoop and pocketed the cash for himself.

Hanrahan soon got his revenge. While hanging round the offices of Southern Investigations, he overheard a conversation about the Paddy Ashdown exposé and the plan to buy the stolen documents.

Hanrahan contacted his mentor, Commander Ray Adams, who in turn tipped off the City of London Police about the rendezvous and payoff. They registered Hanrahan as an informant, and arrested the man trying to sell the Ashdown files to the tabloids.

Having lost a lucrative and politically important scoop for the *News of the World*, the directors of Southern Investigations were furious. 'Fillery suspected

a leak,' wrote Flynn and Gillard, 'and put up a sign in the office warning his staff and visitors, "WHAT YOU HEAR IN HERE STAYS IN HERE".[15] But the damage to the reputation of the Liberal Democrat leader had already been done, and no one was ever prosecuted for the burgling of his solicitor.

* * *

Southern Investigations was also an early adopter of the new technology of miniaturised camera recorders and covert video recording, and this is how they first came to play an important role in the creation of the 'King of the Stings' – Mazher Mahmood.

Mahmood had entered the world of journalism when he betrayed his own brother, Waseem Mahmood, a BBC producer, for moonlighting and shooting wedding videos with the Corporation's cameras. His brother lost his job.

News International recruited Mahmood at the age of 21 as a staff reporter on the prestigious *The Sunday Times*. But he was discovered trying to doctor computer evidence that would have revealed inaccuracies in one of his stories. Mahmood was about to be sacked, but handed in his resignation letter first.

By 1992, after a stint on David Frost's *Sunday* programme, Mahmood was back at Murdoch's other Sunday paper based in Wapping – the *News of the World*. One of his first jobs was working with deputy news editor Alex Marunchak on what he himself describes as the 'most lurid scandal since the Profumo affair'.[16]

After his surprise election victory in 1992, the Prime Minister John Major created a new ministry, the Department of National Heritage (now renamed the Department of Culture, Media and Sport), and appointed a close ally, David Mellor, the MP for Putney, as the first 'Minister for Fun'.

Not only was Mellor a member of a government that many in the press thought owed their election success to newspaper coverage ('IT'S THE SUN WOT WON IT' declared the newspaper the day after Major's election victory), he had also suggested stricter regulation after another of the recurrent British press scandals. 'The press – the popular press,' he told BBC's *Hard News* in 1991, 'is drinking in the last chance saloon.'

By July 1992 Mellor was openly suggesting a government review of the new Press Complaints Commission. A politician making a direct threat to the business model of the tabloid press was inevitably a prime target for *Kompromat*.

Under the supervision of the *News of the World*'s news editor, Alex Marunchak, Southern Investigations deployed their video surveillance and bugging

expertise in the rented flat of an actress, Antonia de Sancha, who was having an extramarital affair with Mellor.

Mahmood was part of the surveillance team. In his autobiography, *Confessions of a Fake Sheikh*, he describes how, with the landlord's permission, de Sancha's phone was tapped, her apartment rigged up with cameras, while he sat outside in a nondescript van monitoring the minister's comings and goings, and recording de Sancha's conversations about the relationship on the phone with friends.

Though the *News of the World* had ample evidence of Mellor's infidelity, the Sunday tabloid's editor, Wendy Henry, had cold feet about using surveillance and subterfuge on such a high-profile political target.

In the end, the smaller, rival Sunday, the *People*, first broke the story of the affair. But Mahmood followed up with much more detail in the *News of the World* with information obtained from the surveillance.

Murdoch's daily *Sun* newspaper then capitalised on the scandal, brokering a deal with the publicist Max Clifford for Antonia de Sancha's kiss-and-tell story.

Though Major refused to let Mellor resign over the de Sancha affair, the Minister for Fun was a consistent figure of ridicule from then on, and tendered his resignation a few months later.

* * *

Within five years of Daniel's murder, Southern Investigations were not only leading the way in the 'dark arts' of press intrusion and corrupting police officers, they were also deploying their suite of services for an important third client base – organised crime.

Former Catford cop Richard Zdrojewski had noted there was something 'bent' about the way Fillery fixed his arrest and bail conditions. Intelligence reports from the early nineties suggest Fillery and Rees were involved in other, more serious, subversions of the legal process.

One uncorroborated but trusted informant claimed Rees and Fillery were in negotiations with a criminal awaiting trial. The plan was to steal a police officer's notebook from a south London police station and destroy key evidence. The fee was alleged to be £20,000. According to the unnamed informant the deal was too pricey, no notebook was stolen, and the penny-pinching criminal was sent down for 12 years.

But the most important piece of intelligence from the early nineties – and the tip-off that brought Southern Investigations back on the radar for the Met – was a link back to south London organised crime.

Various sources alleged that Southern Investigations were trying to help Joey Pyle, the south London gangster mentioned in several anonymous tip-offs around Daniel's murder who was, by 1992, finally on trial for drug dealing.

Pyle had eluded police many times in the past. He escaped a murder conviction in the sixties when jurors were 'approached' at the Old Bailey. In the seventies he'd also managed to avoid charges of helping a murderer escape. Since then he had built up a major extortion and protection racket in the pubs of south London. In 1987, the year of Daniel's murder, he was arrested for a £5m cannabis deal, but that case also collapsed when a key witness refused to give evidence.[17]

Justice finally caught up with Pyle in 1992 when he was arrested for masterminding a multi-million pound drugs ring. An undercover police officer codenamed 'Dave' offered to buy from him thousands of ampoules of morphine and opium painkillers stolen from a Ministry of Defence consignment during the first Gulf War. As a result of the investigation, Operation Gallery, 40kg of heroin was recovered from a warehouse in Wimbledon.

Pyle's first trial for these charges, at Southwark Crown Court, was dramatically aborted when three jurors claimed they had been offered money to return not guilty verdicts, and threatened with violence when they refused. For the second trial at the Old Bailey the new jurors were given 24-hour police protection and an armed police escort.[18]

The intelligence reports suggest Pyle tried to disrupt this second trial by attempting to track down the undercover officer 'Dave', whose evidence was crucial. The reports claim that Fillery and Rees were asked to use their bailiff and process-serving skills to locate 'Dave' so that Pyle's associates could 'either kill him or persuade him not to give evidence'.

Pyle was jailed for 14 years for masterminding the drugs operation, but Rees and Fillery carried on without so much as a caution.

Southern Investigations were not only corrupting police officers and perverting the press, but starting to subvert the entire criminal justice system too.

CHAPTER 18	Wilderness

1990-1993

ALASTAIR: After the Hampshire Inquiry had failed to bring Dan's killers to justice I was in almost utter despair and the family were at a complete loss as to what to do.

We'd tried protesting to the PCA. Mum had written to two home secretaries and even Margaret Thatcher, to no avail. The only avenue now that we could think of was the media.

None of the local media in Hampshire seemed interested, so Mum approached Harlech Television, the independent TV company in Wales. Here, she found immediate interest, particularly as her local MP, Richard Livsey, had offered his support. Because of our Welsh background, HTV had a local angle and were keen.

HTV came to Hampshire to interview me for *Wales This Week*. The programme was broadcast early in 1991. It was disappointing that it was only shown in Wales, but the fact that it was made at all gave us credibility. I sent a copy to my MP, Michael Mates, with a letter. He didn't reply.

Even though the impact was limited to Wales, we felt buoyed up because we were able to do something about Dan's murder.

And I kept on cleaning windows. My income was small, but I was managing to scrape by. But being interviewed on TV had given me confidence and I felt I could do something more challenging. I had an unusual insight into the citizen–state relationship and I wanted to redress the balance so I decided to try and become a journalist myself.

In 1991 I applied for a Higher National Diploma course at Farnham Art College and was formally accepted after an interview. I'd left much unfinished in my life up to then. Now I was determined to finish two things: I was going to complete a degree and make sure that the people who had killed Dan were brought to justice.

I began my studies in the autumn of 1991, four years after Dan's murder. I was now 41 and I was very nervous on the first day of term. Some students were still in their teens, others were in their twenties and a few in their thirties. Only two, including myself, were over 40.

For the first year at Farnham I was a bit of an outsider. I only met the other students during classes and breaks. There wasn't much socialising after college hours. I had to drive back to Liss each day and at weekends I also worked, cleaning windows. Life was busy and this took my mind off the problems with the police to some degree. But I kept four of five of my brother Dan's shirts, which I wore regularly. I don't know quite why, but it made me feel closer to him. He was almost always on my mind.

* * *

Dan and I were born in Singapore. I arrived in December 1948 and he came along 11 months later. I was a normal healthy baby, but Dan was premature, weighed only a little over five pounds and had problems with his legs.

Our parents were both in the Army and met in Singapore. Dad was a 23-year-old war veteran who'd served with the Parachute Regiment at Arnhem. He'd been badly wounded by shrapnel to the legs and a bullet in his shoulder. After being taken prisoner he spent the remaining nine months of the Second World War in a POW camp in Germany. He told me he survived on potato peelings and that at Christmas 1944, he'd finally been able to move his toes for the first time since he'd been wounded: he knew from that moment that he would walk again.

After being liberated, Dad was commissioned and promoted to lieutenant and posted to Singapore. There, he met Mum, the daughter of an English woman and an Aussie First World War veteran. She was 19 at the time.

By the time we left Singapore Dad had been promoted to captain, one of the youngest in the British Army. He'd also been moonlighting as a sub-editor on the *Singapore Times* to pay for Dan's expensive medical care. But my brother's club foot and orthopaedic problems needed expert surgery which was not available there. Dad had to resign his commission and leave our cook, housekeeper and Malay nanny behind.

Dan had problems with his legs right from the start. From the age of about three, he wore a shiny metal calliper on his right leg. He was generally a placid, good-tempered child with a round, cherubic face and a happy nature. I was

more volatile and rebellious. As the eldest of three, I think I was jealous of the attention that was naturally given to my younger siblings.

Dan was an outgoing kid. By the time he was nine or ten he'd had a series of operations on his right leg and no longer wore a calliper. One leg was normal for his age, the other was much thinner, like his forearm with a tiny foot and a lumpy ankle, scarred by surgery. My parents always had to buy him two pairs of shoes – his right foot was a couple of sizes smaller than the left one.

Dan never tried to hide his leg – he wore short trousers like all the other kids. He also wasn't afraid of adventure.

One of our friends was a Hungarian boy called Zoltan whose parents had fled Hungary after the uprising against the Russians in 1956. Zoltan had the estate's best 'bogie', basically a plank with two sets of wheels and a steering arrangement at the front. Dan and I constructed a copy of Zoltan's luxury version, which was upholstered for extra comfort.

One of our favourite pastimes was to take our bogies to the top of the hill, career down and around two bends to see how far we could go along the flat. In winter, if we were lucky enough to get some snow, the bogies would be replaced by toboggans – there were plenty of steep slopes on which to take insane risks.

There was only 11 months between us, but I always felt like the big brother. Not that Dan was at all incapable of looking after himself. Anyone who picked a fight with him in junior school would have his hands full. He never used his leg as an excuse – he was a game kid. But now he was gone, unarmed and killed in a cowardly attack from behind.

* * *

That year there was a general election and we were desperate for a change of government. Mum had written to every home secretary about the case. Each time, a home office official wrote back, telling us what we already knew in the most infantile terms: that the Hampshire Inquiry had found no evidence whatsoever of police involvement in the murder.

We were hoping that a new government might actually listen to what we had to say, but Labour lost the election. The opinion polls had given them a small lead. Prior to the election, there had even been talk of a hung parliament, with the Lib Dems waiting in the wings to form a Lib/Lab coalition if the result was close enough. These plans took a severe knock a couple of months

before the election when Lib Dem leader Paddy Ashdown was exposed by *The Sun* newspaper for having an affair with his secretary.

The 1992 election also brought another setback for us. Mum's MP, Richard Livsey, who had supported us from the beginning, lost his seat to a Tory.

* * *

After my first year at Farnham my sister Jane invited me to spend that summer in Germany. I'd seen very little of my sister since the murder and when she did come to the UK to visit Mum, inevitably we spent most of the time together talking about Dan or the police. Sometimes, for short periods, we could switch off and do normal things, even enjoy life a little, but then something would spark it off again.

That summer was the first time Jane and I were able to talk of anything other than Daniel. As the wife of an Army officer, Jane was in a difficult situation. Once we'd discovered that the police were involved in the murder, she told me that everything changed for her.

'I don't want to deal with this Army stuff anymore. I don't feel the way I used to about Britain, her Majesty the Queen, the UK government and toasting the Queen Mother and pretending to come from one of the greatest democracies in the world. People aren't listening, they're treating us like lunatics.'

Jane's attitude was clearly influencing Justin's career – 'I said to him, "I'm not going to the mess with you anymore and beat the drum for Britain and Britannia Rules the Waves and all that stuff. I said if you want to do it, you must do it, but you must do it alone."'

Jane had withdrawn from Army life and stayed on the farm with their animals, where she felt secure. Back at the officers' mess, Justin was being asked questions like 'Where's your wife?'

He'd reply how Jane had just chosen to stay at home. Then it would get difficult and Justin would have to say to the MOD: 'Look, it's not a package deal. You pay me and I do what's expected of me. She doesn't interfere with my military career.'

'They'd pretend that this was okay,' Jane told me. 'But now it's started to appear on his annual assessment in a sly way. Oh, he's very competent at his job, but I would get a mention like "his wife is never seen and does not support the army ethos".

'He's been a major so long now,' she claimed, 'he should have been promoted to lieutenant colonel, by now.'

Justin never blamed Jane. He wasn't resentful – he was his own man and although Jane's stand was backfiring on him, he understood that what the Army was doing was wrong. But you can't run away from the ugly trauma of murder. Like me, Jane was so full of anger.

'I snap at the drop of a hat,' she confessed. 'It's like there isn't any room in my body to absorb any more pain on top of what I'm already dealing with. I just collect my eggs and walk the dogs. I only have limited contact with my neighbours because my German isn't that good. When I'm working for the coach company, I have to rehearse what I'm going to say to the passengers.'

She was experiencing the same alienation as Mum and me. We belonged to a minority who had lost relatives to murder, and an even smaller number where it looked like the state was involved in the crime. To make matters even worse, that state, our state, was telling us that it hadn't happened.

* * *

Back in Farnham I looked for new accommodation. All my efforts to raise the case in the national media had failed and this frustration made me impatient with some parts of the course.

As far as I was concerned, the purpose of journalism was to hold authority to account. To me, some parts of the course seemed frivolous and I was outspoken in my views. I was even reprimanded by the principal of the college for criticising and walking out of a lecture, but I didn't care. I could be a difficult student at times in Farnham. Other students used to describe me as 'Mad Al' because of my anger.

Nevertheless, I'd begun to make some friends among the students, including a couple called Pete Taylor and Andrea Bolitho, who had grown up in Hampshire. By the end of the second year I'd got to know some of my contemporaries quite well. But I was still restless and agitated. Current affairs were always in focus. Policing issues came up regularly and my mind was preoccupied again with Dan's murder.

Near the end of my second year, a 17-year-old black teenager was stabbed to death in Eltham in south-east London, only a few miles from Sydenham. His parents were furious over the Met's investigation of the murder and began campaigning to bring it to the attention of the government. The young man's name was Stephen Lawrence.

I felt great sympathy for the Lawrence family, but I didn't know at the time that there were important connections in the corrupt circle of cops who so

badly botched the investigation of Stephen's murder, and that of my brother Dan only five years earlier.

At the end of that second year, I passed my Higher National Diploma in journalism. The college was simultaneously approved for a degree course, and in September I rented a spare room in a house in St James Avenue with Pete Taylor and Andrea Bolitho for my third year. I had the front room on the ground floor. The furnishing was basic – a bed, desk, chest of drawers and a wardrobe. We all shared a kitchen and a small sitting room with a TV.

* * *

I remember clearly the first time I set eyes on Kirsteen Knight. I was queuing to buy myself a drink at the bar of the Wheatsheaf pub in 1993. The last day of the autumn term had arrived and the pub was heaving with large gangs of students congregating there for a pre-Christmas drink.

In the middle of this scrum, I remember turning around and seeing a young woman in a striking scarlet dress with a head of dark ringlets and large dark brown eyes. I remember thinking how well the red dress set off her hair.

Manoeuvring my way out of the crowd with my Guinness, I scanned the bar for a spare seat. The crowd was too dense to push through, so I stood there and took a couple of sips of my pint.

The young woman in red moved towards a table in the corner of the bar and I noticed she was leaning on an aluminium crutch with a grey plastic ring that fitted round her forearm. 'She's probably sprained her ankle,' I thought.

A group of people sitting at her table stood up and moved towards the door. I made my way over and took a seat at the other end of her table. Two of the other girls from my course were also sitting there. I said hello and took the opportunity to say hello to the girl in the scarlet dress too.

'Have you hurt your ankle?' I asked her, glancing at the crutch leaning against her seat.

'No, I'm disabled,' she said casually and started talking to the other girls, whom she appeared to know. I can't remember how the conversation developed, but I soon discovered that she was a friend of Andrea. Not just friends, they had been best friends since they were eight or nine years old.

'Andrea's parents live near Hay-on-Wye,' I pointed out. 'My mother lives there too. What's your name?' I asked her.

'Kirsty,' she told me.

I soon learned that Kirsteen and Andrea had attended the same ballet school and had been determined to be dancers. Kirsteen had left home aged 16 to attend the Italia Conti Academy of Performing Arts in London. In her second year, she began to notice that her coordination was not quite right and she began falling out of pirouettes. Gradually, she began to have difficulty walking.

Kirsteen was eventually diagnosed with multiple sclerosis. She graduated and despite the MS had found work in contemporary dance and with a dance company that included disabled dancers, touring and performing at the Edinburgh Festival and Sadler's Wells.

'What are you doing now?' I asked.

'I've just got a job at the BBC today.'

'Wow!'

'I don't want it,' she confessed. 'It was an accident.'

'I wish I could get a BBC job by accident!' I laughed.

'It's just that I was talking to somebody in the Diversity Department about what work there might be,' she explained. 'They jumped on me because there was a special disabled position that needed filling. Not my idea of equal opportunities, but I didn't know how to say no. It'll look good on my CV though.'

Kirsteen made a big impression on me. After about an hour she left with Pete and Andrea. I didn't tag along as I didn't want to appear pushy, I just hoped that I would see her again.

The next time I saw Kirsteen was late January the following year. I'd come back late at night to find Pete, Andrea and our two other housemates were all drinking beer and watching a late-night music programme. Andrea was already half-asleep on the sofa. I took a beer from the fridge and joined them. It was only when I sat down that I saw another body in the room.

One female leg was pointing out from under the table. As I moved forward, I saw there was another leg at a 180-degree angle. It was Kirsteen, lying on the floor with her legs at 180 degrees to her face and stomach on the floor. She appeared to be asleep.

I nearly fell over; I was so astonished. Andrea noticed my amazement.

'Don't worry. Kirsty can't drink very much and often falls asleep like that.'

I sat down, unable to take my eyes off Kirsteen, who appeared to be sleeping peacefully in a position that would leave most people needing immediate surgery.

The next morning, Kirsteen was completely unaffected. I was delighted when they invited me to join them for a pub lunch. Kirsteen had driven down from London. The four of us piled into her little white Peugeot and drove to a country pub for a roast beef lunch. After lunch, Pete suggested we play Trivial Pursuit.

'The last time I played Trivial Pursuit someone put an axe in my brother's head,' I said as we started to play the board game.

Pete and Andrea knew what had happened to my brother, but this was news to Kirsteen. I could see that she was surprised by this bizarre revelation. Almost six years had passed since the murder.

'What are you doing, Al?' Pete pointed at my hands. I looked down and saw that I was smoking two cigarettes – I had one in each hand! The game was obviously affecting me, but we all burst out laughing.

We drove back to Farnham all chatting and joking and spent the rest of the afternoon back at the house. Before long, Kirsteen had to drive back to London and started to get her things together to go to her car. She said good-bye, pulled herself to her feet, grabbed her crutch and made for the front door.

'Need any help?' I asked.

'No, I'm fine,' she replied.

I sat down again. Did I have the guts to ask her out?

Andrea walked to the front door with her and said goodbye. Pete was sitting on the sofa, watching telly and enjoying a bottle of beer. 'It's now or never, Al,' I thought, and made my way out to the hallway just as Andrea was returning. I opened the front door just as I heard Kirsteen slam her car door shut. As I hurried down the road she was putting the keys into the ignition. She looked at me, obviously flustered, and wound the window down.

'Er … I was just wondering if you'd let me take you out for a meal some time?'

Her cheeks coloured. I felt panicky.

'But you're too old!' she blurted out.

I wanted the ground to swallow me up – I felt like an actor who'd forgotten his lines in front of an audience of thousands. I was two inches tall.

'But what does age matter?' I heard myself saying.

'I didn't mean that,' she replied. 'It's just that you took me completely by surprise. I wasn't expecting it.'

'Oh … sorry … Er … well … Would you like to …?'

'Okay, telephone me in the week and we can arrange it. Andrea's got my phone number.'

The following weekend, after an anxious week I took the train to Waterloo and then a tube to Soho. Kirsteen arrived in a taxi. We chose a Chinese restaurant, ordered a meal with some wine and chatted as if we'd been friends for years. She told me about her life as a dancer, that it was all she'd ever wanted to do, and that she hadn't really bothered at all with normal school. She'd taken O level English a year early then didn't get any qualifications in the final year.

'When I got MS, I had no Plan B,' she confessed. 'But actually I'm glad I have no real qualifications. If I had, I might have got another job before I realised that I could work as a dancer who just happened not to walk very well.'

I felt there was some kind of complicity or kinship between us. Maybe I was just trying to put a gloss on it. 'Okay, I'm almost twice her age,' I thought, 'but she's been to the edge.'

'I've enjoyed your company,' she said, and took the last sip from her wineglass. 'Thanks for inviting me out.'

'It's been great,' I replied. So great I didn't want the night to end. 'Fancy going somewhere else for a drink?'

'I've got to tell you something,' she said, immediately puncturing my balloon. 'I don't want a boyfriend at the moment, there's no point. When I finish my stint at *That's Life* I want to do more dance work and that'll take me all over the place and it just wouldn't work.'

'That's fine,' I said, inwardly cursing my luck.

I walked her down to Shaftesbury Avenue, where I hailed a taxi for her.

Rejection made me reflect on my life. How had I ended up in the position I was in? Most people had established careers and families at my age. Why was I such a misfit? How had I messed up so badly? And in the end, what could I do about the past? Nothing!

All I could do was move forward, carry on with my degree and hope that things would work out. There were only five months left before we finished our degrees and a real sense of urgency was beginning to build up. Even so, I was always scanning the newspapers, looking to see what the police were up to.

* * *

A couple of weeks after our London date Kirsteen came back down to Farnham. I'd been dreading the potential awkwardness, but to my surprise she seemed relaxed about it. Her visits became more regular, almost every other weekend.

One weekend, I suggested that we go for lunch at a country pub out on the South Downs. Kirsteen wanted to drive. The landlord was one of my window-cleaning customers and I knew the pub served good food. Kirsteen drank a glass of wine with her meal.

'I get drunk on one glass of wine,' she said. She was very small, only five feet two, and the pills she was taking made the alcohol go to her head quicker. We sat in the pub garden for a couple of hours after the meal before she was able to drive.

'I wasn't really being honest about why I didn't go for a drink with you after we met in London,' she suddenly said.

'I can understand, you know, me being a lot older than you.'

'It's not just that. You see, I'm a bit wary of people. I mean I stand out a bit with my MS and men often think I'm some sort of hero because I'm pretty well at ease with being disabled. It's that "triumph over tragedy" thing. I hate it. Once I went to buy an ice cream and the ice cream man gave me a free one. It was as if he gave me it just because I'd dared to come out!'

'Yeah ... I mean, that's ridiculous, but at the same time I don't know how I would have taken it – the MS, I mean. I have to say that I'm pretty impressed. I think lots of people would be too ...'

'No, but it's not that simple. See, lots of men who've had difficult lives tend to believe that I've been through some sort of awful trauma and can share their pain.'

'She means me too,' I thought. Kirsteen was sitting on the grass. I reached out to give her a hand up. She took my arm as we walked back to the car.

Back at St James Avenue, Pete and Andrea were celebrating a win on the quiz machine in one of the local pubs with a takeaway and copious amounts of booze from the off licence. Kirsteen and I joined them for the evening, playing music, laughing and drinking. Pete's a large man, over six feet tall and 15 stone. When he finally fell asleep on the sofa none of us had the strength to move him. This was where Kirsteen normally slept when she came down at weekends.

'Look, Kirsteen, I don't want you sleeping on the floor in one of your crazy positions,' I told her. 'You can have my bed tonight and I'll sleep on the floor.'

I could hear the insincerity in my voice as I spoke – she didn't raise any objections.

| CHAPTER 19 | Serpico Haslam |

1993-1987

The scandal around the murder of black teenager Stephen Lawrence in April 1993 had a much closer connection to the Daniel Morgan murder than either the Morgan family or the public would realise for another 20 years.

The two murders are both milestones and millstones in the modern history of Scotland Yard. Daniel was killed during an interregnum before a new Metropolitan Police Commissioner, Sir Peter Imbert, took over in August 1987. Stephen Lawrence's murder took place just before Imbert's successor, Sir Paul Condon, replaced him in February 1993.

That corruption was still prevalent in the nation's largest police force, especially among plainclothes detectives and specialist squads, was acknowledged by Paul Condon. Indeed, it was the key plank of his manifesto to become commissioner.

Within days of taking office, Condon commissioned a scoping report looking at the flaws in the internal complaints division, CIB 2, and how to 'tackle what was perceived to be a substantial corruption problem within pockets of the MPS [Metropolitan Police Service]'.[1] This marked the beginning of a controversial anti-corruption drive under a new unit, CIB 3, and a highly secretive cell within it, which would become known as 'the Ghost Squad'.

* * *

A few weeks after Condon's arrival as head of the Met, on the night of 22nd April 1993, a 19-year-old black architecture student, Stephen Lawrence, was waiting at a bus stop in Eltham, south-east London with his friend, Duwayne Brooks, when five youths approached them, shouting racist abuse.

Brooks fled, but Lawrence stumbled and was overcome by the group and fatally stabbed. The five attackers were well known locally and with connections to organised crime.

Just as in the case of Daniel Morgan, the area major incident team called out to investigate Stephen's murder drew on the available pool of detectives and police officers in south-east London – some with undisclosed connections to the murder suspects.

Just as in the case of Daniel Morgan, the early days of investigation were tainted by organised incompetence, as the police were given numerous descriptions and intelligence on the suspects, but no arrests were made, or crucial forensics gathered.

And just as it was for the Morgan family, the Lawrence family was left to pick up the pieces of a botched investigation and appeal for justice. Unlike the Morgan family, however, the Lawrence family quickly found a very powerful and persuasive advocate for their cause.

On 6th May 1993, two weeks after the murder, Nelson Mandela, on a state visit to the UK, met with Stephen's parents and listened to their concerns. The iconic South African President spoke out at a press conference comparing the Lawrence family's call for justice with the struggle of black parents who had lost their children in the battle against apartheid. 'It seems black lives are cheap,' he told the family, 'racism threatens the world and must be fought.'

Mandela's intervention made national and even international headlines, and though the police denied they were acting under pressure, on 7th May they swiftly arrested three of the main suspects: James and Neil Acourt and Gary Dobson. Three days later, David Norris, the son of a well-known south London gangster, Clifford Norris, surrendered to police with his solicitor.

Thanks to Mandela, the state of policing in south-east London was under the spotlight. On 30th April, Commander Ray Adams' name had appeared at the bottom of a letter to the dead teenager's family about liaison with the police. Four days later Adams suddenly took sick leave. He'd never return to work again at Scotland Yard.

To *Untouchables* author Laurie Flynn, the intervention of Mandela and the departure of Ray Adams are directly related. To understand the threads that link this back to Daniel Morgan's murder, we have to return to 1987 and the suicide of DC Alan Holmes.

* * *

In early February 1987, only four weeks before the murder of Daniel Morgan, Commander Ray Adams was given the plum job of head of C11, the Criminal

Intelligence unit in Scotland Yard. The circumstances around his appointment and its timing remain perplexing and troubling to this day.

Raymond Charles Adams joined the MPS in September 1962. Over the next 25 years he served in some of the most sensitive posts within policing, including supervising policing in Brixton during the riots of the early 1980s.

It was back in 1971 that Adams had first joined Regional Crime Squad No. 9 – a cross boundary plainclothes detective unit that covered the whole of south-east England, including constabularies outside the Metropolitan Police which would later be reorganised into the South East Regional Crime Squad (SERCS).

When, promoted to the rank of Detective Chief Supertintendent, Adams became the coordinator of the No. 9 Regional Crime Squad in August 1985 and he was soon joined by DS Sidney Fillery, who had been seconded from Catford. If Fillery was the 'King of Catford' then Ray Adams was the Emperor of the South, with a bailiwick that included London and the prosperous Home Counties.

Adams seemed to live a charmed life. He was handsome and charismatic – contemporaries recall he would talk to senior- or junior-ranking officers in the same direct and personable way. He was also married to a Norwegian model, Inga. The couple lived in a huge £450,000 house on the south London equivalent of 'millionaires row' in Shirley, backing on to Addington Golf Course. They reportedly owned a villa in Portugal. Inga ran her own boutique shop, Caesars, just down the road from the Golden Lion in Sydenham, an area Adams frequented for staff parties.[2] Adams would explain that their relatively lavish lifestyle was because his wife was independently wealthy.

According to his police driver from 1983–1985, Adams would regularly visit CID offices in south London to be greeted like a rock star by subordinates, including DS Fillery, DS Alec Leighton and DC Duncan Hanrahan, who would remain a close associate for years. They were all also prominent Freemasons: Adams at the Blackheath Lodge, Hanrahan and Leighton in Norbury, and Rees and Fillery jointly attended a lunch club at Croydon Masonic Halls for serving and retired police officers called 'Brothers in Law'. Meanwhile, Alan Holmes was Master of the Bensham Lodge, to which he recruited Derek Haslam.

In the spirit of support and fraternity, it is standard practice for Freemasonry lodges to share dinners with each other, and other members. But this

networking is also open to abuse by unscrupulous groups who can abuse its rules of confidentiality.

When Adams was made a commander in 1985 in his early forties, he was described as the youngest (or second youngest) Met officer of that rank. After he was appointed head of C11 in 1987, Adams was – in effect – one of the most senior detectives in British policing. This was an extremely powerful role because it not only oversaw the handling of high-level informants, but most covert operations too.

It was also a controversial appointment. Adams had already been subject to 11 complaints between 1965 and 1985, unsubstantiated, withdrawn or not proceeded with. He was renowned as an informant handler. His most celebrated informant was the gangster Kenneth Noye, who was under investigation for helping to launder millions of pounds' worth of proceeds for the Brink's-Mat bullion heist from Heathrow in 1983.

While under surveillance in 1985, Noye had stabbed to death an undercover officer hiding in his property, PC John Fordham. After his arrest Noye had told officers that Ray Adams was his handler and could testify he wasn't a violent man. Adams then met Noye in the cells at Lambeth Magistrates' Court when he appeared on remand for the murder. Noye was acquitted of the charges at an Old Bailey trial in 1985.

Adams' appointment to head of C11 also came as a shock to the officer who had been appointed to the job.

At the beginning of 1987, Commander Thelma Wagstaff thought she had been given the job heading up criminal intelligence mainly because of her stellar track record but also partly because – being a woman – she could not be a member of the Freemasons. But when Wagstaff moved into her new office in February 1987 and began to unpack her belongings, she was told to leave by mid-afternoon. A prominent Freemason, Ray Adams, was replacing her.

Adams would remain in the post for less than four months. Within days of Daniel's murder, he would be subject to an internal investigation that would lead to another violent, untimely death.

* * *

Detective Constable Alan Holmes, nicknamed 'Taffy' because of his Welsh origins, joined the police in 1961 and was promoted to detective in 1972 based in Addington, near Croydon. In 1984 he'd been seconded to the Flying Squad

in Barnes, south-west London, after the Brink's-Mat robbery of gold bullion from a Heathrow Airport warehouse the previous year. After that he moved to the Serious Crime Squad based in Tottenham Court Road in Central London to track down the £25m or so proceeds from the heist, which had been melted down and processed through various branches of organised crime.

Known more for his networking abilities than his detective skills, Holmes was a dedicated Freemason and openly admitted to friends his plum jobs were partly due to the influence of Freemasonry.

Though Holmes was a gregarious host who was known for providing cuts of meat for Friday night barbecues with senior officers, the Welsh-born detective was troubled and police reports claim he often drank to excess. Married with two adopted young boys, he was having a not-so-clandestine affair with Jean Burgess, former wife of a convicted armed robber, Henry George Burgess.

Holmes had arrested 'Chick' Burgess for safe blowing in 1968 but it wasn't until 1980, after Jean Burgess had divorced, that the seven-year-long relation-ship began. Jean Burgess was 50 and Taffy Holmes was 44. By this time, the robber Chick Burgess had been a long-time informant of Holmes' mentor, Commander Ray Adams.

Then came the events of 1987.

The most important connection between Taffy Holmes and Daniel Morgan was the allegation that, at the beginning of that year, both had been touting a story to the British national press of a multi-million-pound cocaine importa-tion overseen by corrupt police officers and customs officials.

But this connection is still mired in doubt. While multiple sources maintain Daniel was about to reveal a large story of police corruption before his murder, there are only three main sources that say Holmes was involved; one of those is Jonathan Rees, who was deemed even back in 1989 as not a 'witness of truth' and the second is hearsay.[3]

At present, only a single source, Derek Haslam, can independently confirm the involvement of DC Alan Holmes.

* * *

PC Derek Haslam had joined the Metropolitan Police Force in August 1973 and was transferred to the CID in December 1975. Two years later, he collided with an intoxicated pedestrian who walked out in front of his car. The man later died as a result of his injuries. Haslam was disqualified from driving for 12

months and was returned to uniform. Within a year, however, he was again in plain clothes and attached to the Addington Crime Squad. Around this time, Haslam became friends with Alan Holmes.

Ten years later, Derek Haslam was part of the circle that included Sidney Fillery, Jonathan Rees and Daniel Morgan.

Haslam had first met Rees through his police work. Rees was a regular feature at Croydon police stations as he was often sent by his lawyer friend Michael Goodridge to sit in on police interviews. Haslam remembers that he 'was very much a police groupie in those days' and was regularly invited to police drinks and retirement parties. In the year leading up to the murder, Rees called Haslam on his car phone.

In the same way, Haslam also met Daniel Morgan on the south-east London pub circuit. According to Haslam, Daniel also met DC Alan Holmes and began a friendship with him in September 1985. Holmes would identify himself as 'Omo' when ringing up – referring to the washing machine powder, which in ads at that time 'washes whiter than white'.

In 1986, Derek Haslam recalls seeing Daniel Morgan and Taffy Holmes together at a south London wine bar called Gossips. Haslam, who had been introduced to Freemasonry by Holmes, understood that Taffy was intending to do the same for Daniel.

Haslam's first encounter of DS Sid Fillery was during his investigation in 1986 into a ring controlling three amphetamine factories in the south-east of England. One of the gang had killed a courier after taking his cash and keeping the drugs. The courier had then been thrown from a moving car, but his leg had stuck in the safety belt and as his body hit a bollard, he was decapitated.

Haslam's inquiries into the murder led him to another amphetamine dealer called Raymond Gray, who was living in Catford. Haslam thought he could be arrested and turned into a useful informant against the gang leaders who had killed the courier. As head of the local crime squad, DS Sid Fillery helped Haslam with surveillance on Gray's address. Fillery also told Haslam he was planning to retire from the Met soon to start a caravan park.[4]

It was around this time that Derek Haslam says he heard from Taffy Holmes of a much bigger drug deal, this time involving cocaine.

They met at an Indian restaurant in Thornton Heath in early 1987 when Alan Holmes claimed he had a story of a £100m cocaine importation from Miami in

four consignments, overseen by two corrupt customs officials and three senior officers at the Met. Daniel was also alleged to have paperwork to back this up.

There is little doubt that Taffy Holmes was in a position to know such a story. By 1987, Holmes was working in Tottenham Court Road on the 'Collection Plan' – an extensive international operation that used satellite tracking and RAF Nimrods to follow cocaine and cannabis shipments from Spain to the UK, and disrupt the economics of the drug-trafficking trade.

Holmes was a heavy drinker and Haslam dismissed the story as a flight of fancy until Daniel was murdered in March 1987. Having previously worked with the lead murder investigator, Haslam personally went to see Detective Superintendent Campbell to pass on this curry-house conversation with Holmes. Though both agreed that the £250,000 fee Daniel was supposed to be negotiating sounded implausible, the chief murder investigator promised to look into it.

Back on the trial of the amphetamine factory bosses who had killed the courier, Haslam and his colleague, PC Jerry Lunnis, a former military policeman, arrested the dealer Raymond Gray and an associate in possession of 3¾kg of uncut amphetamine on 3rd April 1987. (Coincidentally the day after the arrests of Rees and Fillery.)

The captured chemicals were relatively pure so Haslam and Lunnis knew they were getting closer to the source manufacturers. They offered Gray a deal: they would lessen the possession with intent to supply charges if he agreed to become an informant and reveal more about the amphetamine gang implicated in murder. Gray accepted their offer.

Because Gray was a 'prolific chatterer', Haslam and Lunnis decided to record the interviews. All in all, ten tapes were made. The first five covered the evidence of Gray's drug dealing and his arrest, but as part of Haslam's aim to find out more about the murder and the ring controlling the amphetamine factories, the next four were 'intelligence tapes' about organised crime and drug dealing in south London.

But then something derailed the debrief: on his way back to the cell after an interview, Gray expressed concern that a corrupt senior police officer he knew of 'could disrupt the operation' and expose him as an informant.

Implicating a senior officer in corruption was a major headache. Haslam and Lunnis were attached to the Serious Crime Squad based in Totttenham Court Road.

They travelled to Central London to speak to a detective chief superintendent from SO1 (7).

But the detective chief superintendent wasn't there, so Haslam asked if his friend DC Alan Holmes, who worked at the adjacent unit SO1 (8), was around. At this point Holmes was working on Operation Wimpey, a major drugs trafficking investigation that had intercepted Garry Vian talking on the phone about Daniel Morgan's murder and the sudden overseas trip of Joey Pyle.

Haslam and Lunnis were (unsurprisingly) directed to a local pub to find Taffy – the White Hart. But by the time they got there, Holmes had gone. Instead they encountered a detective inspector who wondered why the two Croydon detectives were being attached to SO1 (7) rather than the Central Drugs Squad.

Derek Haslam explained that there was an officer – they didn't know who – in the Central Drugs Squad who could potentially expose their informant and disrupt their inquiry.

Both Lunnis and Haslam heard the detective inspector exclaim: 'Not that bastard Ray Adams again! He has fucked up so many jobs, it's untrue. There are operations which we would like to mount but he would blow them out.'

The senior officer then went on to talk of allegations of a £2m bribe offered to police dealing with one of Adams' key informants since 1979, the notorious gangster Kenneth Noye.[5] Lunnis recalled the officer saying he couldn't understand 'the most senior detective in London, having access to all criminal intelligence, frankly being a bent copper'.

Derek Haslam and Jerry Lunnis returned to south London to interview Raymond Gray, who was due in court the next day to face the amphetamine charges. On 8th and 9th April, they recorded a fifth tape just in case Gray could identify the corrupt officer so that they could protect their investigations.

To their surprise, Gray proceeded to catalogue dozens of alleged crimes, including numerous named serving police officers. Among his allegations of corruption was none other than Commander Ray Adams.

In Gray's account, in 1972, prior to an armed robbery, he had been arrested by Adams who was then a detective inspector in the Regional Crime Squad. In detention in South Norwood Police Station, Gray said he was told by another detective sergeant that if he paid money to the 'guv'nor' his charges would be reduced from conspiracy to rob to conspiracy to steal scrap metal.

Gray maintained he didn't have the means to proffer the bribe, but eventually the charges were reduced anyway because the others 'paid'. Gray claimed Adams kept up a vendetta against him for the non-payment, and even tried to frame him for a burglary.

The following morning Haslam took the fifth tape to his immediate boss in Croydon. Detective Chief Supertintendent Bernie Davies was head of the Area Major Incident Pool (AMIP) for the Met's area 4 of operations adjacent to area 3 which had responded to Daniel Morgan's murder. He was considered, after the promotion of Commander Adams, to be the most senior officer in the south-east.

According to Haslam, Davies looked 'really uncomfortable' at Gray's allegations and insisted on hearing the tape. About a third of the way through he switched off the tape machine and asked, 'Am I mentioned in this tape?' Haslam told him that his name had not been mentioned. 'Where is Gray now?' asked Davies.

When Haslam explained he was still downstairs in the police station, Davies rushed down to the cells without putting on his uniform tie and pulled the 'wicket' back on the cell door to demand of the sleepy informant. 'You know what you are saying?' Davies asked. 'You can't say that,' he told Gray, according to Haslam. 'What have you got to back all this up?'

'Do you recognise me?' Davies persisted. 'Have you seen me before?' Gray said he hadn't.

Because of the seriousness of the claims, DS Bernie Davies said he would have to refer the matter to more senior officers.[6] 'I'm gonna have to ring Tottenham Court Road about this,' he told Haslam.

Because the allegations of corruption were becoming more specific, Haslam was instructed to take Gray up to the Complaints Investigation Bureau (CIB 2) at Tintagel House on the south bank of the Thames opposite Parliament so that Gray could be properly interviewed by the Met's internal affairs department.

Haslam recalls telling Gray his claims of police corruption would neither help police investigations into the amphetamine trade, nor lead to any proper action. Because 'he's a Commander' the internal affairs department would never take the word of a drug dealer like Gray against Adams: 'But it's your decision, it's totally up to you.'

'In that case,' Gray replied, 'I'll tell them fuck all. I'm not interested.'

Haslam booked Gray into CIB 2 and then went to have a coffee... Then another coffee. Two hours later, Gray walked out of the interview with the internal affairs officers. Haslam took him back to his car and noted: 'For someone who said they weren't interested in helping, you took a long time to say "no".'

Criminal Intelligence

1987–1993

The internal inquiry into Raymond Gray's allegations would lead to a second violent death in 1987: that of DC Alan 'Taffy' Holmes, only four months after Daniel Morgan's murder. The inquests into both deaths would take place within weeks of each other the following year, but strangely, Holmes' would come first.

To Laurie Flynn, co-author of *Untouchables*, the timing of Holmes' inquest was 'staged' to sever any connection with Daniel, and any reference to allegations of police corruption.

Operation Russell began on 16th April 1987 with the following terms of reference: 'To investigate all aspects of police corruption and malpractice arising from interviews held with Raymond John Gray'. It soon widened to include the allegations made in the White Horse pub about Ray Adams' connections to Kenneth Noye.

The internal affairs investigation would become one of the most contentious in the history of Scotland Yard, and was described by Commander Thelma Wagstaff, who took over part of the related inquiries, as 'the worst allegation of corruption ever to be levelled at the Metropolitan Police'. This was mainly because of the seniority of its main subject – Commander Ray Adams – who was investigated for 12 criminal allegations mainly focused on his relationship with senior underworld figures and eight disciplinary complaints.[1]

For the next three years the internal inquiry would look at dozens of allegations of police corruption going back over 15 years to 1972. In total, 25 criminal allegations were looked into, including perjury, bribery, corrupt association, theft of drugs, and conspiracy to pervert the course of justice. Eighteen disciplinary complaints were also investigated, involving over a dozen officers.

But back in April 1987, at the outset of the inquiry, the immediate personal problem for Derek Haslam was his friendship with Taffy Holmes, who was

also close to Commander Adams. Holmes had told Haslam that becoming head of C11 in 1987 had been Ray Adams' lifetime ambition 'because it was like being given keys to the sweet-shop'. Now that was in jeopardy.

Taffy Holmes first learned of the allegations against his mentor Adams when he met Derek Haslam on the night of 13th April at a prearranged training session at a Masonic Lodge of Instruction on Oakfield Road in Croydon, where Taffy was officiating as Master. Now the tragic triangle was set.

Given his friendship with both the officer who had initiated the corruption probe, and the main target of it, Holmes tried to act as a 'linkman'. 'He wants the tapes, he wants the tapes,' Holmes pleaded with Haslam on behalf of Adams over Gray's allegations. 'He's a commander, you know. He's a Mason too.'

Derek Haslam kept trying to tell Alan Holmes to 'keep out of it'. 'Nothing will happen,' he tried to reassure the Welsh detective. 'This complaint will go nowhere because Raymond Gray is a convicted criminal. No one will believe him. End of.'

When debriefed a few days later, Haslam told two of the internal affairs, CIB 2 officers, without revealing Taffy Holmes was the intermediary, Adams' offer of a meeting.

'It's totally unethical for a commander as clean as the driven snow to set up this approach,' Haslam told Detective Sergeant Paul Turrell and Detective Superintendent Banks on the 29th April. 'If it speeds up your investigation, I'll meet him and wear a wire because it will be all sorted then. If he agrees to the meeting, he's disciplined,' he added.

The CIB 2 officers refused.

By this point, Derek Haslam's colleague, Jerry Lunnis, thought the internal investigation was just 'inept', but Haslam suspected CIB 2 had a more focused agenda, to undermine the allegations: 'handed a complaint, they were working to see how they could destroy the essence of that complaint'. Nevertheless, the internal complaints branch did devote considerable resources to the Adams' investigation.

On 8th May a police helicopter caught an illicit meeting between Taffy Holmes and Commander Adams on the golf course behind his house. Holmes was carrying a shotgun, as he had a licence to shoot rabbits there. By this time, Adams had received notice of the internal investigation, a Form 163 setting out Gray's allegations, and CIB 2 had photographed him for their records.

Nine days later, Taffy Holmes happened to 'bump into' the amphetamine dealer Raymond Gray and told him not to cooperate with the investigation.[2] Gray was by now receiving death threats and refused to talk to the internal affairs detectives any further. But Holmes' attempt to protect his commander would backfire, badly.

The attempt to fix the internal investigation was only creating more to investigate. While still protecting his friend Alan Holmes as a source, Derek Haslam warned the CIB 2 officers at a debrief on 3rd June that their investigation was not 'watertight'. The internal affairs officers objected – they had kept a 'sterile corridor' between themselves and any other police operation – but when Haslam told him he'd heard how the police helicopter had flown over Ray Adams' house and taken photographs, they were outraged: 'How do you know that?'

'Perhaps you're not as watertight as you think you are,' Haslam replied.

On 9th July, Alan Holmes visited Derek Haslam's home address in a distressed state. He'd learned from Ray Adams that their illicit meeting had been photographed from a police helicopter; he also had information from his girlfriend, Jean Burgess, that her ex, the safe blower and armed robber Chick Burgess, had set up a meeting with Adams at Selhurst Park railway station.

Throughout July 1987 Haslam kept in contact with Alan Holmes, partially to gain advance intelligence about the moves Adams might make against him. Haslam was right to be suspicious: he was warned that his personnel file had been found in an anteroom outside Adams' office with the inference that the commander was planning to 'put a retrospective derogatory comment in there' to explain why Haslam might get an informant to 'bad-mouth' him.

Then the threats began.

At a Thornton Heath curry house soon afterwards, in front of his lover, Jean Burgess, Alan Holmes relayed an ultimatum to Derek Haslam: 'Unless you start cooperating with Ray Adams, something nasty could happen to you or a member of your family.' Haslam recalled Holmes followed this up with the rider: 'If you think you derive any pleasure from the thought that he would be caught, he said I can assure you he'd be a million miles away when anything happens.'

Haslam knew the Metropolitan Police commander had 'dangerous connections'. Ray Adams had been caught in Spain playing cards with a famous north London crime family – the Adams family (no relation) – and had excused himself with the alibi: 'I was just cultivating informants'.

But Jean Burgess responded forcefully to the intimidation of Haslam with a threat of her own: 'If anything happens to Derek or his family,' the former wife of the armed robber said, 'I'll personally go to the Yard, and tell them what a bent bastard Ray Adams is, and how I paid him out on his own doorstep on behalf of Chick.'

* * *

The detectives leading Operation Russell were obsessed about the leaks from their investigation. These weren't just a disciplinary offence. Given the criminal nature of many of Gray's allegations the contact could constitute perverting the course of justice – a crime in itself.

There was more than one connection. Given that Alan Holmes was having an affair with Jean Burgess, who was the former partner of Chick Burgess, a known informant of Commander Adams, it didn't take CIB 2 long to work out who the 'linkman' was.

Though Derek Haslam had refused to identify Alan Holmes, the internal affairs detectives talked to another police officer in whom Haslam had confided, who was promised relocation out of London in return for revealing Adams' intermediary.

Two days later, on Saturday 17th July 1987, having been up most of the night on a surveillance operation, Derek Haslam was asked to call Tintagel House, where DS Turrell began talking about a 'mutual friend' who had 'joined the police after 1960' and 'had two children and he lives in Shirley, you know who I'm talking about?'

Haslam replied he'd been up all night in a car park in Kent 'trying to read car numbers by braille. I'm a bit tired and over-stressed, I don't really want to play games.' But there was no doubt the CIB 2 officer was talking about Alan 'Taffy' Holmes.

'Mr Winship's a bit cross with you because you haven't told him the name before,' said Turrell, referring to the deputy assistant commissioner who was then head of both CIB 1, which dealt with discipline, and CIB 2, which investigated complaints. 'What he wants you to do,' he continued, 'is contact Alan Holmes this morning and tell him that if he doesn't present himself voluntarily to DAC Winship at Tintagel House by 2pm this Sunday, he will be arrested the next day in front of his wife and family on Monday morning in Shirley. Will you pass this message on?'

'Have I got any choice?' asked Haslam.

'No,' Turrell replied.

Derek Haslam called Tottenham Court Road and later that afternoon tracked down Taffy Holmes outside Scotland Yard 'somewhat inebriated'. He got into Holmes' car.

By this point Haslam believed the car had been 'bugged up anyway' so he passed on the message from DAC Winship about contacting the Internal Affairs Bureau tomorrow or being arrested for corruption on the Monday morning.

'I don't know who you're involved with, what you're involved in,' Haslam said. 'What's more, what I would say to you is: I shouldn't be asked to pass this message on, it should come from your senior officer.' He also advised Taffy: 'Before you say anything, I'd speak to your senior officer and also seek legal advice.'

Mortified, Alan Holmes wanted to stop at the White Swan pub in Crystal Palace, run by a former detective sergeant, Lionel Peacock. His face was such a picture of distress that Peacock exclaimed as he entered: 'What the fuck's happened to you?'

'Ask him,' Holmes replied, gesturing to Haslam. 'Looks like I'm going to get nicked.'

'I've just been asked to pass on a message,' Haslam explained to Peacock, 'I've passed the black spot on telling him he's got to contact CIB regarding his relationship with Adams.'

Lionel Peacock went to pick up Jean Burgess from her work at the Gas Board in Croydon. When they returned, Haslam explained what had so upset her boyfriend: 'It's to do with Ray Adams.'

'Oh, that fucking Adams!' Haslam recalls Burgess saying, 'he's been the bane of my family's life. When Chick went away [to prison] what did I get out of it? Two manky shell suits from his wife's boutique!'[3]

Holmes' reaction to this criticism of Adams was protective: 'Jeanie, Jeanie, he's a commander.'

Derek Haslam reminded Jean Burgess of her threat to reveal all if Adams continued with his intimidation: 'Perhaps now's the time?'

'I will and all,' she replied.

'You can't do that,' protested Taffy.

Haslam left the pub to phone the CIB 2 officers to tell them he'd passed on the message. They insisted on meeting him outside the Met area, and on

arrival at the White Horse pub in Warlingham, he was surrounded by detective chief inspectors and superintendents.

At Caterham Police Station, it seemed as if half of Scotland Yard's senior officers had turned up to debrief Haslam. Haslam signed a statement relaying what had happened, but suggested if they really wanted to get Ray Adams they should talk to Jean Burgess, who'd now said twice she was a witness to corrupt payments. 'If you're gentle with her, and let her think she's helping Taffy,' he added, 'you'll get what you want.'

As he was heading back to his car, Haslam banged his head on the door frame and needed plasters. He took the time out to tell the CIB 2 officers that although Alan Holmes looked hard on the outside, inside he was quite soft: 'If you are serious, what I said about Jean Burgess is the way to go.'

Meanwhile, Burgess and Holmes had gone on from the pub meeting to the Warren Sports Club, where they met one of Ray Adams' associates and Taffy's colleague in Tottenham Court Road – Detective Sergeant John Davidson, otherwise known as 'OJ': 'Obnoxious Jock'.

* * *

On 19th July 1987, both Jean Burgess and Alan Holmes were interviewed voluntarily by the internal affairs department at their Tintagel House base. Burgess gave more details about Adams' relationship with Chick Burgess, which went back to 1971 when he had arrived as a detective inspector at the Regional Crime Squad and arrested Burgess and two others for a £62,000 heist. Chick had fled to Canada briefly and avoided prosecution for this, despite many previous convictions. Within a year, Ray Adams and his family were holidaying in Portugal with Chick and Jean, hiring a car together. She was also quizzed about the alleged £6,000 payout on his doorstep.

Soon after, Taffy Holmes was interviewed about the various meetings he had had with Adams since Raymond Gray's allegations had initiated Operation Russell. His statements were cross-checked with those of Commander Ray Adams.

There were contradictory answers given by Holmes and Adams about the dates, timings and content of their meetings. Adams conceded that Holmes had turned up at his house in May with a shotgun to shoot rabbits: 'He made some excuse about losing his pipe and they both went onto the golf course, where he "sensed that something was troubling" Taffy.'[4]

The team also confirmed that Adams had met Chick Burgess, and that Holmes had 'accidentally' bumped into Raymond Gray and had told him, on Adams' behalf, not to cooperate with the investigation.[5]

The investigators concluded that Alan Holmes tipped off Ray Adams after Derek Haslam had told him of Gray's allegations and had then kept him informed of key stages of the internal inquiry.

With a potential conspiracy emerging, CIB 2 now went in hard.

On 23rd July Jean Burgess was arrested on suspicion of conspiring to pervert the course of justice and bribery. According to Haslam she was locked up in Holborn Police Station for eight or nine hours with no representation until her former partner's solicitor was sent over.

Haslam believes that Burgess' life had been threatened at this point. 'They'd been given the can opener' to the can of worms around Adams, but 'instead used a hammer'.

Jean Burgess clammed up on the second interview under caution. This time round, she denied witnessing the payout to Adams, but did admit she had been approached by Chick Burgess to keep quiet.

'Were you frightened by your husband when he came round to see you last Sunday?' Burgess was asked by one of her interrogators.

'I won't say frightened, no,' she replied.

'But there was an argument,' the detective persisted, 'and it got unpleasant, and he told you he ought to be loyal to him [Adams].'

'Well, that was his attitude, yes.'

'So, he was supporting Ray Adams and didn't want you to cooperate with anything we were doing?'

'Yeah.'

The inquiry team concluded that Chick Burgess 'still has a great deal of influence over his ex-wife'. Jean was later released without charge.

This left only Taffy Holmes himself on the hook for Adams' career and quite possibly something worse.

Holmes was also interviewed under caution on the same day as his girlfriend. He was in a much trickier situation because the unauthorised meetings with Adams were at the very least a serious disciplinary offence. His conversation with Gray also left him open to a much more serious criminal charge of perverting the course of justice.

After the interview, Holmes was described as in a 'very distressed state'. Suspended pending further investigation and barred from contact with Adams, he spent much of the rest of the time with a joint friend, DS John Davidson.

* * *

Detective Sergeant John 'OJ' Davidson joined the Met in June 1970 and was an experienced detective in several high-profile units, including C8 Flying Squad and SO1 Organised Crime task force. Like Taffy, he worked on the Brink's-Mat squad, and was another close ally of Adams. He would also appear as a channel of influence in the notorious Stephen Lawrence murder inquiry six years later. For the next few weeks he became Holmes' main minder.

The last time Derek Haslam saw Alan Holmes alive was at a pub in Shirley on 20th July 1987, where he 'glowered at me over the bar'. Haslam was surprised – he hadn't assisted the anti-corruption investigation into his friend Taffy in any way, only passed the message on.

Because the threats to himself and his family 'were connected to organised crime at a serious level', that July of 1987 Haslam sold his house and bought a place in Norfolk 'to create distance from London'. Until that purchase completed, he lived in his mother's maisonette while his wife Susan and four kids stayed with his mother-in-law in Carshalton. But the day after Derek and his family moved out of south Croydon, a neighbour saw a man fitting Taffy Holmes' description hanging around his old address, wielding a shotgun. The neighbour called the police.

The Welsh detective was on the hook for several offences and the pressure was beginning to tell. The official Met report states that Holmes 'broke down in front of Superintendent claiming that CIB were holding his mistress Jean Burgess hostage and were blackmailing him to say things which were not true. He was particularly concerned his colleagues would consider him a "grass".'

By now Holmes was convinced that his friend Haslam 'had tried to fit them up', leaving him no choice but to 'inform on Adams'. Because Jean Burgess had also been interviewed, Holmes told his wife about his continuing affair. She had learned about Burgess 18 months previously through her husband's confession, but had thought the relationship was over.

On 25th July, according to a later statement from Jean Burgess, Holmes told her that he felt suicidal and spent some time trying to locate the position of his heart. He left the following morning. She never saw him alive again

That same Sunday morning, Holmes told his wife Leonie that he was in disgrace and was expecting to be asked to resign both from work and the Freemasonry. He was concerned that if he resigned he would lose his police pension and was worried about how the family would live.

On 27th July, Holmes spent the day with DS Davidson who noted that he was quieter than usual but feared he would be forced to resign from the Freemasonry and stated again that he had done nothing wrong and that Haslam was a liar. That night Taffy read his children stories before they went to bed.

At 6:50am on the morning of Tuesday, 28th July, Holmes' wife came down from her bedroom in the early morning and noticed both the kitchen light was on and the television in the back extension. She also spotted various notes, a diary, cash and a wallet containing Taffy's credit cards on a small table.

When Leonie Holmes opened the curtains to the garden she saw her husband lying on a chair with blood on his chest, his shotgun by his side. Holmes had died from a gunshot wound to the heart; he was 44-years-old. Among the papers on the table was a note: 'Under different circumstances I would never have left you and the children. But by the actions of Haslam and CIB I have been forced to inform on a CID police commander,' the note said.

On the reverse of his last message Taffy Holmes added: 'I trusted Haslam completely but tell them all he is a Serpico.'

Taffy's widow called a friend, who, when she woke up her two young sons, distracted them from the awful scene in the garden and led them out of the house.

Derek Haslam heard of the apparent suicide when he turned up for duty at Addington Police Station. He immediately rang DS Turrell at CIB 2, who told Haslam his life was in danger: 'Get out of there, go somewhere safe. We'll be in contact.'

On his way out of the station another uniformed officer updated Haslam with more information: 'I shouldn't tell you this, but you're mentioned in the suicide note.' He also revealed how Holmes had shot himself in the chest in his garden, with the shotgun laid under his right arm.

'Straight away, this didn't ring true,' Haslam recalled. 'Most policemen have been to suicides that have gone wrong, possibly involving shotguns. Worldwide, if a policeman commits suicide they "eat the barrel" [they put it in their mouth]. They don't shoot themselves in the chest because so many things can go wrong.'[6]

The arrangement of the gun also didn't sound right. 'He's gone into the garden with a full-length shotgun and pulled the trigger with his toe, with the gun pointing into his chest,' Haslam explained. 'The kinetics of the recoil of a 12-bore shotgun would normally mean an unsecured shotgun would either catapult forwards or backwards. It's most unlikely that someone's grip would be strong enough to let it just slip by their side.'

The fingerprint officer attending the scene, Christopher de Berg, could find no fingerprints on the shotgun.

Haslam was out of the picture now, put on gardening leave for his own protection.

* * *

'COP KILLED HIMSELF TO SAVE PALS IN THE MASONS – YARD MEN'S FURY' ran the headline in the *News of the World* on Sunday, 2nd August 1987. The article was credited to the newspaper's news editor, Alex Marunchak, and Gerry Brown (a surveillance expert who – like his son Conrad – would work extensively with the 'Fake Sheikh' Mazher Mahmood).

Without naming Adams or Haslam, the article detailed the Masonic links between the officers and laid the blame on 'cop killer Kenneth Noye' – a line the newspaper would pursue for the next two decades.

Alex Marunchak went on to describe how the dead detective 'wouldn't give evidence against Masons involved'. A senior officer, Detective Superintendent Bob Green, had made a formal complaint against CIB 2 'in effect accusing the anti-corruption squad of driving Taffy Holmes to his death'.

On 3rd August 1987 a new Met Commissioner, Peter Imbert, was sworn in. At his press conference Imbert pledged to root out corruption. However, he also went out of his way to emphasise to the press pack that Taffy Holmes was 'not in any way suspected of any wrongdoing' even though his subordinates knew Holmes was the major target of one of the Met's most serious corruption investigations for years.

The same day, in a front-page headline 'POLICE CHIEF IN PROBE', *The Daily Express* reporter Norman Luck gave many more details about a 'massive dossier on a senior officer' and his luxurious house in 'millionaires' row' and an expensive 'villa in the sun'.

Without naming Adams, the report suggested the officer was one 'of the class of '71 – all members of the squad headed by the officer under investigation'

and repeated the allegations that a £2m bribe was offered to a top policeman in the inquiry into the Brink's-Mat bullion robbery at Heathrow in 1983'.[7]

The Express did name 'DC Haslam' for the first time though, with allegations he was the target of a £5,000 contract on his life. It also quoted sources at Scotland Yard saying that Haslam had been 'unjustly victimised' and was a 'straight copper'.

'FUNERAL DILEMMA AS YARD FIGHTS SCANDAL' ran the headline in The Daily Express the next day. Norman Luck finally named Commander Ray Adams as the senior officer under investigation and outlined the pressure being put on the new Commissioner, Peter Imbert, to authorise a police funeral with full honours for Alan 'Taffy' Holmes as if he had died performing his duty.[8]

Holmes did indeed receive a full-service funeral at a cremation ceremony on 11th August 1987 with orations and an honour guard to 'keep up the illusion that Holmes died untainted by scandal'. 'Five hundred detectives turned up to pay their last respects,' Norman Luck reported in The Daily Express the next day, noting a wreath describing Holmes as a 'shining light to what a police officer should be'.

Though Haslam believed his presence at the sombre event might be a distraction, he planned to visit the cemetery afterwards to pay his respects. A female colleague who had worked with him in the past (and now worked with CIB 2) invited him out for lunch instead, but he refused the offer. He could tell they were trying to keep him away.

Meanwhile a campaign of misinformation was spreading through the press. The Sun newspaper claimed Derek Haslam had taken Alan Holmes for a game of golf and secretly tape-recorded him confessing to being involved in corruption – describing Haslam, just like the suicide note, as a 'Serpico', based on the true story of a New York Police Department whistle-blower, Frank Serpico, who had been shot in the face for exposing police corruption. His story was turned into a hit movie with Al Pacino and directed by Sidney Lumet in 1977.

That Sunday Alex Marunchak covered the funeral in somewhat more lurid detail. 'YARD THROW PARTY FOR SUICIDE COP'S LOVER' was the News of the World's headline, focusing on the party held for Jean Burgess at the Prince of Wales pub in Thornton Heath, and a wreath from her estranged husband, Chick Burgess: 'To you from me. Thinking of you always'.

Marunchak estimated 1,000 police officers were in attendance. The two-page splash reiterated the claim that the dead detective was a 'high-level Mason' emphasised the Brink's-Mat connection and noted that Kenneth Noye was under investigation by the Grand Lodge of England for using his Masonic influence to try and bribe detectives.[9] But the main focus of the story was Holmes' complicated love life. The article led on the revelation that there were two wakes on the day of his funeral: the first for his widow, Lee, and his two young adopted sons; the second an unofficial drinking session for his mistress, Jean Burgess, whose 'husband Chick has a record for armed robbery'.[10]

Like its sister paper, *The Sun*, the *News of the World* spread the false rumour that 'Serpico' Haslam had 'secretly taped' Holmes, further increasing Haslam's isolation and risk of reprisal.[11]

Alex Marunchak wasn't just operating as a journalist at this point, but also as a police informant. On 12th August, a day after the funeral, as he was writing up a report for the *News of the World*, Marunchak rang the Met's Central Office of Information with a potentially incriminatory tip-off.

He told the Met that Commander Adams was recognised by a police driver making a rendezvous with a Detective Superintendent Bernie Davies at a pub in Croydon. Davies was a person of interest to Operation Russell, as he was alleged to be close to Ray Adams and to have attended the birthday party of Joey Pyle, a senior figure on the south London crime scene. He was also Haslam's overall commanding officer and this was, potentially, further illicit contact for senior officers under investigation.[12]

When later questioned about this by the Operation Russell team, Marunchak 'declined to disclose his source or assist in any way'. The report went on: 'This left the two alleged participants who both vehemently deny the meeting took place and indeed, both professing to dislike each other'.[13]

* * *

On leave of absence for over a month, Derek Haslam feared for his life. After taking his kids on a day trip to the Warren Wildlife Area, he returned to his Austin Allegro only to find the car had been tampered with. Someone had cut through the hard rubber attached to the manifold with a sharp blade, with flammable petrol flowing all over the engine: it was a ticking fire-bomb.

By now another investigation had been launched, this time into CIB 2 and the allegations that they had driven Alan Holmes to an early grave.

Heading up that internal inquiry into the Met's own internal inquiry team was none other than Thelma Wagstaff,[14] who had been peremptorily jettisoned from the job as head of criminal intelligence in favour of Ray Adams six months before. She began the lengthy process of interviewing Derek Haslam about his role in the affair.

Haslam himself had become suspicious of CIB 2's real motivations. They had undermined Gray's credibility by speaking to a doctor who wrote a report saying his patient was 'deranged' and a drug user – even though the doctor added he did not think Gray's evidence was fabricated. They also denied asking Haslam to pass any ultimatum to Taffy.[15]

Ray Adams himself was interviewed several more times that August and alleged that Gray had only made his false accusations because he was involved in a murder related to his drug dealing. (At the same time in August 1987, Jonathan Rees was suggesting a similar story with his press contacts that Daniel Morgan was killed by an axe-wielding drug enforcer because Dan was trying to buy drugs for his older brother.)[16]

For his safety, Haslam was reassigned to the CPS office in Norbury, which liaised with the Crown Prosecution Service, checking case papers before trial. He got a retraction from *The Sun* for the claim he had taped and betrayed his dead friend, Alan Holmes.

In the meantime, Haslam received frequent visits from an old associate, DC Duncan Hanrahan, who would ask how he was getting on and probe as to the progress of Operation Russell.

Not long after, Derek Haslam walked into his Norbury office to find an anonymous hand-written message on his desk: 'You Judas rat. You're fucking dead'.[17]

Wagstaff's report on Taffy Holmes' death on 5th November exonerated Haslam from any suggestion that he'd deliberately betrayed his friend. Haslam recalled that Wagstaff also told him the coming inquest would skip over the ongoing corruption investigation and that 'domestic reasons' for Alan Holmes' suicide would be put forward to the coroner.

* * *

The coroner's inquest into the death of DC Alan Holmes took place on 11th March 1988, only a day after the first anniversary of Daniel Morgan's murder – and when Alastair Morgan first met Derek Haslam at the Victory pub.

Most of the corruption evidence was withheld from the jury and the well-rehearsed lines about a domestic falling-out were cited as the most likely cause of Taffy's suicide, even though Haslam recalls Holmes' wife 'was well aware of his continuing affair with Jean Burgess, and he used to sleep in the room downstairs'.

Extraordinarily, Taffy's suicide note was not entered into evidence and Haslam was not called as a witness.

The jury at Croydon Coroner's Court reached a verdict of suicide on 14th March 1988. Three days later, on 19th March 1988, DS Sidney Fillery, who had been on leave since his arrest the previous April, formally retired from the police force on 'medical grounds'.

With his family relocated to Norfolk, and still under suspicion as far as most his colleagues were concerned, Derek Haslam sought help from the Metropolitan Police psychiatrist about his predicament. By this time the psychiatrist, Dr Farewell, was so concerned about the number of traumatised officers detailing police corruption that he wrote to the commissioner, asking him, 'What the hell is going on in your force?'

Derek Haslam recalled: 'There were other people telling him similar things about similar people… [It] was almost like I had to counsel him.'

Haslam was offered another job at the Met, but no guarantee of any kind kind of protection. 'I'd have always felt I was on offer,' he told his senior officer. 'Some people could fit me up or stick something in my drawer or something in my locker. I think, well, it was just the attitude in those days that however bad something was, you shouldn't be seen to be a whistle blower.'

After 17 years' service Haslam retired from the MPS on health grounds on 19th October 1989. His certificate of discharge from the MPS shows his conduct to have been exemplary.

* * *

The premature death of DC Alan Holmes removed the key witness who could substantiate the perversion of the course of justice strand of Operation Russell, and several allegations Commander Ray Adams had links with organised crime.

In 1990, the Director of Public Prosecutions announced that there was no evidence to support any charge against Adams regarding corruption allegations, and he did not face any subsequent disciplinary action. Adams was not,

however, reinstated in his role in Criminal Intelligence, but worked on the Emergency Hostage and Kidnapping Unit.

Haslam got to know of Adams' exoneration through an odd route. He claims he was called on his ex-directory secret number by David Leppard, Home Affairs correspondent for *The Sunday Times*, who had talked to Alastair Morgan about the murder furtively in 1988. Asked for his reaction about the clearing of Ray Adams, Haslam enquired how Leppard had got hold of his secret number. When the *Sunday Times* journalist refused to explain, Haslam retorted: 'Well, I've got nothing to say to you – full stop.'

To this day, Derek Haslam believes David Leppard could only have known about the report so quickly from Adams and that Rupert Murdoch's *Sunday Times* was a conduit for stories from Adams.

The commander certainly had connections with the press. Two years later, Adams was behind the sabotage of the *News of the World*'s exclusive on Liberal Democrat leader Paddy Ashdown's affair with the help of DC Duncan Hanrahan.

But it was the Stephen Lawrence murder, in the same part of London as the Daniel Morgan murder, and with some key lieutenants involved in the investigation, which would coincide with the sudden termination of Commander Adams' long police career.

* * *

One of the lead investigators in the Stephen Lawrence investigation was none other than DS John 'OJ' Davidson, who was Taffy Holmes' last close colleague and joined the murder squad less than 36 hours after the fatal stabbing in April 1993. Davidson performed numerous important roles in the inquiry, including supervising a vital early witness who had information that the black teenager had been killed by a white gang who named themselves after the notorious sixties East End gangsters, 'The Krays'.

One of the ringleaders of the gang, David Norris, was the son of a well-known underworld figure called Clifford Norris, who was associated with Kenneth Noye, a registered informant of Commander Ray Adams. Like Noye, Norris seemed to have police protection, and he escaped arrest in 1987 when a Customs and Excise raid captured a large consignment of drugs attributed to him. But that October, a Customs and Excise officer noticed

a Met Flying Squad officer, DS David Coles, meeting Clifford Norris and exchanging packages.

After a disciplinary hearing, Coles was required to resign.

Coles appealed. Despite being under investigation himself, Ray Adams intervened in the disciplinary and appeal process. Instead of leaving the force DS Coles was reassigned to surveillance duties. Bizarrely, Coles was assigned to guard the key prosecution witness, Duwayne Brooks, when the Lawrence family launched a private prosecution into Stephen's murder in 1996.

A secret intelligence briefing for a Met task force three years later concluded: 'Coles is connected with the following suspected corrupt serving and former officers... Ray Adams'. The same report concluded that Davidson, a key investigator in the Lawrence murder, was also connected to Adams. Davidson was later accused of being in a corrupt relationship with Clifford Norris (which he denies).[18]

In the light of this, Commander Ray Adams' letter to the Lawrence family offering police liaison services less than two weeks after their son's murder was highly suspicious. Troubling too was the fact that Adams would go on sick leave with an unidentified fracture of the spine only three days later, on 4th May 1993, and retire permanently from the Met that August.

| # Co-Habitation

1994-1997

ALASTAIR: There was no clear point when I moved in with Kirsteen. I went up to London a couple of times over that spring and she visited Farnham regularly. But I was always thinking of ways of reopening the investigation into Dan's murder and was getting behind in my studies. This meant that I'd left writing my dissertation to the last minute. I wasn't alone in this as there was a battle for the limited number of computers at college.

Kirsteen had a computer in her flat. She was much more expert than me at using it and she suggested that I work from there. I came to stay for a few days and never moved out.

By the end of the spring Kirsteen decided to quit her job fielding audience calls for the BBC programme *That's Life*. This meant we had a lot of time together. For the first few weeks we ate out almost every night. I felt like I was on another planet. I'd always been almost broke at college and before that my window-cleaning business barely paid my rent, my car and the exorbitant phone bills I'd run up, badgering the police. This was paradise after what I'd experienced. Frankly, I was amazed at my luck.

I really wanted to give something back and show Kirsteen how much I appreciated her, so I hoovered, cleaned the windows, did the shopping and started cooking. I was worried about her eating habits. Her home diet, unsupervised, consisted of Crunchy Nut Cornflakes and Pot Noodles. I decided to change that and began to introduce her to vegetables, salads, curries, shepherd's pie, stews, roasts, pasta and other normal food.

* * *

Days stretched into weeks. I finished my degree course with an undistinguished 2:2. By this time, Kirsteen and I felt like an established couple. That summer we both travelled down to Wales to meet my mother. She and Mum

got on well from the start – Kirsteen's a good listener and can talk to just about anyone. The conversation quickly turned to Daniel.

Mum's a night owl and the talk went on into the early hours of the morning. The later it got, the angrier and more frustrated Mum became. She said that if the police didn't get Jonathan Rees and Sid Fillery then she'd kill them herself. She talked about how she could get a gun and how she would attack them.

'I'd just give myself up afterwards,' she said. 'I don't care. They'd send me to jail, but I'd get an easy time at my age.'

'But how do you think I'd feel?' I protested. 'I don't want to have to visit you in prison for the rest of your life.'

Kirsteen was horrified and tried politely to point out the pitfalls in the scheme. She told me years later that it was only after she'd sat through several of these late-night scheming sessions that she realised it was just a way of venting frustration. It gave us the illusion that we had some kind of choice. In reality, we felt totally powerless.

Our first Christmas together was by far the happiest I'd experienced since the murder. I hadn't seen my son Ian since I'd started my studies. Kirsteen suggested that I invite him over to see us.

Kirsteen was nervous about meeting Ian. She was, after all, only three years older than him. I just said he's Swedish and it won't bother him in the slightest. And thankfully, it didn't.

In the New Year we took Ian to see his Aunt Iris, Daniel and Sarah. He was only 11-years-old when Daniel was killed but he remembers him clearly. Ian and his mother, Britt-Marie, were both devastated by his death.

* * *

I was so happy living with Kirsteen. The only thing that wasn't working well was finding work.

I'd wanted to go into journalism because I'd seen how the media had played a role in outing corruption in the police and government. Naïvely, I believed that my extreme experience would give me a head start. I envisaged myself getting a research job at somewhere like *The Guardian* or Granada's *World in Action*. I wanted to do something important; some investigative journalism that would make a difference.

The traditional route into journalism starts with a job as a junior reporter on a local newspaper. I hadn't considered that it was unlikely a news editor

would take on a junior reporter who was older than him or her. So, slowly and painfully, I came to realise that my ambition of working in the media was dead.

It had taken me three attempts to get a degree and now I'd finally got one it was worthless. I had to think of something else to do – but what?

Kirsteen suggested that I work as a translator. Oddly enough, I'd never even thought of this possibility. I looked in the Yellow Pages and found that there were literally dozens, possibly hundreds, of translation agencies in London.

Within a week I had an offer of a full-time job with a company in Ascot. A couple of weeks later, I got my first job offer from an agent. It was a company report to be translated from Swedish for Merrill Lynch, the merchant bankers. Gradually, over the next few months the amount of work slowly increased.

As soon as I moved to London I felt it was an ideal opportunity to lobby a new MP. Living in Islington, I was the constituent of Chris Smith MP, so I decided to contact him at one of his surgeries. On my first visit, I met one of his assistants, who recommended that I write a short report on the case and send it to Chris. I produced a ten-page report the following day and posted it to Chris immediately.

Chris is gay and had come out in 1984, a year after entering Parliament. I expected him to be more progressive than most MPs and after reading my report he was immediately supportive. I'd also gained an ally in Duncan Campbell, a journalist on *The Guardian* – I'd been phoning him for a year, trying to get him to write something.

In August 1994, when two of the Met officers arrested after Dan's murder won undisclosed damages against the Commissioner of Police, Duncan decided to use it as a news-peg to write an article.

'WHO KILLED DANIEL MORGAN?' was the headline on the front page of *The Guardian*'s G2 supplement. This was the first time in a decade that a national newspaper had written about the murder. I also felt vindicated by the fact that a respected journalist had taken up the case.

Duncan told me that the article definitely wouldn't solve the case. Naïvely, I thought it would force the police to reopen the case. Kirsteen didn't have the benefit of seven years' experience and she thought it would all be over soon. This didn't happen, but the article gave us credibility with Chris Smith and he started a letter-writing campaign.

It was a long campaign. Chris wrote to the Home Secretary, the Commissioner of the Metropolitan Police, the Police Complaints Authority, the Attorney General, the Crown Prosecution Service, and the Coroner, Sir Montague Levine.

The replies were so uniform that I could have written them myself. The Home Office said it couldn't comment on the case as they had no authority to intervene in the way the police handle criminal investigations. This was even though the Met was the only force in the land that didn't have a police authority to hold it to account. Such was the fiefdom of the Home Secretary.

Chris wrote again pointing out this anomaly and repeating that the case should be re-examined.

I'd also started writing letters to Peter Moorehouse, the new chairman of the Police Complaints Authority. Their replies contained the usual formulaic response 'this matter has received very full and thorough investigation'. In one letter Moorehouse actually wrote: 'If I do not reply to your further letters please do not take this as a discourtesy, merely as an indication that this Authority has nothing further to add to what has already been said.'

In another letter he complained that I kept ringing his secretary and wrote: 'I would be grateful if you would cease telephoning my office in the future'.

I was making a nuisance of myself, but what else could I do?

We were so annoyed with non-responses from the PCA that we planned a demonstration outside their offices. The eighth anniversary of Dan's murder was coming up, so we decided to do the demo on 10th March for maximum media impact. Mum got onto HTV in Wales and they covered our protest. I got the local ITV news, *London Tonight*.

Kirsteen came along to offer her support. We stood on Great George Street outside the PCA's offices holding the banner that I'd made. I had a picture of Dan with the words 'Stop police investigating police'. We got a real lift when drivers hooted their horns or gave us the thumbs-up as they passed by.

Mum wanted to go into the offices and see if Peter Moorehouse would meet her so I stayed holding the banner while she went in. When Mum returned, she had a glint in her eye that told me she'd enjoyed stirring things up.

'What happened, Mum?'

'I went straight up to what looked like the head receptionist and demanded to see Peter Moorehouse. When I said I had to see him, he wanted to know

why. I told him that wasn't any of his business. He didn't like that at all and said in the haughtiest manner, "We don't just let people in like that" and told me to leave the premises. I told him that he had the most appalling manners and left the building.'

'They won't let you in there without an appointment, Mum. That's for sure!'

But Mum just laughed. 'I knew before I even asked that I wouldn't get to see Moorehouse. I was surprised that I got through the revolving doors.'

Mum wasn't intimidated by anyone. She was pushing 70, but she was out on the streets of Hay late every night walking her dogs. And she wasn't afraid to tell the local youth off if she felt they were misbehaving. Kirsteen and I would often warn her about confronting people. I was worried that she might upset a drunken yob carrying a knife, but Mum wouldn't listen.

At the demonstration Chris Smith gave an interview in which he said that he believed we'd been badly let down. After it was over, we went home for some lunch and watched the demonstration on the ITV *London News*.

* * *

Chris continued writing letters and I began badgering the Met's Complaints Investigation Bureau on the phone. Eventually I was put through to the director, Commander Ian Quinn. He told me he would ask his staff officer to review the case. I told this officer about Fillery's actions and the attitudes of the Met and Hampshire squads.

Mum had also written to Ian Quinn. On 22nd May 1995, he wrote back to her, saying there had been an exhaustive review of the investigations and that the Hampshire Inquiry had been 'as thorough as is possible'.

'I do understand how you and Alastair feel,' Quinn wrote, 'and indeed recognise that you feel suspicious of the parts played by a number of people associated with these investigations. However, your concerns have been examined in great depth, but without evidence, suspicions cannot be the basis for criminal proceedings.'

I kept on lobbying and Chris Smith decided to write to Ian Quinn, asking for a meeting. A meeting was agreed for 23rd June 1995.

Mum travelled from Wales and we met up with Chris in the foyer of Tintagel House. When we entered Ian Quinn's office, we were amazed at the number of people waiting to see us. Lined up behind a desk sat Quinn, Paul Blaker and Sergeant Kennedy from Hampshire Police and the solicitor to the

Metropolitan Police. Stacked on two chairs in the middle of the office were half a dozen large red document boxes, obviously containing the papers on Daniel's murder. They wanted to show us how much paperwork the case had generated, but I wasn't impressed.

When the introductions were over, I read out a prepared statement, flatly accusing the two forces of a cover-up. I went over my reasons for this, detailing Fillery's actions before and during the murder inquiry and the failure of Hampshire Police to take a statement from me. The police representatives sat in stony silence as I made my argument.

I showed Ian Quinn a spider chart I'd drawn, linking half a dozen corrupt officers to Southern Investigations. Quinn's reaction was strange: he casually remarked that he'd be able to add another dozen corrupt cops to my list.

During the meeting, Chris said that he would contact the Attorney General, Sir Nicholas Lyell, to raise the matter with him. We said our goodbyes and he left for Parliament.

A few days after the meeting, I received a copy of Chris Smith's letter to the Attorney General. After outlining the case he asked two questions: firstly, whether the evidence really was insufficient to proceed, and secondly, whether the search for additional evidence might usefully be resumed.

He asked for a QC to be appointed to look at the case papers and answer these questions. Then he wrote again on 11th July. I can find no record of any reply. Early in November 1995 I wrote to Hampshire Police, objecting to their conduct. I received a reply from Sergeant Kennedy, who had attended the meeting with Ian Quinn earlier in the year. The letter typified their position.

'The alleged telephone calls,' for Quinn wrote about Fillery's attempt to get me out of town, 'were the subject of examination and cross-examination by Counsel during the inquest into your late brother Daniel's death. At that time Mr Fillery denied making those telephone calls.'

This reasoning drove me crazy. The fact that Fillery denied making the calls was enough in their opinion. It wasn't even necessary to interview my mother, sister, or Joe Harty. None of them had given evidence at the inquest. All three were material witnesses and yet Hampshire's 'due consideration' didn't extend to checking this out.

* * *

The endless setbacks had an effect on my mental health although I didn't like to admit this. Kirsteen once mentioned how much the case had damaged me and I went ballistic. In the first few years we were together we split up on several occasions. It never lasted long, partly because when Kirsteen chucked me out, I had nowhere to go so I just ended up sleeping on the sofa.

There were times when the case took over all my waking thoughts. I'd pace around our small flat like a caged animal. Kirsteen would listen to my rants until late into the night. We'd been together for a couple of years by this point and there wasn't much about the case that she didn't know. Despite this, I'd go over the story again and again as if she'd never heard it before.

Most of the time she was patient with me but I know it really annoyed her when there was a good programme on the television and she would miss vital bits. Political programmes were always risky, particularly if I'd had a drink. I'd rant at the politicians who seemed to be living in a parallel universe. One night I lost control and kicked the television so hard it never worked again.

Somehow Kirsteen put up with me. She was still working very hard at finding work. She'd started a course in television production in Brixton, hoping that it would help her find permanent paid work. Things weren't at all bad in that respect, but I often wondered whether it was fair to have dragged her into all this.

One Sunday night I was reading the last chapters of a book that I'd been engrossed in. It was past midnight. Kirsteen was asleep and the telephone rang. Nervously, I made my way to our study and picked up the receiver.

'Hello?'

After a short silence, a woman's voice replied: 'We are going to kill you, like we killed your brother!' she said in a phoney Italian accent.

I almost stopped breathing. Despite the ridiculous accent, this woman wanted to scare me. There was silence at the other end of the line.

After a few seconds, I hung up. The call had shaken me. At the same time, I was ashamed that I hadn't laughed at her threat. Could someone attack us that night? Common sense told me this was unlikely, but common sense can't always be relied on. I woke Kirsteen and told her about the call – I wasn't the only person who could be in danger.

The obvious thing to do was to call the police. It was a strange feeling calling on the organisation that had caused us so much grief over the best part of a decade.

Within half an hour, two uniformed officers were at the door. We invited them in and told them about the call and our campaign for justice, including our concerns about police involvement in Daniel's murder. I was nervous about how they would respond, but they were polite and attentive. We locked the door very carefully after the police left and went to bed for a few hours' uneasy sleep.

The next morning I rang Chris Smith's office and told his assistant what had happened. Later that day another police officer called and I described what had happened. He replied that he would arrange for any 999 calls from my address to be treated with high priority; he also gave us two personal alarms, but I was still sick with worry.

'Kirsteen, what if the call was just a warning and they come back tonight?'

She was dismissive, which made me even more stubborn.

'How stupid would that be, Al? Anyway, we now have police priority. The last thing they're going to want is for something to happen to you. How bad would that look for them?'

'Okay, okay, I can see that, but I'm not having you go out on your own.'

'Don't be stupid, Al. I'm not going to be locked up here all day or forced to have you escort me everywhere.'

'But you can't run! They could easily run you down crossing the road.'

'Don't make this about me being disabled,' she answered angrily. 'If they really wanted to get us they could shoot us. You can't run away from a bullet. Whether I can run or not isn't the issue, you're just being paranoid!'

It didn't matter what Kirsteen said, I wasn't prepared to take the risk. After all, my brother had been killed for knowing less than I knew. These people were private detectives. It would take minutes for them to find out where we lived.

I rang Chris Smith's office again, asking if some kind of safe house could be arranged for us. Chris quickly contacted Islington Council and we each packed a small bag and drove off to an address in the northern end of Chris's constituency.

By the time we arrived there, some of the adrenaline had subsided and we realised we were facing a very dreary reality. We were shown up to a shabby room with a clapped-out double bed, a chest of drawers and a wardrobe. For the first time since the threat I had time to sit down and think calmly.

It was depressing. We'd been driven out of our home by a death threat and found ourselves in an area that we didn't know, in a room that wasn't our own, with only a handful of our own belongings.

I knew Kirsteen had no intention of staying there. She probably knew that she had to come with me and let me decide for myself that we would not be moved out of our home. It felt like they were winning if we let them change the way we lived our lives. We thanked the people from Islington Council for their help, picked up our bags and drove home to our flat.

When I told people I met about my campaign, one of their first reactions would be to question how safe I was. I'd always reasoned that keeping the case in the public eye actually kept me safer as it meant it would be stupid for the suspects to harm me. I now had a MP who would speak on the news or bring it up in Parliament if anything happened.

But it was different now I thought Kirsteen could be in danger. Up to this point I'd been careful to keep her out of the media spotlight when my family were campaigning. For many weeks afterwards, though, I was concerned when she left the flat.

Kirsteen assured me that she was completely behind me in my efforts. She never wavered.

| Dark Side of the Moon

1994-1997

The decision of the Metropolitan Police Commissioner Paul Condon to investigate police corruption around the time of the Stephen Lawrence murder rapidly yielded results.

Begun in 1993 primarily as an intelligence gathering and 'scoping' inquiry, Condon's task force had a target-rich environment in the cross-boundary crime squad by then rebranded as SERCS (South East Regional Crime Squad).

Under its previous incarnation as Regional Crime Squad No. 9, run for many years by Ray Adams, SERCS had been a training ground for many police officers associated with the Daniel Morgan murder, particularly former Detective Sergeant Sid Fillery, who was seconded there for two years from his Catford base.

Ten years later, many names in the Fillery and Adams' circle were still active in SERCS. They would come under intense scrutiny.

Detective Sergeant Alec Leighton was, like Adams and his former bagman Duncan Hanrahan, a Freemason from south-east London. He was close to Fillery and Rees, and knew Daniel before he was murdered.

Leighton provided evidence to the first two Morgan murder investigations, mainly about Daniel's trip to Malta to recover luxury cars and vague, unsubstantiated allegations that the murdered detective was worried about the repercussions from Maltese organised crime.

By 1993 Leighton was based at the Surbiton office of SERCS when an investigative TV documentary exposed his junior, Detective Constable John Donald, receiving bribes from organised crime.

The story began in September 1992 when a south London wheeler dealer called Kevin Cressey was arrested in Streatham on suspicion of drug dealing. Cressey bribed DC Donald with £18,000 to make him a protected informant

and negotiated a series of payments to his new police handler to pass on police files, even destroying incriminating surveillance logs. DC Donald also agreed to act as a 'linkman' selling top-secret information on police operations to Ray Adams' former informant, Kenneth Noye.

Growing disaffected with DC Donald's demands, Cressey went to the BBC to expose his corrupt handler.

The BBC investigative team didn't shirk from the challenge. For six months from March 1993, *Panorama* recorded 14 meetings between Cressey and his SERCS police handler. They caught DC Donald on camera receiving money in a carrier bag and recorded him offering to help steal Cressey's surveillance logs from a police station. The price was £30,000 because, as Donald explained, he'd also have to pay his boss at the Surbiton SERCS office – Detective Sergeant Alec Leighton.

The prime time BBC *Panorama* documentary, 'The Case of India One', proved that investigative journalists were better at catching bent coppers than the Met. Eight other officers were investigated and six criminal cases in which DC Donald had given police evidence collapsed.

DC John Donald was charged with perverting the course of justice and admitted to four charges of corruption during his Old Bailey trial, two years later. The juries for his and Kevin Cressey's trials were placed under 24-hour police protection and DC Donald was sentenced to 11 years in prison, while Cressey received a seven-year sentence.[1]

DS Alec Leighton was suspended from duty while awaiting an internal affairs inquiry. While suspended, he went to work with another ex-detective and associate of Ray Adams, Duncan Hanrahan, at his newly formed private investigations company, initially based in Leighton's garage.[2]

Under a cloud of disciplinary matters, Leighton left the Met in 1995. He went on to form his own private investigations company, Mayfayre Associates, which would employ both OJ Davidson and Donald, and all three would continue a long association with Rees and Fillery.

* * *

Soon after the Donald case, in May 1994, Condon's anti-corruption team produced a 32-page 'secret' document, which analysed the corruption problems and laid out a strategy to deal with them.

Called 'The Dark Side of the Moon' and subtitled 'Everyone knows it is there but not many can see it', the report concluded that organised crime syndicates had recruited a small but dedicated network of corrupt officers from different ranks who had successful penetrated police organisations and systems.

The report detailed how this internal crime network subverted police investigations. They run unauthorised checks on the Police National Computer and flag up any covert operation or advance intelligence on the secret INFOS system which flagged up ongoing operations, also known as the 'box'. Operatives could provide copies of official police documents or operations, and weaken or lose crucial evidence.

The reward for this corruption was the substantial wealth that could be acquired. Officers would work with informants to plant drugs and firearms on rivals, or steal their drugs and cash. They would act as agents provocateurs with informants to entrap or provoke criminal activity for reward money. Or they would simply conspire with major criminals to commit very serious criminal offences, such as large importations of illegal drugs.

To counter such professional criminals within the highest ranks of the Metropolitan Police, the report concluded that a revived anti-corruption unit, CIB 3, would have to take over from the moribund CIB 2 complaints investigations department, and use all the surveillance technology, intelligence gathering the covert operations usually reserved for organised crime.

'The Dark Side of the Moon' was an important document. It became 'the blueprint' for Operation Othona – named after an old Roman fort in Essex – a massive four-year investigation into corruption. The members of this new secret unit were sealed off from most Scotland Yard operations, and its members given false legends, identities and jobs to conceal them from their targets.

Because of the secrecy of the operation, and the sensitivity of the subject matter for the entire British criminal justice system, the new unit became known as the 'Ghost Squad'. Very quickly, Southern Investigations, and the nexus of corrupt police officers, press and organised crime would become a target.

In February 1994, the Conservative MP for Eastleigh and former journalist, Stephen Milligan, was found dead at his home, asphyxiated after an auto-erotic accident. The lurid details of the 45-year-old's death were quickly leaked to John Ross, the ex-detective who appeared in the Daniel Morgan murder incident room on the night of the first arrests in April 1997.

Ross was a close confidante and colleague of Alex Marunchak at the *News of the World*. On this occasion, Ross was alleged to have received £50,000 from another tabloid for the shocking details of the MP's death.

The Met's anti-corruption unit investigated the Milligan leak, but only disciplined a press officer. This leniency did not go unnoticed among journalists, police officers or private detectives. Nor did the potential bonanza ahead.

At a Press Club party to celebrate John Ross' windfall, guests turned up with bin bags, suspenders, and oranges in their mouths to mock the dead MP. It was this party, and the promise of both money and impunity that, according to contemporaries, convinced Rees and Fillery that the British tabloid press was a much more lucrative customer for their services than local councils or organised crime.

* * *

This rich trade in police leaks, led by Alex Marunchak and John Ross, was known to senior Met officers, according to Nick Davies in his book, *Hack Attack*, who either turned a blind eye or directly benefited.

As for senior newspaper management, facing a growing demand for salacious celebrity stories, the dark arts of Southern Investigations were impossible to resist.

Piers Morgan took over the editorship of the *News of the World* at the age of 28, just a week before Milligan's death. His only journalistic experience beforehand was writing the 'Bizarre' celebrity column at *The Sun*. He appointed an even younger Rebekah Brooks to become features editor that spring.

Given his inexperience with reporting, Morgan relied heavily on the older guard at the newspaper, especially his news editor, Alex Marunchak, whom he described as having a 'deadpan, half-Ukrainian, moustachioed visage'.

Marunchak's police sources would soon land Morgan in trouble.

In his autobiography *The Insider*, Morgan explains how in August 1994 Marunchak and chief crime reporter Gary Jones walked into his editor's office in Wapping and explained: 'Got rather a big one here, boss. Diana's a phone pest.' Marunchak went on to elaborate: 'The cops are investigating hundreds of calls she has made to a married art dealer called Oliver Hoare.'

Gary Jones backed up his news editor with 'a read-out from the police report' which he then quoted verbatim.

Oliver Hoare had received hundreds of silent, anonymous phone calls and reported them to the police. With the help of British Telecom, the police had traced the calls to Kensington Palace, the home of Princess Diana.

When Hoare was informed of the source of the calls he told police officers that he and his wife were friends of Charles and Diana and he had been (according to the police report) 'consoling her and becoming quite close to her' after her separation from Prince Charles, the heir to the throne.

The *News of the World* called the antique dealer for comment. Hoare did not deny there had been an investigation. So, with the bylines of Gary Jones and Royal reporter Clive Goodman, the *News of the World* splashed the story over the front and four inside pages.

The details in the exclusive could only come from the police documents: the date of Hoare's first complaint, the involvement of British Telecom's specialist Nuisance Calls Bureau, the special code BT was given to trace the calls, the activation of the code on 13th January 1994, transcripts of six silent calls, and then the tracing equipment which linked the calls to a private number used by Prince Charles – all this could have only been sourced from the police.

The next day, in a long interview in *The Daily Mail*, Princess Diana denied the story. Piers Morgan began to worry he had made a huge career blunder. There were calls for him to resign. Alex Marunchak tried to reassure the *News of the World* editor: 'We've had the report read to us, she's lying,' he told him. But Morgan still feared the document could be a forgery.

'I felt sick to the pit of my stomach,' Morgan recalled. 'I couldn't eat or even drink a cup of tea, it was hellish.'

The only thing that finally put his mind at rest was a call from his proprietor, Rupert Murdoch.

'Hi Piers,' Murdoch said. 'I can't really talk for long but I just wanted you to know that your story is one hundred per cent bang on. Can't tell you how I know, but I just know.'

He then instructed his editor to get on TV and tell the world that Princess Diana is 'a liar', and to promise more material in the Sunday tabloid the following week.

Though relieved, Morgan couldn't help admitting to his proprietor that he didn't have any more material. But Murdoch replied: 'Oh, you will have by Sunday, don't worry. Gotta go. Good luck.'

How did Rupert Murdoch independently verify the story? It was Alex Marunchak who had seen the police report. Would the proprietor check with his veteran news desk editor?

Others who worked at the *News of the World* at the time have doubted whether Murdoch would have broken protocol and gone over an editor's head to talk to a more junior – if much more experienced – news editor. But Piers Morgan was new to the job, young, and untrained in hard news stories. Unless he had a direct connection at the Palace or another senior officer, there are few other places Murdoch could check the validity of Marunchak's police report other than the veteran news editor.

At the Leveson Inquiry into the practices of the press in 2012, Murdoch explicitly denied even remembering meeting Alex Marunchak though – in careful legal language guarding against any surviving photos – he added, 'I might have shaken hands, walking through the office.'

By that point Marunchak had served in a number of senior roles at the *News of the World* from his first days in the Wapping dispute, attending parties with the News International CEO and senior police officers, to being made editor of the Irish edition, two decades later.

Steve Grayson, a freelance photographer who worked at the Sunday tabloid in the late 1990s, recalls Marunchak explicitly saying he had a direct call from Murdoch on one occasion. Despite his growing global influence, there is no doubt during this era the media mogul still called senior management at the paper most Friday or Saturday nights to check what stories were coming up.

And there's more evidence that Rupert Murdoch was well aware of his senior executive, who served his company for over 25 years.

In correspondence from September 1997, the then Taoiseach of Ireland, Bertie Ahern, wrote personally to Rupert Murdoch to thank him for the *News of the World*'s coverage of the recent general election and particularly 'appreciated the very professional approach of your Associate Editor Alex Marunchak'. The Irish Prime Minister asked Murdoch to pass on 'my thanks and best wishes to Alex'. Murdoch replied on 30th September: 'I shall be delighted to pass on your comments.'

Whatever Rupert Murdoch's uncertain memories of Alex Marunchak, the ultimate source of Piers Morgan's scoop was a confidential police file and – like the Milligan leak – large sums would have been paid for the material.

Later, Morgan was careful to say the source wasn't a 'serving police officer' – partly because that would have opened him and any police officer to criminal charges. But that limited admission doesn't exclude the source being an officer who recently retired or brokered through a middleman.

Nobody was censured or sanctioned for the phone pest story. In fact, it was quite the opposite. Gary Jones went on to win the Press Gazette's Reporter of the Year Award partly due to his *News of the World* exclusive about Diana's anonymous calls. Criticised by the Press Complaints Council for another intrusive Royal splash, Morgan would leave the Murdoch tabloid Sunday in 1995, to an even more senior position editing the rival, *The Daily Mirror*. He would soon bring over Gary Jones and, with him, the dark arts of Fillery and Rees.

Meanwhile, the most senior officer from the SERCS network, former Commander Ray Adams, who had left the Met after the Stephen Lawrence murder, was also gravitating towards the media. After just over a year working for Kroll, the private investigations agency favoured by big law firms and banks, Adams procured an even more prestigious and well-paid post: European head of Operational Security for National Datacom Service (NDS), an Israeli company that secured Rupert Murdoch's global television network with satellite smart cards.

NDS wasn't only vital to the survival of Murdoch's News Corp, which had almost collapsed under the weight of debt in the early 1990s due to the expansion into satellite TV, it was – according to Australian journalist Neil Chenoweth – an internal security agency for the whole of the company.

Adams' direct boss, as global head of Operational Security, was Reuven Hasak, a former deputy head of the Shin Bet, the Israeli security services.

Both Hasak and Adams reported direct to the chair of News Corp: in other words, to Rupert Murdoch himself. Hasak was dubbed 'Murdoch's spy' while Adams would soon become known as 'Murdoch's Yard Man'.

* * *

Just as the techniques of Southern Investigations were beginning to spread from the *News of the World* to other papers, the corrupt nexus of bent cops around Rees and Fillery came under even more scrutiny from the Ghost Squad.

Detective Chief Superintendent Dave Wood took over as operational head of the anti-corruption unit in December 1996. One of the first things he did was recruit former police officer Derek Haslam as an undercover informant.

Haslam had not done much professionally in the intervening seven years since leaving the Met and moving to Norfolk. His wife Susan had returned to a job in banking and since he had not seen much of his children when he'd been a policeman, Derek became a 'house husband'.

In 1996 Duncan Campbell wrote an article 'A Question of Blood' in *The Guardian* about two brothers, fighting for justice for murdered siblings. One of them was Alastair Morgan. Publicity about the case caught Derek Haslam's attention, and he contacted the team with his suspicions the murder was connected to the suicide of DC Alan 'Taffy' Holmes. Detective Chief Inspector Tom Smith, who'd known Haslam from years before, then made his move.

Smith said he'd been trying to contact Haslam about some 'unfinished business' and wanted to introduce him to 'someone important who was very interested in what he could possibly know'. He and Haslam agreed to meet at a neutral location, a hotel in Downham Market in Norfolk, a week later. It was there that DCI Smith introduced Haslam to the man who would become his handler, Detective Chief Superintendent David Wood, who was then running the Ghost Squad.

The first bit of the pitch was to explain to Derek Haslam how he had been betrayed by Duncan Hanrahan and Ray Adams.

'Have you ever wondered why you didn't get that security manager's job at British Telecom?' Haslam recalls DCS Wood asking him.

'Well, I did wonder,' Haslam replied, 'because I thought I did reasonably well in the interview.'

Haslam claims that Wood then excused himself to go to the toilet. After he'd gone Derek Haslam confided in DCI Smith: 'So, what is he actually after? The only reason he'd got for telling that is to make me annoyed and perhaps want to help him.'

When DCS Wood returned, it became clear to Haslam what the internal affairs boss was after: a reinvestigating of the violent deaths from the summer of 1987 – those of Daniel Morgan and Alan Holmes.

For the previous ten years, questions about whether the two violent deaths of Daniel Morgan and Alan Holmes were connected had been raised but never substantiated. Now the senior member of the Ghost Squad, described to Haslam as 'more a spook than a police officer', seemed to the retired detective to be firmly linking the two.

They discussed the revelation that Holmes' blood alcohol came back from the post-mortem results as less than the equivalent of half a pint of beer. Holmes was also a heavy drinker, and they both agreed it 'didn't ring true': 'Alcoholics don't give up drinking to commit suicide. If anything, they start drinking more,' Haslam suggested.

DCS Wood also emphasised the link between Daniel and Taffy, picking up on Haslam's recollection that the private detective was 'negotiating' selling a massive story of police corruption to the press for DC Holmes. As Haslam recalled, Wood had corroborating evidence from a journalist that 'shortly before his murder Daniel was seen with a Welsh detective in a Fleet Street news room'.

Haslam's mission was clear. Since he was once of friend of Rees', and had kept in sporadic contact since he left London, he was now being asked to renew the friendship. Acting as a Confidential Human Intelligence Source (CHIS), he was to gather evidence on Fillery and Rees with a view to reopening an investigation into the murder of Daniel Morgan and also the death of DC Alan Holmes as 'possible murder... at best an assisted suicide'.

At a follow-up meeting Derek Haslam signed the Official Secrets Act and developed his legend as a former officer now disaffected with the Met, who was working in private security for the Life Sciences Institute in Cambridge. At the meeting, Haslam asked for full protection and Wood agreed. He would remain an undercover informant for nearly a decade, only receiving out-of-pocket expenses for his work.

It took two years for Haslam to become 'fully embedded' in the Southern Investigations circle. He recalls Rees was 'pleased to see me' when he began making more visits to London in early 1997 on the pretext of wanting to set up his own private investigations company. His claim to be angry at the Met made sense in the light of what had happened to his career after Holmes' suicide. Haslam also had a good alibi to protect his family, saying he had split up from his wife Susan.

Within weeks of re-establishing contact with Rees, the anti-corruption command targeted the SERCS/Southern Investigations circle with another arrest.

* * *

Duncan Hanrahan had been out of the Met for six years, and after a brief collaboration with Alec Leighton he had set up his own private security firm

with another ex-Scotland Yard detective, Martin King, who was introduced to him by Ray Adams.

King had retired in 1971 but owned a snooker club, a restaurant and night-club, and lived in a large house in south London and had an expansive flat next to Harrods in Kensington too. He was also a friend of solicitor Michael Relton, who used to own John Ross' Briefs wine bar, and had been jailed for involvement in the Brink's-Mat money laundering. Together they formed Hanrahan Associates in 1994.

Despite forming his own company, Hanrahan would still work alongside Rees and Fillery, brokering deals – especially among SERCS detectives – at the now infamous Victory pub around the corner from Southern Investigations in Thornton Heath. They were joined regularly by former DS Alec Leighton, who had been suspended after the arrest of his junior, DC Donald.

By now, SERCS was jokingly referred to as the 'News of the World Regional Crime Squad' because of the volume of information it passed onto the newspaper. But though media contacts were lucrative, they were also jealously guarded and highly competitive.

After a period trying to broker stories to the *News of the World*, Hanrahan was using police connections to provide information from the Police National Computer. Yet, perhaps from what he had learned investigating the Belmont Car Auctions scam a decade before, Hanrahan soon made his specialty the 'inside job'.

Private security provided a fertile field for rip-offs like this. On one occasion Duncan Hanrahan and Martin King offered to provide security to a Lebanese courier at Heathrow who had been robbed of £1m in 1994. But as they scoped out a 'protection detail' for the courier, Hanrahan and King planned to repeat the robbery using their police and criminal contacts. The planned heist failed twice, however, when the courier didn't show and then the police and gangsters fell out.

Hanrahan's other source of income was stealing money or drugs from drug dealers who, for obvious reasons, were unlikely to complain to the police. One of these schemes led directly back to the Daniel Morgan murder, and would provide important new details about the night he was killed.

It was through Jonathan Rees that Hanrahan was introduced to Barry Nash, known to that circle as 'Barry The Fish'. Nash, like his friend Jimmy Cook, was a repossession expert who worked regularly for Southern Investigations.

Through Barry Nash, Duncan Hanrahan was introduced to another wheeler dealer, Steven Warner, who had connections to the north London crime scene. Together they planned to take advantage of a police raid on a rival drug dealer by pocketing some of his product. But this required the collaboration of the arresting officers. Hanrahan brokered the deal with police contacts, who would bust the rival dealer.

It all went to plan. During a police raid on 11th October 1995 on a house in Chiswick, 40,000 ecstasy tablets disappeared. Hanrahan passed the tablets on to Warner for a £6,000 commission – 1% of their estimated street value of £600,000.

Both would have got away with this had Hanrahan not been caught two years later when he tried to cultivate the CIB officer in Norbury, Chief Inspector Peter Elcock. The CIB officer tipped off his superior, Detective Superintendent Tom Smith, who had just helped recruit Haslam and knew all about Hanrahan's connections.

Over the next three months in early 1997 a covert investigation recorded 40 hours and a dozen meetings with Hanrahan and King and the CIB officer who was posing as a bent cop. Operation Eden obtained hard evidence of all kinds of corruption.

On the tapes, Duncan Hanrahan was caught offering £1,000 for papers on a car fraud case. Martin King was recorded paying £7,500 to subvert a prosecution. Hanrahan Associates also paid to destroy police notebooks in a grievous bodily harm case. In May 1997, King even proposed a plot where they would lure a prosecution witness to a building, who would then be thrown to their death.

Unaware of the trap he was walking into, King bragged that he was in league with dozens of policemen, council officers and others. He was apparently still close to former Commander Ray Adams, even though the latter was now installed as Murdoch's head of European security. King acted as a middleman for the former commander and Operation Eden caught them plotting to return a stolen Henry Moore statue in return for a £10,000 reward.

* * *

While CIB 3 were on to King and Hanrahan, two preliminary operations, Landmark and Hallmark, conducted 'lifestyle surveillance' on Rees and Fillery and their associates.

The first static observations on Southern Investigations, to check the movements of the suspects and gather intelligence on those who visited or worked there, took place over a week in mid-May 1997, around the time of Hanrahan and King's arrest.

As Derek Haslam relayed back in his intelligence reports to DCS Wood, the arrests caused consternation in the Southern Investigations circle. Rees and Fillery were immediately concerned that Hanrahan might be turned into a supergrass by CIB 3, and cause problems for them.

It was a justifiable suspicion. Within a month, Duncan Hanrahan agreed to become an informer.

DCS David Wood and his second-in-command, Detective Superintendent Chris Jarrett, began to debrief Hanrahan at a 'supergrass suite' nicknamed 'The Dorchester'. Because he was at risk of attack from criminals associated with corrupt officers, Hanrahan had round-the-clock armed police protection when he was back at his home.

Derek Haslam's undercover reports to David Wood coincide with this moment in June 1997 when Hanrahan became an informant. Haslam would meet his handlers once every couple of weeks at a remote location, having made handwritten reports. His debriefers would copy the details under a code-named informant, while the originals in Haslam's handwriting were destroyed.

In August 1997, Haslam revealed that Rees had been told Hanrahan was informing only on Ray Adams, and not talking about Southern Investigations or Alec Leighton. In return Rees told his source that Hanrahan was 'on bail but has to return to a Police Station each night to sleep'. Rees and Leighton somehow knew that 200 tapes had been used in Hanrahan's interview. Both were also reported to be wanting to target Detective Superintendent Chris Jarrett, either with compromising 'dirt' on his private life or indeed a physical assault.

'It was a serious vendetta,' Derek Haslam would recall. They tracked Jarrett's car, obtained accommodation receipts and his CV, and even found details of the pictures on the walls of his house. Jarrett took over as Haslam's handler that October. According to Haslam, Jonathan Rees also seemed to know a lot about the connection between Martin King and Ray Adams, passing on information that Adams had visited King's wife while her husband was in prison and paid her cash, which would also include her children's school fees.

Duncan Hanrahan's debrief suggested more than 50 officers from his circle alone were involved in corruption. He confirmed that information from the Police National Computer was being sold to criminals, that police were taking bribes to destroy evidence, and that there was a network of police detectives distributing cocaine.

Hanrahan went on to suggest that a 'former Scotland Yard commander' was linked to a network of corrupt officers. He also had more information on the Daniel Morgan murder, saying he had been murdered to prevent him exposing corrupt police practices.

* * *

Operation Othona's initial success with Duncan Hanrahan was most probably the cause of Commissioner Paul Condon's infamous statement, in the autumn of 1997, that there were around 250 corrupt officers in the Metropolitan Police. Though it caused uproar in police ranks and consternation in the press, this was actually a low estimate given the 40,000 or so employees of the Metropolitan Police.

What was not revealed at the time, and would come as a surprise to Haslam and a shock to his handlers, was the extensive involvement of the British press in this corruption.

Surviving samples of invoices from May 1997, and Southern Investigations' phone records from March and February of the same year, confirm that Sid Fillery and Jonathan Rees were billing Alex Marunchak over £150,000 a year,[3] and were regularly working with the *News of the World*'s top journalist, Mazher Mahmood.

Fillery was still supplying his video surveillance for councils like Hackney, Highgate and Tower Hamlets. In 1993, Mahmood had hired Conrad Brown as his freelance video technician, assisting with covert recordings, and watching and following targets.[4] But having trained him in the dark arts, Fillery and Rees were often helping Mahmood out, providing transport and backup.

In just one month's sample of Southern Investigations' invoices, in May 1997, Rees and Fillery billed the *News of the World* for at least five stories with Mahmood, who was now billed as chief investigative reporter.

Sid Fillery acted as an 'extra' in several of Mazher Mahmood's celebrated stings, posing as a private secretary during one of the Fake Sheikh's abortive stings against a friend of the Prince of Wales at The Dorchester hotel on

London's Park Lane. The *News of the World* was billed several times in May 1997 for providing personnel for Mahmood's attempt to crash Sylvester Stallone's wedding at The Dorchester.

Mazher Mahmood's connections to the upper echelons of the Murdoch empire were fast growing and by now he'd become close friends with the deputy editor of the Sunday tabloid, Rebekah Brooks. According to Christine Hart, a journalist posing as the Fake Sheikh's girlfriend for the Stallone wedding caper, Brooks was speaking on the phone to Mahmood four times a day.

It's hard to believe that Rebekah Brooks and Mazher Mahmood, two rising stars who would both soon have protected status in Rupert Murdoch's media empire, never discussed the roles of Rees or Fillery during the newspaper's long association with them. But there was even more concrete evidence that these individuals had access to the highest editorial levels of Rupert Murdoch's flagship tabloid Sunday paper.

When the former child actor, comedian and *London's Burning* TV star, 21-year-old John Alford, became a target of Mahmood in August 1997, he spotted a man he later identified as Sidney Fillery among the Fake Sheikh's entourage at The Savoy hotel.

Under extreme duress, Alford bought a small amount of cocaine for the Fake Sheikh.

There is no suggestion that the Class A drugs were provided by Mahmood and his circle on this occasion. However, intelligence reports at the time record that Rees and Fillery would provide drugs for newspaper stings, which would have to have been sourced by either their underworld or corrupt police contacts.[5] James Ward, a colleague of Garry Vian's, was also under the impression that Southern Investigations had planted drugs for Mahmood.

During the trial two years later, John Alford – who conducted his own defence – managed to procure Mazher Mahmood's billing records for the time in The Savoy hotel when the sting was set up. These showed the Fake Sheikh regularly calling his driver and another central London number connected to Fleet Street – 020 7583 9454.

This was an odd number. News International had moved out of Fleet Street in 1985. The Wapping office of the *News of the World* had various numbers, but from a completely different local exchange near the old Fleet Street headquarters.

The mystery of that number was solved by Greg Miskiw, a *News of the World* journalist and editor for nearly 20 years. He recalls this old Fleet Street number was patched through to the news desk at Wapping. It was a special phone – a kind of bat phone – which took priority over any other calls to the many phones on the news desk. This special *News of the World* hotline was only for the use of senior editors and reporters, like Rebekah Brooks or Mazher Mahmood. If that phone started ringing, you dropped everything else.

Extraordinarily, in the surviving mobile phone records for March 1997, Fillery was also calling this number every other day, especially in the lead up to stories involving Mazher Mahmood, Neville Thurlbeck or Royal reporter Clive Goodman. In 1999, while Rees was in frequent phone conversations with either Alex Marunchak or Mazher Mahmood, Southern Investigations' main office would also call the hotline to News International's best-selling paper.

Given the amount of publicity over the last ten years from the arrests over Daniel Morgan's murder, through the Stephen Lawrence murder, and the convictions of John Donald and Duncan Hanrahan, the criminality of Southern Investigations would have been apparent to any newspaper executive or journalist. Yet for all this Rees and Fillery had access to the *News of the World* hotline reserved for the highest editorial levels of the newspaper.

Despite its well-known connections with corrupt cops, underworld gangsters and a gruesome unsolved murder, Southern Investigations had a hotline to the heart of the Murdoch publishing empire in the UK.

1997–1998

ALASTAIR: On 10th March 1997, ten years had passed since my younger brother was killed. Still no action had been taken by the police.

There was nothing we could do but keep on fighting. The sad fact was that we didn't seem to be getting anywhere. But there was an increasing media focus on police misbehaviour. The Stephen Lawrence case was causing lots of problems for the Metropolitan Police. By this time the Labour opposition had promised a public inquiry if they won the election.

The Lawrence murder definitely warranted a public inquiry, but at the same time I couldn't understand why the same group of politicians were reacting so coolly to Dan's murder.

In Britain the whole population was waiting for the general election in May 1997. Everyone was certain that the Tories would be kicked out. On the day of the election, we went down to Pete and Andrea's flat in Kingston.

We all bought in drinks and spent the evening watching the Tories lose seat after seat as we cheered and laughed at the outgoing government's catastrophic results. As the night wore on and the Labour lead became overwhelming, Kirsteen kept asking, 'Are you sure they really have won?' She could hardly believe it was happening. She was 28 years old and the Tories had been in power for as long as she could remember.

It was a time of hope for everyone. Chris Smith had been tipped for a cabinet post. He was appointed the arts brief, Secretary of State in the Department of Culture, Media and Sport, and we now had the support of a cabinet minister.

Chris had written to the Metropolitan Police Commissioner, Paul Condon, asking for a meeting in February 1997. We were finally offered an audience with Condon that November after the election.

A SON, A BROTHER

Above; Daniel aged 10, and below; Alastair, Jane and Daniel.

GROWING UP

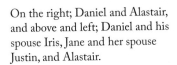

On the right; Daniel and Alastair, and above and left; Daniel and his spouse Iris, Jane and her spouse Justin, and Alastair.

GROWING UP

The siblings with spouses in the garden of Daniel's flat,
and above right; Iris, Daniel, Britt-Marie, Alastair and Jane.

DAN AS WE REMEMBER HIM

THE LONG BATTLE

Alastair 30 years ago, and with Isobel and Iris outside the Old Bailey in 2011, below.

Alastair and his mother, Isobel, and with Kirsteen below.

Alastair and Jane, and right with Isobel.

THE CRIME SCENE

Above; the Golden Lion pub in Sydenham, and left; the car park where Daniel was murdered on 10th March, 1987.